DEATH OF THE OLD WORLD

SIGMAR'S BLOOD
The Prequel to the End Times
Phil Kelly

LORDS OF THE DEAD
Book One of the End Times Omnibuses
Contains the novels *The Return of Nagash* and *The Fall of Altdorf*

DOOM OF THE ELVES
Book Two of the End Times Omnibuses
Contains the novels *Deathblade* and *The Curse of Khaine*

GOTREK & FELIX: KINSLAYER
Book One of the Doom of Gotrek Gurnisson
A novel by David Guymer

GOTREK & FELIX: SLAYER
Book Two of the Doom of Gotrek Gurnisson
A novel by David Guymer

ARCHAON: EVERCHOSEN
A novel by Rob Sanders

ARCHAON: LORD OF CHAOS
A novel by Rob Sanders

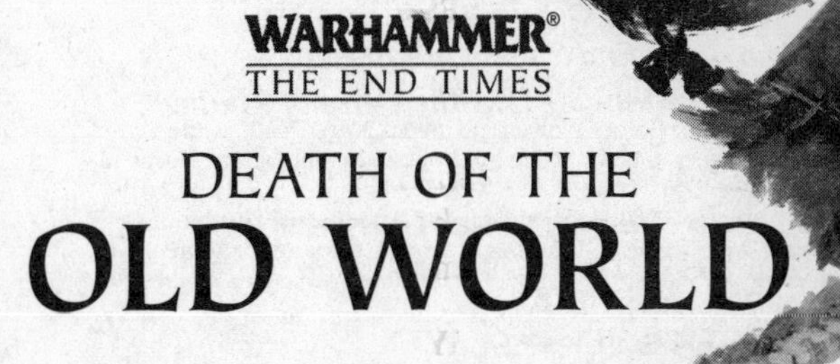

DEATH OF THE OLD WORLD

A BLACK LIBRARY PUBLICATION

The Rise of the Horned Rat first published in 2015.
The Lord of the End Times first published in 2015.
This edition published in 2016 by
Black Library,
Games Workshop Ltd.,
Willow Road,
Nottingham, NG7 2WS, UK.

10 9 8 7 6 5 4 3 2 1

Produced by Games Workshop in Nottingham.

A CIP record for this book is available from the British Library.

UK ISBN: 978 1 78496 175 6
US ISBN: 978 1 78496 176 3

Printed and bound by CPI Group (UK) Ltd, Croydon, CR0 4YY

The world is dying, but it has been so since the coming of the Chaos Gods.

For years beyond reckoning, the Ruinous Powers have coveted the mortal realm. They have made many attempts to seize it, their anointed champions leading vast hordes into the lands of men, elves and dwarfs. Each time, they have been defeated.

Until now.

In the frozen north, Archaon, a former templar of the warrior-god Sigmar, has been crowned the Everchosen of Chaos. He stands poised to march south and bring ruin to the lands he once fought to protect. Behind him amass all the forces of the Dark Gods, mortal and daemonic. When they come, they will bring with them a storm such as has never been seen.

And beneath the world, the ratlike skaven have united for the first time in many centuries. Their numbers are beyond counting and with the daemonic verminlords leading them to glory, their ascension is assured. In the western lands of Lustria, Clan Pestilens launch an all-out assault on their ancient foes, the lizardmen, an assault that the cold-blooded servants of the Old Ones cannot weather.

The southern countries of Tilea and Estalia have been devastated, and Skavenblight expands to create a capital city for the skaven from which they can rule the surface world as well as their Under-Empire. Further north, they swarm into Sigmar's Empire to finish what the hosts of the Glottkin began and drown the remaining cities of man beneath a tide of fur.

And in the Worlds Edge Mountains, the most hated foes of the skaven, the stalwart dwarfs, fortify their holds, preparing for the onslaught that they know is coming. Their time is coming to an end and the time of the skaven is at hand.

These are the End Times.

CONTENTS

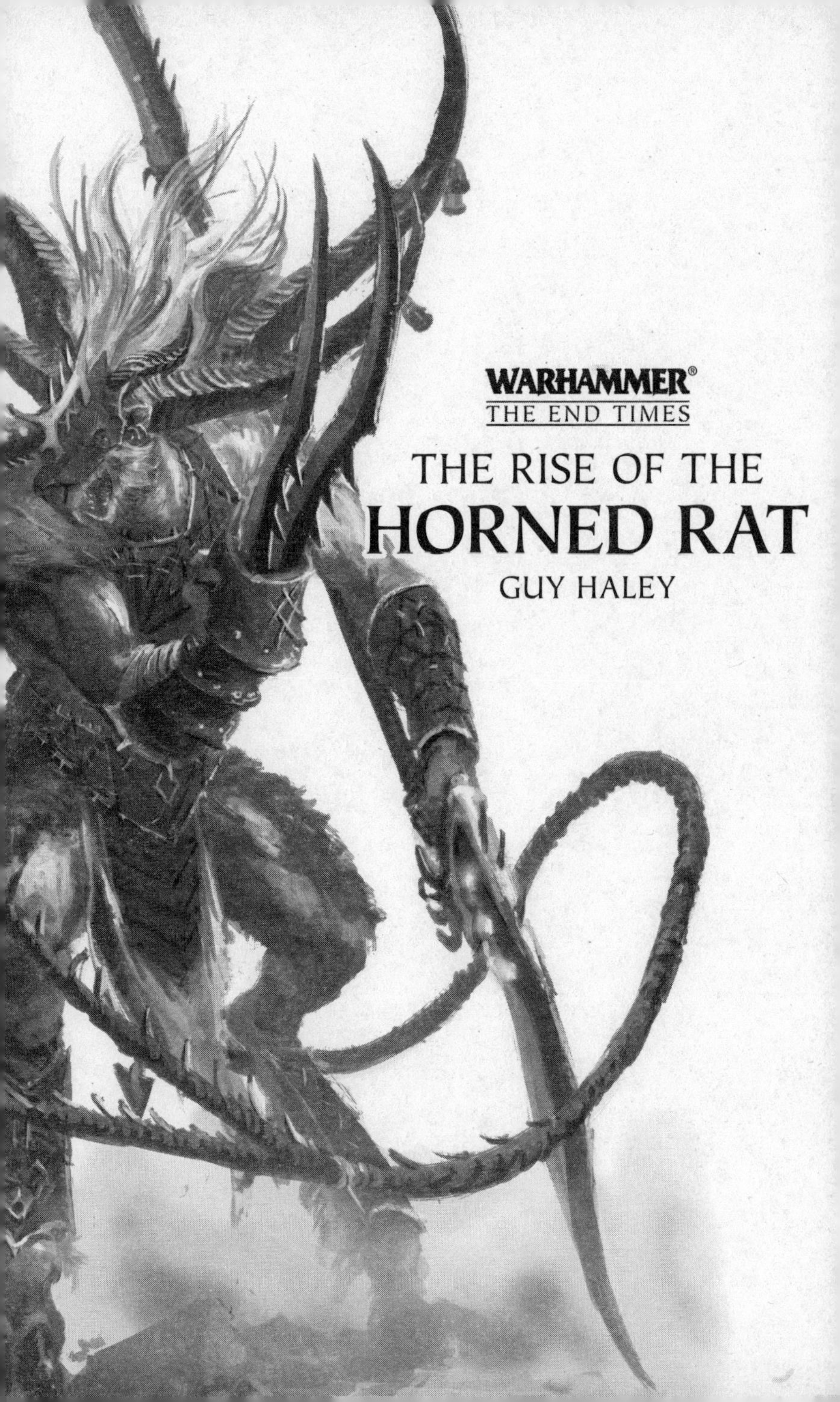
WARHAMMER®
THE END TIMES
THE RISE OF THE
HORNED RAT
GUY HALEY

THE RISE OF THE HORNED RAT

The end of the world is coming, and few realise it. In the mountain realm of the dwarfs, even the stoutest longbeard is starting to doubt that they can weather the coming storm. Orcs, goblins and skaven swarm the Underway in ever-growing numbers. A vast exodus of all sorts of vile creatures from the barren lands to the east tests the defenders of the mountain passes, and allies are scarce as war and horror falls across the lands of man. And in the skaven Under-Empire, a new power is rising – the great rat-daemons known as verminlords walk the world in ever greater numbers, and they have a plan that will ensure the dominance of the skaven over all. The Rise of the Horned Rat has begun.

PROLOGUE

The Realm of Ruin

In the darkest of places, in the most timeless of times, the twelve Shadow Lords of Decay convened in dire assembly.

They came swiftly on foot, scurrying through the rotting refuse that choked their domain. Their high horned heads bobbed furtively, now visible, now hidden by mounded rubbish: the wealth and wisdom of myriad ages taken, gnawed, despoiled, tasted and inevitably discarded. One could find all manner of treasure buried in the stinking filth, but it meant nothing to the creatures who possessed it. It was only to be coveted for the sake of having, ruined for the sake of ruination, and quickly forgotten.

Such was the way of this young race. Scavengers, usurpers, content to squat in the desolation of better peoples, their unnatural vitality and ingenuity nought but engines for entropy. The skaven were the true children of Chaos, and this place, this foetid reek under a glowering sky, was theirs alone – a nowhere realm nibbled out of the Realm of Chaos, given shape by the spirits of the ratmen that came to dwell there. A dismal place, the Realm of Ruin, a hell its inhabitants dearly desired to remake upon the mortal world.

A verminlord is a huge creature, tall as a giant, but in the wrack of the Realm of Ruin there is no scale a mortal mind can make sense of. Thus, although the Shadow Lords walked on two feet, although their heads were capped with mighty horns - and although all possessed some obvious, uncanny power - when seen from afar they appeared small and timorous, resembling nothing so much as the lowly creatures from whom they had descended. They moved like rats and they were cautious like rats, stopping every hundred paces to lift their noses and sniff at the air with a rat's sly mix of boldness and fear. Rats - rats cavorting in the rubbish of worlds.

In ones and threes, but never twos - for two lends itself too readily to betrayal - they came to the place of gathering. Verminhall, the great hall of the Realm of Ruin. The immortal lords of skavenkind converged upon the building. Once close, they broke into a scurrying run, when they were sure no others could see them scamper. They entered the portals of the vast edifice with unseemly haste, keen to clear the open space around its walls and the terrible things that hunted there.

A grandiose, overstated mirror to the Temple of the Horned Rat that stood in the living world, Verminhall was dominated by a tower that soared impossibly high. Sprouting from the uncertain centre of the building, thick and ugly, it disappeared into the churning purple clouds. Its top was lost to the sky, and its filth-encrusted walls flashed to the violence of emerald lightning. As with all things the children of Chaos possessed, it had doubtlessly been stolen from forgotten creatures - some race that had regarded itself as finer and worthier, only to fall in surprise to the vermintide. After all, this chain of events was set to repeat itself forever. In a sense, it already had. Time has no meaning in the Realm of Chaos.

The greater powers sneered at the Horned Rat, seeing him as

one of the infinite array of petty godlings whose insignificant domains marred the purity of Chaos. They were wrong to do so. The Horned Rat was no longer some minor creature, for he had grown mighty. His children were legion. Long-fermented plans were at last coming to fruition.

If this terrible place taught any lesson at all – to those few able to survive here long enough to receive it – it would be this: one should not dismiss the offspring of the lowly.

The hour of the Horned Rat was at hand.

The daemonkind verminlords, first among the servants of the Horned Rat, were as numerous as their mortal counterparts, countless in their multitudes and ubiquitous in the culverts and gulleys of creation. But of them, only twelve were deemed truly great. The greatest of these twelve was Lord Skreech Verminking. He who had once been many, and was now one.

Causality had no meaning in the Realm of Ruin, not in any sense that a mortal would understand. But Verminking's intention was to arrive after his peers, in order to underscore his own importance, and he always performed as to his intent.

The interior of Verminhall was a cave, a monument, a howling void, a place of life and of death, a temple, a palace – all, none and many more of these things besides. The laws of nature were openly mocked. Braziers burned backwards, green light glinting from Verminking's multiple horns as warpstone condensed from the very air. Fumes pulled themselves into dented brass firebowls, adding second by second to the mass of the solid magic growing within them. The lump of warpstone embedded in the daemon's empty left eye socket flared with sympathy at its brothers' birth pangs as the verminlord passed.

There was no sense to the geometry of the great hall. Stairs went on infinitely to nowhere. Black rivers flowed along walls.

Within round cages of iron, cats roasted eternally in green fire without being consumed. Windows opened in midair, looking upon places neither near nor far, but most definitely not within the bounds of the Realm of Ruin. The squeaking of a billion times a billion anguished skaven souls made a painful chittering that obliterated all other sound. Verminking moved through it as one long accustomed to visiting, taking unexpected turns and secret ways precipitately and without warning, the ultimate rat in the ultimate maze.

The other eleven great verminlords awaited their lord in the Chamber of the Shadow Council, a room that was at once endless in size and claustrophobically small. A hollow, thirteen-sided table, as wide as forever, dominated the floor. A pool of noisome liquid was at its centre, in whose oceans strange images stirred.

As they awaited their chief, the Shadow Lords of Decay bickered and schemed with one another, or sat grooming their remaining patches of fur with long tongues, content to listen to their peers, hate them, and secretly plot their undoing. All the others were present, and thus only two places were empty: Verminking's own, the first position; and that next to his, the thirteenth. The head of the table, in a sense, this was the seat of the Horned Rat himself – a massive throne carved of warpstone, big enough for a god. The likeness of its owner glared in baleful majesty from its canopy's apex.

It was said that the Great One could watch them from the unblinking, glowing eyes of his facsimile. Verminking suspected he watched them all the time; he was a god after all, the verminlord reasoned. Such was the burden of being the most favoured of the Horned Rat's many children.

Lord Verminking was not alone in his nervousness, although he hid it better than most. As was usual at such gatherings, each member of the assembled Shadow Council broke regularly from his bluster, blagging and threats to glance at the place of the Horned Rat. The god was known to attend the meetings himself – infrequently perhaps, but thus always unexpectedly. When he did attend, the musk of fear hung heavy on the air, and often as not a new opening became available upon the Council. In their own fear of the verminlords, no mortal skaven would have ever suspected that the rat-daemons felt terror for any reason, but they did. Their hearts were as craven as those of lesser ratkin.

'Lord, I have come!' announced Verminking. As he made for his chair, he kicked aside dozens of the blind white rats carpeting the floor. From the mouths of these pathetic vermin came the mewling excuses of fallen skaven lords, their souls condemned to recount their failures forever.

Verminking's musk glands clenched as he squeezed past the Horned Rat's throne to gain his own seat. When he reached his place, a lesser verminlord – one of the elite guard of the Shadow Council – appeared from the gloom and pulled Verminking's chair out for him. The daemon gave it a cursory examination before sitting. One could never be too careful in the domain of the Great Horned One. The verminlord guards in service to the Council had their tongues ripped out so that they could not relay what they heard, but that was no barrier to ambition – nor, in that place of sorcery, to speech.

'You are late, Lord Skreech,' hissed Lurklox, the shadow-shrouded Master of All Deceptions. He was Verminking's opposite number and, therefore, his second greatest rival. At least that was the case bar every third meeting, when Lurklox was replaced by Lord Verstirix of the fourth position in ceremonial opposition to Verminking. All this was enshrined on the Great Black Pillar growing in the tower. The rules governing the mortal Lords of Decay were maddeningly complex, but as nothing to those that dictated the politics of their hidden demigods. The Black Pillar in Skavenblight had been inscribed by the Horned Rat himself. The Great Black Pillar – the *real* sum of the Horned One's knowledge, the verminlords liked to think – was eternally updated. It grew constantly from the root like gnawing-teeth as more edicts were added to its hellishly contradictory catalogue. Rarely a day went by without some new ruling. The pillar was already over one hundred miles high, and the text upon it was very small. Only Verminking confidently claimed to know the full scope of the Horned Rat's teachings. He was lying.

'We are entitled to be late, yes-yes, Lurklox. It is our right!' insisted the lord of all verminlords. 'Many places we must go, many things we must see, so that you might see them too.'

'You dishonour us,' said Lurklox. One could never quite catch sight of the assassin, he was so swathed in shadow.

Vermalanx the Poxlord waved a diseased hand at Verminking. 'Yes-yes,' he said thickly. 'Mighty-exalted the great Skreech is, he of the many minds and many horns.'

Vermalanx dipped his head in a bow that could have been mocking, but so much of the Poxlord's face had rotted down to brown bone that it was impossible to tell. The more sycophantic members of the Council clapped politely. From lumps of warp rock, empty eye sockets and multiple eyes randomly arranged around malformed heads, they gave sidelong looks to their fellows, determined not to be out-fawned.

The shard of warpstone embedded in Verminking's face flared dangerously. 'Do not mock-mock, do not tease!' He slammed his hand-claw down on the table. 'We are the greatest of all of you. The Great Horned One himself whispers into our ear.' Among Verminking's many untruths, this statement had the distinction of being mostly true, even if it was disconcerting for him when the Horned Rat did actually whisper in his ear.

'Oh, most assuredly you are the greatest, O greatest great one, most pusillanimous sage, O most malfeasant malefactor,' said Verminlord Skweevritch. The metal prosthetics covering the upper part of his body hissed green steam as he twitched submissively.

'Lickspittle,' chittered the Verminlord Basqueak.

'I say vote Skweevritch off-away! We have no time for such sycophancy,' said Lord Skrolvex, the fattest and most repugnant, to Verminking's eyes, of their number.

'Silence!' he shouted, his multiple voices covering all frequencies audible to skaven ears, to deeply unpleasant effect. 'Silence,' he said again for good measure. Long tails lashed. Ears quivered in discomfort. 'There is business afoot, yes. Business we must watch, oh so carefully, my lords. In the mortal lands, great Lords of Decay meet, great Lords of Decay plot-scheme. They meet, so we the Shadow Council, great *Vermin*lords of Decay, the *true* Council, must meet too-also.'

Chattering and insults were traded. Verminking silenced them with a hand-claw, and pointed his other at the pool. 'Listen! See-smell! Look-learn!' he said. Greasy bubbles popped on the surface as the pool became agitated. In slow circuit the liquid turned, swirling around and around, faster and faster, to form a whirlpool, whose funnel plunged deeper and deeper until it surely must have surpassed the limits of the water. A black circle appeared at its bottom, and the whirlpool went down forever. The other verminlords looked at it in askance, lest it drag them in, but Verminking had no such fear. He stared eagerly into the depths of eternity. Fumes rose from the liquid, sparking with warp-lightning, before settling down as a glowing mist. Within the mist, the following image formed.

A room not unlike the Shadow Council's, though not so grand. A table like the Shadow Council's, though not so ornate. Thrones around the table, like the Shadow Council's, though not so large. In the twelve thrones sat twelve skaven lords of great power, though not so powerful as the twelve who watched them unseen.

Verminking's skin twitched. The Verminlords of Decay watched the mortal Lords of Decay. Who watched them? Where did it stop? Were there conclaves of rats, squeaking in the sewers observed by gimlet-eyed beastmasters? Were there layer upon layer of ever greater rat-things plotting and interfering with those below? He chased the thought away, but it lingered at the back of his fractured mind, insistent as a flea in his ear.

The mortal skaven were in full debate. Things were not going well. Shouting and squeaking raised a clamour that shook the room. Many were standing to wave accusing forepaws at one another. Some squeaked privately to one another, or shot knowing looks across the table as deals were silently struck and as quickly broken.

Just as Verminking had silenced the Shadow Council, so Kritislik the Seerlord silenced the Council of Thirteen, although nowhere near as majestically. He was white-furred and horned, and that should have ensured him supremacy. He was chief of the grey seers, the wizard lords of the skaven, blessed by the Horned Rat himself, and nominal chief of the Council in his absence. But the others were in rebellious mood. Kritislik was agitated, squeaking rapidly and without authority. He had yet to squirt musk, but the look of fear was on him, in his twitching nose, widened eyes and bristling fur.

'Quiet-quiet! You blame, shout-squeak! All fault here. Great victories we have were in manlands of Estalia and Tilea.'

'Many slaves, much plunder-spoils,' said Kratch Doomclaw, warlord of Clan Rictus. 'All is going to plan. Soon the man-things will fall. Listen to the white-fur.'

'No!' said one, huge and deep voiced. He was black as night and unconquerable as the mountains. Lord Gnawdwell of Clan Mors. 'You take-steal too much, far beyond your scavenge rights. You test my patience, thief-thief, sneaker. I will not listen to your prattling one heartbeat longer.'

'My clanrats, my victory,' said Kratch, making an effort to keep his voice low and slow. 'Where is Lord Gnawdwell's trophy-prize? I shall squeak you where – still in the hands of the dwarf-things, who you have not yet defeated.'

Squeaking laughter came from several of the others, including, most irksomely for Gnawdwell, Lord Paskrit, the obese warlord-general of all Skavendom.

The lords of the four greater clans scowled at this display of indiscipline among the warlord clans. Lord Morskittar of Clan Skryre, emperor of warlocks and tinkerer in chief, was not impressed.

'Many devices, many weapons, many warptokens' worth of new machines you of the warlord clans were given-granted in aid of the Great Uprising. What have we to show-see for it? Yes-yes, very good. Tilea-place and Estalia-place gone-destroyed.'

General noises of approval interrupted him. Morskittar held his paws up, palms flat, and bared his teeth in disapproval. 'Fools to cheer like stupid slave-meat! The weakest human-lands destroyed only. Frog-things still in their stone temple-homes. Dwarf-things still in the mountains. And Empire-place not yet destroyed!' He shook his head, his tail lashing back and forth behind him. 'Disappointing.'

'What you squeak-say? Where are your armies?' said Lord Griznekt Mancarver of Clan Skab. 'Guns no good without paw-fingers to pull triggers.'

More uproar and shouted accusations. All around the room, the elite Albino Guard of the Council stiffened, ready to intervene on the winning side should open conflict erupt.

'No! No!' said Morskittar. 'I will speak! I will speak!' He slammed a skull carved of pure warpstone down onto the table. It banged like a cannon, the report buying him silence. 'Why point-indicate me with paw of blame?' said Morskittar slyly. 'I say the grey seers are the ones who shoulder responsibility. Clan Scruten are those who bring everything to ruin.' He pointed at Kritislik.

'Yes-yes!' chittered the others immediately, all of whom had their own reasons for loathing the priest-magicians. 'The seers, Clan Scruten!'

'Outrage! Outrage!' squealed Kritislik. 'I have led this council long ages-time! I led great summoning many breedings ago! I speak for the Horned Rat!'

'You speak for yourself,' said Paskrit the Vast, gruffly. Sensing weakness, he heaved his bulk up to face Kritislik on his footpaws. 'You speak for Clan Scruten. Always scheming, always plotting. Always say do this, do that! Why is it Clan Mors find itself fighting Clan Rictus? Why Clan Skurvy lose half of thrall clans the day before sea-battle of Sartosa-place?'

'Grey seer is why, Clan Scruten! Clan Scruten are to blame,' croaked Arch-Plaguelord Nurglitch.

They all shouted then, except for the inscrutable Nightlord Sneek, master of Clan Eshin, who watched it all with hooded eyes half hidden by his mask and no scent to betray his thoughts.

'It is not our fault! Your incompetence and greed-grasping stops the obeying of our rightful orders! We are the horned rats. We are the chosen-best of the Great Horned One! You fight-fight, scrapping like common rat-things on human middens. Listen to us, or suffer,' shouted Kritislik.

'No! Lies-deceit. You pit us against one another when all we wish to do is work in harmony for the betterment of all skavenkind!' said Lord Gnawdwell.

The others nodded solemnly. 'Truth-word!' they said. 'We would conquer, but for you. Grey seers make us fight-fight!' They would all happily have knifed each other in the back at the least provocation, whether a grey seer was pulling the strings or not. That the grey seers usually *were* pulling the strings complicated matters enormously.

The Council of Thirteen erupted into a cacophony of squeaked accusations. The scent of aggression grew strong.

The Shadow Lords looked on with growing disapproval.

'See-see,' said Verminking. 'Great victories they have, and now they fall to fighting.'

'They are what they are, and no more,' said Vermalanx disinterestedly. 'Children yet, but mastery shall come to them. Then true greatness we shall see-smell in due course. I care not for this – my Nurglitch's plans are well advanced.'

'Yes-yes,' said Throxstraggle, Vermalanx's ally and fellow plaguelord. 'What care we for these pup squeakings?'

'Your grave error to set aside Clan Pestilens from the doing-aims of the others. You are not apart from this, poxlords,' said Verminking. 'You and yours distance yourselves, but Clan Pestilens is nothing alone. You think-remember that.'

Vermalanx chirred angrily.

'No mastery will come. They fail! They fail!' spat Basqueak. 'Fool-things! Squabbling while the world slips from their paws. Always the same, civil war comes again. Skavenblight will ring to the sound of blade on blade. Man-things and dwarf-things will recover, and skaven stay in the shadows. Always the same.'

'Yes-yes,' said Verminking. 'They fail. But watch...'

In the mortal realm, Kritislik stood, waving a fist at the other Lords of Decay, admonishing them for their stupidity. From the look on his face, he thought it was working, for the others suddenly fell silent and shrank back in their seats, eyes wide. A few bared their throats in submission before they could catch themselves. Someone shamefully let spray the musk of fear. It hung heavy over the crowd, an accusation of cowardice.

Kritislik began to crow. The mightiest lords of Skavendom, and he had them in the palm of his paw. Now was his chance to stamp his authority all over this rabble again!

Or maybe not. Kritislik was so taken by his own oratory that he had completely failed to notice the shape growing behind him.

Black smoke jetted from the seat of the Horned Rat. The wisps of shadow built into a cloud that writhed and began to take the form of something huge and malevolent.

'Ah! Now! Order, is good, yes! You listen-hear good, you...' Kritislik stopped mid-sentence. His nose twitched. 'You are not listening to me, are you? You do not hear-smell me good?' he said. He was answered by eleven shaking heads, the owners of which were all trying to look inconspicuous.

He turned around to see a horned head forming from darkness more complete than that found in the deepest places of the world.

Kritislik threw himself to the floor in outright obeisance as the manifested Horned Rat opened eyes that flooded the room with sickly green light. Words of power rumbled from some other place, the voice underpinned by hideous chittering – the death-squeaks of every rat and skaven ever to have drawn breath.

'Children of the Horned Rat,' he said, his voice as final as a tunnel collapse, *'how you disappoint your father.'*

'O Great One! O Horned One! Once more I welcome you to the–'

'No one summon-bids I, Kritislik. I come, I go, wherever I please. I have no master.'

'I... I...'

'You squabble pathetically. This will cease now. Your plans are sound, your alliances are not. I will not countenance another failure. Long have Clan Scruten had my blessing. I have given you my mark, great power, and long life.' The head bore down on Kritislik, lips parting to show teeth made of crackling light. *'You have wasted my favour.'*

Without warning, a hand formed from the smoke, scrabbling as if seeking purchase on an unseen barrier. Fingers and claws pointed forwards. The air warped as the hand pushed against an unseen skin, then burst its way into common reality and reached down.

Kritislik squealed in terror as he was plucked from the floor by his tail. His fine robes dropped down to cover his head. The musk of fear sprayed without restraint, followed by a rich stream of droppings.

'The others are right-correct, little Kritislik.' A second hand reached out from the darkness, where now a muscular torso had also formed. A gentle claw-finger lifted the hem of Kritislik's upended robes to reveal his petrified face, and stroked along his horns. *'So much I have given you, and yet you scheme for more. Greedy, when there is enough for all to feast upon. Your avarice stops now.'*

The mouth of the Horned Rat gaped wide. Kritislik was hoisted high by the tail over a maw swirling with terrible possibilities. Kritislik stared down and gibbered at what he saw there.

'M-mercy! M-mercy, O Great One! We will double our efforts! Triple them! Quadrupl–' His pleas ended in a scream as his tail was released. The grey seer fell into the eternally hungry mouth of his god. The Horned Rat's jaws snapped shut. His eyes closed with pleasure, and when he opened them again they burned with a cold and terrible light.

'Thirteen times thirteen passes of the Chaos moon I will give you. Thirteen times thirteen moons I will wait. Go to your legions and your workshops! Bring me victory. Bring me dominance over this mortal realm! You must be as one, work as one, as single-minded as a swarm pouring from a cracked sewer-pipe – all rats scurry-flood in same direction. Only then will you inherit the ruins of this world, only then will you rule. Thirteen times thirteen moons! Fail, and all will suffer the fate of the seer.'

With a crackle of green lightning and the tolling of a bell so loud the room quaked, the Horned Rat vanished. Kritislik's bones lay black and smoking upon the floor.

The tolling bell faded and stopped. The Lords of Decay uncovered their ears, picked themselves up off the floor and sniffed the air.

The ensuing silence lasted for all of fifteen swift skaven heartbeats.

'I move,' said Morskittar, swallowing to moisten his dry throat, 'to vote the grey seers from the Council. Clan Scruten will sit-rule no more!'

For only the fourth time in skaven history, a vote was passed unanimously. As soon as it was done, the clanlords immediately fell to arguing again: over what to do, and more importantly, over who should occupy the empty seat.

In the Realm of Ruin, the twelve Shadow Lords of Decay managed a shocked silence for a little longer.

Skweevritch broke it. 'But the Great Horned One has not gone abroad in the mortal realm for many-many years. Centuries!' he wailed.

'What-what? What?' squealed Soothgnawer, white-furred as the unfortunate Kritislik. He was the champion of Clan Scruten and was dismayed, but he did not voice his objections too loudly in case the Horned Rat became aware of them. 'No seer on the Council? No seer? Unthinkable.'

'And what of us, what do we do?' said Skrolvex. They all glanced nervously at the throne, in case their god should pay them a visit also. The Horned Rat's appetite was notoriously insatiable.

Verminking spoke, cunningly and persuasively. 'Pups need guidance. Who becomes slave, who becomes lord. The strongest decides. The Horned Rat! The Great Horned One has shown us the way. Is it not clear? We must follow his example. We must go to them, into the mortal realm. We will guide them.' He pointed at the bickering mortal skaven.

Lord Basqueak twitched. 'Mortal realm? We are vulnerable there! Danger! Much peril.' His tail twitched.

They were all immortal, chosen of the Horned Rat. And yet certain rules applied to them, as they did to all inhabitants of the higher realms. To suffer death and banishment for a hundred years and a day back into the Realm of Chaos was not a terminal experience, but their places on the Shadow Council would be forfeit, and no verminlord could countenance such a loss of power.

'Coward!' squealed Kreeskuttle. He stood tall with a rattle of armour. Kreeskuttle was the mightiest of arm upon the Council, if not of intellect.

Basqueak hissed, jutting his head forwards. 'Then you, Lord Kreeskuttle, shall go to the mortal lands and take the risk! Show-tell how brave you are.'

Kreeskuttle growled, and sank back into his chair.

'I will go,' said Vermalanx arrogantly. 'I have no fear. I will go to the land of the frog-things, there to guide the great plagues.'

'Yes! Go-go!' burbled Throxstraggle enthusiastically, notably making no promise of his own to follow.

'I too,' said Soothgnawer. 'It wrong-bad no seer sits on the Council. I will help them win their place again. We must atone for our sins against the Horned Rat.'

They eyed each other with quick, suspicious eyes. Plots were forming, plans being drawn up. No doubt others would go without declaring their intentions. Outrageous risk for ephemeral gain wobbled yet again on the balance of the skaven soul.

'Soothgnawer is right,' said Verminking. 'The grey seers hold the key.'

The mist over the pool shivered, clearing away the bickering lords of the mortal skaven. The image wavered, and a narrow alleyway materialised, one of thousands within the crammed confines of Skavenblight. Noses twitched, teeth bared. The verminlords recognised it instinctively, although it changed daily. The home of all skaven.

'Here-here, valued lords. Here-here is our weapon!' said Verminking.

A white-furred figure scuttled along, constantly looking over his shoulder. A massive rat ogre paced along beside him, taking one step for every fifteen of the grey seer's.

'Is that...' asked Vermalanx.

'It isn't...' said Kreeskuttle.

'It is!' gasped Basqueak.

'Thanquol!' squeaked Poxparl.

'Why him-him?' said Grunsqueel, moved finally to speak. 'He is useless! Great power has been gifted-given to this horned one, and what has he done? He has squandered-wasted it. Of all of them, he is by far the worst.'

'Used it no good.'

'True-true. How many times has Thanquol, great grey seer, failed us?' said Lurklox. 'The Horned Rat should eat him too!'

'Many-many times!' chittered the others. 'Failure! Liability!'

'See-watch, how weak he is! He goes always tail down, the musk of fear never far from squirting. He is weak. Excuses, excuses and never success,' said Basqueak.

'He is a coward!' said Skweevritch, which was a little rich, as he was no hero himself.

'Fool-fool. The dwarf-thing and man-thing have thwarted him alone many-many times!' said Kreeskuttle.

'The disaster at Nuln.'

'The shame of his failed summoning!' said Basqueak. The others nodded in emphatic agreement. More than one of them had been ready to step into the mortal world that day, only for Thanquol to botch it.

Verminking held up a hand-claw and hissed. 'He is all these things and more. Failure! Dreg! It is in part because of him no grey seer sits upon the Council in the world below.'

'Failure!' the others squeaked.

'Fool-fool! He should be destroyed-killed, not aided,' said Throxstraggle.

'Yes, failure. Yes, fool-fool. But in him is our greatest tool.'

'What-what?'

'Lord Skreech squeaks madness,' said Verstirix. The warrior verminlord puffed up his chest. 'Enough! Veto right is mine.'

'Do you challenge us, the greatest of our number?' said Verminking.

Verstirix looked to his colleagues for support; they pointedly looked away.

'Grey Seer Thanquol has much service to render. Yes-yes,' said Soothgnawer.

'Too much faith you have in him,' said Basqueak. 'Fool-thing, Throxstraggle is correct. We should slay-kill very slowly. Then find another.'

Verminking stroked the surface of the foetid pool, his long black claw sending ripples across its surface and the image shimmering above it. 'No-no. It is he, it is he.'

'Who make you decide-determine? Vote! Vote!' screeched Verstirix.

'Yes, vote-vote. Ten against two. You lose, Soothgnawer, Skreech,' bubbled Vermalanx.

'Not two against ten, not that at all. You count bad.'

'Two! Two! I see only two, fool-things!'

'*Three* against ten,' said Verminking quietly. He looked meaningfully at the Horned Rat's throne. It could have been a trick of the light, but it appeared that the warpstone eyes of the effigy atop it glowed more brightly.

A silence fell over the Council. Tails twitched. Beady eyes darted beneath horns that shook, just a little, with fear.

'I say,' said Poxparl calculatingly, 'that we give Thanquol another chance. Mighty Lord Skreech has moved-touched my heart.'

'Yes-yes,' squeaked Basqueak very loudly, talking directly towards the vacant throne. 'I vote yes-yes.'

'I too,' said Throxstraggle.

'If it is so, it is so,' muttered Vermalanx.

One by one, the verminlords voted. The motion was passed by a narrow margin – there had never yet been a unanimous vote on the Shadow Council. Verminking looked to Verstirix, challenging him to use his veto. The ex-warlord looked at the empty throne, then found something on the surface of the table that needed his urgent attention.

'It is done, then,' said Lord Skreech Verminking triumphantly. 'Let us rip the veil between worlds. Let us stalk mortal lands again! Skitter-disperse, go to your favourites.' He peered hungrily into the pool. 'Go where you will, as quickly as you can. We shall go to Thanquol.'

Thanquol's nose twitched, his famous sixth sense giving him the itchy feeling that he was being watched. He looked around the stinking alley, into crooked windows, along the skyline, black against the foggy night, into alleyways where sagging duckboards crossed open sewers. He saw no threat, but shivered nonetheless. His musk gland clenched.

'Sssss! Jumping-fear at own shadow! At own shadow!' he scolded himself. He jerked an angry paw at his bodyguard. 'Boneripper, on-on!'

And so, unknowing of the attention focused upon him at that moment, Thanquol continued with his furtive passage through Skavenblight.

PART ONE

The Lords of Ruin
Autumn–Winter 2523

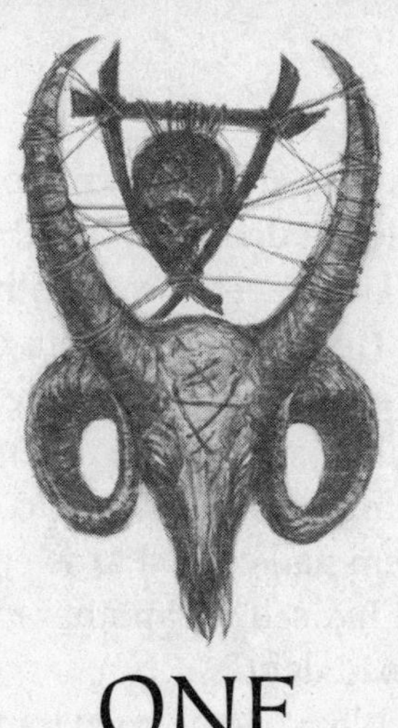

ONE

Kingsmeet

The kingsmeet was over, and Belegar was glad. Soon he could go home.

The dwarf kings met in Karaz-a-Karak, Everpeak, home of the dwarf High King. Everpeak was the last place in the world where the ancient glory of the dwarfs shone undimmed. No matter that only half its halls were occupied, or that the works of its forges could never recapture the skill of the ancestors. The place teemed with dwarfs in such multitudes that one could be forgiven for thinking that they were still a numerous people.

Being there made Belegar miserable. In the distant past his own realm had been Karaz-a-Karak's rival in riches and size. His inability to return it to glory filled him with shame.

He sat in an antechamber awaiting the High King, nursing a jewelled goblet of fine ale. He had been born and raised in Karaz-a-Karak, but half a century of dwelling in the dangerous ruins of Vala-Azrilungol had blunted his memory of its riches. The opulence on display was astounding – more value in gold and artefacts in this one, small waiting room than were in his own throne room. He felt decidedly shabby, as he had done all the way through the kingsmeet. Two months hard travelling and fighting to get here. He had to sneak out of his own hold, and he would have to sneak back in. Now here he was, kept behind like a naughty beardling after all the other kings had been sent to feast. Nothing Thorgrim would have to say to him would be good. The two of them had ceased to see eye to eye some time ago. Belegar steeled himself for another long rant about failed obligations and unpaid debt.

He rolled his eyes. What had he been thinking, telling the others he occupied a third of Karak Eight Peaks? From a strictly technical point of view, it could be deemed truthful. He had opened up mines, captured a good part of the upper deeps, and held a strong corridor between the surface city and the East Gate. But in reality his holdings were far less. The East Gate itself, the citadel, the mountain halls of Kvinn-wyr. Everything else had to be visited in strength. And he had promised military aid. With what?

Not for the first time, he cursed his pride.

The doors to the far end of the chamber opened wide. A dwarf in the livery of Thorgrim's personal household bowed low, sweeping his hood from his head.

'Majesty, the King of Kings is ready for you.'

Belegar slid from the rich coverings of the bench. A second servant appeared from nowhere, a fresh mug of ale on his silver tray. Belegar downed his first, until that moment untouched, and took the second.

'This way,' said the first dwarf, holding out his hand.

Belegar was shown into a chamber he knew only too well. One of Thorgrim's private rooms high in the palace, it was large and impressive, and consequently used by the High King when he was going to dress down others of royal blood. It had grand views of the approach to Karaz-a-Karak, seven hundred feet below.

Summer sunlight streamed in through the tall windows. A fire of logs burned in the huge hearth. A clock ticked on the wall.

'Belegar,' said Thorgrim levelly. The king wore his armour and his crown. Belegar tried to think of a time he had seen him without it, and failed. The latest volume of the Great Book of Grudges sat open on a lectern. A bleeding-knife and a quill rested in specially cut spaces by it. 'Please, take a seat.'

Thorgrim gestured to one of a number of smartly dressed servants. They disappeared, returning moments later with a tall jug of beer and a platter piled high with roast meats.

Belegar sat down opposite the High King with resignation.

'I do not mean to keep you from the feast. Please, help yourself, sharpen your appetite for when you join the others,' he said.

Belegar did as asked. The kingsmeet had been long, and he was hungry. Both food and ale were delicious.

'We'll wait a moment before we get started,' said Thorgrim. 'There's another I wish to speak with.'

The door opened again then. Belegar turned in his seat, his eyebrows rising in surprise at the sight of Ungrim Ironfist. The Slayer King strode in and took up a seat. He nodded at Belegar as he sat. His face was stony. Ungrim always had been angry. Belegar had no idea how he managed to survive caught between two oaths so contradictory. And he had just lost his son. Belegar felt a stab of sympathy for Ungrim. The safety of his own boy was never far from his thoughts.

Thorgrim pressed his hands on the desk before speaking, formulating his words with care. 'All this business with the elgi and the walking dead has got me unsettled,' said Thorgrim. 'Things are happening of great portent, things that speak to me that...' He shook his head. He looked even more tired than he had in the meeting. 'We discussed all that. I am grateful for your support.'

'Of course, my king,' said Belegar.

'Why wouldn't I want to march out and destroy our enemies? You've heard all I have to say on this matter,' said Ungrim.

'I have,' agreed Thorgrim. 'Summoning the throngs will not be easy. You have heard Kazador and Thorek's objections. They are not alone. The argument between attack and defence is one I have had all my life, and I fear it is too late to win it.' Thorgrim paused. 'I have asked you both here as you are, in your own ways, special cases. Ungrim,' he said to the Slayer King, 'to you I urge a little caution. Do not throw away your throng in the quest for vengeance for your son's death, or in order to fulfil your Slayer's oath.

Ungrim's face creased with anger. 'Thorgrim–'

Thorgrim held up his hand. 'That is all I will say on the matter. I do not criticise you, it is a plea for aid. We will need you before the end. Should you fall marching out to bring war upon our enemies, the others will follow Kazador's advice and lock themselves away. That way, we shall all fall one by one. By all means fight, old friend. But use a little caution. Without you, my case is weakened.'

Ungrim nodded curtly. 'Aye.'

'And you, Belegar,' said Thorgrim. His face hardened a little, but not so much as Belegar might rightfully have expected. 'Long have you struggled to keep your oaths. Loans have gone unpaid, warriors have been unforthcoming, and your hold swallows dawi lives and dawi gold as if it were a bottomless pit without any noticeable gain.' Thorgrim stared hard at him. 'But you are a great warrior, and the proudest of all the kings here. You and I have our differences to be sure, but of all the others, I think our hearts are most similar. Of them all, only you have set out to reconquer what was once ours. I respect you for that far more than you realise. So what I am going to ask of you will cut hard and deep. Nevertheless, it must be asked.'

'My king?' said Belegar.

Thorgrim sighed. 'Against all my own oaths and desires, and against yours, I must ask you to consider abandoning Karak Eight Peaks. Take your warriors to Karak Azul. Aid Kazador. If you do, I will consider all your debts repaid.'

It was a generous offer, and sensible advice. Karak Eight Peaks was weak, besieged, a drain on the other holds.

Belegar did not see it that way. All his misery at his plight flashed at once into anger. When he stood, which he did quickly, his words were spoken in haste and fuelled by more than a little shame at his failure to secure all of Vala-Azrilungol.

When he had finally stopped shouting and stormed out of the room, his path was set. That very day, he left Karaz-a-Karak for the final time. He brooded on the High King's words all the way to Karak Eight Peaks.

They would haunt him to his grave.

TWO

Lord Gnawdwell

In the underbelly of the mortal world, a flurry of activity was set in motion. Rarely had the ancient Lords of Decay moved so quickly. A febrile energy gripped Skavenblight. Messengers scurried from place to place, carrying missives that were, in the main, far from truthful. Conspirators struggled in vain to find a quiet spot to talk that was not already full of plotters. Assassinations were up, and a good killer became hard to find.

The doings of the Council were supposed to be of the utmost secrecy, but on all lips, squeak-talked on every corner, were tidings of the death of Kritislik, and of who would inherit the vacant seat on the Council of Thirteen.

Into this stewing pit of intrigue Warlord Queek, the Headtaker, came, thronged by red-armoured guards. Through the underway, into the seeping bowels of Skavenblight, he marched to see his master, Lord Gnawdwell.

Queek avoided the streets, coming to Gnawdwell's burrows without once having a whisker stirred by Skavenblight's dank mists. This suited Queek, who was no lover of the surface world or the crowded lanes of the capital.

Gnawdwell's palace was a tall tower rising over multiple layers of cellars and burrows at the heart of the Clan Mors quarter of the city. That he had summoned Queek to the underground portion of his estates was a subtle reminder of power, an accommodation to Queek. Gnawdwell was saying he knew Queek was more at home under the earth than on it. Gnawdwell was highlighting weakness.

Queek knew this. Queek was no fool.

Queek and his guards took many twisting lanes from the main underways to reach the underpalace. Great doors of wutroth barred the way to Gnawdwell's domain. At either side were two times thirteen black stormvermin. Their champions crossed their halberds over the door. Not the usual rabble, these. They were bigger than and outnumbered Queek's Red Guard.

Queek's nose twitched. There was no scent of fear from the guards. Nothing – not even in the presence of mighty Queek! Was he not the finest warrior the skaven had ever pupped? Was his murderous temper not the stuff of nightmare? But they did not fidget. They stood still in perfect imitation of statues, glinting black eyes staring at the warlord without dismay.

'State-squeak business and rank-name,' one said.

Queek paced back and forth. 'How stupid-meat not know Queek! Warlord of Clan Mors, Lord of the City of Pillars?' His trophies rattled upon the rack he wore on his back, a structure of wood akin to half a wheel, every spoke topped by a grisly memento mori. His forepaws twitched over the hilts of his weapons, a serrated sword and the infamous war-pick Dwarf Gouger.

'We know you, Queek,' responded the guard, unmoved. 'But all must state-squeak name and business. Is Lord Gnawdwell's orders. As Lord Gnawdwell commands, so we obey.'

'Stupid-meat!' spat Queek. A quiver of irritation troubled his fur. 'Very well. I Queek,' he said with sing-song sarcasm. 'Let me in!'

The corridor was so quiet Queek could hear water dripping, the constant seepage of the marshwaters above the undercity into the tunnels. Machines churned night and day to keep them dry. Their thunder reverberated throughout the labyrinth and the streets above, and their heat made the tunnels uncomfortable. They were Skavenblight's beating heart.

'Good-good,' said the guard. 'Great Warlord Queek, mightiest warrior in all the Under-Empire, slaughterer of–'

'Yes-yes!' squeaked Queek, who had no time for platitudes. 'In! In! Let me in!'

The guard appeared slightly deflated. He cleared his throat, and began again. 'Queek may enter. No one else.'

Chains rattled and the doors cracked with a long creak, revealing a gang of panting slaves pushing upon a windlass. Queek darted towards the gap as soon as it was wide enough.

The guard champions crossed their halberds to block the way.

'No, Queek. Queek leave trophy rack at door-entry. No one is more glorious than great Lord Gnawdwell. No insult. Be humble. Arrogance in the face of his brilliance is not to be tolerated.'

Queek bared his incisors at the guards aggressively, but they did not react. He wished greatly to release his pent up aggression on them. Spitting, he undid the fastenings and handed his trophies over to the stormvermin. He growled to hide his own disquiet. He would miss the counsel of the dead things when he spoke to Lord Gnawdwell. Did Gnawdwell know? Stupid Queek, he thought. Gnawdwell know *everything.*

The guards also demanded his weapons, and this made Queek snarl all the more. Once divested of them, Queek was allowed entrance to the first hall of Gnawdwell's burrow. A fat and sleek-furred major-domo with a weak mouse face came to receive Queek. He bowed and scraped pathetically, exposing his neck submissively. The scent of fear was strong around him.

'Greetings, O most violent and magnificent Queek! Red-clawed and deadly, warrior-killer, best of all Clan Mors. O mighty–'

'Yes-yes,' squeaked Queek. 'Very good. I best. All know. Why-why squeak-whine about it all day? You new or you know this,' said Queek. 'Guards new too.' He looked the little skaven up and down contemptuously. 'You fat.'

'Yes, Lord Queek. Lord Gnawdwell gain many scavenge rights in Tilea-place and Estalia-place. War is good.'

Queek bared his teeth in a hideous smile. He rushed forwards, a blur in scarlet armour, taking the majordomo by surprise. He grabbed the front of the slow-thing's robes in his paws and jerked him forwards. 'Yes-yes, mouse-face. War good, but what mouse-face know of war? Mouse-face stupid-meat!'

The musk of fear enveloped them both. Queek drooled at the smell of it.

'Mouse-face fear Queek. Mouse-face right about that, at least.'

The fat skaven raised a hand and pointed. 'Th-this way, O greatest and most marvellous–'

'Queek know way,' said Queek haughtily, shoving the other to the floor. 'Queek been here many times. Stupid mouse-face.'

Many years had passed since Queek was last in Skavenblight, but scent and memory took him to Gnawdwell's private burrow quickly. There were no other skaven about. So much space! Nowhere else in all of Skavenblight would you be further from another skaven. Queek sniffed: fine food and well-fed slaves, fresh air pumping from somewhere. Gnawdwell's palace disgusted him with its luxury.

Queek waited a long time before he realised no servant was coming and that he would have to open Gnawdwell's door himself. He found the Lord of Decay in the chamber on the other side.

Books. That was the first thing he saw every time. Lots and lots of stupid books. Books everywhere, and paper, all piled high on finely made man-thing and dwarf-thing furniture. Queek saw no use for such things. Why have books? Why have tables? If Queek wanted to know something, someone told him. If he wanted to put something down, he dropped it on the floor. Not bothering about such things left more time for Queek to fight. A big table occupied a large part of the room. On it was a map quill-scratched onto a piece of vellum, made from a single rat ogre skin, and covered in models of wood and metal. Poring over this, an open book in one brawny paw, was Lord Gnawdwell.

There was nothing to betray Gnawdwell's vast age. He was physically imposing, strongly muscled and barrel-chested. He might have lived like a seer, surrounded by his stolen knowledge. He might be dressed in robes of the finest-quality cloth scavenged from the world above, fitted to his form by expert slave-tailors in the warrens of Skavenblight. But he still moved like a warrior.

Gnawdwell put down the book he was holding and gestured at Queek to come closer. 'Ah, Queek,' said Gnawdwell, as if the warlord's arrival were a pleasant surprise. 'Come, let me see-examine you. It is a long time since I have seen-smelt Clan Mors's favoured general.' He beckoned with hands whose quickness belied their age. Gnawdwell was immeasurably ancient to Queek's mind. He had a slight grizzling of grey upon his black fur, the sign of a skaven past his youth. The same had recently begun to mark Queek. They could have been littermates, but Gnawdwell was twenty times Queek's age.

'Yes-yes, my lord. Queek come quick.'

Queek walked across the room. He was fast, his body moving with a rodentine fluidity that carried him from one place to the other without him seeming to truly occupy the space in between, as if he were a liquid poured around it. Gnawdwell smiled at Queek's grace, his red eyes bright with hard humour.

Awkwardly, hesitantly, Queek exposed his throat to the ancient rat lord. Submission did not come easily to him, and he hated himself for doing it, but to Gnawdwell he owed his absolute, fanatical loyalty. He could have killed Gnawdwell, despite the other's great strength and experience. He was confident enough to believe that. Part of him wanted to, very much. What stories the old lord might tell him, mounted on Queek's trophy rack, adding his whispers to the other dead-things who advised him.

But he did not. Something stopped him from trying. A caution that told Queek he might be wrong, and that Gnawdwell would slaughter him as easily as he would a man-thing whelp.

'Mighty-mighty Gnawdwell!' squeaked Queek.

Gnawdwell laughed. They were both large for skaven, Gnawdwell somewhat bigger than Queek. Ska Bloodtail was the only skaven that Queek had met who was larger.

Both Queek and Gnawdwell were black-furred. Both were of the same stock ultimately, drawn from the Clan Mors breeder-line, but they were as unalike as alike. Where Queek was fast and jittery, Gnawdwell was slow and contemplative. If Queek were rain dancing on water, Gnawdwell was the lake.

'Always to the point, always so quick and impatient,' said Gnawdwell. Old skaven stank of urine, loose glands, dry skin, and, if they were rich enough, oil, brass, warpstone, paper and soft straw. That is not what Lord Gnawdwell smelt of. Lord Gnawdwell smelt vital. Lord Gnawdwell smelt of power.

'I, Gnawdwell, have summoned you. You, Queek, have obeyed. You are still a loyal skaven of Clan Mors?' Gnawdwell's words were deeply pitched, unusually so for a skaven.

'Yes-yes!' said Queek.

'Yes-yes, Queek says, but does he mean it?' Gnawdwell tilted his head. He grabbed Queek's muzzle and moved Queek's head from side to side. Queek trembled with anger, not at Gnawdwell's touch, but at the meekness with which he accepted it.

'I have lived a long time. A very long time. Did you know, Queek, that I am over two hundred years old? That is ancient by the terms of our fast-live, die-quick race, yes-yes? Already, Queek, you age. I see white fur coming in black fur. Here, on your muzzle.' Gnawdwell patted Queek with a sharp-clawed hand-paw. 'You are... how old now? Nine summers? Ten? Do you feel the slowness creep into your limbs, the ache in your joints? It will only get worse. You are fast now, but I wonder, do you already slow? You will get slower. Your whiskers will droop, your eyes will dim. Your smell will weaken and your glands slacken. The great Queek!' Gnawdwell threw up a hand-paw, as if to evoke Queek's glory in the air. 'So big and so strong now, but for how much longer?' Gnawdwell shrugged. 'Two years or four? Who knows? Who do you think cares? Hmm? Let me tell you, Queek. No one will care.' Gnawdwell went to his cluttered table and picked up a haunch of meat from a platter. He bit into it, chewed slowly, and swallowed before speaking again. 'Tell me, Queek, do you remember Sleek Sharpwit? My servant I sent to you to aid in the taking of Karak Azul?'

The question surprised Queek; that had been a long time ago. 'Old-thing?'

Gnawdwell gave him a long, uncomfortable look. 'Is that what you called him? Yes then, Old-thing. He was a great warlord in his day, Queek.'

'Old-thing tell Queek many, many times.'

'Did you believe him?' said Gnawdwell.

Queek did not reply. Old-thing's head had kept on telling Queek how great he had been since Queek had killed him and mounted him on the rack. Skaven lie.

'He was not lying,' said Gnawdwell, as if he could read Queek's thoughts. A shiver of disquiet rippled Queek's fur under his armour. 'When Queek is old, Queek's enemies will laugh at him too because Queek will be too weak to kill them. They will mock and disbelieve, because the memories of skaven are short. They will call you Old-thing. I, Lord Gnawdwell, have seen it many times before. Great warlord, master of steel, undefeated in battle, so arrogant, so sure, brought low by creeping time. Slower, sicker, until he is too old to fight, devoured by his slaves, or slain by the young.'

Gnawdwell smiled a smile of unblemished ivory teeth. 'I am

much older than Sleek was. Why am I so old yet I do not die? Why you do think-wonder? Do you know, Queek?'

'Everyone know,' Queek said quietly. He looked at the small cylinder strapped to Gnawdwell's back. Bronze tubes snaked discreetly over his left shoulder and buried themselves in Gnawdwell's neck. A number of glass windows in the tube allowed observation of a gluey white liquid within, dripping into Gnawdwell's veins.

'Yes!' Gnawdwell nodded. 'The life elixir, the prolonger of being. Each drop the essence of one thousand slaves, distilled in the forge-furnaces of Clan Skryre at ridiculous cost. It is this that allows me to live now, to stay strong. That and the favour of the Horned Rat. For many generations I have been strong and fit. Perhaps you would like to be the same, Queek? Perhaps you would like to live longer and be young forever, so that you might kill-kill more?'

Queek's eyes strayed again to the cylinder.

Gnawdwell chuckled with triumph. 'I smell-sense a yes! And why would you not? Listen then, Queek. Serve me well now, and you may win the chance to serve me well for hundreds of years.'

'What must I do, great one?'

Gnawdwell gestured at the map. 'The Great Uprising goes on. Tilea is destroyed!' He swept aside a collection of model towns carved from wood. 'Estalia followed, then Bretonnia.' He nodded in approval. 'All man-lands, all dead. All ready to accept their new masters.' Many other castles, fleets and cities clattered onto the floor.

'Queek know this.'

'Of course Queek knows,' scoffed Gnawdwell. 'But mighty though Queek is, Queek does not know everything. So Queek will shut up and Queek will listen,' he said with avuncular menace. 'The Great Uprising has been many generations in the planning, and soon the war will at last be over. Clan Pestilens fights to the south, in the jungles of the slann. But the Council is full of fools.

All fight at first sign of success. They do not listen to I, Gnawdwell of Clan Mors, even though I make claim to being the wisest.'

'Yes-yes!' agreed Queek. 'Wiser than the wisest.'

'Do you think so?' Gnawdwell said. 'Listen more carefully, Queek. I make claim to be wise, I said. But I am not so foolish as to believe it. As soon as one completely believes in his ability, Queek, then he is dead.' He scrutinised the warlord. 'Over-confidence is ever the downfall of our kind. Even the wise may overreach themselves. This was Sleek's greatest error. His self-belief.'

'Lord Gnawdwell believes in himself,' said Queek.

'I am one of the Thirteen Lords of Decay, Queek. I am entitled to believe in myself.' He spread his paw fingers and looked at his well-tended claws. 'But I always leave a little room for doubt. Think on the current status of Clan Scruten. The grey seers never doubted themselves. Then the Great Horned One himself came and devoured the fool-squeaker Kritislik.' He tittered, a surprising noise from one so burly. 'It was quite the sight, Queek. Amusing, too. Now no white-furs are meddling in our affairs. They are gone from the Council with their sticky, interfering paws. The Lords are united. For a short while there is an empty seat on the Council, free for the first time in ages. It will not be empty for very long. I intend to put one of our clan allies in that seat.'

'How-how?' said Queek. He struggled to concentrate on all this. He understood all right, but he found intrigue tedious compared to the simple joys of warfare.

'Why do you think you are here, most noted of all skaven generals? Even Paskrit the Vast is an amateur by comparison. Through war, Queek! War on the dwarf-things. We have let them live for too long. They died twenty thousand generations ago, but are too stubborn to admit it. Now is the time to inform them of their demise. We will kill them all. See-look! Learn-fear how deadly skaven are when united!' he squeaked excitedly, his careful mode of speech deserting him momentarily.

'Here.' Lord Gnawdwell pointed at a set of models, these made from iron, sitting on the map. 'Clan Rictus and Clan Skryre have deal-pledged, and attack together the holdfast of Karak Azul.' He gave Queek a penetrating look. 'I think they will be more successful than you. You remember-recall Azul-place, yes, Queek?'

'Queek remembers.'

'Here, Clan Kreepus attacks Kadrin-place. They have raised many-many warptokens in trading man-thing food-slaves. So now Clan Moulder brings much strength to their paws. Many beasts, great and horrible. There, at Zhufbar-place, the dwarf-things have Clan Ferrik to fight.' Gnawdwell's long muzzle twitched dismissively. 'Weak they are, but many rabble clans flock to them, so their numbers are great. Enough to occupy them, if not prevail. Finally, at Barak Varr sea-place, Clan Krepid joined with Clan Skurvy.'

Queek's eyes widened, his expression settling into an appreciative smile. 'All dwarf-things die at same time. They not reinforce each other. They not come-hurry to each other's aid. They all die, all alone.'

'Very good. Tell me, what do you think? Is this good, Queek? Is this bad?'

Queek shuddered. This was so boring! Queek would gladly go to war! Why did Gnawdwell tell him these pointless things? Why? But Queek had wisdom, Queek was canny. Gnawdwell was one of the few living beings he feared to anger, and Gnawdwell would be angry at his thoughts. So he kept his words back. Only his swishing tail gave away his impatience. 'Good-good that we attack everywhere at once. Then all the beard-things sure to die. Bad that Queek not get all the glory. Queek want to kill all the fur-face king-things himself! Queek the best. It not right that other, lesser skaven take trophies that rightfully belong to Queek!'

'You have half the answer, Queek.'

Half? thought Queek. There was no component to his thinking other than Queek.

Gnawdwell sucked his teeth in disappointment. 'It is not only you who matters, but our clan, Queek! Clan Rictus wants to discredit us, yes-yes! Take our glory, take our new seat from our allies. And Clan Skryre and Clan Moulder and Clan Rictus, and all the rest. It was Clan Mors that brought the dwarf-things down first. This is our war to finish!' Gnawdwell slammed his paw onto the table, making his models jump. He gestured at various positions on the map. 'This will not happen. I have taken precautions to ensure our glory. And many of our loyal troops wait with the others. To help, you understand.'

Queek didn't see. Queek didn't really care. Queek nodded anyway. 'Yes-yes, of course.' When could he go? The skin of his legs crawled with irritation.

'They wear the colours of our comrade-friend clans. We do not wish them to be confused, to think, "Why Clan Mors here, when they should not be?"' Gnawdwell mimicked the piping voice of a lesser skaven.

'No. No! That would be most bad.'

Gnawdwell glanced at Queek's thrashing tail. He bared his teeth in a skaven smile.

'You are bored, yes-no? You want to be away, my Queek. You never change.' Gnawdwell walked back to his general and stroked Queek's fur. Queek hissed, but leaned into his master's caress. His eyes shut. 'You wish to kill, hurry-scurry! Stab-stab!'

Queek nodded, a sharp, involuntary movement. Calmness of a type he felt nowhere else came upon him as his master groomed his sleek black fur. The needles of impatience jabbing at his flesh prickled less.

'And you shall!'

Queek's eyes snapped open. He jerked his head back.

'Queek is the best! Queek wish to kill green-things and beard-things! Queek wish to drink their blood and rip their flesh!' He gnashed his incisors. 'Queek do this for Gnawdwell. This is what Gnawdwell wants, yes-yes?'

Gnawdwell turned back to the map. 'You disappoint me, Queek. To be a Lord of Decay is not to stab and kill and smash all things aside. You lack circumspection. You are a killer, nothing more.' Gnawdwell's lips peeled back in disappointment. He stared at his protege a long time, far too long for Queek's thrumming nerves to stand. 'You were so magnificent when I found you, the biggest in your litter, and they were all large before you ate them. I raised you, I fed you the best dwarf-meat and man-flesh. And you have become even more magnificent. Such courage. There is none other like you, Queek. You are unnaturally brave. Others think you freakish for leading from the front, not the back. But I do not. I am proud of my Queek.'

Queek chirred with pride.

Sadness suffused Gnawdwell's face. 'But you are a blunt tool, Queek. A blunt and dangerous tool. I always hoped you would become Lord of Decay after me, because with one so big and so deadly as you as master of Clan Mors, all the others would be afraid, and the air would thicken with their musk.' He sighed deeply, the threads of his clothes creaking as his massive chest expanded. 'But it is not to be. Gnawdwell will remain head of Clan Mors.' He paused meaningfully. 'But maybe Queek can prove me wrong? Perhaps you might change my mind?'

'How-how?' wheedled Queek. He desperately wanted to impress Gnawdwell. Disappointing the Lord of Decay was the only thing Queek truly feared.

'Go to Karak Eight Peaks. Smash the beard-things. But not in Queek's way. Queek has brains – use them! We will bring down their decaying empire and the children of the Horned Rat shall inherit the ruins. I will see that it is Clan Mors that emerges pre-eminent from this extermination. Finish them quickly. Go to help the others complete the tasks they will not be able to finish on their own. Clan Mors must look strong. Clan Mors must be victorious! Bring me the greatest victory of all, Queek. March on Big Mountain-place. It may take years, but if you are successful there... Well, we shall see if you shall age as other lesser skaven must.'

Queek cared nothing for councils. Queek cared nothing for plots and ploys. What Queek cared for was war. Now Gnawdwell spoke a language he could understand. 'Much glory for Queek!'

'Do-accomplish what you do so well, my Queek. Finish the beard-things, and we will shame-embarrass the others when you bring me the head of their white-fur High King and the keys to their greatest city. Clan Mors will be unopposed. We will deliver the final Council seat to our favoured thrall-clan, and then Clan Mors rule all the Under-Empire, all the world!' said Gnawdwell viciously, his speech picking up speed, losing its sophistication, falling into the rapid chitter-chatter used by other skaven. He clenched his fists and rose up. All vestiges of the thoughtful skaven disappeared. A great warrior stood before Queek.

'Queek is the best!' Queek slammed his fist against his armour. 'Queek kill the most-much beard-things! And then,' said Queek, becoming wily, 'Queek get elixir, so Queek not get old-fast and Queek kill-slay more for Lord Gnawdwell?'

Gnawdwell sank back into himself, the fires going out of him. His face reassumed its expression of arrogant calm. 'That is all, Queek. Go-go now. Return to the City of Pillars and finish the war there once and for all. Then you will march upon many-beard-thing Big Mountain-place.'

'But-but,' said Queek. 'Gnawdwell say...'

'Go, Queek. Go now and slay for Clan Mors. You are right – Queek is the greatest. Now show it to the world.' He retreated into the shadows away from the map, towards an exit at the back of the room. A troop of giant, albino skaven, even bigger than the guards of the outer gate and clad in black-lacquered armour, thundered out of garrison burrows either side of Gnawdwell's exit, forming a living wall between Queek and his master. They came to a halt, breathing hard, stinking of hostility.

Queek scurried over to them. They lowered their halberds.

Queek vaulted over the weapons and landed right in front of the white-furs.

'Queek is the greatest,' he hissed in their faces. 'I kill white-fur guards before. How many white-fur guards Queek kill before white-furs kill Queek?' whispered Queek. He was gratified by a faint whiff of fear. 'But Queek not kill white-furs. Queek busy! Queek will do as Lord Gnawdwell commands.' He screech-squeaked over the heads of the unmoving guards, turned upon his heels and strode out.

'Silence be!' screeched Lord Thaumkrittle.

The coven of grey seers stopped arguing and turned to look at their new leader.

'This is not the place to argue and fight. It is much-very bad that Clan Scruten is no longer on the Council, worse that our god has shown his disapproval. We must work to regain the favour of the Horned Rat.'

More than one emission of fear's musk misted the air. The grey seers chittered nervously.

'We are his chosen! We bear his horns and have his powers!' said Jilkin the Twisted, his horns painted red and carved with spell-wards. 'This all a trick by Clan Mors, or Clan Skryre! Tinker-rats want all our magic for themselves.'

'No. That was the Horned Rat himself, not some machine-born conjuring trick,' said another, Felltwitch. He was older than many, tall and rangy. One of his horns was missing, reduced to a stump by a sword swing long ago. 'And we have disappointed him.'

'It not our fault,' said Kranskritt, once favoured among the other clans, now as despised as the rest. 'Other clans plot and scheme against us, make us look bad to the master.'

'Yes-yes!' squeaked others. 'Traitors everywhere. Not our fault!'

'No,' said the old Felltwitch. 'It is our fault, and only our fault.'

He stepped around in a slow circle, leaning on his blackwood staff. 'If we blame-curse other clans, we not learn anything.'

'What to do? What to do?' said Kreekwik, marked out by his deep-red robes. 'Grey Seer Felltwitch squeak-says we have failed? How to *unfail* the Great Horned One? Will any more grey seers be born? Are we the last?'

Panic rushed through the room, forest-fire quick, taking hold of each grey seer's limbs and sending them into a storm of tail lashing and twitching. Pent up magic added its own peculiar smell to the thick scent of the room.

'We should pray,' said Kranskritt. 'We are his priests and his prophets. Pray for forgiveness.'

'We should act,' said Felltwitch.

'Let us wait them out!' said Scritchmaw. 'We live much longer than they.'

'It is not possible. Clan Skryre has the secret of longevity-life elixir. Lords of Decay live too long – no one lives longer than they. No waiting, no waiting!' said Thaumkrittle. He too was nervous. It was one thing to become chief of Clan Scruten, another to become chief immediately after their god had eaten the previous incumbent. Thaumkrittle was on edge, his emotional state veering between great pride at his elevation and a suspicion that he had only got the job because no one else dared to take it.

'We have lost-squandered the favour of the Great Horned One! What are we to do?' said Kranskritt, the many bells on his arms, wrists, ankles and horns rattling.

'Win it back! Win it back!'

'How do you propose to do that?' A familiar voice came from the back of the room. The entire assembly turned to look. There, at the back, Boneripper hulking behind him, was Thanquol.

'Grey Seer Thanquol!' shrieked Kreekwik.

'It is him! All this is his fault!' said Kranskritt.

A hiss of hatred went up from every seer present. Magical auras fizzed into life. Eyes glowed.

'How my fault-guilt?' said Thanquol, as calmly as he could. 'Many times I am this close to victory.' He held his fingers a hair's-breadth apart. 'But treachery of other clans stop my winning. They are all at fault. It is not me, friends-colleagues. Not me at all!'

Thaumkrittle shook his head, sending the copper triskeles depending from his horn tips swinging. 'You clever-squeaker, Thanquol. Always it is the same. Always it is the lies. Always we believe. Not this time. The Horned Rat himself came forth at the meeting and devoured our leader.' Thaumkrittle pointed his staff directly at Thanquol. 'Fool-thing! We no longer pay listen-heed to your squeak-talk. Go from here! Go!'

'Yes-yes, go-go!' the others chittered.

'You will listen to me,' said Thanquol. 'Listen to my speakings. I have a way!'

'No!' shouted Kreekwik. 'Squeak-talk of Thanquol grandiose lies.'

'Cast him out!' said Felltwitch. 'Cast him out! Banish him!'

Light fled and shadows deepened as each and every grey seer began to cast a spell, bringing a taste of rot and brimstone.

'No-no!' said Thanquol. He backed up to the door, only to find it inexplicably locked. He cursed the guards he'd bribed to let him in. Cornered, he summoned his own magic.

Boneripper. Boneripper was there. Sensing his master's peril, the rat ogre snarled out a thunderous roar and ran at the other seers, chisel-incisors bared.

A dozen beams of warp-lightning intersected on his powerfully muscled body. They flayed the skin from his chest, but Boneripper kept on coming. The muscle underneath smoked. Still he kept on coming. He reached the first grey seer and reached forwards with a mighty claw. Green fire blazed from the seer's eyes, reducing the rat ogre's hand to ash. He roared in anger, not in pain, for Boneripper was incapable of feeling pain. He punched forwards with one of his remaining fists, but this was snared in a rope of shadow and teeth that fastened themselves into his flesh.

'No-no!' Thanquol shrieked. He countered as many spells as he could, draining magic away from his peers, but there were too many. His glands clenched.

With a mighty howl, Boneripper was dragged to his knees. Magic writhed all over him, burning and tearing pieces from him. Jilkin the Twisted, a particularly spiteful seer, reached the end of his convoluted incantation. He hurled an orb of purple fire at the injured construct, engulfing its wounded arm. The fire burned bright, then collapsed inwards into warp-black with a sucking noise.

Boneripper roared, his arm turning into a slurry of oily goo, which fountained over the other seers. A deafening thunder-clap of magical feedback had them squeaking in agony. Many were blasted to the floor by the sudden interruption of their own sorcery.

When they got up, horned heads shaking out the ringing in their sensitive ears, they were grinning evilly.

'No-no! Wait-wait!' chittered Thanquol as they advanced on him. 'Listen-hear my idea!' He looked to them imploringly. 'I am your friend. I was master to many of you. Please! Listen!'

Thaumkrittle drew himself up. 'Grey Seer Thanquol, you are expelled-exiled from Clan Scruten. You will scurry from this place and never return.'

The other rats fell on him, sharp claws tearing, teeth working at his clothes, ripping his robes and charms from his body. Thanquol panicked. Drowning in a sea of hateful fur, he felt his glands betray him, drenching him in the shame of his own fear.

'No-no, listen! We must... Argh! We must summon a vermin-lord, ask them what to do! We are the prophets of the Horned Rat! Let us ask-query his daemons how to pass this trial-test he has set us.'

The seers hoisted Thanquol onto their shoulders and bore him from the room. The door's sorcerous locks clanked and whirred at their approach, the great bars rattling back into their housings.

The night of Skavenblight greeted Thanquol indifferently as he was hurled bodily into it, followed shortly after by the embrace of the mud of the street.

Thanquol groaned and rolled over. Unspeakable filth caked him.

'Please!' he shouted, raising a hand to the closing doors.

They stopped. Thanquol's tail swished hopefully.

Thaumkrittle's head poked out of the crack, the head of his staff protruding below his chin. At least, thought Thanquol, they were still wary of him.

'If you return, once-seer Thanquol, we will take-saw your horns,' Thaumkrittle said.

The large, messy figure of Boneripper was flung out magically after him. Thanquol barely dodged aside as the unconscious rat ogre slapped into the mud.

The door clanged shut. Thanquol snivelled, but his self-pity lasted only seconds before self-preservation kicked in. Interested red eyes already watched from the shadows. To show any sign of weakness in Skavenblight was to invite death.

'What you look-see?' he snapped, getting to his feet unsteadily. 'I Thanquol! I great seer. You better watch it, or I cook you from inside.'

He set off a shower of sparks from his paws, then stopped. The light showed his beaten, dishevelled state all too clearly. The shadows drew nearer.

Clutching the remains of his robes to preserve his modesty, Thanquol checked over his bodyguard. Boneripper had lost two of his arms and much flesh, but his heart still beat. He could be repaired. Thanquol spent some time rousing the construct, his head twitching with intense paranoia this way and that. But though his glands were slack, his heart hardened. Eventually, the rat ogre hauled itself to its feet. To Thanquol's relief, there suddenly appeared to be a lot fewer shadows in the street.

'If Clan Scruten does not want me, then maybe Clan Skryre will,' he said to himself. With all the haste he could manage, he headed off to their clan hall.

Inside the Temple of the Grey Seers, dull-eyed skaven and human slaves mopped at the mess that had been part of Boneripper. The grey seers resumed their places and recommenced their debate.

'I have an idea,' said Jilkin. 'Let us summon a verminlord.'

'That great idea,' said Kreekwik. 'Ask-beg the great ones from beyond the veil.'

'Yes-yes,' said Thaumkrittle up on his platform. 'A great idea of mine. I am very clever. That why I your new leader-lord, yes? So, who want to follow my great idea and speak-pray to the Horned Rat for one of his servants?'

The grey seers looked at one another. Such blatant claiming of Jilkin's suggestion was majestic. They could respect that.

'Of course, O most mighty and powerful caller of magics,' Kranskritt said. He bowed.

The others followed.

THREE

Karak Eight Peaks

Skarsnik, the King under the Mountains, looked out over the greenskin shanty town filling the dwarf surface city. In ruined streets, between ramshackle huts of wood and hide, raucous orcs drank and fought one another. Goblins squealed and tittered. On the slopes of scree studded with broken statuary, snotlings gambolled, throwing stones at passing greenskins, oblivious to the cold that turned their noses pink.

Autumn was halfway through, and the first flakes of the year's snow already drifted on the wind.

Skarsnik shivered and pulled his wolf pelt closer about him. He was old now – how old he wasn't quite sure, for goblins took less care in reckoning the years than men or dwarfs did. But he felt age as surely as he felt the grip of Gork and Mork on his destiny. He felt it in his bandy legs, in his creaking knees and hips. His skin was gnarled and scabbed, thick as tree bark, and he leaned more often on his famous prodder for support than he would have liked. His giant cave squig, Gobbla, snuffled about around his feet, equally aged. Patches of his skin had turned a pinkish-grey, for he was almost as old as his master.

Skarsnik wondered how long he had left. It was ironic, he thought, that after years of wondering whether it would be a skaven blade or dwarf axe that finished him, it would be neither. Time was the enemy no one could fight.

In truth, no one knew how old a goblin could get because they did not usually last that long. Most of them would not even consider dying of old age. Skarsnik considered lots of unusual things because Skarsnik was no ordinary goblin, and what went on in his head would have been entirely alien to other greenskins. Lately, old age had occupied Skarsnik's thoughts a lot.

'Must be fifty winters and more I seen. Fifty!' he cackled. 'And here's another come on again. Still, stunty, I reckon I got another few to come.' Skarsnik was all alone on the balcony, save for a couple of mangy skaven skins and several dwarf heads in various states of decay, spiked along the broken balustrade. It was to his favourite, its eyes long ago pecked out, skin desiccated black in the dry mountain air, nose rotted away, that he addressed his words. A sorry-looking head, but even in death it had a magnificent beard. Skarsnik liked to stroke it when no one was looking. 'Duffskul's still knocking about, and he's well older than me.'

He grumbled and spat, muttering thoughts that not one of his underlings would understand, and drew his long chin into his stinking furs.

'What a bleeding mess, eh, stunty? Them zogging ratties done driven me out of me stunty-house. I am not happy about that, no, not one little bitty bit.'

He looked forlornly at the ruinous gatehouse marking the grand entry to the Hall of a Thousand Pillars, heart of the first of Karak Eight Peaks's many deeps. 'Once upon a time, stunty, that was mine. And everything under it. Not any more. On the other side of the great doors I won one of me greatest victories, and the stunty-house was me kingdom for dozens of levels down. Think about that, eh? Kept hold of it longer than your lot did, I reckon!' His laugh turned into a hacking cough. He wiped his mouth with the back of his hand. His next words came out all raspy. 'Gobboes, beat them all and sorted them out. Ratties. Beat them, and then I beat them, and then I blew them up, drowned them and beat 'em some more. Stunties came back. Beat them too,' said Skarsnik wistfully, looking across at the citadel that dominated the heart of the city. 'Look at that will you, stunty! That's all your king's got. Nuffink. I'm the king around here. I am. Right?'

He paused. The dwarf's beard stirred in the wind. Fat, wet flakes of snow splatted against its taut skin. It was coming down thicker, and the temperature was dropping.

'Well, I'm glad you agree.'

Not that that changed anything. Skarsnik was still dispossessed, and he was not happy about it. He watched another tribe of greenskins straggling into orctown from the west gate. His eyes narrowed, calculating. They were weedy little 'uns, worn by hard travels. Within seconds of coming into the gate they were rapidly set upon by orcs and bigger goblins, who stole everything they had, leaving them naked and shivering in the cold. 'Always more where they came from,' whispered Skarsnik. 'Always more.'

'Ahem!' A high-pitched cough demanded Skarsnik's attention. Behind him, standing ramrod straight, was his herald, pointy hood standing as diligently to attention as its owner.

'What you want, Grazbok?' said Skarsnik, squinting at the small goblin. The sky was overcast, brilliant grey with pending snow, and the glare of it hurt his eyes. 'You keep sneaking up on me like that, I'll have to send you out scouting for ratties. And you,' he said, kicking Gobbla in the side with a leathery *thwap,* 'are losing your touch.'

Gobbla snuffled and waddled off, the chain connecting him to Skarsnik's leg rattling as he licked scraps of dried dwarf flesh from the floor. Grazbok gave Skarsnik a sidelong look that suggested he was going to make more noise next time.

'Your highnessness,' the herald squeaked, 'I have da great Griff Kruggler here to sees ya!'

Skarsnik's lips split in a wide grin, yellow as the moon talismans dangling from his pointy hat. 'Kruggs, eh? Send him up! Send him up!'

Kruggler was a long time coming up the steps from the halls under the Howlpeak. A pained wheezing came first, followed by the click of unsteady claws on stone.

Skarsnik's eyes widened as Kruggler came out into the pale day upon the back of a staggering wolf. He had become fat. Enormously, disgustingly fat. His wolf mount gasped under him as it heaved itself up onto the balcony. Kruggler swung his leg over its back – with some difficulty – and slid to the flagstones. The wolf let out a huff of relief, dragged itself off into a corner and collapsed.

'Been a long time, boss,' said Kruggler.

Skarsnik took in the rolls of flab, the massive hat and the greasy gold trinkets festooning his underling.

'What the zog happened to you?'

Kruggler was abashed. 'Well, you know, living's been good...'

'You is almost as fat as that... what was he called? That boss. That one I killed of yours?'

'Makiki, the Great Grizzler-Griff.'

'Yeah! Only thing great about him was his size.' Skarsnik laughed at his own joke. Kruggler just looked puzzled. Skarsnik scowled at his confusion. Trouble was, Skarsnik was a lot brighter than every other greenskin he'd ever met. It was depressing. 'Gah, suit yerself. How you been?'

Kruggler pulled a face. 'Not good, boss, to tell da truth.'

'And there you was saying living was good.'

Kruggler looked confused. 'Well, I did, er – well, it was, boss, it was. But things... well, they is not no good no more.'

'What do you mean? Look at all these greenies come to join the Waaagh! Good times, Kruggs, good times. Soon there'll be enough to kick the ratties out and take back the upper halls!'

Kruggs gave him a puzzled look.

'Stop looking so zogging thick, Kruggs! Did I make an idiot king of all the Badlands wolf tribes?'

'Well, er, no, boss, but...'

'Go on, go on, spit it out!'

'Well, I said things is no good,' said Kruggler anguishedly. 'I mean it! Dead things everywhere, fighting each other. Dwarfs on the march, fire mountains spitting fire and such. And the ratties, boss. The ratties is all over the place! I ain't see so many, not ever. They's taking over the stunty-houses, all of 'em, and not just a few. They's slaughtering the tribes wherever they find 'em. Something big's happening, something–'

Skarsnik was nose to nose with Kruggler before the plains goblin realised he'd moved. Skarsnik's sour breath washed over his face.

'Careful there, Kruggs. Don't want you starting to bang on about the end of the world. Had a bit too much of that kind of talk lately from a few too many of the lads. Everything's going on as normal here. We fight the rats, the rats fight the stunties, the stunties fight us, got it?'

Kruggler made a funny noise in his throat. 'Got it, boss.'

'Good.' Skarsnik turned away from his vassal. 'So what's you saying then, Kruggs? You think they's going to come here too? Better not, because they'll have old Skarsnik to deal with and I–' He coughed mightily. The fit held him for a minute, his hunchback shoulders shaking with it. Kruggler looked around, his tiny goblin mind torn between helping his boss, stabbing him, and wondering if there was anyone that could see him do either. Paralysed by indecision, he just stood and watched.

Skarsnik hawked up a gob of stringy phlegm and spat it onto a skaven hide rotting on a frame. 'Because if they do, they'll have me to deal with, and I ain't no bleeding stunty! Anyways, look at all them. They's come here to help *me*. They hears I'm the baddest and the bestest. Old Belegar and his mates up there in his stupid tower might have done for old Rotgut, but he can't get me, can he? No zogging ratty or stunty is kicking me out of these mountains, you hear? You hear!'

He shouted loudly, his nasal voice echoing from the ruins of the dwarf surface city. Orcs and goblins looked up at him. Some cheered, some jeered. Some wandered off, uncaring.

'See, with this lot coming to join da Waaagh! I'll kick them ratties out and take it all back for good.'

Skarsnik had, of course, said this many, many times before. But it never happened. The balance of power between the greenskins and skaven swung backwards and forwards viciously; sometimes the goblins had the upper hand, sometimes the skaven – sometimes the stunties stuck their beards in for good measure. So it had been for time immemorial. But lately that had been changing. Skarsnik would never have admitted it to anyone but Gobbla, but each time he was victorious, he was able to hold less of the city, and for shorter periods of time.

'But, boss! Boss!' said a dismayed Kruggler. Cowardice nearly made him stop, but his loyalty to Skarsnik ran deep. He was one of the few who could tell the warlord what he didn't want to hear. At least that's how it'd been in the old days, and he really hoped it was that way still because he couldn't stop himself. He plunged on, gabbling faster as his panic built. 'They're not here to help you, boss. They ain't here for no Waaagh! That's what I'm trying to tell you, boss.'

Skarsnik's prodder swung round and was pointed at Kruggler's face. Green light glinted along its three prongs. His expression became vicious. 'There you go again! What do you mean? End of the world is it, Kruggs, because if you keeps it up, it will be for you.'

Kruggler held his hands up. He leaned back from the prodder so far his boss helmet slipped from his head to clang on the floor. 'I means, boss, they is coming here because they knows you is here and you is da best.'

'Exactly, exactly!' said Skarsnik. He put the prodder up and nodded with satisfaction.

'Yeah, boss. Yeah,' said Kruggler with relief. 'You is the cleverest. I knew you'd be clever and see.' He came to stand next to Skarsnik and looked out. He smiled idiotically. 'They isn't coming here to fight. They think you can protect them! They is running away.'

Kruggler realised what he had said and clapped his hands over his mouth, but the fight had gone out of Skarsnik. He was staring out into the thickening snow at something Kruggler could not see.

'We'll see about that, we'll see,' he said sullenly.

A couple of miles away over the orc-infested ruins, King Belegar, the *other* king of Karak Eight Peaks, looked out into the gathering storm, engaged in his own contemplation. Abandon the hold indeed. Thorgrim's request dogged his thoughts still. But now, six months later, a small part of him feared that the High King might have been right...

Like Skarsnik, Belegar was troubled by what he saw. Something dreadful was afoot.

He pounded his mailed fist on the rampart of the citadel, causing his sentries to turn to look at him. He huffed into his beard, shaking his head at their concerns, although he was secretly pleased at their vigilance.

'Something dreadful is afoot,' he said to his companion, his first cousin once removed and banner bearer, Thane Notrigar.

'How do you know, my liege?'

'You can stop it with that "my liege" business, Notrigar. You're my cousin's son and an Angrund. Even if you weren't, we've fought back to back more times than I care to recall. Besides,' he added gloomily, 'a dawi has to be a real king to get the full "my liege" treatment.'

'But you are a real king, my liege!' said Notrigar, taken aback.

'Am I?' said Belegar. He gestured into the snowstorm, now so thick it had whited out everything further away than one hundred paces from the citadel walls. 'King Lunn was the last real king of this place. History will remember that it was he, not I.'

'There will be many more after you, my liege,' said Notrigar. 'A long and glorious line! Thorgrim is a grand lad. He is coming into his own with every day. You could not wish for a finer son, and he'll be a fine king, when the time comes.'

Belegar was mollified for a moment. 'A fine king, but one of rubble and ruination. And he needs to wed, and sire his own heir. Who will have him, the beggar king of Eight Peaks?'

'But my liege! You are a hero to every dawi lass and lad. Send him back to Everpeak and there you shall have dawi rinn of every clan begging for his hand.'

'What did I say to you? Belegar will do, lad. Or cousin, if you must.'

Notrigar, although now many years in the Eight Peaks, did not feel he knew his cousin well at all, raised as he had been in distant Karaz-a-Karak. Belegar was a legend to him, a hero. He could not countenance calling him by his name, cousin or not. He settled on 'my lord.'

'Yes, my lord,' he said.

Belegar rolled his eyes. 'Beardlings today,' he said, although Notrigar was well past his majority and a thane in his own right. 'All right, all right, "my lord" if it makes you feel better.'

'Thank you, my lord.'

'Don't mention it. What you said, just then. That's the problem, isn't it? He'd have to go back. He'd have to risk the journey. It took me nigh on four months to get to Karaz-a-Karak for the kingsmeet and back, and that in the summer. Things are worse now, mark my words. What if he's taken by grobi or urk? What if the thaggoraki steal him away. Then that'll be that, won't it? What we've all fought so hard for gone. A kingdom of ruins with no king. Fifty years! Fifty years! Gah!' He punched the stone again. His Iron Hammers had more sense and honour than to mutter, but they exchanged dark looks. 'When Lunn was king, this was still the finest city in all of the Karaz Ankor. What is it now, Notrigar? Ruins. Ruins swarming with grobi and thaggoraki, with more coming every day.'

'But you have been here for fifty years, my lord. You are successful.' Notrigar had never dreamed to see his lord and kin in such poor temper, or to confide in him in such an open and upsetting manner. He did not know quite what to say. Reassurance did not come naturally to a dwarf.

'Right. Here I am in my glorious castle,' Belegar said sarcastically. 'I came here hoping to take it all back. I came hoping to look upon the far deeps, on the ancestor statues of the Abyss of Iron's Dream. I dreamed of opening up the Ungdrin again, so that armies might freely march between my, Kazador's and Thorgrim's realms. I dreamed of reopening the mines, of filling the coffers of our clan with gold and jewels.'

They both became a little misty-eyed at this image.

'But no. A few weapons hordes, a few treasure rooms and a lot of failure. We can't even keep our master brewer safe,' he said, referring to one of the more recent entries in Karak Eight Peaks's Book of Grudges. 'Six months since the damn furskins took Yorrik and I've not had a decent pint since.'

'We have the will and the resolve, my–'

'You've not read the reports, have you?' said Belegar. 'Not seen what the rangers are saying, or what those new-fangled machines of Brakki Barakarson are saying.'

'The seismic indicators, my lord?'

'Aye, that's them. Scratchy needles. Thought it was all a lot of modern rubbish, to tell you the truth. But he's been right more than he's been wrong. There's a lot going on underground, down in the lower deeps. Never did get very far on the way to the bottom. Grungni alone knows how many tunnels the thaggoraki have chiselled out down there. Gyrocopters coming in, telling me every inch of Mad Dog Pass is crawling with ogres, grobi and urk. No message from half the holds in months, no safe road out, and no safe road in. I'll bet that little green kruti Skarsnik is out there right now too, standing on the parapets of Karag Zilfin looking over at us as we look over at him. It's been that way for far too long. If it only weren't for that little bloody...' He trailed off into a guttural collection of strong dwarfish oaths. 'One enemy,' he said, holding up a finger. 'I think I could have handled one. If it weren't for him I'd have driven the grobi off years ago and cleared the skaven out of the top deeps. Trust me to get saddled with the sneakiest little green bozdok who ever walked the earth.' He sighed, pursing his lips so that his beard and moustaches bristled. 'And now it's all gone quiet. Too bloody quiet. I'll tell you what this silence is, Notrigar.'

'What is it, my lord?' said Notrigar, for Belegar was waiting to be prompted.

'It's the beginning of the end, that's what it is. Or so those thaggoraki probably think.'

Notrigar looked around for help. The ironbreakers, hammerers and thunderers manning the ramparts were staring studiously off into the middle distance. He raised a hand, started to speak, then thought better of it. To Notrigar's dismay, the king began to hiccup, his chest heaving.

'My lord?' said Notrigar. Oh Grungni, thought the thane, please don't let him be... crying? Belegar's shoulders heaved, and he turned away. Notrigar reached an uncertain hand out for his kinsman.

He leapt back as Belegar burst out laughing, a sound as sudden and surprising as an avalanche, and to the unnerved Notrigar, just as terrifying. The king's mirth rolled out from the ramparts, wildly bellicose, as if it could retake Vala-Azrilungol all on its own.

'That's right, you green bozdoks! King Belegar is laughing at you, and you, you vicious thaggoraki! I am laughing at you too!' he bellowed. His shout was blunted by the snow, the lack of echo unsettling to Notrigar, but Belegar did not care. The king wiped a tear of mirth from his eye, flicking it and a finger's worth of snow crystals away from his moustache. He clapped his arm around his cousin, his face creased with a grim smile. 'Oh don't look so glum, lad. I've always been a sucker for a lost cause, me. We'll show them, eh? We can hold out. We always have, keeping our heads down until more reinforcements come and the bloody fun can start all over again. They'll never get through the fortifications we're planning, no matter how many of the little furry grunkati come – there'll be a trap for each and every one of them, eh, lad? Don't worry, I haven't gone zaki. You see, lad, you have to know what you're fighting, and be certain you're not underestimating it before you can crush it. Once you know what's what, nothing is impossible, and you can shout your cries of victory right in the face of your enemy. Furry or green, or in our case both, it doesn't matter, lad. This is the Eternal Realm. We'll never fall.'

'Yes, my lord.' The other dwarfs were chuckling at their king's good humour, laughing at Notrigar for not seeing the joke. Belegar's arm was like a stone lintel on his shoulders. Notrigar had a sudden urge for an ale. A strong one.

'That's right!' Belegar bawled, making Notrigar's ears ring. 'I'll be ready for you, Skarsnik! Send everything you've got. It will never, ever be enough. Cheer up, Notrigar. Why,' said Belegar, 'I'm just beginning to enjoy meself.'

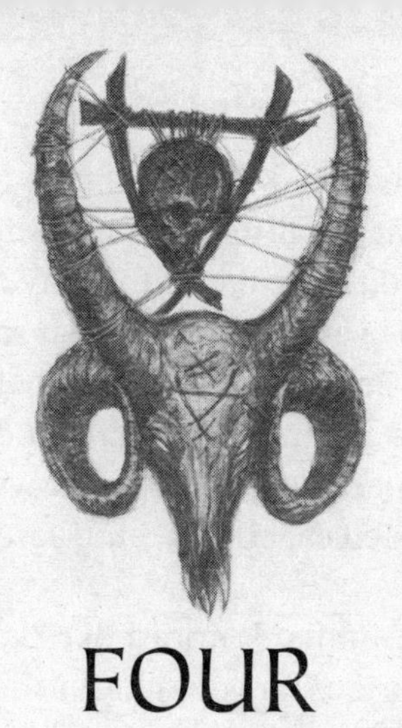

FOUR

The City of Pillars

The upper deeps of Karak Eight Peaks were heaving with warm fur. Every corner, every cranny, from the Trench at the very bottom to the Hall of a Thousand Pillars once inhabited by Skarsnik and his lackeys. The noise of so many ratmen's squeaks and pattering feet close together merged into a sussuration so pervasive the very rocks seemed to be speaking with skaven voices.

Within the Hall of a Thousand Pillars, atop the pinnacle that had once housed the dwarf king's throne, and for fifty years until recently that of Skarsnik, Queek inspected the first clawpack of the warhost of Clan Mors, and he was not happy about it.

Queek paced up and down as block after block after block of skaven marched out of the tunnels around the base of the soaring throne pinnacle, wove their way through the forest of pillars and went back out again, banners waving, their leaders proudly bringing up the rear.

'How long this going to take? Queek bored,' said Queek. 'This boring!'

Thaxx Redclaw twitched his armoured neck, briefly exposing a patch of fur at his throat. He was the leader of the first clawpack, and appointed ruler of the City of Pillars in Queek's absence. With such overlap between their roles, Thaxx felt especially vulnerable. 'Great and deadly Queek, you are best and most perspicacious general! A cunning and mighty war-leader such as the incomparable Queek would want to inspect-smell troops?' Thaxx nodded eagerly, inviting agreement. He received a cold stare.

'There are many,' added Warlord Skrikk, Queek's supposed right claw. 'How glorious for your gloriousness to feast nose and eye on such an army, all gathered solely for you, O great and deadly, violent Queek!'

'Dull! Boring! Queek see hundreds of thousands of millions of skaven in his life,' snapped Queek. 'They all the same. Furry faces, pink noses. Some die, all die. There are always more. What need mighty Queek see all rat-faces?'

Thaxx snickered and bobbed his head, a poor attempt to hide his fear. The other clanlords atop the dais, out of Queek's sight, backed away until they ran into Queek's Red Guard and the massive body of Queek's chief lieutenant, Ska Bloodtail. He stared down at them and shook his head.

'But mighty Queek, O most cunning and stabby of all ratkin, how will stupid warrior-things know how to follow mighty Queek's orders if glorious warlord is not there? See how their faces look upon your most awesome countenance with fear and, er, awe,' said Thaxx.

'You speak-squeak badly, Thaxx. Too long running this city without mighty Queek to keep you in your place. All things scared of Queek! Why is this useful for Queek to see-smell what he already knows?'

Skrikk and Thaxx glanced at each other.

'There are questions of strategy and disposition, great fierce one,' ventured Warlord Skrikk.

'Oh? Oh? Strategy and disposition for Queek. Forgive ignorant Queek for asking, what use is there for you in this case?' said Queek. 'Gnawdwell say you Queek's right claw.' Queek narrowed his eyes. 'Gnawdwell write-say "Take Skrikk! He your right claw!" Queek says he already has right claw. It good for holding Dwarf Gouger!' He held up his paw and clenched it. 'And Queek has Ska! Loyal, good Ska! So, Queek has two right claws. One for Dwarf Gouger, one for punching enemies. But Gnawdwell order Queek needs *another* right claw, so Queek obey. Queek think, maybe Skrikk good! Maybe Skrikk good for boring things, boring things that tire Queek and make him angry. Boring things like counting skaven clanrats.' He leaned in close to the clanlords and twisted his head to regard them one at a time, causing them both to flinch. 'But now Skrikk squeak-says, "Queek must think strategy!" What? Queek fight. Queek command. Queek does not count stupid-meat.'

Skrikk hunched over, looking sideways at Queek nervously.

'Who Skrikk think he is? Queek does think strategy, stupid-meat. Queek greatest warlord there is! Queek think-scheme peerless battle plans. Queek the best strategist you will ever meet, weak-meat. You will see. But what does Queek need to know colours of every stupid-meat rat-flag for if he has Skrikk? Too much pointless knowing clouds Queek's mind.' He leaned back with a dangerous look in his eyes. He greatly relished the fear in Skrikk's. 'If Skrikk can't count or Skrikk can't see-smell clan banners and tell Queek how many rats, how many slaves, how many clan-things and Moulder-things left before Queek run out of battle-meat for victory, perhaps Queek not need Skrikk after all? Queek be very unhappy if Queek has to do all counting and scritch-scratching himself.'

'O mighty one is correct!' squeaked Skrikk, far more shrilly than he had intended. 'Skrikk count. Skrikk has counted very well! I have noted all banners and numbers. See-read!' He beckoned a slave bearing a pile of dwarf-skin scrolls forward. The warlords at least had the will to clench their musk glands, terrified of Queek as they were. But the slave shook uncontrollably, and the fear-stink was heavy on his fur. 'See-look. Skrikk make all these himself. All is in order. I have everything written down so I know, mighty Queek. And what humble, unworthy Skrikk knows, most cunning Queek can know too! By asking! By asking!' he added in a panic. 'Of course you should not weary your piercing eyes reading such dull-tedious reports.' He shooed the skavenslave away and bowed repeatedly.

Something big in the parade let out a long, mournful low. There were many Moulder-things in the army.

'Battle-meat, battle-meat to get Queek close to the beard-things. Five thousand, ten thousand, one hundred thousand, it not matter to Queek,' Queek muttered. He stared at the skaven tramping by and became suddenly still. He no longer saw the troops. In his mind, he watched images of past slaughter.

The others cringed, each subtly trying to be the rat at the back of the crowd, but not too close to the giant Ska. When Queek's constant twitching stilled, someone usually died.

Queek clenched his fists and rounded on them all. 'Bah! This place still stink-smell of goblin-thing. Queek hate it. Queek still smell Skarsnik-thing squatting on his throne.' He pointed to where Skarsnik's throne had once been. 'It so strong, Queek see him!' His quick red eyes darted about, taking in the goblin's defacement of the giant statues lining the walls of the Hall of a Thousand Pillars. The goblins' shanty had been cleared, but signs of the greenskins were everywhere. What wreckage had not already been scavenged was still piled along the walls. Every inch of the place stank of goblin. He longed to kill green-things. He stared at the great dwarf gates to the surface city, opening mechanisms improved with skaven engines by the tinker-rats. On the other side of the doors were thousands and thousands of greenskins. One word would open the gates and the relief of battle could be his. Somewhere out there was Skarsnik, and he hated Skarsnik more than anything else in the world. Killing dwarfs was business, but his feud with the green-thing king was personal. His muzzle quivered with temptation.

'Gnawdwell's orders, remember Gnawdwell's orders!' squeaked the voice of Ikit Scratch from his skeleton impaled upon Queek's back. 'Kill beard-things first, green-things later.'

'Queek go now,' he said quietly, 'before he choke on Skarsnik stink. What new boring thing has Thaxx and Skrikk to show mighty Queek?'

They had more of the same to show him, but neither dared say. 'To the fourth and fifth deeps, O wicked and savage Queek,' said Thaxx, spreading his arms and bowing low. 'To the second and third clawpacks, who await your merciless majesty with much fear and anticipation.'

'Yes-yes,' added Skrikk, not to be outdone. 'They are rightwise awestruck.' The three-week journey here from Skavenblight had been somewhat detrimental to his nerves, and he jumped every time he thought Thaxx bettered him in flattery.

Three days it took to see the next two clawpacks. Queek only stopped to eat – which he did savagely and messily – or to sleep, which he did in short, rapid-breathed bursts. The finest burrows were set aside for him, the best flesh-meat. He did not care.

Much to his annoyance, nobody tried to kill him. His legs spasmed with impatience when he lay down. His hands itched to hold Dwarf Gouger. Everyone around him feared his fury. Murder was imminent, they were sure. Each warlord and clan chief he greeted showed their necks and squeaked in most pitiable homage. Each one half expected to die. Thaxx and Skrikk had it worst by far, for they had to accompany Queek everywhere. They were both sure it was only a matter of time before Queek killed one or the other, and their attempts to outdo each other in their obsequiousness became more outrageous by the hour. Their wheedling only angered Queek more.

But no one did die. They could all see-smell Queek was bursting with the need to kill, but he raised a paw against no one.

'Steady, steady,' said the dead beard-thing Krug to Queek. 'You muff this up, lad, and you'll not be getting Gnawdwell's potion.'

'The beard-thing is correct, mad-thing,' added Sleek Sharpwit's annoying voice. 'Be careful, or you will perish.'

Queek shot Sleek's fleshless skull a murderous glare. 'Do not call Queek mad-thing, dead Old-thing!'

'Steady!' said Krug. 'Steady.'

'Yes-yes,' mumbled Queek, cradling the dwarf king's skull to his chest one sleep. 'Krug right, Krug wise! Time only enemy Queek cannot kill. Only Gnawdwell help with that.'

'And so the mad-thing listens to the dead dwarf, but not to the wisdom of the living. You are a poor warlord, Queek, no match for me at my peak,' said Sleek.

'I alive, you dead. I better,' said Queek acidly.

And so Queek set all his will to restraining his considerable temper, resolving to add Thaxx and Skrikk's heads to his trophy rack in due course.

Clawpacks two and three were led by Skrak and Ikk Hackflay, ex-lieutenants from Queek's Red Guard. These stormvermin were known to him, and respected by him as much as he could respect any skaven. They were braver than most, and Queek was almost civil to them, bringing much prestige to their names. For all his hatred of machination, he changed the status of skaven simply by looking at them wherever he went. This in turn upset alliances and friendships, led to back-stabbings and new pledge-bonds. His passage through the ancient dwarf city rippled outwards, rewriting the architecture of treachery and false promises that underpinned any skaven society.

He was aware of it, but tried his best not to think about it. It only made him angrier.

Clawpacks two and three were much like the first. The second bigger than the third, half of each made up of Clan Mors warriors, the rest a selection of scruffy rabble clans.

'Queek not see-smell slaves. Where slaves?' he demanded shortly after visiting the third clawpack.

'This way, O most terrible one!' said Thaxx.

They cut across the city in the fourth deep, emerging below the stone-pile the beard-things called Karag Rhyn, and the goblins White Fang. There were many long tubular caves deep below this mountain, each carpeted with bones, some full to the ceiling with brittle skeletons. Queek looked repeatedly to the curved roof. Up there, somewhere, was Skarsnik. The imp had taken refuge in the northern range after finally, *finally* being chased out from the deeps. Queek sighed happily as he imagined gnawing his way up through the rock, to emerge in the imp-thing's own room, where he would bite him to death. He tittered to himself, but his amusement turned to anger as the scenario's impossibility rudely intruded. Queek's tail flicked in agitation.

Laired in the bone caves were so many skavenslaves that Queek could not count them. He was dizzy on their scent. They shrank back into side tunnels at his approach, tripping over their chains to get out of his way, their eyes downcast.

'There is many-many slave-meat?' he asked, peering into a tunnel packed full of eyes glinting as they looked away.

Thaxx and Skrikk fought to be the one to deliver the information.

'Over one hundred thousand, O lordly Queek!' said Thaxx, cutting Skrikk dead. 'We have bred them especially quickly, raising them in unprecedented time with black–'

'Many are from Thaxx's breeding pits, masterful Queek,' butted in Skrikk. 'He must be so proud, to make so many weak-meat for Queek. Poor, lowly Skrikk only provide clanrat warriors and stormvermin for Queek's armies. Skrikk sorry!'

Thaxx scowled at his colleague. Skrikk returned a cocky smile.

'Many weak-meat?'

'Many-many!' said Thaxx through gritted chisel-teeth.

'Good-good!' said Queek. 'Then Thaxx not miss these.'

Queek could restrain himself no longer. He leaped into the tunnel, drew his weapons, and vanished into the gloom.

'But they my slaves...' said Thaxx.

'If you like,' said Ska, lounging on a rock and picking his claws, 'you go stop him. I sure-certain that work out just fine for clever Warlord Thaxx.' Queek's Red Guards tittered.

The squeal of panicked ratmen blasted from the tube. They blundered out into the dimly lit corridor, but could not go far, caught by their chains.

One tripped and fell at Skrikk's feet. He looked up at the clanlords pleadingly.

'You go quick-quick now,' said Skrikk. 'Back in there so mighty Queek may kill-slay.'

'He very bored,' said Ska. 'You be good and make him happy.'

The skavenslave stared at them piteously as he was dragged back into the cave, knocking a pile of bones out of the way. He grabbed a skull, but it did not arrest his progress and he disappeared into the dark still clutching it.

A short and noisy time later, during which the cave's stale air ripened with the reek of blood, bowels and musk, Queek emerged from the tunnel, dripping with gore. He panted lightly.

'That no fun,' he said. He licked his lips free of blood and smiled with cruel joy nevertheless. 'No challenge for Queek to slaughter slaves.' He looked speculatively at Thaxx. Skrikk nodded enthusiastically behind his back, jiggling his eyebrows at Thaxx and making a pantomime of how formidable a warrior Skrikk was.

'Skrikk greater warrior!' said Thaxx in a tumble.

'Not so great as mighty Queek!' said Skrikk, his tail twitched nervously.

'Who is?' said Queek with a shrug. 'Now, where final clawpack? If it far, Queek not happy. Maybe we see how good Skrikk and Thaxx are...'

'Not far! Not far, mighty Queek!' said Thaxx, bowing low. 'A half day, then all inspections done.'

Skrikk shot Thaxx a warning look. Thaxx caught it.

'Er, but Warlord Queek must be tired, so much travelling. He should go rest-sleep to increase his strength so that he might kill-slay beard-things and green-things better.'

'You say Queek is sleepy-tired, less-brilliant-than-Queek Warlord Thaxx?' said Queek.

'Oh no, your deadliness, of course not. All know that Queek could kill all things half asleep and with a small feeding spoon. It is just that you are right...' Thaxx took a step backwards as Queek reared up over him.

'You say sometimes Queek not-right?'

'No! No! Queek is always right! Every time! Everyone knows!' squealed Thaxx.

'Yes-yes, Queek the mightiest. Queek also the most correct and cleverest,' said Skrikk. Queek was mollified.

Thaxx relaxed a little. 'You say boring. It boring looking at so many rat-things.' He flapped his paw dismissively. 'They look all the same. Perhaps we go back now? Meet fifth clawpack later?'

Queek's eyes narrowed. 'What Thaxx hide? What Thaxx think Queek not like about fifth clawpack?'

'Hide?' said Thaxx, his eyes wide with wounded innocence.

'Never,' said Skrikk.

'You quite insistent, both of you, that Queek see boring rats. And now, all of a sudden, you not want Queek to see boring rats. Queek not stupid. You think Queek stupid?'

'No,' wailed Thaxx.

'You better tell Queek now,' said Ska.

Thaxx abased himself upon the floor. 'It is not Thaxx's fault. Stupid-meat minions make mistake. He told by great lords to do it.'

'Do what?' said Queek. He hefted Dwarf Gouger and gave it a pleased lick.

'It better,' said Skrikk with a resigned expression, 'if Queek see-smells with his own eyes and nose.'

They went downwards from the bone caves into old skaven ways, gnawed by teeth long before the invention of tunnelling machines. These cut a slope across the outermost edges of the dwarf deeps under the Great Vale. Innumerable shafts and stairways joined the halls carved into the mountains to the undercity proper. The skaven tunnels cut across them all. They came to a winding stair, and went down this for many thousands of paces – round and round, until Queek felt dizzy. He had lived most of his life in Karak Eight Peaks, but this stair was new to him. The Eight Peaks was so vast that it was impossible to know it all, although the hated green-imp claimed to.

Down and down, passing into areas of the city that had collapsed. Some skaven, like Sleek Sharpwit, heretically said that beard-things were not stupid and built well. Queek laughed. Here was proof it was not so! There were many cave-ins and collapses that had sealed off whole sections of the beard-things' burrows before quicker minds had rejoined them.

'Earthquakes, poor skaven engineering undermining good dwarf work,' said Sleek's dead voice sulkily.

'Stupid beard-things,' said Queek.

His underlings, as always, pretended not to notice Queek's one-sided conversations with his trophies.

They skirted the edges of the City of Pillars, the main part of the skaven domain in the Eight Peaks, where the last of the dwarfish deeps gave way to broken mines and endlessly convoluted warrens of skaven burrows. The journey took three feedings before they emerged at the very bottom of the world.

Deep in the deepest reaches of the City of Pillars, hundreds of fathoms below the lowest of the old dwarf deeps, was the Trench.

Who knew what cataclysm had torn this gap into the bowels of the earth? Nearly a mile deep and half a mile across, it went further into the living rock than even the skaven wished to go, and they were the children of the underworld. Along its base were dozens of cave mouths. These were not natural formations. They were carved by living creatures, but only a portion of them by the skaven. Down there were strange things, blindwyrms, deep trolls, scumbloids, mad-things and worse. Skaven who went into those tunnels often did not come out again.

Not today. The tunnels had been pressed into use as barrack burrows and every one crawled with armed skaven. Nothing that did not squeak or bear fur would dare come into the Trench. From end to end and wall to wall, the floor of the canyon was a seething mass of ratkin bodies.

'The fifth clawpack, your most mightiness,' said Skrikk, bowing.

Queek's mouth opened. He shut it with a click. He was reluctantly impressed. There were dozens of warrior clans – none of the greater ones, admittedly, but some of the more respected names among the rabble clans were present. More arresting were the large numbers of Moulder-beasts, far more than in the other formations. He spotted a great number of rat ogres, thousands of giant rats and, most impressively, a pair of caged abominations. Far more monsters than Queek had seen in the rest of the city.

'Who lead-bring such an endless rat sea to the City of Pillars?' asked Queek quietly. Both his lieutenants ducked their heads submissively.

'It hard to say, most subtle and dangerous–' began Thaxx.

'That is, it not easy to put into words, great and–' interrupted Skrikk.

'I do,' said a voice from the shadows. A shape was there, lurking where the dark was too thick even for skaven eyes to see through. Queek smelt the identity of the squeaker before he threw back his hood to reveal the silhouette of horns.

'White-fur!' said Queek, his sword hissing free from its scabbard.

'O mighty, terrible and great warrior Queek! I am Kranskritt, servant of the Horned Rat and emissary of Clan Scruten.' Kranskritt stepped out of the dark and bowed to the jingle of small bells. A bunch of flunkeys came skulking out behind their master. They had precisely none of his poise and threw themselves down to the stone hurriedly for fear of Queek.

Thaxx and Skrikk scuttled backwards, banging into Ska.

'Where you go?' said Ska mildly. He arched an eyebrow. He enjoyed the effect Queek had on the warlords.

Queek laughed horribly. 'White-fur, white-fur! What you squeak-say?' He pointed the rusted blade of his sword at the grey seer, but Kranskritt walked directly towards Queek, his back straight, muzzle smooth and glands closed.

'I say I am the chosen of the Horned Rat, his emissary here in the City of Pillars, and master of the fifth clawpack.' He looked at Queek's swordpoint, hovering inches from his nose. 'I am not frightened of your sword.'

'Oh? Why-tell? You have few heartbeats before I kill-slay. Give me entertainment with last pathetic breaths, stupid-meat. Scruten no longer have favour of Horned Rat. Horned Rat say so himself. I hear he squeak-say it very forcefully to white-fur Kritislik.' Queek giggled a rapid, twittering series of squeaks.

The grey seer came fully into what little light there was. His eyes glowed a dull warpstone-green. He wore purple robes embroidered with arcane sigils. Bells were round his ankles, his horns and his wrists. They tocked and clonked with his every movement. Strangely, none of the skaven present had heard him approach.

'I am not frightened, because we work together for greater quick-death of beard-things. Allies not be frightened of each other, foolish, yes?' said the seer mildly. 'And Gnawdwell, he tell you to work with all, to make quick work of beard-thing pathetic fort-place? It would be a big shame if you kill me for supposed insult and all Kranskritt's warriors go home. Queek's job is then so much harder.' He shook his head sadly, rattling his ornaments.

'Gnawdwell a long way away from here, white-fur. I chop-kill and no one know.'

'Oh everyone will know, most indubitably dangerous and most martial Queek. I doubt-think you care much. But I will tell you a secret.' Kranskritt leaned in close. 'I not care either. You kill-slay me, I go to Horned Rat quick-fast. There perhaps I can explain why Clan Scruten has been wronged, and why Queek is a big danger to all his children. And then you can come too and tell him yourself, because without my clawpack, Queek not get what Gnawdwell promise. Big, big shame and sorrow for mighty Queek as age and time make him weak. And dead. Yes! Dead-dead!' He laughed weirdly.

Queek was outraged. His eyes bulged and veins stood out on his neck. His heart hammered so quickly its beats blurred into one constant note. Equally swiftly, Dwarf Gouger was in his hand. Kranskritt's lackeys shrank back on their bellies. But not Kranskritt.

Kranskritt tilted his head. 'Ah, the real Queek. Kill me then, I do not care.'

Queek squeaked. A paw held back his arm.

'Who dares touch Queek?' said Queek, trembling with fury.

'He is right,' hissed Skrikk. 'Gnawdwell. Remember what Gnawdwell said!'

Skrikk was shaking. Queek wondered what inducements their lord had given him to be so bold as to touch Queek's fur! But this other, he was even more troubling. He exhibited no sign of fear at all, and in the face of the mighty Queek. Queek let his weapons drop and paced around the grey seer, examining and sniffing the stranger from every angle. The seer's servants backed away, still on their bellies.

'You very brave, white-fur. I respect that. But there are no seers on the Council now.'

'We are being tested by the Horned One,' said Kranskritt. 'That is all. You will see. Observe the might I bring to your army!' He swept his paw behind him at the masses in the Trench.

'No power, no influence.' Queek sniffed suspiciously. Warpstone, yes, name scent, yes. Food, old filth and fresh-licked fur. But no fear! No fear at all. 'You are not scared! Why you not scared of Queek?'

'Come and see. I will show you what I have brought, yes? Then Queek know why I know you will not kill-slay Kranskritt, and so Queek will know why I am not scared. Simple, yes?'

Kranskritt gestured to the skaven waiting in the canyon. 'No seat on the Council for Clan Scruten, no-yes. But still have power and influence we do, yes? See! I have warriors from thirty-eight clans, and many-much Moulder-beasts.'

Queek looked sidelong at the grey seer. Still he was unafraid. He held up a delicate white paw and gongs sounded. The skaven below began to march in procession. The hubbub of their gathering became a roaring, the tramp of soft feet and rattle of weapons overwhelming, and the skaven lords struggled to be heard over it. Surely even Belegar high up above could hear this doom that approached him. Queek hid a smile under his scowl.

The fifth clawpack was vast. Kranskritt rattled off the names of units and clans as they went past and into their garrison-burrows, their leaders coming nervously forward from the back of the shelf to be introduced. Despite his avowed disinterest in military minutiae, Queek recognised most of the banners. Some of them were far from home: Clan Krizzor from the Dark Lands, Clan Volkn from the Fire Mountains, for example. He snarled as the banners of traitor-Clan Gritus wobbled past. Only recently they had turned on their Clan Mors masters. Their appearance there was a slight.

'How white-fur get so many warriors?' demanded Queek.

'Have power! Have influence, many-mighty horde of ratkin, yes? See! Many-much veterans, scavenge-armed from sack of Tilea-place and Estalia-place,' shouted Kranskritt.

Queek sneered. 'Stupid man weapons. Stupid man armour. This boring! Ska Bloodtail!'

'Yes, O Queek?'

'We go-depart now. Skrikk will stay. He write down all clan-things. Thaxx stay-listen to stupid white-fur boast-squeaks too. Punishment for not say-squeaking about white-fur.' Queek stepped in close. Thaxx stood his ground as best he could, quailing at the stench of old blood and death coming from Queek's armour. 'Queek bored. Queek go think.'

Skrikk and Thaxx bowed repeatedly.

As Queek swept irritably from the Trench, Kranskritt smiled at his back.

FIVE

Treachery in the Deeps

Queek, Ska and Queek's Red Guard jogged upwards. The din of the fifth clawpack mustering in the Trench was amplified by the tunnel, hurting their sensitive ears. Time and distance diminished it, until the trumpets and stamping of feet joined with all the other mysterious echoes that haunted the City of Pillars, and they found they could talk again.

'This not good-good,' said Queek to Ska. The latter ran as fast as his master, but his great size – for he was a giant among his kind, as tall as a tall man, and bigger than the mighty Gnawdwell himself – made him seem plodding next to Queek's swift movements.

'No, great Queek,' said Ska.

'Thaxx and Skrikk sneaky-sneaks. Not like good and loyal Ska.'

'Thank you, great Queek.' Ska had fought by Queek's side for many years and was of a similar age. Where his arms were visible between his plates of scavenged gromril, his black fur was spotted with patches of brilliant white. Many battles had left their mark upon his face in a pattern of pink scars. One of his ears had been torn off. Already intimidating, he was made fearsome by his war wounds.

They passed onto a wide dwarf-built way. Once a feeder road for the lower mines, it led directly back to the lower levels of the skaven stronghold. Even there, there was little space left, most of the width of the road taken up by sleeping clanrats atop unfolded nesting rolls. From top to bottom, Karak Eight Peaks heaved with vermin. They ran along this for a quarter of a mile, kicking skaven out of the way, then turned into a lesser-used tunnel.

'If white-fur here, much scheming. Queek hate tittle-tattle squeak plots! Queek only wish to fight.' He gnawed at his lower lip as he thought. 'Send-bring me Grotoose, leader of Clan Moulder here, and master assassin Gritch of Clan Eshin. Queek question them both. I find out who behind this, who try to trick Queek.' He squeaked with annoyance. 'Queek happier if Queek bury Dwarf Gouger in Kranskritt's stupid horned head.'

'That is not a good idea, great Queek,' said Ska cautiously.

'Stupid giant-meat Ska! Queek know this! Queek make joke! Queek only wish for sim–'

A tremendous rumble cut their conversation dead. The roof caved in, and a tumble of boulders rushed from the ceiling, clacking one atop the other until they filled the way. Ska pushed Queek aside, but his Red Guard were not so lucky. They squealed in pain and fear as three of them were crushed, and the rest cut off from their master.

Queek rolled with Ska's shove and was back on his footpaws instantly, sniffing the air. Fear musk, blood, the sharp scent of rock dust, registered on his sensitive nose.

'Where Ska?'

'Here, mighty Queek!' said his henchman from the ground. He lay with his feet trapped by rocks.

'Ska better not be hurt – big rat with crushed feet no good to Queek!'

Ska grunted. 'I am not hurt, only trapped. I will dig myself–Queek! Look out!'

Queek was moving before Ska had finished squeaking. He somersaulted backwards as three razored blurs sliced through the air where he had been standing – throwing stars, which clanged from the rock fall leaving smears of bitter-smelling poison on the raw stone.

Queek landed sure-footedly on a boulder. He drew his weapons as he leapt, pushing himself off with his back paws and tail. Ahead of him, a black shape detached itself from the tunnel wall. Its cloak was patterned to match the stone and no name-scent came from it. An assassin. They had their glands removed as part of their initiation. Only they among the skaven carried no smell.

'Die-die!' squealed Queek. He landed in front of the assassin, who promptly flipped backwards, hurling two more stars from quick paws at the apex of his jump. Queek's sword moved left then right, sparking as it deflected the missiles. Queek jumped after his attacker, bounding on all fours, the knuckles of his clenched fists hitting the floor painfully. The assassin turned to face him, brandishing a pair of daggers that wept a deadly venom.

Queek lashed his tail from side to side, aiming to wrap it around the assassin's ankle, but the killer stepped over it as easily as if it were a jumping rope and came in, daggers weaving. Queek parried rapidly, his and the assassin's blades making a network of steel between the skaven. Ska watched his master helplessly, moaning and tugging desperately at his feet. Metal sparked and rang. Suddenly, it stopped.

The assassin's arms sagged, his blades fell to the tunnel floor. Queek dropped Dwarf Gouger and grabbed the assassin by the throat. He struggled feebly in Queek's grip, his pathetic choking noises making Queek smile until they stopped.

The assassin's body followed his daggers to the floor as Queek withdrew his sword from his chest.

'Stupid-meat! No one beat Queek! Queek the best!' He licked his sword clean with a long pink tongue, working out chunks of gore from its serrated edge with his gnawing teeth. He smacked his lips and frowned at his friend. 'What Ska doing there, lying around? Lazy Ska! Come-come! Help Red Guard dig through. Hurry-scurry.'

'Yes, great Queek,' said Ska resignedly, and recommenced tugging at the lumps of rock trapping his legs.

Queek waited in his trophy den for his minions to arrive. Racks where runic axes and dwarf mail coats had once hung displayed skulls and battered armour. Piles of smashed objects and trinkets were heaped all over the floor, a chieftain's spoils gathered over a lifetime of war. He was ten! Ten years! He could not believe it. Time had gone so fast. His muscles twitched, setting his fur quivering. Not from fear, no, never that. But soon he would be old, and he did not like to think about it.

Queek had not been in his trophy room for over thirteen moons. He was gratified that it remained untouched. 'Queek the best,' whispered Ikit Scratch in the back of his head. 'Everyone fear Queek!'

'Yes-yes!' Queek said. 'No one dare touch Queek's trophies.' He ran his hands over a manticore skull, enjoying the memory of the beast's death. 'No one touch Queek's trophies but Queek.' He licked the skull and chirred with delight.

Krug Ironhand, Sleek Sharpwit and Ikit Scratch's eyeless skulls looked on from their shelf of honour. The pickled hands of Baron Albrecht Kraus of Averland had joined his head next to them. This had not been preserved and had mummified in the chamber's dry air, its browned flesh dried into a perpetual, lopsided grin.

'I must say that it is good to have my hands with me,' the baron said. 'You know, I always say that you should have my head with you. Do I not say that, chaps? When the mighty Queek is not here?'

A chorus of ghostly groans came from Queek's trophy collection.

'Yes-yes! Others right! It because you always say "I always say" that your head stays here and is not with Queek and hands are!' snapped Queek. '"I must say this," and "did you know" and "I suggest"! Very boring. Hands not talk. Hands come with Queek, head stay here.'

'My dear fellow...'

'Silence!' Queek was more irritable than ever. He rapidly read the source of his annoyance again, a parchment lately arrived from Skavenblight. On it were direct orders from Gnawdwell. Here he said that Queek should engage the dwarfs in a war of attrition, wear them out with the slave legions of Thaxx Redclaw.

He bared his teeth at it. The hand looked to be that of Gnawdwell, but it made no mention of their earlier conversation and Gnawdwell's orders to finish the beard-things quickly. He held it up to his nose. The scent mark was right too.

'This not right,' he said for the third time. 'Forgery. Must be trick.'

'Trick-trap!' suggested Ikit.

'Maybe,' Queek shrugged. 'Maybe Gnawdwell change his mind, not want Queek to go to other clans.' He sniffed the parchment again. 'Name-smell is Gnawdwell's,' he reassured himself.

'Your kind are traitorous vermin,' suggested Krug. 'Anything is possible. I'd watch out if I were you.'

'Yes-yes, true,' said Queek. 'Maybe Gnawdwell sick of Queek. Maybe Gnawdwell send white-fur to check my power.'

'Yes-yes!' agreed the ghost of Ikit Scratch. 'White-furs have no power. Someone else is behind this happening. Why not Gnawdwell?'

Queek stopped pacing, his tail swishing back and forth metronomically as he thought. The orders were contradictory, but in contradiction was latitude, freedom to act as he saw fit.

'Very useful. Very useful indeed. Queek...' He stopped and raised his nose into the air. 'Shhh,' said Queek, holding up his paw. 'Everyone silent! Someone coming.'

Even with his back turned, Queek knew who it was. He smelt them before they came. One of the reasons he had chosen this old armoury was that the prevailing air currents blew in, not out. One of the approaching skaven had a heavy reek of beasts and skalm, the other very little scent at all. Their footsteps gave them away in any case – the light pad of a stabber-killer from Clan Eshin and the heavier tread of a hulking beast-handler.

'Greetings, O most malevolent of potentates, O sovereign of mighty Mors. I have hurried quick-quick at your summons,' said Gritch, his cloak whispering as he bowed. 'My watch-spies have already told me much-much. So sorry for cave-in. Assassin not one of mine.'

'Hail, great Headtaker,' said Grotoose.

Queek smiled. Grotoose was gruff, to the point, and a deadly fighter – the qualities Queek admired the most. He almost trusted him. Gritch was a useful spy, but as with any Clan Eshin member, he favoured intrigue and was likely to be playing more angles than he had claws. Queek pointedly kept his back to them for a moment, showing he had no fear of a dagger between the shoulder blades. Besides, he could rely on the dead-things to warn him.

Queek placed the manticore skull upon the floor in front of him and stepped around it, acknowledging his minions by turning to face them. Without greetings or preamble, he went to the heart of the matter. 'A grey seer! What is the meaning of this? Did Queek not squeak-tell Lord Gnawdwell about the grey ones' interfering ways? Did either of you know that the fifth clawpack is led by a horned one?'

Grotoose looked Queek in the eyes and bared his fangs. 'I not know,' he said. 'My Moulder-brothers tell me nothing. Big secret.'

Gritch drummed his nervous, twitchy fingers against themselves, scratched his whiskers, and looked at his shuffling feet.

'Gritch? Speak-squeak,' coaxed Queek.

'Yes, yes-yes. I knew. Not for certain, O terrible one,' he said, looking up quickly. 'I hear rumours, I hear whispers. I wait-wait to tell Queek, when next we met.'

'You come see Queek earlier next time!'

'We meet-greet now,' said Gritch with a shrug.

With a swift flick of his wrist, Queek sent Dwarf Gouger to split the manticore skull before him.

'Ska!' shouted Queek.

'Yes, great one,' said Ska from the mouth of the tunnel.

'Fetch Skrikk! Queek want to know what he has to say about this. One look from Queek's eye and he squirt musk and tell all!'

'Yes, great one.'

'And send for Clan Skryre tinker-rats. Time for them to report to Queek. Much-much needs finishing before great signal.'

Queek snarled. He hated all this, hated, hated, hated.

'Queek want to bury Dwarf Gouger in beard-thing's head!' he said.

'Patience!' said Ikit Scratch. 'Soon the time come for death-slay and end of all dwarfs.'

Queek tittered. 'Yes-yes. You right. You clever warlord. But not so clever to kill Queek! Now be quiet, others here.'

Grotoose gave Queek a concerned look. His tail twitched. 'My lord?'

'Nothing! Nothing squeaking for your ears, beastmaster. No! You return to your beasts, Grotoose,' snapped the Headtaker. 'Gritch tell Queek everything he knows about this. This is the Council's doing. But,' he added thoughtfully, 'was Gnawdwell the paw behind it? That is the big question.' He let this last statement hang a moment, knowing full well it would reach eager ears. If they thought the rat was out of the bag, then his opponents might panic. Gritch's face stayed studiously neutral. 'Tell Queek about Kranskritt. Squeak-tell me everything.'

* * *

Kranskritt leaned hard against the burrow wall, his head pounding to the merciless beat of his heart. Every sphincter he had twitched, threatening to flood his robes with urine and musk. He shook all over and his paw-pads sweated. The potion was wearing off. Soothgnawer had warned him that the after-effects were unpleasant. Naturally, he expected the verminlord to lie to him, or not tell him the whole truth at least, but in this one thing he had been truthful – the sensations of withdrawal were awful.

It was horrible down there in the Trench. He hated being at the bottom of the pit. Every sleep he had he was woken by the screams of half-mad Clan Moulder-things. Every time it happened he thought they were coming from him. He was too hot and shook, as if all the fear he should have felt while under the potion's influence were merely delayed, and afflicted him all at once.

With palsied hands he pulled a soft man-skin pouch from under his robes, fished out a piece of dully glowing warpstone and nibbled at it. A surge of wellbeing coursed through him, driven on by his racing heart. Frantically, he dabbed at the crumbs on his front and licked them from his fingers.

Kranskritt closed his eyes and pressed his back and palms against the cool rock, letting the rush of the warpstone chase away his discomfort. He stayed like that until his heart slowed and his glands gave one last twitch. Feeling weak but better, he staggered the remaining way into his burrow, using the wall as a support.

Crates and boxes, some opened and their contents half spilling into the room, filled his chambers. He had not known how much to bring, not knowing how long he would be in the City of Pillars. In the end, he had packed everything, worried he might leave something important behind. But the crammed state of his burrow meant he couldn't lay a paw on anything, and it made him anxious.

He sought a reason other than his own weakness – or Queek, for he was so frightened of him he didn't want to think about it – for his disquiet.

'Soothgnawer, yes-yes. He is too strong!' chittered Kranskritt. 'It is him! So tricksy and sneaky. Never a straight word for poor, honest Kranskritt.'

He paced back and forth. 'A binding, a binding. That must be it. Make him my servant, not the other way around. I am too strong for him!' he snickered. 'Guards!' he called. An unacceptable number of heartbeats later, three mangy stormvermin sloped into the room. Kranskritt missed the elite white-fur guard that usually accompanied seers of his rank, but all that had gone with Kritislik's death and Clan Scruten's disgrace. At least these, being of Clan Gritus, were unlikely to betray him to Queek and Clan Mors.

Probably.

'Clear the floor,' he squeaked imperiously. 'Make me a space! And carefully! No more breakages.'

The stormvermin rolled their eyes but did as they were bid, working until the floor was clear and the crates were stacked more or less safely along the burrow walls. Kranskritt dismissed the stormvermin and hunted about for his warpstone stylus. He couldn't find it. Forgetting his admonishment to the guards, he lost his temper and upended three crates before he seized upon it with a screech of triumph.

'Now,' he said, kicking packing straw and broken possessions to the edge of the room. 'Where to begin?'

Kranskritt spent a happy bell scuttling around his chamber, sketching out his circle in chalk then filling in the design with his stylus. Where the lines met, they glowed with the non-light of warpstone. The atmosphere of the room changed, growing pregnant with power. And then he was interrupted.

'Greetings, Grey Seer Kranskritt, O most wise and malign. I gather-bring news of the Headtaker.'

Turning from the writhing runes he was scratching into the chamber floor, Kranskritt glowered at his messenger.

Bowing profusely, the skaven gave his report to the floor, not daring to look upon the seer. 'A boulder trap missed Queek. Three of his Red Guard were smashed-slain, but the Headtaker leapt aside.'

Kranskritt's muzzle twitched. 'He will know it was a set-trap, yes-yes,' said the grey seer. 'Who will he suspect-blame? Tell me who has he questioned about my presence?'

'Grotoose of Clan Moulder, Gritch of Clan Eshin and Warlord Skrikk, my lord,' responded the messenger without raising his eyes.

'Hmmm, but not Gnarlfang?' said the grey seer, musing to himself. 'Strange-odd. Send Gritch to me immediately.'

Twitching his head to listen, Kranskritt waited until the sound of the messenger's footsteps had receded before returning to his circle.

'Your circle will not work,' said a whisper from the shadows. 'You are inscribing it wrong.'

Kranskritt froze. 'Why don't we tell-explain to the Headtaker that it is not us? Clearly he will come after me soon,' said Kranskritt to the darkness.

A soft and altogether evil laughter filled the room, a sound as palatable as nails scratching on polished slate. 'Of course he suspects you, but it would be no good to tell him that the one behind the attempts is Lord Gnawdwell. He suspects this to be the case, but he would not believe you. And yes, his agents are already on their way.'

After a long pause, the voice spoke again. 'I could protect you, little Kranskritt, but there must be no more attempts to bind me.'

Kranskritt stamped his footpaw in frustration and threw down his stylus. 'You tell me not to be scared of Queek. I not scared of Queek, but Queek almost kill this poor, stupid-meat. Then potion wear off and I am plenty-scared! Why did you not tell me how bad I would feel?'

'But I did,' which was true, 'and you were not scared, little horned one,' which was also true.

Kranskritt drew a breath in to whine and dissemble, but he stopped, puzzled. 'No. I was not scared.'

'And so you are still alive. My potion worked. Stop-Fear! No gland will betray you. Fear is weakness. When will you learn-understand that what I say is truth?'

Whenever you start telling the truth consistently, and not only when it suits you, thought Kranskritt, though he did not say it. He cringed. How did he know the verminlord could not read his mind? He hurriedly composed a fawning apology in his head.

A mist gathered in the centre of the circle, coalescing into the form of a verminlord with white fur and many horns sprouting from its bare skull. Soothgnawer stepped daintily over the bounds of the binding circle, eliciting a squeak of annoyance from the grey seer. 'I did say you were doing it wrong.'

Kranskritt slumped into a sulk, arms crossed. The first time he had seen the verminlord, taking shape in the magical fumes of the Temple of the Grey Seers in Skavenblight, he had collapsed in fear and adulation. He had been even more frightened when Soothgnawer had chosen him as the catspaw for his schemes. Not any more. Familiarity really did breed contempt. Now what he felt mostly was petulant, the verminlord treated him like a favourite slave. From under its impressive rack of horns, it gazed down at him with a wholly infuriating mixture of indulgence and smugness, like it knew it knew far more than Kranskritt ever could, and although it kept most of its knowledge to itself, it was secretly pleased when Kranskritt figured out a part of the greater picture. Most patronising, most infuriating!

'Queek is angry, little seer,' the verminlord said. 'He travels repeatedly from clan to clan, despite his irritation with the role. Soon he will visit you – you cannot hide from him forever.'

Kranskritt's tail twitched. His glands clenched. 'Queek has his paws full. Many clans, all together. Bad recipe for big trouble. He is a mad-thing, always talking to himself.'

'His name is enough to quell any revolt, little seer. He is not as mad-crazed as he pretends to be. When he talks, voices answer him.'

'Whose? Who speak-squeaks to Queek?'

Soothgnawer laughed, a velvety evil sound. 'That I will not tell you, for you do not need to know.'

'Then what do I need to know?' whined Kranskritt, and he threw himself flat on the floor, his forehead and the full length of his muzzle flat against the stone. 'O great and powerful malicious one! Give-tell humble servant of the Horned Rat instructions so he might further great verminlord's master's schemings.'

'Hush! Hush!' said the verminlord. It reached out a massive claw. Kranskritt forbore to be tickled between the horns. 'Be calm, little seer. You must keep Queek on your side, for now. Do as he says until I instruct-command otherwise.'

Kranskritt looked up into the currently skeletal face of Soothgnawer. His appearance was inconstant, and changed worryingly.

'Do not fear, little seer. Soon there will be opportunity for Clan Scruten to regain influence. That is what we both want-desire, yes-yes?'

'Of course, of course,' said Kranskritt.

'Your fellows labour upon the Great Spell in Skavenblight. Already they draw the Chaos moon nearer to this world. This has been revealed to the remaining eleven Lords of Decay. The disturbance its presence will have upon the earth will be the signal to attack.'

'But the tinker-rats? What if they are successful with their rocket and our spell is not?'

'Clan Skryre attempt the construction of their rocket to destroy the moon. This contest between the clans becomes heated. Much turmoil in Skavenblight, many assassinations.' Soothgnawer paused. 'And Grey Seer Thanquol helps Clan Skryre.'

'Thanquol?' said Kranskritt in surprise.

Soothgnawer nodded. 'It is not my doing. He has proven his lack of worth time and again. He is deservedly outcast. You are my preferred instrument to restore the fortunes of Clan Scruten.'

Kranskritt grovelled in appreciation.

'The head of our Council has plans for him, as I have plans for you, little seer. Thanquol will succeed in his venture, but Clan Skryre will fail. The Great Spell must succeed!'

'Why cannot Kranskritt join in this most holy of sorceries, great one?' said Kranskritt, who really would have been anywhere else but near Queek.

'Because, little seer, there is more than one task to be done. The beard-things must die. All of them.'

Kranskritt, still abased on the floor, felt the air stir the fur on his neck as Soothgnawer bent low. 'And do you really think,' the verminlord said, his hot breath washing over the seer, 'that we can trust a mad-thing like Queek to accomplish that? No.' Soothgnawer often answered his own questions. 'Without you, he will fail. And without you, he might survive.' Soothgnawer's fleshless smile grew wider on his skull. 'And we can't have that, can we, little seer?'

SIX

The Breaking of the Mountains

Morrslieb loomed, bigger than it had ever been, peering over Karag Nar like a glutton eyeing a honey cake. Sickly light shed from its mournful face reflected from the snow, painting the world a disturbing green.

'As you see,' said Drakki Throngton, loremaster of Vala-Azrilungol, 'the Chaos moon waxes huge, my lord.'

'What does this all mean?' whispered Belegar. 'Other than it's got bigger,' he said sharply, remembering Drakki's endless lectures on precise speech during his youth.

'I do not know,' admitted Drakki sorrowfully. His breath misted his half-moon spectacles in the cold night air. 'All I can do is check the measurements of our ancestors against our own observations.'

'And?' said Belegar.

'Technically, my lord?'

'Aye! Technically. I'm no beardling.'

'I apologise, my lord,' said Drakki. 'Well, see here.' He flopped open a book over his forearm. The moonlight, cursed though it was, was ample illumination for a dwarf to read by. 'The Chaos moon waxes and wanes according to its own whim. Sometimes there is a pattern, often there is not. It has grown larger and smaller in the past.' He licked an ink-stained finger and flicked back a couple of hundred pages, two centuries' worth of measurements. The handwriting was the same as in the recent pages. Drakki was old. 'Such as here. That was when it was at its largest.'

Belegar glanced up from the page. 'The years of the Great War Against Chaos.'

'Indeed, my king.'

'And the numbers?'

'Well, my liege. There we have the most troubling news. These indicate that this is the largest it has ever been. Diameter, illumination, frequency of transit...' His voice trailed away. 'All higher numbers even than during the Great War.'

'Hmph,' said Belegar. He leaned against the parapet. In the city in the Great Vale, greenskin campfires burned insolently. 'And what if I were to request the non-technical version?'

Drakki shut the book with finality. 'Then I would say we were in a great deal of trouble, my liege. And not just us. Everybody.'

'Now that's putting it mildly,' said Belegar. He drummed his fingers on the stone. 'I've had requests, from the other holds, asking for their warriors back. Even, would you credit it, from High King Thorgrim.'

'Yes, my liege.'

'What kind of world is it, where even a dwarf can't keep his word any more? A few weeks ago I was up here with Notrigar, winding him up.'

'Oh, he is a little on the sparse-chinned side when it comes to recognising a good joshing, sire,' said Drakki, his aged face crinkling with mirth.

'That he is,' said Belegar, no humour in his voice at all. 'But I don't feel it now. I look out at this place, Drakki, and all I can see is my dream slipping through my fingers.'

'We will prevail, sire.'

'That's what I told Notrigar.' Belegar huffed. The breath strained through his frosty beard to break free in clouds. 'We do what we can. We're as fortified as we can be. All we can do is wait for them, because as sure as gold is in the ground and khazukan crave it, they are coming. The only question is *when*.'

They looked out over the vale for a while, until a rumbling from the earth had them both casting their eyes downwards. Fragments of stone jumped like frogs from shelf to shelf on the outside of the citadel, click-clacking all the way down. A louder grumble took up with the first, then another and another, all eight mountains ringing the city protesting the failures of the world, sorrowful as longbeards deep in their ale. The ground convulsed, once, then again. The grating of stone on stone from the city told of ruins collapsing.

Belegar and Drakki swayed, their flat dwarfish feet keeping them upright. Alarms went off up and down the citadel, horns and clanging triangles.

'Earthquake! Earthquake!' dwarfs shouted.

The citadel's masonry ground block on block, sending showers of ancient mortar down on the dwarf king, but the dwarfs were wise to the ways of the earth and built accordingly. The citadel did not fall. Hammerers ran to his side, pitched across the wavering battlements like sailors on a stone ship. 'Protect the king! Protect the king!' their leader, Brok Gandsson, bellowed. Shield rims clacked into one another as the dwarfs formed a barrier of gromril and steel to shelter their lord, half of them angling their shields upwards over his head. Fragments of masonry bounced off them.

'Get back! I'm no beardling frightened by a little shiver,' Belegar shouted, shoving at his protectors. They stood solid as the stones themselves.

'Not until this is over, my king,' said Brok.

The earthquake went on for long minutes, dying only gradually. Belegar waited under the shield roof while the earth gave one more heave. No more aftershocks came, and he shoved his men aside. Drakki followed him from the knot of hammerers.

A wind, unnaturally hot, stirred their beards, the runes on their weapons pulsing with blue light as it ran over them. Out in the ruins came the clamour of panicking orcs and goblins.

'My lord, look!' Drakki was pointing south. The winter skies were stained orange by distant fire. 'Karag Haraz is erupting most fiercely.'

A distant boom rolled over the mountains, reflected from every rock face, until it seemed they clamoured in despair. Far to the north, more flamelight tainted the sky, colouring the high vaults of night.

'And Karag Dronn,' said Belegar.

'They have been spouting fire for long months now, but these latest eruptions must be immense, if we can see them from here,' said Drakki, unconsciously reaching for a notepad to mark the phenomenon down. 'Karag Dronn is over one hundred leagues away.'

'If they both speak, then doubtless Karag Orrud and the Karag Dum do.'

'And east,' said Drakki quietly. A gentle aftershock shook the ground, causing the hammerers to tense again. Drakki nodded to the eastern night sky. A haze of red coloured it as far as they could see from north to south.

'Grungni's beard,' Belegar said. 'All of them?' The others remained silent. Such troubles from deep in the earth had brought the Karaz Ankor to its knees in the distant past and heralded the beginning of the dwarfs' long decline. Nobody needed reminding of that.

'Is it over, loremaster?' asked Brok.

'There will be further small earthquakes, but I expect the

strongest have passed, for now.' He looked to the Chaos moon, crowding its once larger brother from the sky. 'There must be some connection. And if it continues to grow, there may be worse to come.'

Belegar nodded curtly. 'Messengers!' he called. Several lightly armoured dwarfs appeared from inside. 'Get yourselves down into the first deep. I want to know of every stone out of place, do you understand?'

'Yes, my liege,' they all said.

'It would be our bloody luck if that lot brought down some of our defences. If there are any casualties, Valaya forfend, you let me know.'

The messengers ran off, heavy boots clumping down the winding stairs leading down from the parapet into the citadel.

'Something's coming, very soon. If this doesn't–'

A sky-shattering explosion tore through the night. The face of Karag Nar leapt outwards with surreal slowness, long cloudy trails of rock dust puffing up like flour from a burst sack. The ruined fortress upon its shoulder tumbled down like a town made of model bricks pushed over by a child, the finely cut dwarf masonry becoming one with the tumble of broken rock racing down the mountain's flanks. Belegar watched open-mouthed as debris arced towards him.

Belegar was unceremoniously shoved to the flagstones of the wall-walk by his guards. This time he did not order them back. Pebbles rattled off gromril armour, the heavier stones that came tumbling soon after eliciting grunts from the hammerers covering the king. More explosions boomed, these muffled by depth.

A rain of boulders slammed down into the city, levelling whole districts. Avalanches of rock poured off the flanks of the mountains, burying further sections.

Silence was a long time coming.

Belegar's hammerers jumped up, hauling the dazed king to his feet. They attempted to hustle him back inside, calling for more of his bodyguard. Belegar was filled with rage and shoved their hands away. He went to the edge of the parapet to see what had been done to his kingdom, ignoring their cries for him to be careful, to get inside.

A choking mist of pulverised rock hung over the Great Vale, biting the throats of everyone who breathed of it. Caught by the wind, it drifted away like rain, to reveal a scene of utter devastation presided over by the grinning moon.

Three of the eight mountains bore wounds in their sides. Karag Nar's eastern face had slumped inwards, while Karag Rhyn had collapsed into a broad fan of rubble, its height reduced by a half.

Belegar stared out in disbelief. Behind him, his hammerers formed up, but none dared approach the king.

When he turned to face them, a tear tracked down one dusty cheek.

'The mountains. They have killed the mountains.'

'That was no earthquake,' said Drakki, blood from a cut on his forehead making red tracks in his dust-whitened face.

Horns sounded again, this time from inside the citadel, answering others blown in the first deep. Belegar clenched his fist.

'Thaggoraki,' he said. 'It is starting.'

'Another war,' said Drakki.

'No,' said Belegar, pitching his voice low enough that only Drakki and Brok could hear. 'The beginning of the end.'

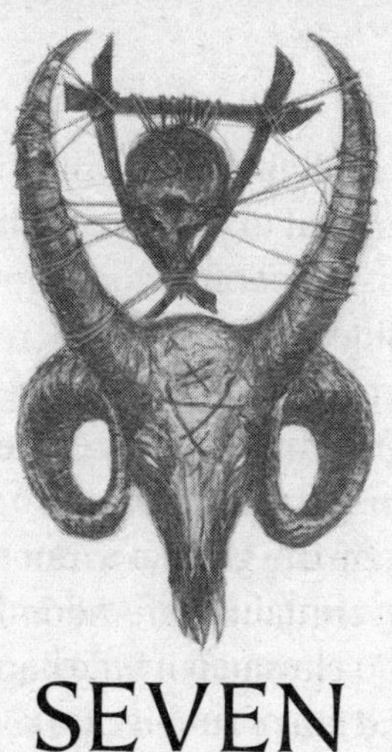

SEVEN

The Hall of Reckoning

Horns sang all over the dwarf-held part of Karak Eight Peaks, echoing down corridors and up forgotten shafts, so that it was impossible to tell where they were coming from.

'That's the signal! Here they come, lads!' cried Borrik Norrgrimsson. His ironbreakers, Norrgrimlings all, held their shields up and locked them together, awaiting the arrival of the ratmen.

'It's about time the thaggoraki got here,' growled Hafnir Hafnirsson, Borrik's second cousin. 'I'm eager to split a few heads.'

'We've been standing in this hall for two months waiting for this lot. I'm sure we can hang on for a few more minutes,' said the Norrgrimlings' notoriously miserable Ironbeard, Gromley. 'Now shut up, or you'll put the thane off. He's on to something.'

Borrik kept a careful eye on all three entrances to the Hall of Reckoning. Two dwarf-made stairwells leading down into the enemy-infested second deep, and a massive pit, gnawed by some unspeakable thing, gaped in the middle of the floor. Not goblin work, or Borrik was an umgi. Other places gave him cause for concern. He had a keen eye for tunnelling, Borrik, and had spent a goodly amount of time tapping at the walls with variously sized hammers. There were more tunnels behind the walls, some of them worryingly new. And if there was one thing 'new' meant to dwarfs, it was trouble.

When Belegar assigned him to the hall, he had examined every inch thoroughly. Four hundred and one half-dwarf paces long, part of a broad thoroughfare that once ran east-west through the first deep to join with the Ungdrin Ankor. Blocked at both ends by rock falls, it would have been of little concern, save one thing. The fall at Borrik's end was pierced by a narrow gap, shored up by a failed expedition many centuries ago. At the other end, in a chamber hacked out of the loose rubble, was a steel-bound door that led into another passageway. This in turn led to the lower parts of the citadel. The door of Bar-Undak was its name, a messenger's access way to the Ungdrin in happier days. Now, in Borrik's seasoned opinion, a bloody liability. Belegar had been determined to keep the hall open, it being one of the more easily defensible ways into the deeps. So it stayed open, as did thirty-nine other ways, thought Borrik grimly. Thirty-nine. Sometimes the king was a real wazzok.

In this tunnel, the Axes of Norr were arranged, two dozen in all, their front rank of ten flush with the low entrance. Seven irondrakes – the Forgefuries – were ranged in front of them.

'If Belegar has one fault, it's optimism,' he grumbled to his banner bearer, Grunnir Stonemaster.

'Aye,' said Grunnir, his eyes fixed like Borrik's on the arched stairwells leading into the hall. 'Like you, my lord, I find anything other than healthy cynicism in a dwarf entirely unnatural. But I'll say this, what other trait would lead a dwarf to try to retake Karak Eight Peaks? There's a lot to be said for bloody-mindedness. I thought you of all people could respect that.'

'If it had been down to me, I would have blocked off this tunnel long since. As I've said to the king a dozen times...'

Grunnir rolled his eyes. He'd heard this opinion a lot recently. Borrik wasn't one to let a point lie.

'...ever since Skarsnik's grobi got pushed out of the upper levels two years gone–'

'It's been obvious the thaggoraki are planning something,' said Grunnir, finishing his thane's words for him, so often had he heard them before. 'You're not the king, Borrik. And you and me and all the rest of us followed him here, didn't we, you grumbaki?'

'So? I've every right to grumble.'

'As has every dwarf with a beard as long as yours, cousin. My point is that we all share Belegar's fault – if it is a fault – in being here at all. So it's not really his fault, is it?'

Borrik sniffed. There was no arguing with that. He was quiet a moment. 'I'd still have sealed this tunnel off, mind.'

'Oh, give it a rest, would you?' said Grunnir. Borrik raised his eyebrows. 'Thane,' added Grunnir.

'That's better,' said Borrik.

There was so much history around them. Ancestor faces at the top of the stairways told of Vala-Azrilungol's glory days. The rock falls recalled its weakening and downfall, the marks of the mason who had chiselled out the tunnel they now defended harked back to one of the many doomed attempts to reclaim it, while the gaping, tooth-gnawed pit before them told them all who Karak Eight Peaks's real masters were now.

A hideous chittering echoed up out of the dark.

'Right, that's it, here they come,' said Borrik. 'Ready, lads!'

A musty draught blew up from the tunnels.

'By Grimnir's axe, there must be a lot of them,' said Grunnir, flapping his hand in front of his face. 'I can smell them from here!'

Hafnir grinned. 'There's always a lot of them, but it doesn't matter how many, because we're here. One hundred or a million of them, they'll not get past!'

'Aye!' shouted the lads.

Stone-deadened explosions sounded down the stairs, sending a brief, fiercer breeze washing over the dwarfs that smelt of gun smoke, sundered rock and blood.

'That'll be the traps, then,' said Hafnir. Grim chuckles echoed from gromril helms.

More explosions sounded, closer now. Any other attacking army might have been discouraged, but the skaven were numberless and were never put off. Borrik hoped they'd killed a lot anyway.

The first skaven spilled into the room, eyes wild with fear. They were scrawny, badly armed if at all, mouths foaming. They saw the dwarfs in their corner. The front rank hesitated but were pushed on, those attempting to go against the tide falling under the paws of their fellows.

'Typical,' said Borrik, indicating the rusted manacles and trailing chains of the lead skaven with a nod of his head. 'Slave rats. They're going to try and wear us down.'

'Don't they always?' said Grunnir.

'Just once, it'd be nice to go straight to the main course,' moaned Gromley.

'In your own time, lads,' said Borrik, nodding at Tordrek Firespite, the Norrgrimlings' Ironwarden leader. The Forgefuries levelled their weapons. The skaven scurried forwards, forced on by the mass of ratkin boiling up out of the depths. The far side of the chamber was a mass of mangy fur, crazed eyes, twitching noses and yellow chisel teeth.

'Fire!' said Tordrek.

Thick blasts of searing energy shot out of the Forgefuries' guns, punching through skaven and sending them sprawling back into the mob. The fallen disappeared under their scurrying colleagues. Many fell into the hole in the centre, forced over the edge by the surging press; others stumbled and were crushed underfoot.

'Fire!' cried Tordrek again. Once more the irondrakes spoke, misting the air with gunsmoke.

'Fire!' he said one more time. The entire front rank of the skaven horde had been smashed, but thousands more came on behind them.

'That's close enough. Part ranks!' shouted Borrik. The dwarf ironbreaker's formation opened up like a clockwork automaton, allowing the Forgefuries to slip through to the back. They went unhurriedly into the small chamber around the door of Bar-Undak, as if there weren't a numberless pack of crazed thaggoraki snapping at their heels.

'Close ranks!' bellowed Borrik. The gromril-clad dwarfs slid back together, presenting their shields as the first skaven hit home.

The skavenslaves were slight creatures, no bigger than grobi and less heavily built. The wave of them crashed feebly upon the shield wall. Rusty blades and rotten spears broke on impenetrable gromril. More and more skaven piled in from behind, pinning the arms of the foremost, crushing the air out of their lungs. The dwarfs stolidly pushed back, unmoved by the immense pressure. The skaven trapped at the front snapped at the dwarfs, shattering their teeth on armour. The dwarfs responded by swinging their axes, chopping the foe down with every swing. They could not miss. Behind the shield wall it was surprisingly peaceful, as if the dwarfs waited out a storm battering the windows of a comfortable tavern.

'This is too easy,' grunted Kaggi Blackbeard, hewing down his fourteenth skaven.

'Aye, but how long can we keep it up?' said Hafnir. 'How long will your muscles hold? This is not a contest of arms, but one of arms!' he laughed.

'I'm just getting warmed up,' said Kaggi. 'And save your puns for when you've a better one, Hafnir.'

Desperate claws scrabbled over the shields held over the front rank by those in the back, as a slave forced itself through the narrow gap between shields and tunnel ceiling.

'Oi! Oi! Up top!' shouted Grunnir. The skavenslave dropped down behind the back rank. It brandished a knife, realised where it was, vented the foulest stink and was promptly chopped down for its troubles.

'Woohoo! Smell that! It's like Albok's been at the chuf again!' said Kardak Kardaksandrison.

'You want to be up front,' said Hafnir. 'Fear stink. It's all over me shield.'

'It'll take an age to clean off,' said Gromley miserably. 'You mark my words. Don't get any of that muck in your beard or you'll run out of water before you ever get it out.'

'Here comes another!' warned Hafnir.

A second and third skaven scrambled over the shields, more intent on getting away from the crush than fighting. They found no escape. One was hewed down in midair, the other gut-barged by Tordrek and stamped to death by the Forgefuries.

The floor became slippery with spilt blood, but the surefooted dwarfs barely noticed. The skaven were not so lucky, skidding over in the viscera of their slaughtered littermates.

'Pressure's easing off!' shouted Hafnir. The proof of his words came as more rotting spears and rusting blades battered against the shield wall as the skaven found room to move.

'Ready,' ordered Borrik. 'Prepare to advance!'

The dwarfs in the front pulled their shields in tighter, while those at the back lowered them from over the front rank's heads.

'Forward!' said Borrik. 'Deep formation!'

Swinging their axes, the Axes of Norr stepped forwards, mowing down skaven. As they advanced, they smoothly rearranged their formation, so that they were arranged into a block four dwarfs deep and five wide, the thane at the front in the middle. Shields overlapped to the fronts and sides, making them a walking fortress of gromril and thickset dwarfish limbs.

'Charge!' yelled Borrik.

'Gand dammaz! Az baraz! Norrgrimsson-za!' The dwarfs shouted the ancient war cry of their clan, and broke into a stately jog. They were not fast, but when they hit they were unstoppable. The skaven parted in front of them, scrabbling over each other to get out of the way. The Axes of Norr ploughed on. The stink of terrified skaven became overpowering, that sweet, old-straw smell of rodent urine mixed with something stronger and far more acrid.

Almost as one, the remaining rats broke and fled. Borrik and his ironbreakers pursued them, still in formation, as far as the pit in the centre of the chamber.

'Halt!' cried Borrik. 'Forgefuries!'

Blazing bolts of energy seared past the dwarfish block, cutting down fleeing ratmen. The skaven tore at each other in their haste to escape, ripping their comrades to pieces. Many were pushed into the hole, or leapt into its fathomless depths in blind panic. Another volley went booming past. The skaven poured back down the stairwells.

And shortly came running back out again, the fleeing, terrified rats who had just exited the room driven back into it by a fresh legion of skavenslaves.

'They're coming again,' shouted Hafnir.

'They always come again, lad,' said Kaggi.

'Pull back, lads. Back to the tunnel!'

The dwarf formation halted and reversed, faces always to the enemy, pulping the corpses of their foes under weighty dwarf boots. Once in the tunnel mouth, they held their ground again.

One more time the dwarfs rushed out. One more time the skaven were cast back. The fighting went on for hours, until the last assault broke, and the skaven fled. Borrik had his panting ironbreakers rest, ordering Tordrek forward with his irondrakes.

That time, the skaven did not come again. The ironbreakers rotated their shoulders and worked aching muscles, complaining loudly that they had not enjoyed proper exercise before the skaven fled. They broke out pieces of stonebread and chuf – the hard survival cheese of their kind. A keg of ale stored by the door of Bar-Undak was broached and leather flagons passed around thirsty lips.

'Oh look at that,' spat Gromley. 'Look at that!' He ran his finger along a tiny scratch in his shield. 'Ruined! Absolutely ruined.'

'Shut up and drink your ale,' said Grunnir.

Gromley stared mournfully from the depths of his helm. 'It's all right for you to say that. Nobody's scratched your shield, have they?' He shook his head. 'No respect for good craft, you youngsters. Happy with umgak work, you are. Now, in my day I'd have got a bit of sympathy. But is one of you reaching for your polish to help an old longbeard grind out the damage? No. And we wonder why we're in this mess!'

'Show some respect, shortbeards,' said Uli the Elder, the oldest of their number. 'Let's not let our standards slip.'

Good natured jeers vied with heartfelt grumbles.

At the front, Borrik conferred quietly with Tordrek.

'When will they come again?' Tordrek asked.

'Too soon. We've been lucky. I reckon we've accounted for about four hundred of their lot, for not a single one of the lads.' He sucked deeply on his pipe. 'Good work, and greater fortune, but it can't last.' He called back over his shoulder. 'Hafnir! Gromley! Get me some blackpowder.' He pointed the stem of his pipe at the doors. 'I reckon it's time to get ready to stop up some mouseholes. The rest of you, we need some clear space to fight. I want these corpses shifted to one hundred paces out.' The others gulped their ale and moved out from the tunnel, wiping suds from their beards with the backs of bloodied hands. 'And be clever about it,' said Borrik. 'Don't stack 'em – we don't want to give the thaggoraki anything to hide behind, do we?' He pointed the stem of his pipe at a young dwarf, barely sixty years old, who was doing just that. 'Call yourself a Norrgrimling, Albok? Think, lad! What would your old dad say?'

'Sorry, thane.' Albok pushed over the pile he'd made with a boot. 'Where do we put them then?'

Borrik grinned and jabbed with his pipe stem. 'Chuck them down that there hole.'

Albok heaved a skaven corpse into the black, his thick arms tossing it as easily as a wet fur blanket. No sound came. Albok cocked his head appreciatively, and began to throw them in quickly.

'That's right, lads, don't tarry. We're not going to have long before the little furry kruti come back for another go.'

Queek paced back and forth angrily. He struck down the messenger, drawing blood from his muzzle.

'Still standing! Still standing! What squeak-nonsense Clan Skryre tinker-speaker bring to Queek? Four mountains were bombed-targeted. Only one collapse! What news of Skarsnik?'

'No sign of him, O most undefeated and puissant of overfiends,' said the messenger. 'The other tall-rock, it also nearly gone. White Mountain-place, half size it was. My masters...'

Queek glared at him so hard the skaven pulled his head all the way back into his shoulders. The sight of it was so pathetic that Queek laughed madly.

'Stupid-meat, or brave-meat, hrn?' Queek bounded over and flipped the Clan Skryre skaven onto his back with a footpaw. He leaned in and sniffed. 'Stupid-meat.'

The skaven squealed in terror, exposing his neck and spreading his arms. Queek had lost interest and walked away. 'And you, rest of you! Why beard-things not dead?'

'It stupid beard-things fault!' said Skrikk. 'Not mine, oh no. Seventy thousand slaves we sent...'

'Thaxx say one hundred thousand!' said Thaxx.

Skrikk shrugged. 'Skrikk count, Thaxx lie. Terrible, terrible shame. And I thought him so loyal. No doubt great and fiercely intelligent Queek can see to the traitor-meat squirming beneath loyal-fur.'

'Thaxx Redclaw the most loyal–' began Thaxx.

'No squeak-tellings! Beard-things!' snapped Queek so loudly Skrikk flinched.

'They are not killing the slaves quickly enough, grand one,' said Grotoose. 'They have chosen good spots for defence and cannot be dislodged. Our slave legions can attack on narrow fronts where they are easily slain. This is not the way to beat them.'

'You tell Queek that stupid-meat beard-things, with their slow and stupid minds, are outwitting the swiftest thinker-tinkers in all of the Under-Empire?'

The assembled skaven looked at one another and pointed fingers. Queek squeaked loudly, stopping the accusations and counter-charges of incompetence before they could begin.

'Enough, enough! Enough with slaves and weak-meat! Send in the clanrats. Call in the stormvermin. Kill the beard-things. Kill them all dead-dead!'

'What of orders?' said Thaxx. 'What of Lord Gnawdwell's commands?'

'I do not care. Queek general here – where is Gnawdwell?'

'In Skavenblight?' ventured one.

'Yes-yes, whereas Queek the Mighty here. We will win. Nothing else is important. We will destroy. Queek will show the whole world that Queek is the mightiest, the best, the most deadly! We will see what Gnawdwell says about orders then.'

The messengers bowed several times and rushed away. The clanlords and potentates of the City of Pillars attempted a more dignified exit. Queek's long mouth split in a hideous grin and he waved his paws at them. 'You too, hurry-scurry! Queek not like sluggards. Loyal Ska tell sluggards what Queek thinks of slow-meat.'

'Queek does not like them,' said the giant stormvermin, 'and I don't like them either.'

'Boo!' shouted Queek, making as if to leap into their midst, and away they fled spraying fear musk, much to Queek's amusement.

The chamber was empty bar the patter of retreating paws and the smell of fear. Queek snickered to himself.

'You see, Ska? This is why Queek is so great.'

There came no reply. Ska was thankfully brief in his praise of Queek. All the bowing and scraping and insincere flattery that characterised skaven social interaction the warlord found tiresome, but Ska usually said *something*.

Queek's nose twitched. Something was wrong. A smell of old fires, rubbish and hot warpstone made him sneeze. The light leached from his surroundings, leaving everything grey. Ska was unmoving, frozen in position. He called for his guards, but they did not come.

Movement in the unmoving world caught his eye. He did not turn to it, not immediately. Something big was in the corner.

He spun around, leaping into the air and twisting his entire body. Dwarf Gouger leapt into his hand, and moved in a blurred arc impelled by all his weight and speed. His serrated sword came up next, aimed directly at the vitals of his giant ambusher.

Queek crashed into the stone. The creature was not there.

'Oh ho! You are as good as they say. But mighty Queek could be the mightiest of all mortal skaven, and he still would not catch me.'

Shadows boiled all around him, darting like swarms of flies over the marshes. Queek hissed and made feints and jabs, but the darkness moved away from him, slipping around his weapons like water.

'Who-you?' he cried. His fur bristled with a fear he would not allow himself to feel. For the first time in years, his glands clenched. 'What you want with Queek?'

The darkness ran together and parted for an instant, affording the warlord a glimpse of a masked, rodent face, ten feet in the air, topped with three sets of horns, two straight, one curved.

The ends of them were twisted into the runic claw-mark of Clan Eshin.

'I am Lurklox, Shadow Lord of Decay, one of the twelve above the twelve. And what I want with you, strutting warlord, is your victory.'

EIGHT

The Hall of Pillared Iron

In the Hall of Pillared Iron, King Belegar took counsel. Between the thick iron columns that gave the place its name, venerable dwarfs of many clans crowded around low tables layered with maps. The hall had been built with the same attention to detail and pride with which the ancestors had built everything. Each of the room's sixty-four column capitals had been wrought in red iron to resemble four straining longbeards holding up the roof. The remainder of the columns were inscribed with runes inlaid with precious minerals, most picked out by rapacious greenskins, but in the more inaccessible places electrum, silver, polished coal and agate still glittered, a reminder of the hall's former glory.

Despite the care and craft of its making, the Hall of Pillared Iron was a foundation, a utilitarian room intended to support the finer citadel halls above. The metal in its walls and pillars allowed the citadel to reach its great and graceful height without compromising its efficacy as a fortress.

That had been then. The upper chambers were mostly toppled

by centuries of war and earthquakes, among them the magnificent Upper Throne Room, whose wide windows and fine art made it the mirror to the Great Throne Pinnacle in the Hall of a Thousand Pillars in the first deep. Unique in all the dwarf realms, at the height of the Karaz Ankor the twinned thrones had represented Karak Eight Peaks's mastery of the worlds under sky and under stone. Of these two hearts, one was rubble and the other had been occupied by a succession of foul creatures.

So low had the dwarfs of Karak Eight Peaks sunk that the Hall of Pillared Iron was their greatest hall. Magnificent though it was, as grand as Belegar's throne looked when viewed down its aisles, the Hall of Pillared Iron was a support. Might as well call a single stone block all the temple. Belegar had refused to have it completely restored, lest the dwarfs of Karak Eight Peaks forget why they were there, and become content with scraps.

Drakki was speaking, addressing his king and his advisors. Brunkaz Whitehair, the oldest dwarf in the hold, was beside him. His beard was so long it looped three times in a complicated plait about his thick gold belt.

'At Bar-Undak the Norrgrimlings are taking casualties. The endless stair is being overrun, half the Zhorrak Blue Caps are dead. Valaya's quay has fallen, our warriors there falling back to the base of the citadel.'

'The Undak?'

'Still running clear,' said Drakki. 'But how long will that continue? The thaggoraki poisoned the river once – now we've lost the quays at the headwater, they could easily do it again.'

'Buzkar,' swore Belegar. He looked from map to map, searching for a sign of hope, some weakness in the enemy he could exploit, some dawi strength he could call upon.

He spread his hands over a portion of the map, caging it protectively in his fingers. 'Kvinn-wyr still holds strong. So long as we hold the mountain, our people will have somewhere safe to stand. We've got the gyrocopter eyries at Tor Rudrum. As long as we have them, we can stay in touch with the other holds. Above all, the citadel is safe. Perhaps it is time to abandon the first line of defence and make our next stand at the Hall of Clan Skalfdon,' said Belegar. He pointed to a great hall in the first deep below the citadel, three quarters of a mile from the collapsed east halls, where many lines of communication intersected. 'Beat them back there and they'll think twice about trying to crack the hold.'

'There's not time to fortify it,' said Brunkaz. 'We need to dig in there, or it'll be a slaughter.'

Belegar laughed. 'The only slaughter I've seen in recent weeks is that of the ratkin! We've slain so many I could carpet the east road all the way to the Uzkul Kadrin in vermin fur.'

'Aye, true enough,' conceded Brunkaz, although his expression made clear his distaste at covering good dawi stone with ratskin. 'But these aren't dregs we're facing – that part's done with. Belegar, you know how they work. The Headtaker is sending in his clan warriors and stormvermin. Our lads are worn down, and we've lost a good number. They'll not last until the defences are ready.'

'They'll have to,' said Belegar firmly.

'There's no time, my king,' said Brunkaz.

'There'll have to be time, or we'll not get the other lines finished!' snapped Belegar.

Drakki cleared his throat, politely interrupting before grudges began to sprout like grobi in a damp cave. 'And what of the way into Kvinn-wyr?'

'That at least is in hand,' said Belegar. 'Dokki,' he called over to an engineer hard at work over his own maps.

'My king?'

'How're the preparations at the Arch of Kings going?'

'Give me three weeks and the dawi I've got, or sixty more engineers and two days and I'll have the fort back in dawr order. Before that...' He sucked in his breath and clucked his tongue. 'You'll be lucky if it's before the end of the month.'

'This is the Eternal Realm! Surely we have time,' said Belegar. 'What about Kolbron Feklisson's miners?'

'Ah! Here we have less dire tidings,' said Drakki, brightening a little.

'We've retaken the western foundries?' said Belegar hopefully.

'Er, no. The miners have lost the foundries, but are still holding the eastern entrance.'

'That's good news,' said Belegar hesitantly, fully expecting the worst. He was rewarded with it.

'For now, my lord. They're going to be encircled here and here – it's only a matter of time,' said Drakki, tracing a series of halls on the map. 'We've rumour of thaggoraki tunnelling teams at work behind them.'

'From who?' said Brunkaz. 'Half our number are sparsely bearded hill dwarfs or umgdawi.'

'Sadly not from them, my lord,' said Drakki. 'From Kolbron himself. No one knows stone better. If he says there's something going on in the rock, you can bet your last coin there is.'

Belegar shook his head from side to side, his beard whispering against the parchment. 'Tell them to withdraw.'

'They won't retreat, Belegar,' said Drakki, a note of pleading in his voice.

'Tell them it's a direct command from me. I'll write it on a bit of paper if it makes them happy. Get them back up here. I want them reporting to Durggan Stoutbelly and helping him fortify the Hall of Clan Skalfdon before sunrise or I'll be writing grudges against the lot of them, is that clear? With their stonecraft under Stoutbelly's direction, we've a fighting chance of establishing the next perimeter.'

'It'll be a hard task,' said Brunkaz. 'Not like the old days.'

'Yes, yes, yes!' said Belegar tersely, only just reining in his temper and maintaining the appropriate level of respect due to the living ancestor. 'It never is like the old days, and it never will be again if we don't give good account of ourselves here. We're in a tough spot, aye, but we'll all be dead if we grumble about it.'

Brunkaz's wrinkled face paled under his beard at Belegar's lack of deference. Belegar regretted his tone. 'Have the messengers set out?' he said, more softly.

'This morning, my lord,' said Drakki. 'Six for each of Zhufbar, Karak Kadrin, Karaz-a-Karak and Karak Azul. No gyrocopters, as you commanded.'

'We need them here.' Belegar ground his broad teeth. Going cap in hand to the High King grated on his honour. What choice did he have? 'The other kings will understand we cannot send their warriors back. They've not failed us yet. We'll just have to dig in. Get Clan Zhudak to the gates of Bar-Kragaz, hold them back at the west tunnel. They'll be coming through from the foundries that way as soon as they discover the miners have gone.'

'Aye, my lord.' Drakki hesitated, words that would not be spoken keen on his lips.

Brunkaz curled his lip at Drakki and made a rumble of disapproval that started deep in his gut and travelled upwards, quivering his moustaches as it came out of his mouth. 'Drakki's too good a dwarf to say it, but I will. We've got no chance. Half of us are dead already. The skaven are numberless. They've never attempted anything like this before. We'd be better off fighting our way out and leaving them to the greenskins.'

'It's a bigger attack, I'll grant you. Nothing we can't handle,' said Belegar, his voice stiffening.

'They've blown up Karag Nar! The sunset mountain, gone! Karag Rhyn's a shadow of itself – half the old farmlands to the south are buried in its rubble. Can't you see? Has pride blinded you so much? The mountains, Belegar, the mountains themselves are in pieces! If they can't endure, what chance do we have?' Belegar stared at his advisor, but Brunkaz had gone too far to stop. 'There's only one reason the Headtaker's done that, and that's to keep the greenskins off his back while he comes to finish us off. Or have you considered, it may not be long before they do the same to us? The thaggoraki have changed. We are not fighting against rats with sticks any more. Some of their machines make the creations of the Dawi-Zharr seem like toys! Why do you think they've left the surface camps alone? Why has Lord Duregar not had so much as a whiff of rat round the East Gate these last months while we're knee deep in them? The answer's simple – they're coming to wipe us out! They don't care. They're massing for a final blow right at our heart, right into Kvinn-wyr.'

Belegar's face grew purple, and his words when they came were quiet, the hiss of rain before the first thunder crack of a storm. 'You will not mention the eastern kindreds in these halls again.'

'All your life you've asked me for my counsel, from beardling to the king I love and serve gladly. I'll give you the truth and aye, unvarnished,' said Brunkaz. 'This is my sooth, king of Karak Eight Peaks. Leave now, before we're all dead. We tried our best. Sometimes we have to retreat a little further than we wish. Let the grobi and thaggoraki fight over the scraps. When the world's troubles die down again, we can come back and take our lands from whoever wins. They'll be weaker for their victory. More importantly, we'll still be alive.'

'Is that all, Brunkaz?'

'Think of your *son*, Belegar.'

'*Is that all, Brunkaz?*' Belegar's shout cut through the quiet muttering of dwarfs at council, so loud the candles and torches lighting the hall wavered before its fury. Only the glimlight of the glowstones was unperturbed.

Brunkaz could not meet his king's eyes. He worked his cheeks, causing his beard and moustache to move around like a live thing. 'Aye. That should just about cover it.'

'Thank you. I suppose you'll be wanting to leave, then? If you do, I'll release you from your oaths, but the others'll not thank you for it.'

Brunkaz went bright red. 'I'll not abandon my oaths! Course I'm staying. Why, if you were a few decades younger I'd put you over my knee and–'

'Very well,' interrupted Belegar. 'If you're staying, I'd appreciate you keeping your words tucked up behind your beard unless they're something to do with defending the hold. Do you have anything useful to add in that regard?'

Brunkaz buried his chin in his chest, considering his next words. 'There are ogres in the pass, my lord,' he said slowly.

'There are always ogres in the pass,' said Drakki dismissively.

'More than usual, Drakki Throngton. Golgfag Maneater leads a great host of them,' said Brunkaz, still not looking at his king.

'The Maneater is in the Uzkul Kadrin?' said Belegar, brightening. He reached his hand, richly gloved, up to his mouth, as if he would hide the smile spreading under his beard.

'You can't be thinking on hiring him, my king? Ungrim nearly killed him. He's a thug, a pirate, a... a... mercenary,' said Drakki, taking his turn to be outraged.

'That's exactly what he is,' said Belegar. 'A mighty one.'

'I beg you, my king, recall Duregar from the East Gate,' said Drakki.

'What, and let Skarsnik have it? And how do we get out then, if it should come to that?' The king shot Brunkaz a warning look not to take up his cause again. 'The East Gate garrison stays where it is, for now. Golgfag is what we need. He's fought many times for the dawi.'

'And just as often against us. And he doesn't come cheap,' said Brunkaz.

'You'd beggar the kingdom for an ogre's sword?' Drakki shook his head so vigorously that he dislodged his spectacles. He pushed them back into place with an ink-stained finger, and squinted expectantly at his king.

'Better a beggared kingdom than a fallen one. I'll promise him the pick of the treasury.'

'There's precious little in the treasury,' grumbled Drakki.

'He doesn't know that, does he?' said Belegar. 'Get a messenger out to him.'

'There's a blizzard rising.'

'Then no one will be able to see him, will they?' said Belegar. 'Do it now, Grungni scowl at you!'

Now both longbeards were taken aback by Belegar's attitude. Belegar supposed he should feel guilty, snapping at these honoured elders like they were callow beardlings, but he didn't. They knew his temper well enough.

The longbeards walked away from the table, chins wagging like fishwives. Belegar ignored the pointed looks they gave him. To keep others from approaching him, he affected an air of bristling bad temper. He didn't have to try very hard. Those dwarfs waiting to petition him – priests, merchants, umgdawi and hill dwarfs – were discouraged, if not by his manner then by his hammerers, who ushered them out of the hall. He heard their complaints well enough; the hall wasn't that big. Fair enough, some of them had been waiting a day or so, but he wasn't in the mood to dispense the king's justice. He feigned deafness and returned to his maps, staring hard at them until his eyes swam. As if that would be enough to turn the red and green parts of the map blue again.

If only it were so simple.

One dwarf, somehow, got through.

'Perhaps now your majesty might consider our request?'

The smell of rancid pig fat and lime was unmistakeable. Belegar looked up from his maps into the magnificently crested face of Unfer, nominally the leader of the Cult of Grimnir in the hold. When the Slayers wanted something, it was Unfer who asked. Belegar assumed he must be their leader, but in truth he did not know. Their ways were closed and mysterious to all who had not taken the oath.

The king tried to look away, but was arrested by the Slayer's eyes. Beautiful eyes, set into a face scarred by cuts and inner pain. They were out of place, clear blue as ice, and as devoid of emotion.

Belegar tugged at his beard and cleared his throat. He waved his hand over his maps.

'I'm loath to let such fine warriors go out. I need every axe we have here.'

Unfer glanced at the maps like they were a carpet he had no interest in buying, and Belegar an overeager merchant. 'That is not the nature of our oath, my lord. We have no desire to retreat until there is nowhere left to retreat to, to find our doom backed into some corner, or worse, to be taken alive. There is no hope in this defence. Let us go, and kill as many of them as we can for you. It is a service we gladly offer you.'

Unfer's glacial gaze bored into Belegar's eyes. The insult to the king's ability as a general was implicit.

'There is always hope,' said Belegar. 'Help might come yet.' He heard the desperation in his own voice; he was afraid that the Slayer was right.

'There is no hope left in all the Karaz Ankor. No one is coming. The Eternal Realm is finished. Best we all shave our heads and take the oath so that we might die with a song on our lips and our shame washed away in blood.'

'Shame?' said Belegar. Unfer shrugged shoulders craggy with muscle. Blue tattoos writhed over them. In hands like boulders, he carried paired rune axes – royal weapons. Belegar often wondered who he'd been. Unfer would never tell.

'The shame of all our kind,' said Unfer. 'That we have failed to restore the glory of our ancestors. Better to fight. Better to wish for a good death than a ragged hope.'

Belegar was tempted. To sally out with his remaining few folk, and kill the thaggoraki until they themselves were killed. Let them taste dawi steel and remember them forever!

He blinked visions of a glorious end away. He could not. He was a king. He had responsibilities. He had a son, the first heir born to the king of Karak Eight Peaks since its fall two thousand years ago. He would not retreat. He would not abandon the legacy of his ancestors, so much dearer now it was the heritage of another.

'No,' he said. 'We wait here. We will defend, and retreat, and defend. And we shall prevail.'

Disappointment flickered over Unfer's face. 'As you wish. It is your kingdom.' The Slayer put one axe over each shoulder and turned away.

'I have not finished,' said Belegar sternly. 'You have my permission to go,' he added with understanding. 'I cannot keep you from your oaths. What manner of king would I be if I did? I wish you would reconsider, but if you must, you have my leave. Fight well, and find the doom you deserve, Unfer.'

Unfer nodded once. 'It is all any of us can hope for any more. Grimnir go with you, King Belegar. If we meet again, may it be in happier times for all dawi.'

'You'll not go yet,' said Belegar. Unfer cast a weary look over his shoulder. The Slayer moved in the way those with deep depression do: slowly, as if through a treacle of despair. 'I may be a poor king, but I'm still a king. You'll get a proper send off. I'll open my cellars to you, we'll say the right words, drink to your deaths.' He smiled awkwardly. 'The old way.'

Unfer gave an appreciative bow. 'Let no dawi say that King Belegar is ungenerous. It is good to hold to the old ways while we still can.'

'Aye,' said Belegar. 'Aye, it is.' He meant it as a good thing, but his troubled face said otherwise. All they had was the past, he thought, and even that was running away from them.

He didn't notice Unfer leave. A commotion at the gates drew his tired eyes. One of the Iron Brotherhood, Skallguz the Short, was pushing his way through. He jogged up to his lord, red faced and out of breath.

'My king!' he said, and dropped to his knees.

'What is it?' said Belegar.

'It is the queen, my lord. The prince...' The dwarf stammered to a halt.

'Spit it out!' Belegar's face went pale with terrible presentiment.

'My lord,' the dwarf said. 'I don't know how to say it... They've both gone!'

NINE

Kemma's Way

Wind sang sadly through the teeth of the broken window, set in the dairy, high up in the side of Kvinn-wyr. A sheer drop of four thousand feet fell away down the mountain outside, ending in broad fans of scree covered by snow. Gromvarl pulled his head back in through mullions worn edgeless by the wind and rain, and leaned against a cracked milk trough. He shook the snow from his shaggy mane of hair and filled his pipe.

He winced at the taste of the tobacco. Once the dwarfs had produced the world's finest smoking weed in the Great Vale, along with much else. The soil of the bowl cupped between the eight mountains was so rich they called it Brungal – brown gold. In Belegar's pocket kingdom there had been plans, and much talk in ale cups, of how the dwarfs were going to clear the farmlands and raise great crops to end Vala-Azrilungol's reliance on the other holds. Of course, like so much Belegar said, it remained an unattainable dream.

A stealthy tread sounded in the old goat way outside. Gromvarl brought his crossbow up one-handed, wincing as he rested the stock in the crook of his broken arm.

He narrowed his eyes, finger on the trigger lever, then relaxed. No skaven or grobi whistled like that.

A deeply tanned dwarf with an expression so cheerful it belonged on the face of no real dawi came in through the door. He doffed his wide-brimmed hat, showing the scarf tied tightly over his ears and under his chin. His name was Douric Grimlander, a dwarf reckoner, a calculator of debts and grudges. Little better than a mercenary, to Gromvarl's eyes.

'Gromvarl! What happened to you?' Douric said, his eyes lighting on Gromvarl's splinted arm.

'An urk happened to it. And then I happened to the urk.'

Douric peered about the small dairy. 'You alone then?'

'What does it look like?' said Gromvarl through teeth gripping his pipe. He had always found Douric insufferable, even at the best of times.

'I told you he'd say no,' said Douric breezily. 'I suppose it's all off then. Belegar's a fool to turn your offer down, but that's that.'

'Listen to me, you scraggle-bearded wazzok,' said Gromvarl. 'Why do you think he said no? This is his hold. Thorgrim is his son and heir.' Gromvarl fixed the shorter dwarf with a beady eye and poked him in the chest with his pipe stem. 'I wonder if you're a real dwarf at all. You've no honour.'

Douric took the insult as a compliment, or so his broad smile suggested. 'I like money. You like money. Who doesn't like money? I have honour, but like my money, I'm just a little more careful than you where I spend it, that's all.'

Gromvarl grunted, wiped the mouthpiece of his pipe on his bearskin, which was no cleaner than Douric's jerkin, and replaced it in his mouth with the clack of ivory on teeth. 'Oaths are worth more than gold, reckoner.'

'I keep mine, unlike your king,' said the reckoner mildly. 'If I combine honour with payment, does it make me all that bad?

Besides,' he said, hitching his hands into his wide belt. 'You're the one who suggested to the king we should steal the queen out of the city against all tradition. So where's *your* honour?'

Gromvarl adjusted the sling holding his broken arm, sliding thick fingers between the fabric and his neck. 'My oath has always been to protect the queen, ever since she was a child. I'm doing that now.'

'Doing that...?' Douric's eyes widened. 'Oh ho ho! Gromvarl! I didn't think you had it in you. She is here isn't she?'

'Not yet,' said Gromvarl grudgingly. 'Soon.'

'Handing her over to me! A mere mercenary. Tut tut, Gromvarl. You'll be coming with us now, I'll warrant. It'll be a mite uncomfortable down there once Belegar finds you've kidnapped his son.' Douric jerked his thumb over his shoulder, back down the passageway in the exact direction of the citadel. Douric always had had a fine sense of direction, even for a dwarf.

Gromvarl grumbled, levered himself up from the tub and took a heavy step forwards, until he was nose to nose with Douric. 'I've other oaths, oaths of service to the king. I'll not break either. I need a dwarf of your... moral flexibility.' He looked the reckoner up and down, his grubby clothes, his odd umgak gear garnered from who knew where. He was right, this was no true dwarf.

'So you're in a bind, then? Who's the more fortunate here – you, all thick with responsibility, or me, who tends to the more cautious side–'

'Self-serving more like,' interjected Gromvarl.

'–of things?' continued Douric, undeterred. 'A philosophy that enables me to help you out now. Who else would, Gromvarl? Who's the better?' He waggled his eyebrows in almost lewd fashion.

'You little krutwanaz...'

'Will you two stop arguing? The pair of you, thicker-headed than trolls!' A sharp female voice speared out of the corridor. Queen Kemma of Karak Eight Peaks emerged into the dairy. She was followed by a very young dwarf, no older than ten or twelve, whose chin was covered in the straggly hairs of first bearding, and a hammerer, who nervously glanced behind them. Both the queen and youngster wore travelling cloaks and the rough clothes favoured by the kruti and foresters who worked overground. When the queen pushed past Gromvarl, her fastenings parted slightly, revealing rich gromril mail beneath. Both of them too had a royal bearing. Gromvarl sighed. No matter how they dressed up, there was no hiding who they were. He just hoped they had not been seen sneaking away.

'I am sorry, vala,' said Gromvarl, who at least had the decency to look abashed. He cast his eyes downwards. Douric, on the other hand, arched his back, and clasped his hands behind his back, an exceptionally self-satisfied look on his face.

The hammerer rubbed at his bulbous nose. 'Here they are. I better get back.'

'Another oath-bender!' said Douric. 'They're popping up like mushrooms.'

'Guard the queen as long as she is in Karak Eight Peaks, that was my oath. Well now she's not,' said the hammerer. 'Nearly.'

'You're a good dawi, Bronk Coppermaster,' said Gromvarl. He held up a small purse, distastefully pinched between finger and thumb, as if it were soiled. 'For your trouble.'

Bronk looked at it in horror. 'You've been hanging around with these here reckoners too long. Just see her safe, that's all I want. If this ends well, then I'll take my chances with Belegar, and we'll still have our prince. If it doesn't end well... Well,' he shrugged, his gromril rattling musically, 'then it's not going to matter very much what Belegar thinks.'

Gromvarl nodded. 'I look forward to fighting alongside you, Bronk.'

Bronk nodded and hurried off back up the passageway.

Meanwhile, Douric was attempting his charm upon the queen. 'Vala Kemma! It has been too long. With every passing year your beauty grows greater.' He bowed his head and reached for her hand.

'Don't even think about it, reckoner,' said Kemma, snatching her fingers back from his puckered lips. 'We have to be away now.'

'Mother, are we sure this is the right thing to do?' said Thorgrim. 'I am the prince of Karak Eight Peaks, my place should be here. Father will be furious.'

Kemma placed her hands on his shoulders, and looked up into his face. Not yet full grown, he was already turning into a fine figure of a dwarf. He was already three feet tall; chances were he was going to be bigger than his father, and certainly as strong. Bryndalmoraz Karakal they called him – the bright hope of the mountains.

'I am taking you to be safe, my son. Is it not your first responsibility to preserve the royal bloodline?'

Prince Thorgrim's young face twisted with inner conflict. 'But I am the prince, mother. I will not be an oathbreaker.'

'You have taken no oaths,' soothed his mother, stroking the lines on his face. 'If you did not believe us to be doing the right thing, then you would have stayed behind. We have already come so far.'

The prince looked doubtful and bit his lip, causing the fuzz of growing beard to puff up. He nodded in what was intended to be a decisive manner, but Gromvarl saw he was still unsure. He was brave for a boy of his age.

'Very well,' said Thorgrim.

'King Belegar for a father and that one there for his mother, I don't envy that youngster,' said Douric quietly.

'You're not wrong there,' Gromvarl replied as the queen and prince talked. 'But he's almost past all that. He'll be his own master soon, mark my words. He's got a strong head, that boy, but with her temperament, thank Valaya. The last thing Karak Eight Peaks needs is another Belegar.'

'I'm not sure the queen's temperament is necessarily an improvement,' said Douric.

Gromvarl snorted.

Strange noises sounded from deep in the mountain.

'We best be away, vala. These tunnels were much fractured in the time of Great Cataclysm. They are unsafe. No one knows where they go,' said Douric.

Kemma's face crinkled with bitterness. 'There is nowhere safe in Karak Eight Peaks – there never has been. I should have left as soon as Thorgrim was born.' She reached into her robes. Douric held up his hand.

'Payment upon safe delivery, or my word is not my bond,' he said. 'Best say your farewells.' Douric tactfully withdrew, drawing the prince after him to leave Kemma alone with her guardian.

Gromvarl gave his queen a bow. He huffed on his pipe like a steam engine building power, filling the dairy with smoke.

'Well, I suppose this is goodbye.'

'Brave Gromvarl. Are you sure you will not come with us?'

'Not with this, vala,' said Gromvarl, lifting his broken arm. 'And even without, I'd have to stay. You know why.'

Kemma smiled her understanding. 'I lack the words to thank you for all that you've done for me.' She leaned through the clouds around him and laid a gentle kiss on his old cheek.

'It's not necessary! Get on with you now, young lady,' said Gromvarl, his voice inexplicably warbly. He coughed. 'Damned tobacco making my eyes water! I'd give my other arm for a pouch of Everpeak Goldleaf.'

Douric led on up the passage, a krut ungdrin, where in better days herds of goats had been driven from their pastures to be milked and overwintered. They went through ways long forgotten, winding up the secret stair to a door high up on the shoulders of Kvinn-wyr.

'Be careful, my lady, my prince,' said Douric. 'It's cold and mighty windy out.'

This proved to be something of an understatement. The three of them were buffeted by a howling gale that drove needles of snow into their faces. The path they found themselves on went down steadily towards alpine pastures arrayed on the mountain's shoulders. Rusted spikes of ancient iron in the rock showed where a safety line had once been anchored, but it was a distant memory. The three of them clung on to the stone for dear life until they turned a corner onto the southern flank of the mountain, where the wind dropped to strong gusts that plucked at their clothes, petulant at its lost power.

'That's the worst bit, for now,' said Douric.

'You know this way well?' said Kemma.

'I know all ways well, my lady. A reckoner's not a reckoner if he can't get in or out of a place where reckoning needs doing. Those with debts are generally shy, retiring sorts. They can be a little tricky to dig out,' he said with a grin.

They went through high fields well above the tree line. Subject to the caprices of the wind, much of the snow had been blown from them, gathering in huge drifts against broken drystone walls and the cairns of piled rocks cleared from the fields by the ancestors. Tumbledown shacks marked the refuges of goatherds, and in one place the walls of a ruined village made straight, soft lines in the snow. All was abandoned, as everything was in the Eight Peaks. Here, however, there had recently been dwarfs tending flocks. The signs of recent occupation were visible in places, especially near other krut ungdrin. Once again, the pastures were empty.

Kemma found it hard to believe, but not so long ago there was an optimism to Karak Eight Peaks, a sense that things were turning for the better. Another cruel joke, and one she had never fallen for herself. This had always been a fool's errand, and in Belegar the errand had found its fool. Nevertheless, she was a dwarf, and the ruination upset her as much as any other. She had never told anyone, but this was why she hated Vala-Azrilungol so much. Every inch of it was a shameful reminder of what her people had lost.

Douric hadn't looked back at them the whole time they'd been outside; if he did she hoped he'd think her tears were brought forth by the biting wind and not from sorrow.

At one corner, they passed a collection of dwarf beard scalps, frozen stiff in the wind and rattling against their posts. 'Thorgrim! Look away!' she said. Her son did not heed her, and gawped at them. Anguish pulsed in her breast that he had to see such things, but it hardened her resolve. This was why they had to leave.

As they threaded their way through a series of terraced fields, the air grew thicker and it became easier to breathe. The tall white finger of Kvinn-wyr, cloaked in winter snow from peak to skirts, raised itself behind them. They were hidden from the feeble sun, trudging through a world of shadow and ice.

'Soon we must go back inside,' said Douric. 'Through another way. We can rest a while at its head before we press on.' He said this for the benefit of Thorgrim, who had a long way yet to go before he developed the full width of his thighs. He was trying his hardest to hide his discomfort like a good dawi, but his pale face and trembling lips told another story.

Kemma went to her son, and fussed over him as mothers do. He was proud enough to shoo her away, and Douric smiled at that. Kemma frowned, which he thought a little extreme, but then she held up her hand. 'Shhh!' she said. 'What's that?'

Douric cocked his head. His eyes widened in concern. 'Curse my ears, I'm getting old!'

Kemma drew her hammer and put herself in front of her son.

'Off the path! To that hut down there, and stay on the rocks. Leave no tracks!' Douric pointed to a sorry ruin thirty yards away. Too late. A party of Belegar's hammerers came around the corner from below, lining up three abreast to block their way down the rocky path.

'Brok Gandsson,' said Kemma. 'Belegar has you chasing mothers who love their sons, has he? Your beard thickens with honour day by day.' She spoke haughtily. There was no point in pretence. There was only one reason he could be here.

'Halt! Halt in the name of the king!' said Brok Gandsson, leader of the Iron Brotherhood. He stood athwart the path, puffing clouds of cold breath. Dressed in full armour, he wore no extra garb in concession to the temperature, and his nose was red and dripping as a result. His expression made it clear that he meant business.

'I'll do no such thing. You'll let me by, Brok Gandsson. The future of the Angrund clan and all of the Eight Peaks is here by my side. Take him back, and you will doom him. Let me take him away from here.'

Brok stood his ground, his face set. Tension showed in the line of his jaw, bunching muscles under beard. He was not enjoying this role. That was something, thought Kemma.

'The mountains are full of grobi and urk, and the tunnels heave with vermin. If I let him off this mountain, it is you who will be killing him, not I. I will not let your mistake weigh on my conscience.'

'It'll be your mistake, not mine. I've made my mind up.'

'She's coming with us,' said Brok to his warriors in an unnecessary display of authority. 'If her highness complains, clap her in irons.'

'I am your queen!' said Kemma, outraged.

'No dwarf is to leave Vala-Azrilungol without the say of King Belegar. Queen or not, Vala Kemma, you'll not be among those who disobey him.'

Douric stepped forwards, hands held in front of him as if they were full of reason, and they would all go away content if only they would look into his palms to see. He wore his habitual grin openly, like they were all sharing a joke that needed a punch line. 'Wait a minute here, Brok. Can we not see our way through to some other solution? The lady only wants what's best for her son, and the Angrund clan.'

But Brok was in no mood for amity. He looked upon the reckoner with undisguised hatred. 'What do you know of the honour of the Iron Brotherhood? Long have you been a thorn in our king's side! Always you reckoners taking a peck of this here, a pick of that there, when you have no right.'

Douric's good humour fell away from his face in an avalanche, showing the cold hard stone beneath. 'I have every right. I am a lawmaster of the High King, my lad – a petty one, I grant you, but I bear his seal and his authority.'

'Then go back to Thorgrim in Everpeak, and steal your ale from his cup for a change!'

Douric took another step forwards. 'You should let them go.'

Brok raised his hammer. 'Do not come another step closer, wanaz. I'm warning you.'

'Let's just talk this out...'

Brok swung his hammer to smack into the side of Douric's head with a final crack. The reckoner spun on his feet and went down hard, falling limp to the ground, where broad red flowers bloomed in the snow. His hat blew away on the wind.

Brok stepped from foot to foot, horrified at what he had done. His dawi murmured. Brok's face hardened. 'A pox on all reckoners and their dishonourable dealings! Gazul judge you harshly, oath worrier, grudge doubter!' He spat on the rock. 'You dawi! Stop your grumbling. Help the queen and the prince here back into the mountain. It's cold up here and there are grobi about.'

Two hammerers came forward, reaching for Kemma.

'Unhand me! I command you to let me by!'

Their hands dropped.

Some of the fury went out of Brok, and he sagged, unmanned

by what he had done. 'Belegar gives me my orders, vala,' said Brok. 'I had no choice. I am oath-given.'

'Dawi killing dawi. Oaths or not, that's a fine sight, not that my husband would care. He's wanted Douric gone a long time. Too stupid to see a good dwarf in front of his nose, like a wattock can't tell fool's gold from gold.'

'For what it's worth, I am sorry.'

'Not sorry enough to take the Slayer's oath.'

Brok stared at her with a peculiar mix of emotions, all strong.

'The reckoner's body?' asked one of his followers. 'We can't just leave it here.'

Brok stared at the dead dwarf. The wind teased his hair and beard, his hands were still open in a display of peace. He looked asleep, but for his caved-in skull. Self-hatred got the better of Brok, and he turned it outwards. 'Yes we can, and we will. He was a traitor. Umgdawi to the core and gold-hungrier than a dragon. Leave him for the grobi and the stormcrows.'

'Thane...'

'I said leave him!' bellowed Brok.

'Shame on you, Brok Gandsson, shame on you,' hissed Kemma.

'We should all be ashamed, vala. We've taken a few wrong tunnels on the way, and now it's too late for all of us,' he said, grabbing her by the elbow and pulling her forwards. Two other hammerers gently helped Prince Thorgrim away with encouraging words and swigs of ale. 'Each and every one.'

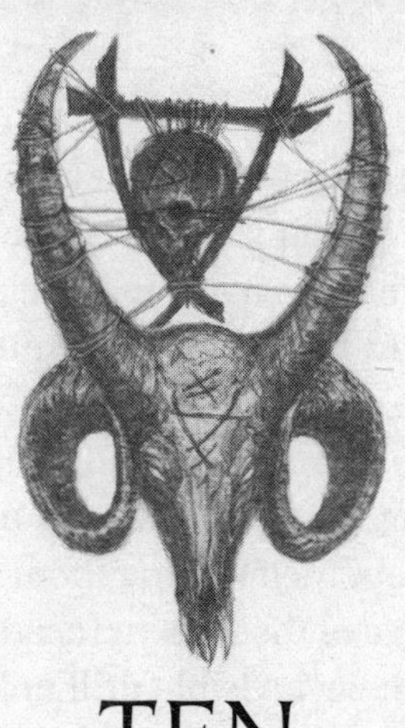

TEN

An Oath Fulfilled

Borrik hewed down the last of the stormvermin still facing him, his runic axe pulsing with power. The pure blue of its magic, clear as brynduraz in the sun, radiated more than light. The axe's blessings brought relief to his burning muscles, drove the tiredness from leaden limbs. This was good, for Borrik could not remember the last time he had slept.

Once the Norrgrimlings had been renowned for sleeping upright while standing guard, taking turns in the centre where they might be held up by their brothers. Borrik yearned for those days as much as he yearned for sleep. Neither would come again. There were not enough Axes of Norr left to attempt their famed feat, and he feared they would never rebuild their numbers enough to do so again. It was a point of pride to his ironbreakers that they never had nor ever would abandon a post given them to guard. Pride had ever been the undoing of dwarfs. Soon it would be the end of them.

'They're falling back,' he said. His strong, proud voice reduced to a hoarse wheeze. 'Forgefuries, forward!'

With a stoicism that would shame a mountain, the remaining four Forgefuries set off with the same skill and speed they had possessed two months ago. Only their faces betrayed their fatigue, pale skin and brown smears under eyes grown small and gritty.

'Fire!' said Tordrek. His dawi reloaded and fired with breathtaking skill, pumping round after round of blazing energy into the back of the skaven, incinerating them as they fled.

The squeaking panic of the ratmen receded down the tunnels. Borrik stared at the near-invisible drill holes packed with powder around each stairwell mouth. If Belegar would only let him blow them… But the king would not. His name was a byword for stubbornness, even among the dwarfs. He cursed the king under his breath.

'Right, lads,' said Borrik. 'You know the drill.'

'Aye aye,' said Albok tiredly. 'Rats in the hole. Come on!'

The remaining Axes of Norr lumbered forward, clenching and unclenching fists that were moulded into claws suited only to holding axes. They betrayed no sign of weariness as they heaved up dead skaven from the floor, save perhaps a certain slowness as they tossed the corpses into the hole at the centre of the chamber. Not scrawny rat slaves these, but skaven elites, black-furred stormvermin equipped with hefty halberds and close-fitting armour. Some of this was dwarf-made. For the first days of the battle against the better skaven troops, the dwarfs had diligently stripped the work of their ancestors from the ratmen and stockpiled it in the chamber fronting the door of Bar-Undak. But there was so much of it, so very much, that they had given up. Now the defiled armour went into the hole like everything else, swallowed up along with their grief at seeing the craft of their ancestors so abused.

What cheer the Norrgrimlings had was gone. Weeks of hard fighting had worn them down, stone-hard though they were, as centuries of rain will wear down a mountain. Their eyes were red with lack of sleep, their beards stiff with blood they had neither the time nor the strength to comb out. Seven of them had gone to the halls of their ancestors, among them Hafnir and Kaggi Blackbeard. Their voices were as missed as their axes. Uli the Elder had lost an eye to a lucky spear-thrust, but refused to retire. Gromley had several missing links from his hauberk to add to the scratch on his shield, and complained bitterly about it. No one teased him for his grumbling any longer.

'Is there any more ale?' asked Borrik. 'My throat's dryer than an engine-stoker's dongliz.'

'There's another delivery due soon, but they're getting tardy,' said Grunnir Stonemaster. There was no way of telling the time in the dark underground, but the dwarfs had an unerring knack for it. 'It's past midday or I'm a grobi's dung collector.'

Borrik managed a grin that hurt his face. 'That you certainly are not. Not only are they late, but the barrels are getting lighter.'

Grunnir shrugged. 'Back in the glory days that would never have happened. Proper brewmasters then, and proper brew.'

Borrik looked at the devastation around him. Nothing was like it was, not any more. 'You're sounding like a longbeard.'

Grunnir tugged his beard. 'It's been well watered with blood these last weeks. It's growing as quickly as my tally of grudges.'

Distant drums sounded. Borrik stood. 'All right, lads! Back in formation – they're coming for another go!'

The ironbreakers tossed another few corpses into the pit and trudged wearily back to their stations. Skaven began filing out into the Hall of Reckoning in organised lines that spread into calm ranks, a far cry from the panicking thralls they had first faced.

'Look at them,' said Gromley, taking in the number of stolen dwarf items in the hands of their enemies. 'Thieving vermin. They're so intent on killing us, they never stop to think who'll they'll steal off when we're gone.'

'Less of that,' said Uli. 'We're not going anywhere.'

'Well,' said Grunnir, settling his standard into a more comfortable position. 'If they do win, I hope the little furry beggars choke on their victory.'

'Borrik! Borrik!' A hand tugged at the mail shirt of the thane. Tordrek had come forward. 'There's someone at the door.'

'Ale?' said Borrik brightening.

Tordrek shook his head. Borrik cast an annoyed look at the marshalling skaven and followed his friend through the thin back rank of the Axes of Norr. There remained a single full line of ten to block the way.

The sound from the skaven was muted in the chamber at the rear. A steady tap-tapping came from the door. Borrik pressed his ear against it.

Borrik counted three different hammer sizes beating out the code, the notes they made identical to anyone but a dwarf.

'Aye, that's the right signal. Open the door,' he said. 'Quickly now, we don't want this gate gaping wide when the skaven come to attack.'

'We're all right for a minute,' came Gromley's sour voice from the front of the ironbreakers. 'They're still trying to get themselves in order.'

Tordrek's remaining Forgefuries, guarding the door, opened it.

What emerged was not ale. A spike of orange hair came around the door. Borrik took a step back, face grim. 'It's come to that, has it?' he said. 'Make way, lads!' he called. 'We've got company.'

Silently, the Slayers came out, more than twenty of them, all stony-faced killers. Their leader, an emotionless dwarf who made Borrik look the size of a beardling, nodded a greeting to the thane. The rest filed out without looking. Borrik didn't look them in the eye, because behind the flinty light that burned there you could catch the darkness of shame. A broken oath, a grandfather's mistake uncovered, a romantic advance rebuffed... Whatever crimes these dwarfs had committed or shames they had suffered, trivial or gross, they all felt the same. They were all broken by their experiences. Through the narrow passage they went. At the far end, the Norrgrimlings parted to let them past.

The skaven were working themselves up into a frenzy, biting at their shields, their leaders squeaking orders from the back, their soldiers squeaking together in response.

'Quickly now, quickly,' said Borrik. 'Close ranks as soon as they're through.'

Gromley gave him a hard stare that suggested that wasn't going to be necessary, but prodded his tired warriors into place with his axe haft.

The Slayers spread out once in the hall, not in a disciplined line but each finding a spot that suited him best. That meant as far away from the others as possible. They said nothing as they waited for the skaven to attack. The ratmen did so cautiously, their eagerness for the fight seeming to desert them when they saw these fresh opponents.

Driven on by furious squeaking and the clang of cymbals, the skaven charged, flowing over the broken, bloodied floor of the Hall of Reckoning as one.

When the enemy were close, the Slayers counter-charged. Some shouted out to Grimnir, some sang, others howled with the pain of whatever shame had driven them to take the oath. Yet others made no noise, but set to with voiceless determination.

They were engulfed by the vermintide like bright rocks in a dark sea. Like rocks, they were not overcome.

'Look at them,' muttered Gromley. The Slayer leader leapt and whirled, his paired rune axes trailing light and blood in equal part.

'This is a rare sight. I'm glad I have one eye left to see it with,' said Uli.

'Look at that one! The big one with the scars!' Albok pointed to a dwarf who was wider than he was tall, his body covered in tattoos, his tattoos scratched through by scars. He wielded a single, double-handed axe with a head as big as his own torso.

'That's the Dragonslayer Aldrik the Scarred, if I'm not mistaken,' said Gromley. He blew out his cheeks and shook his head. 'If you live to be five hundred, you'll be half the warrior he is.'

Aldrik was a solid presence amid the churning mass of skaven. They were far quicker than him, but he moved aside from every blow. His axe strokes were deliberate. Not a single one missed. Every swipe cut a skaven in half.

The Norrgrimlings relaxed. It was plain to them all that they were not going to be needed in this engagement. The Slayers were butchering the skaven, and the ratmen were close to breaking. Already, their back ranks were becoming strung out from the mass at the front.

Of a sudden, the skaven had had enough. They fled, squealing frantically. The Slayers let out a shout and chased after them. Surrounded by piled bodies were three orange-haired dwarf corpses. The remainder disappeared down the stairheads after the fleeing skaven.

The Axes of Norr let their guard drop.

'That's that, then. Time for a rest,' said Grunnir.

'Aye, and more besides,' said Thane Borrik, pushing his way to the front with a metal message scroll in his hand. 'We've got new orders from the king. Time to pull back to the Hall of Clan Skalfdon.' He pointed over his shoulder with his thumb. 'Got a herald back there, so it's as official as it gets. Tordrek, blow those doors up before we go.'

'What about the Slayers, Thane?' asked Albok.

'Three groups of them have gone out,' said Borrik. 'It's shameful to say, but we won't see the likes of this for a long time. They've got their wish. Let's take their dead back. The least we can do is lay their axes on the shrine of Grimnir, and let him know they fulfilled their oaths.'

As the Norrgrimlings tenderly retrieved the dead Slayers, Tordrek stepped up with his dawi and headed for the centre of the room. Once there, they opened fire and ignited the charges packed around each stairhead. The explosion in the Hall of Reckoning sounded like the end of everything. Dust blew out, coating the surviving members of the Axes of Norr so they appeared like the ancestors, freshly awoken at the roots of the world. Bright eyes peered out from grey faces.

'That should keep them back a bit,' said Borrik, when the last rock had clattered to a standstill. 'Come on, lads, let's see if there's any ale left in the citadel. This has been a thirsty couple of weeks.'

ELEVEN

A Confrontation

'A messenger is coming,' said Soothgnawer's voice, as yet unattached to a body.

Kranskritt startled. It was unnerving how the verminlord came from nowhere. He looked around for Soothgnawer, nose working frantically. He caught a whiff of the otherwordly creature, but the scent was faint and all around him, and Kranskritt could not see him.

'There is always a messenger coming. Who? What-what?' responded the grey seer testily.

'One of the Red Guard,' came the reply. Soothgnawer had still not manifested. Kranskritt saw a darkening against the wall, a shadow out of place. He stared fixedly at it, determined not to be surprised.

'Queek will give the orders I foresaw,' said Soothgnawer smugly. 'Queek has guessed the deception. It is to the peaks you will go, hunting goblins. He wishes your clawpack to engage Skarsnik and keep him away from the main assault upon the beard-things.'

'Pah! Mad-thing does great insult to me,' Kranskritt said. 'I should be with him, I should whisper-command in his ear! He is mad and foolish-stupid.' Kranskritt shivered. The bells on his ankles, wrists and horns tinkled with fury.

'Hush, little seer! Do you remember our plans? You will have what you wish.' Soothgnawer's voice was poison-perfumed velvet, smooth against the senses, beguiling, yet smothering.

Kranskritt bridled. They were most assuredly not his plans. He did not like this situation. It was typically he who had foreknowledge and he who did the manipulating. This creature was always two scurryings ahead of him, possibly more.

'Not our plans!' he said, wringing the hem of his robe. 'Yours! What happens if Queek discovers? What if he say-accuses me? He has no fear of the Horned Rat. He has no fear of me!'

'Patience!' said the voice, now from right behind him.

With a yelp, Kranskritt spun on the spot. From the shadows between unpacked crates, a space far too small to accommodate the verminlord, large eyes full of an ancient malevolence regarded him. Half concealed in this too-small space, yet there nonetheless, the creature's triple rack of horns seemed to grow and twist sinuously. At that moment skin and fur clothed his skull, and he looked like a grey seer grown vast on magic and evil. A clawed hand thrust out, holding an enormous gazing globe.

'You are right to fear the future, Kranskritt. If Queek suspects, then die long and horribly you will, and lower the status of Clan Scruten becomes. Look-look! There are many paths to follow. All bad but one. In life I too walked as a grey seer. Now I am more. Much more. I scry beyond space and time – the future is downwind. And I tell you, there is no other way.'

The voice left the room, burrowed directly into Kranskritt's mind. It was at once compelling and threatening. Soothgnawer had a way of posing questions that provided their own answers, which, when examined later, posed more questions. The endless conundrums this generated in Kranskritt's agile mind was threatening to drive him as mad as Queek. He turned an involuntary blow at his own head into a scratch of his ear so furious it drew blood, and glanced into the ball.

'Yes-yes, I see-scry that now.' He saw nothing, but wished to appear wise before this creature. He instantly regretted the hesitancy in his voice. Verminlords could smell deception.

'You see nothing.'

Kranskritt wailed. 'I cannot see!'

'Look harder.'

The grey seer turned away, shaking his head, but the voice would not be dislodged. 'Tell me, why-why is my clawpack not ordered into the fight?' demanded Kranskritt. 'Why must I chase the green-thing? I have the largest clawpack.'

'Patience, little seer. Queek was confounded. Two sets of orders from his master demand his action in opposing manner.'

Kranskritt tittered. 'A good trick-treachery on the arrogant mad-thing! Who is behind it? Is it your doing, horned master? Such a trick is worthy of your unsurpassed intellect,' he said, remembering his manners under the verminlord's gaze.

Soothgnawer emerged a little further into the material world, huge and terrifying. 'Little seer must learn to listen more closely. Both sets of orders come from Lord Gnawdwell. The lord of Clan Mors tires of his general.'

Kranskritt wrinkled his muzzle. 'Then why two orders? Why not bad orders, or simple kill-slay? It makes no sense!'

Soothgnawer eased himself out of whatever hellish realm he inhabited and into Kranskritt's burrow. The laws of space-time asserted themselves, and he popped into existence. Fully manifested, he filled the room, his horns scraping fragments of stone from the ceiling. He pushed crates over and sat down on one. Still he towered over Kranskritt. 'Is this the level of the grey seers' intelligence in these times? So sad. No mystery to me why the Great Horned One punished Clan Scruten.' Soothgnawer spoke with infinite paternal patience to the seer. 'Gnawdwell wants to see what Queek will do. He is too attached-fond to the warlord. In his head, here,' the verminlord tapped between his eyes, 'he thinks that he confuses Queek to make him hesitate, to anger his underlings so that they will kill-slay him and replace him. But in his heart Gnawdwell has become too sentimental. His attempts on Queek's life are poorly planned and half-hearted, and so is this scheme-plan. He does not admit it, but he gives Queek another chance, a way from death. If Queek is successful here, Gnawdwell will not kill him. He knows Queek is unworthy as his successor, that a creature as insane as Queek can never sit upon the Council of Thirteen, but he has deluded himself that the Headtaker might change, and so Gnawdwell's heart wars with his mind.'

Kranskritt spat. 'The heart is quick and treacherous. Great thinkings only come from the mind. Is it not established that the skaven are the most intelligent of all races? We grey seers do not listen to our traitor-hearts.'

'This is so. This is right. Make sure you stay that way, little seer.'

'Tell-squeak me, how you know what Gnawdwell think-feels, great and wise Soothgnawer?' asked Kranskritt, half afraid of the answer, for if the verminlord could read minds as he suspected, Kranskritt would have a lot of grovelling to perform. His glands twitched.

'To be a master of our kind, as I am, little seer, you must look beyond what each ratkin does to another, and into the mind behind the scheme. Within all of you there are many reasons and many desires, and these vie and plot one against the other as surely as you fight one another.' The creature paused. Its white-furred face lost all flesh and skin to appear as an eyeless skull, turning back into a grey seer's face without appearing to change, even to Kranskritt's magic-sight. Kranskritt felt very weak indeed and flinched from him. 'Now Queek reacts with open violence. It is what Queek does. He is as unsubtle as his Dwarf Gouger. Look-look into the ball and see.'

Reluctantly, Kranskritt stared into the verminlord's over-sized gazing glass. If he had put his arms around it, his paws would not have met. Now he saw. In its uncertain depths were crystal-clear images of skaven marching all over the City of Pillars, all going upwards. The burrowing machines of Clan Skryre worked tirelessly to bore them new routes. Massed ranks of skaven confronted lines of glowering dwarf-things, the long-fur on their faces bristling. Skaven war machines opened up on them, killing the stupid creatures by the score.

'The dwarfs will soon retreat. The future is changing. We come to a nexus in the way. At the right moment, you must be in place to act and seize the right path. See why, little seer. Watch now and witness a fate that will be yours and all grey seers' if you are not successful,' said Soothgnawer, his voice lodged still in the space behind Kranskritt's eyes, more irritating than a tick. 'Watch-watch.'

Kranskritt gave a startled squeak. He was no longer in his burrow, but in a hall choked with many skaven dead. A large hole was in the centre, and two piles of shattered stone were to either side. Rock dust drifted on air currents, the smell of freshly broken rock and blackpowder was choking, but although he could smell it, although he felt he should be coughing hard, he breathed easily. He looked about for Soothgnawer. He could not see him, but could feel his presence.

'You are here and not-here, little seer. This is the Hall of Reckoning, as the dwarf-things call it. Great things happen here very soon. Be calm and watch.'

Kranskritt tried his best not to think about where he was or how he was there. On the edge of his perception was the endless, anguished squeaking of millions of voices that he did not care to hear.

Fortunately for him, the burring noise of heavy machinery soon troubled the chamber and drowned out the squeals of the damned. The ground shook. A short distance from the leftmost blocked tunnel, a fall of dust sheeted away from the rock. Small stones skittered from their position on the rock falls as the vibrations grew louder, until with the crack of broken stone, a giant drill head breached the wall, multiple toothed grinding heads all turning in separate directions. The Clan Skryre machine jolted as it drove out of the tunnel and dropped six inches to the floor of the hall. A platform on tracked wheels followed the drill head, two goggled and masked warlocks tending the mass of sorcerous machinery mounted atop it. They pulled levers, flicked switches. Lightning burst from the tops of brass orbs. Fluids bubbled in long glass tubes protected by copper latticework. The drilling machine drove off to one side, pulping skaven corpses under its truckles. The drill ceased spinning and the machine came to a halt, powering down with a teeth-wounding whine.

A score of heavily built stormvermin came from the new corridor, a thunder of pounding, muscular legs and thick armour. Stones pattered from their shoulders as they emerged, but the tunnel held. They fanned out, forming a solid square in the middle of the chamber. Kranskritt drew back into the shadows.

'Foolish little seer, they cannot see you,' laughed Soothgnawer in his mind. 'Do not fear!'

Their leader, a mid-ranking member of Clan Mors whose name-smell was Frizloq, came next, entering the Hall of Reckoning as warily as a common rat might dare a night-time kitchen. He sniffed the air, stepping delicately down the spilled rock to survey the room. Whatever he expected to find there was gone, and he grinned widely at its absence. He prodded one of his minions with the butt of his polearm, gesturing that he should enter the tunnel in one corner. The skaven cringed at being separated from the warmth and protection of his littermates, but obeyed. He disappeared into the tunnel with a wary backward glance.

A second passed. The stormvermin re-emerged.

'Empty!' he squeaked triumphantly. 'Broken beer keg. Slain skaven, but beard-things gone!'

'The door?' asked the leader.

'Locked-barred. No traps,' reported the scout.

The clawleader rubbed his hands together. 'Locked, you say? Barred, you squeak? We shall see-see. We shall see! Get it open! Get it open for the glory of Clan Mors! We shall be first into the citadel!'

A flurry of activity followed. At first the skaven tried to beat the door down themselves, but the gate of Bar-Undak was too strong and they were too feeble to breach its steel.

The leader pulled his warriors back, generously rewarding them for their efforts with the battle corpses littering the floor. As they settled down to eat, he conferred sharply with the warlocks, pointing and chittering something lost under the noise of the idling machine. The engine roared, black smoke tinged by green flecks puffed from its chimney, and it ground around to face the tunnel to the chamber. The drill picked up speed and the machine chewed through the thirty feet to the door chamber in short order, widening the original tunnel considerably. As soon as it backed up, Clan Moulder packmasters brought in two monstrously built rat ogres. Their masters gestured to the stones on the floor by the rock falls. The rat ogres understood, taking up a hefty lump of rock in each fist. They loped then into the widened tunnel and thence the chamber. There, under the direction of their masters, they battered at the doors, snarling as they grazed their knuckles and banged their heads on the ceiling in the cramped space. Their handlers goaded them with sparking prods and the rat ogres squeal-roared, bashing harder with their improvised tools. The door shook on its deep-set hinges.

For an hour, during which time Kranskritt continued to watch from his shadow-place, the door refused to give. The rocks scarred the steel, little else. But slowly the strength of the rat ogres began to tell, and the door became loose. They pounded out a bowl in the middle and a rent appeared. The rat ogres cast aside their stones to work their claws into the gaps and tug and pull at it.

At this juncture, Warlord Thaxx Redclaw arrived at the front, stepping imperiously from the tunnel mouth with an honour guard of equally arrogant stormvermin.

'Masterfully canny Thaxx arrives at the most opportune moment, as no doubt his incomparable planning intended,' squeak-greeted the skaven leader. 'Humble Frizloq has great news. This door is soon to be destroyed. Come-see!' He beckoned to his lord excitedly. 'You are just in time to witness the opening of the way!'

'You have done well, Frizloq,' said Thaxx coolly, looking down his muzzle at the clawleader. 'Four-score weak-meat I will pledge-give you for your adequate efforts on my behalf.'

Frizloq dipped his head in gratitude.

A bellow came from the door chamber, then a crash as the door was torn from its hinges and cast down.

Frizloq called out to his warriors, all of whom were feasting or sleeping, grabbing the opportunity to rest while the rat ogres worked. 'To arms! To arms!' he squeaked. 'To the beard-thing citadel, and there to victory!'

Thaxx Redclaw grabbed his underling's arm and shook his head. 'No-no! Wait-wait.'

Frizloq became confused. 'Why-why? The door is broken, the door so many died to breach. Why we not press on? Catch the beard-things unawares? If we hurry-scurry, we might disrupt them. Surely they fortify-build as we squeak? That is their way.'

'No-no,' repeated Thaxx. 'Warlord Queek's orders. All attacks on this front must halt. He does not wish Clan Mors warriors to die-die in dwarf-thing traps. First clawpack will wait, wait for slaves, for weak-meat.'

Frizloq opened his mouth, for Thaxx's command directly contradicted his earlier orders from Queek himself, but he thought better of it. He twitched meekly and exposed his throat as a display of his utmost subservience. 'As great Thaxx demands, so shall it be!'

'Not humble I, but mighty Queek,' corrected Thaxx. 'We must thank to his strategic pre-eminence for this clever-smart move. Thaxx is but his worthy message-bearer.'

As if in direct challenge to Thaxx's statement, a clanking came up the corridor. Frizloq's skaven were shoved aside. Red-armoured stormvermin burst into the room, their mouths twisted into snarls, tails swiping with pent-up aggression. At their head came the biggest skaven in the City of Pillars, Ska Bloodtail. Thaxx's nose quivered. He swallowed rapidly and blinked. Where Ska went, Queek was close behind.

The Headtaker bowed low to enter the Hall of Reckoning, saving his precious trophies from damage on the ceiling.

'Who speak-squeaks on my authority?' he demanded. 'Why this front not press on? Mighty Queek say all stormvermin attack! All clanrats to move forward! The time for weak-meat is done. Why Thaxx say otherwise?'

Thaxx curled his lips, exposing his teeth all along his muzzle. In his shadow-space, Kranskritt shrank back, terrified by the murderous glare burning in Queek's red eyes. The Headtaker bullied his way through the crowd, skaven scrambling over each other to get out of the way. He confronted Thaxx. Redclaw stood tall and held his ground.

'What bribe-gift you take to betray Clan Mors?' asked the Headtaker, tail swishing back and forth.

Those around the two powerful war-leaders spread out, forming a large challenge ring. Fear musk sprayed from the lesser members of the crowd. The stormvermin watched intently, but others were desperate to find elsewhere to be. Walking sideways, the two combatants began to circle each other, their muscles tensing to spring.

Excuses, denials and renewed pledges were the tried and true ways of skaven avoiding, or at least delaying, such confrontations. Thaxx Redclaw had known Queek Headtaker too long to attempt such pretence. He knew what was coming next, had planned for it. He had not expected it to happen now, necessarily, but no scheme was mad-thing proof, and he was ready. Baring his teeth in a hissing grimace, the warlord of the first clawpack drew his sword, its cruelly serrated edge glistening with warp venom. Yet how did Queek know? Thaxx had told no one of his dealings with Clan Skryre. And how did the Headtaker get here so quickly? Both things were impossible – but now was not the time to think upon it.

The Headtaker sneered. 'You wonder how I know? Mighty Queek has informants you could never dream of, fool-thing... No one bests Queek!' He drew his sword and weighed Dwarf Gouger carefully in his other hand, his gaze fixed on Thaxx's head. Thaxx glanced nervously at the new spike of pale wood lashed to the Headtaker's trophy rack. 'Now, tell Queek, Thaxx traitor-rat, what was the promise-pact? No warptokens or breeders – you have too many of those already,' said Queek. 'Yes-yes, don't look surprised. Queek knows what you hide in your under-warrens. No, the great Thaxx would not be tempted by what he already has. The offer was to be first warlord of Clan Mors, wasn't it? Yes-yes? Replace great and mighty Queek in City of Pillars? Delay long enough until Queek failed and a replacement was in order, unless there was an accident first?' Queek tutted. 'Queek say Thaxx has been left alone for too long in City of Pillars. Now Thaxx learn highly unpleasant lesson from good teacher Queek.'

Thaxx leapt forwards, his sword hissing down at Queek. Queek dodged out of range with ease, and Thaxx went right past him. But Thaxx's attack was merely a feint, giving him space to draw a hidden warplock pistol with his free hand. He spun past the Headtaker, turning his failed lunge into a graceful turn.

'Die-die!' shrieked Thaxx, squeezing the trigger over and over.

Queek laughed. Thaxx should never have reached for another weapon. Without that, he stood more of a chance. Against the mighty Queek, Queek thought, that was still less than no chance, but he might have died with dignity.

With the agility of a warrior born, Queek leapt aside. Knowing he would never close the distance in time, he hurled his sword.

Thaxx had time to fire off three quick shots from his repeater pistol. Two of them dented Queek's armour, sending showers of warpstone-impregnated dust from it. The third missed, and then Queek's blade slammed into his pistol. The sword severed one of Thaxx's fingers, the digit still locked upon the trigger as the pistol clattered to the floor. Thaxx squealed with pain. In shock, the wounded warlord looked down first upon his bleeding hand, and then to the fallen pistol, to find his missing finger. This was his final mistake.

Queek crossed the gap between them in a single bound. He brought Dwarf Gouger down and then up, catching Thaxx under the chin with the blunt side.

Thaxx's jaw shattered, and he was sent sprawling onto his back. Queek pounced so that his feet were spread either side of Thaxx's chest. He thrust his yellow incisors close to Thaxx's face.

'Tsk tsk, foolish Thaxx. Queek knows a bribe from Clan Skryre when it is fired at Queek,' hissed Queek. 'But tell-say, who else is involved? That venom on your sword-blade smells like Clan Eshin good stuff. Tell-squeal and Queek will end it quick-quick.'

Queek leaned in, so that Thaxx's burbling, blood-choked words were audible to him alone. But Kranskritt, aided by Soothgnawer's magic, heard them too, mangled though they were through the Redclaw's wounded jaw.

'The Horned Rat skin you forevermore, mad-thing.'

To Kranskritt's surprise Queek laughed and nodded with satisfaction. He drove Dwarf Gouger down point first into Thaxx's belly, and ripped upwards, disembowelling Thaxx.

Straightening up, the Grand Warlord of the Eight Peaks surveyed the skaven gathered around him in the Hall of Reckoning. 'First clawpack,' rang out Queek's voice. 'Thaxx betrayed Clan Mors. I will lead you now.'

'Queek! Queek! Queek!' the others shouted. Frizloq prostrated himself with admirable alacrity. His officers, then the lesser rats, did the same, all chanting the Headtaker's name.

'Loyal Ska!' yelled Queek over the adulation.

'Yes, O mighty Queek?'

'This not over. Bring me Skrikk, bring me Kranskritt, bring me Gritch.' He snickered evilly. 'It is time all traitor-things dance with Queek!'

'See now?' said Soothgnawer to Kranskritt. 'This is what you face.'

Kranskritt nodded.

'Good. Back we go!'

The Hall of Reckoning faded from view, and Kranskritt found himself in his burrow once more.

The grey seer gathered what little courage he had and thrust out his horns. He closed his eyes – a skaven show of confidence. This time he spoke more boldly. 'Yes-yes. How could perfect Soothgnawer be anything but correct?'

'Indeed,' said Soothgnawer.

'I will find the goblin and make the offer. Goblin kill first clawpack, Kranskritt save the day with fifth clawpack. Grey seers look like heroes.'

And so, Kranskritt dearly hoped, Kranskritt could avoid his meeting with Queek.

When he opened his eyes once more, he was alone. Soothgnawer was gone, but the verminlord's voice rang still in the secret spaces of his skull. 'I know,' it said.

Kranskritt threw together a variety of magical ingredients. He called in his servants. 'Gather fifth clawpack! Into the mountains! Send-scurry message to mighty Queek.' Kranskritt smiled as his scribe fetched quill and man-skin parchment. 'Tell him unworthy Kranskritt follow mighty Queek's orders to the letter, loyally and without question.'

TWELVE

Skarsnik's Big Deal

The halls under Karag Zilfin had once belonged to a powerful dwarf merchant family. In the glory days of the Eternal Realm, the place was plaqued with gold, its dark ways lit with glimlight glowstones and runic lamps whose oil never ran dry. Not that Skarsnik, the current occupant, knew that. Vala-Azrilungol had been stripped thousands of years before Skarsnik had sprouted. He had to contend with walls that ran black with mould, water that dripped from the ceiling all the time, and the constant blast of the mountain winds whistling in through glassless windows and empty door frames.

'I hates this. It's rubbish,' he muttered as he walked to his chambers. He passed through his audience room, which was embarrassingly tiny compared to the Hall of a Thousand Pillars he'd once called his own. Tribute lay heaped chaotically everywhere. 'Really rubbish. Nowhere near enough room for all me presents. I miss it in the proper underground, Gobbla. Nice and warm.' He cut down a long corridor, perfectly carved in the stunty way with not a curve or kink to halt the wind blasting in from outside. Treasuries, store rooms and steps leading down opened up either side of him. At the end were his private quarters. He wasn't too happy when he got there and came upon the moonhat guards and phalanx of little big 'uns trusted with his safety, all of whom were sprawled about the place snoring and not at all doing a good job of guarding. He was too annoyed to kick them awake. Instead, he let Gobbla eat one. His screams woke the others and they ran, mismatched armour rattling, to their posts.

'Zogging idiots!' he shouted. 'There's a bleeding war on!'

He muttered darkly and scowled at them. Gobbla burped. The goblin elite shook so hard their knees knocked.

There was, at least, a door across the entrance to his rooms. He went in and shut it behind him with a sigh. A fire of bigshroom stalks burned in a long stone trough in the fireplace. He looked at the filthy furs heaped on his bed, and thought of sleeping.

He shook his head. 'Nah, never no time for sleeping. Sleep when you's dead, eh, Gobbla?' He chuckled. 'Got work to do. First mind, I reckon it's time for a little drinky.' On a table piled high with parchment covered in his spidery handwriting were numerous bottles. He shook them until he found one that was full. He held it up critically, grumbling that he had to tilt it this way and that to read the label. His eyes weren't as good as they used to be.

'*Produzzi di Castello di Rugazzi,*' he said. He shrugged at it. Castello di Rugazzi had been burned down along with the rest of Tilea a couple of years before. He wouldn't have cared had he known, but what Skarsnik held in his hands was quite probably the last bottle of wine from that vineyard, if not from Tilea. Skarsnik's stash had once had brews from all across the Old World, purloined from caravans braving the trek over to the Far East. But once Gorfang was killed and the rats infested Black Crag, there was no one to police Death Pass. Then the wars had started. No one had come that way he could bully or rob for a long while, and Skarsnik's cellars were running dry.

'Gotta be better than Duffskul's brew,' he said sourly. He found his goblet on the floor, groaning as he stood up straight and his back cracked. He tipped a spider out and peered in. The goblet was filthy, so he spat in it and cleaned it with his ink-stained thumb until he was satisfied.

He bit the top off the bottle with his needle-teeth and poured. As it glugged into the goblet, Skarsnik smacked his lips in anticipation. He pulled a snotling out of a cage and made it drink some. He watched it for a moment. It smiled stupidly, and obligingly did not die, so he shoved it back into its prison.

'Cheers, snotties,' he toasted his tasters, and slurped down a mouthful of wine. Then he lit a candle of dwarf fat and sat down to his work. 'Now then, now then,' he said, rubbing his hands. He was determined to update his list of tribes currently squatting in the surface city and the Great Vale. 'Got to be organised, eh, Gobbla? Where are you if you's not organised?'

Gobbla growled. That was not the correct response. Skarsnik stiffened. His ears prickled.

A ball of black lightning burst into being behind Skarsnik, caused him to spin round so fast he lost his face in the back of his hood.

'Not this again! Ratties, they never learn!' he said, wrestling with his bosshat. 'You've tried this fifteen times before, ya dumb gits! Garn! Get some new ideas!' He stood up violently, sending his papers onto the floor. His goblet he caught deftly in one hand as the table toppled from underneath it. With the other hand he snatched up his prodder, and pointed it at the fizzing orb.

Black energy throbbed, sending arcs of greenish-black sparks earthing in his possessions. Much to his annoyance, his papers caught fire. 'Oi! Oi! Oi!' he yelled. 'You want to come and talk to me, use the zogging front door like everyone else! You's burning all me stuff up! Bleeding ratties! Got no manners!'

The whirling energies settled down. Through a dark portal, an arrogant horned rat-thing, fur white as snow, robes suspiciously clean, stepped into Skarsnik's bedroom. The grey seer surveyed the room as if it owned it, and that really annoyed Skarsnik. Actually, that was kind of the entire problem with the Eight Peaks. When would they learn that the place was his!

The rat sniffed the air and pulled a face at what it found. 'I great Grey Seer Kranskritt. I come-skitter with deal-tidings, green-thing.' It spoke in accented orcish, higher than a gobbo, but perfectly intelligible. Skarsnik was used to that.

'Well, well, well – a horny rat!' said Skarsnik back in Queekish, the language of the skaven, and that took the grey seer by surprise, to Skarsnik's delight. 'Tinkle-tankle little bells too. Very nice, very pretty. Learn that off an elf? Cut above the average squeaker, ain't ya? But it's not like your lot to turn up yerselves. Usually get some poor rodent to do your dirty. You can't be that important.'

'I very-very much-important, green-thing!' said Kranskritt, eyes boiling with outrage. 'You show me respect!'

Skarsnik leered a yellow grin and slurped upon his wine. 'Yeah? Or what? I'll tell you what, you goat-rat... fing, whatever you is. You'll get angry and then I'll blow you up with me prodder, that's what'll happen. It's happened before. It's getting late and I've got a lot on, so be my guest. Tempt me, and then I can gets on with me work.'

Kranskritt clashed his incisors together, eyeing the prodder nervously. Its power was well known by his kind, and feared.

'I suppose you want to make a deal, then? Your lot don't do well in deals with me, you realise that?' said Skarsnik.

'You very annoying-pain, green-thing,' admitted Kranskritt.

'You could have just sent me a messenger.'

'We did. His skin-pelt now your new bedding,' said Kranskritt, pointing disdainfully at Skarsnik's bed.

Skarsnik looked sidelong at the fresh rat pelt serving as a

coverlet. 'Oh. Right. Yeah. He did try to tell us something, to be fair. If it makes you feel better, he was very tasty. Right then. I got things to be doing. Stuff to write. Plans to make. You know, you burneded all me papers up. Took me ages to do that. I'm not happy.'

'Pah! Green-thing plans little plans. I know-know much more.'

'So you said.' Skarsnik had another drink. The wine wasn't too bad. 'Actually, you haven't said much of anyfink apart from how important you is.'

The grey seer hissed and clenched its fists. This meeting was obviously paining it. 'Tomorrow, Lord Queek of Clan Mors begins the next stage of the great war of extermination against the beard-things. He attacks in the Hall of Many Beard-Things.'

'In the citadel?'

'Big beard-thing fortress, yes-yes!' snapped Kranskritt. His tail lashed.

'Funny really, don't know the citadel well. Even before the stunties came back, didn't really go there. Full of traps. Nasty little stunties. I quite like being alive, y'see. No idea what you're talking about.'

'I show-show!' snapped Kranskritt.

'All right, all right, keep your horns on.' Skarsnik giggled at the skaven as it bristled. 'What's the point?'

'It would be good-proper if Lord Queek is not successful. Tunnel teams dig-melt their way upwards. I show. You take them, good quick-fast, yes? You come up into citadel. You kill many dwarf-things, many, er, stunties, you stop Queek's easy victory.'

Skarsnik set his drink down. 'Why? I ain't no patsy for ratsies.' He laughed again. He was on form today.

Kranskritt clawed his hands. 'Foolish green-thing! Now your time is done, but still you making stupid joke-laughs! The children of Chaos rise! The Under-Empire will rule over all! You be destroyed, swept-aside like leaves in storm! You do it, and you live. Not enough for you, green-thing? You die now, if you prefer.'

'Yeah, right. Blah, blah, blah. Squeak, squeak, squeak.' With his teeth on his lips, Skarsnik mimed a little rat mouth jabbering. 'I have heard it all before!' he said, suddenly angry. 'Year in, zogging year out! It's always the same with your lot! Ooh, we is so clever. Ooh, we is the best. If that's the bleeding case, how comes I'm the king of Karak Eight Peaks?'

Skarsnik stood tall. He was very large for a night goblin, bigger than the seer. The prodder thrummed with orcy power. 'I ain't no idiot. If you are so powerful, you don't need me, does you?'

Kranskritt growled in irritation. He and his kind were used to skaven grovelling before them, squirting the musk of fear as soon as a seer showed its face. This goblin's cool insolence was deeply disrespectful. 'Very well! You help my faction, you help yourself. Hand-claw to hand-claw. Friends-alliance! No war! You take back upper deeps when beard-things dead.'

'That's more like it,' said Skarsnik. 'All the deeps to the third, and no poking yer little pink noses out of yer burrows for four winters.'

'Skweee! Done-done,' said Kranskritt.

'All right then. Yeah. I'll do it.'

'Tomorrow! Third bell.'

Skarsnik shrugged. 'Sorry?'

Kranskritt squealed. 'New-day sunrise! Be in the west foundry, fifteen scurryings down-up-down-north of the Hall of a Thousand Pillars!'

'Lots of ratties down there. In my house, I might add,' said Skarsnik. 'I'll bet you know some of them. They'll probably try to kill me. I'm not all that popular with your lot.'

'I know you know-have ways in. Be there!'

Kranskritt disappeared with a squeak of annoyance and a burst of purplish light.

Skarsnik let out a long breath and shook his head. After a moment, he went to refill his goblet and gathered up the remains of his work. He frowned as he stared at the still-smouldering edges. 'So then, Gobbla, rats is fighting rats again. Always the way. And when they is fighting, there's some space for the likes of me to make something of it. Get me house back, get me halls back. Get some of them greenboys from up top down there to keep it, and for good this time! Be warm again!'

He flopped into a chair. The chamber rumbled with yet another tremor. They had never really stopped since the days the mountains had exploded. Gravel pattered onto his head. Gobbla waddled up and snuffled for a scratch. Skarsnik obliged, massaging Gobbla's favourite spot between his eyes. 'Of course, boy, it's all a big trap. It always is.' He slurped his wine. 'But,' he added thoughtfully, 'why does I have this feeling this time things is a teeny bit different? And not in a good way...'

He sat there a long time rubbing Gobbla's leathery skin, thinking thoughts no other goblin could, alone as always.

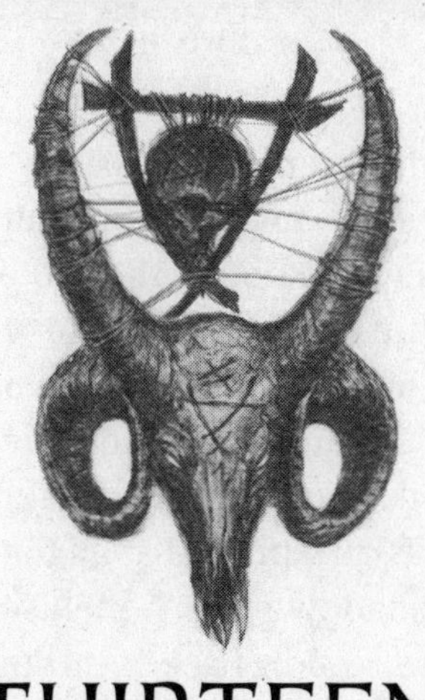

THIRTEEN

Payment for Services Rendered

Duffskul flapped his sleeves manically until his grubby green hand was free to press the stunty face. The fist-sized carving made a click, and the secret door it activated rumbled back into the wall. Duffskul puffed on his pipe and clucked his tongue with appreciation. It never ceased to amaze him how long the stunty-stuff kept on working.

Cold wind keened through the crack of the door, became a moan as the gap widened, and then a blast of winter that put out his pipe. Duffskul frowned and tapped the ashes from the bowl. He tucked the pipe into his belt, muttered some words to Mork and Gork, and waved his hands around desultorily. It was a poor effort, but lately the world had been so heavy with the essence of the Twin Gods, he barely had to try any more. The spell came on quickly, flattening him out, deepening the darkness of his robes. Soon all that was visible of him was a shadow like all the other shadows, excepting perhaps a greenish smear that might have been a face until you looked right at it.

The door finished its grinding recession, leaving the shaman's way clear. Duffskul stuck his head out into the day. He was a night goblin and therefore not at all fond of daylight, but what little effort the sun put forth through the winter sky, choked as it was with ash and magic, was weak and unimposing.

He hopped out of the door. The odd flake of dirty snow splatted against his hood. Snow had been falling for weeks in the mountains, and Duffskul squinted at all the brightness of it, but wrapped up in his shadow cloak he felt safe enough from the Evil Sun. Besides, he couldn't see it through all that cloud, so it couldn't see him, could it? The thickest runt knew that. Even if the ground shone like silver. Humming tunelessly for courage, Duffskul tottered off, out onto the flanks of the Silverhorn.

Seventeen treacherous switchbacks later, a quick dart past a fresh skaven tunnel, and a hairy moment when a dozen rocks the size of cave squigs bounded inches past Duffskul's nose, the aged shaman reached the bottom of the mountain. There the path joined a wider dwarf way, its cobbles much split by tree roots, which in turn descended through scrubby pine woods to join the main old road that ran through Death Pass.

Duffskul came out in a place not far from the Tight Spot, where the road went through high moorland. The dwarf road was heaving with greenskins of every kind, passing in long scrap trains out of the Dark Lands. They had started coming a few years ago, fleeing some upheaval out there and heading into the Badlands. Goblins first by the thousand, because they don't like fighting. But lately there had been many orcs also. They had their fiercest faces on, but Duffskul was canny, almost as canny as Skarsnik, and he could see they were afraid. Duffskul wondered what was happening in the wider world. He had tried staring out through Gork and Mork's eyes, but there was so much magic bleeding into everything that it made him dizzy just to try. Most troubling was that on the western side of the pass, where most of this lot were heading, the greenskins were coming back again. Life in the Badlands wasn't too good either, Kruggler kept saying. All fine news for Skarsnik, thought Duffskul, as the majority of the greenskins, having nowhere else to go, were ending up in the Eight Peaks. But what did it mean? Through his persistent fug of intoxication, the old shaman couldn't help but be concerned.

The ground rumbled. Rocks pitter-pattered down from the heights. It was not, reflected Duffskul, a question that needed answering. Earthquakes were frequent. They'd always had a bit of the old heave-ho coming from the ground, but nothing like this. Over the eastern peaks of the mountains the sky was black as night, and the sun never, ever shone there any more. The Dark Lands had become a whole lot darker.

'The world is changing, that's what,' he muttered to himself. 'A sorry sight, and no mistake, oh yus.' A group of wolf riders bolted as his shadow popped, turning him back into his usual solid self. He giggled at the sight of the riders struggling to control their mounts, causing chaos in the already fractious crowds of greenskins marching west. It took his mind off being exposed to the light.

'Can't be helped,' he muttered. 'Get trod on if I is a shadow.'

He plopped himself down on a dwarf milestone. From under his filthy robes he produced a puffball flask. He guzzled down the contents, some of his own special brew. Courage fortified, he refilled his pipe with shroom-smoke fungus, and took in the view.

At this point past the Tight Spot, Death Pass opened up. Here it stretched ten miles wide, the far side blued by distance. Much of it thereabouts was inhospitable moorland, broken by humps of rock, little streams and the grey stumps of pines hacked down by the greenskins for their fires and rickety constructions. Only the old dwarf road offered good travel, and that's where the traffic was.

In a state of disrepair, the road of Death Pass still held the power to impress. It went dead straight as much as possible, burrowing through such minor inconveniences as mountain spurs without stopping. There were ditches to either side, deep and lined with stone, although all that was visible this time of year were indentations in the snow and hairy yellow grass poking through. Every eight hundred yards, paired statues of stunty gods stood guard over it. Most had been broken aeons ago by orcs, but a few were more or less whole, glaring at the usurpers marching under their noses. Duffskul scuttled by these intact ones whenever he encountered them, because they gave him the creeps.

The pass had long been the domain of the orcs. The way had been tightly controlled for years by Gorfang Rotgut down in Black Crag. But the Troll-Eater was gone, killed by the king of all the stunties, so they said, and no one collected his tolls any more. Duffskul supposed sudden freedom of passage hadn't helped the traffic levels.

He watched the endless caravans groan past. Most of the greenskins were wolf tribes, not much use for Skarsnik's battles underground, but they had at least a number of ferocious beasts in their rickety cages. He even saw a group of much-battered hobgoblins chained up in one.

What is the world coming to, he thought, if even them treacherous backstabbers aren't being stabbed first chance? They don't even taste very nice. Why keep 'em?

He scowled at them. Cowardly at the best of times, they were beaten and downcast, and did not return his gaze.

He smoked awhile with his eyes closed to shut out the horrid glare of the sun until he felt suitably fortified by smoke and brew. He opened one eye, then the other, hiccupped and slid off the rock.

'Suppose I better be getting on,' he said. He let his finger rise up of its own accord, snaking around in the clouds of pungent shroomsmoke until it had found the right direction. 'Ah,' he said, 'that way.'

He headed east, and the crowds parted for him. Now he was far from the ratties and stunties, he could trust to his status as a shaman of Mork and Gork to keep him safe. It wasn't just a matter of respect due him for his ability to commune with the Great Twins, but one of fear. Not even the biggest black orc wanted turning into a squig, a magic that was well within Duffskul's considerable capabilities.

When Skarsnik had called Duffskul in, he hadn't needed to ask what had happened; Skarsnik's rooms still stank of magic and rat.

'You had a visitor, boss?' he'd said.

'Them ratties are trying to make a deal,' Skarsnik said. And then he had told Duffskul what the deal was, and who had made the offer.

Duffskul wasn't fazed – the ratties were always trying some-such nonsense or other. 'Yus, boss,' Duffskul said. 'They is always trying to do that, isn't they, boss? Do deals and that, oh yus.'

'Yes, yes, they are. But I'm not having any of it. Not this time!'

'You not going to do it, then? Not make the deal?'

'Of course I'm going to do it!' Skarsnik said. He had paced up and down his room with his hands behind his back, head bowed in thought. Gobbla waddled faithfully behind him, the chain that connected them clinking. 'There's always more to it with them furry little zoggers. There'll be some nasty surprise for us in there. And the chances of them giving us back the upper stunty-house like what they said they would are about as big as Kruggler's brain.'

They both laughed, Duffskul's eyes spinning madly in his ancient face.

'What we need is a plan of our own. I says we do what that magic ratfing says. We go in and take these burrowing gizmos off of them rats, burst up through the floor as planned. But...' Skarsnik held up a finger. There was always a 'but' with the king of Eight Peaks, you had to hand it to him. 'But, we have a few alterations. Make a plan of our own, so to speak. They have a plan, and so I has a plan.'

'Oh yus, boss, right you are, boss,' said Duffskul, leaning on his staff. He'd never known Skarsnik not to have a plan. 'What plan would that be then, boss?'

Skarsnik grinned slyly. He pulled out a heavy-looking sack from under his bed and dropped it on one of his many work desks. It hit the wood with that kind of rich clunk only solid gold makes. He whipped back the filthy material to reveal a battered but still impressive crown. Five types of gold, stunty runes, some really finickity chasing work and an awful lot of big gemstones.

'Ooh, that's nice, that's lovely that is.' Duffskul reached out a hand; he couldn't help himself, but snatched it back when Gobbla fixed him with his one good eye and growled.

'Ogres, Duffskul! Ogres is me plan. Been saving this for a special occasion,' the boss said. 'Now's as good a time as any.' He nodded at the sack. 'I've heard Golgfag is nearby.'

'What, Golgfag the incredibly large and famous ogre chieftain, boss?'

'That's the one. Golgfag the incredibly large and famous ogre chieftain, Duffskul.'

'And what do we wants with this incredibly large and famous ogre chieftain? He's known for not playing it straight, if you gets me, and he often fights for the stunties.'

Skarsnik smiled broadly, Duffskul smiled back. 'And those two reasons, me old mate, is exactly why we want him, isn't it?'

'Oh yus, boss! Oh yus! I gets ya!'

The pair of them had laughed long and hard together. Skarsnik's snotling food tasters joined in from their cages, not a single idea as to what they were laughing at in their empty little heads.

Now Duffskul pushed on to where his finger told him Golgfag could be found – a trick he'd learned long ago, from the somewhat mad Tarkit Fing-Finga, back in the... Well, there was no telling how long ago it was now. Greenskins swore and cursed as he went against the tide of the migration, moving their wagons aside just the same. Wolves snapped at each other as they were whipped out of the way. The road got progressively narrower as he approached the Tight Spot, where the pass was squeezed hard between two mountains.

Then a wolf was before him, snarling and drooling. Duffskul squeaked with shock, but it yelped as reins tugged its head back. A wall of mangy fur and stinking, bandy-legged goblin raiders flowed into being in front of him.

'Shaman! Which way to the Eight Peaks?' a goblin warchief with gold teeth shouted at him, his accent all funny. Duffskul giggled at him, he sounded so stupid. 'Where do we find Skarsnik the Great?'

The Great? thought Duffskul. He'll like that. 'That way!' he said. 'Follow the big road up into the mountains. Big city, huge stunty-house. You really can't miss it, to tell the truth, oh yus.'

The goblin chief wheeled his steed around and let out an ululation, waving his hand around his head. He shot forwards and his band followed, leaping over the ditch, over the uneven ground at the roadside, and scrambling onto the loose rocks and snow that lined the pass. They must have been from the mountains somewhere, because they were quickly away on the rough ground, drawing annoyed shouts from the other goblins forced to trudge along.

A scrapwagon pushed by grumbling stone trolls creaked by next, the slave-cage atop it empty of prisoners but heaped with ragged possessions. A fat goblin on the top waved a couple of snotlings on a stick in front of the trolls to make them move. He looked unspeakably glum, as did the tribe behind. They were all injured, some seriously, many with burns and blackened faces.

There came a blast of brazen horns resounding off the pass's sides. Gruff orc voices shouted, huge black orcs moving forward in the crowd, shoving lesser greenskins out of the road. 'Make way! Make way for Drilla Gitsmash! Make way, yer lousy runts!' They backed their words with slaps and worse, spilling dark red blood on the setts. They stamped forward, until one was right in front of Duffskul, staring down at him with furious eyes. It snorted plumes of steam into the chill mountain air.

'Get out da way, wizlevard, or you'll be sorry.'

'Will I now?' said Duffskul. He cocked an eyebrow over one mad eye. The black orc roared and hammered its axe against its breastplate, but moved on just the same.

Around the corner came the biggest orc Duffskul had ever seen. That would have been enough to make him shift, but the contraption the orc rode decided it. Duffskul lifted the skirts of his dark robes and hopped over the ditch like he was a hundred years younger. He took up position well out of the way at the foot of a fan of scree.

Drilla Gitsmash's mount was a clanking, mechanical boar, its black iron spell-marked with the runes of the curly bearded tusk-stunties of the Dark Lands. Steam hissed from its pistons as it trotted by, hooves cracking the slabs. Four banner bearers came after him, holding high icons fashioned from steel. Further along the pass, the black orc heralds were shouting at the goblins and their troll cart, cursing them off the road. Trolls moaned, goblins wailed. A snap cracked off the mountainside, and the cart sagged on a broken axle. Shouting angrily, the black orcs cut the traces of the trolls, put their shoulders to the wagon bed and heaved it over, ignoring the shrill protests of its owners. It toppled into the ditch and broke apart.

Drilla's brigade of black orcs marched past Duffskul in perfect step. They held their heads high, the tusks of their visors jutting towards the sky. They were disgustingly clean, their armour immaculate. On and on they went. There must have been over three hundred of them. Screams sounded from further up the pass as they ran into the thick press of greenskin refugees, but they did not slow, they did not stop.

The last rank of black orcs went by. A final blast of brazen horns resounded off the pass's sides, and the black orcs disappeared round a shoulder of the mountain.

For a few minutes the pass was clear. Duffskul scrambled back onto the roadway to take advantage of the lull, and jogged as fast as his old legs would carry him. The crowds thickened soon enough, but when they caught sight of the shaman, his dirty robes held high over his knees, face determined, they got out of the way no matter how cramped the road was.

The ogres were camped at the Tight Spot. There were two old stunty-houses there, both forts, on knolls either side of the road. One was so tumbledown it looked like part of the mountain, the other was whole and, consequently, full of ogres. On the other side of the Tight Spot the pass rapidly widened again, becoming heavily wooded and sloping steeply down towards the Dark Lands. Duffskul left the road and puffed his way up the broken track to the gates, flanked by large ogre banners depicting that big gob of theirs. He paused in his ascent for a look out east. The line of greenskins went on forever. He tried counting them – and he could count, properly; not quite as well as his boss, but not far off. He had to give up. There were too many.

He didn't get much further up the hill before he was noticed.

'Ooh looks, it's a shaman, zippety zap!' gnoblars jeered from behind rocks in accented greenskin.

Duffskul waved his staff at them, and they ran away shrieking in terror. 'I dunno, only kind of greeny worse than you lot is the zogging hobgobboes!' he shouted. 'Gnoblars! Hill goblins! No sort of gobbo at all!'

A pair of bored ogres stood guard at the dead-eyed gatehouse to the stunty fort. They stood taller and gripped the handles of their swords as he approached.

'What you want?' one demanded, his voice thick, clogged with fat and anger.

Duffskul leaned on his staff like he didn't have a care in the world and stared up. 'You Golgfag's lot?'

'Yeah, what's it to you?' said the ogre.

'Got a job for him.'

'From who?' said the second ogre. 'We already got employment.'

'So I hear, but I's got an offer for your boss he might find very interesting. Money's a wonderful thing, ain't it?' He leaned forwards and whispered behind his hand, 'And we got lots. Let me in, let me see Golgfag.'

The ogres looked at one another. One shrugged. The other jerked his head into the camp. 'Can't do any harm. Go on then. You'll find him easy enough. He's having his dinner.'

For some reason that made them laugh deeply. Duffskul shook his head. Ogres were such fat idiots.

The place was better organised than a greenskin camp would have been, but only just. Piles of bones, scraps of half-cooked flesh still stuck to them, littered the place, filling the courtyard with the stench of decay even in the cold. Ogres went about their business heedless of everything below gut level, forcing Duffskul to dodge out of the way frequently. Despite the chill, nearly all of them were naked from the waist up. A semicircle of heavy wagons filled the back half of the fort. Giant shaggy draught beasts and mounts were corralled by a fence made of tree trunks nearby.

Golgfag was indeed hard to miss. He sat at the centre of the camp upon the top half of a broken stunty statue, next to a roaring bonfire. Bigger than every other ogre in the place, his head seemed disproportionately small atop the mountain of fat and muscle that was his body. A maul and sword were propped up next to him, an iron standard depicting a circular, toothed maw thrust into the ground behind. A pair of halfling cooks worked nearby over a smaller fire. Whatever they were cooking smelt much tastier than the gnoblars being roasted over smaller fires.

Golgfag was munching on one such cooked gnoblar. The outside was burned to a crisp, the inside pink.

'When's my stew ready, Boltho? I'm nearly done on my starter!' Golgfag shouted in grumbling Reikspiel.

'Coming right away, gutlord!'

Duffskul licked his lips, at both the halflings' food, and the sight of the halflings themselves.

The ogre tore a mouthful of meat off, white strings of tendon hanging from his mouth.

'Ahem,' said Duffskul.

Golgfag turned round, searching at ogre height for his interlocutor, greasy moustaches flapping. It took him a moment to look down.

'Ah, another course,' said the mercenary brightly. 'Thanks for delivering yourself.'

'Nah, you's not going to eat me,' said Duffskul. 'Got a business offer.' He sat down and began to fill his pipe.

'Oh yeah?' said Golgfag. 'Already got a job. I don't see what a hole-skulking cave runt goblin like you can offer me that the king of Karak Eight Peaks can't. Go on, get out of here, or I will eat you.'

'No you won't,' said Duffskul. He clamped his pipe in his mouth. His eyes glowed green and it ignited. 'Because I'm here from the *real* king of Karak Eight Peaks.'

'I'm not worried by no scrawny goblin magician!' laughed Golgfag. 'And I'm not too impressed by this Skarsnik either. If he's so great, how comes he's always fighting? He's been at war for half a century! I would've beaten them all by now.'

Duffskul shrugged. He pulled out an object wrapped in oilskin from under his cloak and put it on the ground. He unwrapped it, revealing the lost crown of Karak Eight Peaks. Ogres were greedy for more than food, and Golgfag's eyes widened comically at the sight. He shuffled round on his seat to get a better look.

'Now that's a pretty trinket.'

Duffskul tittered. 'It is, ain't it? From Skarsnik. You like it?'

'What's not to like?' The ogre leaned forwards, face alight with avarice.

'You can have it. Payment. We just need a little favour. Carry on like you is, be all friendly like with the stunties...'

'What, then when the time comes turn on them and give 'em a nasty surprise? That old trick? What do you say I don't just rip your head off and eat you and take that there crown off you right now? I'm getting sick of gnoblar. Goblin's got an altogether gamier flavour. Very nice your lot taste, underground greenies. Hint of mushroom to you. Delicious. I like a nice wizard too, sparkles on the tongue.' A different kind of hunger showed upon the ogre's face. His gut rumbled, twitching behind its horned belly plate.

'Because, fatty, this ain't it, is it?' Duffskul passed his hands and the crown dissolved into a handful of old leaves.

Golgfag sat back and belched out a reek of uncooked meat. 'Right. So in that case, how do I know you have actually got it? Your boss ain't exactly known for his upright nature.'

'Oh, we've got it all right.'

'King Belegar has promised me one tenth of the treasure in his treasure chamber. That's a lot of gold. Now that's a pretty crown. But worst case for me is that you've no crown, and when I pull the old switch on the stunties I get no gold at all. And that is not happening.'

'Lot of gold? Belegar? It ain't a lot of gold,' countered Duffskul – now it was his turn to laugh – 'because he's having you on! Old Belegar ain't got no gold!'

'Nah, he's a dwarf, they've always got gold,' said Golgfag, flapping the shaman's stinking smoke away from his face.

'Not this 'un. Poorer than a snotling, he is. Not much more sense either. Tell you what, do this for us and you can have *half* of Belegar's stunty-hoard. And the crown.'

Golgfag took a bite from the gnoblar's haunch and pondered for a moment. 'Seems fair enough. If you make it three-quarters. Got me overheads – not cheap running a mercenary band like this, and the price of grog is way up. If your lot lose, I'll get only the crown and Belegar's downpayment, nothing else. You understand.'

Duffskul made a sympathetic face. 'Times is hard. That crown is worth a lot, though.'

Golgfag smiled, the gaps in his teeth jammed with bloody meat. 'If you say so.'

'I do says so, and you heard me say it. Now tell me, what do we get for the crown then?'

'The real crown?'

'Course,' said Duffskul.

Golgfag stood up and stretched. He tossed the remains of his first course into the fire. 'See them gutlords marching?' He pointed a greasy finger at heavily armoured ogres sparring with hooked swords as big as an orc. 'You'll get them. And me other lads. The whole lot. I'd throw in a few gnoblars for you as well, but Belegar's messenger was quite insistent on us not bringing them in.' He belched and scratched under his belly plate. 'He didn't want any greenskins in his hold at all. As if gnoblars count! Ain't that the ironic thing? Anyways, we ate all the fighting ones. It doesn't matter, because they're useless at fighting. We only bring 'em along to distract the enemy. No great loss. Still got me pets.'

'They is not gobboes, that's the truth, oh yus.' Duffskul could not agree more on that score. 'Also, you promise no double-double crossing!'

'Hah!' said Golgfag. 'Now that's funny coming from you. Don't you worry, Belegar would never give us more money. Too tight, them dwarfs, especially if he's as skint as you say. It'll be the end of them, if you ask me.'

'And what about the other party?' said Duffskul obliquely.

'The ratmen? Nah, can't stand them myself. Vermin. Always getting into my larder.' He nodded at a couple of spitted skaven roasting on a fire. 'Caught them trying to sneak into the pay wagon three nights ago. When they pay you, half the time they don't pay you, if you know what I mean. If I told you how many of their cash deliveries turned out to be magicked, the chests full of rats in black cloaks that go all maniac on yer with their little stabby knives, you'd be surprised.'

Duffskul hiccupped. 'Nah, I don't think I would.'

Golgfag laughed. 'Right. Your lot's got experience there. Let's shake on it then.' He gobbed a truly impressive mouthful of spit into his palm and held out his hand to shake, humie-style. His fingers were thicker than Duffskul's limbs, and smelt of roast greenskin. 'We got a deal?'

Duffskull took a finger on the proffered hand and shook it carefully. 'We have got a deal.'

'See you around, little greeny. I'm off to finish my dinner. I'll send word to the lads not to eat you on the way out.' The general's vast bulk shifted around. It was like watching a hill move. 'Send us the details later. We'll need some kind of signal. You have a little think about that, all right?'

'All right.'

'Until later, shorty,' said Golgfag.

'Until later, fatty,' giggled Duffskul.

FOURTEEN

The Hall of Clan Skalfdon

Atop a mound of rubble, King Belegar stood at the front of his Iron Brotherhood, Notrigar beside him bearing the clan banner of the Iron Hammers. The dwarf battle line stretched from the eastern side of the hall to the west, the high ground of an ancient rock fall at the north-western end held by Durggan Stoutbelly and the grand battery of Karak Eight Peaks. Past the Iron Brotherhood, the east end of the rubble pile was occupied by the Clan Zhorrak Blue Caps, and beyond that the rubble shelved off. From there to the walls of the hall, the ground was level, the flagstones uncovered by detritus. Two hundred yards behind Belegar's position was the Gate of Skalfdon, one of the last fine things remaining in the derelict hall, a massive portal barred by a rune-carved stone gate five feet thick.

To the south, the Hall of Clan Skalfdon stretched away, the ancestor statues carved into its far walls lost in the gloom. A few lonely glimlights still burned up in the high roof a full twenty centuries after the fall of the city, stars lost in a stone forest of pillars supporting the vaulted sky. Most of the light came from less grand sources – torches and lanterns in the main, held by the dwarf host.

Belegar looked up and down the ranks of his people. Six hundred of them, pretty much all the strength he had, barring Duregar's garrison holding the East Gate at the end of the Great Vale. Clan Skalfdon's hall swallowed them up, built at a time when a thousand times six hundred dwarfs had dwelled within Karak Eight Peaks. That glory was long gone, like the Skalfdon clan itself, the last of whose scions had perished in one of the many attempts to retake the Eight Peaks before Belegar was successful.

Successful. He snorted. This wasn't success. Already the skaven were creeping out of their holes, coming in through the dozen archways at the southern end of the hall.

'Something troubles you, my king?'

'Aye, Notrigar, a great deal,' said Belegar. 'I look at them and my blood boils. This is their domain, not mine. Look at how at home they are in the ruins, skulking about in the graves of better people. Look at them! Look at their dirty feet scrabbling on the faces of our ancestors. Look at the weapons they carry. They value nothing, not hard work, or craft, or skill – all they wish is to tear down and destroy, and disport in the remains. They thrive on blight and decay. They don't build anything to last. They don't build anything fair to look upon. All their kingdoms are but the debris of dying civilisations. It is unfair that such as these should inherit the world while better folk perish.'

'It strikes me as so, my king,' agreed Notrigar. These depressing rants of Belegar's had become more frequent, his moments of humour seldom as the war wore on.

'It strikes me that the gods are a bunch of baruzdaki,' said Belegar, 'by whom our own great ancestors were sorely mocked. Everything's gone, diminished. Look to this battle, one of the great acts of our days, and I see the pale reflections of the Karaz

Ankor in pools of blood. Our ancestors battled the lords of misrule themselves, forcing them step by step out of this world and back into their own. What would Grimnir, who holds to this day the hordes of Chaos at bay, think of his descendants smashing rats into the dirt in their own homes?' He shook his head.

Mutters of agreement came from the ranks of the Iron Brotherhood.

'Still, we'll give them a pasting to remember, eh, lads? It ends here! One way or another, or I'm no dawi.' Belegar pointed, past the carpet of giant rats and slaves seeping into the hall like rising floodwaters. Glints of metal could be seen coming through the gateways, blocks of troops forming up behind the wretches in the vanguard.

'See, brave khazukan!' shouted the king, so all could hear. 'See how our great foe comes! See how he marshals all his strength against us! The Headtaker is here!'

A wail of fury went up from the dwarfs. They clashed their axes against their shields and roared. Belegar continued to speak, his anger powering his voice through the clamour raised by his warriors.

'He comes to see us die, to see an end to dawi in the great city of Vala-Azrilungol! Well, I say, let him come. Let him break his vermintide upon the shields and axes of the sons of Grungni. Let him be disappointed! Khazukan! Khazuk-ha!' he bellowed.

'Khazukan! Khazuk-ha! Grungni runk!'

Durggan added the voices of his war machines to the dwarfish war cry. At various points within the hall, range-markers had been secreted, white stones that told Stoutbelly exactly who he could hit from where, and with what. The lead ranks of skaven-slaves now passed the first of these.

Cannons boomed thunderously, tearing long holes in the ranks of the slaves. They squealed in terror, and doubtless those nearest the carnage would have turned to flee if it were not for the endless swarms pushing them on. At the back, whips cracked. In reply to the cannons, streaks of green whistled into the dwarf ranks, felling warriors along the length of the line.

'Jezzails!' shouted their officers. 'Shields up!'

'Garrak-ha!' shouted the dwarfs. Triple-forged dwarf steel rippled upwards along the dwarf line, locked together with a clash. Bullets still punched through, but fewer dwarfs fell.

'Belegar! My lord! Get down!'

Belegar stood at the front of the Iron Brotherhood shouting his defiance. Warpstone bullets pinged off his rune-armour and the Shield of Defiance, disintegrating into puffs of nose-searing green smoke. 'Let them try, Notrigar. I am no skulking ratman to hide at the back of his warriors. Let them come! Let them come! Queek, I am here! I am waiting for you!'

Dwarf crossbows twanged as the skaven came into range. Shortly after, the popping reports of handguns joined them. So tightly packed were the skaven that every bullet and bolt found its mark. Those who fell were pulped under the feet of those following. Bolt throwers skewered them in threes and fours, cannons blasted them to pieces. Grudge-stones rained down, sailing between the columns of the roof on perfect trajectories. But there were thousands of skaven, and no matter how many died, there were always more. The tunnels leading back into the lower deeps were thick with them, their red eyes shining in the dark.

At the appropriate time, Durggan unleashed the fiery horror of his only flamecannon, incinerating a wide cone of skaven. They squealed in fear and pain, and the air was thick with the smoke of their burning.

'Here they come, lads!' bellowed Belegar. He gestured forwards with his hammer. 'At them!'

Shouting the war cries of their ancestors, the Iron Brotherhood ran into the mass of skavenslaves.

Queek watched patiently from a broken statue, squeaking orders when he felt his minions were letting him down. These were carried off by rapid scurriers, who forced their way into the ranks to seek out Queek's officers.

'You wait, little warlord, this is good,' hissed a voice only Queek could hear. The shadows cast by a pillar danced with more than the flamelight of battle. Queek's trophies were unusually silent, cowed by the verminlord.

'Pah! Queek hate waiting. Queek want to smash-kill dwarf long-fur and take head! But Queek is no fool, Lurklox-lord,' he said, the honorific unpleasant on his tongue. 'Dwarfs outnumbered ten to one. And this is but the first clawpack! They have no reserves. Queek guess that no dwarfs are anywhere else nearby, except sick, young and old.' He tittered. 'Young very tasty. Not so tough as old long-furs!' He sneered. 'Dwarfs are stupid, slow-thinking – not quick-clever like skaven – but they are strong. Very good armour. Fine weapons. Much singing.' He shuddered; the grinding-stone sound of the dwarfish battlesongs hurt his sensitive ears. 'No matter.' He waved his hand-paw dismissively. 'Under enough pressure, even dwarf-forged steel will snap. Soon will be time. Loyal Ska!'

'Yes, great Queek,' said Ska from the foot of the statue, where he restricted access to the mighty Queek.

'Ready my guard. Tell Grotoose now is time to loose his monsters.'

Queek watched the dwarf line. Having made a space at the front of the king's position, Belegar's Iron Brotherhood were retreating with mechanical precision from their initial foray to the safety of the line. Slaves scattered in the opposite direction, many shot down as they tried to flee. Others surged forwards, drawing themselves right onto the dwarfs' guns, where they died in droves. 'Pah!' said Queek. 'That is what slaves are for, yes-yes, Lurklox?'

There was no reply. The shadows were empty.

'He has scurry-gone,' said Ikit Scratch from his position along the central run of spikes on Queek's trophy rack.

The dead-thing sounded afraid.

From the gates behind Queek came an unpleasant bellow as Grotoose, the Great Packmaster of Clan Moulder, prodded his creatures into the fight. First to come were packs of slavering rat ogres, starved for the battle. They ran at the dwarf lines, barely directed by their packmasters.

Behind them came two gigantic Hell Pit abominations, their naked, maggoty skin rippling as they heaved themselves forwards, their many heads snapping at the air. The creatures, a hideous mix of flesh and machine, moved surprisingly quickly. Cannonballs slammed into the foremost abomination, and it howled in idiot rage. But its unnatural vitality saw its skin knit back together almost instantly, and it continued onwards. They squashed hundreds of slaves as they went towards the dwarf shield wall, but that did not matter. Queek had thousands and thousands more of such weak-meat. Every dwarf killed could never be replaced. He snickered as the first then the second abomination burst into the dwarf line, punching a big hole in it. No slaves followed into the openings, too terrified of the beasts. But the abominations were mighty enough alone. The entire dwarf east flank became bogged down fighting only one, while the other abomination turned at right angles to the beard-thing's battle line and began to work its way up towards the west flank, scattering those dwarfs it did not kill.

The rat ogres, meanwhile, loped forwards, giant hands grasping, swatting aside any slave that did not move away quickly enough. Queek watched as they swiftly arrived at the front of the battle. The largest pack was sent against a weak spot in the dwarf line hard by the king, a group of blue-capped beard-things wielding slow-loading crossbows. Such a pathetic weapon, typical of the dwarf-things: powerful but ponderous. Obsolete and doomed as their owners! The beard-things had time for three shots and no more before the rat ogres went raging into them. These dwarf-things were lightly armoured and did not last, the surviving few breaking and running, allowing the rat ogres to pile into the flank of Belegar's bodyguard.

Queek's eyes narrowed. This was the moment he had been waiting for. He bounded down the side of the statue, towards the front of his Red Guard.

'Now, Ska, now! Sound the advance!'

Skaven gongs rang. The slavemasters ceased cracking their whips, allowing the slaves to flee. They needed little prompting, their ragged remnants trickling away from the hall, leaving space for Queek's advance. The second line of skaven readied themselves, these well armed and armoured. Gongs clashed, bells rang. They started forwards.

At their centre went Queek Headtaker.

Belegar's hammer crushed the skull of his opponent, spattering all those around him with skaven brains. His fellows threw down their arms and ran for it, affording Belegar a moment's respite. From his vantage point, he could see up and down the line of his warriors. All were embattled. In two places his line had been breached by the abominations, and more deadly creatures were coming to attack them. Rat ogres were headed right for Clan Zhorrak. Belegar swore. The Blue Caps were no match for the beasts, and their supporting units were thoroughly occupied with the reeking monstrosity rampaging through his rear echelon.

'Blue Caps, bring them down!' he shouted, gesturing with his hammer.

The dwarfs shot numerous quarrels into the rat ogres, felling several. But there were well over a dozen of them, and most barrelled forwards ignoring the missiles sticking out of their bodies. With a hissing roar, the rat ogres bounded up the rubble pile, right into the Blue Caps. The dwarfs dropped their crossbows to pull out their double-handed axes. Bravery was not enough against the creatures, and the quarrellers were lightly armoured. Sword-long claws ripped the quarrellers apart. The rat ogres pushed through their formation, slaying many. By the time the Blue Caps of Clan Zhorrak broke, there were few left. Without stopping even to feed, the rat ogres pivoted and slammed right into the flank of the Iron Brotherhood. Signal flags fluttered on the opposite side of the cavern. Skaven war-gongs and bells tolled. Seeing the king's guard assailed, and the dwarf line sorely pressed all along its front, the skaven elite pressed forwards.

'Queek.' Belegar pointed towards the approaching skaven.

The rapidly thinning horde of slaves fled. Those who were slow were pushed forwards onto the axes and hammers of the dwarfs by the bigger skaven coming from behind. With horrifying speed, Queek and his Red Guard were upon the Iron Brotherhood.

The dwarf hammerers were holding their own against the rat ogres, smashing skulls, ribcages and knees with typically dwarfish efficiency. But they were pinned in place by the monsters, and could not react effectively to the charge of Queek's favoured.

'Protect the king! Protect the king!' shouted Brok Gandsson. A knot of hammerers hurried forwards, and surrounded Belegar. The Red Guard smashed into the dwarf front, huge ratmen almost umgi-tall, their sleek black fur rippling with muscle. They wore the tokens of their might: the teeth of black orcs and giants, stolen dwarfish talismans, beardscalps and skulls. Tirelessly the Iron Brotherhood fought them back; for every one hammerer who fell, three elite skaven paid with their lives.

Queek had not yet entered the fight, but that was about to change. He scurried up the rubble like it was a set of shallow steps, the hated Dwarf Gouger and his serrated sword held out either side. He launched himself skywards, spinning as he went. Using the momentum of his somersault, he punched the spiked side of Dwarf Gouger through a hammerer's helmet. Queek landed on the shoulders of another, his sword flashing down to end the dwarf's life before he could react, then leapt again.

Hammers aimed at him seemed to move through treacled ale, so slow were they in comparison to the Headtaker. He leapt and spun and killed and killed and killed, unhindered by his heavy armour and unwieldy trophy rack. Without gaining so much as a scratch, he was in the middle of the Iron Brotherhood's formation, killing his way towards Belegar.

Belegar roared. 'Now, Notrigar! Now! Sound the horn! Sound the horn!'

The dwarf horn-bearer lifted the Golden Horn of the Iron Brotherhood to his lips. Bejewelled, ancient and honoured, the Golden Horn was among Clan Angrund's most treasured relics.

A bright note lifted over the battle, pure as fresh-cut diamond. The dwarfs took heart at its sounding, singing their songs of grudgement louder and fighting harder. But that was not the purpose of its winding.

A noise like a giant drum came from the Gate of Skalfdon, followed by the rattling of chains so heavy their movement could be heard through the thickness of the gate. The gate slid upwards, the stone moving smoothly over its ancient mechanisms, flooding the hall with golden light.

Roaring out the name of their leader, Golgfag Maneater's mercenary band marched into the hall. The dwarf line near to Durggan Stoutbelly's position opened, and the ogres barged their way into the fight, mournfang cavalry and sabretusks going before them, driving wolf rats away from the artillery battery. Skaven were flung high into the air by the force of the ogres' impact, and the mercenaries penetrated many yards into the seething fur before they were slowed. The ogres were untroubled by the skaven's weaponry, and killed the creatures easily, their cannon-wielding warriors slaughtering whole units with each blast. Golgfag's disciplined force then turned to the left, and began fighting their way down the front of the dwarf line, their cavalry pushing their way deep into the horde. The pressure came off Durggan's position, and the dwarf artillery intensified its fire, blasting, spearing, roasting and squashing hundreds of clanrats.

Belegar smiled. His eyes gleamed. He pointed his hammer at Queek. 'Come on then, Headtaker! Match your skill against mine. There is one head here you will never have!'

'Charge-kill!' screeched Queek. He leapt from rock to rock, then into the dwarfs.

Time slowed in his quick skaven mind. He reacted without thinking, relishing his skill. In battle he was free of scheming lords and underlings and verminlords. Here he was the mightiest, unmatched Queek, the greatest skaven warrior who had ever lived! No more, and no less.

He bounced and slaughtered his way through the clumsy beard-things, killing them with ease. Their hammers moved so slowly! His Red Guard, not so mighty as he, fared less well against the long-face-fur's elite, but it did not matter. All he needed was a little time, and for now the Red Guard were full of courage, scrambling forwards up the piled stone to replace those slain. Ska Bloodtail fought at their fore, knocking down dwarfs with every swing of his mighty paws.

Queek had come up the hill some way from the dwarf king. Once within the packed ranks of the dwarfs he started to kill his way towards Belegar. Jammed together, the beard-things were easy prey and handy stepping stones both.

A horn rang out several yards from Queek, the horrid nature of its tune hurting his ears. There was the sound of a gate lifting, and shortly the music of the battle changed. Queek was too involved in his own melee, too intent on the dwarf king, to take notice of what it betokened.

Belegar turned to face the Headtaker, a triumphant look on his flat, funnily furred face. He shouted a challenge at the warlord. Queek grinned.

He bounded from the shoulders of one of the king's tough-meats, killing him and two others before his paws touched the ground. Queek ducked an arcing hammer, and three more dwarfs died.

Then Queek was before King Belegar. The beard-thing glared at him, his eyes ablaze, the reek of hatred leaking from his body. His long-fur twitched on his patchy-bald face, his hand gripped his hammer tightly.

'So, Belegar beard-thing. You want to fight Queek? Good-good! Queek is here!' said Queek. He always used Khazalid when he spoke with the dwarf-things. It upset them so much.

Queek launched himself at the dwarf king so quickly it was hard to see him move. Belegar was ready, side-stepping the warlord's rush and landing a heavy blow on Queek's shoulder guard. Queek rolled with the hit, saving his shoulder, but his armour split with a shower of glinting, green-black motes of metal. He squealed at the shock. Belegar reeled, blasted back by the magic of Queek's warpshard armour.

The pair circled each other for a moment, Belegar with his guard up, his shield in front of him, hammer at the ready. Queek held both his weapons wide, his sinuous body low. He hissed and giggled, and his tail twitched behind him with excitement.

'So long I have waited for this!' he said; his use of the secret tongue of the dwarfs clearly riled the king.

'I too, filth. Today will be a great day when your entry might be stricken from the Dammaz Kron of Karak Eight Peaks!'

Queek attacked without warning, hammering Belegar with a flurry of blows from both his weapons. But slow and stolid though the beard-thing was, he was always in the right place, always ready with a block when Queek thought he had a killing blow. Queek twisted around Belegar's replying strikes, acrobatically evading blows that would have shattered his body had they connected. Five times Queek was sure he had landed a final blow on the king, five times Belegar deflected them. Queek was quick, Belegar skilled. After two minutes of fighting, all Queek had to show for his efforts were a series of small scratches on Belegar's shield.

Battle raged all around them, the dwarf and skaven ranks now thoroughly intermixed. The din of battle in the hall was amplified by the stone walls. Fire, blood and death were everywhere. Queek boiled with irritation. He hid it behind a wicked smile.

Queek wiped his mouth on the back of the paw holding Dwarf Gouger. 'Belegar-king good warrior! This is most satisfying for mighty Queek. Too many famed killers die too quick-quick. That very boring for Queek.'

Belegar glared back at him.

'But beard-thing king not as good as Queek! He cannot stand against mighty Queek for long. Already, Queek has slain many beard-things. See?' He waggled his back, sending a dried dwarf head's beard swinging atop his trophy rack. 'Beard-thing king's littermate. He was very poor. Not so good as strong-meat Belegar, but Queek kill him anyway. Now I kill-slay you. I bring him out specially from Queek's trophy room, so he see you die-die. Soon your head will sit next to his. You will have long-ages to discuss how mighty Queek is. Won't that be nice for long-white face-fur?'

To Queek's frustration, Belegar did not react as so many beard-things would at his taunting – with a wild bellow of rage and a foolish attack. Instead, he warily circled the skaven.

And then he made his mistake. The tiniest opening. Belegar's eyes flicked involuntarily up to the head of his brother impaled upon the spike.

Queek reacted instantly. Belegar was ready again, catching the blow of Dwarf Gouger upon his shield, but he was distracted and the block was not as true as his others had been. The shield was slightly too far out; it would take a fraction of a second longer to reposition. Queek made as if he were to make a second swipe. Belegar tensed to react. Queek swept Dwarf Gouger up and away, pirouetting past the king's shield, putting all his weight and momentum into a backhand blow that sent Dwarf Gouger's vicious spike through the king's gromril and into his side. Queek yanked it free, and danced backwards, but too slowly. Belegar slammed him in the face with his shield, denting Queek's helmet. A following blow from his hammer drew sparks from the rock as Queek rolled aside. He was licking dwarf blood from the maul as he regained his feet. He tittered, although his head rang like a screaming bell.

'Mighty Queek!' bellowed Ska. He was throttling a dwarf in ornate armour in one hand. The creature's face went purple, and Ska cast it aside with a clatter. 'We are in much-much danger!'

Queek's eyes darted about. Ska was correct. Big-meat ogres and dwarf-things had pushed back the skaven line. The left flank was melting away. The dwarfs were occupied in containing the Hell Pit abomination there, and that was all that was saving his clanrats from destruction. How long it would hold them back was uncertain; it was surrounded on all sides by angry beard-things and was being hacked into pieces by their axes. The other abomination continued to wreak havoc, but elsewhere ogres pushed deep into the skaven horde with seeming impunity, while the dwarfs' cannons were firing freely into Queek's army. Worse still, the last rat ogre went down as Queek watched, its head smashed into a bloody pulp. The king's guard were now free to concentrate on Queek's Red Guard. Their formation tightened up, they began to push forwards, and the Red Guard were dying quickly, their morale wavering. Queek was in danger of being surrounded, and cut off.

Queek took all this in an instant. He made his decision to retreat just as quickly. He backed up. Belegar screamed at him, charging forwards with his hammer raised. Queek leapt out of the way, landing on the edge of the rubble pile's cliff-like face.

'Run-retreat!' he squeaked. 'Fall back, quick-quick!'

Gratefully, the Red Guard fled, more of them bludgeoned to death as they showed their tails.

'We meet again soon, long-fur,' chittered Queek, dodging hammer blows as dwarfs interposed themselves between him and the king. 'Until then, Queek takes another trophy.'

He jumped from the circle of dwarfs, pushing off with one foot-paw from the helmet of one of Belegar's warriors. He aimed himself at the king's banner bearer, fending off the warrior's hopeless parry. Queek relished the look of surprise and fear in the beard-thing's face as his sword descended, cutting perfectly into the weaker mail at his neck and severing the dwarf's head. The head toppled along with the standard, the metal icon painted red by fountaining blood.

Ska scooped up the fallen prize, and together they fled the stony mound.

'Notrigar! Notrigar!' howled Belegar.

'Oh dear,' said Queek to Ska as they scurried away. 'Look like long-fur beard-thing lose another littermate.'

The dwarfs cheered as the skaven fell back, hurling insults after Queek. Some of the skaven army retreated in good order – Queek's guard and his other stormvermin units held firm – but most did not and scrambled for the exits. Ogres ran them down without mercy, knocking handfuls of them flying with each swing of their massive clubs and swords. Green trails in the air marked out where jezzail teams aimed for the mercenaries, but the toxic bullets seemed not to affect them much, and it took several rounds to bring even a single ogre down.

The battle-dirges of the dwarfs changed. Victory songs erupted along the line at the flight of the skaven.

At the centre, the Iron Brotherhood found themselves unengaged. They yelled insults and banged their hammer hafts on the rock and on their shields.

Brok Gandsson sought out his lord, who stood at the brink of the cliff, looking down upon the scattering of bodies and blood-washed rock.

'A great victory, my king!' said Brok, his eyes bright, the shame of his murder of Douric forgotten for the moment.

Belegar looked with hollow eyes at the headless body of his cousin.

'My lord?' said Brok. He gestured for another to take up the fallen standard.

'It is not a victory, not yet. If we prevail, and I say "if" carefully, Brok Gandsson, a dozen of our finest lie dead around us. Grungni alone knows how many others have fallen.'

'Shall we pursue them? We stand a chance of catching the Headtaker,' said Brok keenly. 'Many are the grudges that can be stricken from the Book by his death.'

'Pursuing Queek is futile,' said Belegar. 'We will be drawn into the mass of troops waiting for us and killed piecemeal. We have other foes of direr nature, and closer to hand.' He pointed his hammer at the second abomination. The first was dead, but in their fury at the losses of their kin, the dwarfs of the Stoneplaits clan continued to hack at it. The second was dragging its vile bulk through the army, mindlessly unaffected by the general rout of the skaven. A bold unit of miners stood their ground in front of its heaving bulk. They buried their mattocks in its sickly white hide, only for them to be torn out of their hands by the convulsions of its flesh. A cannonball smacked into it, as effectual as a child's marble impacting dough. 'There is yet one more task for our hammers.'

'My king!' Brok bowed. He ordered the Iron Brotherhood to come about face. The king marched with them, his wound concealed by his shield. He gritted his teeth against the pain and told no one of it.

The abomination reared over them, stinking of decayed meat and warpstone-laden chemicals. The weapons of half a dozen clans were embedded in its flabby sides, its underside slick and red with the blood of those it had crushed under its enormous weight.

Upon seeing their king and his guard arrive, the remaining miners fighting the creature took heart and shouted their war cries anew. Those without weapons took up whatever they could find to assail the creature.

'The heads! Destroy the heads,' ordered Belegar.

'They're high up for a killing stroke,' said Brok.

'Then let's get its attention,' said Belegar, 'and make it bring them nearer our hammers.'

He strode forwards. Shouldering his shield, he swung the Ironhammer two-handed, smacking the thing hard on the rump. Waves rippled away from the impact. A second blow shattered a leg, a third a wheel grafted to its rear.

Finally recognising what it felt for pain, the abomination howled and reared up, dragging a pair of dwarf miners off their feet. They hung on to their picks for grim death as it lumbered around to face this new irritation.

'Khazuk! Khazuk! Khazuk-ha!' shouted Brok.

The hammerers advanced. Their numbers had been whittled down by a quarter in their earlier fight, and they had been battling for a good part of the morning without rest or refreshment. Lesser creatures would have been weary, and suffered for it. But these were dawi, many highborn, all warriors of the finest mettle. In their endurance they were indomitable, and they swung their hammers as if taking them up for the first time that day. Like triphammers in the forges of Zhufbar, the hammers of the Iron Brotherhood fell in a wave, pounding upon the skin of the horror, snapping bone and mashing flesh. The creature roared, swiping with one of its many arms. The first rank of hammerers were knocked down like pins in a game of skittles, but thanks to their armour few were hurt. The second rank stepped up to deliver another rippled blow. A grasping hand was shattered, a bloated paw burst. Brok Gandsson bellowed a challenge and ran at the side of the creature, pushing himself up the shattered machinery crudely grafted to its limbs. His feet bounced on its rubbery hide, but he kept his footing, ran to the top and cracked it hard over one of its nine heads. The neck attaching it to the sack of its body cracked, and the head sagged, dead. The abomination flung its upper portion to and fro, sending Gandsson flying.

Shouting mightily, the hammerers followed their champion, surrounding the creature and smashing at it furiously. The abomination thrashed, howling horribly. It killed but a few of the dwarfs, and its lower portion was soon so pulverised that its unnatural vitality could not heal all the tears in its flanks. Crying, it sank low, biting at its tormenters, allowing the hammerers access to its heads by doing so. These the dwarfs smashed to pulp one after another as soon as the snapping jaws came near.

Finally, the last head was split. With a tremendous shudder and a pitiful moan, the abomination breathed its last through pulverised lips and broken jaws.

The hammerers gave a ragged cheer.

'Well done, Brok Gandsson,' said Belegar, as the Iron Brotherhood helped their bruised but otherwise unhurt champion to his feet with many a clap on the back. 'A deed worthy of the ancestors.'

Brok bowed his head. 'My thanks, my king.'

'Now blow the Golden Horn once more. It's time we left this battlefield and retreated to the next defence.' Belegar looked around sadly. To do so meant leaving the deeps completely in the hands of his enemies. From now on, they would be fighting for the citadel's roots alone.

The war for the underhalls was lost, probably forever.

The horn blower lifted the sacred relic to his lips, but did not blow.

'What...?' said Belegar. All dawi eyes looked to the ground.

Through the ground came a rumbling sensation that built steadily until the floor itself vibrated. No dwarf could mistake it for an earthquake. The sensation was too regular, too localised for natural perturbation of the rock.

'Tunnelling machines,' gasped Brok.

'Reform!' bellowed Belegar. 'Reform... ahh.' He gasped, and clutched at his side. Red blood dripped upon the floor. His head swam. A strange, unholy heat radiated from his wound.

'My lord,' said Brok in dismay. 'You are wounded!'

Belegar shouted back, annoyed at himself for betraying his injury. 'It is nothing – a scratch. I gave the Headtaker more to remember me by than this, believe me. I commanded the army to reform. Look to them, not me. Be about it quickly, or all is lost!'

'Yes, my lord.' Brok relayed the order, and his orders were passed on by others. Dwarfs were efficient in all things, and very shortly horns sounded as the dwarfs called back their warriors from the pursuit.

A sound came from behind the Iron Brotherhood's new square.

'My king!' shouted Brok.

Brok pointed at the abomination. Its skin shuddered. Three of its mouths worked. Bones cracked as jaws reset. Eyes grew bright. Flesh knitted together. It vomited freely from all of these mouths, and with a pained squeal, it jerked fully back into life and hauled itself up once more.

FIFTEEN

Enter Skarsnik

Queek's scampering slowed. He looked to the ground and giggled. 'Halt-stop!' he called, holding up his hand-paw.

The Red Guard tittered, recognising the rumbling for what it was – the anticipated arrival of their reinforcements from the third clawpack. They formed up. Other units were slowing, their flight turning. For a moment they stood in a state of stilled disorganisation, before flowing back together, units consolidating almost magically from the chaotic mass of the rout. From the gateways into the hall more skaven issued. This was the remainder of the first clawpack, ordered to join battle by Queek only when the tunnelling machines made their presence known.

'Hehehehe,' snickered Queek. 'Now we see who is the best, Belegar-king. See, loyal Ska, how the dwarf-things have broken their line in their foolishness. Too quickly they are to believe Queek would run-run! They have fallen for mighty Queek's trap! They will all die-die, no matter how fast they stump-run to find their clawpacks again!'

Ska frowned. To his simple mind, it had looked like they were about to lose. Ska wasn't particularly quick, but he was smart enough to know saying so would not be wise. 'Yes, mighty Queek,' he said instead.

The vibrations grew stronger, a bone-shaking grinding joining them. The entire hall rumbled. Just when it seemed they couldn't possibly get any louder, the tone of the noise changed and piles of splintered rock mounded up in various places in the hall.

Queek leapt onto a boulder and brandished his weapons. 'Be ready!' shouted Queek, his voice barely carrying over the noise of the tunnelling machines. 'Third clawpack arrives! Today, mighty Queek take long-fur's head!'

'Queek! Queek! Queek!' squeaked his army.

The snout of a drilling machine appeared from one of the oversized molehills to the north, fifty yards short of the rapidly reforming dwarf army. The drill poked a few feet overground, then withdrew. With nothing to support it, the centre of the hillock collapsed, leaving a gaping hole in the ground.

Queek waited gleefully, his tongue searching out fresh scraps of dwarf flesh and blood in his fur.

Green light issued from the hole. Smoke poured after it. Other machines were poking up out of the floor and walls, and retracting, leaving fresh tunnel mouths behind them. One by one they fell silent and the tremors dwindled.

'Not long now, loyal Ska. Truly is Queek the most cunning of generals.'

'The most cunning of the cunningest,' agreed Ska.

Something emerged from the hole. It was a long way to see for Queek's weak skaven eyesight. He squinted hard and made out a bouncing, round shape headed for the dwarf lines.

'That not third clawpack...' said Ska in dismay.

'Queek can see that!' squeaked Queek loudly. 'Queek know!'

The hole burst outwards as dozens more of the creatures came boinging out, their powerful hindlegs propelling them at great speed into the air. They slapped into the ground, rolling and bouncing, shoving themselves off with their legs to repeat the process. The mushroom stink of green-things blew from the holes.

'Skarsnik!' chittered Queek, stamping from foot to foot. 'Skarsnik! What is this? How does he know? How does he still *live?*'

As if invoked by the name of their king, the green-things poured in great multitudes from the holes in the ground. Regiments of night goblin archers came first, firing as they ran, the new tunnel mouths wide enough to let them come out four abreast. The skaven, expecting allies to come from the ground, were taken by surprise, and some among the newly rallied army were seized again by panic. Black-fletched arrows fell among them, bringing forth many death-squeaks. The massed skaven retreated from the holes, allowing legions of goblins to flood the hall.

There were many tribes, and many kinds of green-thing. Queek narrowed his eyes and hissed. 'Imp-thing been busy!'

The greenskins wasted no time in attacking both armies. From a hole opened right before the Gate of Skalfdon, ranks of tittering spearmen, drunk on fungus beer, marched out. They jogged into position on the far side of the dwarfs. Staggering fanatics carrying massive iron balls were pushed from their regiments. They blinked and stared around themselves, laughing and drooling. And then they began to spin.

Faster and faster they went, round and round, the drugs coursing through their veins allowing them to drag the huge weapons they carried up and get them airborne. In a blur of metal and spinning pointed hoods, they connected with dwarfs turning to face the goblins behind them.

The fanatics moved quite slowly, but such was their momentum that they smashed the dwarf shield wall apart, caving in the best armour and pulping bodies. If their initial impact was bloody, their lives after were short. Some spun through into the skaven on the far side; others wavered unsteadily along the dwarf line or turned back upon their frantically shrieking comrades. Ultimately, they came variously to throttle themselves on their chains, collapse exhausted or crash into the pillars and rubble piles that made the hall so hazardous for them.

It did not matter, the damage was done. The goblins followed their fanatics quickly, charging the disordered dwarf lines.

Squigs were running amok through the dwarf army, gobbling down a dwarf with every bound. Queek's quick mind followed his quick eyes and nose as he judged the situation. 'Now would be a good time to fall back, lad,' said Krug, from his perch.

'Oh, good time for you to talk now, dead-thing,' muttered Queek. Still, he was of half a mind to follow the dwarf king's advice, retreating while the beard-things were occupied with a new enemy. Let them wipe each other out. Queek would come back for whoever was left later.

He would have done so too, had Skarsnik himself not appeared.

Skarsnik rose from a hole in the ground in the very middle of the hall. Explosions and flashes of magic surrounded him, the indescribable noise of squigpipes played him in, making sure all saw his grand entrance. He walked cockily from the hole, his attendants carrying banners stuck with the heads of the leaders of the third clawpack. He walked to a pile of fallen rock, and climbed unhurriedly to the top, his rotund pet obediently following. Queek squealed in annoyance. The sheer arrogance of Skarsnik enraged him. He behaved like he was the best, when who was the best? Queek was!

'Listen, youse lot!' shouted the green-thing, his voice carried on the magic of the smelly lunatic who always accompanied him. Sure enough, he was there, blowing foul fumes from his pipe not far behind the king's right shoulder. 'I's the king here, so why don't all you furboys and stunties zog off. Give to Skarsnik what belongs to Skarsnik, and we'll call it quits.'

With that inspired piece of oratory, Skarsnik held aloft his prodder and let a stream of violent green energy streak into the roof.

Razor-sharp shards of rock blasted out from the impact, slicing into whoever was below. Which was mostly goblins, but Skarsnik, true to form, didn't care about that.

This was altogether too much for Queek.

'Skarsnik! Imp-thing! Kill-kill!' he shrieked. He ran forward, leaving his guard behind. They milled about confused until Ska Bloodtail squeak-ordered, 'After him! After the mighty Queek!'

Seeing their lord and his guard surge ahead, the skaven clan leaders, clawpack masters and other officers decided they had better advance. Their ragged charge became organised as more of them came to the same conclusion and followed.

The skaven were so intent on the goblins that they didn't notice the ogres change sides.

'Keep up the fire to the front there!' shouted Durggan Stoutbelly.

The cannons boomed over the heads of the Axes of Norr, detailed to guard the battery. It was an honourable task, given to them in thanks for their heroic efforts at the door of Bar-Undak.

Borrik ducked as a bolt of green lightning blasted past his face. He snarled in the direction of Skarsnik. The goblin king was stood upon a pile of rock in the centre of the battlefield, capering madly.

'He looks pleased with himself,' muttered Gromley.

'Aye,' said Grunnir, spitting on the floor. 'Little green kruti.'

This is not looking good, not looking good at all, thought Borrik. The goblin ambush had surprised both armies, but the dwarfs suffered the most for it. Their flank, anchored by Durggan's war machines, had become cut off from the bulk of the dwarf throng as a prong of the greenskin ambushers pushed its way through the army. Worse, although Belegar was sounding the orders for retreat, their way from the cavern was blocked by hundreds of grobi and no small number of urk emerging from at least two fresh tunnels.

And there were the ogres as well. This wasn't a very good day.

'Here they come again, honourless fat baruzdaki,' said Borrik. 'Norrgrimlings-ha!' he shouted.

A regiment of swag-bellied Ironguts ran up the slope at the much-depleted battery. Only two cannons remained. The others were silent, destroyed by magic or their crew all slain. Dead goblins, skaven, dwarfs and ogres were intermingled around the battery, their corpses dangling from the earthworks and drystone walls erected before the battle.

'Fire!' shouted Durggan. With a deafening bang and gouts of smoke, the cannons unloaded two lots of grapeshot right into the teeth of the ogre charge. The last few Forgefuries added their hand-cannon shots to the fusillade. The front rank, four ogres wide, stumbled and fell.

Gromley cocked his eyebrow. 'Now I don't say it often, but that was impressive.'

'Well I live and breathe, at least for a few moments longer,' said Borrik, shouting over the ogres' deafening war cry. 'Gromley impressed by something! I reckon I can die happy, and maybe not a little surprised.'

Gromley's sour response was lost to the clatter of ogre gutplates hitting gromril. The thin line of the remaining Axes of Norr, five all told now, bowed but did not break. 'At 'em, lads!' shouted Borrik, and hewed an ogre's foot away with a single blow of his rune axe. The ogre hopped about, crashing down when Gromley took his other leg off at the knee.

'Serves 'em right for being so tall,' he said.

The Axes of Norr hurled back the charge. The remaining ogres broke and fled. The dwarfs let out a small cheer from tired throats.

'I'd kill for some ale right now,' said Borrik.

'You are killing,' said Gromley, 'but I don't see any ale at the end of this.'

'There might have been more, if the rats hadn't done for poor old Yorrik,' said Grunnir. 'Oh, look at that, they got Albok.'

'Grungni curse those treacherous ogres,' spat Gromley.

Albok lay dead, his head open from the crown to his nose, his brains glistening inside his broken helmet. Four Axes of Norr remained standing.

Insane tittering came at them. A pair of fanatics spun into view. Two shots rang out, and both goblins fell with smoking holes between their eyes. Borrik looked up to see Durggan blowing the smoke from his pistols.

'Aye, good lad, Albok,' said Borrik. He lifted his shield. Every sinew and muscle twanged with fatigue. There wasn't much more to say to it than that. They'd grieve properly later, if there was a later.

Goblins milled about just out of grapeshot range, the corpses of the three previous failed charges buried now under dead ogres. 'That's right,' said Gromley. 'You stay down there.'

'Hang on, lads, this might be us,' said Grunnir.

Golgfag was marching up the hill, his maneaters behind him.

'They're a mean crew and no mistake,' said Gromley.

Borrik looked down his meagre line of clansmen, four Axes, three Forgefuries. Where had they all gone? He remembered a time when the Norrgrimlings had been a large and prosperous clan. He was going to have a lot of explaining to do when he got to the Halls of the Ancestors. 'Grunnir, Gromley, Uli, Fregar, Tordrek, Gurt, Vituk... I'd say it's been an honour...'

'Not living, breathing and fighting with this lot of grumbaki!' said Grunnir.

'Hush! The time for jesting's done.' He gave Grunnir one of his sterner looks. 'It's been more than an honour,' continued Borrik. 'A lot more. I could say more, I could wax lyrical, but you know what I mean. We're dawi, aren't we? I'm not an elf to collapse into tears and give everyone a cuddle.'

'Dawr spoken,' said Gromley.

Golgfag's ogres were breaking into a charge.

'Norrgrimling khazuk! Khazuk-ha!' Borrik said. His warriors

repeated the words. He wondered what each was thinking here, at the last stand of the Axes of Norr.

He supposed it didn't matter. What mattered was that they stood by him until the end.

Durggan was lining the cannons up to get one last shot on the ogres. One of his crew let out a cry and fell, a black-fletched grobi arrow sticking from his throat. Another died, slumping over the gun with a warpstone bullet embedded in his chest.

'Keep it up! Keep it up!' barked Durggan. 'We'll not fall without one last blast, eh, lads?' He helped the remaining crewman of the cannon to line up the barrel. The second was ready, the last dwarf of its crew grasping the firing string, but Golgfag raised a pistol as big as a dwarf handgun and blasted him off his feet. As he was thrown backwards, the dwarf jerked the cord. An ogre took the ball to his gutplate, sinking to his knees with blood gushing around his hands. The other ogres hurled themselves into the Norrgrimlings. Golgfag singled out the thane, and attacked.

As proud and skilful a warrior as Borrik was, he could not stand against the Maneater. Golgfag quickly put him down with a punishing blow to the head. Through blurring vision, Borrik saw his remaining clans-dwarfs smashed down, barged off balance by fat stomachs, then bludgeoned by umgi-high clubs.

The maneaters wheeled and went for the cannon. Durggan, working on his own now, struggled to get the last piece aligned.

'Not today, stunty,' said Golgfag. He drew another pistol and blew out Durggan's guts with it. So died the chief engineer of Karak Eight Peaks.

The ogres halted. There were none left alive on the high ground except Borrik. He couldn't move.

'Look at this lot,' said Golgfag waving his giant hand out over the battlefield. 'This is madness! Nobody's going to win this. Stunties in the north-east, skaven to the south, gobboes in the middle. It don't make sense.'

'They are not soldiers, not like we are, captain,' said one ogre, almost as massive as his master and dressed in outsized Imperial finery.

'What now, Captain Golgfag?' said another.

'I reckon we're done here. Fulfilled our side of the contract. We're never going to see that dwarf king's gold if we stick around for the end of this mess. It don't matter whose side we're on. Besides, I got a healthy down payment.' He patted a bulging pouch at his side. A gold object was poking out of it. Even through his near insensibility, Borrik recognised the crown of Vala-Azrilungol, lost for ages. He added that to his growing mental list of grudges.

'Kulak, shout the withdrawal. We're leaving.'

'Captain! What about that one? He's still alive,' said someone Borrik couldn't see.

Golgfag swung around and looked right at Borrik. The ogre chief walked towards him, his boots filling Borrik's vision. A rough hand grabbed his mail and rolled him over. Borrik found himself staring into the lumpen face of the world's foremost mercenary captain.

'Tough little buggers, your lot,' said Golgfag. 'I really hate fighting dwarfs. You take ages to kill. All that armour! Haha! Ha!' he laughed, as if to include Borrik in his joke. A gale of halitosis swept over Borrik, rank with poorly cooked meat. 'It ain't nothing personal, stunty. Business is business.' Golgfag patted Borrik's chest with a massive hand.

'The lads are coming, captain,' said the finely dressed maneater.

'Right then,' said Golgfag, looking away. 'West tunnel, third in. Looks very badly guarded. We'll fight our way out that way. Any objections?'

None came.

'Good.' Golgfag hitched his trousers into a more comfortable position and stood, his gut obscuring Borrik's view of his face.

'What about him?' said an ogre. 'You not going to kill him?'

'The stunty? Nah,' said Golgfag, leering down at Borrik. 'It's your lucky day, shorty. Like I said, I've fulfilled my part of the contract. I've finished here.'

The ogres left Borrik lying in the shattered remnants of his clan.

If I ever get out of this alive, he thought, I'm donating my entire treasury to the priesthood of Valaya, and then I'm taking the Slayer oath.

Queek butchered goblins by the score. Spears of wood and toughened mushroom stalk shattered under the blows of his weapons. He snarled and spat as he slew them, squeaking in frustration as his blades became fouled in their filthy robes. He was attempting to reach the hated imp, Skarsnik, the so-called king. But for every goblin he slew, there seemed to be a dozen more. They tried to retreat from him, and wisely, but could not for they were packed into the hall so tightly. The dwarf artillery had been silenced, but Skarsnik was still blasting skaven and dwarf-things alike with impunity with the prodder. Queek had witnessed Skarsnik's magical trident at work many times in the past, but never like this. It glowed with green light so bright it was nearly white. The glare of it left painful after-images streaking across his vision. The energy bolts it threw seemed many times more powerful, and more numerous, than ever before.

'Let me pass! Get out of Queek's way!' shouted Queek at a group of skaven who found themselves in his path. They were lowly clanrats, scared beyond comprehension. They stared at him stupidly as he yelled at them to move. They did not, so he cut them down where they stood. Skarsnik was now only one hundred and fifty scurries from him. The goblin had seen him and was gesticulating obscenely. A bolt of green light came after his gestures, singeing Queek's whiskers as he threw himself out of the way.

'You wait-wait, green-thing. Today you die-die!'

Queek leapt onto a pile of rubble, and from there threw himself into the melee swirling around its base. He cleared himself a space, slaughtering combatants from both sides. An ogre was close, isolated from his fellows a few yards further on. Queek launched himself at it, slamming his pick's spike into the creature's forehead. He used this to arrest his leap – curving over the ogre's back, he yanked Dwarf Gouger out in a spray of blood and brains. Landing nimbly, he found himself alone on bare rock, as skaven, goblins and the ogre's comrades fled from him.

The way to Skarsnik was clear.

Queek gathered himself for another leap, tittering evilly.

The ground shook. Light blasted around him and he fell to the floor, Dwarf Gouger clattering from his grasp. His ears rang from the blast. When he looked up, goblin and skaven corpses smoked all around him.

At first he thought he had been hit by Skarsnik, but the goblin was gone from his rock pile. Away to the right of where Skarsnik had capered, Queek caught a glimpse of pale grey fur, almost white.

'White-fur!' hissed Queek. 'You pay for this with your head!'

Kranskritt rose from a tunnel in the centre of the cavern, arcane power crackling around him, and came to rest on the side of a toppled pillar. He snarled imperiously and flung out one hand-paw. The ground rumbled. Fissures opened like hungry mouths, swallowing creatures of all kinds indiscriminately. Queek started, meaning to run-scurry at the white-fur and strike him dead. But there was something else with him, a shadow behind him, half hidden by the black glare of Kranskritt's magic.

Verminlord. Queek snarled. At first he thought it the same one as had come to him, but it was not. The horns were different, for one, and it was less hidden in the shadows than the other.

'Two verminlords in the City of Pillars?' he whispered to himself, ill at ease. 'Unprecedented.'

The ground shook regularly as Kranskritt and his master – for the verminlord was almost certainly the weak-willed sorcerer's ruler – unleashed a storm of earthquakes, sending even the agile Queek staggering. Snarling, he ran towards Kranskritt.

'Fool-fool! Stop-stop!' shouted Queek.

To his surprise, Kranskritt heard him and looked down. An expression of pure, malicious calculation crossed his face. His hands rose. Queek tensed, ready to dodge. His warpstone amulet pulsed with protective magics.

The moment passed and Kranskritt performed a deep bow. One without any sign of submission, the sort of acknowledgement given to an equal! Kranskritt was getting too confident. Another reason to kill him.

'Do not despair, mighty Queek!' the sorcerer shouted over the noise of his patron's continuing magical barrage. 'I came from my hunt in the mountains as quick-quick as I could. Clan Scruten will aid mighty Queek and save the day from greenthing treachery!'

The verminlord loomed over Kranskritt. The grey seer's tail swished easily, given confidence by the proximity of the daemon. Queek snarled. His mind worked fast. If he killed Kranskritt now, it would be in front of everyone at a time when the sorcerer was helping turn the battle. Furthermore, he had a verminlord stood right behind him. Queek fleetingly considered matching his blades against it, but wisely decided not to.

He shouted instead. 'Fool weak-meat! You send the greenimp scurrying away from mighty Queek's blade! You will pay for this!'

'And mighty Queek was doing so well without me,' said Kranskritt sarcastically. 'See! The goblin tunnels collapse. They are trapped! You win-win, mighty Queek. You are correct – I should be paid for this. I should be paid many-much warptokens, not with unkind bite of steel.'

Queek bared his fangs and held his serrated sword up in

challenge to the seer. Then with a swift turn he sprang away, seeking others to vent his anger upon.

He would kill Kranskritt later. He promised himself that he would.

A great tremor ran through the ground as the skaven daemon and his pet sorcerer unleashed another earthquake. The goblins' tunnels fell in, opening long trenches in the floor. Warriors from all sides fell into the gaping pits.

Belegar's plans were in tatters.

'A thousand times a thousand curses on Golgfag and his honourless ogres,' said one of his bodyguards.

'Yes,' said Belegar absently. He watched the skaven sorcerer. He was troubled anew. Daemons were abroad in Vala-Azrilungol.

'They are ogres. It was a gamble, a poor roll of the dice, no more, my lord,' said another.

Belegar shook with anger. 'It's not that. I don't understand,' said Belegar. 'How did Skarsnik know? How did he speak with them?'

Behind his back, the hammerers shared glances. This was an oft-repeated story: bold King Belegar outwitted by a goblin.

The abomination was finally dead, for good this time, but the price had been high. The crushed corpse of Brok Gandsson leaked its life-fluids onto the bare rock, pinned under the bulk of the twice-living monster. Only thirty or so of Belegar's elite hammerers remained.

Belegar looked at the disaster unfolding in the hall. Durggan's battery was shattered; all his men and those set to guard him were dead. The sorry remnants of the flank the artillery had anchored were surrounded on all sides, cut off and beyond hope. The horns sounded the retreat time and again, but many of the dwarfs of Karak Eight Peaks were mired in battle with one faction or the other and could not retreat. Either that or they had fallen into all-consuming fits of hatred, desperate to bury their axes in their despised foes. These dawi had lost all reason and did not heed the signals. Worst of all, the path to the doors of Clan Skalfdon was thick with goblins.

'Sire, sire!' said a familiar voice.

'Drakki?' Belegar said flatly. 'Why aren't you with the rearguard, recording our...' He wanted to say defeat, he should have said defeat, but somehow he couldn't. He was bone weary, not merely from today, but from fifty years of chasing an impossible dream. Defeat was too big a word to fit into his mouth.

'The rearguard *are* with you, my king. The lines have collapsed. We have been pushed together.' He gestured at the shrinking knot of dwarfs, units fighting back to back. 'Bold dawi await your command, my king.'

Belegar was dazed. 'I...'

Drakki grabbed the king's shoulder and squeezed. 'Do something,' he whispered.

It was thanks to the mercy of Valaya, Belegar supposed, that the ogres were leaving the hall, killing anyone of whatever army who got in their way. He blinked. The fuddle of emotion clouding his mind receded.

'Blow the charges,' he said.

'My king?' said Drakki.

'I said, blow the charges,' Belegar repeated, more clearly. He hefted his hammer. His warriors breathed easier seeing their lord return to them.

'Are you sure this is wise?' said Drakki.

'No. But they are rigged to collapse the hall to the south. If Durggan did his work well – and when did he ever not? – we should be able to retreat through the gate.'

'Dawi of Karak Eight Peaks! Dawi of Vala-Azrilungol that was! To arms to arms! Make for the gate!' called their thanes.

Horns blew loudly. The dwarfs checked their aggression, forming up into squares and blocks.

'Do it now,' said Belegar.

A complex tune played from the Golden Horn of the Iron Brotherhood.

'To the fore! To the fore!' shouted Belegar's clan lords.

The dwarfs, now in a broad column, lurched like a train of ore carts beginning their journey. Slowly they gained traction, and then they were away, axes and hammers falling, carving a red path through thaggoraki and grobi alike towards the great doors of Clan Skalfdon.

Three minutes later, long fuses burned their way to the charges hidden around the bases of the pillars to the southern end of the hall. Twelve explosions followed one another quickly, their reports amplified to deafening levels by the enclosed space.

The pillars ground on shattered bases. Broken at top and bottom, they tumbled with apparent slowness, an illusion created by their great size and weight. They broke into many pieces as their toppling accelerated, falling on the hordes of Belegar's enemies as effectively as bombs and bringing torrents of stone from the ceiling with them, killing hundreds more.

The dwarfs fought on, too occupied to pay much attention to the roof falling in behind them. The collective scream of skaven and goblins being crushed chilled even boiling dwarf blood.

'My king,' shouted Drakki. He pointed upwards. Belegar followed his arthritis-knobbed finger to the ceiling. 'Something has gone wrong!'

A crack was opening across the sky of stone, dislodging glimstones that had shone for five thousand years. The fissure spread with ominous leisure, slowly, as if it were sentient, and choosing for itself the most devastating route. Stones rattled down on the column of embattled dwarfs.

Shouts rose from along the force's length 'Ware! Ware! Cave-in!'

The dwarfs raised their shields over their heads, as the roots of the world fell in upon them.

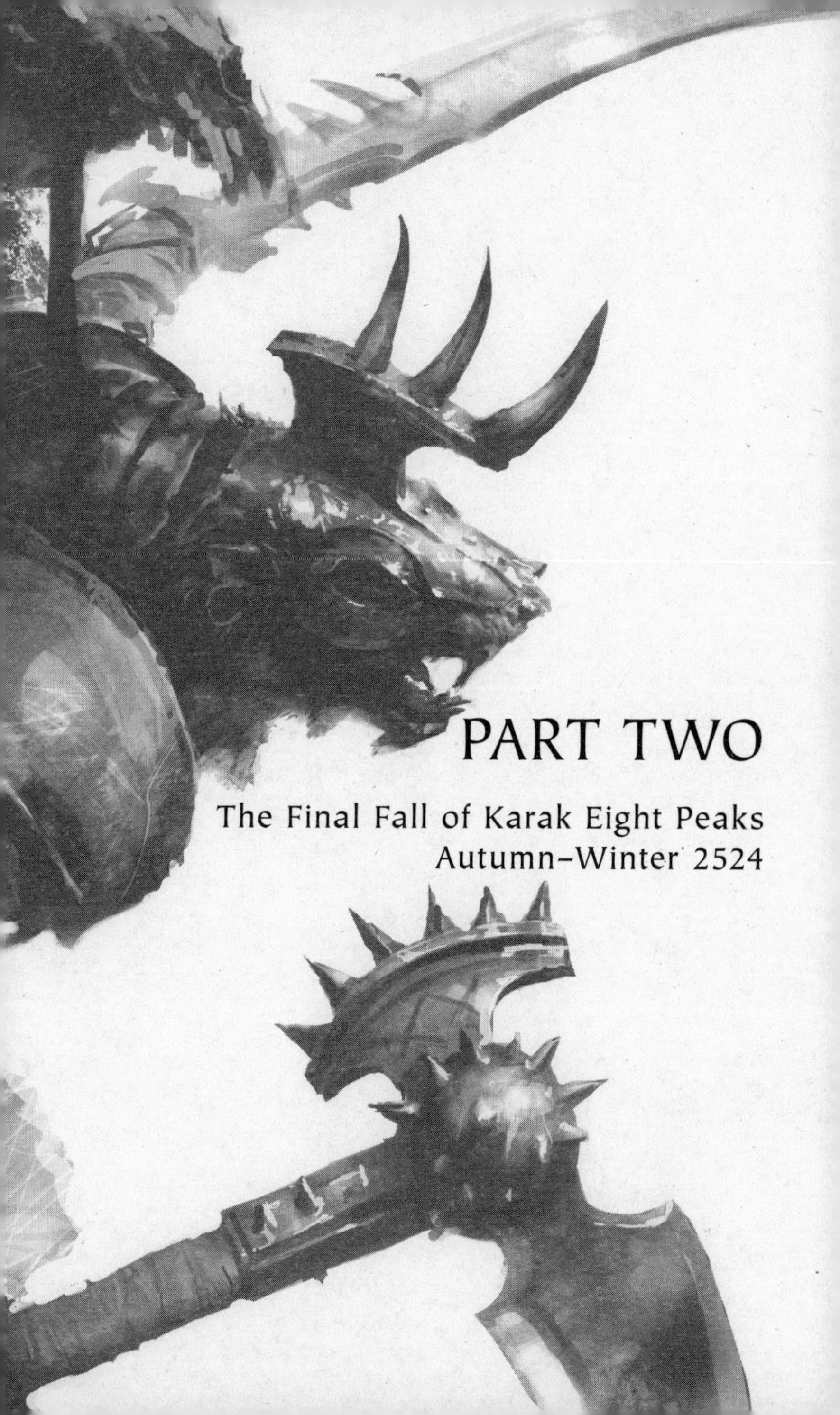

PART TWO

The Final Fall of Karak Eight Peaks
Autumn–Winter 2524

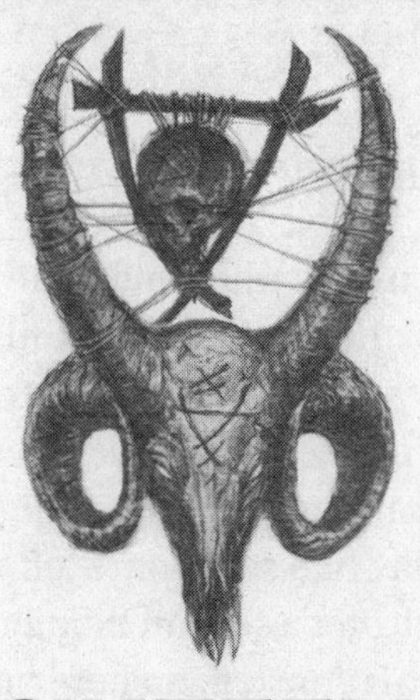

SIXTEEN

Queen Kemma's Oath

'Tor Rudrum is gone, vala,' said Gromvarl.

Queen Kemma set down her riveting pliers and sagged over her metalwork. She did nothing but thread mail links to one another all day every day, because there was nothing else for her to do. Belegar would not let her out, nor would he see her.

'We are trapped, then,' she said.

'Aye, lass,' said Gromvarl. He reached out awkwardly to pat her back. 'That's about the size of it. A flight of gyrocopters came in yesterday.'

'That's good, isn't it?'

'Only one got through, Kemma,' he said gently. 'The rest were shot down by the thaggoraki. They've overrun all the peaks, those that are not in the hands of the grobi, at any rate.'

Kemma gave a sad nod, staring at the shining hauberk, perfectly crafted although not yet finished, in her lap.

'The last one, pilot by the name of Torin Steamhammer, just got in before the ledges were taken by grobi on spiders.'

'Spider riders? I thought they lived in the forests in the lowlands.'

'They did,' said Gromvarl, wheezing as he sat down on a three-legged stool. He took his pipe out from his jerkin and filled it. He thought to take a half-bowl, for there was precious little tobacco left in the Eight Peaks, just like there was precious little of anything fine remaining. But with things the way they were he figured he probably had scant days left to smoke what small amounts he had, and after a second thought rammed it full with his thumb. 'All sorts of monsters up here now. Things I've never seen in the mountains before. The world's in turmoil, vala.'

'Do you have to call me that?' Kemma said sharply. A booming played under their conversation, deep and monotonous, never stopping – the beat of an orcish battering ram on the great gates of the citadel. The greenskins had been at it ever since they'd driven the dwarfs back from the outer defences. Belegar's warriors did what they could to keep Skarsnik's hordes back, but they were low on everything bar rocks to drop on the besiegers. 'You're my only friend, Gromvarl. My only link with home.'

Gromvarl looked at her fondly. How much she's grown, he thought. Such a pity the way fate falls. 'Aye.'

'He still won't talk to me, will he?'

Gromvarl shook his head, sending his clouds of smoke shifting about his head.

'My son?'

'Thorgrim's fine, my lady. He's fretting about you. Keeps asking his dad to come and talk things through, but Belegar's having none of it.' He didn't tell her that Belegar had precious little time for his heir either. He had become withdrawn, pale. He wasn't sleeping, he was sure of that. Dawi were tough, and Belegar tougher than most, but that wound he was trying so hard to hide from everyone was not only obvious, it was not healing. Gromvarl was worried, very worried, but he did his best to hide it from Kemma behind an air of grave concern.

'My husband is an arrogant, prideful fool, Gromvarl,' said Kemma.

'He's one of the best, if not the best, warrior in all the Karaz Ankor, va- Kemma.'

'He's an idiot, and we'll all die because of him.'

Gromvarl couldn't disagree in all honesty, so he harrumphed and looked around the chamber, searching for the right thing to say. It was austere, cold, lacking a womanly touch. He found it depressing that such a good-hearted rinn as Kemma should have been brought to this. He was glad he did not have daughters. He was glad, in these awful times, he had no children at all. Still, he had not finished imparting his run of bad news. He mulled over how much he would say, but he had promised to keep her up to date.

A promise is a promise, he reminded himself. Without honour, and trust, what did they have left? An oath lasted longer than stone and iron.

'There's more, Kemma,' he said quietly. Kemma fixed him with her eyes, expressionless, waiting patiently. 'The gyrocopter brought a message from Karaz-a-Karak. After he read it, the king sat on his own in the Hall of Pillared Iron all day, bellowing at anyone who came near. He only told us what it said this morning, when he'd calmed down. A bit. Most of the holds are under siege, it can't be much longer before they all are.'

'And?' said Kemma. 'There is more, isn't there, Gromvarl?'

The longbeard sighed. She always was far too clever. 'Karak Azul has fallen.' His heart pained him to speak it aloud. 'King Kazador and Thorek Ironbrow were both killed, an ambush in the high passes some time ago.'

Kemma drew in a sharp breath. Ironbrow in particular was a terrible loss. None had his wisdom and skill with the runes. Much sacred knowledge was lost with him.

'The hold was overrun not long after,' continued Gromvarl. 'The message from the High King was the same as all the others the king has had these last weeks.'

Kemma clutched at the hauberk. The rings tinkled. Gromril, by the look of it. 'This is for Thorgrim,' she said. 'He's outgrown his last.'

'He's getting a good girth on him,' said Gromvarl approvingly. 'He'll be a strong lad, and a good king.'

Much to Gromvarl's dismay, Kemma burst into tears.

'He'll never be king! Can't you see? It's all over. They're coming to kill us all. They'll kill you, and the king, and my son!'

Gromvarl reached out his hand uncertainly. A year on, his arm still pained him. Though it had set true, it had been wasted from weeks of disuse, and half-rations were no aid to building its strength back up. 'Come on now, lass, there's no need for that. It's worse than it was even in the time of King Lunn, I grant you, and yet your husband is holding out. There's not many who could do that. The runes might no longer glow upon the gates...'

'Why?' demanded Kemma. 'The magic of the ancestors deserts us.'

Gromvarl clucked his tongue and rattled his pipe on top and bottom teeth. 'No one knows. No one knows anything any more.' It was a poor answer and did little to satisfy her. He blundered on. 'My point is, they're strong still. They're tall, made of stone, steel and gromril. Made to last forever. They have not fallen yet. Why,' he forced a smile, 'the urk have been at it for days and they've not even dented them.'

'There are many things like that in the dwarf realm, supposedly eternal, and they are failing one by one,' said Kemma. She wiped her eyes, angry at herself for her lapse in control. 'I'm sorry, but this is my son! A curse on dawi heads and the blocks of stone they call their brains. We should have gone months ago. Pride will kill us all.'

'You'll see,' said Gromvarl. 'Things are bad, but we'll prevail. We've less ground to cover now the surface holdings are gone. Duregar's finally been called back from the East Gate. We've some strong warriors here. Good lads, and brave. Most are veterans. I've not seen such a lot of battle-hardened dawi in my life. With them at our backs we've every chance. We've still got our defences. Kromdal's line is the strongest yet. There are only four ways through that: the King's Archgate, the Blackvault Gate, Varya's Stonearch and the Silvergate. Hundreds of dawi wait there, and they're all spoiling for a fight. And if they get through that there's the Khrokk line, and after that...'

'After that they're into the citadel,' said Kemma harshly. 'Belegar is waiting for our enemies to fall on each other, or to wear themselves out. But they won't. Ogres, greenskins and thaggoraki have us under siege. There's never any less of them, and fewer of us every day. We've nowhere left to run. My husband's too set in his ways! He can't see that they're not going to kill themselves on our shield walls – they're going to keep coming until they break through and destroy every last one of us.'

'It's worked all the other times.'

'This isn't like all the other times! Valaya preserve me from the thickheadedness of dawi men!' she said. 'You've already told me there's no help coming. We've not changed, Gromvarl. It's why we are going to fail. Doing the same thing over and over and over... All it has to do is not work once. It didn't work at Karak Azul. Why should it work here? They killed the reckoner. Dawi killing dawi! Do you know why?' She didn't give him a chance to respond but answered for him. 'They killed him because he knew. Because he wasn't a tradition-bound fool.'

'Because he was helping you leave,' said Gromvarl. He deliberately avoided the word escape.

'It could have been you,' she said in a small voice. 'I'm glad it wasn't.'

Gromvarl sighed around his pipe stem, and patted her hand. She was right. Kvinn-wyr was overrun, all the surface outposts, the East Gate three weeks back. The citadel was all they had left, and only the part above the ground at that.

'It'll all be fine, you'll see,' he said.

Kemma grasped his hand. She smiled through her tears. 'You have been a loyal servant. You are wise beyond the length of your beard, and a fine warrior, Gromvarl, but you are a terrible liar.'

He humphed and clicked his teeth on his pipe.

'Don't get into a huff! I'm no beardling to be coddled. If we're to die, then I'll do it with my hammer in my hand,' she said. Her smile hardened with resolve. 'This I swear.'

SEVENTEEN

Ikit Claw at the Eight Peaks

'Patience, Queek, patience. You cannot kill Kranskritt, not any more.'

Queek hissed and gripped the arms of his throne. He didn't like this new advisor of his much. For a start, the dead-things he had so carefully collected over his bloody career would no longer speak with him while Lurklox was around. Secondly, the verminlord showed no deference or fear towards him whatsoever. Kranskritt's daemon ruled him utterly. Queek was determined the same would not be the case with him. He had the sneaking suspicion he wasn't succeeding.

'Pah! What sneaker-squeaker know?'

'I killed many thousands for the Council while I still lived, little warlord,' said Lurklox menacingly. 'Deathmaster Snikch's skill is a poor imitation of my glorious ability.'

'What you know of killing in plain view, Queek means! You hide and hide before stab-strike. Too cunning, too cautious. Mighty Queek sees an obstacle, mighty Queek destroys it! Hidey in the dark is not my way.' Queek grumbled and settled into his throne. 'Why all this pretence-pretending! It boring! Queek bored!' He cast a look at his favourite trophies, arrayed upon a massive rack fanning across the back of the throne. Dwarf Gouger and his sword were in a lacquered weapon stand taken from some Far Eastern place to his right. All down the aisle leading to the throne-burrow mouth were heaped piles of dwarf banners. The right claw of Clan Mors liked to boast he had more dwarf standards than the dwarf king himself. But to have them all on display made him uneasy. These were Queek's private things! Not to be seen or touch-sniffed by any other. Mine.

'You will do as I say, small creature,' said the voice, coming first from near, then from behind and then to his left, 'or I will devour you as surely as the Horned Rat himself devoured Kritislik. Arrogance is a virtue, but too much of a good thing is still too much.'

Queek glanced about. Lurklox had disappeared completely; the twitching shadows that betrayed his presence were not visible. Queek felt the first stirrings of fear. He shifted on the throne, acutely aware of his musk glands for the first time in years.

'You are right to be afraid, O most mighty and invincible Queek,' mocked Lurklox's voice, coming from nowhere in particular. 'I know you are wary of the Deathmaster, and yet perhaps one as talented as you in kill-slaying might best him in open combat. Yes-yes,' the voice turned to musing. 'That would be a good-fine match to watch. But I am not the Deathmaster. I am Lurklox, the greatest assassin ever to have been pupped in Skavendom! In my mortal years my name alone could stop a ratkin's heart. In open battle you would stand no chance against me then, and now I am the immortal chosen of the Horned Rat himself. You could never beat me.'

Queek's ears twitched.

'Oh I know-smell you think of it, and that a part of you wishes to try. Against the lesser verminlords of the Realm of Ruin, you might even triumph.' The voice hissed close to his ear, startling

Queek. 'Never against me! And if we were to come to violence-conflict, it would never be face to face. You would die screaming in your sleep, mad-thing Queek, and I would place your head upon your trophy pole to rant at those you killed, for no one else would hear your words. This would be my kindness to you, for the pain would be great but the humiliation worse. Do as I say-command. You are important to my plan-scheme, but no one is indispensable. You should know that. You should understand. Do you understand, Queek?'

Queek stared straight ahead, unblinking. 'Yes-yes,' he said through clenched teeth.

'Good. Now listen-hear to what I say-squeak. You cannot kill Kranskritt. You know why. News of his success has already reached Skavenblight. My brother in darkness aids him. They seek to regain the seers' position on the Council. I suspect this to be the will of the Horned Rat, to test his chosen. The seers of Clan Scruten always were his favourites. I see no reason why they are no longer. My advice is that it would be foolish to disturb this test.'

'Kranskritt is powerful, useful-good,' said Queek. 'You say this Soothgnawer wanted to create good impression with Kranskritt's victory by helping mighty Queek? This is nonsense. He wants Queek dead, to take all glory for his scheming white-furred self. When Kranskritt is no longer useful, he is no longer good. Then Queek slay-kill. If you try stop me, then we will see if mighty-dark Lurklox say-squeaks the truth about supernatural battle-prowess.'

'You are not as mad as they say.'

Queek giggled. 'Mad or not, Queek still mighty.'

'That you are, Queek of Clan Mors, although you have many enemies. Too many for even you.'

'Kranskritt, Skrikk, Gnawdwell, Soothgnawer and Lurklox,' he said rattling the names off quickly. 'Queek does not care.'

Lurklox did not speak, Queek knew he was reading his body language and scent for the lie in his words, probably his mind too, and he knew also that Lurklox would find none.

'I withdraw,' the daemon said presently. 'Ikit Claw comes. Do not reveal my presence! It will be worse for you than would be-is for me.'

Queek chittered his acknowledgement, irritating though it was to be beholden to the verminlord.

The hall fell silent. Lurklox allowed none near Queek while they spoke. Not even the dead-things. Not even loyal Ska!

Queek could hear the clanging iron frame and steam-venting hiss of the approaching Ikit Claw long before he could see him. It was not by accident that the dignitary was forced to walk the lengthy corridor. Queek watched the warlock slowly approach. He did not move fast, being more machine than rat, but there was a solidity to him, a stolidness too, that was lacking in other ratkin. He reminded Queek of a dwarf-thing. Queek suppressed a titter at the thought.

Ikit Claw did not speak until he had finally clanked to a stop before Queek's towering trophy throne. A voice rasped behind his iron mask. 'Greetings, O great Queek, Warlord of the City of Pillars. I bring-carry tidings. Yes-yes, I have slain many beard-things – I have broken Iron-Peak!'

Queek had heard that the rival Clan Rictus had as much to do with bringing Azul-place low as Ikit had, but he was too canny to mention it. What Ikit Claw said was as much provocation as delivery of news; Queek's own failure years ago to destroy Karak Azul was widely known.

Queek squeaked in annoyance as Ikit drew in a long metallic breath, presaging a long flurry of ritual greetings and mock-flattery. Queek went straight for the point.

'Why-tell are you here?'

A menacing green glow emanated from Ikit's iron mask. 'I bring great Queek tribute. The Council bid I gift you Clan Skryre weapons. Very kill-kill, these devices.'

Ikit paused. If he was expecting gratitude, he was disappointed. 'Where-tell are they? Show mighty Queek!'

A grating clunk sounded from Ikit's metal face that might have been a noise of regret. 'Clan Mors will not be granted direct usage of these weapon-gifts. Much work has gone into their creation by Clan Moulder and Clan Skryre, although mostly hard-work thinkings of Clan Skryre. Trained teams of Clan Rictus direct them where Queek needs.'

'I see-smell,' said Queek coldly. 'Is cunning Ikit Claw also to remain, to hold Queek's hand-paw all the way to victory?'

Ikit raised his paw to his chest and bowed slightly. 'Unfortunately not. As mighty Queek doubtless knows in his most labyrinthine and devious mind, the chief servants of the Council must hurry-scurry on and on. I cannot stop-stay,' he said. 'I am bid-go to the mountain of the crested beard-things, there to make much war-killing, and end another infestation of dwarfs for betterment of all skavenkind. Fool-clans besiege Kadrin-place for many months, and cannot break it. I have much fame, much influence. I killer of dwarf-places. They call for me to come here. But mighty Queek does not need much help, does he? Not like weak-meat fighting the orange-beards.'

Without waiting for a reply, the master warlock engineer turned tail and began clanking his way back. 'But I will be back if Queek cannot do the task,' he said. 'So speaks the Council of Thirteen.'

'We shall see-see,' said Queek softly as he watched Ikit painfully clatter his way out again. 'While fool-toys of Clan Skryre face beard-things, Queek will deal with his other enemy, and then we see-smell who is the greater. Tomorrow, Skarsnik imp-thing dies on my sword.'

'Wait, Queek, there is another way...' said Lurklox. The shadows thickened once more, and a rank smell of decay filtered into Queek's nose from behind his throne. Ikit Claw left the throne-burrow and the door slammed shut. Queek levered himself out of his chair and gathered up his things. He felt better once his trophy rack was on his back. He lifted his weapons. 'Yes, there always another way, rat-god servant. There is Queek's sword, and there is Queek's Dwarf Gouger. Two ways is enough choice for Queek! Skarsnik die by one of them. Which, Queek not care.'

'Queek!' said Lurklox warningly. 'We must be cunning...'

But Queek was already scampering away, calling for his guards and the loyal Ska Bloodtail.

At the Arch of Kings, dwarfs waited.

A tributary of the Undak had once run through the cavern, and the arch had been built to bridge it. In its day, the cavern was among the most glorious places in Karak Eight Peaks, a cave of natural beauty enhanced by dwarf craft. The river had gathered itself together from six mountain streams in a wide pool below a small hole some half a mile upstream. The dwarfs had channelled the flow into a square trough five dwarfs deep and sixteen wide, coming into a broad grotto of cascading flowstone. Lesser channels led off from the river to aesthetic and practical purpose, flowing in geometric patterns around stalagmites, before exiting the cavern through various gates and sluices to power the triphammers of the western foundries.

The river was long dry, the streams that fed it blocked by the actions of time or the dwarfs' enemies, the natural columns and peaks of the stone smashed. The trough had become instead a dry ditch, the rusted remains of the machinery that had once tamed the river broken in the bed. But the walls were true, sheer dwarf masonry still flawlessly smooth, affording no purchase to the most skilful of skaven climbers, and so it still presented a formidable obstacle to invaders. For fifty years the Arch of Kings had aided Belegar in keeping the ways open between the citadel and the dwarf holdings in Kvinn-wyr. Additionally, it provided an easily defensible choke point to fall back to, should need arise. Now the dwarfs had been driven out of their halls in the White Lady, that need had arisen, and the ditch kept the enemy from coming any closer to the citadel from the mountain. The Arch of Kings was the key defence for the west.

Belegar's enclave had erected a gatehouse on the eastern side of the riverbed, modest by the standards of their ancestors' works, but sturdy enough. As the road descended from the apex of the bridge's curve, it encountered thick gates of iron and steel that barred the way to the citadel. A wide parapet with heavy battlements hung over the road, overlooking the river beyond. The wall-walk was machiolated over the foot of the bridge, to allow objects to be dropped onto the heads of attackers. Similarly, murder holes pierced the stone of the gate's archway before the gate and behind it. A portcullis was set behind the gate, behind that, another gate, and behind that was a regiment of ironbreakers, well versed in the arts of war and irritable with the lack of decent ale.

Ikit Claw's weapons went there first.

'Movement!' called Thaggun Broadbrow, the lookout that fateful day. His fellow quarrellers immediately started on the windlasses of their crossbows, drawing back the strings. They were practised; their bows were drawn quickly and the sound of bolts slipping into firing tracks clacked up the battlement.

'See,' said one to another, 'I always held that crossbows are better than guns. Where are the handgunners, eh? Out of powder, that's where. Whereas me, my lad, will always have a missile to hurl, as long as there's a stick and a knife to sharpen it with to hand.'

'Aye, true that, Gron, too true.' Gron's companion tapped out his pipe on the wall and carefully stowed it before fitting his own bolt into his bowstock. 'Always be able to send a couple of them away, no matter what the situation.'

'Grim. That's what it is, Hengi. Grim.'

'Aye. Grim comments for grim times.'

'Rat ogre!' called the lookout. 'Rat ogre...?' Thaggun's voice trailed away into astonished query.

Gron peered out into the dark. 'Now what by the slave pits of the unmentionable kin is that?'

'Big, that's what,' said Hengi, sighting down his weapon at the beast approaching.

Big didn't cover it. This was the largest rat ogre any of them had ever seen, and being dwarfs oathsworn to defend Karak Eight Peaks to the bitter end, they'd seen more than their fair share of the things. This one was a head higher than the biggest, covered all over in iron and bronze armour. Grafted to each arm was a pair of warpfire throwers, the tanks feeding each thick with plating.

'I don't like the look of that,' said someone. 'Why isn't it charging?'

'Ah, who cares? We'll have it down in a jiffy,' said another.

'Not before it goes crazy and kills half its own!' said someone else.

But the rat ogre plodded forwards, showing none of the snarling, uncontainable antipathy its kind usually evidenced.

'Quarrellers of the Grundtal clan! Ready your weapons!' shouted Gron.

The clansdwarfs rested their weapons' stocks on the battlements, secure in their position behind the thick stone.

'Take aim,' called Gron.

They each chose a point on the rat ogre.

'Loose!' said Gron, who would never be caught dead saying 'fire.'

Artfully crafted steel bows snapped forwards on their stocks, sending bolts of metal and wood winging at the rat ogre, by now halfway across the bridge. A unit of skaven bearing the banners of Clan Rictus ran cautiously behind it.

Not one of the bolts hurt the creature. They hit all right, but clattered off its armour. A couple punched through or encountered weak spots and stuck in the creature's flesh, but it was unaffected.

'Reload! At it again!' cried Gron. 'You lot down there better be ready,' he shouted through a hole to the gate's ironbreaker guards.

Quickly the dwarfs wound back their bows and fitted fresh missiles. Again they fired, to similar effect. Several clanrats fell screaming from the bridge, felled by wayward bolts, but the rat ogre stomped along, blinkered by an eyeless helm. There was a smaller rat riding its back, Gron noted. The rat ogre's arms came up to point brass nozzles at the gates.

'Everyone down!' yelled Gron.

With a whooshing roar more terrifying than dragon-breath, green-tinged fire belched from the rat ogre's weapons. It washed against the gates and melted them like wax. Backwash shot up through the murder holes onto the parapet. Several quarrellers were hit this way, spattered by supernatural flames that would not go out. They screamed as the fire burned its way through cloth, armour, flesh and bone.

The sharp smell of molten metal hit Gron's nose. The Axes of Clan Angrund below were shouting, orders to form up and sally forth echoing up. It did no good.

The warpfire throwers blazed again. The rat ogre held them in position for a long time, melting its way through the portcullis and the second gate. The stones warmed under Gron's feet. Screaming came from below as the ironbreakers were engulfed. A terrible way to die – Gron had seen it before. They would be cooked alive in their armour, if not outright melted.

'Bring it down, lads!' he bellowed. 'Get it away from the bridge!' Doing so was suicidal, but this thing had to be stopped.

His warriors stood up and crossbow bolts rained down. At this close range they had greater penetrative effect, and the rat ogre roared in pain. It took a step back and raised its arms.

'Down!' shouted Gron, and once more the quarrellers hit the stone flags. The battlements could not save them. Green fire washed over and around them, setting the quarrellers ablaze.

Gron felt the diabolical heat of it as a patch stuck to him, charring its way into the skin of his left arm. A gobbet of it hit his right thumb. He gritted his teeth; no one suffered like a dwarf. But try as he might, the agony was unbearable and he screamed.

The fire abated. His arm and hand no longer burned, but were useless. His left arm he could not feel at all aside from an awful warmth. His right hand was clawed and blackened. His dawi were all dead or mortally wounded. The stone of the parapets glowed red-hot, the crenels melted back to rotten-toothed stumps.

Hengi rolled onto his back, groaning.

'Hengi! Hengi!'

'My eyes... Gron, my eyes!'

Gron looked out. The rat ogre had moved aside. Skaven waited for the ruined gates to cool. He saw then that the rider of the rat ogre was nothing of the sort, but some hideous homunculus grafted to its flesh.

'Hengi, Hengi, take my bow.' He thrust his weapon at his blinded kinsman as best he could with his ruined limbs. Hengi's hands were sound, but his upper face was a red raw mess, his eyes weeping thick fluids. Lesser creatures would have been howling in agony, but they were dawi. Pain could not master them. 'They've something controlling the rat ogre, some creature of theirs. If we can kill it, we might be able to stop it.'

'Shoot then,' said Hengi, his voice thick with bottled pain.

'I cannot, my arms are ruined. You will have to do it. Let me aim it for you, here!'

Gron guided Hengi to a crenel whose merlons were not red-hot, pushing him with his shoulders into the gap. The pair were hidden by the smoke of stone burning beneath them, allowing Hengi to fumble the crossbow onto the wall. Gron got behind Hengi and sighted down it as best he could.

He squinted. 'Left a touch. Up, up! No, down. Easy, Hengi. Now,' he said.

The last discharge of a dwarf crossbow upon the King's Arch-gate occurred, sending a bolt fast and true to bury itself in the wizened creature on the back of the rat ogre. The monster reacted immediately, shaking its head as if coming out of a drugged sleep.

It roared. Clanrats squeaked in fear. The warpfire throwers belched again and again, fired by the furious monster without thought. Gron looked on with satisfaction as the rat ogre spun round, setting the regiment alight. Presently its fuel ran out and the skaven brought down their wayward creature eventually, but only after one regiment of thaggoraki had been entirely destroyed, and three more fled.

Gron looked back over the dry river. The darkness was alive with movement and red eyes. As soon as the rat ogre was dead, they were on the move again.

He sank back against Hengi. Soon the skaven would be coming for them.

'Let's not let them take us alive, eh? Lad?' said Gron. 'You'll have to go last, I can't move my hands at all.'

Hengi nodded. His knife slid from his belt.

All along the third line of defence, similar things were happening. Rat ogres armed with ratling guns, upscaled poisoned wind mortars and other terrible weapons came against the dwarfs. One by one the gates fell, with such speed that the dwarfs of the Khrokk line had no time to prepare, and this too fell the same day.

The way was open to the citadel.

EIGHTEEN

A Gathering of Might

Duffskul hiccupped and waddled along the corridor to Skarsnik's personal chambers in the Howlpeak. He hummed to himself as he went, trailing clouds of stinking shroomsmoke behind him. He was wearing his best wizarding hat – a once very bright yellow, now so grubby it was almost green – and a collection of charms that hummed with Waaagh! magic.

The little big 'uns and moonhats by Skarsnik's chambers scrambled over themselves to open the doors.

'A fine welcome, oh yus. You got the right respects for your betters, grotty boys,' he said. They simpered gratefully at his praise.

In the corridor it was freezing; the constant winds whistling through the windows gave the mountain its goblin name and its hurty-bit biting temperatures. In Skarsnik's rooms it was a different matter, swelteringly hot from the fire blazing in the hearth. Duffskul brought in a gust of sharp-smelling winter with him, but it was swiftly defeated, carried off by the vapours steaming from his robes in the sudden heat.

'Duffskul, me old mate,' said Skarsnik, looking up from his work. As usual papers tottered around him, and on many other desks too, to which he flitted as he worked. He wrinkled his eyes, holding a parchment at arm's length.

'Too much reading's bad for you, boss, oh yus.' Duffskul kicked old bones, rags and bottles out of the way as he made his way over to a sturdy dwarf chair near the fire. Gobbla lay asleep on the filthy rug before the flames, whiffling gently in his sleep.

'Someone's got to keep these zogging idiots in line,' said Skarsnik. 'Can't do it if you's not organised...' His words trailed away as he deciphered whatever it was that he had written there.

'I always said you was a funny little runt. Done us proud you have wiv all that thinking there in the old brain box.' Duffskul rubbed his hands together in front of the fire and sighed contentedly. His heated robes gave off the most noxious smell. 'Ooh, that's nice, ooh, that's very nice!' He smacked his lips and pulled out his gourd of fungus beer. He sloshed it around disappointedly. 'If only I had a little drinky to help meself really enjoy it.'

Skarsnik had gone back to his work, the enormous griffin quill in his hand scratching over his parchment.

'Wanna drink? Help yourself,' he said distractedly.

Duffskul didn't need telling twice. He grabbed up the nearest bottle and uncorked it. 'You is running low.'

'And you is going to have to brew up a lot more fungus beer. And preferably stuff that don't taste of old sock!' said Skarsnik. 'Precious few stunty barrels to nick, and none of the grapey goodstuff coming out the west these days, so don't you go gulping it all. I needs me drinks to thinks,' he said, and giggled quietly.

Duffskul guzzled anyway, glugging priceless Bretonnian wine right from the bottle until it had nearly all gone. 'Ahh! Now that is better. Ooh, that is a lot better.'

'Right. Now you is all nice and comfy, why don't you tell me what you is doing here,' said Skarsnik, finally looking up and laying down his quill. 'I am a very busy goblin.'

'Ain't you just, ain't you!' giggled Duffskul.

'Get to the point, you mad old git,' said Skarsnik affectionately. Duffskul had been with him right from the very start, and had stuck with him when others had wandered off, turned traitor or inconsiderately died.

'Well, we has questioned the ratty scouts.'

'Yeah?'

'And we has kept careful watch on their doings and all that, oh yus.'

'Tolly's boys?'

'Best sneaks in the peaks,' said Duffskul. 'And I has been trying to speak with da Twin Gods! Gork and Mork, what you has visited and who is the mightiest greenies of them all.'

'Right. And? Are the ratboys going to attack, then? They've got them stunties well bottled up. Only a matter of time before they make their move on me. When and where, that's what I want to know, when and where.'

'And you shall know, king of the mountains!' Duffskul swivelled in the armchair, and leaned on its torn, overstuffed arm. 'The rats are going to try and drive us out for good, starting with orctown in the old stunty city and da camps outside the walls.'

'Right,' said Skarsnik, who had expected as much. 'East Gate?'

'Drilla's boys went to kick out the stunties yesterday. Empty. Well, it was – full of black orcs now.'

'Hmm.' Skarsnik drummed his fingers on the table. 'Well, let's ambush the little furry bleeders.'

'They'll be expecting that,' said Duffskul.

'Course they will! That Queek's not an idiot, even if he is as mad as snot on one of your better madcap brews. But what he's not gonna be expecting is a *special* ambush, and so I's going to make it a very special ambush. He'll definitely not expect that!'

'Oh no, oh yus,' said Duffskul.

'The Waaagh!'s building, Duffskul, greenies coming to me from left right and centre.' He paused, and looked down at his lists, running ink-stained fingers down the parchment. 'I reckon I should meet with this Snaggla Grobspit. Drilla's lads have already come over. Time to take that cheese-stealing maniac to task, don't you fink?'

'Oh yes, boss! Oh yes. Oh yus,' said Duffskul, his eyes spinning madly in his face. 'And I've got a cracking idea meself.'

'Have you now?' said Skarsnik. 'Right then, tell me all about it, and we'll figure out exactly what we is going to do...'

The paired skaven warpsteam engines at the gates of the Hall of a Thousand Pillars chuffed madly, whistling as they vented pressure to equalise their efforts. Masked Clan Skryre engineers looked out from the haphazardly armoured embrasures holding their machines, then scuttled back to their charges, fiddling with knobs and tossing levers. Satisfied that their pistons were synchronised, the tinker-rats blew whistles at one another, then set about yanking more levers into the correct positions to open the doors. The tone of the engine's voices deepened as their gearing wheels thunked into position, engaging with the massive cogs that worked the door mechanisms. Huge gear chains twanged as they came under tension. Machinery hidden high in the roof of the Hall of a Thousand Pillars rattled, and the great gates of the underhalls of Karak Eight Peaks creaked open.

The skaven massed behind the doors shrank back in terror of the sunlight. Few of them had ever been overground, and the prospect of a world without a roof sent a chitter of nervousness through their ranks.

'Hold-hold!' their masters ordered, cracking whips and punching the most timid.

The gates crushed rubble and other detritus to powder as they opened. Ponderous but unstoppable, they were one hundred feet tall. The tired sun picked out their decoration as they swung inwards, the runes and clan marks of the beard-things that made them still fresh as the day they had been carved.

'Forward!'

The first claws of skaven scurry-marched up the ramp leading into the surface city.

All around Karak Eight Peaks, skaven emerged blinking and terrified into the sunlight, pale though it had been made by the choking ejecta of the world's volcanoes and the endless, uncanny storm that wracked the skies. At the fore of the warriors emerging from the Hall of a Thousand Pillars into the surface city went Ikk Hackflay, a rising star in Queek's entourage. He was a logical replacement for Thaxx and Skrikk, whose heads now graced the Grand Warlord's trophy room.

From the skaven-held mountains, more warriors emerged. Four of Queek's five clawpacks. Reduced by months of war, they still numbered in the tens of thousands. Over one hundred thousand warriors marched forth. Every column flinched as it walked out into the day, and not just for the frightening lack of a ceiling. They all expected to be ambushed as they came out, no matter how well hidden or supposedly secret their burrows were.

They were not ambushed. The immediate fighting they had planned for never came. They surfaced instead to a ghost town. The thickly packed orc-shacks and tents in the city were empty, as were the encampments in the weed-choked farmland beyond the city walls.

Queek surveyed all this impatiently from the top of part of the rubble slope created by the collapse of Karag Nar.

'Careful, Queek,' said Krug from his trophy rack. 'He's a wily one, that Skarsnik.'

'What news?' he said to his gathered lieutenants. 'Grotoose?'

'Nothing, great Queek.'

'The fifth clawpack has found not one of the green-things, exulted Queek,' fawned Kranskritt. Queek gave him a hard look.

He still did not trust the grey seer. Only Lurklox's insistence kept the wizard alive.

Skrak reported the same, as did Gnarlfang and Ikk Hackflay, who had been furiously stomping from place to place in search of something to kill.

'There is no one here,' said Gritch, his assassin's voice pitched just over the wind soughing through the dry winter grasses. There had been precious little snow that year, though it was bitingly cold. 'The siege camp is empty. They have abandoned their attack on the gates. There is a new idol in the main square of the beard-thing city. Stone and iron, it stares-glares with skull-eyes at dwarf-thing fort-place.'

'So good your scouts are. Well done! So skilled to find big stone giant, but not little things,' Queek said. 'What about scouts sent to the mountain halls and peaks? Where is the Skarsnik-thing, where are his armies?'

'Many scouts not scurry back, great Queek,' said Gritch, bowing low.

'Queek very impressed.'

Gritch began to protest, but Queek cut him off. 'Big-meat ogre-things?' said Queek.

'Gone with the gold,' said Skrak.

'Fools,' said Queek. 'Why they so obsessed? Gold soft, useless.' He held up his sword and looked up its length. 'Not hard-sharp like steel. They like to eat, more than a skaven gripped by the black hunger.' He shrugged. 'Maybe they eat it.'

'Skarsnik has gone then,' said Grotoose. 'He has fled the wrath of mighty Queek!'

Queek rounded on him, raising Dwarf Gouger. 'Oh no, do not be mistaken. Little imp watches, little imp waits to see what we will do. Little imp thinks he will beat Queek in very-very cunning-clever trap. But little imp will not trap Queek.'

'Will he attack in the day?'

'Skaven love-like the night. We scurry under the big roof now that is no roof at all. Skaven not like it, pah! But Skarsnik's little soldiers no different.'

Kranskritt glanced nervously up at the sun, shining pale yet still menacing through the thick cloud. 'What do we do then, mighty one?'

Queek wondered if he could strike the seer dead now. He could, he thought. Lurklox was not there, and he did not see Soothgnawer – nor did he think he was near, for his trophies whispered their wisdom to him, something they did not when either verminlord was close by. He refrained from acting upon his whim.

'We clear the city as planned, Queek decrees! Tear it all down, break it to pieces, smash the imp-thing's little empire on the surface as we smashed his town in the Hall of a Thousand Pillars. Then we will see if he can be tempted out or not.'

Orders were given, and the army split into its various components to cover the vast area encompassed by the bowl sheltered by the eight peaks. Clan Skryre engineers set up their war machines near the mostly securely held skaven mountains in case of attack, while the armies subdivided further and began the work of demolishing the greenskins' settlements. In ruined fields covered by scrubby forest, greenskin shelters were kicked down. Clanrats clambered over the crumbling dwarf city, levering stones out of the walls of rough-built huts. Warpfire teams torched entire villages of tents, while wind globadiers tossed their poisons into ruins and caves that might hold monsters. Teams of rat ogres tackled the bigger structures, clawing down idols of stone, wood and dung.

None, however, could bring low the great idol of Gork staring fixedly at the citadel in the centre of the city. Queek followed the line of its gaze. Glints on the battlements of the citadel showed dwarfs powerlessly watching as the skaven rose up to take control of yet more of their ancestral home.

'Soon, Belegar long-fur, it will be your turn,' hissed Queek.

The idol was as tall as a giant, but much more massive, its

crude arms and legs made of monoliths stacked on top of each other and chained in place in crude approximation of orcish anatomy. A huge boulder with crude eyeholes hacked into the face topped it off, a separate jaw of wood hanging by more rusty chains from its face. It looked as if it should be pushed over easily, but would not fall. Warpfire splashed off the rock and iron. Warp-lightning crackled across it without effect. More powerful explosives were sent for. All the while the idol hunched there, apish and insolently strong as the day wore on.

Still Skarsnik did not come.

From his position atop the parapets of Howlpeak, Skarsnik watched the skaven go about the business of wrecking orctown. Fires burned everywhere.

'They is behaving like they own the place, burning our houses down,' said Skarsnik. 'Old Belegar is probably loving every bit of this.'

'Should we go and get them now, boss?' said Kruggler. Crowds of orc and goblin bosses hung around him, the lot of them sheltering under nets and swags of cloth covered with dust and dyed grey to hide them from the skaven's eyes.

Skarsnik snapped his telescope shut; the skaven weren't the only ones to steal from dwarfs. 'In a minute, Kruggs.' He swept his hand out towards the eastern peaks. 'We'll wait until they're nice and spread out, then we'll attack, smash the centre, rout the rest and have a nice big ratty barbecue.'

'I is not for waiting!' grumbled Drilla Gitsmash, king of the Dark Lands black orcs. What with his thick accent, he was almost unintelligible behind his heavy, tusked visor. 'We should get out there and smash 'em good now. I is not for waiting!' he repeated.

'Oh yes you is, if you want to win,' said Skarsnik, looking up at the black orc as if he weren't twice his size and four times his weight, before re-extending his telescope and turning back to the view.

'But if you wants to go out there on your own and get chopped up to little itsy bitsy pieces, then go ahead. I is sure my boys could do with a laugh. No?' Drilla said nothing. 'Good idea that. Best to wait until we're all going out. Is everyone in position?'

'Yes, boss,' said Kruggler.

'Tolly Grin Cheek?' This was not the original supporter of Skarsnik from way back, but the fourth murderous goblin to bear the name, and the facial scars that went with it.

'He's up behind them, boss.'

'And that Snaggla fella? Not sure about him. Tell you, spiders is fer eating, not riding – and what's this nonsense about some spider god? How many gods are there, boys?'

'Gork and Mork,' said one. 'That's four.'

'Five?'

'Definitely more than one!'

'One,' grumbled Drilla. 'Mork don't count.'

'There's two!' said Skarsnik, his voice becoming shrill. 'Two. Gork and Mork. Not three, or lots, or twenty-two thousand.'

Goblin faces creased in pained confusion at the mention of this incomprehensible number.

'I told you, boss, I fought wiv some of them forest boys up north in the Border Princes,' said Kruggler. 'They is real sneaky. Morky as you like. You'll love it.'

'Right,' said Skarsnik. He gave the vista one last pass with his telescope. He squinted at the sun. Noon, as near as he could reckon it. Not good for his night boys, but it couldn't be helped. 'Now or never,' he said. 'Positions, lads. And get the signal to Duffskul sent!'

Skaven passed under Duffskul's nose. From the shoulder of the idol he was looking right down at the top of their pointy little heads, and some of them looked right back at him. He pulled faces at them and laughed at how close they were. They couldn't see him, couldn't smell him, didn't know he was there at all. They milled about, trying one thing after another to destroy his idol, arguing over how it had got there. Duffskul knew the answer to that, of course.

It had walked.

It had taken him ages to ride it back down from old Zargakk the Mad's wizlevard cave, way up over the Black Crag. A risky journey, but funnily enough, he hadn't been bothered by anyone at all on the way back.

A single puff of smoke, black as a night goblin's robes, rolled up into the sky over the tumbled parapets of the Howlpeak's Grimgate. Duffskul laughed. He did a little dance. He whispered horrible things in the general direction of the skaven.

And then he did his magic.

'What-what is that noise?' said the skaven warlock nearest to the idol's foot.

'What noise?'

'Deaf-deaf, you are! A scream-shriek, getting louder.' The pair of them looked left, looked right and all around them, turning in circles to find the source of the rapidly loudening cry.

'I hear now!' said the second, exactly half a second before a goblin smashed itself to paste yards from their position. All that was left was one twitching foot, a shattered pair of canvas wings, and the echoes of its scream.

Only then did the skaven, born and bred in a world with comfortably low skies, think to look upwards.

Goblins were arcing through the heavens in long lazy curves, swishing their wings back and forth like birds. The illusion was impressive. One could almost think a goblin could fly, so at home the doom divers seemed in the clouds.

They were, unfortunately for the goblins, as aerodynamically gifted as boulders, and their flights lasted only marginally longer.

Unfortunately for the skaven whose regiments they steered themselves onto, they did about as much damage as boulders too. A goblin's head was uncommonly dense, especially when crammed into a pointed helmet.

'Look-look!' The second skaven tugged upon the sleeve of the first.

'Yes-yes, I see! Flying green-things, very peculiar.'

'Not there,' he said, grabbing hold of his colleague's head and pointing his gas-masked face at the head of the idol, their field of vision being somewhat restricted. 'There!'

The skaven looked up at the idol. The idol, eye-caves glowing a menacing green, stared back.

'*Waaaaaghhhhhh!*' the idol shouted.

The skaven shrieked as a heavy rock foot ground them out of existence.

Atop its shoulders, Duffskul whooped. By way of reply, the mountains and ruins of Karak Eight Peaks resounded to the blaring of horns and the clanging of cymbals, the roll of dwarf-skin drums and the tuneless squeal of the squigpipes.

With a rapid clacking, the Grimgate swung open, splitting the grimacing orc-head glyph painted over the ancestor runes in two.

Out marched legions of greenskins. They headed right for the centre of the city.

'All right, Mini-Gork, I believe we'll be needing to go thataway!' said Duffskul.

With rumbling strides accompanied by the grinding of rock, the Idol of Gork swung about and set off towards the enemy.

'He is coming! Green-imp shows his hand-paw! Foolish greenthing. Loyal Ska, sound the advance!'

Skaven cymbals clashed, and the entirety of Queek's first claw-pack rose up from its hiding places. Forming rapidly into claws, the elite of Queek's army made a wall of strong, armoured rat-men across the widest of the Great Vale's shattered boulevards.

'Forward!' shouted Ska. 'Forward for the glory of Queek! Forward for the glory of Clan Mors! Forward or I'll kill-slay you myself!'

Ikk Hackflay's Ironskins were off first, the fangleader eager to prove himself. Queek had had his eye on the skaven ever since he had raided Belegar's lower armouries months ago, taking enough dwarf armour to equip his entire claw, changing their names from the Rustblades to the Ironskins afterwards. From the speed he set off at, he evidently felt Queek's scrutiny upon him.

Lightning blasted skywards from the ground, bursting goblins apart in the air. Some got through, some of those shattered the scaffolds the lightning cannons were mounted upon, and so the goblin doom divers and the best of Clan Skryre occupied one another.

'That's good, that is,' said the dead dwarf king Krug. 'Stops them from smashing your lads up.'

Queek hissed irritably. 'Of course, Queek knows this. It is all part of Queek's plan!'

Down the slopes of the mountain, innumerable hordes of goblins poured. Queek glanced nervously around the mountain bowl, across the city and out beyond where the lower reaches of the further peaks were hazy. His eyesight was as good as any skaven's, which is to say at distance, not very good at all. But he saw no sign of movement elsewhere, and heard no sound of battle.

'Ska!'

'Yes, masterful Queek.'

'Send messengers. Be sure to warn our lieutenants. This is not the fullness of the green-things' force.'

Ska nodded, detailing his own minions to fulfil the orders.

Meanwhile, Skarsnik's vanguard were jogging forwards to form a broad front. Queek ordered the slaves ahead, and with a terrified chittering, caused as much by the snarling packmasters at their rear as fear of the enemy, they surged across the mounded ruins of the dwarf city towards their greenskin foe. As the slaves neared, the goblins laughed loudly and shoved out whirling fanatics towards them. Queek had seen this so often by now that the tactic no longer held any surprises for him, but he remained wary of them. They spun round and round, laughing madly, hefting giant metal balls at the ends of long chains that should have been impossible for a goblin to lift.

He could not see their connection with his slave legions directly. The bodies of weak-meat tossed high in the air by the goblins' swinging balls informed him of when it happened anyway.

'Pick up speed! Hurry-scurry!' shouted Queek. The Red Guard broke into a jog, their wargear clattering. 'Mad-thing green-things will come through, kill-slay slaves – we must be through before they can turn and chase Queek!'

Queek's elite burst through their screen of slaves, hacking down those who did not get out of the way. The goblins had advanced some three hundred yards from the Grimgate, filling the wide road and spilling into the ruins either side. The city here had been much reduced, piles of rubble with twisted trees poking out from them or greened mounds showed where once workshops and homes had stood. It made for difficult ground to fight over.

The town sloped downwards from Queek's position, following the contours of the Howlpeak. Above was the still-open Grimgate. Ikk Hackflay's Ironskins pushed their way out of the slaves there, slightly ahead of Queek's formation. From his vantage, Queek saw the broad, bloody lanes through the skaven created by the fanatics. These wobbled in uncertain lines, some looping right the way back round towards the goblin lines. The casualty numbers were horrendous, but all were slaves and of little worth. Queek snickered; they had performed their role excellently. The fanatics were falling one by one, smashing into low walls, dropping from exhaustion, or becoming hopelessly tangled with the slaves, their miserable deaths aiding the skaven cause far more than the ratkin ever could in life.

The slaves were thinned by panic, fanatics, bow-fire and doom divers. Clanrats came through them to support their general. Poisoned wind globadiers ran before them, approaching perilously close to the goblin lines before heaving their spheres of gas into their foes' tight-packed ranks.

Queek sniffed the air. The wind was rank with greenskin. Neither his nose nor his eyes could pick out Skarsnik. 'That way!' he shouted, pointing directly at the centre of the greenskin force. 'Come-come, quick!'

With a fierce cry, the Red Guard ran forwards. They burst through their screen of slaves and into the goblin vanguard, where they hacked their way through two mobs of goblins in short order. Queek's view of the battle became restricted. He heard rather than saw the charge of Hackflay's Ironskins, and the following clanrats. The first line of goblins bowed under pressure, nervous of the stormvermin carving their way through and the masses of clanrats coming next.

Deeper into the greenskin army Queek pushed, spinning and leaping, effortlessly felling the feeble warriors. Another goblin regiment parted before him, throwing down their shields and crooked spears rather than face him. His Red Guard skidded to a halt, momentarily cowed by the massive mob of black orcs they saw on the other side.

'Oi! Squeaker!' shouted their leader, a massive brute of an orc. 'I'm gonna have you!'

The black orcs executed a flawless turn to the left, and charged.

'Kill-slay them all!' squealed Queek. 'Breeding rights to the three who kill most big-meat!'

Spurred on by his generous offer, Queek's Red Guard broke into a run. The two elite units met with a clash of metal that drowned out all else.

These were no goblins, but the ultimate orcs, bred by magic in the slave pits of Zharr-Naggrund. They smashed down the Red Guard with their huge axes. The Red Guard duelled with them, seeking to keep the black orcs at arm's length with their halberds. The skaven felled a good number, but there were many, and they were fearless. The Red Guard's advance ground to a halt. Their leader pushed his way forwards, levelling his massive two-handed axe at Queek.

'Come on then, Headtaker! I've heard a lot about you. Nonsense, I reckon.'

The greenskin's accent was outlandish, but Queek understood. He replied in the beast's own language.

'Come die then – always space for more trophies for Queek!'

The orc roared and charged, bowling over a Red Guard who got in the way and trampling him down into the dirt. Queek spun round, allowing the orc to pass him, then smashed the spike of Dwarf Gouger through its chest. The orc made a noise of surprise. Queek finished it with a thrust through its visor slit with his sword, skewering the orc's small brain. It fell over heavily.

Queek wasted no time, prising off its tusked helmet and sawing its head off. He handed it to one of his guard, who jammed it upon a free spike on Queek's rack. He'd left many empty for today.

Seeing their leader cut down disturbed the black orcs, and the Red Guard pressed their advantage, surrounding them and hewing through their thick mail with their halberds. Clanrat regiments had cut through the shattered goblin vanguard, joining Queek. They pressed back at greenskins moving to fill this potential gap in the line.

'Ska! Break them!' called Queek, cutting down two more of the black orcs.

Ska nodded, slammed a black orc out of the way, and leapt at their standard bearer.

The black orcs' metal icon wobbled in the air as Ska attacked, then fell.

The orcs, reduced to a knot surrounded by ferocious skaven, broke. Queek and his warriors cut many of them down. Predictably, the greenskin centre collapsed around them. Seeing their toughest regiment destroyed, and well aware that their destroyers lingered still in their midst, a huge tranche of weaker greenskins broke.

'The way to the gates are open!' squealed Queek, forgetting in his exultation exactly who he was dealing with. The clanrats surged forwards after the fleeing goblins.

Horns sounded from all across the city. The left and right flanks of the goblin army angled inwards, coming at the mass of skaven from both sides. A fresh wave of doom divers began to rain down from the sky, unsettling the skaven with their shrieks. They plummeted into the horde of ratmen with final wet splats, their broken bones and flying harnesses shattering into spinning shrapnel that cut down many ratkin. Under the ferocity of this suicidal bombardment, the clanrats' advance slowed and began to break up.

'No! No!' shrieked Queek. 'We have them!'

He bounded up onto a ruined wall, the last corner of a building torn down who knew when. The age-worn stones were cold under his bare foot-paws.

Queek hissed at what he saw. Goblins were pouring out of the mountains to the west, encircling his rear. The huge idol they had discovered that morning had come to life, smashing its way through the skaven centre, some sorcerer atop it flinging bolts of green lightning from its shoulder. Queek wished for a screaming bell, or an abomination or two, but the dwarf-things had slain both of his. From caves thought cleared came a stream of squigs, including one big as a giant. It squashed as many skaven as it ate. Lesser round shapes bounded around its feet. A collective squeak of terror drew Queek's attention to the foot of Karag Zilfin, where mangler squigs carved red ruin through his army.

Queek returned his attention to the fleeing goblins. Skarsnik had lured him into a trap, that much was certain, but it was not going to plan. The green-imp's bait force had not rallied and fled still.

Even so, the skaven army was at a disadvantage.

Squeaks from the foot of the wall called to him. His minions had caught up with him. A gaggle of messengers stood there, waiting expectantly to carry fresh orders away.

A final messenger, its fur matted with drying blood, came to a panting stop. 'Great Queek! Much terror-slaughter on the east. Giant spiders attack.'

'How big? Fist-paw big?'

The messenger shook his head and swallowed. 'Wolf-rat big and... Much-much bigger.'

Queek bared his teeth in anger. Away out beyond the outer edges of the city, into the derelict farmland to the east, many death-squeaks were being voiced. He narrowed his eyes. In his blurred distance vision, large shapes lurched against the pale horizon.

Just as he thought he was getting a paw on the situation, a terrifying screech rent the air and there was a snap of leathery wings. A dark shape swooped overhead, bringing with it a carrion stink and a sharp, reptilian smell.

A wyvern bearing an orc warboss landed heavily right in the middle of the clanrat regiments behind Queek.

A fresh wave of panic rippled through the clanrats around his position. This proved too much for them. Predictably, they ran. A huge section of the skaven centre collapsed. There was now a large part of the central battlefield devoid of combatants, each side running from the other. Queek was left alone with his Red Guard, who held fast about the Great Banner of Clan Mors.

'Stand! Stand! Cowards!' squealed Queek. He turned to his messengers with a snarl.

He pointed to one.

'Kranskritt!' he commanded. 'Go to him! It is most important he kill-slay the idol!'

He spared a look for the rampaging rock construct. Warp-lightning crackled around it with no effect.

To another he said, 'To the Burnt Cliffs with you – call out the reserves.' He spoke then directly to Ikk Hackflay and Grotoose. 'Ironskins and rat ogres, pursue green-thing rout.'

'And you, mighty leader?' rasped Ikk.

Queek scanned the sea of black-robed goblins, seeking out the tell-tale splash of red that would reveal the location of Gobbla, and therefore his master. Queek could not find him! The imp-thing would have to wait. He turned his face to the wyvern flapping about the battle and slaughtering clanrats.

'Queek has other matters to attend to.'

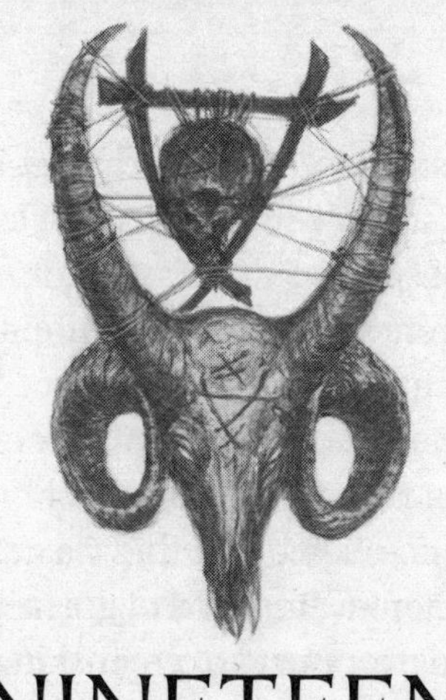

NINETEEN

War in the Great Vale

'Waaagh!' cackled Duffskul madly. He danced a little jig and threw bolts of green lightning from his fingertips, blasting skaven to pieces with every shot. His knees popped as he danced, but he was too excited to care. Swarms of ratmen fled before the feet of the Idol of Gork, squealing in terror. Wherever the stone monster went, skaven units burst apart like ripe puffballs, disintegrating into individual warriors who ran in every direction like mice fleeing an orc. 'That's right, ya little ratties! That's right! Run away!'

Duffskul's eyes glowed with the surfeit of Waaagh! energy washing over the battlefield. From atop his idol he could see right across the Great Vale for miles and miles. The main scrap was right there, in the old dwarf surface city, but smaller skirmishes were going on right the way across the entire bowl. Outside the walls, wolf riders ran down blocks of skaven infantry. Streaks of green whizzed down from on high where jezzail teams discharged their guns. Doom divers plummeted from even higher up. Batteries of goblin artillery duelled with skaven lightning throwers, sneaky gobboes dripping in night-black squig oil fought running battles with groups of skaven assassins. Right at the back, mobs of spider riders ran amok, unopposed by anyone. The ratboys were trying to bring their lightning cannons about, but weren't having much luck. Not long now and they would smash up the skaven artillery. There was a lot more to see than just the big ruck at the centre, oh yus.

Duffskul liked a nice fight, and this was the biggest and best he had ever seen. There were loads of greenies! Lots of lots, boys from every tribe and every kind of greenskin you could think of – except sneaky hobgobboes and stupid gnoblars, naturally – while there were so many ratties on the other side that he couldn't even begin to count them, and Duffskul could count pretty high for a goblin. It was a proper Waaagh!

'Waaagh!' he screeched. 'Waaagh!' The powers of Gork and Mork flooded through him and out his arms and toes and nose, the great idol of mad old Zargakk filling him with power.

What had happened to Zargakk, Duffskul had no idea. No one had seen him in years. He was probably dead. Good thing too, or there'd be no way Duffskul would have got his hands on the idol.

'Come on, Gork!' he called. A phantom foot formed from the magic spilling from Duffskul's skin. With a screech he sent it smashing into a unit of ratties, squashing them flat. He laughed uproariously, so hard he cried. Orc magic that one; Duffskul might be crazy, but he was deeply in favour with the Great Green Twins.

The idol lurched to one side, nearly tipping Duffskul from his perch on its shoulder. With desperately scrabbling hands, he caught himself on the rough stone. Sucking his lacerated fingers, he cast about for his attacker.

A flash of black lightning crackled against the idol, making it moan. It stumped around to face its tormentor, a white-furred skaven sorcerer who was hurling magic of his own at Duffskul's new pet. Unlike the blasts from the skaven cannon, this was hurting it.

'Oi!' he shouted, responding with a crackle of his own destructive magic. He screamed in triumph as it fizzed towards the skaven, but the rattie waved a dismissive hand, and the green light of Waaagh! power dissipated. The sorcerer raised his hands and hurled twin blasts of blacklight at the idol's knee. Duffskul countered, but the magic got through, weakened, but still effective. With a tinkle, the chains binding the menhirs of the idol's left leg burst apart. The idol took another step, reaching out crude hands to grab the sorcerer, but its foot was left behind.

'Watch out! Watch out!' Duffskul said in horror as the footless leg descended once more.

The idol let out a moronic bellow as it fell. The ground rushed up at Duffskul.

'Heeeeeellllllp!' he wailed. The idol crashed down, breaking into a dozen pieces of bouncing rock that rolled all over the place, trailing wisps of dying magic.

The sorcerer stood triumphantly, sure of his victory.

Duffskul was having none of that. Bruised but otherwise undamaged, he stood and rolled up his sleeves. 'Oi! Ratty! Who do you think you are?'

The rat snarled, exposing the tiny needle teeth either side of its flat incisors. Its eyes went dead-black. Smoke tinged with purple flares poured from its mouth.

Duffskul threw up his own hands. Giant green fists formed around them. He held out his hand, a hand that had become the magic-wreathed, crackling fist of Gork himself. He swung at the sorcerer, who warded off Duffskul's magic with his dark mist. Duffskul swung again. The skaven responded too late, and Duffskul grabbed him hard.

'How you like that, eh, ratty? Orc magic that. I know it because I is the chosen of Gork and Mork, their teller of fings to Skarsnik, who was raised up high because of me!' He squeezed hard. The skaven squealed.

'We make deal-deal?' it said in mangled greenskin.

'I don't fink so.'

Duffskul sucked in deep, inhaling the winds of magic rushing over the excited orcs and goblins. Power filled him. So much power! He could drink it all in and then he'd be the bestest wizlevard who ever lived, mighty as the gods themselves!

Duffskul's head hurt with the strength of it, a good pain, deep and satisfying, like the kind of itch it is a pleasure to scratch. The magic-light flaring in his eyes bleached out his vision.

Duffskul giggled. The skaven white-fur shrank in his magic fist. 'I'm gonna do this proper, you squeaking cheese-thief,' said Duffskul. Determined to make a show of it, Duffskul fished inside his robes and pulled out a piece of shamanshroom. He taunted the skaven with it.

'You know what this is, ratty? This is a shamanshroom. From da deep caves, where only those in da know can go. An old shaman, taken root, you might say, gone into da great green! But they leaves some of their magic behind, leaves it for the likes of me to eat up and squish ratties like you. Oh yus.'

Duffskul popped the leathery fragment in his mouth and chewed hard with black teeth. Something of the dead shaman's residual power flooded into him, augmenting the magic coursing through Duffskul to catastrophic levels. Everything went far away. He could hear the laughter of the Twin Gods in the distance. Sometimes that was a good sign. But not always, far from it.

'Now I is... Now I is...'

He hiccupped. Something went *pop* deep inside his brain. Duffskul frowned.

'Whoopsie,' he said.

With a wet splotch, his head exploded, fountaining a great deal of blood and a lot less brain all over the remains of the idol and the skaven sorcerer both.

The green fists evaporated into mist, and Kranskritt fell, taking in a deep and welcome breath to his bruised lungs.

'Heh heh, green-thing. Very good. Very interesting. But you dead now.' He frowned and leaned in to check. The green-thing's head had gone, what was left soaking messily into his dirty yellow robes. 'Yes-yes, definitely dead.'

Trying to salvage his dignity, Kranskritt brushed as much brain off his clothes as he could and walked away, checking all the time that no one was looking.

Skarsnik held up his prodder and waved it. Horns sang out all through the fleeing tribes. The regiments immediately stopped and turned around. A few of the more enthusiastic lads carried on going right through the city and up the mountain slopes; others were too far gone in panic to heed the rallying horns, but the majority – and all of these were Skarsnik's own boys, he noted proudly – reformed their ranks. A fresh flood of night goblins poured out from the gates to reinforce his back line.

Skarsnik peered under the black cloth covering Gobbla. 'You all right under there, mate?' he said. Gobbla snuffled back. 'Good.' Skarsnik looked up and down his lines. All in order. 'Let's see what we can see,' he said and unsnapped his telescope.

The skaven army was in total disarray. Split up by Skarsnik's ambushes, large parts of it were isolated into groupings of a few hundred strong. He watched with satisfaction as the foreigner Snaggla Grobspit and his giant spiders tore apart the skaven war machines. But it wasn't over yet. The Headtaker had a strong force about him, and was heading for that cocky big head Krolg Krushelm on top of that big lizard he was always riding about. Well, Skarsnik would wait to see what happened there. Either way, Krolg's loss would be no great one. The orc hadn't been in the Peaks long, and hadn't yet learned to show the proper respect. That was the usual way with the orc bosses, but this one was more uppity than most, and making the other orcs behave badly.

He turned his spyglass elsewhere. In other parts the battle was in balance, not going quite as well as he had hoped. The manglers had run out of steam over by the Burnt Cliffs and been killed, allowing skaven reinforcements to pour out of the rat holes there and strengthen the flank about the base of Silver Mountain. Big Red the giant squig was stomping far from the main fight, chasing down a dwindling pack of ratmen, but was effectively out of the battle. A flare of magical energy drew his attention to the Idol of Gork rampaging around the skaven rear. A sympathetic 'Oooh!' went up from the army as the magically animated statue lost a foot and pitched forwards flat on its face. Skarsnik saw Duffskul fall with it, then lost him amid the ruins. 'He'll be all right,' said Skarsnik to himself, although he was worried – not for Duffskul, but mainly because he had expended his store of secret weapons and the skaven still weren't broken.

Still, neither was his army.

He turned his telescope to the front, where, through the magnified points of goblin hats, he saw Ikk Hackflay's Ironskins and a bunch of massive ratboys closing with his position. Furry ogre-things came with them, driven on by a fat, mean-looking skaven. Two of Queek's best, he thought. Be good to get rid of them. 'Ready, lads! We've got big furry lads coming in, one mean looking fella leading them, and some ogre-fings with a fatty ratty. We's gonna kill them both. Everybody ready?'

'Waaagh!' they responded.

'I'm glad you said that,' he said, with a crooked smile.

Queek ran at full scurry towards the wyvern and its stupid-meat rider. The wyvern charged about on the ground, smashing prey down with its heavily armoured skull and gulping them down whole. Gore hung from its mouth. The bloody remains of skaven were scattered everywhere, along with piles of the wyvern's dung.

As it moved, it toileted, clearing room in its bulging stomach for more meat. Given enough time, it would eat itself into a torpor, but wyverns had big appetites and that time would be too long in coming.

The orc speared a clanrat, dangling the still-squealing creature in front to the mouth of his mount. The wyvern's beady eyes fixed on the morsel, and snapped at it as the orc snatched the skaven out of the way. He laughed uproariously as he teased the beast.

Queek signalled to his guard to halt, and strode out. He banged his weapon hilts on his breastplate to get the orc's attention.

'Big-meat! Queek the Mighty, ruler of City of Pillars, will fight you.'

Hearing this, the orc heaved on the wyvern's reins, pulling it around to face Queek.

'Headtaker,' he spat. Krolg eyed the stormvermin twenty paces behind Queek carefully. They made no move to come forwards, or he might well have flown off. That's why Queek had ordered them to stay where they were. The wyvern spread its wings and bellowed. Its tail arched high over its back, in the manner of a scorpion. Black venom dripped from the point of it sting. The vinegary stench of it made Queek's eyes run.

Krolg dug long spurs into the tender skin under the wyvern's wings. It leapt into the air, gliding the short distance at Queek. The impact of the beast's landing shook the ground. The orc thrust at him overhand with his spear, a clumsy blow that Queek parried easily, riposting with a powerful backhand against the wyvern's head. Queek had never fought one of these creatures before, and its iron-hard scales took him by surprise. The blow jarred his arm so hard his teeth clacked together. The wyvern barely registered it, snapping at him from one side while the orc drove his spear at him from the other. Queek sprang back, only to expose himself to a punishing strike from the wyvern's poisoned tail. Queek barely threw himself aside. He skidded as he landed, vulnerable for a moment, but the orc and his mount were too slow. The stinger plunged into the ground, whipping back almost as quickly.

Queek wiped spatters of burning venom from his muzzle. The orc atop the wyvern chuckled at him and urged his mount on.

The rock here was harder to gnaw than it appeared, so the old saying went.

The goblins stumbled backwards, pushed by the fury of the stormvermin. A massive rat-leader slew a brace of goblins with each sword stroke. Skarsnik levelled his prodder at him and let fly with a blast of raw magic. Some sixth sense caused the rat-leader to leap aside, and Skarsnik burned up half a dozen of his fellows instead.

'I'm going to have to sort this out myself, aren't I?' said Skarsnik. 'Come on, Gobbla.' He pulled on his squig's chain, and the pair of them shoved their way down to the front.

Skarsnik's prodder emerged first, punching through the gap between two goblins and spearing a stormvermin on its triple prongs. Skarsnik grunted as he pushed, shoving the dead rat back off its feet and tripping those in the ranks behind it. The rat was big, but Skarsnik was strong. Under his robes he was a mass of knotted muscle, his success such that he had grown huge for a night goblin – for a goblin of any kind, for that matter. Only Fat Grom had been bigger, but as Skarsnik liked to say, that was all fat and it didn't count.

'Come on, you ratties!' shrilled Skarsnik. Recognising their master's arch nemesis, the stormvermin scrambled over each other to get at him, eager to be the one to take his head. He stabbed and blasted with his prodder. Gobbla fought at his side, snapping the heads off halberds that might have speared his master, snapping the hands off that held the halberds, and snapping off the heads of the vermin that guided the hands. Skarsnik was old and thoughtful, but when roused he was mean as an orc warlord after a heavy night on the fungus brew. With Gobbla by his side, he was well nigh unstoppable. By his own efforts, he opened a wide circle in the front ranks of the stormvermin. 'Go on! Get on at ya!' he shouted, whirling the prodder round his head and whooping with delight. The goblins pushed forwards after him, chanting his name.

Skarsnik brought his prodder in a wide arc, aiming to decapitate three stormvermin with one blow, only to find it intercepted by a black sword. A terrible strength was behind it. He pushed, and a fat, heavily muscled skaven pushed back. Skarsnik did not know his name, but it was Grotoose. A pack of rat ogres moved in and boxed in Gobbla, leaving the King under the Mountains to face Grotoose alone.

The Clan Moulder war-leader leaned in close to Skarsnik, both of them grimacing with hatred and effort. With a flourish, Skarsnik disengaged, flinging Grotoose's sword arm wide. Skarsnik reversed the prodder, sending the weighty ferrule on its base driving into Grotoose's flabby stomach. Air exploded from the skaven's mouth, and he doubled over. Skarsnik stepped in, but Grotoose was shamming. As Skarsnik approached, Grotoose slammed his sword hilt into Skarsnik's head, and again. Driven back, Skarsnik stumbled, his feet fouled in the chain attaching Gobbla to him.

Grotoose loomed over him, blotting out the pale sky.

He raised his sword. 'Now you die-die!'

Grotoose never landed his blow. Gobbla came from the side, a bolt of crimson death, teeth snapping. He swallowed the claw leader of Clan Moulder whole.

Skarsnik got to his feet and patted his pet. 'That was close! That was too close,' he muttered. 'Good boy, Gobbla.'

Gobbla burped.

Skarsnik took a moment. The stormvermin and rat ogres had been driven back, the flow of battle moving away from him.

Annoyingly, the stormvermin's boss was still alive and kicking, but he was on the defensive. 'They don't need us no more, come on. We got some strategising to do,' he said. His speech was peppered with bastardised Reikspiel and Khazalid words he used for concepts Orcish lacked the capacity to express. He led his pet back to his vantage point to begin said strategising.

He extended his telescope again. The battle was much as it was before. Then he saw something he had never seen, a blurring shadow that leapt all over the battlefield. One instant it was in one place, in another elsewhere. A disk of metal whirred out from this darkness, curving through air and flesh alike without interrupting its course. It banked around and flew back to its starting point, being snatched out of the air by a huge clawed hand.

'That's weird,' said Skarsnik. 'That looks a bit like one of them...'

Gobbla whined. Skarsnik looked down.

'What's wrong, boy?'

Gobbla's nose snuffled. He looked up into Skarsnik's eyes with his one good one.

'Gobbla?'

A dribble of blood collected at the corner of the squig's mouth. Skarsnik knelt down, concerned. A squelching sound came from Gobbla's innards. Skarsnik put his ear to the squig's side.

Gobbla whined again.

A knife burst through the top of the squig's skull. Gobbla's eye rolled back into his head, and the squig collapsed, deflating. His bulk wobbled and shook, and the knife cut downwards.

'Gobbla!' screamed Skarsnik.

Grotoose hauled himself from a long slit in the squig's side. His skin was blistered from Gobbla's potent stomach acids, fur falling out in clumps. Half his face had been melted off. Groaning in pain, he dragged himself away with fingers whose flesh came away from the bone as he scrabbled at the rock.

Skarsnik looked on in speechless horror. Grotoose raised a head with eyes that had been burned to whiteness.

'I first Clan Moulder beastmaster in Eight Peaks,' he said thickly. 'It take lot more than stupid red-ball, fungus-thing to kill me.'

His face contorting with rage, Skarsnik raised the prodder high and drove it down through Grotoose's back so hard it shattered the stone beneath. Grotoose shuddered, as if he'd still planned on getting up, before he finally realised he was dead.

'Gobbla,' said Skarsnik, in a small voice. The battle forgotten, he dropped his prodder and fell to the squig's side. The squig sagged in on itself, its capacious body pooling like a half-empty wineskin. Skarsnik knelt and hesitated, eyes surveying this most cruel ruin as if he could bring it back to wholeness by wishing it otherwise.

It didn't happen. It couldn't happen. Gobbla was dead, his small, faithful brain leaking out through the hole in the top of his head.

Skarsnik laid both hands on the leathery hide of his closest companion.

'Gobbla,' said the Warlord of Karak Eight Peaks, with a catch in his throat. 'Gobbla!'

Queek dodged another thunderous blow from the wyvern, tripping on a half-buried lump of masonry as he did. He was panting heavily, bleeding down one arm from a lucky spear-thrust.

'Getting tired, incha, little rattie?' rumbled the orc. 'You're a tasty fighter, that's what they all say. Down in the Badlands they say that. That far away. Yeah, that's right. Ain't you proud?' The orc laughed. 'Broken Toofs, my tribe. We heard that all right, we heard all about da Headtaker.' He widened his eyes in mock fright. 'But I reckoned it was all bluster, all talk. Load of nonsense. No rat going to outfight an orc every day of the week like what they say you can, though I see you got a couple of blackies up there on your spikes. Idiots, they are. No fun in them. I ain't one of them snaggle-toothed stunty slaves. I'm a free orc – you'll never beat me.'

Queek kept his distance from the circling wyvern. He spat on the ground. Let the orc talk himself into an early grave. The ones with the big mouths always spoke too much, leaving themselves open to Queek's mightiness.

This fight had gone on too long. If he didn't finish it soon, the green imp might win!

How to end it? How to end it? Queek burned inside.

'My name,' said the orc, 'is Krolg Krushelm! You hear that, now. I wants you to be thinking it when I guts ya! I'm a real greenskin, not like this sneaky little git here. No wonder you ain't been beat yet. As soon as I'm done with you, I'm taking that cave runt down. It's about time the Eight Peaks had a real boss.' Krolg spurred his mount.

The wyvern roared, spraying Queek with foul-smelling spittle. The tail swiped down, jaws coming at him from another angle, Krolg's spear from a third.

Queek had the measure of his opponents. A good fight, a fine challenge. A pity to finish it.

He ducked the sting, batted the spear tip aside with his sword, rolled under the wyvern's head, sprang to his feet and, with a powerful swing, buried Dwarf Gouger in the wyvern's eye. The spike on the pick punched through the soft eyeball and the thin bone at the back of the socket with ease.

The wyvern bellowed in agony and spread its wings. It wrenched its head back from the source of its pain. Queek kept tight hold of Dwarf Gouger's haft, letting go only when the time was right. As he arced through the air, Krolg's mouth formed an 'o' of surprise below his twisting body.

Krolg was still wearing the expression when his head toppled from his shoulders and rolled into the dirt.

Queek landed on his feet in a crouch, a gleeful smile on his lips.

He waited until the wyvern's death throes had ceased before retrieving his favourite weapon.

* * *

'Boss! Boss!'

Skarsnik heard the words only dimly. His entire attention was fixed on the dead Gobbla, his hands still pressed into his gradually sinking flesh.

A hand grabbed him. 'Boss!'

Skarsnik whirled round and snarled into the face of Kruggler.

Kruggler took a step backwards, both hands raised. 'Boss! Now ain't the time. Don't let them see you like this, boss. The lads need bossing, boss! What are we going to do?'

Skarsnik shivered. The skin around his eyes felt tight. A strange emotion he'd not felt before... Nah, nah, that wasn't right. Once before, long ago, when Snotruk had killed Snottie, his loyal companion in his lonely days as a runt. Hollow like, all empty inside, like nothing really mattered any more.

He shook it off, but it clung on, clamping around the quivery bit of meat inside his chest like it would crush it with cold, cold ice.

'Ye're right, ye're right.' He nodded at Gobbla. 'Someone take that away!' he said, trying to sound like he didn't care. The goblins that came forward were wise enough to handle the dead squig very carefully indeed. Kruggler helped the goblin warlord up while one of Skarsnik's little big 'uns smashed the chain with his long axe.

The weight gone from his foot felt weird. He wiggled it around speculatively. Definitely weird.

'Boss!' said Kruggler in exasperation.

'What? Yeah, sorry, the battle, the battle.' Skarsnik raised his hand to his eyes. He couldn't see very well because they kept filling up with water and he didn't know why. He blinked it away and took stock of the battle.

Towards Silver Mountain, a fresh horde of clanrats running down the remainder of the squig teams there.

To the east, the now very distant form of Big Red trumpeting his way towards the evening. To the south, a mighty arachnarok spider being dismembered by the mysterious shadow.

To the centre, the broken Idol of Gork – or was it Mork? He really couldn't be sure – and an additional item: one slaughtered wyvern, topped with a headless orc. The Headtaker's troops were forming up, gathering stragglers back into solid formations. The formation that Skarsnik's little big 'uns had broken was being bullied back into shape by its leader.

'I've seen enough,' said Skarsnik.

'What?' said Kruggler.

'It's a bust. We've lost. A good scrap, but we couldn't pull it off, because there really is a lot of them, ain't there?' said Skarsnik to himself. 'Farsands, and farsands.' He did a quick mental calculation, the kind that would make a normal goblin die of a brain infarction. 'That's actually a lot more of them than there is of us...' He looked to the citadel. 'Old Belegar's next. We need to scarper.'

'What?!' repeated Kruggler.

'Kruggs, mate, we have lost! Can I make it any simpler for you? If we don't shift, Queek'll have our heads on that poncy bedstead he wears on his back quicker than he'll have Belegar's. I don't think I want to stick around for that. Sound the retreat!' he shouted.

'What about the rest of the boys?'

'What? Out-of-towners, weird scrawny runts wot smell of old leaves and ride about on spiders, and deadbeats? Nah, they played their part. Leave 'em. Besides, if we all go at once, then the rats might attack us before we can get away, mightn't they?' Skarsnik tapped his grubby forehead with a bloody finger. 'Always thinking me. That's why I is king and you is not.' He addressed his signallers again, before they commenced their flag-waving and horn-blowing. 'And by retreat, I mean walking back inside carefully with your weapons ready, not running for the hills so we's can all get out of breath, run down, chopped up and et by ratsies! Got that?' he bawled.

His horn-blowers and flag-wavers nodded. At least some of them understood. They relayed his orders as best they could. Some of the greenskins even obeyed them. All in all, thought Skarsnik, as he watched his tired tribe and its allies about face and march up to the gates of the Howlpeak, things could have been a whole lot worse.

Once he'd regained the gates himself, he went up to the broken battlements atop it. Through his telescope he watched the skaven break into a desperate run as the last of the Crooked Moon tribe withdrew to the safety of the Howlpeak. For a long time, he kept his spyglass trained on Queek's furious, furry face and watched it get madder and madder. He kept watching, in fact, until the gates clanged shut.

Now that was funny.

'Gobbla,' he said, meaning to share the moment with his pet. 'Gobbla, look at that, eh? Boy? Boy?' Skarsnik looked down at his side.

But, of course, there was nobody there.

TWENTY

Lurklox's Deal

Skarsnik went into his private rooms as quickly as he was able. That was not very quickly. He had to patrol the borders of his much-reduced kingdom to make sure the lads were watching out properly, and that there were units ready to see off an attack, and that the outsiders who had come into the Howlpeak didn't cause any bother. That went double for any who were orcs. He had a few challenges now Gobbla was gone, but that was not such a bad thing. He needed to put a couple of orcs down to keep the rest in line. Without Gobbla, they found him still extremely dangerous, and the fact that he could still break an orc with his bare hands without his giant pet had quietened them down real quick. But Gobbla's loss was telling on him in other ways. Without the squig, he'd lost his skaven assassin early warning system. He might as well leave the door unlocked, dismiss all his guard and go to sleep with a knife conveniently laid out next to his bed.

Once inside, he locked the door and commenced pacing, the butt of his prodder clashing on the floor. He banged it harder and harder as he got more and more worried. Skarsnik was no stranger to dilemmas, but this one was a real pickle and no mistake.

'Got to get organised, got to get organised!' he muttered to himself. 'Where is I if I don't gets organised?' He glanced to his papers, but this time they didn't hold the answer. 'Gotta fink!' he said, and worried at his fingers with sharp goblin teeth. 'Item one,' he said to himself. 'Old Queek's going for conquest. Item two, there's loads more of them than there is of us. Item three, them stunties aren't going to be there much longer, and when they is not, old squeaky Queeky's gonna come knockin' on me door with all his monsters and such. So what to do? Need Duffskul, yeah.' He made to call the shaman, but remembered he was dead too. Who else could he call on? No one had seen Mad Zargakk in years, Kruggler was the brightest of the gobboes to hand but still very thick, and there was no point at all in asking an orc...

He caught something from the corner of his eye, a flicker in the room where one shouldn't be.

'Oh, come on. Not again!' he groaned. He levelled his prodder at the globe of black lightning crackling into being. 'I'm not in the mood today, ratboy! Buzz off or get a face full of Morky magic!'

But as the visitor manifested, Skarsnik's expression of defiance turned to a gape. His intention to zap the rat dissipated. This wasn't your usual rat with horns, magicking himself in to have a pop – although it did, he supposed, have horns. And it did look like a rat, only not that much. Bigger, it was. Everywhere.

'Rats,' he said, 'aren't usually that big.'

Skarsnik took a step back as an immense shape stepped out of the shadows. Although, that wasn't right, because the shadows came with it. They writhed over the thing, whatever it was, stopping Skarsnik from getting a good look at it. He got an impression, nothing more – long, hairy arms lined with thick tendons, black claws, and a head crowned with an impressive rack of horns above a masked face where terrible eyes burned.

For the first time in a long time, Skarsnik gulped fearfully. The thing! The weird thing from the battle that had taken out Grobspit's spider monsters, right there in his bedroom! The creature was huge, bigger than a troll, all wiry muscle and patches of fur. It had claws bigger than Gobbla's teeth. Then Skarsnik recognised it for what it was, and recovered his wits. Better the daemon you know, and he knew this kind well enough.

'Oh. Right. It's one of *those.*' The stink of rodent and glowy green rock was unmistakeable. 'Ratfing daemon, one wiv lots of extra shadow, but a ratfing daemon you is. Well, ain't I honoured,' he said archly. 'Oi, back off,' he shouted, holding his ground. His prodder crackled with power. 'I ain't no snotty to be pushed about.'

'I am a lord of the Thirteen in Shadow!' scoffed the rat-daemon. 'I am master-assassin! That cannot hurt me. You cannot hurt me!'

'Yeah, right. Shall we give it a little try? I reckon a blast of Mork magic'd put a very big hole in you, you... you... ratfing. Don't you?'

'This is no stand-off, green-thing. I mighty-powerful. I show you mercy. If I wanted you dead, tiny and most vexing imp, dead you would be.'

'Who's showing who mercy? You want to test?' He jiggled the prodder. 'Fzapp!' it went, very quietly but menacingly. Skarsnik sniffed at the sharp smell of discharged magic. 'What is it you want, anyhow? Not seen one of your like for a while.'

'I am verminlord! Master of skaven. You have glimpsed-seen my kind?' said Lurklox, catching his surprise just a moment too late.

Skarnsik nodded the tip of his pointy hat to a large skull mounted over the fireplace. 'Yeah. You could say that. Bagged that one about fifteen winters back.'

Lurklox looked at the yellowing skull then back at the prodder. Skarsnik grinned evilly.

'So now we got that out of the way, what do you want, then? Get on with it, I haven't got all day. Just lost a battle, and I need to do something about it.'

Skarsnik's bravado rather put Lurklox off his stride, and spoiled his grand entrance. He stood taller, but the goblin would not be intimidated.

'Green-thing!' said Lurklox portentously. 'You are beaten-defeated. The indefatigable Queek has smashed your army for the last time.'

Skarsnik looked off at his heaped stuff, disinterested. 'Has he now? There's a lot more where those boys came from.'

'Lie-lie! Green-things like strength. You beaten, you not strong. They leave soon, and you die-die.'

'Right,' said Skarsnik. 'I'm no quitter though, and I've won a lot more battles than I have lost.'

'Already your large and bouncing beast-thing is no more.' Lurklox pointed at the broken chain still manacled to Skarsnik's ankle. 'We kill-slay it, we kill-slay you.'

'You wait a minute,' said Skarsnik with sudden and dangerous anger. 'The fight ain't gone out of me yet, you big horned rat... rat... What was it you said you was?'

'I great verminlord!' shrieked Lurklox.

'I don't care what you are, you're in my bedroom and I'm not happy about it!'

Lurklox sniffed the air and made a disgusted noise. 'Neither of us are. To business, then! I come offer-give with mighty gift-offer for green-thing Skarsnik! In possession of Ikit Claw, arch-tinker rat, is a very powerful bomb.'

'A bomb?' said Skarsnik.

'A bomb! The greatest bomb ever made by rat-paw and skaven ingenuity.'

Lurklox waved a paw, and a scene wreathed in warpstone-green smoke shimmered in the air before Skarsnik. It showed a vast and busy workshop. Skaven in strange armour worked at cluttered benches. Atop one of these was an intricate brass device the size of a troll's head.

'Yeah?' said Skarsnik, careful to hide his surprise at the

workshop, the likes of which he'd never seen before. He rapidly factored its existence into his calculations, allowing for it being an illusion, but he reckoned it probably wasn't. 'So what? Why are you telling me this? Gloating, are we? Going to blow me up? Didn't work last time, did it?' He decided the towering rat god wasn't going to kill him just yet, and he sat down on his filthy bed with a groan. It had been a testing day.

'No-no! I give-bring to goblin warlord! A fitting gift-prize for worthy foe.'

'And what the zog exactly am I supposed to do with this giant metal egg, eh?'

'There are many dwarf-places left. See!' Lurklox brandished his shadowed claws again. An image of a strong dwarf citadel surrounded by a siege camp. 'Zhufbar-place! Impregnable, undefeated. Many skaven die here. Perhaps you could win great glory for yourself by bringing it low?'

'Looks like you've got plenty of furboys there right now. What do you need me for? And come to think of it, why not just get one of your sneaky pink-nosed little pals to do it? You don't need me at all.' Skarsnik's eyes narrowed. 'Why not just off me now? I'm not buying this at all.' Skarsnik emphasised his words with the prodder.

'You are as much boon-thing as problem-trouble, green-thing. Many pieces on the board-game. I prefer to keep you alive. The skaven at Zhufbar-place are weak. You are strong. Dependable.'

'That's nice to know,' said Skarsnik.

'You do as I squeak-say, green-thing?'

Some of the defiance went out of Skarsnik. He felt older than ever. He was tired. Outside a sea of rats awaited him, Queek wanted his head and might just get it this time, he'd lost his only useful advisor, and then there was Gobbla. The next time this big rat paid him a visit, he might not survive. Skarsnik slumped a little, it was time to face facts. 'I don't see I got much choice,' he said quietly. 'But it's going to cost you more than the big boom boom,' he added sharply.

'Yes-yes?'

'If I can't kill Queek,' he spat the name, 'I'll not be happy leaving both them gits alive. Bring me Belegar's head for me collection, and I'll do as you say. Skarsnik will leave the Eight Peaks,' he smiled. 'Although it's more like six and a half peaks now, ain't it?'

'You swear-swear, and you go to Zhufbar? Lead your mighty armies there?'

'And then I'll never come back. I swear it. Although you know that means nothing, right?'

Lurklox's masked face appeared for a moment in the swirling green-black fog surrounding his form. Something like a smile wrinkled the skin visible around his eyes.

'I see why we have not beaten you yet. You are almost like a skaven.'

'Oi!' said Skarsnik. 'There's no need to be rude.'

There was much to be done upon the surface. Queek's desire to see the green-things' shanty totally demolished and their burrows stopped up bested his patience, and it was growing dark before Queek, still besmirched and begrimed with the filth of battle, marched back towards the comforting darkness of the underworld. His troops lined every street on his route, squeaking out his name. He went slowly, letting them see him, his head held high and chest puffed out, his trophy rack bloody with new heads. Ska went behind him, his Red Guard marching in perfect step after Ska.

'Another victory!' Queek said. 'Another victory for mighty Queek! Queek brings Clan Mors only victory!'

'All hail mighty Queek!' shouted Ska.

His guard clashed their halberds on their shields and shouted. The army cheered, bowing and fawning over their leader as he walked past them.

Once inside, Queek made straight for the burrows he had requisitioned as his base for this war on the surface. His servants awaited his coming. Blind, weak and castrated, they were feeble examples of the skaven breed, and that suited Queek perfectly.

He went to be cleaned, allowing the quaking slaves to unstrap his armour. They licked blood from his fur, bit out tangles and scabs, and gingerly cleaned his few scratches. His armour was given the same attention. Once upon a time, Queek had been lax in his hygiene, allowing the muck of battle to cake his armour for weeks at a time until he stank. Not any longer. He had resolved not to go abroad filthy as a plague monk. He told himself it was all about appearances, but deeper down, and as Sleek Sharpwit's head kept telling him, it was because the smell of death reminded him that he was getting old.

As his servants worked on him, he relaxed. Some of the murderous tension went from his muscles. To his followers he had delivered a great victory, but all he could think about was the green-thing retreating back through his gates to the safety of the Howlpeak. Queek's lip curled, his fists clenched. Belegar was easy-meat now, dead-meat weak-meat, but his extermination of the dwarfs would give the imp time to retrench, and Queek had not slain as many of his goblins as he had hoped.

If he were truthful, he was lucky to have won at all.

The torches in Queek's chamber flickered. In the corner he had a pile of looted glimstones, their cold light forever constant, but these too stuttered. The presence of his dead-thing trophies, always tentative of late, receded entirely. A shadow gathered. It would be behind Queek. It always was. He did not give Lurklox the pleasure of turning to greet him.

'Little warlord preening, good-good. Sleekness is stealthiness,' said the verminlord's voice, as Queek had predicted, from behind him.

Even blinded, the thralls felt the powerful presence and scurried to get out. The shadow grew around Queek, making everything black. Queek alone remained illuminated, alone in the dark.

Lurklox stepped through into the bounds of this world, gracefully uncoiling himself from nothing into something. Although he had seen it many times now, Queek was unnerved by the way the towering verminlord stepped out from the shadow.

Queek did not care for the way Lurklox spoke to him, nor did he like the way his fur stood on end in the rat-daemon's presence.

'What have you found out?' demanded Queek.

'Impudence, haste-haste. Always the same. Either too much greeting, or none at all. The warlord clans never change.'

Sensing that Queek had steeled himself against such provocations, the verminlord got to the point.

'The grey seer needs you as an ally. Your Lord of Decay Gnawdwell moves to ally with Clan Skryre. It is he that makes the attempts upon your life. It was he that bid-told Thaxx to delay. It was he that called upon Ikit Claw to shame you. You are being used, Headtaker. Gnawdwell grooms many replacements for you.'

Queek burst into laughter. Lurklox's anger grew thick, a palpable, dangerous thing, but Queek did not care. 'Great and stealthy Lurklox talk as if this not known to Queek!' He dissolved again into giggles. 'None of this news to Queek. Every lord tests his lieutenants. So what? Most die, some live to be tested tomorrow. And Queek has lived to see many tomorrows! Gnawdwell will not be disappointed by Queek disappointing him.'

Lurklox loomed, growing bigger. Queek stared defiantly up at the shadowy patch he judged the verminlord's face to occupy.

'Then what of Gnawdwell's prize, long life and forever battle?' said Lurklox, and Queek's blood ran cold. 'Does it still stand, or was Gnawdwell only lying to Queek? Queek is a fool-thing, mad-thing. Queek does not know everything, but I do.'

Lurklox let his words hang, making sure he had asserted dominance over the warlord before continuing. Queek wanted to know if the offer was real; Lurklox could taste his incipient fear at his growing age. Good. Let him be afraid.

'Time runs on,' said Lurklox, hammering the sentiment home. 'Time Queek no longer has. I have come from council with Skarsnik. I have struck a deal with the goblin-thing for you. The war here will soon be over. Queek is needed elsewhere.'

The shock on Queek's face was a further reward for the verminlord.

'Yes-yes!' said Lurklox, encouraged. 'Deliver the dwarf-king's head by sunset tomorrow and Skarsnik will leave the City of Pillars.'

Queek snorted and licked at a patch of fur his slaves had missed. 'What else did you give-promise Skarsnik? Queek's lieutenants make uncountable bargains with the goblin king, and he breaks every single one. What make Lurklox think this time will be any different?'

'Queek guesses well. Clever warlord. There was something else. The promise of that head... and something Ikit Claw does not yet know is missing. A threat-gift. If the imp-thing not take, then we use it against him.'

'Why not use this thing-thing against him in first place, mysterious Lurklox? Simple way best. Skaven too stupid to see.'

Lurklox did not answer.

'Very well,' said Queek. 'I will slay the beard-thing and hand over his head to the imp. Queek has-owns many dwarf-thing trophies already. What does Queek want one more for?'

On rickety shelves, nearly two dozen trophy heads looked at him with empty eyes.

Queek refrained from explaining to Lurklox just how tricksy the goblin was. It would give him a great deal of amusement to see the verminlord upstaged by the imp. There was no way that the so-called king would give up the kingdom he had been fighting over for his entire life. And when he broke his deal, Queek would kill him and take back Belegar's head and Skarsnik's into the bargain. Queek tittered.

'A great-good deal, clever high one, most impressive.'

TWENTY-ONE

The Final Saga of Clan Angrund

In an out-of-the-way cellar of the citadel, Gromvarl stood in a pit in the floor and tugged at an iron ring set into a flagstone. Unprepossessing, lacking the adornment of most dwarf creations, a slab of rock hiding a secret. There was a finality to it.

'Someone give me a hand here!' grumbled the longbeard. 'It's stuck.'

'It's the differentiation in air pressure – sometimes does that, sucks it closed. It's murder to get open,' said Garvik, one of Duregar's personal retainers. 'Come here. Ho ho, Frediar! Hand me a lever.'

Garvik's nonchalant manner turned to swearing. Soon there were four of them in there, arguing over the best way to prise the door open. Finally, after much effort, it budged. Air whistled around the broken seal. They tugged hard, and a fierce draught set up, building to a shrieking wind that settled into an eerie moan once the stone had been set aside.

Gromvarl looked down the narrow shaft the trapdoor covered:

big enough for a dwarf, no more. He held his lamp over it. Red iron rungs stretched down into the blackness. The shaft descended thousands of feet. That it had not been uncovered by the thaggoraki or the grobi was a wonder. Only weeks ago, a handful of rangers had set out from this place to guard the refugees fleeing the sack of Karak Azul. There had been hopeful talk of their numbers swelling those of the dwarfs of Karak Eight Peaks, but Karak Eight Peaks had become a place of wild hopes. None of the dwarfs of Ironpeak had ever arrived, and the warriors sent out to help them were lost.

A double-or-nothing gamble for the king, and the dice had come up poorly once more. The dice these days were always loaded. Douric could have told him that. The king rolled now in desperation, a dawi down to his last coin.

'Gromvarl! Get yourself out of there. The king's coming.'

Gromvarl disdainfully allowed himself to be helped up out of the pit, like he was doing those who helped him a favour, and not the reverse. Truth was, he was not so spry any more, but he hid it under a barrage of complaints.

Once out, he stood among a group of fifty dawi gathered in the cellar, three dozen of them dressed for hard travelling, all armed. The room was crowded, the damp air fogged by their breath and the heat of their bodies. Longer than it was broad, with a tapering roof of close-fit stone, the cellar was flawless work, but all unembellished as the escape door. No such place of shame should be decorated. No carven ancestor face should look upon the backs of dwarfs as they fled. That was the reasoning. A shame that ordinarily ale barrels and cabbage boxes hid.

Several of those present were proper warriors, rangers and ironbreakers. They stared at the floor, humiliated beyond tolerance by the king ordering them to leave. They understood that what they had to do was important, all right, but Gromvarl would bet his last pouch of tobacco – and he was down to the very last – that every one of them wished some other dawi had been selected and told to go in his place. They chewed their lips and moustache ends and fulminated. Gromvarl could see at least three potential Slayers among their number.

A dwarf matron rocked a babe in arms. The child, its downy chin buried in its mother's bosom, snuffled in its sleep. Gromvarl smiled sorrowfully at the sight. There were too few unkhazali in these dark days, and there was no guarantee this one would survive. His expression clouded. Dwarf babies were as stoic as their elders, but they still cried from time to time. One misplaced call for milk and ale from the bairn could spell the end for the lot of them.

Better out there than in here. His thoughts turned to others, whose parents could not be swayed to leave. He thought too of Queen Kemma, shut up in her tower. As merciful as Belegar had been in permitting, and in some cases ordering, others out, he could not be swayed to release his queen and his prince. Oaths, said the king. Sadness gripped Gromvarl. Some oaths were made to be broken.

With that in mind, he clutched the key in his pocket.

Torchlight glinted from artful wargear. The king and his two bodyguards entered the small cellar where the dwarfs waited to flee.

The king was wan, his eyes heavily pouched and bloodshot. He tried to hide the stiffness in his side, but Gromvarl was too old to be fooled. The rumours of the king's injury told of a sad truth. That was far from the worst of it, however. Gromvarl could tell from the look on Belegar's face; he had finally given up on the slender hope of aid from elsewhere. He was prepared to die.

'I'll not make a meal of this,' said Belegar softly. 'I know none of you made this decision lightly, and some of you didn't want to go at all. Let it be known that I release you all from your oaths to me. Find some other king, a better king. Under his protection and in his service, may you live out more peaceful lives.

'Warriors,' he said to those handful of such. 'I have not chosen you to go because I can spare you. I cannot. I have chosen you because you are among the finest dawi left alive in Karak Eight Peaks. These are your charges. They need you more than I do. I release you also from all your oaths to me, and consider them fulfilled two and a half times over. Had I gold to give, you would have it by the cartload and in great gratitude. Instead, I place upon you one final burden – guard these last few of the clans of Karak Eight Peaks with your lives and your honour. Do not let the bloodlines of our city die forever.'

At these words dwarf resolve stiffened. Gazes were no longer downcast. Lips trembled with new emotions, and spines straightened.

'Aye, my king,' said Garvik, then the others repeated this one after another, some of the shame at their departure leaving through their mouths with the words. Belegar held the eye of each one and nodded to them.

'Now go, go and never return. This was a glorious dream, but it is over. We wake to the darkest of mornings. May you all see the light of a better morrow.'

Gromvarl stood back. Garvik wordlessly indicated that they should begin. A ranger went first, the group's guide, spitting on his hands before he reversed into the dark hole and took grip of the first of the iron rungs. The moan of the wind changed tone as he blocked the shaft.

'Four thousand feet,' he said, his words bearing the soft accent of the hill dwarfs who had once ranged above the ground of the Eight Peaks. 'Your arms will hurt, dawi or not. Keep on. After me, leave ten rungs, then ten rungs between each that follows after. Anyone thinks they're going to fall, call a halt. Pride will kill everyone beneath you should you slip. Remember that. Don't talk otherwise. This way is as yet undiscovered by our enemies, let us keep it that way.'

His head disappeared into the shaft. They counted ten ringing steps.

'Next!' whispered the ranger from the ladderway.

The first went, then the next. As they disappeared into the dark, wives bid farewell to husbands, children to fathers, warriors to their master. Then they were all gone, swallowed up by the ground as if they had never been.

Gromvarl watched them all go into the hole, one after the other, his heart heavy and a lump in his throat. So went the last sorry inhabitants of Karak Eight Peaks, to a doom none within would ever know.

When the last had gone, the king nodded. Gromvarl beckoned to two others. With their help, the trapdoor was replaced. Runes of concealment flared upon it. As the marks faded back into plain stone, the trapdoor went with them. The inset iron ring disappeared, as did any sign of a join with the pit floor. Then the dwarfs levered the flagstone that concealed the pit wherein the trapdoor nestled back into place. Masons hurried forwards, swiftly mortaring it back into place. Within a couple of hours, it would look like any other slab in the floor of the cellar.

Barrels were rolled back in, filling up the room.

The escape route disguised, the dwarfs filed out in silence.

'And here we come to the end of it all,' said Belegar. 'Fifty years of dashed hopes and broken honour. Was it all worth it?'

Never numerous, there remained only two hundred fighting dwarfs left in all of Karak Eight Peaks, a sum that included those untried warriors previously restricted to garrison duty, and those elders honourably retired from the front lines. A shattered people remained, drawn in to this last toehold from every part of the kingdom that had been so painfully retaken. Too few to adequately defend the doors into the Hall of Pillared Iron, Belegar had ordered them into a square at the centre of the room.

'Do not lament cracked stone, cousin,' said Duregar. 'If you swing the hammer so clumsily, the chisel slips. Best learn to swing it better.'

Belegar laughed blackly. 'There has to be a next time for the learning to take, Duregar.'

Duregar shrugged, working his mail into a slightly more comfortable position. 'Then others will learn from our errors, if errors they were. There's no harm to be found in trying to do something right and failing. Better to chance your arm than never risk failure at all.'

'Your words are a comfort to me.'

'They are intended to be, my king.'

'To the end, then, Duregar?'

'As I swore, to the end. For the Angrund clan, and for the chance at a more glorious future.'

Duregar gripped his cousin's hand tightly. The king squeezed back.

'Whatever it is I have achieved here,' said Belegar, 'I could not have done it without you, Duregar.'

A black masked face appeared around the main doors at the far end, and quickly withdrew.

'A scout, lord!' shouted one of the lookouts.

'Leave it be. Get back into formation. At least we know they'll be here soon. A small surprise seeing us stood here rather than behind more barred doors, eh?' Belegar paused. 'I'd make a speech, say words of encouragement to you all, but you need none of that. You know what is coming, and will fight boldly all the same. I could not be prouder of you all. I...' He stopped. 'This is something better said with ale rather than speech.'

The hogshead of ale at the centre of their formation was cracked open. To the last the dwarfs were fastidious in all they did, carefully tapping the barrel with a spigot, lest any go to waste. Foaming tankards were passed around, each dwarf given as much as he desired. The days of rationing were ending along with all else.

They drank quickly, wiping suds from their beards with satisfied gasps. This was the king's ale, the best and last. In quiet ones and twos they clasped arms and said their farewells, toasted kinsmen fallen in battle or treacherously murdered by the thaggoraki and grobi. Fond reminiscences were aired, and particular grudges recounted.

Belegar counted his men again. Of the Iron Brotherhood, fourteen remained. Duregar's bodyguard swelled their ranks to twenty-nine. They had only three cannons pointed at the two main gates, precious few guns or other machines, and just a smattering of crossbows.

'Like the last days of King Lunn,' said Belegar. 'Traditional weapons, tried and tested – none of your new fangled gear. Iron and gromril and dwarfish muscle.'

'Personally, I'd be glad of a flamecannon,' said Duregar.

'Aye,' admitted Belegar. 'So would I.'

Noise echoed up the corridors leading from the lower levels of the citadel.

'Here they come! Dawi, to arms!' shouted Belegar. His wound twinged as he climbed atop his oath stone and took his shield and hammer from his retainers. He tried not to wince.

Explosions rippled out, their distant rumbles carrying billows of dust into the hall. Worthless slave troops, sent to their deaths in the dwarfish traps. That was always the skaven way. Belegar wished that Queek would get on with it.

The battle was short by recent standards. Four waves of skaven came in and were thrown back, broken upon the unyielding steel of the shield walls. Poisoned wind globadiers scurried in the wake of the clanrats to be shot down by dwarf quarrellers with tense trigger fingers. This last time the skaven's poisons choked their own. Ratling guns and warpfire thrower teams met the same fate, every one felled by pinpoint shots. The dwarf cannons fired until their barrels glowed.

But the dwarfs were few, and the skaven many. In ones and

twos the final brave defenders of Karak Eight Peaks fell. The defensive ring around Belegar grew smaller and smaller. The skaven pressed their attack. The cannons fell silent. The number of dwarfs shrank steadily from two hundred, to a hundred, to fifty. The fewer they were, the harder they fought, no matter how tired they were, no matter how thirsty for ale. Each kinsman dragged down fired the dwarfs with righteous anger, driving every one on to acts of martial skill that would have been retold in the sagas and noted in books of remembrance, if only there were survivors to carry their stories away.

It was clear there would be none.

The latest skaven attack flowed back from the dwarfs, but there was no rest. A flood of red-armoured skaven bearing heavy halberds came streaming into the room.

'Queek Headtaker's personal guard,' said Belegar. 'He is coming.'

'This is it, then,' said Duregar, who stood side by side with his cousin still. 'You and he will meet for the final time. Strike him down, Belegar. Send him back to whatever hell sired him.'

Belegar set his face and hefted his hammer. The crust on his wound opened again. Blood dampened his side under his armour.

The stormvermin of Queek's Red Guard crashed into the remaining two-score dwarfs. The stormvermin were fresh and fired with vengeance. Long had the Iron Brotherhood been a ratbane. They hacked down the dwarfs, although the folk of the mountain gave good account of themselves. The last dozen dawi crowded round their lords, sending the Red Guard back time and again. Belegar and Duregar fought back to back, hammers crushing limbs and heads.

One by one the last of the dawi were dragged down, until only Belegar and Duregar remained. All round the kinsmen, skaven fell upon the fallen, tearing at dwarf flesh in their feeding frenzy, or wrenching trophies from the corpses. Duregar was attacked by six of the creatures at once and pulled down, his last words in that life a defiant war-shout to Grimnir.

'Come on! Come on!' bellowed Belegar. 'Take me too, then, you miserable vermin!' He brandished his hammer, sweeping it about him, but the skaven withdrew to a safe distance, imprisoning him in a circle of spearpoints. 'Where is the Headtaker? I would show him my hammer!' Belegar wept freely, tears of sorrow mingled with tears of anger.

The ring opened, and in stepped Queek.

'Here I am, dwarf-thing. Eager-keen to die?' he said in high-pitched Khazalid. This was too much for Belegar. To be confronted with this theft of the innermost mysteries of the Karaz Ankor at the very end was one insult too many.

'Still your tongue! The language of our ancestors is not for you to profane! Bring your head here so that I may crack the secret of our speech from your skull. Attack me, Headtaker, and let us see how well you fare against a king!' roared Belegar.

Queek hefted Dwarf Gouger and his sword. 'Queek kill many kings, beard-thing. Your head joins theirs today, yes-yes.' He tittered, then sprang into a spinning leap, the infamous Dwarf Gouger and sword whirling with deadly speed.

Belegar parried them with stolid economy. Queek curled over a hammer strike that would have flattened a troll and landed behind the king. Belegar faced him.

'And I thought the Headtaker a master of combat,' said Belegar quietly. All emotion save hatred and defiance had bled from his face. He stood on legs weakened by his wound and battle fatigue, but he stood nonetheless. 'If you are the finest warrior your kind has to offer, no wonder you must resort to cheap tricks to bring your enemies low.'

Queek snarled and ran at Belegar. He punched forwards with the head of Dwarf Gouger, intending to make Belegar sidestep onto the point of his sword. But Belegar moved aside a fraction of an inch, evading the maul. He stamped down on Queek's sword, though it moved almost too quickly to be seen, wrenching it from Queek's grasp. A hammer blow of his own caught Queek by surprise. The skaven warlord moved aside awkwardly, holding only Dwarf Gouger. The hammer grazed him nonetheless, bruising his sword arm and driving his own armour into his flesh. Queek jumped back, swordless, blood matting his fur.

'Pathetic,' said Belegar. 'Flea-ridden vermin, swift and twitchy. There's not a dwarf alive who isn't worth twenty of you.'

'Queek has killed many hundred beard-things,' said Queek. He shook his arm. Agonising pins and needles ran from his shoulder to his hand, jangling the nerves of his fingers. His shoulder was numb. 'Queek kill one more very soon.'

'Probably. I am tired, and I am beaten, and the memory of our last encounter festers still in my flesh. But even as you hack the head from my neck, Queek, you will know that you could never best me in more honourable circumstances.'

Few skaven gave a dropping for honour, but Queek was one of this unusual breed. His honour was not as a dwarf would see it, but it was there, built of arrogance though it was. Queek became enraged at this slur upon it.

The duel that followed was swift, its outcome inevitable, but Belegar was not done yet. Queek spun and ducked, casting a deadly net of steel about the dwarf with his terrible maul. Belegar smashed it aside several times with his shield, but with each swipe he became weaker. Queek hooked the king's shield with the spike of his weapon, yanking it free from Belegar's arm with a squeak of triumph. A following blow smashed into Belegar's side, causing the king to cry out as his wound burst wider, but Queek overreached himself and the dwarf's hammer hit his left side, rending apart his warpstone armour and cracking his ribs. Agonised, Queek staggered, only at the last turning his stumble into a spin that had him facing the long-fur again.

He and Belegar panted hard. Belegar bled freely from the wound Queek had given him in their last encounter. Blood pooled about his feet. He had other wounds, some small, others graver. He could not see it himself, but his face was ghostly white.

Queek smiled in spite of his pain. The end approached.

'Greet-hail your ancestors when you meet them, beard-thing. Queek will come for them next. Death is no refuge from the mighty Queek!'

Again Queek charged, putting all his cunning into a complicated swipe reversed at the last moment to send Belegar's hammer spinning away from him. Another blow took the dwarf king in the knee, shattering it, and sending the dwarf down. But to Queek's amazement, the king arrested his fall. Holding himself in a kneel, his weight on his undamaged leg, he glared at the skaven, his eyes poison.

Queek swung Dwarf Gouger a final time. The spike connected with the side of the king's helmet, punching through the gromril. Queek squealed at his victory, but his cries turned to pain. He looked down. The dwarf had somehow got Queek's own sword up, and now it pierced him at the weak shoulder joint of his armour. He stepped back, and Belegar fell over with a crash, his eyes never leaving Queek's face.

Queek screamed as he pulled out his sword from his armpit, the weapon's square teeth dragging lumps of his own flesh with it. Ska rushed out from the ranks of the Red Guard, but Queek shoved at his massive chest with his unwounded hand.

On shaking legs, Queek walked over to the dwarf king. He plucked Dwarf Gouger free, casting it onto the carpet of dwarf bodies. With a yell, he swung his sword over his head, severing the king's head with one blow.

He dropped his sword and bent over, then held aloft Belegar's head with his good arm. He stepped up onto the dwarf king's oath stone.

'The City of Pillars is ours, from deepest deep to loftiest peak! Queek brings you this greatest of victories, only Queek!'

His guard squeaked out their praises, and Queek showed them

all the lifeless head of Belegar. Such a fine trophy. Such a shame he had to give it up.

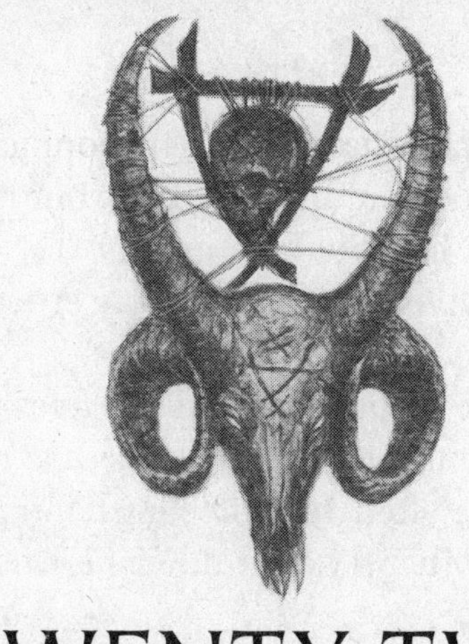

TWENTY-TWO

The Last King of Karak Eight Peaks

Gromvarl staggered up the stairs. Black spots swam in front of his eyes, crowding out what little light there was left in the citadel. The poisoned wound in his back throbbed a strange sort of pain, at once unbearable yet simultaneously numb. He fought against it with all his dwarfish will, forcing himself on in the fulfilment of his first, last and most important oath.

The protection of Vala Kemma.

The sound of fighting still sounded from below, but it was that of desperate, lonely struggles fought in dark corners against impossible odds, and not the regimented clash of two battle lines. Screams came with it, and the stink of burning. There were only the old, the sick, and the young in the upper levels. The skaven were coming for Karak Eight Peaks's small population of children.

Gromvarl stumbled on the steps, his feet failing to find them. He broke a tooth on the stone. Five thousand years old, and still a sharp corner on the step edge. Now that, he thought, was proper craftsmanship.

Kemma was up above, locked in her room and forbidden to fight. Gromvarl had one of the only keys, but had been forced by the king to swear he would not use it.

The king was dead. As far as he was concerned, the oath died with him.

He staggered his way upwards, his progress growing slower and slower as he went. The fiery numbness had taken hold of his limbs. He had to rest often, his unfeeling hand pressing against the stone. He knew that if he sat down he would never reach his destination.

Finally, he arrived, one hundred and thirty-two steps that had taken a lifetime to climb behind him.

The door wavered ahead of him, its black wutroth shimmering as if seen through a heat haze. He fell to his knees and crawled towards it, the poison in his blood overcoming his sturdy dwarf constitution at the last.

With a titanic effort of will, Gromvarl slid the key home in the lock. Only his falling against the door enabled him to twist it at all.

The door banged open and he fell within. He moaned as he hit the floor. He slid into blackness. To his surprise, it went away again, and he managed to heave himself up to his knees. His head spun with the effort.

'Kemma!' he said. 'Kemma!' His throat was dry. A fire raged in it, consuming his words so they came out as insubstantial as smoke.

The queen was not there. The room was too small for her to hide. There were sounds coming from her garderobe, smashing, a frantic scrabbling.

A black-clad skaven came out, a scarf wrapped around its muzzle. It was a wonder it hadn't heard the door; then Gromvarl realised that the sounds of battle were very close behind.

Upon seeing him, the skaven assassin leapt over him, and pulled back his head sharply by the hair. A blackened dagger slid against his throat, the venom that coated it burning his skin.

'Where dwarf-thing breeder-queen?' asked the skaven. Like all of its kind, its voice was surprisingly soft and breathy. Not a hint of a squeak to it when they spoke the languages of others. Gromvarl found this rather funny and laughed.

The skaven twitched behind him, agitated.

'What so amusing, dwarf-thing? You want to die?'

'Not particularly, you thieving thaggoraki.' He burst out laughing again.

'Very good. You die-die just the same.'

A loud bang filled the room. The skaven slid backwards, its poisoned knife clattering to the floor. Gromvarl tossed the smoking pistol away.

'Never did like guns,' he grumbled, 'but I suppose they have their uses.' He fell onto his hands and knees. 'Not long now, eh, Grungni, eh, Grimnir? Soon I'll be able to look you in the eye and ask how I did. Appallingly, I'll bet.' He coughed, and bloody froth spattered from his mouth. Before he fell face down onto the floor, he smiled broadly.

Vala Kemma had always been as particular as any dwarf. Even in this prison in all but name, she'd kept her mail well oiled and her armour shining.

The mannequin that it had sat upon was empty.

Kemma had got away.

'That's my lass,' he said into the stones of the floor. They were cool, welcoming. His breath dampened them with condensation. 'That's my lass,' he whispered, and the stones were damp no more.

Kemma ran through the upper storeys of the citadel, her secret key clutched in her hand, not that she needed it now. Poor Belegar, he always underestimated her. Leaving her shut up behind a simple lock? She felt a moment of anger; it was almost like he didn't think her a proper dwarf, probably because she was a woman.

But she was a dwarf, with all that entailed. Dawi rinn, and a vala too. More the fool him for not realising. He had always been so blinkered! Look where that had got him. Look where that had got them all.

People were running, those few warriors stationed in the top floors of the tower towards the sounds of fighting coming from the stairs, the remainder away to the final refuge with as much dignity as they could muster.

Only now, at the very end, were some of the dwarfs succumbing to panic, and not very many of them at that. Most were shouted down and shamed by their more level-headed elders, and there were plenty of them up there to do the shouting.

She caught sight of a familiar figure, bent almost double by the weighty book she had chained about her neck. Magda Freyasdottir, the hold's ancient priestess of Valaya. Even at the end she was dressed up in the lavender finery of her office, her ankle-length, silk-fine hair bound in heavy clasps of jet.

'Magda! Magda!'

The priestess turned, her face surprised. Kemma ran right into her arms.

'Steady, my queen,' she said ironically, and rightly so, for Kemma's kingdom was by now much circumscribed. 'I am not so steady on my feet as I was. I have someone here who might better appreciate your hugs. My king!' she called. 'Here he comes,' she said to Kemma. 'The last king of Karak Eight Peaks.'

Thorgrim came through the door, fully armed and armoured, his wispy beard hidden behind a chin-skirt of gromril plates. The sight of it made Kemma's heart swell. Next month he would have been eleven years old, nineteen years until the majority he would never attain. In his boy's armour he looked ridiculously young. In the visor of his helmet, his soft brown eyes, so like his father's in particular, were wide with fear but hard with duty. My son, thought Kemma. He would have been a fine king.

'Mother!' he shouted with undwarf-like emotion. The others looked away at the boy-king's unseemly display. They embraced. Someone tutted.

'I thought you were dead.'

'I too,' said Kemma. She looked him deep in the eyes. His return look said he knew it too, that soon they would be.

'Where are your Valkyrinn?' said Kemma to Magda, looking about for the priestess's bodyguards.

'Gone. Gone to fight, and now doubtless dead.'

'The king is dead?' she asked, although she knew the answer.

'Fallen. We are the last few dawi of Karak Eight Peaks. Thorgrim is our lord now.'

'Whatever you say, mistress Magda,' said Thorgim.

Magda chuckled. 'You're the king! You don't have to defer to me.'

'I think I will,' said Thorgrim gracefully. 'If it's all the same to you.'

The last few dwarfs were running down the hall towards the room, heavy boots banging sparks from once fine mosaics. Worryingly, this included the last few warriors. Bloodcurdling screams and a horrible squeaking pursued them.

'We better get in, and quickly,' said Magda. She produced from under her robes a heavy object wrapped in oilcloth and offered it to the queen. 'You'll be wanting this.'

'My hammer?' guessed Kemma.

'Of course. No queen should stand her last without her weapon. Are we dawi, or are we umgi females to go screaming into the night?'

Kemma nodded and took the oilcloth from the priestess; there indeed was the hammer.

'Thank you.'

'I took it from the armoury. I had no doubt you would need it at the end. Valaya provides for her champions.' She gave a weary sigh, and steadied herself on Kemma's shoulder. 'I fear she has one final task for you before the end.'

Freya beckoned her through the door. The few dwarf warriors outside nodded their heads grimly and slammed it shut. A key turned in the lock from outside, and those inside barred the door as best they could, nailing planks across the door and frame that had been left there for that purpose.

What a last stand. Here were the young and infirm, the very, very old. Those beardlings old enough to fight or who flat out refused to leave, those young unkhazali who were too young to chance the journey. Their parents' choice, not theirs. Kemma wished Belegar had ordered them all to go.

A room mostly full of those who never would or could no longer swing an axe. But all of those strong enough to lift them held one. Cooks, merchants, beardlings and rinn. All dwarfs had warrior in them, but some were more warlike than others, and the dwarfs in that room were among the least. They were down to the very last. She and Thorgrim were the champions of the room, the last heroes of this failing land.

She looked out of the room's small window. Snow swirled around the tower, but it could not obscure the hordes of greenskins camped outside, insolently within gunshot of the walls. It made her sick to see them. Within hours, she reckoned, they would be fighting with the skaven over her bones.

The door shook. The beardlings tried their best to be brave, the younger children were openly terrified, the unkhazali cried in their mothers' arms. There were not many children there; Karak Eight Peaks had never been a kind environment to raise beardlings. And here they all were, Karak Eight Peaks's hopes for the future, trapped like rats and waiting to die.

The warriors in the corridor called out their battle-cries. From beyond the door a clashing of blades and the squealing of dying skaven set up. Thorgrim looked to his mother.

'Don't hold your axe so tightly,' she scolded gently. 'It will jar from your hand, and then where will you be?'

'Sorry, mother,' said Thorgrim.

Kemma smiled at him sadly. 'Don't be sorry. You have never done a wrong to dawi or umgi or anyone or anything else.' She reached up to pat his face as she always had, a mother's gesture for her child. But, she realised, he was not a child any more, despite his years. He was a king. She grasped his arm instead, a safe warrior's gesture. 'You would have been a very great king, my boy.'

The sound of arms abruptly ceased. There was a thump on the wood and a dying gurgle. Blood pooled under the door. Queekish squeaked outside. Silence. Then the door began to shake.

The door bounced in its frame. The wood splintered. The nails in the planks worked loose, and the first of them clattered to the floor.

'They're coming!' screamed Kemma. 'They're coming!'

The fight was short and bloody. Kemma barred the way, keeping her son behind her, but he was singled out, and he was among the first to die. Kemma held back her grief and fought them as long as she could, a succession of untried warriors taking the position at her side. The skaven were stormvermin, strong and cunning warriors, but she was a queen, her hammer driven by a mother's grief. They stood no chance. Ten she slew, then twenty. Time blurred along with her tear-streaked vision.

Kemma felt relief when the poisoned wind globe sailed into the room over the stormvermins' heads, and shattered on the stone walls behind her. The choking gas poured with supernatural alacrity to fill every corner. The skaven in front of her died, white sputum bubbled at its lips, eyes bulging. Kemma held her breath, though her head spun and eyes stung and blurred. She ran forwards, hoping to buy time enough for the dwarfish young to die. Better a quick death by gas than the lingering torment of enslavement that would await them should they be taken alive.

'Dreng! Dreng thaggoraki! Dreng! Dreng! Dreng!' she shouted, swinging her hammer wildly. Her lungs burned, she could feel them filling with fluid. She was drowning in her own blood. Still she fought, sending the skaven breaching party reeling. Behind her, the cries and coughs subsided. Good, she thought. Good.

'Za Vala-Azrilungol!' she cried, holding her runic hammer aloft. The runes on it were losing their gleam, the magic leaching away, becoming nought but cut marks in steel. 'Khazuk-ha! Vala-Azrilungol-ha! Valaya! Valaya! Valaya!' She swung her hammer for one final swing, bloodying a stormvermin's muzzle, but she was dying, her strength fleeing her body, and they brought her down. They pinned her to the floor, and she spat bloody mouthfuls at them. She panted shallowly, but could draw no sustenance from the air. The world and all its cruelties and disappointments receded. A golden light shone behind her as the halls of her ancestors opened their doors. Before she passed through, she flung one last, panting curse at her murderers.

'Enjoy your victory. I hope you live to regret it.'

The column of greenskins toiled up the slopes of the mountains, into the bitter chill of the unnatural winter. They were led by a toothless, wrinkled old orc clad in nothing but a pair of filthy trousers and a stunty-skin cloak with the face still attached. The head of the stunty sat on the orc's scalp, moustaches hanging either side of the orc's face, beard tied under his chin. Consequently the dangling arm and leg skin of the dead dwarf only came halfway down the orc's back. He had on no shoes, no shirt, no nothing, and it was freezing cold.

'This way, this way!' said Zargakk the Mad, for that was who the orc was. 'No it ain't!' he scolded himself. 'Oh yes it is!' he replied.

'Just where have you been these last years, Zargakk?' said Skarsnik. 'Funny you just turning up this morning like that. We could've used you in da fight.'

'Yep, yep,' yipped Zargakk. 'Could have, could have. But I's been busy. Yep, very busy. Part of it I was, er, dead. Yeah. I forget, um, the rest. But you got me Idol of Gork, dincha? That was a help! And I'm here now. Whoop!' His eyes blazed green. Smoke puffed from his ears. Duffskul had been nutty, but Zargakk was totally crazy.

'Funny, ain't it,' said Skarsnik, half to himself, 'in an ironical kind of way, that we is using the same little hidden ways to gets out that them stunties used to get in.'

'Suppose,' said Zargakk. The goblin and orc chiefs marching with them shared perplexed looks.

'But there's no stunties there now, boss, none at all. They's all gone!' said one, who was either braver or even thicker than the rest.

Skarsnik shut his eyes tight and shuddered.

They had marched out in the morning, after a nervous-looking skaven had delivered the king's head. Zargakk had been sitting on a toppled stunty statue in front of the Howlpeak, the citadel burning behind him. All across the skies were clouds of blackest black, so black the night goblins didn't really notice it was day at all. In the east, south and north they were lit red by the fires of the earth. Only to the west was there a hint of blue, and that was pale and scalloped by roils of ash.

Up, up onto the slopes they went, chancing the high passes. The main road out of the Eight Peaks to the west was buried in rubble from the skaven's detonation of the mountains. Although large numbers of skaven had departed to the north, some remained, and the East Gate was most likely in the hands of the ratmen by now. Skarsnik wasn't banking on them keeping their word, so up into the cold they went.

From high above the Great Vale, Skarsnik turned to take one last look at his former domain. His entire army stopped with him. Most of it did, anyway, those elements that did not tripping over the ones that had, and no small number of them slipping to their deaths as a result.

'Garn! Get on! Get on!' yelled Skarsnik, planting his boot in the breeches of a mountain goblin. 'Blow the zogging horns, you halfwits. Do it! Get 'em moving! Just cos I is stopping don't mean *everyone* should!'

Horns blared, the mountains answering sorrowfully. Drums rolled like distant thunder in the forgotten summers of the world. Skarsnik thought there might never be a summer again.

'Look at that. Would you look at that,' said Kruggler, peering out from under his dirty bandages. He'd been wounded across the forehead during the battle, but his skull was particularly dense and he seemed unharmed. 'Seems such a waste, leaving it all behind.'

'Yeah,' said Skarsnik. 'Don't it just? All them zogging rats just upped and left an' all. Ridiculous. It's empty. Empty after all this time.'

'The greatest stunty-house in all the world!'

'Second greatest,' corrected Skarsnik, holding up a grubby finger. 'Second greatest. And it was all mine.'

'Why they going?' said Kruggler.

'Search me,' shrugged Skarsnik. 'Don't make no sense.'

'Why don't we just go back then?' said someone.

'Nah,' said Skarsnik. 'We do that, they'll come back. Besides, new vistas, new worlds to conquer. All that.'

'Stupid rats,' grumbled Dork the orc, current boss of Skarsnik's bigger greenies. Skarsnik had lost so many of his chieftains he wasn't sure who was who any more, and he couldn't exactly stop to check his lists.

'Mark my words, it'll be full of trolls soon enough,' said Tolly Grin Cheek the Fourth.

'Maybe,' said Skarsnik, raising his eyebrows. 'Wouldn't be the first time, except, it won't happen.'

'How you know that, boss?' said Dork.

Skarsnik plucked a human-made watch from his pocket and screwed up his eyes to peer at it. 'I just do. Should be about now.'

'What, boss?' said Tolly Grin Cheek.

'You don't think I'd let those ratboys have the place, did you? You don't think I'm beat do you? Eh? Eh?'

The goblins and orcs looked at each other searchingly. No one wanted to hazard a guess at the right answer to that one.

'Course not!' said Skarsnik. 'Y'see, those ratboys are too zogging clever by half.'

'Not like us, eh, boss!' said Dork. The others laughed at their own cleverness.

'No. No. Definitely not,' replied Skarsnik flatly. 'Anyways, that big ratfing promised me two things. Old Belegar here.' Skarsnik patted his dwarf-hide pouch, wherein languished the severed head of the king. 'And one of them fancy machines the ratties are always meddling with. I had a mob put it down there, set it off to go, then run away.'

'What was it, boss? What was it?' they shouted excitedly.

Skarsnik pulled a pained expression and shuddered. 'Can't one of you zogging morons have a guess, just one guess?'

'A super trap!' said one.

'A big axe?' said Dork hopefully.

'A troll!'

'A dragon!'

'Two dragons!'

'Lots of dragons!' someone else shouted, getting carried away with the whole dragon idea.

'It's a bomb, you snotlings-for-brains. Our boss here got a big bomb off them, didn't he?' Zargakk the Mad said. 'He did, he did!' he added, nodding in enthusiastic agreement with himself.

'That's the truth, right there,' said Skarsnik. 'A bomb. Apparently, they was going to blow up the big dwarf mountain up north where the king of all stunties live. Well, not now they ain't!'

They all shared a good laugh at that.

'This big rat god fing showed up, and offered it to me. Tried to talk me into blowing up Zhufbar with it! So I said yes.'

'But we ain't at Zhufbar, boss!'

'Yeah, Zhufbar's, like, miles away.'

'It's at least three.'

'More like loads.'

'Will you just let me finish?' shouted Skarsnik. 'Zhufbar's one thousand and eighty-four miles away, if you must know. So I thoughts to meself,' he continued at normal volume again, 'I ain't walking all that way on the say-so of a ratboy! Then I finks, well, if I ain't going to have the Eight Peaks, and the stunties aren't going to have the Eight Peaks, then the zogging ratboys certainly aren't going to have it. I'm going to be the last king of the Eight Peaks. Me,' he said, low and growly. 'Not some mange-furred rat git with cheesy breath! I tells you, it's the biggest bomb what ever there was. Huge! All brass and iron and wyrdstone.' He had to exaggerate its size. The goblins would never have believed something small as a troll's head could do so much damage.

'Weeds toe what?'

'He means the glowy green rock what the ratties likes so much,' said Dork, glowing almost as much as said rock himself with self-satisfaction.

'Yeah, that's right. The green glowy. About a ton of it, I'd say, all packed about with black powder.'

'What's an "aton"?'

'Lots! A ton is lots! Very heavy! It's lots, all right?' said Skarsnik, his hood vibrating with irritation. 'So lots it'll make them little bangs what the ratties brought down Red Sun Mountain with look like squigs popping on a fire. And I made 'em give it to me! Me!'

A tinny chime sounded from out of the watch, strange music to play out the destruction of their home, accompanied by the slap-tramp of goblin feet as the tribes wound their way upwards.

'And that's the timer,' said Skarsnik. He chuckled evilly.

They all stared expectantly at the city. Big 'uns and bosses had to lash the lads to stop them from gawping at what their betters were looking at.

Nothing happened. Nothing at all.

'Was that it? Has it gone?' asked a particularly thick underling, who was staring right at Karak Eight Peaks's desolate ruins.

'No. No. No! That wasn't it, you zogging git!' Skarsnik roared. He spun round and blasted the gobbo with a bright green zap of Waaagh! energy. The goblin exploded all over everybody else.

An uncomfortable silence fell, punctuated by the drip of goblin blood. Karak Eight Peaks remained resolutely, undemolishedly there.

'Er,' said Kruggler, tentatively tapping Skarsnik's shoulder. 'You know them skaven gizmos, they don't always work, do they, boss?'

'Mork's 'urty bits,' said Skarsnik. He sniffed. He spat. He shuffled about a bit. The chain that Gobbla used to be attached to clanked sadly. He couldn't bring himself to take it off. 'Not with a bang, but with a whimper,' he muttered to himself.

'Sorry, boss?'

'Nothing, Krugs,' said Skarsnik with forced bonhomie. 'Nothing. Just something I read in a humie book once.' Skarsnik shook his head and waved his sorry band onwards. 'Come on, boys. Nothing left to see here. Nothing left at all.'

''Ere, boss,' called someone. 'I got a question.'

'Yes?' said Skarsnik. 'Dazzle me with your piercing insight, Krugdok.'

'Just where exactly are we going?'

'And I remain undazzled,' said Skarsnik with such sharp sarcasm you could have trimmed a troll's nose hair with it. Besides Zargakk, not one of the goblins or orcs, excepting perhaps Kruggler - and then only perhaps - noticed. 'To tell you the truth, and I really mean it this time...' The goblins dutifully tittered. The orcs scowled. '...I haven't got a bleedin' clue.'

And with those eternal words, the last king of Karak Eight Peaks turned from his kingdom for the final time, and trudged over the mountain shoulder. Ahead of him the lowering volcanic skies hid an uncertain future.

TWENTY-THREE

Twelve in One

Thanquol splashed through shallow puddles on the walkway by the sewer channel. He had given up trying to keep his robes clean. They were roughly made anyway, not like the finery he was used to.

'This not good-good,' he grumbled. 'Grey seers fall low, Thanquol lowest of all.'

He scurried along, head constantly twitching to look behind him. He missed the comfort of Boneripper's presence. He got more done when he wasn't constantly watching his own back.

Not very far over him were the warrens of the man-things, the city-place they called Nuln. He was here to take it for Clan Skryre, and things were not going very well at all.

If he'd known how much the clan would expect of him, then he probably wouldn't have thrown himself on their mercy.

Probably.

Not so long ago, Thanquol and his fellow seer Gribikk – how annoying to find him here too! No doubt he had already reported

Thanquol's presence back to Thaumkrittle – would have been in charge of the expedition, and it would all have been over some time ago. But it was Skribolt of Clan Skryre who was in charge, his large contingent of warlocks supposedly fighting alongside Clans Vrrtkin, Carrion, Kryxx and Gristlecrack. Naturally, the entire expedition was unravelling.

It was all Skribolt's fault, not his. The Great Warlock was a fine inventor, Thanquol could see that, but he lacked vision, and his strategies lacked scope. How was it Thanquol's fault that Clan Vrrtkin and Clan Carrion had turned on each other? How was it his doing that they could not even take a warehouse full of gunpowder without fighting among themselves?

Of course, he was being blamed. Poor Thanquol, once the darling of the Council, now a scapegoat for a tinker-rat of limited vision. He gnashed his teeth at the terrible injustice of it all. He was desperate. The plans to raid the man-thing's city for gunpowder and a working steam engine had come to nought. The Council of Thirteen had made it very clear the mission would succeed, or heads would be forfeit. As things stood, that meant *his* head, and that would not do at all. The emissary from the Council had been quite specific, in a roundabout way. Thanquol still could not believe that the grey seers had fallen so far. The shame of having to explain himself for something that patently was not his fault made his ears burn. Worst of all, it had been a lowly warlock who had come all puffed up and guarded by the Council's elite Albino Guard to deliver the ultimatum. That was a grey seer's task.

Skribolt was close to ridding himself of Thanquol. He was in league with Gribikk – it was the only explanation. They'd taken Boneripper from him not long afterwards, ostensibly for repairs, but Thanquol knew the truth of it. Another attack on the surface failed shortly afterwards, again due to the treachery of Clan Vrrtkin. Ordered to report his own 'failure' by farsqueaker, he had sabotaged the machine and fled to the sewers. The uprising was going wrong all over the Empire, and they couldn't blame him for all of it. But they didn't have to. He was at last resorts. He didn't know whether to be more angry than afraid, or more afraid than angry. If this didn't work...

Thanquol reached the door he sought and glanced about himself, nose twitching with nerves. The bundle he carried mewled, and he shushed and patted at it. A splash sounded up the river of filth flowing sluggishly past him. He stayed deathly still, ears pricked for any sound, but nothing came to him but the steady drip of water, and a far-off rushing sound from where the sewer discharged into the river.

He unfroze, tail moving first and then his whole body melting into nervy activity. With his free hand he drew forth the key for the door, stolen from the city sewerjacks many years ago.

They hadn't missed the key. The lock was so clogged with rust it was patently obvious no one had been here since his last visit. He had to place the squirming bundle on the floor to turn it. The squealing it made set his heart pumping and glands clenching. The door groaned louder still when he pushed it open. He paused again, holding his breath until he was satisfied.

He scooped up the bundle and scurried in, pushing the door slowly to behind him.

As he suspected, the chamber was undisturbed. The man-things definitely hadn't been there, and he breathed a little easier. Cobwebs thick with dust festooned the domed ceiling. A lesser drain ran diagonally through the circular room, cutting off a third of it from the rest before disappearing through a culvert in the walls. Thanquol absently patted the bundle again, and set it down in the corner as far away from the stream of human waste as he could. To summon the verminlord, it was important his offering was as pure as possible.

He flexed his right hand-paw. The grafting scar around his wrist itched. He held both of them, regarding their mismatched nature. 'Gotrek!' he hissed, recalling the moment his hated nemesis had severed the paw. He clapped his left hand over his muzzle. Who knew if the dwarf-thing were here, lurking in the shadows and ready to foil him yet again?

Thanquol took a generous pinch of warpstone snuff to calm his nerves. His head pounded at the effect, his brain strained against his skull. His chest rose and fell expansively. His vision cleared, and he saw revealed the straining tendrils of magic crossing the room. So much of it in the world!

Enough perhaps for success. His eyes narrowed, and he allowed himself his most diabolical chuckle.

Thanquol set to work.

First, he brushed as much dust away from the centre of the room with his foot-paws as he could, revealing the stone beneath. Though segments of the walls dripped with moisture, and filth ran through it, the room was otherwise wholesome, and surprisingly dry. With a shard of sharpened warpstone, he scratched out a double circle and filled the band between inner and outer layers with intricate symbols. He fought the urge to nibble on the warpstone shard, at least until he was done. When he had, he munched on the blunt end as he scrutinised his work. He nodded, and turned to the bundle.

He unwrapped it quickly.

'So ugly!' he hissed. 'Not like skaven pups. Come-come! You sing for Thanquol now.'

Thanquol drew his knife and placed the squealing bundle in the centre of the circle.

When he was done, Thanquol carefully dripped the blood into the gouges in the floor. His usual frenetic movement became measured as he carefully filled in each. This had to be done precisely. Messing it up didn't bear thinking of. He whispered words of summoning under his breath, hoping it wouldn't be like the last time, hoping that...

Skarbrand...

Do not think-recall the name! he told himself. It was probably still listening. He calmed himself, waited until the memories of the bloodthirster he'd accidentally called up the last time faded, then continued.

He placed the pup's remains and its bloodied rags outside the circle, and held up his hand-paws.

Although his past efforts had ended in disaster, once more the white-furred sorcerer attempted to slice the veil between realms. Once more he attempted to bring forth a verminlord. He spoke-squeaked the words of power, calling upon the Horned Rat and the mightiest daemons of his court. Green fire crackled from his eyes and between his upraised paws.

'Come-skitter! Join me in the realm of the mortal! I command you! I, Grey Seer Thanquol so squeak-say!' he said. There was a blast of power and the fabric of reality rippled.

He stood there exulted, hands still upraised. It was working!

Nothing happened.

He let his arms drop, and looked around. The room was unchanged. He was alone.

Once more Thanquol had failed. This time, at least, he had not done so with the same disastrous consequences as his previous attempt. He groaned. His paws clenched.

'Why-why?' he said. The temptation was to storm out, destroy the circle, and find someone else to blame. But he could not. He was the one being blamed – entirely unjustly – by others. He had to succeed.

Tail swishing, the grey seer paced out of the circle, careful not to scuff the marks. He went around and inspected them all.

'Perfect! Perfect! They are all perfect! The Horned Rat himself could not have drawn them better. Why-why does it not work?!' he squealed angrily. The bloody rags caught his eyes. Maybe *two...?*

It was then that Thanquol perceived a shadowy hand reaching out of the blackness gathered in the chamber's vaulted ceiling. The claws ripped through reality with a screech that sent pain running down his spine. The enormous hand headed unerringly for him. He found that he could not move, not even when the hand grabbed him by the ankles and lifted him upright, dangling him upside down as its owner stepped out of a black abyss of shadows. Remembering the fate of Kritislik, Thanquol liberally vented the musk of fear.

But he was not consumed. The entity stepped through into the realm of the mortal, casually bestriding Thanquol's protective circle. It examined him with curiosity, peering at him this way and that.

Thanquol could do nothing but squeak in wide-eyed wonder. He had seen verminlords before, of course, but never anything like this. No horns had ever sprouted so majestically as the ones upon its head. Multiple sets curved and entwined the daemon's face. They seemed to sinuously curve and move as Thanquol watched them. Beneath the horns one eye was missing. In its place was not an empty socket, but a warpshard, or if the angle was correct, a black hole of endless nothing. Thanquol's head throbbed as he looked into it.

'Ahhh, Thanquol, you took your time. Perhaps you are not so gifted as I thought?' it purred. 'I have waited for you to call me. Yes-yes, we have much to do.'

'Who-what are you, O great master?' shrilled Thanquol.

The creature placed him gently alongside the channel. Only then did the grey seer notice that one of the verminlord's foot-paws was in the drain. It did not sink into the river of filth but hovered above it.

The ancient being stooped to Thanquol's level.

'Our name is Lord Skreech Verminking,' said the verminlord. 'There are many of us, and one.' As he spoke, Thanquol saw before him – or perhaps he imagined it – the verminlord's visage flicker, revealing many ghostly aspects that together somehow made the face the creature wore: the contagion-ridden body of a plague priest, the shadowy assassin, the hungry hordes, the tinkering weaponsmith, the future-gazing seer. 'The ruins, the decay, they give me power. I was called here by blight and destruction. There is much in the world in this time, and it is good,' it said, sniffing the air and craning its neck. 'And by you, Thanquol.'

Thanquol swallowed in awe. Could it be? The grey seers had long spoken in whispers of 'the One,' a Rat King – a conglomerate evil. As mortal skaven had their hierarchies of clan, caste, and rank, so too did the verminlords above them. There was one, an entire Council of Thirteen elevated by the Horned Rat in the past to daemonhood as one creature. He was their ruler, the lord of the supposed Shadow Council of Thirteen. Had Thanquol really just summoned forth the most powerful of all verminlords? He had always known he was special, but this was pleasing confirmation. Pleasing indeed. He smiled.

The grey seer looked up into that strange face staring back at, and possibly through, him. It seemed to have read his thoughts, for it looked down upon him indulgently, its enormous claw reaching out to ever so gently stroke his horns. 'I am who you think I am, yes-yes, little seer. You have a purpose. I have need of your singular talents. Together we shall conquer.'

Thanquol's heart soared. With this creature at his side, none could stand before him! He couldn't wait to see Skribolt's face, or to smell him squirt the musk of fear.

'Nuln-place first?'

The verminlord nodded its head, pleased with the seer, or so it seemed to the conceited Thanquol. 'And much more besides. We have many tasks ahead of us. But first, gifts!'

Impossibly, a huge shape was in the corner of the room, half shadowed, like it had been there all the time and was patiently waiting for its cue. Thanquol's eyes widened. The largest rat ogre he had ever seen stepped out of the shadows.

Thanquol's whiskers twitched with glee.

'Many thanks-gratitudes for such beneficent generosities, O

great and unplumbably wise Lord Verminking!' Thanquol's eyes narrowed, his imagination alive with much smashing and kill-slaying. 'I shall call him Boneripper,' he said.

In the war council of the Nuln-place clawpack, all was not well. For hours the skaven assailing the city had hurled accusations at each other by the dimly flickering light of warp-braziers. The room the council occupied was a small one, built and forgotten by humans long ago, and pitifully insufficient in size to contain so many over-weaning egos.

'I say-squeak you are a worthless weak-meat, and all Clan Vrrtkin are puny-small and shifty!' squeaked Warlord Throttlespine of Clan Kryxx. He had drawn his sword and pointed it at Warlord Trikstab Gribnode of Clan Vrrtkin. 'You are at fault for our lack of success, tricking and lying and attacking when we should fight together.'

'Lies, lies! Not good lies either,' squealed Gribnode. He pulled his own sword. The other members of the war council stood hurriedly from the table, upsetting their chairs. 'All knows Thanquol-seer is weak link in rusty chain here, and you are next weakest, Throttlespine. Banish Thanquol, great and cunning Warlock Skribolt! Banish him, so we not have to suffer the stink of his slack musk-hole! It is this that foils our efforts! Then let us banish Throttlespine. He is in league with Thanquol! His cowardice too is legendary.'

Throttlespine growled and jumped onto the table. 'Coward, am I? I lead from the back of my ratkin as every true warrior should-must, whereas you, where are you? Skulking and hiding off the battlefield! You are to blame, and seek to smear my good-true name with ordure of failure. I am a loyal servant of the council!'

'No, I am the loyallest servant of the council!' retorted Gribnode.

'Stop-cease, halt!' squeaked Skribolt. 'This is too much!' Unable to get anyone to listen to him, he began to crank the handle of his warp-lightning generator.

Throttlespine was tensed for a leap when the sound of fighting came from outside.

'Stop-stop!' squeaked a stormvermin beyond the door. 'Many-much council leaders exercise deep and important thinkings. Go aw–' The guard's order was cut short. The sound of armoured bodies clattering off the walls took its place. A terrifying roar had them all looking at each other, and struggling to control their fear glands.

A single blow felled the plank door so hard it hit the flagged floor with a bang like a cannon shot. On the other side was the largest rat ogre any of the council members had ever seen, even Grand Packmaster Paxrot of Clan Moulder, and he knew his rat ogres very well. The four-armed behemoth doubled over to squeeze its bulk through the doorway. Following the monster came Grey Seer Thanquol.

'Thanquol?' said Skribolt, his hand slowing on the warp-lightning crank, then speeding up again. 'You are banished!'

'Good-good, all still here? I bring news from the Council,' said Thanquol, who was puffed up and obviously very pleased with himself.

This proclamation was most stunning to Great Warlock Skribolt, whose claw still churned the handcrank on his warp-energy generator. His muzzle twitched as he grasped for what to say.

'Yes-yes, after so much incompetence,' and here the grey seer paused to look at Skribolt, 'I am to be in charge. Any disputes can be directed to my bodyguard, Boneripper.' At this, Thanquol nodded at the hulking beast stood snarling behind him, surveying the gathering with hate-filled eyes.

'But that is not...' Skribolt started to say, but the grey seer cut him off.

'My *new* bodyguard, Boneripper,' said Thanquol. 'The old one was mostly dead,' he added dismissively. 'This one better. Now that the element of surprise is gone-lost,' Thanquol continued, 'I feel it is time to switch tactics. My plan is to–'

At last Skribolt found his tongue. 'Enough! No more! Halt-stop!' said the Great Warlock, the last words coming out perhaps more shrilly than he had wished. 'On whose orders were you gift-granted authority? Why-tell was I not informed?'

Skribolt was standing, lightning wreathing him as his whirring contraption sucked in the winds of magic. All the other skaven – warlords, a top assassin, and a master moulder – took a step backwards away from the two.

When a voice spoke from the shadows all turned, finding a terrible sight. The blackness strained with life, and an awful shape moved there. Such was the power inherent in it that several of the lesser warlords let their musk glands loose.

'On our authority, Great Warlock!' said the shadow. The room went black, lit only by dancing chains of lightning. A long, elegant claw reached out, snuffing out the sparks between Skribolt's backpack conductors. In the blackness a single terrifyingly evil eye radiated green over them, holding them each in its turn, leaving none in any doubt that his most treasured schemes had been exposed, digested and dismissed as the work of fools.

As suddenly as it appeared, the blackness was gone. The war council was alone again.

'What do you bid-command, O great and exalted leader Thanquol?' intoned Warlord Throttlespine, bowing low. The rest of the skaven followed suit, although they did subconsciously shuffle away from those who had befouled themselves.

Thanquol had already surmised that Throttlespine was the smart one, yet it was gratifying to be proven correct. Nodding his head slightly in acceptance, Thanquol began again. 'As I was squeal-saying, my plan...'

PART THREE

Eternity's End
Autumn 2527

TWENTY-FOUR

The King's Head

The world had changed.

No longer could the dawi count the mountains as their own. They teetered on the brink of extinction.

Thorgrim Grudgebearer ground his teeth together. The Dammaz Kron lay under his hand. It had glutted itself on woes, growing thicker faster than at any other time in the High King's remarkable reign.

He stared at the Granite Gate two hundred feet away. Massive twin doors of stone, imposing despite being only half – and it was exactly, precisely half – the height of the tall, vaulted corridor they barred. The gates shuddered under an impact from the far side: a quiver in the stone so small that only a dwarf, stone born and stone master, could see. Bands of runes carved into the gates glowed intensely with inner blue light, their magic striving to keep the gates whole and closed.

The skaven were coming. As sure as Thorgim's chin wore a beard, they would get through. The ratkin had burst every defence, arcane and otherwise, that the dawi of Karaz-a-Karak had thrown up.

Thorgrim thought on the horrors that afflicted his people.

Karak Azul overthrown.

Karak Eight Peaks lost a second time.

Zhufbar swarmed by an endless tide of vermin.

Barak Varr pouring smoke from its great dock gates, the pride of the dwarf fleet broken in the sea before it.

The holds of the Grey Mountains overcome and lost in three horrific nights of bloodshed.

Karak Kadrin poisoned.

Karaz-a-Karak besieged for years now, cut off on all sides above and below. The streams of refugees pouring into the dwarf capital from other kingdoms had given Thorgrim much anguish. At a time when he thought his dream might be fulfilled, that the lost realms of the Karaz Ankor would be reclaimed, it had all come to nothing. The fleeing dwarfs brought with them tales of proud strongholds cast down, and not only in dwarf lands. Many dwarfs of the diaspora had fled back to their ancestral homeland from human cities – their habits and speech strange; some of them even trimmed their beards! – telling of similar woes beyond the mountains. But what was more horrifying than the incoming flood and the dire tidings they brought was that it had stopped. No dwarf had come into Everpeak for months.

Tilea, Estalia and Bretonnia ashes. The Empire devastated. The moon cracked in the sky, invasion from the north, and ratmen swarming from everywhere.

'We stand alone,' he said into his beard, his unblinking stare locked upon the door. It shuddered again.

'The runes will not last, my liege,' muttered Hrosta Copperling. A runesmith, but a mere beardling compared to the likes of Kragg the Grimm and Thorek Ironbrow. Their kind would never come again into this world. Hrosta was loyal and dedicated to his task, but his store of knowledge was paltry.

Thorgrim did not grace Hrosta's obvious statement with a reply, but continued to stare at the Granite Gate.

Forty feet wide, fifty tall, the gate was a lesser portal of Everpeak. Leading onto a once-safe and well-travelled section of the Ungdrin Ankor, it had become, like all the other many gates into the mountain, yet another way for the skaven to attack them.

'Thaggoraki,' Thorgrim growled. He thought of what he had seen from the Rikund, the King's Porch at the summit of Karaz-a-Karak. The endless seas of enemies, whose bodies stained the roads leading to his kingdom brown. There were so many of them, more than there had ever been before.

'My king, I implore you to return to the Hall of Kings,' said Gavun Tork, the most venerable of his living ancestors.

'You leave, my friend, we have lost too many heads full of wisdom. Go back and be safe. My duty is here. The time for counsel and talk is done. The Axe of Grimnir will speak for me.'

'Thorgrim, please!'

Thorgrim jerked his head at the living ancestor. Two of his hammerers broke from the ranks of the Everguard. 'Escort Loremaster Tork back to the eighteenth deep. Keep him safe.'

'Aye, my king,' said his warriors.

Tork gave the king a helpless look, his rheumy blue eyes brimmed with concern that threatened to spill into the deep lines on his face. 'If I were but two hundred years younger...'

'You have swung many axes for the glory of Karaz Ankor, my friend,' said Thorgrim. 'Let those younger take your place. Yours is a different burden.'

'I...'

'Go!' said the king.

The living ancestor shook off the hands of the hammerers. 'Very well. But stay safe! This is foolishness. You should not risk yourself.'

'You are wrong, loremaster,' said Thorgrim, his flinty eyes returning to regard the door. 'It is exactly what I should do.'

The clink of the Everguard's armour receded. Silence regained its hold over the throng. One hundred ironbreakers, irondrakes in support, and three score of his Everguard.

It should be enough, thought Thorgrim.

The doors' runes flickered and went out. The rock at their centre glowed bright orange, a pinprick at first that spread out in a perfect circle. The stone of the Granite Gate had been chosen well; there was not a flaw in it.

'Close secondary portcullises!' bellowed the gatewarden of the Granite Gate.

Three sets of heavy iron portcullises descended simultaneously from slots in the roof, their machinery noiseless. Only when they met the ground, and their heavy-toothed bottoms slid into matching holes in the floor, did they make the faintest clink.

The glow in the doors spread to engulf their middle, top to bottom. The light of it glowed redly from the ceiling and polished floor, catching in the eyes of ancestor statues, whose faces, changed by shadowplay, took on horrified expressions. A dribble of molten rock ran from the gate's centre, creating a hole that grew as the rock collapsed outwards, a hole that guttered a plume of fire.

'Irondrakes!' called the gatewarden. 'Airshaft doors ready!'

Fifty runic handcannons were levelled at the door.

The Granite Gate sagged all at once, its perfection lost in a pool of cooling slag.

'Fire!' bellowed the gatewarden. Tongues of flame burst from the irondrakes' guns, aimed at the centre of the hole. Whatever was on the other side exploded noisily before it could withdraw. Green-tinged fire rolled out, licking at the irondrakes' enchanted armour without effect. Squeals of dismay came from the other side of the doors. The stink of skaven fear and burning rock washed over the throng, and the air became stuffy and difficult to breathe.

The stone skinned over and cooled to a dull, ugly grey. A thick vapour obscured whatever lay on the far side of the broken gate.

Next came a hissing noise, as a green mist issued from the breach.

'Gas! Gas! Gas!' shouted the gatewarden. 'Airshafts open!'

The noxious fog rolled towards the dwarfs, sinking low to the floor. The clink of rolling glass and its shattering followed. Lesser plumes of poison sprouted as short-lived mushroom clouds around the front of the dwarf line.

The gatewarden's orders were quickly obeyed. Dwarfs cranked open large steel flaps, revealing shafts that stretched far up the mountain. Steam engines churned on levels above, creating a ferocious wind that blew downwards, exiting from angled horns to blow the gas back towards the door. More squeaking came.

Thorgrim smiled to hear them panic. The dwarfs were slow to embrace the new, but when they did, you could be sure it would be perfect.

The gas dissipated, misting the air. It was in danger of choking the dwarfs, and so the doorwarden ordered the steam engines disengaged. The pumped wind ceased, and the natural pressure difference between the low halls and the high mountain sucked the gas away, venting it harmlessly high above the tree line many thousands of feet above their heads.

Only then did the skaven come. As usual, the frantic squealing of slaves being driven at the dwarfs preceded the main assault. These were shot down without mercy, the blasts of the irondrakes' handcannons immolating them by the handful.

'No matter what they do, they are not coming through this tunnel,' said Thorgrim.

In that, the High King was wrong.

What should have come next was more slaves, thousands of them, sent to die solely for the wasting of the dwarfs' ammunition.

Through the reek of battle came no slaves. Instead the smoke curled around a great shape, horned and tall as a giant. Light warped around it, as if recoiling from the unnatural beast, shrouding it in a flickering darkness.

'Verminlord,' called out Thorgrim. 'This one is mine!'

The rat-daemon strode forwards. Jabbering in some unholy tongue, it swept its glaive in a wide arc, allowing its hand to slip far towards the counterweight at the bottom, and extending its reach to well over fifteen feet. Trailing green fire, the weapon impacted the first portcullis with a thunderous clash. The steel was sundered, deadly shrapnel from its destruction slicing into the ranks of irondrakes. 'Fire!' called the gatewarden. Handgun fire from embrasures in the walls joined the shorter-ranged bursts of the irondrakes. All were stopped by the cloak of shadow that wreathed the daemon. The second portcullis was broken. Thorgrim ordered his thronebearers forward. They obeyed instantly, bearing the great weight of the High King's throne without complaint. The ironbreakers parted ranks to allow their king passage.

'Shield wall!' roared the gatewarden. A line of overlapped steel formed to the front of the ironbreakers. The irondrakes withdrew, leaving the ironbreakers facing the monster before them. The third portcullis was thrown down, its refuse clattering off the ironbreakers' shields. The verminlord threw back its head and squealed.

Then the skaven attack began in earnest, a rush of clanrat warriors pouring through the ruined gateway. As they reached the heels of their demigod, the daemon broke into a run, glaive thrumming around its head.

Thorgrim raised up his axe, and roared out a challenge. The creature came right at him. It brought its weapon down in an overhead sweep that would have slain a rhinox. But the mystic energies of the Throne of Kings responded and a flaring shield of magic stopped the blow three feet above Thorgrim's head. He shouted his war cries, voicing the unyielding defiance of the dwarfs, and struck back. The Axe of Grimnir clove through the shadow protecting the creature and into its evil flesh. Blackness like ink spilled in water escaped from the wound, bringing with it the scent of rot. Thorgrim's beard prickled at his proximity to the thing. He bellowed again, and swung again, and the creature blocked, spinning its glaive around the axe, nearly tearing it from Thorgrim's grasp.

The skaven were upon his warriors. Driven to a great fervour of war by the presence of their god's avatar, they slashed with their weapons with strength beyond their feeble bodies, and bit so hard they broke their teeth. But they did not care. Thorgrim's bearers hewed about them, keeping the creatures from their lord while he duelled with the daemon.

The verminlord struck again, thrusting with the point of its glaive, spear fashion. The rune of eternity blazed again, but the warpmetal – greenish black and as unearthly as its owner – slid through the protective magic. The great strength of the verminlord punched it through the Armour of Skaldour, ripping open Thorgrim's side. The poisonous pain of warp contamination burned in his blood, but his roar was one of anger for the damage done to his panoply, for the skills to repair it had long been lost. The verminlord regarded him with amusement glittering in its red eyes. It assumed a guard posture, ready to strike again.

A fey feeling came upon the dwarf king. The settling of some great power about him. He felt it first as one feels the breath of another upon the cheek, perhaps unexpected, often welcome. His beard crackled with energy. This was magic, or he was umgdawi, but it was a clean sort, heavy with age, and if dwarfs respected anything at all, age was foremost. His doughty mind rebelled against it, yet against his will his heart welcomed it, and it came into him without resistance.

The world glowed golden. The metal of his throne gleamed in a way he thought impossible. The gold took on a most amazing lustre, a warmth pooled about his wounded side, and he felt the metal move there.

Infused with this glamour, Thorgrim lurched to his feet, his bearers expertly accommodating the movement of the king in combat as they fought themselves. He ran to the prow of his throne, and it felt as if the stuff of his wargear helped him – the metals that made it lending power and purpose to him above and beyond the already mighty measures he had of both. He came up level with the beast's head. Before the power upon the king, the dark magic that pinned the rat-daemon to the fabric of the earth unravelled, the glow going from its glaive blade, the shadow wafting back as surely as the gas attack had been dispersed by the ingenuity of the dwarfs. The verminlord understood what was coming at it and recoiled. The thing was slowed somehow, and the king brought the axe down hard, splitting the skull of the creature before it could move out of reach. It died with a shriek that had warriors of both sides clutching their ears in agony. A jet of noxious black spewed from its shattered head as it fell backwards. The glaive dropped and vanished, while the body collapsed into its own shadows, boiling away to nothing before it could crush the ratmen scurrying at its feet.

Seeing their godling so decisively bested, the thaggoraki wavered, even though they were hundreds deep and outnumbered the dwarfs many times over. Their cowardice had ensured the dwarfs' survival time and again.

'Forward!' shouted Thorgrim. 'Retake the gate. Allow not one of them to set paw upon the sacred stones of the inner mountain!'

With a great shout the ironbreakers pushed forwards. Thorgrim's Everguard led the charge, bludgeoning skaven with looks of murderous determination. The waver turned into panic, then into rout.

Almost as one, the skaven turned tail and fled, many dying on the axes and hammers of the vengeful dwarfs as they scurried to escape, and leaving their wounded to their fate.

'Victory!' shouted Thorgrim. 'Victory!'

'My king, of course the traps are primed,' said Chief Engineer of the Cogwheel brethren, Bukki 'Buk' Ironside, 'but we are...'

Buk was not an easily intimidated dwarf, not by a long measure of beard, but he wilted nonetheless under Thorgrim's furious stare. Not the boldest dawi, nor the oldest, nor the wisest, could weather the king's glare. His advisors stood in a semicircle before the Great Throne, all of them deeply interested in their beard ends.

'There is no place for "but" in my kingdom!' said the king. His eyes were red with unexpressed emotion and lack of sleep.

'We stand ready at your command, my king,' said Buk hurriedly, bowing several times as he shuffled from the king's displeasure back into the safety offered by his engineering peers.

'Good!' snapped Thorgrim.

'My king,' began Gavun Tork. He stood at the head of a dozen other living ancestors, all grim and uncomfortable-looking in their gold-thick finery and elaborate beard plaits. 'We have advised you several times on this matter. We counsel that we should weather this storm as we always have...'

'As I have heard your counsel!' said Thorgrim. He patted the Dammaz Kron. 'So we sit and we sit and we wait, while our defences are weakened and our numbers dwindle.'

Nockkim Grumsbyn, a short but headstrong dwarf, tired of Tork's moderate attitude and pushed his way forward. 'Defence has guaranteed our continued existence for many millennia, what you propose is suicide.'

'Hiding behind our walls has all but doomed us!' roared Thorgrim, all deference to the ancestors' age and wisdom burned away by his furious despair. 'For the entirety of my reign I have desired to march out with the axe-hosts of the dawi kingdoms and exterminate the skaven. Time and again I argued that this alone would save our kind. But you counselled against it, you and your like, Nockkim. And so we find ourselves skulking like trapped badgers in our hole, while our enemy, allowed to grow unchecked to uncountable numbers, plots our final demise. No more!' he roared again. He stood. 'Get out! Get out, all of you! I am king of the dawi nations. Your advice is flawed. For too long have you filled my ears with the whispers of caution, keeping me from reclaiming the glory of our ancestors, dwelling instead upon their dwindling legacy. Well now it dwindles to the point of extinguishment. Get out, I say!'

The entire gaggle of king's councillors stepped back in horror. Never had they seen Thorgrim fly so brashly in the face of traditional respect.

'Sire, there is something amiss.' Tork gestured at Thorgrim's throne. 'The throne, your words – there was an odd light upon you in the battle and although it may have gone...'

'Out! Get out! All of you!' Thorgrim slammed his fist down on the Dammaz Kron. 'Out,' he said, his voice subsiding. 'Get out.'

Thorgrim's Everguard stepped forward. 'Clear the throne room! By order of the High King of the Karaz Ankor! Clear the throne room!'

The Everguard, all fifty of them on honour duty at that moment, formed a line in front of their king and marched out slowly, shepherding the king's council out before them.

All around the mighty hall, whisperings and rustlings spoke of servants and other attendants withdrawing.

It took a full five minutes for the scandalised court, its servants and Thorgrim's bodyguards to leave the room. The great doors swung to with a soft boom.

Thorgrim stared down the aisle between the columns for a while. When he was completely sure he was alone, he stood up, gasping at the pain from his wound.

Whatever the strange power was that had settled on him had healed his armour, but not his flesh. Many dawi had seen him struck, but none had seen his armour rent. Consequently, none knew of his wound but a select few of his closest retainers and the priestesses of Valaya who had treated him. From all of them he had extracted oaths of silence on the matter. Among this select few, only the priestesses knew that it was not healing, poisoned by warp metal. He would let no one else know. If he began griping about every scratch, then how were his people to feel? Dwarfs were of adamant; nothing could break them. They needed to see that quality exemplified in him.

He gritted his teeth against the pain as he stepped from the Throne of Power, steadying himself on its dragon-head decorations for a moment before going on. He had already been weak before the wound. Writing so many grudges into the great book had demanded too much of his blood.

He went to the back of the throne and bent down. Agony stabbed him afresh and he choked back a cry. It was partly to deny the others the sight of their king in pain that he had sent them away, but mainly because Tork had been wrong. The light in the throne had not gone.

It had faded. The gold gleamed still, but only as bright as dwarf gold should. The magic had hidden itself away, that was all. Thorgrim could feel it all about him, and the king knew where it might be.

Sure enough, the Rune of Azamar was glowing with a steady light, more brightly than it had for centuries. The rune of eternity had been carved, it was said, by the ancestor god Grungni himself at the dawn of time. So powerful was it that only one of its type could exist at a time. It was also said that so long as it was whole, the realm of the dwarfs would endure. Thorgrim placed his hand upon it, and the rune's pulsing could be felt through the metal of his gauntlets. He let his hand drop. This magic was alien to him, not of the dawi at all. But it was not malevolent. Cautious though he was in most matters, he somehow knew this for an unassailable fact.

He missed his runesmiths more than anything then. Kragg the Grim had died months ago during the Battle of the Undermines there at Karaz-a-Karak. The only other who had exceeded his knowledge had been Thorek Ironbrow, and he was also dead, slain years before. No other had their knowledge. He considered asking the younger runesmiths, or the runepriests of Valaya, or the priests of the ancestor gods, but that was a risky course of action. They would likely be as baffled as he, and the tidings would get out. In that time of threat and upheaval, there was only so much more the dwarfs could take. The last thing Thorgrim wanted were whisperings of fell powers in their king's throne, or, perhaps more damaging, wild hopes of the ancestor gods' return. Was this not Grungni's own rune? Did it not guarantee the persistence of the dawi race while it was still whole? Thorgrim felt the first stirrings of such hope himself.

No one was coming. He could not risk the crash in morale that could follow the revelation of this hope being false.

He would wait and see. That was the proper dwarf way. Only when he was satisfied would he reveal this new development.

His mind made up, he wearily got into the throne. He sighed. He supposed he had better apologise to the longbeards. Tork at least needed to know what was happening.

Before he could summon his servants, a long, mournful blaring filtered down sounding shafts into the hall. Thorgrim sat forwards, listening intently. Up on the tops of Everpeak's great ramparts, the karak horns were sounding. The immense tusks of some ancient monster, the twinned horns were blown whenever danger threatened. From the notes played by the hornmasters, the entire city could be informed of the nature and size of the enemy force.

They played ominously long and low.

The doors at the end of the hall cracked open. A messenger huffed his way up the long granite pavement to the foot of the throne. Red-faced, he executed a quick bow and began to speak.

'My king, a fresh force of thaggoraki is moving to reinforce the besieging ratkin outside the gates.'

'Who brings this news?'

'Gyrocopter patrols, my liege. They report a massive horde on its way.' The messenger's face creased with worry. 'They fill the Silver Road with their numbers for twenty miles and more. Clans Mors is here, Queek Headtaker at their head. Banners of the warlock clans and their beastmasters also. Clan Rictus too. They have many hundreds of war engines, my lord. Also in the deeps, my king. Traps give forewarning. Mining teams report much stealthy movement.'

'This is it,' said Thorgrim, clenching his hand. 'This is it! Bring me my axe! Thronebearers! Everguard! Marshall of the Throngs, call out the dawi of Karaz-a-Karak! We skulk no longer behind our gates! Open the Great Armoury. Take out the weapons of our ancestors. Let them sit in prideful peace no longer! Dawi and treasures both to war! To war!'

As the king lifted his voice, more horns played out their alarms from the many galleries of the Hall of Kings. Within minutes, the entire city was abustle, called to the final battle.

The electric flea-prickle of the skitterleap tormented Thanquol from horn curl to tail tip, and then the sensation was gone. He clutched his robes about him with the sudden chill.

From Nuln to Lustria to the man-thing place of Middenheim, Thanquol had followed Lord Verminking. He had been dragged about the world only half willingly, skitterleaping unimaginable distances. He did not trust the verminlord, because he was not a fool. Thanquol knew he was being used. He was arrogant enough to think initially that he was the master in his relationship with the Verminking, but wise enough to quickly reach the correct conclusion. Thanquol was merely a pawn in the mighty daemon's game.

Once he had accepted that, everything did not seem so bad. Surely it was no bad thing to serve the most powerful rat in existence after the Great Horned One? And he was learning a great deal from the creature. More, perhaps, than Verminking intended to teach.

He examined their new location. It was an unusual place for a meeting, thought Thanquol, but the symbolism was hard to miss.

Even with its head blasted to rubble, the statue of the ancient dwarf-thing was enormous. Once this great stone king would have watched over the Silver Road Pass, an image of the strength of the dwarf kingdom. Now, in its ruin, it made rather the opposite statement.

'They come,' hissed Verminking. 'Be silent, be deferential, or even I will not be able to protect-keep you!'

Clouds of shadows blossomed all around Thanquol and Lord Skreech. Ten more verminlords towered over him, gazing down, their ancient eyes gleaming with malice.

'Why-tell the little horned one here?' asked one of two diseased Lords of Contagion among their number.

Not knowing what to do, Thanquol gave the sign of the Horned Rat and bowed low before each. This seemed well received by the entities. Only the two foulest-looking of them gave tail flicks of displeasure.

'You know why, Throxstraggle,' answered Verminking, his own twin tails flickering menacingly. He glared intently at the greasy rat-daemon for a long moment before continuing, addressing the circle of verminlords. 'We asked-bid you here so that we all agree. The Council of Thirteen decree is that the clan that delivers the dwarf-king's head name-picks the last Lord of Decay. We are as one on this agreement, yes-yes?'

This was news to Thanquol. From Verminking's feet he tried to gauge the reaction around the circle. Most of the verminlords bowed their heads in assent. A few of them looked irritated and abstained. It was with some pride that he noticed that none of the verminlords had horns as twisted or as magnificent as did the mighty Lord Skreech.

'We are but eleven in number – where-tell is Lurklox?' asked one, a grossly inflated parody of a skaven warlord.

'Here,' said a voice from behind them. Thanquol startled, but was pleased not to have leaked out anything regrettable.

A black-shaded Lord of Deception joined the circle, its face masked and body hidden in curling shadows. 'As we anticipated,' it said in a whispering voice, 'the end of the dwarf-things approaches.'

'All goes to plan-intention?' asked Verminking.

'What plan-intention?' said a white-furred verminlord of inconstant appearance. 'We agree-pledge that Clan Scruten will be reselected to the Council. This is our plan.'

Again, general indications of assent from the circle, with some dissension.

'Quite right, we all declared it to be so. Why fret-fear?' said Verminking reasonably.

'My candidate is ready. Tell-inform me how the head will be won, and how it will be delivered to Kranskritt.'

'You doubt our purpose?' said Lurklox.

'Lord Skreech takes new-pet Thanquol with him everywhere. He is a grey seer. I suspect-think Lord Skreech intends to gift-give the head of the long-face-fur to him.'

Verminking bristled. 'You doubt my word, Soothgnawer?'

Soothgnawer laughed. 'I would be a fool weak-meat to give any credence to your words at all.'

Verminking dipped his head in appreciation of the compliment. 'Be easy. Thanquol has been very useful, very cunning. He will win great reward for his efforts, but...' He looked down. 'His place is not to be on the Council. We need his many talents elsewhere.'

Thanquol inwardly shrank. Until the fateful words were said, he had felt privileged; now he felt like a serving-rat. He kept up his outside appearance of interested confidence, behaving as if he often attended gatherings of such august personages, but inside he seethed.

'Is this true, little grey-fur? Tell me the truth! I will know otherwise.'

Several of the giants crowded over him. Thanquol's glands twitched. 'Mighty lords! The fine and most infernal Lord Skreech Verminking has not told me of any plans to gift-grant me the fine and high most honourable exalted station of a seat among the Thirteen.' This was exactly the truth. Verminking told Thanquol very little, only revealing his intentions when the outcome was already unfolding.

Soothgnawer sniffed the air as Thanquol spoke, then stood straight.

'He speaks the truth, the precise truth, although he is very much disappointed to hear he will not sit beside the other little Lords of Decay. Very wise, very clever not to tell the little one of your plans, Skreech.'

'The wise and cunning Thanquol knows everything he needs to know,' said Verminking.

Thanquol looked up to the verminlords talking around him. That they could smell untruth and knew the mind of any skaven was an established fact. But it suddenly dawned on him that these gifts did not work upon each other. To all intents, in their own company they were as reliant on bluff and double-dealing as any other skaven. He wondered how. He wondered if he could possibly replicate their methods...

Thanquol remembered this for later use. Already ideas were forming. He wasn't yet decided on how he could wring an advantage out of this information, but he would. He was certain of that.

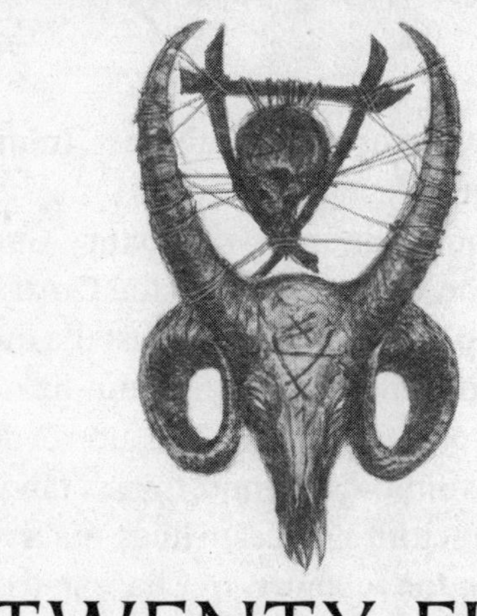

TWENTY-FIVE

Queek's Glory

Queek was old. He felt it in his stiffening limbs. He saw it in the grey that grizzled the blackness of his coat all over, a coat once sleek and now broken with dry patches, whose coarsening fur revealed pink skin crusted with scurf.

Decrepitude surprised him suddenly, coming on swift as an ambush. He had thought to suffer a slow decline, nothing like this. Only three years after his great victory at Eight Peaks, and look at him. Beyond the limits of his arms' reach, his sight grew dim and unreliable. Through the mists of age, the marching lines of his army blurred into one mass, losing colour around the edges. His smell and hearing remained sharp, but into his limbs a weakness had set, one that made itself more apparent with every passing day in the numbness of his fingers and the stiffness of his joints. The cold made it worse, driving him into frequent murderous rages that his troops had learned to fear.

It was always cold now, no matter where they went. It had been since the night the Chaos moon had burst, circling the world with glittering rings that obscured the stars. In the mountains it snowed all year round.

So much had happened. The swift victory Gnawdwell had wanted had not come. In many places the Great Uprising had not gone to plan, and the Great War against the dwarfs dragged on and on. The land of the frog-things and lizard-things had been annihilated, most of Clan Pestilens along with it, while in the lowlands in the ruins of the man-thing's lands, the skaven conquered, only to fracture along clan lines. Such was the way of skaven. Alliance with the followers of Chaos had come, a move that made many on the Council, Gnawdwell included, deeply uneasy.

That was politics, and it was not for Queek. During that time Queek had fought the length of the Worlds Edge Mountains, destroying dwarf strongholds one by one, and exterminating their inhabitants wherever they were to be found. Clan Mors had grown rich on the plunder.

Finally, Queek had been ordered to Beard-Thing Mountain-place, where all attempts to take the dwarf capital had failed. Gnawdwell, inscrutable as always, continued his attempts on Queek's life, simultaneously releasing the full might of Clan Mors and ordering it to go to Queek. Queek had not been back to Skavenblight in the years since their last meeting, wary of Gnawdwell's intentions, but for the time being Queek seemed to be in his lord's favour. All Clan Mors's allies and thralls, from the Grey Mountains, Skavenblight and beyond, came with the Great Banner of Mors. Karak Eight Peaks had been emptied, leaving it an empty tomb for the many warriors who had fallen there in the long years of war.

The dwarf realms had been reduced to but one, the mightiest, the greatest. Karaz-a-Karak, Everpeak, as dwarfs and men respectively called it. Beard-Thing Mountain, as the skaven called it. A name supposed to convey their contempt, but uttered always with fear. Under skies perpetually darkened and striated with the sickly colours of wild magic, the skaven marched to bring their four thousand-year war with the Karaz Ankor to its end.

'This whole pass stinks-reeks of dwarf-thing,' said Queek, sniffing tentatively. His tail twitched. The scent of the dwarfs had become inextricably linked with bloodshed in Queek's mind, and thus with excitement. It never failed to arouse his sluggish pulse, to excite his aged heart.

'What does the mighty warlord expect it to smell of?' said Kranskritt haughtily. The presence of Ikit Claw made the grey seer arrogant. Despite the long enmity between their clans, the two of them were knot-tailed much of the time, constantly tittering and squeak-whispering just out of Queek's earshot, or so they thought. Queek's hearing was better than he let on.

Queek growled by way of reply. He was in no mood to bandy insults with the seer. Kranskritt still smelt youthful to Queek, granted unnaturally long life by the Horned Rat. Even those grey seers without alchemical or mechanical aid could be known to reach the ridiculously advanced age of sixty. Not like Queek. Queek was old, he felt it. Kranskritt could smell it. Weakness.

'It will smell of burrow and home soon enough,' said Ikit. 'We will smash the beard-things and take their heads. No more dwarf-things! All done. All ours.'

'This is true. Once enough failures accrue, they call for Queek. No one is better than Queek at killing dwarf-things. Queek will end this siege. Queek will win this war!'

The dead things on his back wailed and gibbered. What they said now made little sense. When their utterances became intelligible, what they said made Queek's fur crawl. Their voices never ceased. The long periods of quiet he had once enjoyed were no more. Even when the verminlords were close, which had been rarely of late, they did not stop their racket.

'Not without my help,' said Ikit. He too, under his mask of iron, had aged better than Queek. Queek could smell the long-life elixir on him. 'I am the pre-eminent slaughterer of dwarf-things. They call me here to finish it – you are only to help.'

'Yes-yes,' said Queek sarcastically. 'Queek hear many times of great Ikit Claw's impressive victory over orange-furs of Kadrin-place. I hear the flesh of the dead so poisonous after Ikit Claw's masterful plan not even trolls would eat it, and even now, three cold-times since big death there, the air is still deadly to breathe. Very good plan, making such a fine mountain-holdfast uninhabitable to skaven clan-packs. Very clever way of denying living space to Clan Skryre's enemies.'

'And the dwarf-things,' said Ikit, his voice ringing inside his iron mask. How Queek had grown to loathe that voice.

Queek found the warlock engineer even more irksome than the grey seer, although he was secretly relieved that the warlock's clanking pace allowed him to walk more slowly. Ikit's war engines were impressive, even if it annoyed him to admit it to himself. A lesser clan might scrape together enough warp-tokens to buy one or two lightning cannons from Clan Skryre. A greater clan might have a dozen. In the siege train of their army there were hundreds, dragged painstakingly through tunnels and mountains to assail this last enduring rock of the dwarf-things. No other warlord clan could access such materiel. As a result of Gnawdwell's manoeuvring, Skryre and Mors were open allies. The supply of sorcerous machines had been cut off to all other clans. Clan Eshin had not been drawn into the pact, but provided Queek's army with their warriors anyway. Clan Moulder backed all sides, so consequently many of their creatures, and specifically the newer rat ogre weapon-beasts bred in conjunction with Clan Skryre, supported his troops. With Skryre came the larger part of Clan Rictus's clanrats. From Rictus, Ikit Claw had his own bodyguard, the Clawguard, war-scarred stormvermin as large and imposing as Queek's own Red Guard. At Queek's back went one of the largest skaven armies ever to brave the surface.

'The fate of more than the dwarfs depends upon this war,' said

Kranskritt. 'Remember, O ignoble and most devious warlords, whoever takes Thorgrim-Whitebeard's head will win the seat on the Council of Thirteen. Most assuredly it will be I, and Clan Scruten will regain its rightful place.'

Queek snorted. Poor-fool Kranskritt. He was naive to the point of idiocy, not like mighty Queek! Gnawdwell had forged a pact with the other Lords of Decay, stipulating this final condition for victory in the struggle for the seat. Tired of the long years of instability the empty seat had provoked, the other clans had agreed. Clan Mors and Clan Skryre had steered events masterfully so far. Together they would claim the head of Thorgrim and break the power of the grey seers forever.

Queek wondered how long Clan Skryre had been working themselves into this position. He had no doubt that the head of the dwarf king, once he took it, would find its way into the paws of Clan Skryre, who would at the last cheat Gnawdwell. Who would stop them? Clan Pestilens were mostly destroyed in the war for Lustria.

Mighty Queek, that was who. He recalled the scratch marks on the order scroll that had arrived six weeks ago, and which he had swiftly eaten. Gnawdwell would allow Queek some of the long-life elixir, if he brought the head of the long-fur to him.

Finally, finally. Queek could not wait. He had tasted infirmity and had no liking for it.

Kranskritt was being cossetted and fooled. Even the verminlords were being played off against each other. Or were they deceiving the Council? The interminable power plays of the skaven court made Queek's teeth ache. Ever dismissive of politics, he had grown careless over the last few years, openly provocative. He set out to deliberately antagonise the heads of other clan clawpacks. Only his reputation, his distance from Skavenblight, and his own skill at arms kept him alive.

He bites his own tail, just to see it bleed, others said of him. 'Doom, doom, doom! Death, death, death!' wailed the chorus of his victims.

Only when he had a battle to fight did the ailments of mind and body recede.

The endless column of skaven crested a rise in the Silver Road Pass, and the capital of dwarf-kind came into view.

Queek was chief general of the most powerful warlord clan in all Skavendom. As such, he had seen Karaz-a-Karak many times before, but never so close. The mountain was colossal, one of the tallest in the world. Soaring above the pass and into the bruised clouds, its peak was lost to the boiling skies, its flanks dappled by the polychrome strangeness of magical winds. The raw stone had been shaped by generations of the dwarf-things, so that giant faces, hundreds of feet tall, glared challengingly at Queek. The main gate was yet many miles away, but even Queek's failing eyesight could see the dark smudge of its apex reaching high up into the cliff face that held it, surrounded on all sides by soaring bastions. The skaven leaders and their bodyguards left the road and mounted a hillock that blistered the side of the mountain. They clambered onto the rubble atop it. The beard-thing watchtower that had occupied the mound had been melted into bubbled slag. Streaks of metal in the contorted stone hinted at the fate of its garrison.

Kranskritt hissed, daunted by the sight of Everpeak. In contrast, Queek felt the confidence only those gifted with supreme arrogance can. Behind Queek stretched more clawpacks than had ever been assembled in one place. Millions of skaven were his to command. They marched by in an endless stream, their fur carpeting the road as far as the eye could see, from one end of the pass to the other. More moved underground, ready to attack from below.

'How will we take-cast down such a place?' said Kranskritt. 'There must be so many beard-things within.'

Ikit Claw laughed, his machinery venting green-tinged steam into the chill noon, as if it shared his amusement. 'The dwarf-things breed slowly. Many breeders produce no young. They were dying even before we challenged them for their burrows,' said Ikit. 'Surely you must know these things, wise one?'

Kranskritt shook his hand at the warlock. The bells on his wrist conveyed his irritation in tinkles. 'The will of the Horned Rat is my interest, not the breeding habits of lesser races.'

Ikit sniggered again.

'Are you sure this plan of yours will work, Queek?' said Kranskritt. He had stopped using the insincere flattery of their kind some time ago when speaking with the Headtaker. This social nicety had always annoyed Queek, but it annoyed him more that Kranskritt had ceased its use. 'It is rather simplistic, attacking directly.'

'Queek's plan is sound. We come on all fronts. Every shaft and hole will be assaulted at once, white-fur. And what does white-fur know of strategy? Thorgrim beard-king will not know where to defend. His forces will be scattered and easily worn down. This is the way of the dwarf-things – to stay behind their walls and fight, fool-meat that they are. We have the numbers, and they have no time. So declares mighty Queek.'

'It is still simple,' said Kranskritt. 'A pup-plan.'

Queek shrugged. 'The simpler the better, white-fur. How many grand schemes fail-wither due to incompetence and stupidity, or treachery? Treachery is so much the harder when there are fewer folds to hide in. Simple plan, Queek's plan, is best.'

'For this once, the mighty Queek speaks wisdom,' said Ikit Claw. 'All weak points are already known. This fortress has been attacked a hundred times, a thousand. There is nothing we do not know about it. Why waste time with cunning ruses to learn what we already know?'

'We have a long wait,' said Queek. 'We must meet-greet the clan warlords here and take command. Too long they have besieged the great beard-king. Thorgrim-dwarf-thing must be very sad at all this. He need not worry, for soon it will all be over. Mighty Queek is here!'

* * *

A day later Queek ordered the attack. Alone atop a newly broken statue, he watched the advance through brass looking glasses - made for him by a foolish warlock, who was dead as soon as he completed the commission. Let not know of Queek's weaknesses!

The slave legions went in first, if for no other reason than Queek had them, and they went in first by tradition. From their thousand gunports, the dwarfs gave fire.

He saw the light flashes of cannons long before he heard the sound. Rolling thunder filled the pass. The vast numbers of skaven looked puny in front of the great gates of Karaz-a-Karak.

The hundreds of lightning cannons in the skaven train were pushed into range and set up under fire. Warlocks squealed frantic orders. The guns elevated and replied.

Soon the vale at the doors of Karaz-a-Karak was thick with gunsmoke lit by discharges of greenish lightning. The skies overhead were dark, polluted by magic seeping into the world from the north. The thunders of the battle vied with those ripping the heavens apart. The imaginings of the most deranged flagellant of the Empire could not outmatch the scene. This was the end of the world, beating its apocalypse upon the stone doors of the dwarfs.

The skaven died in howling masses at the gate, the machines they dragged with them to penetrate it smashed to pieces before they ever reached the stone and steel. Slaves surged back and forth, waves on a beach capped by froths of blood as they were cut down by dwarf and skaven alike.

So it went. So Queek expected it to go, until one of the many attacks he had ordered from the underworld broke through and skaven got into the soft underbelly of Beard-Thing Mountain-place, silenced the guns one by one, and allowed his siege engines to approach unmolested. Queek had killed many examples of the myriad creatures that crowded the world, but his greatest pleasure, and his greatest skill, lay in killing dwarfs. He knew their minds well. They would sit behind their stout walls until nearly dead, and then likely as not they would march out, determined to kill as many of the enemy as they could before they themselves were killed.

'It will cost you many lives,' said the voice of Krug. Queek's ears stiffened. The voices had been constant yet incoherent for a very long time. Krug spoke clearly, without the respect he once had. Queek glanced behind him. From a spike on Queek's rack, Krug's eye sockets glimmered with wild magic.

'Yes-yes, but I have meat to spend. The dwarf-things do not,' said Queek.

'They will make you pay,' said Krug, and there was a note of pride and defiance in his voice.

'Do not be so sure, dead-thing!' Queek snapped. Krug's voice melted into gruff laughter, before rejoining the howling chorus of the others.

Queek scratched at his head; it was bloody from his constantly doing so. The voices receded eventually.

The battle did not proceed as he expected.

The dwarf bombardment ceased. The last thunder of their discharge rolled and died. Queek watched, fascinated, as smoke puffed from the gunports and blew away. The lightning cannons went on firing unchallenged, blasting showers of rock from the mountain and its fortifications. Surely his infiltrators had not succeeded so quickly?

The great horns mounted high up the mountain blared: first one, then the other, their mournful, bovine hooting joined by hundreds of others from every covered walkway and battlement carved into the mountain. The noise of it was dreadful, and Queek flinched from it. Under it there came a great groaning creak.

'The gates! The gates!' he said excitedly, moving his field glasses from the gunports to the doors.

He fiddled with the focusing wheels, cursing their maker as the vista became a blur. He pulled the view back into focus in time to see a gleaming host emerge from the gates of Karaz-a-Karak.

The king went at the fore upon his throne. He looked as if he rode a ship of gold upon a sea of steel.

From out of the gates, the last great throng of the dwarfs marched to meet their doom.

Queek lowered his glasses for a moment. His nose twitched in disbelief. His fading eyes did not deceive him. From the vale, the sounds of gruff beard-thing voices in song drowned out the crack of lightning cannons, and the clash of arms was louder still. Loudest of all was the voice of the king. Queek raised the glasses again. Thorgrim stood upon his throne platform, one finger tracing the pages of his open book. His words, though faint, were heard clearly by Queek even from so far away.

'For the death of Hengo Baldusson and the loss of ninety-seven ore carts of gromril, five hundred thaggoraki heads. For the loss of the lower deeps of Karak Varn, two thousand thaggoraki hides. For the cruel slaying of the last kinsfolk of Karak Azgal, nine hundred tails and hides. For the...'

His recitation of his grudges roared from him, the atrocities of four thousand years of war driving his warriors onwards. Queek watched in disbelief. For the dwarf-things to sally out so early was unheard of! He panned across the column. There were hundreds of beard-things. Thousands! He gave a wicked smile.

'The whole army of Beard-Thing Mountain comes to make war on Queek!' he tittered. 'Very kind, oh very considerate, of Thorgrim dwarf-king to bring his head to Queek's sword!'

As the dwarfs advanced into the seething mass of skaven, the guns of the walls spoke all at once. Cones of fire immolated hundreds of slaves, while cannon balls streaked overhead, the guns' aim recalibrated, to shatter dozens of the lightning cannons.

A good loss, thought Queek. He laughed as he watched Clan Skryre's pride battered by the vastly superior dwarfish artillery force. No matter how many war engines they dragged up here, the dwarf-things would always have more. Open space before the gates became a killing field, a zone of destruction advancing in front of the dwarfs in a devastating creeping bombardment.

The skavenslaves predictably broke. They fled away from the vengeful dwarf-things only to be slaughtered by the skaven stationed behind them. They went into a panicked frenzy, tearing each other apart, gnawing on anything to escape. This was a fine exploitation of the explosive violence of the skaven's survival instinct, and had won many battles on its own. But every dwarf was armed and armoured in fine gear. The weapons they carried glowed with runes, Thorgrim's dread axe brightest of all. The Axe of Grimnir shone as if sensing the rising tide of war, emitting a radiance that could be seen far down the gloomy pass. The throng of armoured bodies shone blue in its reflected effulgence.

The dwarfs waded through the frenzied slaves regardless of their snapping mouths and their insensate fighting. Weapon-light pushed back the twilight of the dying world. Queek had never seen so many magical weapons deployed in one place. He would not have thought there so many in the world. Queek's triumphal squeaking quieted as the dwarfs cleaved their way relentlessly through the slave legion and into the clawpacks waiting behind. Skaven died in droves. Soon enough, the dwarfs were through the slaves and trampling Clan Rictus and Clan Mors banners underfoot.

A titanic boom rumbled from a few miles up the pass. Queek swung his glasses around, catching sight of the sides of the pass collapsing along a good mile of the road. The rocks peeled away either side to bury thousands of his troops, and his better ones at that, in deadly avalanches. Pale new cliffs shone in the war-choked gloom, menacing as bared fangs.

No, this was not quite as good as he first thought. Still, the inevitable was happening. The dwarfs drove forward. Caught up in their hatred, they were moving further and further away from the gates. The guns would soon stop for fear of killing their own. Something Queek himself had no qualms about.

Making his decision, Queek secreted his seeing aid within his robes.

'Loyal Ska!' he called.

The great skaven limped around a boulder that had until recently been the nose of a dwarf king.

'Coming, O mighty one,' he said. Ska too was old and slow, but his arm was still stronger than that of any other.

'Order up the next clawpack! Make the dwarf-things rage. Soon-soon they go out of range of their guns, fool-things. Ready Queek's Red Guard. When the beard-things are tired, when they are alone, then Queek will attack and add the head of the last king to his collection!'

'Yes, great one,' said Ska with a curt bow.

'Ska?'

'Yes, O mightiest and bloodiest of warlords?'

Queek looked back into the valley, the battle a shifting blur without his glasses. The noise from below told him all he needed to know. He had seen many dwarf armies at bay before, fighting to their last out of sheer, stubborn vindictiveness. A sight that was as glorious as it was terrifying. 'The long war is nearly over.'

'For the slaughter of the miners of Karak Akrar, fifty thaggoraki hides!' roared Thorgrim. The power of the throne was in him, the pain of his wound dulled by his hatred. The stink of the rat creatures surrounding him angered him further. Only their blood could slake the terrible thirst for vengeance he felt. 'For the deaths of Runelord Kranig and his seven apprentices, and the loss of the rune of persistence, nine hundred tails!' The Axe of Grimnir hummed with power as it bit into worthless furry hides.

'Onward, onward! Crush them all! Queek is impudent – we shall meet him head on and take his head!'

His army, initially reluctant, were overcome with their loathing. Every dwarf fought remorselessly.

Thorgrim spoke of Karak Azul, and Zhufbar, and the sack of Barak Varr, and the endless litany of unpaid-for wrongs that stretched back to the Time of Woes. The orders he gave were few and barked impatiently. Always he read from the Great Book of Grudges. He became a conduit for grudgement; millennia of pain and resentment flowed out from its hallowed pages through him.

The slaves were all dead. By now the dwarfs had pierced deep into the skaven army, moving away from the gates to where the vale was wider. The outlying elements reached the thaggoraki weapon positions. At the vanguard went the Kazadgate Guardians. These well-armed veterans had pushed into the war machines and were cutting their crews down. Their irondrake contingent, the Drakewardens, drove off reinforcements coming to save the machines with volleys from their guns. Their handcannons crippled the war machines, and warp generators exploded one after another in green balls of fire. The surviving warlocks squealed in anguish to see their machines destroyed.

A clashing of cymbals heralded a counter-charge led by a skaven in an armoured suit that hissed steam. Thorgrim, up on his throne, had a fine vantage point and recognised him as Ikit Claw.

'For the warpstone poisoning of the Drak River, the life of Ikit Claw!' he said, pointing out the warlock.

Claw came with a thick mob of stormvermin, but these were cut down easily by axe and forge-blast. Ikit Claw attempted to rally his followers, casting fire and lightning from his strange devices at the ironbreakers and irondrakes. But the Drakewardens walked through the fire unscathed. Their return fire blasted the stormvermin around Claw to bits. He wavered,

Thorgrim thought, but a terrific racket drowned out the battle-chants of the dwarfs as a dozen doomwheels came barrelling over a rise. Too late to save their cannon, the doomwheels exacted revenge for their loss, running down a good portion of the Kazadgate Guardians.

At this insult, Thorgrim took pause. He had come right out in front – too far in front. In the wider vale, the dwarfs had no way of protecting their flanks, and his army was being encircled, broken up into separate islands of defiance. They were gleaming redoubts in a universe of filth. Thorgrim could count the warriors remaining to him, and their numbers dwindled. The skaven were effectively infinite.

Thorgrim looked from side to side. His Everguard and throne stood alone, one of the smallest of these islands. His fury was the greatest and had carried him furthest.

The Great Banner of Clan Mors, festooned with obscene trophies, was approaching him at the head of Queek's Red Guard. Alongside it came rat ogres of a new and vicious kind, bearing whirring blades instead of fists, smoke belching from the engines upon their backs.

The High King and his bodyguard were cut off. The nearest group of his army had noted the peril he was in and were fighting desperately to come to him. They hewed down skaven by the hundred, but there were always more to fill the gap. They might as well fight quicksand. By the time the other dwarfs reached the High King, it would be too late.

'Bold dawi,' said Thorgrim. 'Queek comes. We shall meet their charge.'

His Everguard reformed into a square, clearing space in the skaven horde for their manoeuvre with their hammers. Thorgrim spied Queek's back banner at the front of the formation moving to attack them.

'Stand firm!' he called. 'In our defiance, eternity is assured!'

Queek broke into a run, coming ahead of his followers, his

yellow teeth bared, the pick that had taken the lives of so many dwarfs raised high.

Queek vaulted over the front line of the Everguard, cutting one of them down. Before he landed, the lines of dwarf and skaven met with a noise that shook the mountain.

Queek had not waited for the best time, thought Thorgrim; he would have been better served holding off for a few more minutes. But it was still a good time, he thought ruefully.

The Everguard were the elite of the dwarf elite, warriors bred to battle, whose fathers' fathers had served the kings of Karaz-a-Karak since the dawn of the Eternal Realm. The Red Guard could not hope to match them.

Queek, however, could. Thorgrim was chilled at how easily the skaven seemed to slaughter his warriors, spinning and leaping. Every thrust and swipe of his weapons spelled death for another dwarf, while their own hammers thunked harmlessly into the spot the skaven lord had been a moment before. There were still many ranks of Everguard between Thorgrim and Queek, but time was not on their side.

'I'll not wait to be challenged by that monster! Forward, thronebearers. Forward! Everguard, you shall let me pass as your oaths to me demand!'

In dismay, the Everguard parted, fearing for the life of their king. They were beset on all sides, the rat ogres chewing through their right flank. The dwarfs killed far more skaven than died themselves, but they fought the same battle every dwarfhold had fought and lost: a hopeless war of attrition.

'Forward! Forward! Bring me to him so that he might feel the kiss of Grimnir's axe!'

The shouts of dwarfs were becoming more insistent. They were far out of the range of their guns. The cannons spoke still, slaughtering every skaven that came close to the gates, but the greater part of the throng of Karaz-a-Karak was isolated, and surely doomed.

Thorgrim reached the front line. His axe sent the head of a rat ogre spinning away. His Everguard cheered as it died. He would not allow that he had doomed his hold and the Eternal Realm. Only victory was on his mind; it was the only possible outcome. The magic in the throne reached up, lending strength to him through the metal of his armour and weapons. Queek changed course. He was twenty feet away, then ten. The square of dwarfs shrank as more of their number fell, Thorgrim's thronebearers stepping back in unison with them.

The end was coming.

'For Karaz-a-Karak! For the Karaz Ankor!' Thorgrim shouted, and prepared himself for his ancestors' censure for his foolishness.

Horns sang close at hand. Dwarf horns.

Thorgrim eviscerated a rat ogre. It went down, teeth still clashing. He lifted his eyes upwards. Against the glow of the shrouded sun, he picked out figures. The silhouette of a banner emerged over a bluff, as down an almost invisible game trail, dwarfs came.

Atop the banner gleamed a winged ale tankard.

'Bugman is here! Bugman comes!' shouted the dwarfs, and swung their tired arms harder.

Bugman's rangers were few in number, no more than a hundred. Vagabonds who roamed the wastelands behind their vengeful leader, survivors of the sacking of Bugman's famous brewery, they were scruffy and ill-kempt. But each and every one was an implacable warrior, as skilled in the arts of death as he was in brewing. Crossbow bolts hissed into the Red Guard's rear. Surefooted dwarfs ran down the steep slope, tossing axes at the greater beasts and bringing them down. A brighter light shone, that of fire, and what Thorgrim saw next burned itself into his memory.

Ungrim of Karak Kadrin was with Bugman's rangers. On him too was a strange, magical glow. His eyes burned with the heat of the forge. The Axe of Dargo trailed flame, the crest on his helmet elongated by tongues of fire. With a desolate roar of rage and loss, the last Slayer King launched himself twenty feet from a cliff top straight into the skaven ranks. Burning bodies were hurled skywards with every swipe of his axe. Behind him came many Slayers, the last of his kin and his subjects, each one orange-crested and bare-chested. They scrambled down rocks and set about their bloody work. Night runners detached themselves from the shadows, hurrying to intercept the reinforcements, but they were slaughtered, flung back, their remnants scurrying away back into obscurity.

'Bugman! Ungrim!' laughed Thorgrim. His face changed. 'Queek,' he said quietly. He ordered his thronebearers to set down his throne. 'Headtaker! I call you! Queek! My axe thirsts for vengeance. Come to me and with your blood we shall strike many grudges from the Dammaz Kron!'

Heaving himself up out of the Throne of Power, Thorgrim marched upon Queek in open challenge.

TWENTY-SIX

The Death of a Warlord

His troops were letting him down again! Queek smelt the fear-stink, heard the calling of beard-thing instruments and the change of pitch in their shouts from despair to excitement.

'Must finish this quick-fast,' he muttered.

The Horned Rat must have heard Queek. Thorgrim approached him, stepping down off his land-boat, bellowing Queek's name.

'Good-good,' snickered Queek. 'Very good! Here dwarf-thing, a spike is waiting, much company for the long face-fur!'

Queek flicked his wrist, spinning Dwarf Gouger, and took up his battle stance. With one finger he beckoned Thorgrim onwards.

Thorgrim shouted at him, his voice deeper than the pits of Fester Spike. 'Queek! Queek! For the death of Krug Ironhand! The head of Queek!'

Queek laughed at his petty grievances.

'Queek flattered that mighty beard-thing not need his special book to recount Queek's fame!'

'For the illegal occupation of Karak Eight Peaks! The head of

Queek!' shouted Thorgrim. The dwarf-thing's eyes were glazed and spittle coated his beard. Quite mad, thought Queek. Good.

'Queek is coming!' trilled Queek, and laughed. 'Queek killed many dwarf-things – soon there will be no more left to kill. This makes Queek sad. Maybe Queek take a few of High King Thorgrim-thing's littermates back to Skavenblight for fighting practice? Truly Queek is merciful.'

Roaring his hatred, Thorgrim charged, just as Queek had anticipated. Dwarfs were a weak race; their affection for their pups and littermates made them easy to goad. Such a pity, Queek had wanted this duel to be one to savour in the long years ahead, when he grew young on Gnawdwell's elixirs and there were no more dwarf-things in the world to slay.

Queek waited until Thorgrim was so close he could see the red veins threading his tired eyes before launching his rightly famed attack. Queek leapt, his age forgotten, his body spinning. He drew his sword and simultaneously swung the weighted spike of Dwarf Gouger at Thorgrim's helmet. Queek's mind worked quickly, so fast the world appeared to move more slowly to him than to those of longer-lived races. He did not know it, but it was a blessing in some ways, this rapid life cycle. Queek could enjoy the sight of his weapon spike hurtling towards the dwarf's face in unhurried slowness.

Queek blinked. Thorgrim swept up his axe. Impossible! The runes on the axe shone as bright as the hidden sun, searing their image onto Queek's eyes. He could not read the scratch marks, but in one terrible moment of understanding their meaning became clear: Death. Death to the enemies of the dwarfs!

Dwarf Gouger met the axe. The rune-shine whited out his vision, and he knew if he survived his eyes would never recover. Dwarf Gouger shattered on the edge of the blade with a bang and discharge of freed magic. Queek landed, panicked. He thrust at Thorgrim with his sword, seeking to make him dodge aside so that Queek could put distance between them. But the snarl nested in the thing's long face-fur grew more ferocious. He grabbed Queek's sword in his armoured fist and yanked him forwards. Queek scrambled to get back, but could not. So unusual was the situation that he did not think to release his sword's hilt until it was too late. Thorgrim dropped his axe and grabbed Queek by the throat, lifting him high into the air. Only then did Queek let his sword go, and Thorgrim flipped it around, using it to cut loose Queek's treasured back banner. The dead things' heads fell, screaming in exultation, free at last.

'For the Battle of Karak Azul, the head of Queek,' rasped Thorgrim, his voice ruined by his screaming.

Queek squirmed and thrashed, his teeth clashing in panic. He braced his legs against Thorgrim, trying to flip backwards. His world turned black around the edges. Queek scrabbled with his hand-paws, raking at the king's face.

'For the killing of Belegar Angrund, rightful king of Karak Eight Peaks, the head of Queek,' spat Thorgrim.

Queek's struggles weakened. His frantic gouging became more precise. He gave up trying to hurt Thorgrim and desperately attempted to pry the dwarf's granite grip loose. The fingers would not shift, and Queek's own bled as his claws tore loose on the king's impenetrable armour. Thorgrim tightened his grip. Queek's choking became wet, feeble as the death croaks of a dying slave-rat.

The king pulled Queek level with his bearded face. 'For the death of many thousand dawi, the head of Queek. Now die, you miserable son of the sewers.'

The last thing Queek ever saw were the eyes of Thorgrim Grudgebearer, burning with vengeance.

Thorgrim shook the skaven. Queek's neck snapped. His body went limp, but Thorgrim continued to squeeze, the litany of woes he shouted at Queek transforming into a long, inchoate roar.

At last, he dropped the body at his feet and stamped upon it with ironshod boots, shattering Queek's bones. He spat on it with disdain.

'You can keep your head upon its neck, thaggoraki. I'll not have it sully my halls.'

Thorgrim retrieved the Axe of Grimnir and gestured to his thronebearers. The skaven were in full flight, mad panic radiating out from the points where Thorgrim stood and where Ungrim slaughtered them. Queek's Red Guard were smashed down as they broke.

'That's right! Flee, you worthless, honourless cowards!' shouted Thorgrim. The sun had sunk below the level of the boiling clouds, and a golden light shone on the battlefield, as if the strange aura of his throne had expanded to take in the whole of the vale.

Satisfied at what he saw, he turned and walked back towards his throne, his bearers kneeling in anticipation. He looked forward to striking out many grudges today.

Unseen by the king, a black-clad skaven flitted from the churning mass of fleeing ratmen and ran at him. Too late, one of his thronebearers called a warning, dropping the throne and raising his axe to protect his lord. His bodyguard were too far away to intercept it, caught up in the merciless slaughter the battle had become. Thorgrim was exposed and alone, surrounded by bodies.

The assassin leapt as Thorgrim began to turn, drawing two long daggers that wept black poisons. It drove them down, putting all its momentum into the strike with a victorious squeal. The blades shattered upon the Armour of Skaldour, and Thorgrim dispatched the creature, opening its body from collarbone to crotch with the Axe of Grimnir.

Thorgrim flicked the blood from his rune axe and remounted his throne as a ragged cheer went up. All around the skaven were fleeing. Trapped by the avalanches unleashed by the dwarfs, they had nowhere to run, only a few making it over the broken mountainside blocking the road back to the safety of their tunnels. They still outnumbered the dwarfs five hundred times, but their flight was unstoppable. Only Queek could have halted them, and Queek was dead.

'Destroy them all! Destroy them!' shouted Thorgrim. 'Let none escape!' Cannon and gunfire slew those who attempted to run towards Karaz-a-Karak in the confusion. Ungrim and his Slayers cut down the warlock engineers, Ungrim's axe blasted fire over their leader. Thorgrim saw Ikit Claw fall. He watched to see him rise again, but he did not. Another grudge answered.

A roaring filled the vale as gyrobombers flew over the king, stirring his beard hair with their progress. They swooped low, bomb racks rattling, blasting the skaven apart. Ungrim's fire consumed those few ratkin who tried to reform.

The battle was over. Thorgrim saw the greatest victory of his time play out around him, and it felt good. But the strange power had left him and his throne. It gleamed only as much as gold could gleam, and his armour felt heavy upon him again. He sent a silent prayer to Grungni for his aid, if that was indeed who had sent it.

'My king!' said a thronebearer. Thorgrim glanced down to the ashen face of Garomdok Grobkul.

Thorgrim felt ice in his heart. Somehow, he knew what Garomdok was about to say before he said it.

'The Rune of Azamar, my king, it is broken!'

TWENTY-SEVEN

Eternity's End

At the edge of the battlefield, three dwarf lords watched their kin go about their sorrowful work.

'I could not save them,' said Ungrim Ironfist. Fire still flickered around him, on his axe and in his eyes, but it could not hide his despair. 'I marched too far from my gates, filled with thoughts of vengeance. They sprang their trap. Three of their abominations breached the gates. They had within them bombs full of gas...' His face contorted. He could not understand why anyone would do such a thing. 'Everyone, everything... It is all gone, gone!'

'Rest easy, lad,' said Josef Bugman, who had a particularly disrespectful way with kings. 'Here, let me get you something for your nerves.'

Bugman beckoned over one of his warriors, a young dwarf already scarred and grim-eyed from many battles. Bugman took a tankard from him and offered it to Ungrim. 'Fit for a king,' he said encouragingly.

The Slayer King stared at him, deep in shock. 'I am not a king any more. I have failed in one oath. Only by fulfilling the other can I make amends.'

All over the battlefield dwarfs worked, retrieving their lamentable number of dead. There were many runic items scattered amid the gore. These were attended to even before the slain, while a large block of troops stood ready, in case the skaven mounted another attack, took them unawares and armed themselves with the treasures of their ancestors. Dusk had fallen. Night came quickly, abetted by the fumes that clogged the sky and kept the sun away.

'Drink,' said Bugman encouragingly.

'No, no, I will not,' said Ungrim. 'I cannot rest, I will not rest. My Slayers and I will go to the Empire, to lend what aid we can to the Emperor, if he still lives.'

'All need light in dark days,' said Bugman.

'Grimnir is with me,' said Ungrim.

'At least let me give you a few casks of ale for your warriors. They'll march further and fight harder with a little of my XXXXXX in their bellies.'

Ungrim nodded, and Bugman gave the necessary orders. The last dwarfs of Karak Kadrin, unsmiling though they were, were nevertheless grateful.

Thorgrim and Bugman watched them go into the fast-falling night, Ungrim's fiery aura making of him a living torch to light the way.

'A kingly gift, Master Brewer,' said Thorgrim.

'I am not a king either, High King,' said Bugman affably. 'But I do what I can.' He sighed. 'A bad business this. A bad, bad time.'

'It is a time we cannot recover from,' said Thorgrim quietly. 'Look at Ungrim. Karak Kadrin fell three years ago and he behaves as if it were yesterday. If we prevail, shall we all be the same? Broken-minded, fit only to roam the lands of our ancestors?'

'Steady now, that's not like you to say so, king.'

'The Rune of Azamar is broken,' said Thorgrim.

To them both, the mountain breeze blew a little more chill. Silently, Thorgrim led Bugman round the back of the throne and pointed out the awful truth. There was no light to the rune, and a long, fine crack ran across it from top to bottom.

Bugman tamped down tobacco into the bowl of his pipe and sat down upon a rock. Behind them, dwarfs shouted and chisels clattered as the stonemasons' guild repaired what damage they could to the walls. Bugman blew out a long plume of smoke. 'Aye,' he said at last. 'I am not surprised.'

'The Karaz Ankor will fall.'

'What about Ungrim? The light of Grungni was on him. Surely that's worth something.'

Thorgrim eased himself down next to the old brewer. 'It's not the light of Grungni. Something similar affected me too, filling my armour and weapons with might. Ungrim is possessed by some fire spirit, and I think something rooted in the spirit of metal came to me.'

'Is it gone now?'

Thorgrim nodded.

'Well,' said Bugman, 'Grungni or not, there's still good in this world, that's for sure.' He gave the king a penetrating stare. 'Will you drink with me, High King? You'll not refuse my brew too, will you now?'

Thorgrim was taken aback. 'A king can refuse many things, Master Brewer, but never a sup from Bugman's own barrels.'

'Good for you,' said Bugman. 'But I can do better than my own barrel. I reckon you could do with a bit of pepping up. Here, drink from my own tankard. You'll never taste its like, I promise.' The dwarf passed over a battered pewter tankard. Once finely worked, it seemed to have taken much hard use and its decorations were worn smooth where they were not tarnished.

The High King took the tankard from Bugman. It brimmed with frothy ale, although the cup had been but moments before hanging empty at the brewer's belt. The colour was perfect: a deep, golden brown, as pure as a young rinn's eyes. And its bouquet... Thorgrim lacked the words to describe it. Just smelling the beer made him lightheaded. He immersed himself in the sensation. It brought back memories of happier days, and he forgot all his woes.

Bugman chuckled. 'Go on then, don't just stare at it! Drink up, I swear by Grungni's long beard you'll feel better for it.'

Thorgrim did as he was told, even though part of him did not want the moment of expectation to pass. He put the pewter to his lips and drank deeply of the ale. Warmed to perfection, it tasted finer than anything he had ever partaken of before, and he'd enjoyed plenty of Bugman's ales in the past.

As he drank it down, a glow as golden and clean as the colour of the beer seeped into his limbs. There was a brief, vicious stab in his side as the wound seemed to fight back, but it was overwhelmed, and the warmth pushed aside the dirty, itching pain the injury caused him. He drank half the tankard down, of that he was sure, before pulling it away. His gasp of satisfaction turned to one of amazement. The tankard was still full.

'Take another pull, O king,' said Bugman.

The king did. When he finished, he patted his side, then prodded it, then poked hard. Nothing.

'The wound is not healed, I'm afraid,' said Bugman. 'It's too far gone for even my old great-granddad's tankard to fix with a couple of draughts. But you won't feel it for a while, and it might just tip it onto the right road to be mended. The curative powers of the mug and my ancestor's best brew. You'll not get that anywhere else now but from my own pot. Count yourself privileged.'

Thorgrim, usually so stern, was wide-eyed. 'It is the greatest honour I have enjoyed in a long time, Master Brewer.'

'Isn't it just?' said Bugman. He looked the king dead in the eye. For all his power and honourable ancestry, Thorgrim felt the battered ranger, born from the dwarf exodus, little better than city-dwelling umgdawi, to be far more than an equal to him.

'When my old dad's brewery burned to the ground, and my folk were all killed, I thought it was the end of the world.' He sighed, a spill of smoke twisting its way from his mouth. 'And it was the end of one. Another began. I am still here. Don't scratch out the dawi yet, High King. There's fight in us all still.'

Bugman hung his magic pint pot, now mysteriously empty again, from his belt. He stood up and offered his hand to the king, like they were two merchants in a bar and not a dispossessed brewer and the lord of all dwarfs. Thorgrim shook it.

'I'll be away now.' He looked into the night, broken only by the dwarfs' lamps and torches and the light streaming from the high windows of the forts. 'There are other dwarfs out there as need me.'

'Still?' said Thorgrim.

Bugman smiled down at the king. 'Aye, and there always will be. Whatever happens next, king of kings, don't ever forget that. We've lost a lot, that's for sure, but there's no use crying over spilt ale. As long as the mountains are made of stone, there'll be dwarfs in them, of that I've no doubt.'

Bugman lifted up his head, and let out a long trilling whistle. The call of the high mountain chough, not heard for years in those parts. It brought a tear to the king's eye.

Dark, solid shapes moved from out of the rocks. Thorgrim rubbed his eyes. He felt quite drunk. Bugman, seconds ago alone, was surrounded by his warriors.

'Look after those of my lads that fell here, king.'

Thorgrim nodded. Bugman winked and vanished into the dark.

Blearily Thorgrim got into his throne. From the vantage it offered, he looked about, but Bugman was nowhere to be seen. He suddenly felt very tired.

'I shall rest a moment,' he said. 'Just a moment.' He sat down, closed his eyes, and drifted off to the sound of dwarfs hard at work repairing the damage others had done.

* * *

Thanquol was nauseous. No matter how he held himself, he felt like he was about to fall over. The walls of the tower – he assumed it was a tower, but who knew if it was or if it was not – did not look right. He felt like he was standing at an angle even when he was quite straight. Wherever Lord Verminking had brought him was not of his world.

'Now we show you, as promised,' said the verminlord.

'What should I see?' asked Thanquol. He stared into the swirling scrye-orb Verminking produced out of nowhere.

'Doom, yes-yes. Doom which will lead to your ascension,' said the verminlord.

This did not exactly answer Thanquol. He had no idea how the swirling clouds within the orb amounted to doom, and how was he going to ascend? The grey seer was about to question the verminlord further when the mists of the globe coalesced into faintly glowing images. He was watching a dwarf-thing.

'The king of all dwarfs!' he whispered. 'How do you do-accomplish this? Dwarf scratch-magic makes see-scrying impossible.'

'Not to us,' said Verminking, tittering. 'We know things you shall never know. Concentrate. Think yourself inside his head. You will know all. You will know his thoughts, his heart, his mind. Breath-breath! Yes, yes, that is right. In, we skaven can steal into anything, why not another's soul? Listen to me, Thanquol, and you learn much, plenty-good magic...'

Thanquol's vision swam. And then he wasn't there any more.

Thorgrim Grudgebearer looked up the first curl of the spiral Stair of Remembrance. The walk to the King's High Porch atop Karaz-a-Karak was always an arduous climb, but right then the stairs were as daunting as a steep mountain slope. He was bone tired. He'd woken a few hours before dawn to find himself exhausted. A clean tiredness, that of the purged, but heavy upon him. He suspected his whole body ached, but could only feel the renewed throb of his wound. Bugman had been right, though. The returned pain was less than it had been before he drank from the fabled tankard. He supposed he should rest more, and he would, but this had to be done first. With his jaw set in determination, the High King began the journey up the spiral stair. Although he longed for sleep, this personal ritual, a way to both commemorate the fallen and ultimately to clear his head, had to be performed.

Despite his victory, his mind was awhirl. Ungrim – grown stranger than ever – had given the High King much to muse over, but that would have to wait. And Bugman, with his never-empty cup and unquenchable hope. Could it be the dwarfs would persist? Now the ale glow was gone, Thorgrim was not so sure, and his oaths to retake their ancient realm seemed laughable.

The stairs demanded his attention, and he turned it upon them. Up and up he wound, each step bringing him pain.

No one but the High King might use these stairs. The lookout at the top and its King's View was his privilege alone. It was High King Alriksson, Thorgrim's predecessor, who had shown Thorgrim the way, and even then he had not been permitted to look out, not until Alriksson was dead, and he had made the journey alone.

With each clumping step, Thorgrim remembered one of the slain from the day's battle. He recalled each dwarf, his name and clan. The journey took hours, yet Thorgrim always ran out of stairs before he ran out of names. The rest of the fallen must await his return trip.

Towards the top, the air grew very thin, and Thorgrim's lungs laboured hard, aggravating the pain in his side. Dwarf blood was thick, but the air was too sparse here even for them. His progress slowed. The last quarter took longer than the rest. He saved the names of the greatest of warriors for this difficult part of the climb.

At last he reached the top, a high dome carved right inside the very tip of the mountain, adorned with carvings unseen by any other eyes and lit with a king's ransom of ancient runic glim-lights. The sight always awed him slightly, a reminder of the power and glory of the old dwarf kingdom. Coming here was like ascending into the heavens themselves.

Outside, there were no longer any stars. Thorgrim pushed open the rune-heavy door to the porch. The stone slid outwards soundlessly.

Wind whistled around the edges. The air this high was icy and incredibly thin. Thorgrim took deep, panting breaths to stave off dizziness and stepped onto the shallow balcony of the King's High Porch. Twelve paces across, seven deep, a small balcony, whose balustrade pillars were fashioned in the shape of dwarf warriors. Cut from a natural bay in the mountain, the porch was invisible from below. When shut, the door behind Thorgrim blended seamlessly with the stone. Below him the high snow-fields of Karaz-a-Karak plunged downwards. The horizon to the east was a dull silver, the rising sun fighting against the murk. In the few clear patches of the night-gripped sky overhead, only rings of black-green could be seen, the whirling remnants of the cursed Chaos moon.

From the top of the world, Thorgrim looked down upon the lesser peaks. They marched away to every horizon, untroubled by the wars of the creatures who lived among them. Only now in this private spot did the High King begin to open and examine the chambers of his mind. Karaz-a-Karak had resisted, but for how long? And how much stock could he put in the legend of the Rune of Azamar? He wished Ungrim had remained behind – he had never expected Bugman to – but perhaps he could do something to aid the realms of men. In some of the few accounts Thorgrim had received, the Emperor was dead; in others he was alive, but his nation was a ravaged ruin. If he still lived, he would need all the help he could get.

Deep in thought, Thorgrim never saw the black shadow unfold from the rocky peak. Spider-like, it crawled down a cliff face before letting go.

'Assassin!' squealed Thanquol in his nowhere place.

'Hsst!' warned Verminking. 'Do not let your excitement alert the king to our presence. We are in his mind!' Then, more gently, he continued, 'This is the culmination of many scheme-plans. Deathmaster Snikch delivers the final blow to the dwarf-thing's empire. It has taken him long-long to work his way to the top of Beard-Thing Mountain-place. No other but he and Lurklox could have achieved it.'

'The king's armour...' began Thanquol doubtfully.

'He bears new knives, they are warpforged, each triple blessed by the retchings of the Verminlord Lurklox, Master of All Deceptions. They can slice through gromril as easily as incisors sink into a corpse. He will not fail, now hush, and watch!'

In mid-air, the dark shape somersaulted and drew forth its three blades - one in each hand and a third in its tail. With all the momentum of his fall, Snikch drove all three blades into his target.

Thorgrim staggered forwards, great stabs of pain coursing through him. Thanquol gasped, sharing a sliver of his agony. As the king fell to his knees, Thanquol fell to his. Through Thorgrim's eyes he could see the points of three blades jutting out of his chest, and for a gut-churning second, Thanquol thought it his own.

Thorgrim's last thoughts were for his people. Like a damned fool beardling he had left the door open behind him. There were so many grudges left unanswered. His last thought crystallised with painful clarity - of course, the hateful cowards had stabbed him in the back.

* * *

Thanquol's consciousness retreated from the dead king, and he observed the scene once again through the scrying-orb.

Tail lashing with excitement, Thanquol watched Snikch saw off the king's head with his tailblade. The Deathmaster kept watch on the open runic door, his tail performing the grisly deed by its own volition.

'That head will come to you, little horned one,' purred Verminking behind him. 'You must take-show it before the Council of Thirteen, Reclaim the grey seers' rightful place.'

'But... but... you told Verminlord Soothgnawer, many praises be upon him, that...'

Verminking chittered, half in amusement, half in exasperation. 'I had not expected such naivete from you, little seer.'

Thanquol, who had long anticipated himself on the Council of Thirteen, let his mind race with possibilities.

In the orb, the asssassin was scrawling runes upon the stone.

Verminking explained. 'He is summoning Lurklox. Dwarf scratch-magic prevents skitterleaping, but his scratch-markings will overcome them. Soon an army of gutter runners will be inside Karaz-a-Karak. They will open the gates for our rabble army. Clan Mors has been all but destroyed, but the lesser warlord clans wait in the deep tunnels, and they will be inside before the dwarf-things know. The dwarf realm will be utterly broken!'

'Then we have won, yes-yes?' asked Thanquol in surprise. The thought of it seemed... odd.

Verminking shook his head solemnly, his majestic horns swaying. 'We have won much, but not all. The lizard-things and their lands are dead-gone – but Clan Pestilens is broken. I sense Vermalanx and Throxstraggle's fury. Although,' he mused, 'we must not forget Skrolk, or the Seventh Plaguelord, for he is hidden within the Under-Empire even from my eyes. Clan Skryre has been humbled, but Ikit Claw just survived and will be dangerous. While more goes on in the minds of the Moulders than you know.'

Verminking looked down upon the grey seer, his enormous claw-hand patting Thanquol's head.

'And our new allies – the Everchosen, Chaos. They are most powerful of all, yes-yes. We need-must not tell you. Yet we, you and us, we will bide our time. One day it will all be ours.'

Thanquol smiled faithfully up at Verminking. The answer to how to conceal his true thoughts had been simple, when it came to him. As he guarded his words, he must guard his thoughts. All day he had been practising at obscuring his intentions from the verminlord behind a wall of sycophantic loyalty he built across his mind. Once he was certain of the method, he had thought the most treacherous thoughts he could. And Verminking did not hear! All through the battle he had done so without repercussion. He was growing in power.

Shielded by this mental redoubt, Thanquol plotted how he would rid himself of the verminlord for good, and use what he had learned to his greater advantage. He was Thanquol! The most cunning skaven who had ever lived. Lord Skreech Verminking would come to regret forgetting that.

'Yes-yes, O great one,' said Thanquol. His eyes narrowed. Soon he would be the master. Soon he would sit upon the Council of Thirteen in the mortal world. But why should he stop there? Unwittingly, the verminlord had opened endless worlds of opportunity to him.

Thanquol's face betrayed even less than his mind did. 'Your wishes are my commands,' he said, and meant not a word of it.

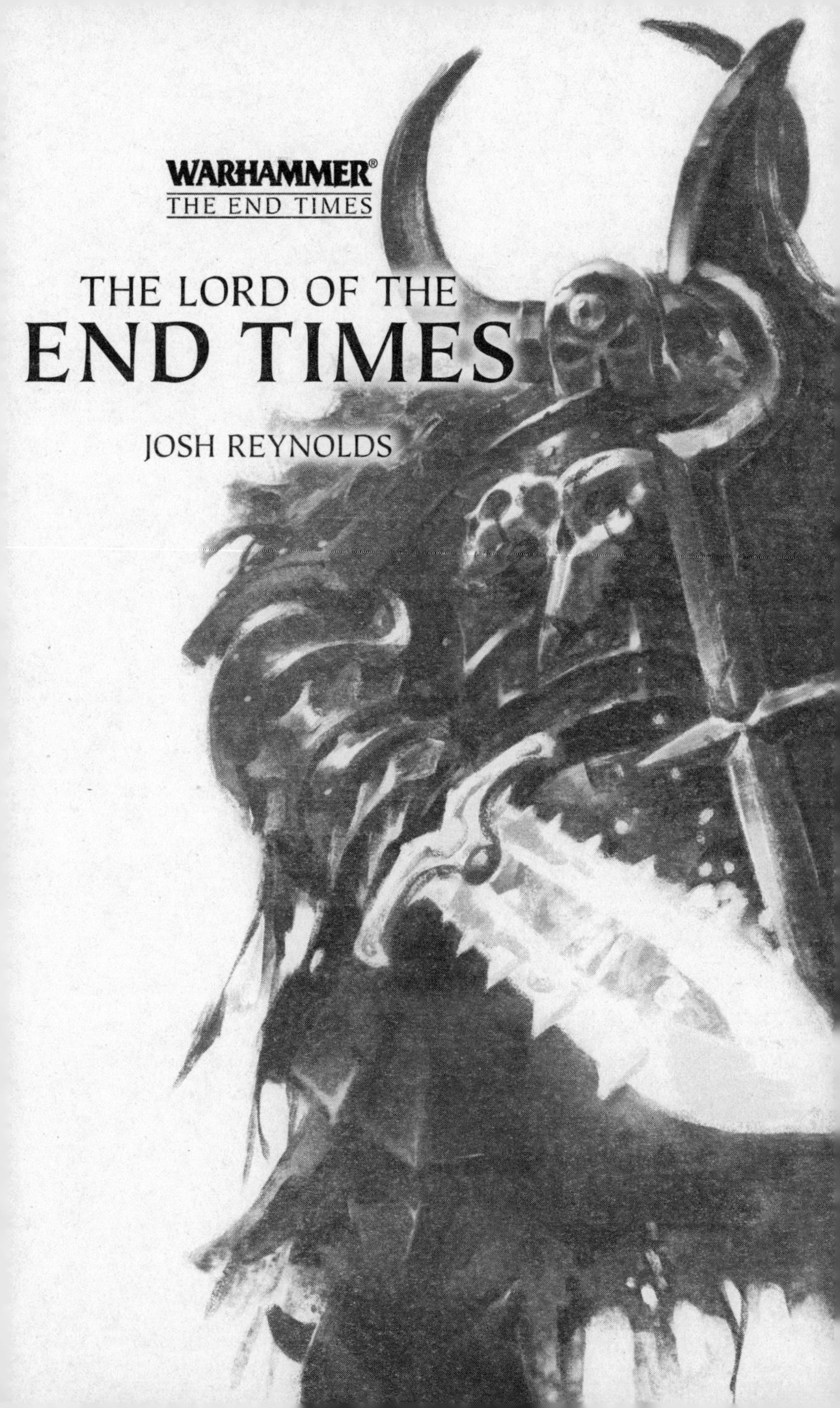
WARHAMMER®
THE END TIMES
THE LORD OF THE
END TIMES
JOSH REYNOLDS

THE LORD OF THE END TIMES

The end of the world is here. Archaon Everchosen, the Three-Eyed King, marches on the city of Middenheim, intent on seizing it – and a secret that has lain hidden beneath it since before the rise of man. In distant Athel Loren, the last heroes of men, elves and dwarfs gather their forces and prepare to wage their final war, to free the world from the tyranny of Chaos or die in the attempt. Their only hope is to harness the power of the Winds of Magic, now earthed in mortal hosts. But can the Incarnates of magic put aside their differences for long enough to save all that they hold dear, or will the world be crushed beneath the heel of the Lord of the End Times?

PROLOGUE

Autumn 2527

 *The Drakwald Forest*

The runefang slid from its sheath with a dreadful hiss. The blade shimmered crimson as it bit into the squealing ungor's neck and removed the beastman's verminous, almost-human head from its scrawny shoulders. The unlucky creature's comrades scrambled to avoid a similar fate, but the sword rose and fell in a display of red butchery, spattering the trunks of nearby trees with gore. The blade's wielder gave a harsh cry and his horse reared, one iron-shod hoof snapping out to catch a fleeing beastman in the back, snapping the wailing creature's spine.

Boris Todbringer, Elector Count of Middenheim, Marchlord of the Drakwald, twisted in his saddle, laying about him with the runefang. The sword, called 'Legbiter', seemed to hum with joy in his hand as it went about its work. It, like its master, took pleasure in the simple things in life and the shedding of blood was the simplest thing of all for such a weapon. Ungors screamed and died to blade and trampling hoof, and Todbringer roared with pleasure as each new carcass struck the soft loam of the forest floor.

'Come on then, come and die, filth,' he bellowed. 'Let Khazrak hear you scream.' An ungor leapt at him, a spear clutched in its hairy hands. The blade drew sparks as it scraped across his cuirass and he brought his shield edge down on the creature's skull, splitting it.

Todbringer smiled fiercely, despite the close call. He felt more alive now than he had for many years. He'd at last shifted the weight of responsibility to stronger shoulders, and was free to do as he wished. And what he wished was to hunt down the foe whose shadow had blighted his life for too long. The creature which had claimed the lives of his sons and taken his eye. The beast which had massacred his people and challenged his authority.

Khazrak would die. Even if the world was coming to an end, even if the Emperor himself fell, Khazrak would die. The beast must die. That certainty drove Todbringer on, and lent strength to his aching limbs as he hewed and slashed at the enemy like a man half his age – or one possessed. The world had narrowed to that singular point, and nothing else mattered. In some part of his mind, Todbringer wondered if killing the beast might not reverse the course the world had taken in the fraught months since the second fall of Altdorf.

The Empire was in flames. Even the most sceptical of men could see that the great kingdom which Sigmar had built was now turning to ash on its death-pyre. The plague-ravaged remains of Marienburg crawled with maggots and rot. Nuln was a rat-gnawed ruin, reduced to a blasted crater by the vermin which even now laid siege to Middenheim. Talabheim was a stinking shell, so poisonous and foul that it was avoided even by the armies of the Three-Eyed King. Even Altdorf, which had weathered the plague-storm that had consumed Marienburg, had fallen at last to the chittering hordes of the ratmen. The Emperor had fled south to Averheim, while others had come north, to the City of the White Wolf. His city.

A crude axe bounced from his shield and he urged his horse forwards into the press, trampling the beasts as they tried to form a ragged phalanx. His runefang, the sign of his authority, of his right of rule, sang a woeful song as he swept it out in a precise arc, lopping off spear heads and malformed limbs alike. 'Fight me, beasts,' he roared. 'Come and die, you spawn of a six-legged goat!'

Even nature itself was in rebellion. The skies roiled with crackling, magic-laden clouds and the birds and beasts had fled. The Drakwald was empty of all life save the mutated aberrations who now died beneath his sword. It was the End Times. That was what Gregor Martak had claimed, when he'd arrived alongside the so-called Herald of Sigmar, Valten – a former blacksmith, of all things! Martak might have been the Supreme Patriarch of the Colleges of Magic, but deep down he was still a country lad from Middenland, with soil in his ears and gloom in his heart, and Todbringer wouldn't have put much stock in his mutterings save for the evidence of his own eyes.

Martak and Valten had come, bringing men and news, and their army of stragglers, refugees and flagellants had breached the zigzag trench lines and burrowed encampments of the ratmen which had ringed Middenheim. Todbringer had welcomed them, though not the news they'd brought. Not at first, at least. They spoke of the fall of the great cities and more besides, of the collapse of the dwarf empire and the slow dissolution of Bretonnia. Tilea, Estalia, all of the great southern states were ashes as well, burned to cinders by the conflagration which even now pressed in on the remnants of the Empire.

The End Times. The thought was enough to send a shiver of uncertainty through him, even as he chopped down on a shield of wood and animal hide. The ungor brayed in fear as the runefang sought its heart. Todbringer grunted and sent the body slewing into its fellows with a flick of one thick wrist. The End Times. That was why he had heaved his responsibilities onto

Valten's broad shoulders, and named him Castellan of Middenheim. Let the Herald of Sigmar fight the war to end all wars. Todbringer had his own war: a smaller war, but of the utmost importance. If the world was coming to an end, then he had one last matter to attend to. One last debt to settle.

It was a pure, just thing in a time when the foundations of the earth seemed to be eaten away and the sky gaped wide and hungry. That was what he told himself. One valorous act to stem the tide of brute corruption which sought to envelop everything. Kill the banebeast, and break the warherds. With the beast-tribes broken, the war in the north could be won easily. Without their fodder, the armies of the Three-Eyed King would find themselves bereft of their numerical advantage. That would be enough to turn the tide. It would be enough. It had to be.

A pulse of guilt shot through him. It wasn't the first time, and it wouldn't be the last, he knew. A small but insistent part of his mind constantly whispered that he had left his city, his people, in the hands of strangers. Only a Todbringer could weather the storm that had come to engulf Middenheim, it said, and he felt determination fade to doubt, and that doubt became a certainty that he had made a mistake.

At least until the band of ungors he was now rampaging through had trampled out of the undergrowth, and doubt had at last given way to the rough joy of vindication. After days of searching, days of threading through the tangled trails of the Drakwald, he had been overjoyed to find the enemy at last. When he'd spotted the semi-human beastmen, he hadn't been able to resist the urge to slake the bloodlust that had steadily built up in him over the weeks of his fruitless hunt. Deaf to the alarmed yells of his entourage, he'd spurred his horse into a gallop and charged right into the midst of the enemy.

Now ungors surrounded him on all sides, shrieking and snarling, and his horse reared, lashing out with its hooves even as Todbringer smashed his runefang down on hideous faces and primitive shields. He roared and cursed as he fought. From behind him, he heard the howl of the Knights of the White Wolf who made up his bodyguard as they laid about them with their brutal hammers, and the rising curses and war cries of the three-score huntsmen who had accompanied him into the baleful recesses of the Drakwald. The battle swirled about the muddy trail, in the shadows of sour-rooted trees, and twisted bodies fell in heaps. At last, the ungors broke and began to stream away. Some dived back into the undergrowth they had emerged from, while others broke into lurching flight along the trail. Todbringer was tempted to pursue the latter at once, but he jerked on his steed's reins, turning about to face the slaughter that was occurring behind him. 'Leave one alive,' he roared, as he watched his men butcher those creatures too slow or frenzied to flee. 'Damn your hides, I need one of the beasts breathing, so it can tell me where its one-eyed master is lurking.' If any of his warriors had heard him, however, they gave no sign.

He cursed himself, as he finally recognised the ruin he had inadvertently wrought. The orderly column of soldiers he had led into the Drakwald had devolved into a disorganised mass of men, milling about in a wild battle beneath the trees. The Drakwald ate men as surely as did the beasts it sheltered beneath its dark boughs, and staying within sight of one another was the only way of not losing men to the shadows and false trails that blighted it. Even then it was no sure thing. How many men had he lost to the Drakwald over the course of his time as elector count? A thousand? More? How many good men had he fed unwittingly to the hungry dark?

The forest seemed to press close to either side of the rutted track. The path was a narrow, muddy thing, barely wide enough for three men to march abreast. There was no space to form lines, no room for a proper charge. He was suddenly aware of how stifling the silence was, beneath the crash of arms, and how thick the dark beneath the trees was. It was as if the Drakwald were holding its breath. Unease strangled his eagerness and he kicked his horse into motion. He needed to restore order, and swiftly.

I hope you're satisfied, old man, he thought bitterly. *You know better!* He began to bellow orders as he rode, trying to shout over the din of battle. In his youth, he'd had one of the best parade-ground voices in the Empire, but age had dimmed his volume somewhat. The flush of combat was fading from him, and he felt tired and old. Every joint ached and the runefang felt heavy in his grip, but he didn't dare sheathe it. Not now.

The enemy was close. He saw that now, and he cursed himself for not thinking about it earlier. How often had his men been led into just such an ambush? How often had they done the leading themselves? He'd allowed his need for vengeance to blind him, and he could feel the jaws of the trap grinding shut about him.

A long, winding note suddenly rose from the trees. The sound of it speared through his recriminations and struck his gut like a fist. He jerked on the reins and turned his horse about, scanning the forest. More terrible groaning notes slithered between the trees and rose above the canopy, piercing the stillness. Brayhorns, he knew. The hunting horns of the warherds. Then, with a suddenness which defied reality, the forest, so still before, was suddenly alive with the sounds of tramping hooves, rattling weapons and snorting beasts.

Arrows hissed out from between the trees, punching men from their feet. Todbringer yanked his horse about. He had to reach his men – if they could form a shield-wall, they might manage an organised defence, long enough perhaps to escape the trap he'd led them into. But even as he galloped back towards his warriors, the beastmen burst through the trees on all sides at a run, slamming into the scattered column like a thunderbolt. There were hundreds of them, more than any shield-wall or line of hastily interposed spears could hold back, and men and horses screamed as they died.

Todbringer howled in rage as he spurred his horse to greater speed. He crashed into the mass of snarling beasts and the force of the impact sent the foe rolling and squealing as his horse trod on those too slow to get out of the way. His runefang quivered in his grasp as he swept it out and chopped down on upraised maws and clutching hands. For a moment he was adrift on a sea of snarling faces, jagged tusks and rusted blades. He cursed and prayed and screamed, matching them howl for howl, as he hewed about himself. Blood hung thick on the damp air, and it dripped into his armour and from his beard. Still they swirled about him, a never-ending tide of bestial fury. He glimpsed his men falling beneath filth-splotched blades one by one, dragged down and reduced to bloody ruin.

The trees nearby exploded outwards in a spray of splinters as a minotaur charged into battle, its bull-like head lowered and its great hooves trampling man and beast alike. The monster roared and swung an axe in a wide arc, cutting a Knight of the White Wolf and his braying opponent in half in a spray of gore. Todbringer kicked his horse into motion and charged towards the beast even as it turned to meet him. The minotaur lurched towards him through the press of combat, its eyes bulging with blood-greed. It swung its axe and the notched blade caught Todbringer's stallion in the neck, killing the poor beast instantly. The animal sagged and the count toppled from the saddle.

He rolled away, avoiding the horse's death-throes. The minotaur lumbered towards him, froth dripping from its champing jaws. Todbringer forced himself to his feet, even as the monster dropped its axe towards him. The runefang shuddered in his grip as he caught the blow, and the crude axe blade shivered to fragments. The minotaur reeled back, shocked from its fury by the loss of its weapon. Todbringer lunged, and his sword opened the brute's belly. The minotaur shrieked and clutched at its guts as it grabbed for him awkwardly. Todbringer avoided its clumsy attack and brought his blade down on its forearm. The runefang bit through flesh and bone with ease, and the severed arm flopped into the mud at his feet.

The minotaur collapsed like a felled tree, its blood steaming as it pumped across the ground. Beastmen pressed in around Todbringer, and he found himself beset on all sides. His breath rasped harshly in his agonised lungs as he moved and fought harder than ever before, seeking to wrestle just a few more seconds of life from the talons of what seemed to be his preordained fate.

Some part of him had always known that it would end this way, with him surrounded by braying herds, his standard trampled in the mud. Martak had been right; this was the End Times. The time of the Children of Chaos, when the cities of man would burn and be torn apart stone by stone. The world would belong to the mewling, goat-faced freaks which gibbered and snarled around him. He set his feet and heaved back against them, using his shield to batter the closest to the ground, where they were easy prey for his runefang.

For a moment, he stood alone. His heart ached with sorrow as he heard the sounds of the last of his men being put to the sword by the milling beast-kin. *Your fault, old man,* he thought. He stared at the snarling faces that closed in around him. These, then, were the inheritors of the world. He snorted and couldn't restrain the laugh that forced its way out of his throat. It rang out hard and wild over the track, and silence fell in its wake.

He swept his arms out as he glared at the beasts that milled about him, inviting them to attack. 'Come on then, beasts. Dogs of abomination, whelps of darkness – curs by any other name. A Todbringer yet stands. Middenheim stands. Come and feel the White Wolf's bite!'

The beastmen lunged forwards. They came at him from every side, remorseless and hungry. Todbringer slashed, hacked and chopped at the horde, and they returned the favour, their barbaric weapons scoring his armour and gashing his exposed flesh. Soon, he could hear the rumble of his heartbeat in his ears and the world seemed squeezed between ribbons of black as he wheezed and staggered. His foot slid in the mud, and he sank down to one knee. The beasts crowded around, and he readied himself for the end.

Horns blew, loud and low and long. The sound shivered through him, and the beastmen pulled back, whining and griping like hounds denied the kill. Something pushed through their ranks and came into view. 'I knew it,' Todbringer murmured.

Khazrak the One-Eye had come to claim his due. The banebeast of the Drakwald was large, and bulky, heavy with muscle and old scars beneath a suit of piecemeal armour. Yellowing skulls hung from his leather belt, and he carried a barbed whip in one giant paw, and a blade covered in ruinous sigils in the other.

The trees rustled in a sudden breeze, and it sounded like laughter. Khazrak spread his arms and the beastmen backed away, making room. Todbringer felt his heart speed up. Khazrak hadn't just come to watch him die. The banebeast had come to kill him.

Mortal enemies, brought together by fate. The thought brought a mirthless smile to Todbringer's face. He glanced up. The clouds resembled vast faces in the sky, leering down through the canopy of branches: like gamblers watching a dog savage rats in a pit, he thought. 'Well,' he croaked, 'here we are again, old beast.'

Khazrak hesitated. The beastman's good eye narrowed. For the first time, Todbringer noticed how much white there was in the other's hair, and how carefully the beast moved. Like an old warrior, conserving strength. Like Todbringer himself. He felt a pang of sadness. For all that the monstrosity before him deserved death, it had been the closest thing he'd had to a friend these past few years. Knowing that Khazrak was out there had given him a sense of purpose. It had given him a reason to live, after his wife's death, even if that reason was for hate's sake. And in a way, he was grateful to his enemy for that, for all that he intended to take Khazrak's head. *Some things are just meant to be,* he thought grimly. Then, he laughed. *At least now I can stop chasing fate.*

Khazrak's thick wrist flexed, and the barbed whip uncoiled. Todbringer took a breath. 'How long, old beast? A decade? Two? It seems a shame to miss the end of the world, but we've never been showy, have we?' he asked. 'No, best to let them get on with it, eh? We know where the real war is, don't we?'

The caterwaul of the gathered beastmen dimmed as he raised his sword. They were no longer important. They never had been. Only Khazrak mattered. The others were animals, and no more or less dangerous than any beast of the forest. But Khazrak was almost a man, and he deserved a man's death. Preferably, a long, lingering one.

Slowly, the two old warriors began to circle one another. 'Oh yes, we know,' Todbringer murmured. 'You took my sons, and I took your whelps. I took your eye, you took mine.' He reached up to trace the scar that cut across the empty socket. Khazrak mirrored the gesture, seemingly unthinkingly. 'The world is on fire, but our war must take precedence. We have *earned* this, haven't we, old beast?'

Khazrak met his gaze, as the question lingered on the air between them. 'Yes, this is our moment. Let us make the most of it.' Todbringer took a two-handed grip on his runefang. Khazrak raised his blade. It might have been a salute, but Todbringer doubted it. No, Khazrak knew nothing of honour or respect. But he recognised the totality of this moment, as Todbringer did. Strands of destiny bound them together, and as the world ended, so too would their war. It was only appropriate. Todbringer brought his sword back and closed his eye. *Guard my city, Herald of Sigmar. May the Flame of Ulric burn bright forevermore, and may its light guide you to victory, where I have failed,* he thought.

Khazrak bellowed, and Todbringer's eye snapped open as the beast lunged for him. Their blades slammed together with a sound that echoed through the trees. The two old enemies hacked and slashed at one another ferociously. They had fought many times before, and Todbringer knew the creature, even as the beast knew him. Blows were parried and countered as they fell into an old, familiar rhythm. Two old men, sparring in the mud, surrounded by a circle of monstrous faces and hairy bodies.

He flashed his teeth in a snarl, and Khazrak did the same as they strained against one another. The faces of his sons, his wives, his soldiers flashed through his mind – all of those he'd lost in the course of his war against the creature before him. He wondered if Khazrak was seeing something similar – how many whelps had the banebeast lost over the course of their conflict? How many of his brutish mates and comrades had Todbringer's sword claimed? Did he even feel love, the way a man did, or did he know only hate?

The mud squirmed beneath his feet, and his heart hurt. His head swam, and his lungs burned. He was old, too old for this. He could smell Khazrak's rank perspiration, and the creature's limbs trembled no less than his own. How many challenges to his authority had Khazrak faced, in his long life? Todbringer recognised some of the beast's scars as his handiwork, but the rest... 'Did they toss you out, old beast? Is that why you're here, and not with the rest, laying siege to Middenheim? Or did you refuse to go, did you refuse to bow before the Three-Eyed King until our score was settled? Were you waiting for me?' he gasped as he leaned against his sword, pitting all of his weight against that of his opponent.

Khazrak gave a bleat of frustration as they broke apart for a moment, and the whip hissed and snapped as the beastman sought to ensnare Todbringer's legs. An old trick, and one that had caught Todbringer unawares many years before. But he was ready for it now. He avoided the lash and stamped down on it, catching it. Even as he did so, he lunged forwards awkwardly, slashing towards Khazrak's neck, hoping to behead the beast. Khazrak staggered back and parried the blow.

Off balance, Todbringer jerked back as Khazrak snapped the whip at his good eye. The tip of the lash tore open his cheek. Khazrak pressed the attack. The beast's sword hammered down once, twice, three times against Todbringer's guard. One blow tore the shield from Todbringer's grasp and sent it rattling across the ground, the second and the third were caught on the runefang's length, but such was the force behind the blows that Todbringer was driven to one knee. Thick mud squelched beneath his armour, and he felt his shoulder go numb as he blocked another blow. Khazrak was old, but strong; stronger than Todbringer. And fresh as well. He had saved himself, gauging the best time to strike. Even as he reeled beneath his enemy's assault, Todbringer felt a flicker of admiration. *What a man you would have made, had you been born human,* he thought. A fifth blow slid beneath his guard, and he felt a pain in his gut. He shoved himself back, and saw that Khazrak's blade was red to the hilt.

The gathered beastmen scented blood and began to bray and stamp in anticipation. Todbringer was nearly knocked off his feet by Khazrak's next swing. He sank back, rolling with the blow. Khazrak charged after him, snorting in eagerness. Todbringer lashed out, and felt a savage thrill of joy as his blade caught Khazrak in the shin. Bone cracked and Khazrak gave a cry. The banebeast fell heavily, and Todbringer hurled himself onto his enemy, knocking the weapons from Khazrak's fists. He raised his runefang over Khazrak's pain-contorted features. 'For my sons,' Todbringer hissed.

Khazrak's good eye met his own. The beastman blinked, just once, and stilled his thrashing, as if in acceptance of what was about to transpire. Then Khazrak snarled, and the runefang descended, piercing the creature's good eye and sinking into his brain. Khazrak's hooves drummed on the ground for a moment, and then were still. Todbringer leaned against the hilt of the runefang until he felt the tip sink into the mud beneath Khazrak's skull. 'This time, stay dead,' he wheezed.

The gathered beastmen were silent. The Drakwald was quiet. But Boris Todbringer was not. He rose wearily, his strength gone, only stubbornness remaining. He was wounded, weakened, and surrounded by hundreds, if not thousands of beastmen. He would die here.

But he had won.

Todbringer tilted his head back and laughed the laugh of a man who has shed the last of life's shackles. For the first time in a long time, he felt no weight on his heart. He had won. Let the world burn, if it would, for he had made his mark, and done what he must.

He looked down at Khazrak, spat a gobbet of blood onto the death-slackened features of his old enemy, and ripped his sword free, even as the closest of the beastmen began to edge forwards, growling vengefully. He was going to die, but by Ulric, they'd remember him, when all was said and done.

'You want the world?' Boris Todbringer growled. Clasping his runefang in both hands, the Elector Count of Middenheim, supreme ruler of Middenland and the Drakwald, raised the blade. He smiled as the enemy closed in.

'You'll have to earn it.'

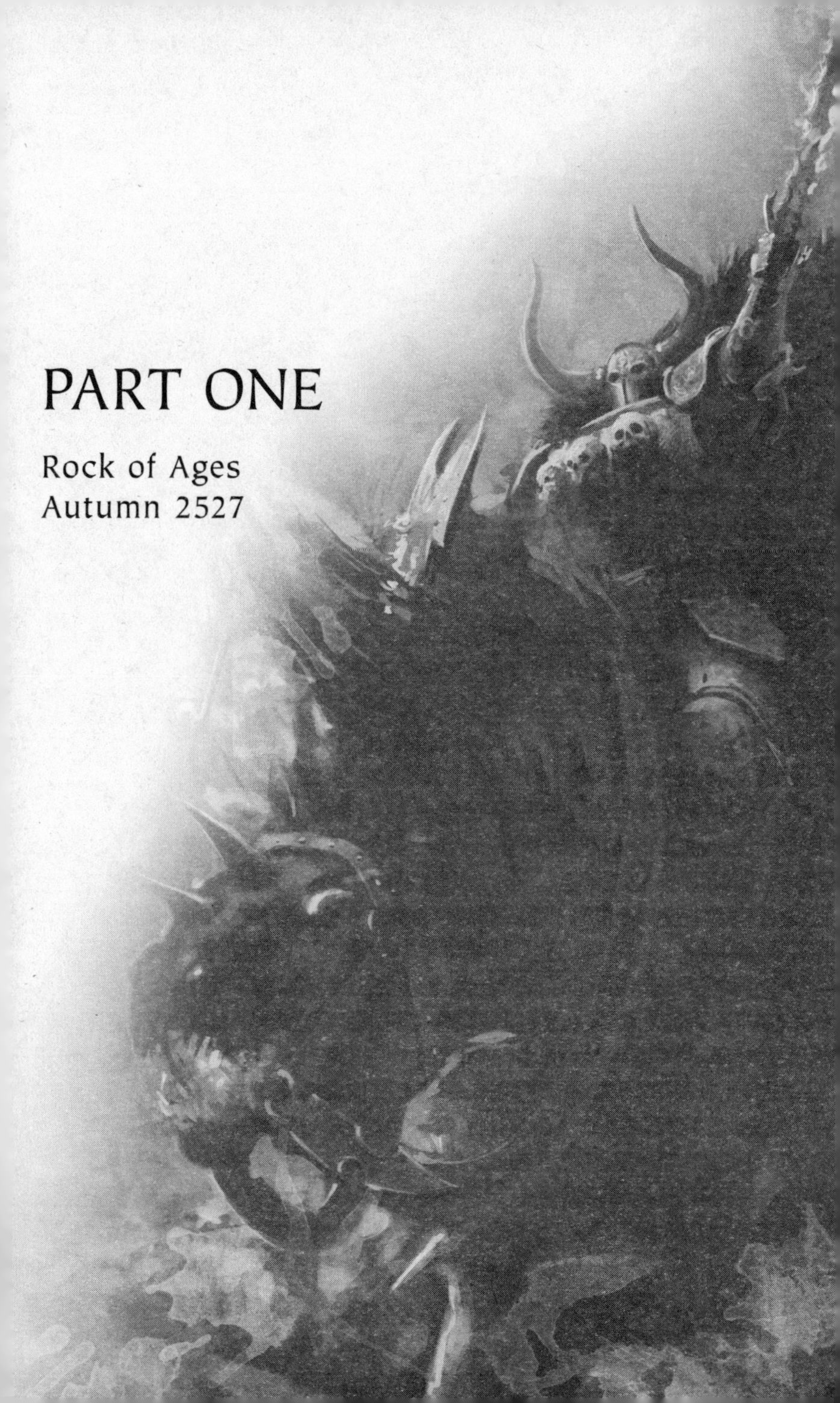

PART ONE

Rock of Ages
Autumn 2527

ONE

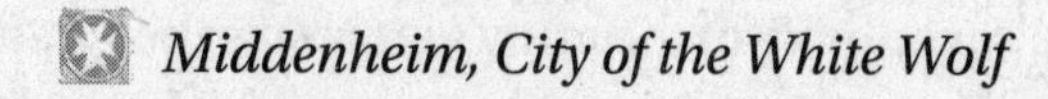

Middenheim, City of the White Wolf

Gregor Martak, Supreme Patriarch of the Colleges of Magic, took a pull from the bottle of wine and handed it off to the man standing beside him atop the battlements of the Temple of Ulric. The temple, fashioned as a fortress within a fortress, dominated the Ulricsmund and the city of Middenheim itself, and was the highest point of the Fauschlag. Martak's companion – clad in the dark armour of a member of the Knights of the White Wolf, albeit much battered and in need of a good polishing – took the bottle grudgingly, after the wizard shook it invitingly. Martak scratched at his tangled beard and looked out over the city. From the temple battlements one could see further than anywhere else in Middenheim, almost to the ends of the horizon. And what Martak saw now chilled him to the bone.

Rolling banks of black cloud had swept in from the north, and hung over the city, blotting out the sun. Every torch and brazier in the city was lit in a futile effort to hold back the dark. Sorcerous lightning rent the clouds. The crackling sheets of lurid energy lit the streets below with kaleidoscopic colours, and mad shadows danced and capered on every surface. But the darkness was no barrier to what now approached the city.

The pounding of drums had been audible to Martak and the rest of the city for some hours before the arrival of the horde which now seethed around the base of the Fauschlag in an endless black tide. The wind had carried the noise of the drums, as well as the guttural roars and screams of the damned who made up the approaching army. Flocks of crows had darkened the rust-coloured sky, and the roots of the mountain upon which Middenheim stood had trembled.

The front-runners of the horde had emerged first, from the edges of the forest to the city's north. Trees were uprooted or shattered where they stood, the groans and cracks of their demise joining the cacophony of the army's arrival as they were battered aside by hulking monsters the likes of which Martak had hoped never to see. Behind the savage behemoths came numberless tribesmen from the far north clad in filthy furs, armoured warriors and monstrous mutants. They poured out of the forest like an unceasing tide of foulness, and the thunder of the drums was joined by the blaring of war-horns and howled war-songs, all of it rising and mingling into a solid roar of noise that set Martak's teeth on edge and made his ears ache.

Now, the horde stood arrayed before Middenheim, awaiting gods alone knew what signal to launch their assault. Thousands of barbaric banners flapped and clattered in the hot breeze, and monstrous shapes swooped through the boiling sky. Beastmen capered and howled before the silent ranks of armoured warriors. The horde's numbers had swelled throughout the day, and even the most sceptical of Middenheim's defenders had realised that this was no mere raiding band, come to burn and pillage before fading away like a summer storm. No, this was the full might of the north unbound, and it had come to crack the spine of the world.

'I hate to say I told you so, Axel, but... well,' Martak grunted.

He swept back his grimy fur cloak and gestured with one long, tattooed arm towards the walls beyond which the foe gathered in such numbers as to shake the world. Or so it seemed, at least, to Martak. His companion, despite the evidence of his senses, didn't agree.

Axel Greiss, Grand Master of the Knights of the White Wolf and commander of the Fellwolf Brotherhood, used the edge of his white fur cloak to wipe the mouth of the bottle clean, and took a tentative swig. 'What is this swill?' he asked.

'A bottle of Sartosan Red. Some fool had hidden it in the privy,' Martak grunted.

Greiss smacked his lips, made a face, and handed the bottle back. 'It's a rabble out there, wizard. Nothing more. You've spent too much time amongst the milksops of the south if that's your idea of a horde. I've seen hordes. *That* is no horde.' He sniffed. 'Middenheim has withstood worse. It will withstand this.' He gestured dismissively. 'Ulric's teeth, they've even chased off the ratmen for us.'

Martak took another pull from the bottle. 'Have they?' The skaven who had been besieging the city prior to the arrival of the horde had abandoned their siege-lines, like scavengers fleeing before a larger predator. Some of the ratmen had gone south, Martak knew, while others had surely scampered into the tunnels below the Fauschlag. Not that he could get anyone to listen to him on that last score. It was Altdorf all over again. What good was being the Supreme Patriarch if no one listened to him? Then, it wasn't as if the Colleges of Magic still existed, he thought bitterly.

Greiss, as if echoing Martak's thoughts, eyed the Amber wizard disdainfully. 'They're gone, wizard. Fled, like the cowardly vermin they were. Do you see them out there?'

'Doesn't mean they aren't there,' Martak grunted. It was an old argument. He had ordered scouts sent into the depths of the Fauschlag, despite the vigorous protestations of Greiss and his fellow commanders. What they had reported had only confirmed his fears of an attack from below. The skaven hadn't fled. They'd merely given over the honour of the assault to Archaon. No, the ratmen were massing in the depths, preparing to assault Middenheim from below. He could feel it in his bones.

'Doesn't mean they are, either,' Greiss said. He shook his head. 'And if they are, what of it? Middenheim stands, wizard. Let the hordes break themselves on our walls, if they wish. They will fail, as they have done every time before. As long as the Flame of Ulric burns, Middenheim stands.' Martak made to hand him the bottle, but Greiss waved it aside. 'Stay up here and drink the day away if you will, wizard. Some of us have duties to attend to.'

Martak didn't reply. Greiss's words stung, as they had been meant to. He watched the Grand Master descend from the battlements, his armour clanking. Greiss didn't like him very much, and if he were being honest, Martak felt the same about the other man. He didn't like any of his fellow commanders, in fact.

Men of rank and noble birth from Averland, Talabheim and Stirland, as well as Middenheim, were all somewhere below in the city, jockeying for position and influence. The world was collapsing around them, shrinking day by day, and men like Greiss thought it was just another day. Or worse, they saw it as an opportunity. The world was ending, but men were still men. Martak upended the bottle, letting the last dregs of wine splash across his tongue. *Men are still men, but not for much longer,* he thought.

He shuddered, suddenly cold, and pulled his furs tighter about himself. He'd thought, just for a little while, that victory was possible. Just for a moment, he'd seen a ray of light pierce the gathering dark, and a spark of hope had been kindled in the ashes of his soul.

He'd seen that light – the light of the heavens – ground itself in the broken body of Karl Franz, and restore him to life in the ruins of Altdorf. He'd seen the foul gardens of plague and pestilence scoured from the stones of the city, and the monstrous things that had grown within them struck down. He'd seen more besides... The broken body of Kurt Helborg, his proud face stained with blood; the regal figure of Louen Leoncoeur, King of Bretonnia, as he stood against daemons in doomed defence of a realm not his own; the shattered statue of Sigmar, weeping blood. The light had washed it all away, in the end.

But only for a moment. Then, the dark had closed in once more. With the Auric Bastion no more, and Kislev turned to ashes, the armies of Chaos had swept south, burning and pillaging. Names out of black legend had returned to bedevil an Empire that had thought itself free of them. And not just the Empire. Bretonnia was shattered into warring fragments; Tilea had been erased by the chittering hordes of ratmen; Sylvania had swollen from boil to tumour, and the unbound dead roamed the land, attacking the living.

Martak stuck a finger into the mouth of the bottle, feeling around for any remaining droplets. Altdorf had survived one assault only to fall to another. Now it was a haunt for scuttling vermin. Karl Franz had fled to Averheim, the only city other than Middenheim yet remaining to the Empire. *And soon it'll be down to one, unless Averheim has already fallen,* Martak thought sourly. Greiss's overconfidence aside, Martak knew a losing battle when he saw one. He'd lived most of his life in the wilderness, and Middenheim reminded him of nothing so much as a wounded stag, surrounded by hungry wolves. Oh, the stag would gore a few. It'd put up a good fight, but in the end... the outcome wasn't in doubt.

Regardless, he had his own part to play. He would see to the tunnels beneath the city, since no one else thought they were worth defending. He could do some good there, he hoped. He had ordered barricades to be pulled into place at the top of the winding stairs that led down into the guts of the Fauschlag, and had demanded, and received, a levy of men from the walls to guard key tunnel junctions. Soon enough, he would go down to join them, in the dark, to wait for the attack.

There were thousands of skaven massing in the depths, whatever Greiss thought. That was where they had all gone when Archaon arrived, but they wouldn't stay below for long. And when they decided to come up, there would be little Martak could do to stop them.

He stuck a finger in his mouth and sucked the liquid from it. He'd never been much of a drinker before all of this, but now seemed as good a time as any to develop a few bad habits. Martak hefted the bottle in preparation to hurl it out over the city, when something made him stop. A voice, strong and sonorous, rose from somewhere below him. He could not make out the words, but he recognised the timbre easily enough.

Valten.

The Word made flesh. The Herald of Sigmar, come to light their darkest hour. He had been a blacksmith once, they said. Martak's father had been a swineherd, and he saw no shame in humble beginnings. Especially when the end result was so… impressive. He lowered the bottle and set it on the battlement. Then, picking up his staff from where it lay, he made to descend. As he headed for the steps, he heard a soft growl behind him.

Martak stopped. He turned, heart thudding in his chest. Something that might have been a wolf, or the shadow of a wolf, sat where he'd stood only a few moments before. It regarded him steadily for the span of a single heartbeat, and then, like a twist of smoke, it was gone. Martak stared at the spot, mouth dry, hands trembling. He was suddenly very, very thirsty. He turned away and left the battlements as quickly as his legs could carry him.

When he at last reached the main rotunda of the temple, Valten's speech was coming to a close. His voice swelled, momentarily blotting out the noise from outside the walls. Martak moved through the large crowd of refugees that had occupied the main chamber of the temple, towards the main doors and, beyond them, the steps that led down into the close-set streets of the Ulricsmund. The huddled masses gave way before him, and whispers of worry preceded him, as well as murmurs of disgust for his unkempt presence. Even the basest peasant had standards, Martak supposed; standards which he obligingly failed to meet as often as possible.

Valten had given some version of this same speech several times since the arrival of Archaon's forces outside the walls. The streets were thick with panicked citizens, and frightened refugees crowded every temple and tavern. But where Valten passed, Ghal Maraz balanced across his broad shoulders, calm ensued. He spoke to crowds and individuals alike, with no preference or bias for province or station. His voice was measured, his words soothing. *Be at peace, for I am here, and where I stand, no evil shall prevail,* Martak thought as he trudged out towards the vast steps of the temple. It was an old saying, attributed to Sigmar. From what little Martak knew of the man behind the myth, he doubted the veracity of the phrasing, though not the intent.

He watched the tall, broad figure of Sigmar's Herald speak words of comfort to the massive crowd of soldiers and refugees occupying the steps, and felt the burden on his heart lift, if only slightly. Valten was taller than any man Martak had met, but he moved with a grace that an elf would have envied. He'd grown a beard since the fall of Altdorf, and now looked more at home in Middenheim than even an old wolf like Greiss.

That was the trick of him, Martak had learned. Valten simply... fit. Wherever he went in the Empire, he found a home. Talabeclanders, Averlanders, Middenlanders, they all claimed Valten as one of their own. He spoke their dialects, he knew their history; he could even sing their songs. It was as if the burly, bearded young warrior were the Empire made flesh and bone. He was everything that was good and pure about the land and its people incarnate.

As he spoke, Valten seemed to shine with an inner radiance

that warmed a man better than any fire. His voice rose and fell like that of a trained orator, and he spoke with a passion that would have put even the late Grand Theogonist, Volkmar, to shame.

Martak paused in the entrance to the temple, so as not to interrupt the speech. The great iron-banded doors had been flung wide at the start of the ratmen's siege, and they yet remained open, welcoming any who sought sanctuary. The entrance itself was a vast stone archway carved in the shape of a wolf's upper jaw, complete with great fangs, and as it rose over him he thought again of the shadow-shape he'd seen on the battlements, and shivered. It hadn't been a daemon; that much he was sure of. While the Flame of Ulric burned, no daemon could set foot inside Middenheim.

He glanced at the Flame, where it crackled in the centre of the immense temple rotunda. The fire burned silver-white, casting its light throughout the main chamber of the temple, warming the crowd and illuminating the enormous bas-reliefs depicting Ulric's defeat of the bloodwyrm, his breach of the stormvault and countless other deeds of heroism performed by the wolf-god. More and more people had begun to seek the comfort of its presence as the unnatural darkness fell. Martak couldn't fault them for it. It was the embodiment of Ulric's strength and rage, and for that reason it provided a beacon of hope to the wolf-god's chosen people. It was said that should the fire go out, winter unending would grip the world.

As the thought crossed his mind, he caught sight of a low, lean shape prowling through the legs of the crowd. The shadow-wolf had followed him, it seemed. Its yellow gaze met his own briefly and then it vanished into the forest of humanity. He was about to follow it, when he heard a voice say, 'It's beautiful, isn't it?'

Martak turned, and looked up at Valten. He grunted and shrugged. 'One fire is much like another, to one used to doing without.'

'I grew up in a forge,' Valten said, simply. 'There's a strange sort of beauty in fire, I think. It is all colours and none, it provides comfort and light, but can kill or blind the unwary. A tool of both creation and destruction... rather like a hammer.' He hefted Ghal Maraz for emphasis. 'Sigmar built an empire with this weapon, and destroyed the works of his enemies.'

Martak smiled sourly. 'Very pretty. Will that homily go in your next speech?'

Valten chuckled. 'I doubt there'll be time for one. Otherwise, you wouldn't have come to tell me that you're about to go below.' He looked at Martak, and the wizard shifted uncomfortably. Valten had a way of staring right into a man's soul. He never judged what he saw there, though that only made the feeling worse.

'Yes, it's time,' Martak said, leaning on his staff. 'Scouts have reported that there are ratmen massing in the depths. And Archaon's rabble didn't walk all the way here just to sit outside and look menacing.'

'I know,' Valten said. He looked up, and closed his eyes. 'It's almost a relief.'

'Not exactly how I would put it,' Martak said.

Valten smiled. He looked at the wizard, and put a hand on his shoulder. 'No,' he said. 'Then, you're a gloomy old bear, and there's no denying it.'

Martak snorted. 'And you're a cheerful lamb, is that it?'

Valten's smile faded. 'No. No, I can feel the weight of this moment, Gregor, as well as you. It has pressed down on my soul and my mind since I first swung my father's hammer in anger at the Auric Bastion. It has sought to forge me into the shape it wishes, the shape it requires, but sometimes... I do not think it will succeed.' He dropped his hand and hefted Ghal Maraz. 'This is part of it, I think. Burden and blessing in one,' he said, turning the ancient warhammer in his hands. 'Sometimes, this hammer is as light as a feather. Other times, I can barely lift it.

I am not certain that it is my hand which is meant to wield it.' He looked at Martak. 'Sometimes I wish Luthor were still here, to tell me that I am wrong, and that my course is set.' He smiled sadly. 'No offence, Gregor.'

'None taken,' Martak said, waving aside the apology. 'I wish Huss were here as well. And while we're wishing, I'll add the Emperor, Mandred Skavenslayer and Magnus the Pious. Because Taal knows that we could use them now.'

Valten's smile turned fierce. 'We shall just have to act in their place, my friend. We can do no less. Middenheim stands. The Emperor and Graf Boris charged me to keep this city and her people safe, and I will do so or die in the attempt.'

Martak was about to reply, when he felt something stir in him. He clutched his head, and heard a great cry which seemed to echo up from every stone in the temple. It was as if a legion of wolves had howled as one, and then fallen silent. Valten grabbed him as he stumbled. 'Gregor, what is it, are you–'

Wordlessly, Martak moaned. He felt as if there were something missing in him, as if someone had carved a portion of his heart out. He heard Valten gasp, and blinked blearily as he tried to clear his head. As he forced himself erect, he saw that the crowd had moved back from the Flame of Ulric. Men and women were wailing and moaning in fear. Valten raised his hands, trying to calm the growing panic. Martak pushed away from him and staggered towards the Flame, staring at it in disbelief.

As he watched, the Flame of Ulric guttered, flickered and died. The chamber was plunged into darkness, and the crowd began to stream away, seeking safety elsewhere. He heard the screams of the trampled, the wailing of lost children, and Valten's voice, rising above it all, trying vainly to impose order on the chaos. And beneath it all, beneath the cries and the shouts, beneath the fear... *laughter*. The laughter of the Dark Gods as Middenheim's hope faded, leaving behind only ashes.

Martak closed his eyes. Something itched at the back of his

mind, like someone speaking just at the edge of his hearing, but he couldn't catch it for the laughter that echoed in his head. He gripped his staff so tightly that the wood creaked in protest. He felt cold and hot all at once, and his skull felt two sizes too small as images crashed across the surface of his mind's eye. There were shapes squirming in the dark behind his eyes, impossibly vast and foul, and they were scratching eagerly at the roof of the sky and the roots of the earth. He saw a shadowy figure confronted by wolves of ice, and heard the moan of a god as the Flame dimmed. He heard the bray of horns and the rumble of drums, and felt his guts clench in protest as the moment he'd feared came round at last.

A hand gripped his shoulder, shaking him out of his fugue. 'Gregor – it's time. The enemy are advancing,' Valten said. 'I must go to the walls.'

'And I must go below,' Martak croaked. He looked at Valten, and as he did, the daemonic laughter crowding his thoughts suddenly fell silent. There were some things that even daemons could not bear to look at. 'The gods go with you, Herald.'

'I know that one, at least, walks with me,' Valten said. He lifted Ghal Maraz and saluted Martak. 'Middenheim stands, Gregor. And so do we.'

'But for how long?' Martak murmured, as he watched the Herald of Sigmar depart.

Northern Gatehouse, Grafsmund-Norgarten District

'That, my friends, is nothing less than a bad day wrapped in fur,' Wendel Volker said, indicating the army that was on the march on the plain below, as he upended the jug and gulped down the tasteless Kislevite alcohol. It was the last of its kind, since Kislev no longer existed, and he intended to enjoy every foul drop in the hours before his inevitable messy demise. He only wished he had a bottle of good Tilean wine to wash it down with.

He stood atop the gatehouse, having shooed the men who were supposed to be on duty back down into the structure. He stood on the trapdoor, so that he could have a few moments of uninterrupted drinking. The taverns were packed, and every wine cellar and beer hall in the city had been drunk dry three days ago. He'd managed to squirrel away the jug of Kislevite vodka, but it was almost as bad as being sober.

Volker had come up in the world since his days as a captain in the fortress of Heldenhame. Now he wore the armour and regalia of a member of the Reiksguard, given to him by Kurt Helborg himself as a reward for salvaging what was left of Heldenhame's garrison and bringing it to Altdorf just in time to bolster the city's defences. It wasn't exactly the sort of reward that Volker had hoped for, but one couldn't look a gift horse in the mouth. Especially in times like these. And the armour had come in handy more than once, for all that it was dratted heavy and rubbing him raw in all the wrong spots.

Volker handed the jug off to one of his companions, a big man clad in sea-green armour, decorated with piscine motifs where it hadn't been battered into shapelessness. 'A bad day, Wendel, or *the* bad day?' the latter said, as he took a swig. Erkhart Dubnitz was the last knight of an order that wasn't officially recognised by anyone with any sense. The Knights of Manann had fought to the bitter end when the plague-fleets had sailed into Marienburg's harbour, but Dubnitz alone had escaped the freistadt; he'd been sent to Altdorf, bearing tidings of warning that had, sadly, not been heeded until it was far too late. Now he was a man without a country, fighting to preserve a nation not his own. It was in Altdorf that Volker had made the acquaintance of the Marienburger, and found a kindred spirit, of sorts. At least where it concerned spirits of the alcoholic variety.

'What's the difference, Erkhart? Either way, we're the ones it's happening to,' the third man standing atop the gatehouse said. He waved aside the jug when it was offered to him. 'No, thank you. I'd rather die with a clear head, if it's all the same to you.' Hector Goetz had the face of a man who'd seen the worst the world had to offer, and hadn't come away impressed. His armour bore the same hallmarks of hard fighting that Volker's and Dubnitz's did, but it was covered in the signs and sigils of the Order of the Blazing Sun. As far as Volker could tell, Goetz was the last templar of the Myrmidian Order left alive. Most, it was said, had died with Talabheim. Goetz had been there, but he refused to talk about it. Volker, a native of Talabecland himself, resisted the urge to press him.

In truth, he wasn't sure that he wanted to know. He'd left his parents, his kin, and several enthusiastic and entertaining paramours behind in Talabheim when he'd been given a commission in the Heldenhame garrison. That they were all likely dead had yet to pierce the armour of numbness which was the only thing protecting his sanity at this point. It was either numbness or madness now, and Volker had seen too much to think that there was any sort of relief in madness these days.

'Suit yourself, Hector. More for me and young Wendel,' Dubnitz said, with a grin. He passed the jug to Volker, who took another swig, and then gave a mournful burp.

'It's empty,' he said. 'Dubnitz, be a friend and go get another one.'

'There isn't another one,' Dubnitz said. 'Gentlemen, we are officially out of alcohol. Sound the retreat.'

Volker cradled the empty jug to his chest. 'Why bother? There's nowhere to go.'

'Nonsense. The horizon is right over there.'

'He's right, Erkhart. There's nowhere to go. The gods are dead,' Goetz said softly. His expression became wistful. 'I thought, for a moment, that they were still with us.' His face hardened. 'Then Talabheim happened, and I knew that they were gone.'

Dubnitz's grin faded. He sighed. 'It's a sad thing, when a man outlives his gods.'

'Aye, and we're soon to join them,' Goetz continued. He glanced at Volker. 'Unless, of course, that Herald of yours has some divine trick up his sleeve.'

'Not that he's shared with me, no,' Volker said. When he'd first seen the Herald of Sigmar in the flesh, he'd been duly awed. The man was everything the priests of Sigmar had promised. A demigod, come down amongst mere mortals to fight at their side and lead them to victory against the enemy. That awe had not faded, in the weeks since, so much as it had matured. There was something about Valten that chased away despair and neutered fear. But he was a man like any other, Volker knew. A good man, a just man, but a man all the same. He was about to elaborate, when Goetz suddenly stiffened and cursed.

'Well... here we go,' Dubnitz breathed softly. 'Time's up.'

Volker saw a flash of polychromatic light below, rising above the horde. The air took on a greasy tang, and he tasted something foul at the back of his throat. He recognised it easily enough, though he wished he didn't. The clouds began to thicken and twist, and howling gales of wind rippled across the city. Goetz's face was pale as he backed away from the ramparts. 'Daemons,' he whispered hoarsely. 'They're calling daemons.' He clutched at his side, as if in memory of an old wound. 'I can hear them screaming...'

'That's not all,' Dubnitz said. He pointed out across the city. 'Correct me if I'm wrong, but isn't that where the western gatehouse is?'

Volker turned and saw a column of smoke rising over the city to the west. His mouth felt dry. 'Oh, gods,' he rasped. He twisted about as a dull rumble filled the air, and saw a second cloud, this one a sickly greenish hue, rise over the city's eastern gatehouse. Then, a half-second later, the world gave a sickening lurch as the whole gatehouse shook, nearly knocking him from his feet. He heard screams from below, and thin trickles of green smoke began to creep around the edges of the trapdoor. 'What the devil–?'

Dubnitz suddenly reached out and grabbed the back of his cuirass, hauling Volker back, even as a blade hissed through the air where his head had been. 'That's the devil,' Dubnitz said conversationally as a strange apparition, hunched and wrapped in black, landed on the rampart and sprang towards them, a serrated blade clutched in its verminous paws.

Volker acted instinctively, bringing the jug up and catching his attacker in the skull. The clay jug exploded and the creature fell twitching. 'Skaven,' he said dumbly, staring down at it.

'Really, and here I thought it was a halfling with scabies,' Dubnitz said, drawing his sword as more of the creatures appeared, scrambling over the edge of the ramparts. 'Where are the blasted guards?' he growled, as he hacked down a leaping ratman.

'Dead, if that gas is what I think it is,' Goetz said. He had his own blade in hand, and effortlessly blocked a blow from one of the black-clad skaven. 'It's poison. Don't let it touch you.' As he spoke, he moved away from the trapdoor, which was fuming steadily.

'That'd explain why the vermin are wearing masks,' Volker grunted as he booted a skaven in the chest and off the rampart. He swung his sword about in a tight arc, driving his opponents back. He heard the muffled squeal of chains and cranks, and knew that the gas had only been a means to an end. 'They're lowering the drawbridge. They're going to let the northmen into the city!'

'Well, sod this for a game of sailors, then,' Dubnitz said. He rushed towards the inner rampart which overlooked the courtyard of the gatehouse below, and, in a rattle of armour, vaulted over the edge, taking a squealing skaven with him. Volker looked at Goetz, and then, as one, both knights followed their companion over the rampart, leaving the astonished skaven staring after them.

Volker screamed until he struck the hay cart, and from there it was curses. He rolled off the cart, every limb aching, and hit the cobbles with a crash. The body of the skaven that Dubnitz had caught up flopped to the ground beside him. The big knight grinned down at him, and offered him a hand. 'On your feet, young Wendel – we've got unwelcome visitors on the way, and our swords are needed.'

Spitting hay, Volker allowed Dubnitz to haul him to his feet. 'Did you know this hay cart was here the whole time?' he asked.

'Of course,' Dubnitz said. 'You learn a lot, being a drunkard. For instance, always make sure you have a soft place to land handy, just in case. Now help me extricate Goetz, before we're knee-deep in murderous daemon-fondlers.'

Northern Viaduct

'Horvath, have you ever wondered about the choices that brought you to this point in your life?' Canto Unsworn rumbled to his closest companion in the press of Chaos warriors, northern tribesmen and howling beastmen moving steadily up the viaduct. There were hundreds of them, moving in a slow but steady lope towards the gatehouse above. An ugly green smoke rose from the ramparts of the wall and the drawbridge had thudded down not a handful of moments before, a sign that their verminous allies had delivered on their promise to knock out the gates.

That the Three-Eyed King had seen fit to trust such creatures was still a matter of some disbelief among the gathered warriors who had flocked to his banners. That the skaven had, in fact, followed through on their promises was even more unbelievable, at least as far as Canto Unsworn was concerned, and it made him wonder what further marvels awaited him, should he survive the carnage to come.

'Blood for the Blood God!' Horvath roared, echoing the cry of the men around him. He glanced at the other and frowned. 'What are you nattering about now, Unsworn?'

'Never mind,' Canto said.

Horvath eyed him suspiciously. The two warriors were a study in contrasts. Both were big, as befitted men who had survived the numberless dangers of the Chaos Wastes, and clad in baroque armour too heavy to be worn by any man not touched by the breath of the Winds of Change and the light of the Howling Sun. Horvath's armour was the hue of dried blood, and bedecked with grisly sigils of murder and ruin. A trophy rack wobbled on his back, cradling an intact skeleton, every bone of which was carved with a blasphemous litany. Canto's black armour, while as heavy and imposing as Horvath's, bore neither sign nor sigil, and he carried no trophies save for the yellowing skulls with strange marks carved into them which hung from his pauldrons and cuirass.

'Why must you always talk, Unsworn? Why must you chatter like a nurgling?' Horvath growled, shaking his head.

'The gods gave me a voice, Horvath. Blame them,' Canto said. 'Crossbows.'

'What?'

'Crossbows,' Canto said and raised his shield as crossbow bolts punched into the front rank of warriors moving up the viaduct. Dozens of men and mutants fell. One, however, remained on his feet. Crossbow bolts jutted from his all-encompassing and face-less armour, but still he staggered on, dragging his sword behind him. As he neared the gatehouse, he seemed to gain strength, and he swung his sword up to clasp it with both hands. With a hoarse cry, he began to run towards the enemy. 'That one is looking to catch the eyes of the gods,' Canto muttered as the lone warrior charged towards the smoky ruins of the gatehouse.

'He already has, Unsworn,' Horvath grunted, plucking a bolt out of his arm. 'Don't you recognise him?' He snapped the bolt in two. 'That's Count Mordrek.'

'The Damned One?' Canto murmured. 'No wonder he seems in such a hurry.' Mordrek the Damned was a living warning to all those who vied for the favour of the Dark Gods. He walked at the whim of the gods, never knowing rest, oblivion or damnation. Mordrek, men whispered, had died a thousand times, but was always brought back to fight again. He was the plaything of the gods: beneath his ornate armour, his form was said to change constantly, as if he were the raw stuff of Chaos made flesh.

'He just wandered into camp last night. He wasn't alone, either. We wage war accompanied by the heroes of old, Unsworn. Aekold Helbrass might be content to play in the ashes of Kislev, but others have come in answer to the Three-Eyed King's challenge – Vilitch the Curseling, Valnir the Reaper, a dozen others. All rallying to the banner of the Everchosen,' Horvath continued. He slammed his axe against his shield with every name he rattled off. 'To march in Mordrek's wake is an honour, Unsworn. We follow in the footsteps of legend!'

Horvath's cry was swallowed up by the roar of the warriors around them. Mordrek's charge had roused the horde, and Canto found himself carried along as the warriors around him and Horvath began to press forwards up the viaduct once more. As they moved, hatches banged open on cannon embrasures to reveal the hollow muzzles of guns ready to fire. Canto felt his heart quicken with anticipation of the noise and fury to come. He was not afraid; not precisely. He knew what cannons could do. He'd seen the war-engines of the *dawi zharr* first-hand, and knew that these guns were but a pale shadow of those terrible devices. Men would die, but not him. Not if his luck held, as it had so far.

Canto had fought his way south with the rest of Halfgir's Headsmen, as they called themselves, when the thrice-damned sorcerous bastion the southerners had erected had come down at last. He'd fought living men and dead ones, and rival champions seeking the favour of the gods as well. The sky was the colour of blood and the moons were crumbling, and sometimes, when he looked up quickly enough, he could see vast faces, leering down at the world from whatever lofty perch the gods regularly crouched on.

The thought gave him no pleasure. They were just watching now, but if it truly was the end of days, if the Last Hour was finally upon them, then the gods might start taking a more direct hand in the affairs of mortals, and Canto didn't want to be around when that happened. The gods were unpredictable and malignant, and no man could survive their attentions.

Middenheim's walls came alive with blossoms of fire. Bolts, bullets, cannonballs and mortar shells fell among the throng. Canto saw a bouncing cannonball carom off Count Mordrek, knocking the Damned One from his feet. A moment later Mordrek was shoving himself upright, the buckled plates of his armour reshaping themselves even as he staggered back into motion.

'He is truly blessed,' Horvath said.

'Don't let him hear you say that,' Canto grunted. All around them, blood and torn flesh sprayed into the air as cannonballs and mortar shells struck the massed ranks of men moving up the viaduct. Canto grimaced as blood spattered across his armour. He'd counselled the others against this, but they hadn't wanted to hear it. No, they wanted the glory, the honour of first blood. And he'd had no choice but to go along with it; to do otherwise was to risk death. They would have cut him down where he stood, and then gone anyway. *Story of your misbegotten life, Canto,* he thought.

Despite the barrage from the walls Mordrek reached the gatehouse intact, Canto and the others dogging his heels. The Damned One struck the defenders like a wolf attacking sheep. His sword arced out, lopping off limbs and opening bellies. Even as the wounded men fell, their bodies began to writhe and change. New, monstrous limbs erupted from them as the newly awakened things within them shed their human flesh. Monsters sprang up in Mordrek's path, and launched themselves at their former comrades.

Monsters within, monsters without, Canto thought, as he broke into a run. He beheaded a whey-faced halberdier, and then he was inside the walls of the City of the White Wolf, an army of the lost and the damned at his heels.

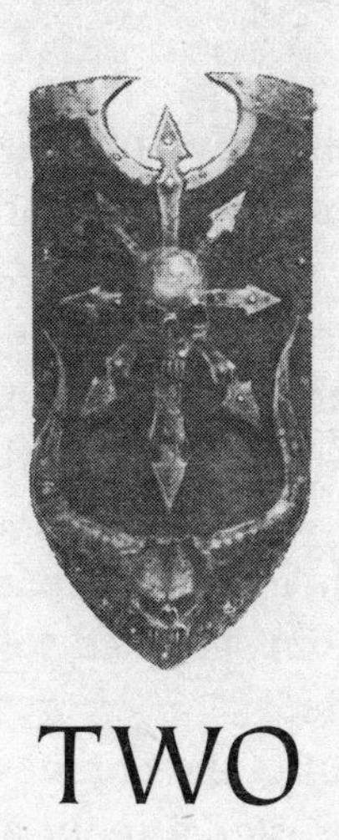

TWO

 *The Depths of the Fauschlag*

Beyond the flickering light of the torches, beady red eyes gleamed. Gregor Martak peered into the dark and frowned. He reached out with his mind, grasping the strands of Ghur which inundated the tunnels. The Amber Wind flowed wild throughout Middenheim, rising from the god-touched stones. The Fauschlag seemed to reverberate with the howling of wolves that only Martak could hear, and he felt a wild, terrible power settle into the marrow of his bones.

'Well, wizard?' Axel Greiss grunted, hefting his hammer. Greiss had come to observe the defence of the tunnels, and had brought reports of enemy contact at the other junctions. A cadre of armoured knights surrounded him, each one a glowering, bearded beacon of Ulric's favour. The presence of the knights and the Grand Master had done much to stiffen the resolve of the common soldiers. Rumours about what had happened in the Temple of Ulric had spread like quicksilver through the city, and Middenheim was in turmoil as priests and templars of Ulric sought to calm the panicked citizenry and soldiery both.

'Hush,' Martak said absently. 'I need to concentrate.' Greiss flushed and growled something, but Martak ignored him. He set his staff and pulled that savage influence into himself, drawing it up, and with a whisper he set it flooding into the packed ranks of troops standing before him, granting courage and strength where there was a deficit of either. As the power flowed out of him, he thought he saw something low and white slink through the legs of the soldiers before him. He felt a wash of hot breath on his neck, and something growled softly in his ear. He shuddered, and the feeling fled.

The skaven poured out of the darkness, a chittering, squealing mass of mangy fur, rusted armour and jagged blades. Men recoiled in instinctive horror, but the whip-crack of a sergeant's voice, loud in the confines of the tunnel, was enough to steady most of them. A second order saw crossbows clatter. A volley of bolts tore through the rapidly diminishing space between the defenders and the encroaching enemy. At such close range, in the narrow tunnel, it was impossible to miss. 'Ha! That's the way,' Greiss bellowed.

Martak watched as the front rank of skaven were punched from their feet. Their bodies, some still twitching, vanished beneath the talons of the next rank as the horde pressed forwards. A hurried second volley proved no more an obstacle than the first, and the skaven ground on, over their own dead and dying, until Martak could hear nothing save their squealing. An order rippled up and down the Empire line and shields were hastily locked, even as the enemy reached them.

'Now you'll see, wizard,' Greiss said. 'This is how a true son of Middenheim fights. With iron and muscle, not sorcery.'

His words stung. Martak looked away. Born in Middenheim he might have been, but he was as much a stranger here as Valten. More so, in fact. Valten wasn't a sorcerer. In the City of the White Wolf, there was no such thing as a good wizard. There was only Chaos, and anyone who practised magic was destined for a fiery end, tied to a witch's stake in a market square, unless the Colleges of Magic got to them first. Even now, they looked at him with suspicion. Even now, they thought he was as bad as the enemy battering at their gates.

If I had my way, I'd tell you to go hang, and take this cesspool with you, Martak thought, watching the battle unfold. He'd always hated cities, and as far as he was concerned, there was no difference between Middenheim and Altdorf. Let them fall. The world would be the better for it. He leaned against his staff, letting it support him for a moment. *But who are you to decide that, eh?* he thought, not without some bitterness. *The gods decided your lot long ago, Gregor Martak. They might be dead and gone to dust, but the course they set for you still holds true. And you'll follow it to the bitter end, because there's no other way out of this trap.*

Screaming ratmen crashed into the shield-wall, and paid a deadly toll. Snouts were smashed to red ruin, and furry bodies were impaled or hacked down by thrusting spears and jabbing halberds. Martak saw a frothing skaven scramble up the surface of a soldier's shield and fling itself onto the man behind him in an effort to escape the deadly press.

Everywhere Martak looked, men and skaven strove against one another. The press of battle swayed back and forth, but the ratmen could not break the shield-wall. Soon, they began to falter. Martak gestured and strengthened flagging sword arms. Unbloodied state troops moved in to bolster the line, and Martak stepped back, pulling his cloak tight about himself, grateful he'd had no cause to enter the fray directly. Ever since the winds of magic had begun to blow so strongly, he could feel the boiling rage that accompanied the Wind of Beasts – a need to tear and bite, to eat and eat and *eat.* He closed his eyes and shivered. When he opened them, he could see Greiss looking at him sidelong, though whether in concern or disgust, he couldn't say.

Pushing the thought aside, he turned his attentions to the

battle. As glad as he was that the skaven were being held at bay, he wondered at the absence of the strange weapons which they had used to such devastating effect during the battle for Altdorf. Where were the gas weapons, the warpstone-fuelled lightning guns? Where were the rat ogres, or even the armoured, black-furred elite of the chittering horde?

'Chaff,' he muttered. 'They're throwing chaff at us. Why?' He stepped back as more troops flooded into the tunnel. Over-enthusiastic commanders were throwing their men into battle with the skaven, stripping them from the garrisons above, trusting in the walls of Middenheim to hold the enemy without while they destroyed the enemy within. And that hadn't been an unreasonable assumption, while the Flame of Ulric had burned. But the fire that stirred the blood of the men of Middenheim and kept daemons out of its streets had been snuffed. 'It's a trick,' he grunted.

'What?' Greiss asked.

'These are the dregs,' Martak said, gesturing. 'They have better troops than this. So where are they? Now is the perfect time to strike, but they are not here.' He looked at Greiss. 'Was it the same in the other tunnels?'

'What's the difference? One rat is much like another,' Greiss said.

'It's a trick,' Martak said. 'They're bleeding us, drawing our eyes away from something else, some other point of attack.' He hesitated. 'We need to fall back. We'll strip men from the reserves in the tunnels above, and bolster the defences along the walls. They're up to something, and we can't let ourselves get trapped down here.'

'Don't be daft,' Greiss said dismissively. 'This is no trick. You said it yourself, man... They're attacking from below, as Archaon attacks from without.' He looked at Martak. 'You were right, wizard,' he said, grudgingly.

'Then how do you explain it?' Martak demanded, knowing

that whatever he'd thought earlier, and whatever Greiss now believed, there was more going on than he could see. He could feel it in his bones.

'I don't have to,' Greiss snarled. He hefted his hammer warningly. 'They attack. So we must defend. Middenheim stands, and while it does, we fight.'

'But what if you're defending the wrong spot?'

'What other spot would you have me defend, wizard? Here is where the enemy is, and– Eh?' The tunnel shuddered violently, interrupting Greiss's outburst. Dust drifted down. Martak looked up. The northern gatehouse was somewhere above them. He blinked dust out of his eyes. Cracks ran along the roof of the tunnel, and his eyes widened.

'By the horns of Taal,' he muttered, as he realised too late what had occurred. He looked back towards the skaven hurling themselves on the swords and spears of the state troops, distracting them, occupying them. He looked back at Greiss. The old knight looked confused. 'Don't you understand? I was wrong! This is a feint! The enemy is in the city,' Martak snarled. 'If you would save your city, Greiss, then you'd best shut up and follow me.'

Northern Gatehouse

Smoke filled the courtyard. Not the greenish cloud from earlier, but black, greasy smoke which vented from the gatehouse and its attached structures. Someone had set fire to something somewhere. The skaven had vanished as quickly as they had appeared. *Small favours,* Wendel Volker thought, as he followed Dubnitz and Goetz across the courtyard. He could still feel the echoes of the drawbridge thudding down in his bones. The sound of it had reminded him of a death-knell, but whether it was for him, the city or the world, he didn't know and feared to guess.

O Sigmar, please take some other poor fool today if you must, but not me, Volker thought as he coughed and staggered towards the raised portcullis that marked the way to the drawbridge. The gatehouse was, in many ways, a small fortress in its own right, and it was far bigger than it first looked. It would take the enemy several minutes to traverse it. He could hear the thudding of feet on the drawbridge, and the creak of the outer portcullis as the enemy sought to rip it from its housings. Stone buckled and burst with a shriek, and men roared in triumph and fear. 'At least we're not alone,' he rasped, drawing his sword.

Those soldiers who had survived the skaven attack on the gatehouse had apparently mustered in the inner causeway between the portcullises, and he could hear some unlucky sergeant screaming for them to hold fast, even as the enemy butchered them. He heard shrieks and cries, and the roars of monsters. Handgunners and crossbowmen on the walls above fired down into the melee. Volker took some comfort in the belch of gunfire, though there was precious little of it to his ears. Where were the reinforcements? Why wasn't anyone coming?

'Probably heading for the eastern gate,' Goetz said. Volker blinked. He hadn't realised that he'd spoken aloud. 'That stuck-up wolf's hindquarters Greiss stripped half the garrison to reinforce the tunnels.'

'Now is that any way to talk about the Grand Master of our honoured brethren in the Order of the White Wolf?' Dubnitz asked. 'What would he think, if he were here to hear you?'

'I wish he *was* here,' Goetz shot back. 'It'd be one more body between us and whatever is bloody well coming across that gods-bedamned drawbridge.' He plucked a shield from the lifeless grip of one of the bodies littering the courtyard and ran the flat of his sword across its rim with a steely screech.

'I'll tell you who I wish were here – a priestess I knew by the name of Goodweather. That woman and her magic shark's teeth would come in handy right about now,' Dubnitz said. His smile faltered for a moment, and his eyes tightened, as if he were seeing something he'd rather not. Then he shook himself. 'Ah, Esme,' he said softly. He shook his head. 'No use wishing, at any rate. We're what's here, and we'll have to make do.'

'Or we could leave,' Volker muttered. 'Make a strategic redeployment somewhere else – preferably Averheim.' Despite his words, he didn't mean it. Not really. He wasn't a coward, though he felt like one at times. He simply wanted the world to slow down, for just a moment, so he could catch his breath.

Unfortunately, the world didn't seem to care what he wanted. Men began fleeing through the courtyard, past Volker and the others. They were bloodied, and looked as if all the daemons of the north were on their heels. Which, Volker supposed, they were. Clawed, incandescent flippers abruptly emerged from the gateway and gripped either side as something squamous and bloated squeezed itself out and gave a deafening screech. A multitude of colourful tendrils moved across its oily skin as it flopped after a fleeing swordsman and scooped him up with an eager grunt.

Before the knights could move, the unlucky man was stuffed kicking and screaming into the monstrous thing's wide maw. Scything fangs reduced the man to silent ruin, and the orb-like eyes of the beast rolled towards them. 'Chaos spawn,' Goetz spat. He swatted his shield with the flat of his sword. 'Come on, ugly. Come to Hector. Come on!' Sword and shield connected again, the sharp sound drawing the monster's attention.

'Goetz...' Volker began.

'Stay back,' Goetz said warningly. He spread his arms, as if inviting the creature to attack. It duly obliged, bounding towards him with a thunderous croak. Its jaws spread like a hellish flower as it flung itself towards him. 'Chew on this,' Goetz snarled as he rammed the rim of his shield into the creature's mouth. He hacked at its protoplasmic flesh, ignoring the lashing tendrils that sought to pull him apart. It grunted and moaned as his sword bit into it. Volker moved to help him, but Dubnitz grabbed his arm.

'Don't worry about Goetz, my friend,' Dubnitz said. 'He once killed a troll with nothing but a broken shield and harsh language. Man was touched by the gods – when there were gods, I mean.' He snatched two fallen shields from the ground and tossed one to Volker, who caught it and slid it on just as the first of the enemy exploded out into the courtyard.

Volker's shock and fear fell away from him as he blocked an axe-blow and brought his sword around and down on the northman's skull. For a moment, the world shrank to the weight of the blade in his hand and the sound of metal biting flesh and bone. He remembered Heldenhame and the long, gruelling march to Altdorf; the retreat north, with roving warbands of skaven and beastmen dogging their heels; the promise of safety which was never quite fulfilled; the faces of friends who'd died on the way.

He stamped forwards, ramming his shield into a marauder's chest, shoving the man back. He drove his heel down on the man's instep, and caught him in the throat with the tip of his sword as he jerked back. In his mind's eye, he saw bodies left lying in the snow and the mud. He heard the crying of children without parents, and the screams of parents without children. And above it all, he heard a booming laughter which he wanted to believe was simply distant thunder, but in his heart knew was anything but.

Nearby, Goetz backhanded a screaming tribesman with his shield, knocking the warrior flat. His sword was a blur of steel, and for a moment, Volker thought that the last Knight of the Blazing Sun might throw back the hordes of Chaos on his own. But more of the howling, wild-eyed northmen slipped past him and charged towards Volker and Dubnitz, the names of their vile gods spilling from their lips.

'There are too many of them for us to hold here,' Volker said. 'Not alone – we can't do it without reinforcements.' He looked around, hoping to hear the tramp of boots or the clop of hooves, but all he saw were the bodies of the dead, and all he heard were the blasphemous cries of the enemy as they made their way over the drawbridge and through the gatehouse. Volker realised with a sinking sensation that he and his fellow knights were the only defenders left. 'This isn't fair,' he whispered, his guts roiling as he lifted his shield to block a wild blow from a frothing beastman. He thrust his sword out instinctively, gutting the creature. He'd come all this way, survived so much – just for it to end here?

'Way of the world, my friend,' Dubnitz grunted, hewing at a Chaos marauder. Blood spattered the big man's face and glistened in his wide, spade-shaped beard. He thrust his knee up between another opponent's legs and opened the warrior's skull from pate to chin.

'What world?' Goetz said, his bronze-hued armour dulled by dust and blood, as he whipped his blade out in a tight arc and opened the throats of three of the shrieking warriors pressing towards them. 'Everything's gone, Dubnitz, and we're fighting over the damned ashes.'

'Speak for yourself,' Dubnitz growled. 'I'm fighting for that last bottle of Sartosan Red I've got chilling in the privy. I'll be damned if one of these barbarians gets to enjoy it before I do. I didn't fight my way out of what was left of Marienburg with it stuffed down my cuirass, just to miss out now!'

'I'm sorry, did you say Sartosan Red?' Volker asked, as he caught an axe-blow on his shield. 'What year is it, then? And you told me we were out!'

'Does it matter?' Goetz asked. 'It's not like any of us will get the chance to drink it.'

'Pay him no mind, Wendel, he's a Talabeclander. Got the taste buds of a radish,' Dubnitz said. He snagged the braided beard of his opponent and jerked the northman towards him. Their heads connected with a dull sound and the Chaos marauder staggered back, eyes wide. Dubnitz gave a laugh and lunged, spitting the man on his sword. He whirled and smashed aside the shield of another warrior, opening the man up to a skull-splitting blow from Goetz. 'There we go – look at that. Just like old times, my friend,' Dubnitz chortled.

'Erkhart – look out!' Volker reached for Dubnitz, even as the Chaos warrior's blade erupted from the other knight's chest. Dubnitz coughed and lurched forwards, pulling himself off the blade. He sank down to one knee, his hand clamped to the wound. Goetz caught the Chaos warrior a blow on the head, staggering him.

'Get him up and out of here,' he snarled, as he moved to confront the warrior who'd felled Dubnitz. The Chaos warrior came at him, roaring something in a guttural tongue. His sword seemed to drink up the blood that coated it, and it glowed with pale flames. Goetz moved quicker than Volker thought possible for a man in full plate, blocking his enemy's blow and countering with one of his own. The two warriors traded blows in the breach, neither giving ground. Behind the Chaos warrior, more northmen mustered, ready to rush the gatehouse when the contest was over. Volker could see that Goetz was tiring, despite his spirited defence. He felt a grip on his arm and looked down into Dubnitz's bloody grin.

'Second privy from the left,' Dubnitz said.

'What?'

'The wine, Wendel. Just in case you live through this,' Dubnitz wheezed. He levered himself to his feet with Volker's help. 'Fall back. They'll need you out there, and no sense in you dying here. Two will do as well as three. We will hold them here, as long as possible.'

'You'll die,' Volker protested.

'Really? Hadn't thought of that. You're right. You stay, we'll go.' Dubnitz caught the back of Volker's head and gave him an affectionate shake. 'Don't be an idiot. My guts would trip me up before I took two steps, and poor Hector has been looking for a place to die since Talabheim.' He smiled weakly. 'It's a funny old world, isn't it? I thought I'd die at the hands of an irate husband. At the very least, I'd do it in Marienburg. Still, one place is as good as any other. Like Hector's late, lamented brothers were wont to say, we do what must be done.' He pushed away from Volker. 'Remember – second one from the left. Don't let it go to waste,' Dubnitz called, as he staggered towards the gatehouse. Along the way he snatched up one of the braziers the sentries had used for light, and hefted it like a spear.

As Volker began to back away, he saw Dubnitz give a shout and lurch into the Chaos warrior, smashing the armoured brute from his feet with the brazier. Goetz was too busy to capitalise on his foe's predicament, as the massed ranks of the enemy gave a roar and charged into the courtyard. Goetz hefted his shield and readied himself to meet them.

The first of the invaders reached him, and their shields slammed together. Goetz was shoved back, but his sword slid across the top of both shields and through his enemy's visor. He wrenched the blade free and shoved the body back, even as a number of slavering Chaos spawn bounded towards him and Dubnitz out of the smoke, their jaws wide. Dubnitz shoved himself to his feet, and for a moment, his eyes met Volker's. He grinned briefly, displaying blood-stained teeth, and winked before he swung around, catching the first of the spawn in the side of its malformed head with the brazier.

Volker turned away. He heard Goetz cry out the name of his goddess, and then he was staggering out of the courtyard, chest heaving. A rank of levelled spears awaited him, protruding from within a wall of locked shields. He stopped short, and then turned as a wild scream caught his attention. A northman charged out of the courtyard, axe raised. And then another, and another. Volker backed away, shield ready. He killed the first of them, grief and anger adding strength to his blow. The second slammed into him, and they fell in a tangle. Volker slammed the pommel of his sword against the warrior's head, and then opened his throat to the bone.

Before he could get to his feet, the third was upon him, axe raised for a killing stroke. Volker tensed to receive the blow he knew was coming. *Sorry, Erkhart,* he thought. *I guess that wine will go to waste after all.*

Moments before the barbarian's blow landed, a warhorse interposed itself, and a hammer sang down, driving the warrior to the ground in a broken heap. Volker looked up into the eyes of the Herald of Sigmar himself, and felt the despair of only a few moments before begin to give way before a surge of hope. 'Are you the last?' Valten asked, his voice carrying easily above the din of battle.

'I... yes,' Volker croaked, trying not to think of the others. *I'm sorry,* he thought again.

Valten nodded brusquely, and turned his head towards the gatehouse. 'Then on your feet, Reiksguard. I need every man who can stand. The enemy is coming, and I would welcome them properly.'

Canto Unsworn strode over the tangle of bodies that blocked the way into the gatehouse courtyard. Dead Chaos spawn, tribesmen and the armoured figures of several of Halfgir's more eager Headsmen were in evidence, as were the bodies of the defenders, one clad in bronze, the other in green. *Two men,* he thought. Horvath strode past him, kicking a plumed helmet aside. 'Two men did all of this,' Canto said, keeping pace with him as they headed for the shattered portcullis at the far end of the courtyard at a fast lope.

'Khorne will welcome their skulls,' Horvath growled. They stepped out of the courtyard and into a melee. Canto saw Count Mordrek wading through the enemy with casual disregard, his blade shrieking in pleasure as it tore the humanity from its victims.

'Maybe so, but I'm not very keen on this invasion if that's the sort of welcome we can expect,' Canto said as he parried the blow of a desperate halberdier. 'These sorts of things have a way of – well, let's be blunt, shall we? – spinning out of control.'

'Silence, Unsworn,' Horvath growled as he chopped through an upraised shield and into the man cowering beneath it.

'All I'm saying is, this just proves that things could go very badly, very quickly. Pivotal moments, Horvath. They're an unsteady sort of foundation to build future endeavours on.'

'By all of the names of all of the gods, would you be silent, Canto? You've been yammering incessantly since Praag,' Horvath hissed. 'If Halfgir were to hear you...'

'Halfgir caught a cannonball in the gut coming up the viaduct. He's not hearing anything any time soon,' Canto said, not without some humour. 'I suppose that means you're in charge of the warband now – Horvath's Headsmen, they'll call us.'

'I said be silent,' Horvath snarled, slapping a swordsman aside. 'By the brass balls of Khorne, do you ever shut up?'

Canto didn't reply. An Ulrican priest circled him, moving lightly across the blood-slick cobbles, hammer raised, wolf-skin cloak flapping. Canto concentrated on the man's sweaty, snarling features, waiting for that oh-so-familiar tightening of skin around the eyes that would betray his next move. Flesh crinkled, and the Ulrican stamped forwards, hammer whirling. Canto twisted aside at the last moment, and the hammer smashed down, shattering cobbles. Before the priest could recover, Canto drove his sword through the man's side. The Ulrican howled, and Canto twisted his blade and shoved, chopping through the man's spine and out of his back in a spray of blood.

He was already moving forwards as the body flopped to the ground. Swords and spears sought him from every direction, and he chopped and slashed, trying to clear himself room. The Empire troops were beginning to waver. Already the rear ranks were retreating. But there were still enough of them to prove troublesome. *Tilea, Estalia, maybe even Cathay, but no – Kislev. You chose to go to Kislev,* he thought. But that was a lie. There had been no choice. He and Horvath and all of the others, the whole innumerable horde-to-end-all-hordes, were like drowning men caught in a maelstrom. There was no way to break its pull, no way to escape. You could only go with the tide, and hope you drowned later, rather than sooner.

Or, in the case of some men, that you drowned at all.

Count Mordrek lashed out with the flat of his blade and his fist, driving back his own allies. Marauders stumbled back in confusion as Mordrek cleared a space between the two sides. The soldiers of the Empire, in contrast to their enemies, seemed only too glad for the momentary respite. Mordrek whirled about and pointed at a figure on horseback with his sword. 'Herald of Sigmar! I see thee, I name thee and I demand thy presence!' he roared, in archaic Reikspiel. 'Count Mordrek challenges thee, son of the comet.'

Canto lowered his own blade. 'So that's why you were in such a blasted hurry,' he muttered. Around him, Horvath and the others had realised what was about to happen. Gore-encrusted weapons began to smash against shields, or thump against the cobbles. Canto examined the warrior that Mordrek had called to, and felt a stirring of recognition as the man urged his horse through the ranks of the state troops. He'd seen that face before, during the battle at the Auric Bastion. And he recognised the heavy warhammer clutched in his hand, as well. 'Skull-Splitter,' he hissed.

'What?' Horvath grunted.

'That's Sigmar's hammer, dolt,' Canto said. 'The Skull-Splitter itself. I saw it used once, a long time ago. Some self-righteous prig from Nuln was using it to put the fear of his god into the enemy at the battle of the Bokha Palaces. Like a thunderbolt wrapped in gold,' he murmured, lost for a moment in images of the past. That was when he'd first set his foot on the path to immortality and ruin. In Kislev, when another Everchosen had been knocking on the door of the world, Canto had been given a choice. And he'd made the wrong one. *But who knew old Wheezy von Bildhofen would become Emperor? Not me. How was I to know? Not a sorcerer, am I? I did my bit,* he thought, centuries of bitterness welling up as fresh as the day he'd chosen not to slip a knife in the back of his old school-mate, out of some misguided sense of – what? – friendship? Pity? Or something else... Fear, maybe.

And now here we are again, Canto. Part of the Army of the End Times, only this time you're being honest about whose side you're on, aren't you? he thought, watching... Valten, that was his name, riding towards them, carrying the weapon of a god. Unease gnawed at his gut as Valten drew closer. It wasn't just the hammer; it was everything about him – the set of his shoulders, the armour he wore, the look in his eyes. All of it screamed 'danger', the same way von Bildhofen had, so many centuries ago.

'On this day, I at last see clearly. The world is once more real to me. The voices of the gods have guided me to this moment. Time, fate and destiny grow thin, and there is only the now. A chance to feel alive,' Mordrek continued as Valten approached. His voice, rusty with disuse, began to grow stronger as he spoke. 'The gods demand that I kill you, Herald, and then they will free me. But they lie. They always lie, even when it serves no purpose.'

Valten slid from his horse and strode towards Mordrek, hammer in hand. As he drew close, Canto felt a quiver of fear blossom in him. He looked around and saw that he was not alone in feeling out of sorts. A shape, larger than any man, at once ghostly and somehow more real than the world around it, crouched within that husk of flesh, and it was *hungry*. It was so terribly hungry. It hungered for split skulls and splintered bones, for battle and cleansing fire. In Valten's footsteps, Canto could hear the rattle of spears, the roar of warriors, the howl of wolves and, above it all, the dull, ponderous rhythm of a hammer slamming down on an anvil. He'd heard that sound before, at the Bokha Palaces, in the words of a man named Magnus. It rang in his skull like the stroke of doom, and he began to edge back.

'What is that? What *is* it?' Horvath growled hoarsely, eyes wide. 'Is it a daemon?'

'Did you think we were the only ones with gods, you blood-drunk fool?' Canto snapped.

A warrior, unable to control himself, broke from the ranks and charged towards Valten, howling out a prayer to the Skull Throne. Mordrek cut his legs out from under him before he'd gone far, and then beheaded the writhing spawn that erupted from the dying man's tattooed flesh. He spun, arms spread, driving them back with the force of his fury. 'This day is mine! I have been waiting for it always. I will not be denied. Not by gods or men or even the Three-Eyed King himself,' he roared.

Point made, he turned back to Valten, who had stopped some distance away, hammer held low. Mordrek lifted his sword. 'I know the fire which snarls in me, Herald. Even in death, it burns. It cannot be extinguished, not even by the gods themselves. It can only be snuffed by the hand of the one fated to do it. By your hand! Never more to be raised up, never more to be kindled anew. Kill me if you can, Herald of Sigmar,' the tall warrior intoned. 'And Count Mordrek, once-lord of Brass Keep, once-elector, once-son of a forgotten Emperor, shall sing your praises in the world to come.' He struck his cuirass with a clenched fist.

'Gladly,' Valten said. That single word sent a ripple of unrest through the men around Canto, and he could not blame them. The word was a promise, and a prophecy. Mordrek made a sound deep in his throat, like an eager dog, and he sprang forwards.

Cursed blade and godly hammer connected in a shower of sparks. A shriek, like that of a dying goat, echoed through the streets as the daemon trapped in Mordrek's weapon felt the touch of Ghal Maraz. They duelled back and forth, moving almost too fast for Canto to follow.

Mordrek lunged, stamped and thrust, wielding his sword two-handed. Valten blocked every blow but launched few of his own, content to prolong the fight for as long as possible. A moment later, Canto realised why. Past the fight, he saw that the Empire ranks were beginning to thin. He felt a smile creep across his face. *Clever,* he thought. No wonder Valten had agreed to the duel. While they were occupied watching Mordrek work out his frustrations, the enemy were slipping away. He considered bringing it to someone's attention, and then dismissed the thought. He wasn't in charge, and it wasn't as if there were anywhere to go. If those men didn't die here, they'd die somewhere else. At this point, it was a foregone conclusion.

Mordrek's blade screeched as it skidded across Valten's pauldron, drawing smoke from the metal. Valten turned into the blow and his hammer smashed into Mordrek's belly, catapulting him off his feet. Mordrek hit the ground and rolled. Valten stalked forwards as Mordrek levered himself up, one arm wrapped around his stomach. Mordrek, still on one knee, extended his sword towards Valten, holding him at bay.

'Pain,' Mordrek rumbled. 'I have felt so much pain. Pain will not kill me, Herald. My will is strong, and I will not be denied.' He lunged to his feet, sword whirling over his head. Valten ducked aside as the blade snarled down, cleaving a cobblestone in two. Mordrek spun, and his sword lashed out again. It connected with a hastily interposed hammer. Even so, the force of the blow nearly knocked Valten from his feet. 'Fight, damn you,' Mordrek roared. 'Fight me, Herald. I am here to kill you – to spare the Three-Eyed King your wrath, and see that the desires of the gods are not thwarted. But I do not care about Archaon, or the petty wants of fate. What shall be or would have been is not my concern. Fight me. Kill me!'

Valten did not reply. He swatted aside Mordrek's next blow and sent Ghal Maraz shooting forwards through his grip, so that it crunched into the visor of Mordrek's helmet. Mordrek staggered back. The terrible hammer licked out and smashed down on Mordrek's sword arm. His blade fell from nerveless fingers and clattered to the ground, where it screeched and wailed like a wounded animal. Valten stamped down on it and kicked it aside before Mordrek could retrieve it.

The hammer snapped out, and Canto winced as one of Mordrek's knees went. Mordrek sank down with a groan, and the world seemed to shudder slightly, as if it were out of focus. The hammer dropped down, crushing a shoulder, then a clawing hand. Canto risked a look up at the howling sky, and saw no leering faces. The gods had turned away from this battle now. Were they disappointed, he wondered? Part of him hoped so. Part of him hoped that here and now Mordrek would slip their leash. He turned his attentions back towards the duel.

Mordrek knelt before the Herald of Sigmar, head bowed, his armour shuddering slightly, as if what it contained were seeking escape. Mordrek made no move to stand. He looked up as Valten's shadow fell over him.

'I never had a chance,' Count Mordrek said. He sounded happy.

'No,' Valten said.

Mordrek began to laugh. The eerie sound slithered through the air, and even the most slaughter-drunk warrior fell silent at its approach. Mordrek bowed his head again. The hammer rose. When it fell, the mountain shuddered. The sky twisted, and the wind howled. An empty suit of armour rattled to the ground. Thus passed Count Mordrek the Damned, wanderer of the Wastes and exile of the Forbidden City.

The Herald of Sigmar turned to face the ranks of the invaders. In his cool blue gaze was a promise of death and damnation. He raised his hammer, and the closest of them drew back. Their gods were not here, and there would be no help. Canto shivered inside his armour, and wondered if there were any champion among them who was equal to the man before them.

Valten held their gaze as the moment stretched. Then he turned, caught his horse's bridle, and swung himself into the saddle. He turned the animal around without hurry, and rode away, after his retreating troops.

The northern gatehouse had fallen to the enemy.

THREE

 *The Manndrestrasse, Grafsmund-Norgarten District*

Gregor Martak flung out his hand. Shards of amber coalesced about his curled fingers and shot forwards to puncture the dark armour of the Chaos knights charging towards the embattled soldiers. He spun his staff in his hands, his fingers bleeding where they had been scraped raw by the rough wood, and a whirlwind full of amber spears roared across the plaza, sweeping up tribesmen and reducing them to red ruin. But it wasn't enough. The enemy pressed his threadbare force from all sides. The air stank of smoke and blood, and the battle cries of Talabecland and Middenland warred with idolatrous hymns to the Lord of Skulls and the Prince of Pleasure. Courtyards and junctions were swept clear of the enemy by cannonades, only to be filled anew moments later.

Guns boomed around him, banners fluttered bravely overhead, and his own magics threw back the enemy time and again, but it wasn't enough. Still the enemy ground on, showing no more concern for their fallen than the skaven had in the tunnels. Black-armoured figures chanting praises to the Dark Gods poured with undimmed enthusiasm towards the men of the Empire. Mingled among them were the hairy forms of loping beastmen, and the abominable, contorted shapes of mutants and worse things besides.

Rage surged in him and he slammed the end of his staff down. Cruel spikes of amber burst through the street, impaling a knot of snarling, scarred Aeslings. His breath shuddered in his lungs, and he cursed himself for the third time in as many minutes.

Stupid old man. Thought you were so clever, didn't you? Well look at where that cleverness has got you now, ran the refrain. It was, he had to admit, not without merit. After realising what the skaven were up to, he had hurried back to the surface, stripping reserves of state troops from the staging points in the upper tunnels as he went. The way he'd seen it, those men would be more useful on the surface, than waiting for an attack that might never come below.

And they had been. He'd led them up onto the streets, and they'd thrown back the Chaos vanguard. Martak had led the way, flinging spears of sorcerous amber, and bellowing orders in his best imitation of Grand Master Greiss. The halberds and crossbow bolts of those following him had butchered northlander tribesman by the score. Knights of the White Wolf galloped down cobbled streets, hammers swinging, driving entire tribes of the enemy before them. Men from every province fought together as one, united in their desire to drive the northlanders from the city.

Unfortunately, his decision to strip the garrisons had proven to be less than inspired when a fresh wave of skaven reinforcements had driven the token force that remained in the tunnels out. Even now, a seething wave of chittering ratmen was flooding down the broad avenue of the Manndrestrasse towards his lines, driving the remainder of the tunnel garrisons before them. He caught sight of Greiss, as the latter crushed a rat ogre's skull with a brutal blow from his hammer. As the beast fell, the old templar glared at him, fury in his eyes.

'It seemed like a good idea at the time,' Martak muttered, though he knew the old man couldn't hear him. If both of them survived this, Greiss would kill Martak himself, and the wizard wouldn't blame him. He thrust his staff out like a spear and a tendril of amber shot from the tip, plucking a Chaos knight from his mutated steed.

Hundreds of ratmen had followed Greiss and the others into the streets, and these were no fear-crazed vermin, but the elite of that fell race. Bulky, black-furred rats clad in heavy armour marched alongside lumbering rat ogres with belching fire-throwers strapped to their long arms and metal plates riveted to their abused flesh. More skaven, Martak fancied, than even had laid siege to the city before Archaon's arrival. By the time he'd understood the full enormity of his error, the skaven had struck his lines from behind.

Now, they were making a last stand on an avenue named for the Skavenslayer himself as the skaven swept through the city, their forces joining those of Archaon to isolate the remaining gatehouses. While the north and east had already fallen, the south and west gates had remained barred to the enemy. But Martak could see the smoke, and runners had brought him word that the gatehouses were surrounded and cut off.

Middenheim would fall. It was not his fault, but that didn't make it any better. Not everyone agreed, of course. Greiss's horse thrust its way through the fighting towards him. 'Was this your plan, then?' Greiss snarled. 'We're cut off from the rest of the city. The enemy is before us and behind us.'

'As they would have been had we stayed below,' Martak rasped.

'So you say,' Greiss snapped. The old man looked fatigued, and blood streaked his features and armour. 'You've doomed us, wizard. We should never have abandoned the Ulricsmund.' He twisted in his saddle and swatted a leaping mutant from the air. The creature fell squalling amongst a group of halberdiers, who swiftly dispatched it. 'And where is the so-called Herald of Sigmar, eh? Where is Valten, when we need him?'

'Fighting for the city, as we are, I imagine,' Martak said. He felt the winds of magic tense and flex beneath the clutch of another mind. He turned, seeking the source of the disturbance. A cloaked and hooded figure crouched atop a nearby roof, worm-pale hands gesturing tellingly.

Martak shoved past Greiss and shouted a single word. The air before them hardened into a shield of amber even as arrows of shadow launched themselves from the curling fingers of the sorcerer towards the Grand Master of the Order of the White Wolf. The amber barrier cracked and split as the shadowy missiles writhed against it. Martak gestured, and the barrier collapsed about the darkling projectiles, sealing them inside. A second gesture sent the amber sphere hurtling away at speed, back towards the sorcerer on the rooftop. The man leapt gracefully from the roof a moment before impact. He dropped to the cobbles, where he was engulfed by the battle and lost to Martak's sight.

A moment later, that part of the street erupted in a flickering balefire. Bodies were hurled into the air or slammed back against the buildings that lined the street. Warriors from both sides screamed as the coruscating flames consumed them. Men fell, wracked with sickening, uncontrollable mutations, their bodies growing and bursting like overripe fruits. The sorcerer, his robes askew, strode through the conflagration, his hood thrown back to reveal a golden helmet covered in leering mouths. 'Malofex comes...' the mouths shrieked as one. 'Bow before Malofex, master of the Tempest Incarnate, freer of the First Born, bowbowbow*bow*.'

'No,' Martak said. He slammed his staff down, and the street rumbled as a ridge of amber spikes sprouted and stretched towards the sorcerer. Malofex stretched out a hand, and the amber turned liquid and rose into the air, becoming globules which began to spin faster and faster about the sorcerer's head. Then, with a sound like the crack of a whip, the globules shot back towards Martak.

Martak's eyes widened and he whipped his staff up and around in a tight circle, carving protective sigils on the air. The globules of amber struck the invisible barrier and exploded, casting razor-edged shards into the melee around him.

'Malofex, who freed Kholek Suneater, Malofex, who uprooted the Gibbering Tower, bids you cease and kneel, hedge-wizard,' the mouths on the sorcerer's helmet ranted. 'Bow to Malofex, and live.' As the sorcerer moved towards Martak, colourful flames sprouted on his robes, rising about him like an infernal halo. The flames swept out and struck the ground, towering around them like the walls of a keep.

Martak set the butt of his staff on the ground, and gripped the haft in both hands. Shards of amber formed and darted for the sorcerer, and were melted by the flames, or caught and crunched by the hateful mouths. He could feel the other's will pressing down on his own. He had surprised his opponent before, caught him off-guard, but now the full force of the sorcerer's attention was on him, and Martak found himself slowly but surely buckling beneath the weight of it. He was tired. He had been since Altdorf. There was no time to rest his mind or body. The war had been gruelling and his strength was worn to the nub. But he would not surrender, not now, not here. He hurled spell after spell at his opponent, and each was blocked or dispelled easily.

Out of the corner of his eye, he could see Greiss trying to break through the flames that had risen to isolate him and his opponent from the battle going on around them. In the flames were faces, moaning, screaming, laughing, and they licked at Martak's flesh, raising weals of strange hues and sending shivers of pain through him. He could hear the chuckles and whispers of the mouths, and the sibilant crackle of the flames rising from his opponent's frame as the sorcerer drew close. But, then, a new sound intruded and the world grew slow around him. The flames seemed to freeze in place, and the colour drained from them as they fell silent.

In their place was the howling of wolves. Martak's breath frosted as the temperature dropped. His skin felt cold and clammy, and he heard the snarls and growls of beasts on the hunt. Lupine shadows stretched across the ground towards him. And then, as it stepped through Malofex's fire, he saw it.

The wolf loped towards him, seemingly unconcerned by what was going on around it. It moved effortlessly, as if it were a thing not of flesh but instead a ghost or phantom. Its jaws sagged in a lupine grin, and the howls grew louder, threatening to rupture Martak's eardrums. He could no longer hear Malofex, and the roar of battle sounded as if it were far away. All he could hear were the howls, and the harsh panting of the white wolf as it closed in on him.

It leapt past the sorcerer, sparing him not a glance. Martak wanted to move out of its path, but some force held him frozen in place. The wolf grew larger and larger, its mouth expanding until its upper jaw blocked out the sky and its lower tore furrows in the street, and then Martak was between them and they snapped shut.

Martak was enveloped in darkness. Frost formed on his shaking limbs, and icicles grew in his tangled beard. The howling grew thunderous, and he sank down to one knee, hands clasped to his ears. White specks swam through the dark, faster and faster, and he thought that they might be snow. He heard the crunch of footsteps: human ones, not the padding of paws, but somehow more terrifying for all of that.

Get up.

Martak peered into the swirling snow. The voice had been like ice falling from the face of a cliff, or the stormy waters of the Sea of Claws as they smashed into the shore. It reverberated about him, surrounding him and filling his head.

Get up, Gregor Martak. A man of Middenheim does not kneel.

Martak shoved himself to his feet. Something massive and terrible lunged out of the whirling snow, and caught his throat in a cold grip. He felt claws digging into his neck, and found himself flung down onto hard stones.

He does not kneel. But he will bare his throat, when it is demanded.

The curtain of snow parted, revealing not a beast, but an old, stooped man crouched over him, one hand locked about his throat. The old man's nostrils flared and he tilted his worn, hairy features up, as if tasting the air. He was clad in white furs and bronze armour, of the kind worn by horse-lords and the barrow kings who had ruled what was now the Empire in the centuries before the coming of Sigmar. His eyes glinted like chips of ice as he dragged Martak to his feet. 'Who–?' Martak croaked.

The old man threw back his head and howled. The sound was echoed by the unseen wolves, and its fury battered Martak like the blows of an enemy. He would have fallen, but for the old man's grip on his throat.

Quiet. Listen.

Martak shuddered, as the gates of his mind were burst asunder and a wild host of images flooded into him. He saw a vast cavern, somewhere far beneath the Fauschlag, though he did not know how he knew that, and saw the roaring light of the Flame of Ulric, stretching upwards towards the Temple of Ulric above. He saw a figure clad in flowing robes step from the shadows and saw ancient wolves rise from the sleep of ages to defend the Flame from the intruder.

In the flashes of sorcerous light which accompanied the short but brutal battle, the figure stood revealed. *An elf,* Martak thought, confused. His confusion turned to horror as he watched the elf thrust his staff into the Flame. The fire shrank away as the head of the staff touched it, and the guardian wolves howled as one and collapsed into shards of bone and ice. A moment later, the chamber fell into darkness.

And in that darkness, something moved and grew. In the ashes of the Flame, something began to stir, and Martak felt fear course through him. 'What is it?' he groaned as he squeezed his eyes shut. There were stars in the darkness, not the clean, pure stars of the night sky but rotten lights which marked the audient void, strung between sour worlds. He could hear voices, scratching at the walls of his mind, and heard the cackling of daemons.

Chaos, Ulric said. *The thief stole my flame, and now the world aches as old wounds open in her flesh. Our mother dies, Gregor Martak, and I die with her. I am the last of the Firstborn, and my power, my rage... fades.*

Martak looked up into the old god's face. There was fear there, but anger as well. The anger of a dying wolf as it snaps and snarls at its hunters, even as the trap crushes its leg and the spears pierce its belly. Ulric released his throat and laid a hand on his shoulder.

But it is not gone yet.

Ulric was not one to waste time. There was a moment of pain, of a cold beyond any Martak had felt, and a tearing sensation deep in his chest, as if something had eaten out his heart to make room for itself. And then, the world crashed back to life around him.

Martak opened his eyes. He could hear the crackle of Malofex's flames, Greiss's shouts, the din of battle. And beneath it all, the heartbeat of a god. Frost slipped from between his lips as time began to speed up. His staff vibrated in his grip as the ancient wood was permeated with rivulets of ice. He released it and it exploded into a thousand glittering shards, which hovered before him. The temperature around him dropped precipitously, and Malofex's flames were turned to ice. The sorcerer stopped and looked around, confused.

The hungry smile of a predator spread across Martak's features. The shards of icy wood shot forwards, punching through Malofex's hastily erected mystical defences as if they were not there, and smashed into the sorcerer's body. He was hurled backwards, and where he crashed down, ice began to creep across the cobblestones.

Malofex tried to pull himself upright, his many mouths cursing and screaming. The shards burrowed into him and tendrils of ice erupted from his twitching frame, coating him in frost and covering the street. Soon, there was nothing left of the sorcerer save a grisly sculpture. Martak turned his attentions to the northmen.

As the Chaos worshippers charged towards him, he raised his hands. He snarled a string of guttural syllables, and the air hummed, twitched and then exploded into a howling blizzard. Those closest to him were flash-frozen where they stood, becoming ice-bound statues, much like Malofex. Martak brought his hands together in a thunderous clap, and the newly made statues exploded into a storm of glittering shards. Hundreds fell to the icy maelstrom. Beastmen, skaven and Chaos warriors alike were ripped to shreds by Ulric's wintry fangs.

Martak lifted his hand, drawing the newly fallen snow and ice up in a cracking, crunching wave, and a moment later, the Manndrestrasse was blocked by a solid wall of ice. The wizard lowered his hand, and turned. Frightened men stumbled away from him, their breath turning to frost on the chilly air which emanated from him. Only Greiss did not fall back as Martak approached. Even so, the old knight flinched as Martak's eyes came to rest on him.

'Your eyes... they've changed,' Greiss said.

'Yes,' Martak said. 'We must fall back. To the Temple of Ulric, where the heart of the city still beats. Valten will meet us there, as will any other survivors.' He strode past Greiss without waiting for a reply.

'How do you know he'll be there?' Greiss demanded. 'How did you do whatever it was you just did?' He lumbered after Martak. 'Answer me, wizard!'

Martak stopped, and turned. Greiss froze. The old man stared at him, and his face paled as he began to at last comprehend what he was looking at. 'Your eyes are yellow,' Greiss murmured. 'A wolf's eyes...'

Martak said nothing. He turned away. A moment later, the first of his men followed. The ranks split around Greiss and flowed after Martak, leaving the Grand Master of the Order of the White Wolf staring after them.

The Ulricsmund

Wendel Volker beat aside the rough wooden shield and drove his sword through the northman's stinking furs. The warrior uttered a strangled cough as he folded over the blade. Volker set his boot against the dead man and jerked his weapon free.

Panting, he looked around. The battle, such as it had been, was winding down. A few dozen had tried to ambush his small troop of handgunners and halberdiers, and had fared accordingly. His mother had always said that northmen had neither fear nor sense, and that combination was what made them dangerous. Volker was forced to agree, given what he'd seen of their conduct so far. It was as if they had all been driven mad, all at once, and unleashed by some ill-tempered caretaker.

Then, perhaps their madness was merely acceptance of the inevitable. The horizon glowed with witchfire, and strangely hued smoke rose above the eastern section of the city. He could hear strange sounds slithering through the streets, like cackling children and grunting hogs. Shadows without bodies to cast them moved tauntingly along the walls to either side of Valten's battered column of men, and sometimes, when Volker glanced at them quickly enough, they seemed to be reaching for him.

Ghosts, he thought. The city was full of ghosts now. Would it become like they said Praag had been, before its final razing, or like Talabheim was now – a haunt for monsters and daemons, unfit for normal men? That was always the bit of the old stories that had stuck in Volker's craw as a child. Even when men won, they lost. It hadn't seemed particularly fair to a lad of six, and the world hadn't done much to change his opinion since.

'Right, lads, back in line,' he called out to the others. They wore a collection of uniforms from various provinces and carried a motley assortment of weapons, and there was at least one woman among their ranks, a narrow-faced sneak-thief named Fleischer. 'Close ranks, wipe the blood off your faces and don't get separated. If you get lost, I'm not bloody well coming to look for you.'

'Not unless we're in a tavern,' one wit grunted, a formidable looking man by the name of Brunner. He wore a dented sallet helm that covered most of his face, and a battered suit of brigandine armour. Bandoliers of throwing knives and pistols scavenged from gods alone knew where hung across his bulky torso.

Volker pointed his sword in Brunner's direction. 'And if you find one that's still standing, and not drier than the Arabyan desert, be sure to let me know.' The others laughed, as Volker had known they would. Even Brunner cracked a smile. He'd known men who commanded through fear, like the late, unlamented Captain Kross with whom he'd shared duties at Heldenhame, and others who seemed born to it, like Kurt Helborg. But for the Wendel Volkers of the world, who were neither particularly frightful, nor authoritative, humour was the lever of command.

A jape and a jest served to keep you surrounded by friends, rather than resentful underlings. Discipline was required, but a bit of honey helped it work its way down. It was especially useful given that he and his motley coterie were the merest nub of the hundred or so men who had followed Valten from the northern gatehouse or been picked up en route. The northmen were pressing into the city from all directions now, and the shattered remnants of the defensive garrisons were retreating before them.

Why exactly he'd volunteered to lead the way and act as the point of the spear, Volker couldn't say. Valten hadn't asked, and there were other men likely better suited to the task close to hand. But he'd needed to do it. He'd needed to prove something to himself, perhaps, or maybe he'd simply needed to *do* something. Something to occupy his mind, something to focus on, to keep him busy while the darkness closed in. When the end came, Volker didn't want to see it. He had a feeling that it wouldn't be any more pleasant for seeing it coming. Not for him a hero's death. Something quiet and relatively painless would suit him fine.

He reached up to rub his shoulder in an effort to ease the ache growing in it, and swore under his breath as his armour snagged painfully. He still wasn't used to it. He didn't know why he'd accepted the commission into the Reiksguard. The Volkers had always been staunch Feuerbachists, rather than supporters of the Holswig-Schliestein family. 'Up Talabecland,' as his father had often used to say, loudly and at inappropriate times. Then, what did political divides matter when the wolf was at the door of the world?

Volker swept his sword clean on his defeated opponent's furs, nose wrinkling in disgust. As he sheathed his blade, he thought again of Goetz and Dubnitz. He wished they were here. Bravery had come easily in their presence. They had been like him – normal men, trapped in abnormal times. *A dying breed,* he thought, as he looked back at the column as it advanced down the boulevard, Valten at its head.

He caught the other man's gaze and nodded once, briskly. Valten returned the nod and raised his gore-stained hammer, rousing his men to the march once more. He spoke of the Temple of Ulric as if it were a source of salvation, rather than a place to make a final stand, and his words instilled courage and drove back fatigue. He wasn't like Volker. Volker had been wrong, before. He saw that now. Valten was something else – not just a man, but an idea made real. Hope given form, and authority. The Empire made flesh. Abnormal times bred abnormal men. Only gods and monsters could survive what was coming, Volker thought. Where that left him, or any of the rank and file, exactly, he didn't know, and didn't care to think about.

He shook himself, and looked at his men. 'Let's go. We've got half the Ulricsmund between us and the temple, and the wolves of the north are snapping at our heels. It'll take the Three-Eyed King time to get them all moving in the same direction, but I'd like to be behind a cannon when that happens. Brunner, take point.' The big man nodded and moved forwards through the smoke, along the ruined boulevard, falchion in one hand and a pistol in the other. Volker had heard somewhere that Brunner had been a bounty-hunter, before the natural order had been overturned. Whatever he'd been, he was a born scout – stealthy, sneaky and utterly vicious.

Volker and the others followed as Brunner loped ahead of them. Volker kept his cycs on the surrounding buildings and alleyways, alert for anything that might signal an attack. He could hear the sound of battle echoing up from the city around him, and the air stank of a thousand fires. A mass of men as large as the one behind him was bound to attract attention. It wasn't a question of if an attack would come, but when – not to mention what form it would take.

Besides attacks by random warbands of northmen, out for slaughter and pillage, the column had had to deal with worse things. The creature calling itself Count Mordrek had been but the first. Others, champions of the Dark Gods all, had hurled themselves at Valten out of the press of battle as he led his men through the reeling city. Volker could not help but keep a tally, for some of those names were nightmares which had frightened him as a child: names like Ragnar Painbringer, Sven Bloody-Hand, Engra Deathsword, Vygo Thrice-Tainted and Surtha Lenk. Names to conjure with, warlords and near-daemons, all of whom seemed intent on taking Valten's head before he laid eyes on Archaon.

Whatever their names or titles, Valten fought them all. Ghal Maraz took a steady toll of shattered skulls and broken bones, and through it all, the light within him shone brighter and brighter. It was as if whatever force drove him was growing stronger. Vashnar the Tormentor fell on the steps of the Middenplatz, and a burly, boisterous warrior calling himself Khagras the Horselord was left broken in the ruins of the Dragon Ale Brewery. The most recent of them, Eglixus, self-proclaimed Executioner of Trechagrad, had fallen mewling and broken-backed in the dust of the Freiburg, as Valten led his men steadily towards the Temple of Ulric.

Volker heard a whistle from up ahead. Brunner appeared out of the smoke, his taciturn features pale beneath his helm. 'How many?' Volker said.

Brunner held up three fingers. 'Three,' he rasped.

'Three what? Three dozen? Three hundred?'

The former bounty hunter shook his head. 'Just three.' He looked at Volker, and then past him. Volker turned, as Valten rode towards them.

'What is it?' he asked.

'Three men,' Volker said. He looked up at Valten. 'Do you want us to go ahead?' he asked, even as he prayed that the other man would say no.

Valten shook his head. 'No.' He smiled, and for a moment, it was as if something older and infinitely more savage looked out at the world from behind his eyes. 'No, I think they are waiting for me.' He turned and signalled for the column to wait. Then he urged his horse forwards, into the smoke. Volker looked at Brunner and the others, shook his head and gestured.

'Well, we bloody well can't let the Herald of Sigmar ride off alone, now can we?'

'Speak for yourself,' Brunner muttered. But he followed Volker as the latter led the others in pursuit of Valten. They didn't have far to go. They just had to follow the sound of weapons meeting, and the harsh curses of the combatants. A large edifice, once regal, now smashed and defiled, rose up before them through the smoke.

Volker stifled a gasp as he recognised the Temple of Verena. The dome of the roof had been cracked wide open, and what appeared to be a Norscan longboat now rose from it. How it had got there, Volker couldn't imagine. The wide avenue before the steps was littered with bodies in the livery of three provinces, all buried beneath clouds of humming flies. The bodies were already beginning to bloat and burst, as if they had been out in the sun for days, rather than hours. He pressed the back of his hand to his mouth, and tried to control the surge of bile that suddenly filled his throat.

Two men duelled amid the heaps of bodies. One was a monster of a man, clad in black, ruined armour, wielding a triple-headed flail. The other, a hairy northman wearing battered armour and more skulls than any self-respecting human ought, fought with a Norscan longsword and a heavy kite shield. They paid no heed to the newcomers, seemingly occupied with their duel.

'They've been fighting for just hours,' a languid voice said. Volker's spine itched as the words reached his ears. For the first time, he noticed the golden-haired man sprawled across the steps of the temple, a polished shield propped up beside him and his feet crossed on the broken body of a priest of Verena. The man was inordinately handsome. Too handsome. Volker felt something in him twitch away from the sheer, monstrous beauty of the speaker.

'You'll have to forgive Valnir and Wulfrik,' the man continued. There was a glow about him, as if thousands of fireflies were flitting about his head and shoulders. 'They are otherwise occupied. Selfish brutes that they are, they have little thought for the boredom such games inflict on others.' He smiled widely and sat up. 'Lucky for you, I am unengaged.'

Valten straightened. He laid his hand on the hammer where it lay balanced across his saddle, as if to calm the ancient weapon. The man on the steps frowned, and Volker felt his guts turn to ice. 'Are you not going to ask who I am?' the man said.

'I know who you are, Geld-Prince. Sigvald, boy-prince of an extinct tribe, monster, cannibal and daemon.' The strange lights surrounding the other man seemed to dim as Valten spoke, and when he took hold of Ghal Maraz's haft and lifted the weapon, the lights faded entirely, leaving only a ghostly afterglow.

'Not a daemon. Not yet. Perhaps never. Such ugly things, daemons. Function over form, as they say,' Sigvald said. His smile returned. 'The gods have tasked we three with killing you, but, well, that is not an honour lightly bestowed,' he purred, admiring his reflection in the polished surface of his shield. He glanced at them, and Volker felt a chill as those radiant eyes swept over him and dismissed him in the same instant. 'I, of course, felt it should have been mine, but, well, my... comrades disagreed. So, the Reaper and the Wanderer fight. Winner gets you, Herald of Sigmar.'

'And you?' Valten asked.

Sigvald laughed, and Volker cringed. He wasn't alone in that reaction. Even Brunner looked uncomfortable, and Fleischer unleashed a flurry of curses beneath her breath. The sound of Sigvald's laughter was too perfect, too beautiful, and nearby, one of Valten's men wept bloody tears as he dropped his weapon and clutched at his ears. He sank down into the dust, and began to whimper. Sigvald smiled, as if the sound were for his benefit. 'I have no interest in you, son of the comet. You are but the appetiser to the glorious banquet to come, and one does not gobble such morsels. This is a very tasty world, and one must pace oneself, mustn't one?'

He sniffed and rose gracefully to his feet. 'No, the Chosen Son of Slaanesh shall not sully himself on the Herald, when he might yet taste the real thing. Am I not deserving of such an honour?' His lips twitched. 'The answer, by the way, is most assuredly yes. I am perfection, and I do not waste my gifts on the imperfect. Thus do I take my leave. There are still pleasures yet to be plumbed in this moving feast of a city, and I shall wallow in them to my heart's content, while I wait the coming of the king.'

Valten watched as Sigvald strode off down the avenue, whistling a cheerful tune. Only when the creature had vanished into the clouds of dark smoke rolling across the street did he turn his attention to the duel. The battle had continued even as he and Sigvald had conversed, and neither warrior seemed to have noticed the new arrivals or have the upper hand.

Every time the armoured hulk wielding the flail battered the hairy giant from his feet, the latter was up again a moment later, cursing and slashing at his enemy, his blows glancing from the other's maggot-ridden suit of Chaos plate.

Finally, the flail tore the heavy kite shield from its owner's grasp. The latter staggered back, apparently off balance. His opponent closed in, stomping forwards. 'Fall, Wanderer, for the glory of Father Nurgle,' the Chaos champion rasped.

'You first, Valnir,' Wulfrik said. He twisted aside, avoiding his opponent's next blow, and drove the broad blade of his sword into the pustule-lined gap between Valnir's helmet and cuirass. Wulfrik leaned into the blow with a grunt, forcing the sword all the way through his opponent's neck. The tip of the blade emerged in a burst of stinking gas and leprous filth. Valnir squawked and dropped his weapon as he reached up to claw at the blade. 'Oh no you don't,' Wulfrik growled. He set his boot against the other champion's hip and wrenched his blade free, out through the back of Valnir's neck.

Valnir's head dropped from his bloated frame and bounced across the cobbles. Wulfrik shoved the twitching body aside and spat after it. 'Say hello to the Crowfather for me, eh?' he said, as he retrieved his shield. Wulfrik turned towards Valten. 'Well, I like a man who's prompt,' he said in crude Reikspiel, spreading his arms. 'Herald of Sigmar, I, Wulfrik the Worldwalker, the Inescapable One, demand that you face me. The gods want your skull on their fire, and I'm of a mind to give them what they wish.'

Valten said nothing. He slid from the saddle, and waved back Volker and the others. It was a command Volker was only too happy to obey. Wulfrik grinned. 'I heard you did for old Mordrek. I killed him once myself.' He blinked. 'Twice, actually, now that I think about it.'

'This time, he will stay dead. Is that what you wish for yourself?' Valten asked, as he moved to meet the Chaos champion. 'Death? I know you, Wanderer, though I do not know how. I know your name, and your fate. I know why you are here, and I know that you cannot stop me. My doom is... already written.' Valten hesitated, as if uncertain. Then, he said, 'And it is not by your hand.'

'No, it wouldn't be, would it?' Wulfrik grunted. He sucked in a deep breath, and released it loudly. 'Ahhhhh. No, I feel the weight of your weird from here, Herald. Not a grand doom, for you. Just a doom. Stupid and small.' He looked up. 'Do you think, at the end, there will be anyone left to sing our sagas?'

Valten was silent. Wulfrik laughed. 'No, I thought not,' he said. He slapped his shield with the flat of his sword. Valten raised his hammer. Wulfrik attacked first. He bulled forwards, attempting to smash Valten flat with the face of his shield. Valten pivoted aside, but before he could bring his hammer around to strike, the other's sword was screeching across his armour. Valten stumbled back, eyes narrowed in surprise.

Wulfrik flashed his grin again and moved round warily, blade balanced on the rim of his shield. 'Come on, boy... Long fights are the stuff of poets' dreams,' he growled.

Valten whirled Ghal Maraz about, and advanced. Wulfrik gave a harsh laugh and raised his shield, but Valten didn't alter the trajectory of his blow. A moment later, Volker realised why – Ghal Maraz connected with the broad face of the shield, and the latter exploded into red hot fragments. Wulfrik was flung back by the force of the blow, and he skidded through the bodies. He was on his feet a moment later, his necklace of skulls rattling.

'*Now* it's a fight,' Wulfrik roared. He caught his sword in two hands and bounded in, hurdling the piles of corpses. Valten met him halfway. Sword and hammer connected again and again, the sound echoing through the streets. Valten made a wild swing, driving Wulfrik back. The Wanderer retreated, but only for a moment, twisting in mid-step to bring his blade around in a blow meant to decapitate his opponent. Valten fell, avoiding the sword's bite but losing his balance. He crashed to the ground, armour rattling, and rolled aside as Wulfrik's blade came down again, drawing sparks from the cobblestones.

Valten, still on his back, swung Ghal Maraz. The head of the hammer smacked into Wulfrik's waiting palm. Volker heard the bones of the man's hand splinter and crack from where he stood, but Wulfrik gave no sign that he felt any pain. Instead, his broken fingers folded over the hammer as his foot lashed out, catching Valten in the chest. As Valten fell back, Wulfrik tore the hammer from his grip and hurled it aside.

Valten shoved himself up on his elbows as Wulfrik approached. 'That hurt,' the champion grunted. 'Maybe your weird wasn't so heavy after all, eh?' He raised his blade in one hand, and brought it down.

Valten's hands shot up, catching the blade. He gripped it tight, even as it bit into his palms. Thin rivulets of blood ran down the tip of the blade. Wulfrik was forced back a step as Valten gathered his feet under him and slowly rose, still gripping the sword. Metal cracked as Valten and his opponent faced one another across the length of sharpened steel. Wulfrik's grin became a grimace of effort.

The sword shattered. Wulfrik fell forwards, eyes wide. Valten, a chunk of the sword still in his hand, slid it into the Chaos champion's throat as he stumbled past. Wulfrik toppled, clutching at his neck. Valten retrieved his hammer and turned back to his enemy. Wulfrik, gasping and choking, lowered his hands and lay waiting. He was smiling again, his teeth stained with blood. 'Good fight,' he gurgled as Valten stood over him. He closed his eyes. Ghal Maraz struck.

Valten made his way back to the others. The blood on his hands had already dried. Volker was possessed by the sudden urge to kneel. An urge shared by his men, and one by one, they did so. Even Brunner. Valten looked down at them silently. Then, a slow, sad smile crept across his face. 'Up,' he said softly. 'The Temple of Ulric is just ahead. And for good or ill, that is where we will make our stand.'

Grafsmund-Norgarten District

Horvath died slowly, and angrily if his frustrated howls were any indication. The Knights Panther, clad in their swirling, spotted skins and dark armour, had ridden out of an isolated cul-de-sac as the horde passed by, moving in pursuit of the retreating state troops. Horvath had been one of the unlucky ones, caught and spitted on a lance in that first charge. But it wasn't until the Knights Panther were joined by halberdiers, spearmen and cross-bowmen, all flooding the wide boulevard, that Canto realised that the Headsmen, and the warbands following in their wake, had been drawn into a trap.

Middenheim, for all that it was undone and doomed, was still a battleground. Every house, every temple, every guildhall and tavern, was a fortress filled with desperate, deadly enemies, all determined to make Archaon's followers pay in blood for every stretch of street. Helblasters vomited volleys of shot from open doorways, and handgunners fired from behind overturned wagons and toppled stalls at the other end of the boulevard.

The warriors of Chaos pressed forwards, into the teeth of the fire, because there was little else they could do. And because the eyes of the Everchosen were upon them. Canto parried a halberd and hacked down its owner, even as he caught sight of the battle-standard of the Swords of Chaos rising above the melee. He couldn't say where they'd come from, or when they'd arrived, but they were here now, and where his Swords went, the Three-Eyed King would not be far behind.

A lead bullet struck his armour and caromed off into the press of battle. Canto spun and rammed his sword through an open doorway, killing the handgunner. He forced his way into the structure beyond, the taproom of a mostly empty tavern. Women and children cowered behind a barricade of tables, as men in the livery of Stirland raced to intercept him. Canto gutted the first to reach him, and beheaded the second. A sword shattered on his daemon-forged armour, and he turned, grabbing its wielder by the throat. He shoved the man back and slammed him against a support beam.

Canto tilted his head, looking up. He smelt smoke, coming from above. Some fool had set fire to the thatch. He looked back at the man he held pinned. The swordsman struggled uselessly in his grip. Ineffectual fists pounded on his arm. Canto considered snapping his neck. Then, without quite knowing why, he released him. 'Get your women and children and go. Out the back. Find a hole and hide, if you can. Or die. It makes no difference to me,' he said, stepping back. The swordsman stared at him. Canto turned away, and stepped back out onto the street. As his foot touched the cobbles, he was already regretting his mercy.

Then, it wasn't really mercy, was it? Middenheim was doomed, and its people with it. There would be no door strong enough, no hole deep enough to keep out the followers of the Dark Gods when the battle was won. When the last defenders fell, then the true horror would begin. Archaon had promised this city to the gods, and the word of the Everchosen was law.

As if the gods had heard his thoughts and wished to punish him, a lance slammed into his side, knocking him to one knee. His armour had been forged by the daemonsmiths of Zharr Naggrund and the mortal weapon merely splintered, peeling away as it struck him. Even so, the force of the blow was enough to rattle his brains, and he reeled, off balance. The knight galloped past, freeing a heavy morning star from his saddle as he did so. The spiked ball crashed down on Canto's helm. He lurched back, slamming into the doorway of the building. The horse reared over him, hooves lashing out. Canto snarled a curse and lunged forwards, driving his shoulder into the animal's midsection.

The horse toppled with a squeal, carrying its rider with it. Canto dispatched both swiftly. But even as he wrenched his blade free of the knight's shuddering body, he saw that his attacker hadn't been alone. The Knights Panther had ploughed through the jammed ranks of the horde, leaving a trail of carnage in their wake. It was a suicidal endeavour, but it had a purpose. Most of them had already been pulled from their saddles, but some still rode on, intent on their quarry – Archaon himself. One of the knights roared a challenge as he spurred his horse forwards, and raised a single-bladed war-axe in readiness for a killing blow.

The Everchosen was mounted upon a coal-black nightmare of a beast, with eyes like burning embers and hooves which split the stones they trod upon. Its fanged maw champed hungrily at its iron bit as Archaon hauled back on the reins and turned the animal to face his challenger. The menace of the steed was nothing compared to that of its rider. It was the first time Canto had seen the Everchosen in the flesh.

Archaon was taller and broader than most who fought under his banner and his armour was far more ornate, its plates covered in lines of scrawled script, strange runes and abominable sigils which made even the most puissant sorcerer weep with fear. Too, it seemed to be of all colours and none, shifting as it caught the light through a vast spectrum of hues wholly unknown to man. Canto had heard that the armour had belonged to Morkar the Uniter, First Chosen of Chaos, in the dim, ancient days of the past.

In his hand, Archaon held a heavy sword – the infamous Slayer of Kings. The blade writhed with barely contained power, and leering faces formed and dissolved on its surface as he brought it up and sent it slamming down through his challenger's shield and into the body below. The knight fell from his saddle as his horse thundered past. His death did not deter his comrades, however. Indeed, it seemed to only spur them on.

Canto watched in incredulity as the Everchosen was surrounded and separated from his bodyguards by the remaining knights. Those chosen to keep the Swords of Chaos at bay did so with reckless abandon, fighting furiously, with no thought for their own well-being. The remaining trio engaged Archaon. Two came at him from either side, while the third hung back. As soon as Archaon had turned to deal with his companions, the knight kicked his steed into motion and galloped towards the Everchosen.

Time stopped. The world grew still and silent. Canto held his breath. Archaon was the Chosen of Chaos, the man before whom all the daemons of the world bowed. But he was still a man. He could still be killed, and a blade to the back would do the job as easily as a cannonball or a warhammer in the hands of the Herald of Sigmar himself.

Against his better judgement, Canto looked up. The sky still moved. The clouds writhed and became faces, before breaking apart and becoming just clouds again. The gods were watching. Now would be a good time to pretend he hadn't seen anything, that he was elsewhere. *Pretend you're not here,* he hissed to himself. *Let the gods look after their own.*

But even as the thought crossed his mind, Canto hurled himself forwards. His blade hewed through the horse's legs, and the animal fell screaming. Its rider toppled from the saddle, but came to his feet a moment later. His sword slammed into Canto's and they duelled over the body of the dying horse, but only for a moment. The man was hurt, and perhaps even dying, even as his sword arm faltered and Canto's sword landed on his shoulder, driving him to his knees. The dawi zharr-forged blade cut through the knight's heavy armour with ease and he flopped across the body of his steed, dead.

Canto jerked his weapon free of the body. 'You have my

thanks, warrior,' a voice rumbled. Canto turned. The Three-Eyed King looked down at him, and Canto wondered how far away Kislev was. Archaon looked down, at the body of the knight, and then back up, taking in Canto's unadorned armour. Canto stepped back, suddenly conscious of the lack of devotional markings on the baroque plates of black iron. He was called 'Unsworn' for a good reason; he had never climbed the eight hundred and eighty-eight steps to the Skull Throne, or hacked his way into Nurgle's Garden looking for a patron. The gods couldn't be trusted. They gave a man everything he wanted, even when he begged them to stop.

'Kneel,' Archaon rumbled.

'Rather not – trick knee,' Canto said, but he was already sinking down even as the words left his lips. The battle still raged about them, but here, in this moment, he felt the weight of a terrible silence descend on him. The clangour of war was muted and dull. He refused to look up, because he knew that if he did, something would be looking down at *him* from the wide, hungry sky. For the first time, the gods would see him. *You've done it now, fool,* he thought. *You've got their interest now, and you know what that means.*

Except he didn't, not really. Oh he'd seen what could happen, but he'd spent centuries avoiding the gazes of the gods. He'd done just enough, but never too much. Just enough to survive, but never enough to prosper. A rat hiding in a midden heap. His heart stuttered in its rhythm, and his armour rattled.

'Canto the Unsworn,' Archaon said. He sounded amused. Canto didn't bother to wonder how Archaon knew his name. The gods had likely whispered it in his ear. 'You rode with the Gorewolf, and before him, Tzerpichore the Unwritten.' Archaon cocked his head. 'They say Tzerpichore's great tortoise of iron and crystal still walks the Wastes, searching for its master.'

'Yes, they do,' Canto said. 'And it does.'

'There are few men these days who do not find sanctuary in

one god or another's shadow. But you stand apart. Is that due to fear or pride, I wonder?'

'Fear,' Canto croaked. Archaon's eyes shone like stars, and he felt the strange heat of a cold fire wash over him. It was as if he were being flayed from the inside out, opened up so the Ever-chosen could examine every nook and cranny of his black and blasted soul.

'What do you fear?'

'Death. Madness. Change.' The words slipped out before Canto could stop them. They hung on the air, like the notes of a song. He felt the hideous interest intensify, and knew what a mouse must feel when it is caught by a cat. Several cats, in fact. And their king was glaring down at him, considering where to insert his claws.

'I was damned from the first breath that I took. All men are,' Archaon said, almost gently. 'We change from what we were with every moment and hour that passes, losing ourselves the way a serpent loses its skin. To hold on to the old, that is madness. To strive against the current, *that* is madness. There is nothing to fear, Unsworn. Not now. The worst has happened. The horns of doom have sounded, and the pillars of heaven and earth come crashing down.' His great blade stretched out. Canto closed his eyes. He saw his life – a life of running and fighting and colours and sounds and somewhere, out there, far away, he thought he could feel the slow rumble of the tortoise as it continued on its way through the Chaos Wastes, and he felt a moment of inexplicable sadness.

There was a soft sound, and he opened his eyes as the flat of Archaon's blade touched his shoulder. 'Rise, and be fearless. Rise, and find sanctuary in *my* shadow, Unsworn. We ride for ruin, and our victory is assured.' Then the sword was lifted, and Archaon's steed reared, pawing the air with an ear-splitting shriek.

Time snapped back into focus. Noise washed over Canto,

staggering him. A howling, wolf-cloaked warrior charged towards him, hammer swinging out, and he rose to his feet smoothly. He swept his sword out and disembowelled his attacker. A riderless horse, its flesh writhing with thorns and its eyes made of smoking gemstones, galloped past, snorting and kicking. *Like a gift from the gods,* Canto thought, even as his hand snapped out to catch hold of its bloody bridle.

FOUR

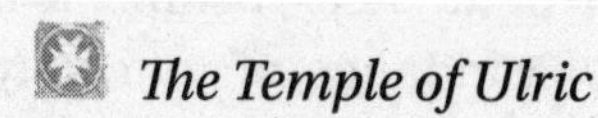

The Temple of Ulric

Gregor Martak climbed the broad steps of the Temple of Ulric, looking about him with satisfaction. Whether that satisfaction was solely his or was shared by the power now inhabiting his body, he couldn't say, but he thought Ulric must approve of Valten's preparations. The Herald of Sigmar was no fool, whatever his origins.

He had garrisoned the cloisters and processionals of the eastern and western wings of the temple with bands of state troops, ensuring that the flanks and rear of their position were well defended. The bulk of the surviving forces under his command now occupied the northern edge of the vast cobbled square which sat before the temple's main entrance. Deep ranks of troops stood before the steps, their lines anchored by the wings of the temple. Men of Averland, Ostermark and the Reikland stood ready to the east, their fire-torn standards whipping in the unnatural wind that curled through the streets of Middenheim. To the west, Talabheimers stood firm alongside the musters of Altdorf and Stirland. The honour of the centre position had been given to their hosts, who stood in the shadow of their god, halberds and crossbows ready for the storm to come.

The survivors of the various knightly orders who had chosen to make Middenheim their burying ground stood behind the centre. The Knights of the White Wolf, the Gryphon Legion, the Knights of the Black Bear, and the Knights of the Broken Sword were all in evidence. There were others scattered throughout the city, fighting a desperate holding action or mounting suicidal counter-attacks. The knightly orders had ever been the mailed fist of the Empire, and in these final hours most seemed determined to get in as many blows as possible, even if that meant their own annihilation.

Deployed at the top of the steps, before the doors of the temple, were the remnants of Middenheim's once-proud Grand Battery. Every gun that could be salvaged from the walls and keeps of the city had been, and they were now arrayed so as to belch fire and destruction into the enemy whose approach even now caused the street to shake slightly.

Martak joined a group of men at the top of the steps, before the battery. A ragtag group of captains, sergeants, and mercenary commanders stood in tense discussion. Martak recognised a few of them, including the raven-haired Torben Badenov, the peg-legged Marienburger Edvard van der Kraal, and the loutish Voland, a hedge-knight from Tilea. Nearby, Axel Greiss was arguing with two of his fellow Grand Masters, Nicolai Dostov of the Gryphon Legion and Volg Staahl, the Preceptor of the Order of the Black Bear. The latter nodded to Martak and said, 'Look, Martak's here. The day is saved.'

Greiss whirled. He glared at Martak, but only for a moment. 'Glad you could join us, wizard,' he muttered, turning back to the others. 'Tell him what you told me, Staahl.'

Dostov and Staahl shared a look. The other man's dislike of Martak was well known, and the wizard wondered if Greiss's sudden desire to include him in their hastily convened war council surprised them. Like Greiss, they were older men. Dostov, a white-moustachioed Kislevite clad in the banded mail and back banner in the shape of a pair of wings which marked a warrior of the Gryphon Legion, was lean and hard-faced. Staahl, on the other hand, was a keg with legs. With his ash-smeared plate armour and ragged bear-skin cloak, he resembled nothing so much as a particularly fat, disreputable bear.

'Achendorf is dead. Took his knights and made a try for the head of the beast, poor fool,' Staahl rumbled. Dostov frowned, but said nothing. Greiss snorted.

'Do not pity him. He gambled, and lost. Would that he had succeeded,' he said.

'It's not him I pity,' Staahl snapped. 'It's us. We could have used him and his men, Axel. Instead, he sacrificed them in a foolhardy attempt at glory. Every sword counts, and he took good men into death with him.'

'Does it matter where they die?' Greiss growled, bristling. He gestured at the men below with his hammer. 'That is why they – why *we* – are here, you fat old fool. To fight and die, so that the Emperor might live one more day. We are *bleeding* them. Nothing more.'

'No.'

They all turned as one, Martak included. The fragment of Ulric within him twitched as he caught sight of Valten ascending the steps. Down below, more men hastily squeezed into the ranks. 'No, we are not just a sacrifice, Master Greiss. In the end, perhaps. When the war is done, and scribes record the events of this day, that is what they might say of us. But here and now, we are so much more.' The trio of Grand Masters stepped aside as Valten strode past them. He looked up at the temple for a moment, and then turned back to them. 'Here and now, we are the Empire of Sigmar. Here and now, we are the City of the White Wolf. Middenheim stands. And while it does, so too does the world.' He raised his voice, pitching it to carry. Down below, the noise of men preparing for war had dimmed. Martak realised that almost every eye in the square was upon them.

As cheers rose up from below, Valten turned back to Martak and the others. Greiss and his fellow knights were staring at him as if, for the first time, they suddenly understood that Valten was not merely a jumped-up blacksmith in borrowed armour, but something else entirely. Valten met Martak's gaze. The part of the wizard which was Ulric recognised the spark of... otherness in the man before him. It was only a spark, but it might grow into a roaring flame. One to cleanse the stones of the Fauschlag of the filth that crept over them. If it was given the time.

But even as the thought crossed his mind, Valten's smile faded, becoming sad. He shook his head slightly, a gesture so infinitesimal that Martak knew he alone had seen it. And in his soul, Ulric howled mournfully.

Greiss cleared his throat. 'A very pretty speech, blacksmith. But speeches alone won't see us safely to another sunrise.'

Valten turned to the old knight. 'No, for that we'll have to trust in Altdorf steel, Nuln gunpowder and Middenheim courage.' He paused, as if taking stock of the situation. Then, he continued. 'We hoped that the Fauschlag would protect us. That the walls of Middenheim would keep the enemy at bay for weeks, if not months.' He looked at each of the gathered officers in turn. 'We hoped that the Emperor might rally the rest of the Empire from Averheim, and perhaps even relieve us here. That together, we could drive the enemy back into the Wastes.' He grinned. 'Doesn't seem very likely now, does it?'

Staahl snorted, and several of the captains chuckled. Greiss and Dostov frowned. Martak couldn't restrain a harsh cackle. He felt Ulric growl unappreciatively within him; the wolf-god wasn't, by nature, fatalistic. Nor did he have a sense of humour.

'The enemy is inside the walls. All we can do now is hope to bear the brunt of his fury, and break his back when he exhausts himself,' Valten continued. He looked at Martak. 'If we can bring

Archaon to battle, then we have a chance. If the Three-Eyed King falls, his army will disintegrate. Middenheim might well be consumed in that conflagration, but that is a small price to pay for victory.'

Ulric snarled in agreement within Martak's soul, and Valten smiled slightly, as if he'd heard the god's voice. Martak wondered just how much Valten saw. If they survived the coming conflict, he intended to ask him. He heard the winding howl of a war-horn, and turned. 'It looks like we'll have no trouble with the first part of that plan,' Martak murmured.

Along the southern edge of the square, the foe had begun to arrive. Black-armoured northlanders chanted and bellowed, clashing their weapons and shaking their shields in furious tumult. Drums boomed back, deep in their ranks. Daemons capered about them, hurling incoherent threats at the men standing before the Temple of Ulric. Beastmen paced at the fringes of the gathering horde, throwing back their heads to add their roars and wildcat screams to the dreadful clangour. But, even as their numbers swelled, they did not move to cross the square and attack.

'They're waiting for their master to arrive,' Valten said. He stared at the gathering ranks of the enemy, as if in search of Archaon.

'Biggest dog gets first bite,' Martak grunted. He could feel the essence of the wolf-god gathering itself in him, ready for the fury to come. His breath came in pale puffs, and those men closest to him stepped back nervously.

Suddenly, the air was split by the sound of beating wings. It was as if a hundred thousand crows had chosen that moment to fill the air above the square. The men on the steps cried out in alarm, and clapped their hands to their ears as the thunderous wingbeats threatened their eardrums. Even Valten staggered slightly as the air rippled with the shadows of diving, swooping birds. Martak alone stood tall.

His eyes narrowed, and his hand shot out to catch hold of the end of a spear moments before it lanced through Valten's chest. The whirring, shifting shadows parted, and the spear's wielder was revealed – a snarling beastman, with wide, black-feathered wings rising from his broad back. *Malagor, the Dark Omen, Best-Loved of the Dark Gods,* Ulric's voice growled in his mind. Martak's lips skinned back from his teeth, and he returned Malagor's snarl in kind. The tableau held for a moment, as man and beast stared at one another. Martak's arm trembled as he slowly forced the spear back. Malagor's wings beat heavily, as it tried to drive the weapon forwards. Then, in a clap of darkling thunder, the creature was gone.

On the other side of the square, the gathered beastmen suddenly broke ranks and pelted forwards, as if Malagor's attack had been a signal. They brayed wildly and brandished crude weapons as they charged in a scattered, undisciplined mass towards the gleaming ranks of spears and halberds.

Valten shook himself, as if emerging from a dream. He raised his hammer. 'To your places, brothers, captains, masters... May Sigmar and Ulric both watch over you,' he said, looking at the others. They snapped into motion, hurrying to their positions, as down below orders rang out along the Empire battle-line, drums rattled and horns blared. Valten looked at Martak. 'They want me dead,' he murmured. 'They do not want their chosen weapon to meet me in combat.'

'Well, let's disappoint them, then,' Martak growled. He looked out over the square, eyes narrowed. Whatever madness had seized the beastherds had not consumed the rest of Archaon's army. Unsupported as they were, and out in the open, the beastmen were being cut to ribbons by volleys of crossbow bolts and gunfire. Behind Martak, the great cannons began to bellow, and soon cannonballs bounced across the square, ploughing into the frenzied ranks of charging beastmen. Mortar shells and rockets hammered the disorganised herds, hurling broken corpses through the smoke-stained air. A looming ghorgon, massive jaws snapping hungrily, toppled backwards as a cannonball smashed through its skull, and crushed a dozen of its lesser kin.

A shriek from above tore Martak's attentions from the carnage being wrought in the square. He and Valten looked up, to see a swirling murder of crows descend on the artillery at the top of the steps. Gunners cried out in fear and pain as Malagor swept through them, plucking eyes and raking flesh. The Dark Omen was monstrous and unstoppable, and his body dissolved into a shower of feathers only to reform elsewhere to wreak more havoc. Even as the bodies of those he'd slain tumbled down the steps, Malagor vanished, the thunder of wings echoing in his wake.

Valten started up the steps, hammer in hand. Martak grabbed his arm. 'No. I'll handle the beast. You see to the battle.' Valten opened his mouth, as if to reply, then nodded and turned to race down the steps. Martak cracked his knuckles, and then closed his eyes. His nostrils flared as he inhaled the stench of Malagor's magics. The creature was ripe with the stink of the swirling energies which permeated the clouds far above. Martak, eyes still closed, turned one way, and then another, following Malagor's twisting, turning pilgrimage across the battle-lines of the Empire. Men died wherever the beast settled, and it seemed to be unconcerned with the savage slaughter being inflicted on its kin, for its attacks were random, rather than calculated to ease the advance of the beastmen.

Nonetheless, the beastmen were possessed by an unmatched ferocity, and down in the square they hurled themselves through the teeth of the artillery and crashed home at last, smashing into the ranks of the state troops. The creatures were outnumbered, and almost ridiculously so, but Martak knew that such concerns no longer held sway over them. The Children of Chaos had been driven into a killing frenzy, and they were determined to taste the blood of their enemies.

There!

The thought sliced through his consciousness, and Martak's eyes snapped open. His head ached with the pounding of wings as he turned and saw a mass of whirling feathers dropping towards Greiss and his knights. Martak raced down the steps, one arm flung back. He stopped, and his arm snapped forwards. A jagged spear of amber, coated in ice, cut through the air with a whistling shriek.

The mass of shadow-crows gave a communal scream and something hairy dropped from their midst to crash down on the steps. Martak pounced, his hands seizing the length of his conjured spear, and he shoved his prey back down as it tried to rise. Malagor howled in agony as it pawed uselessly at the ice. Its blood had splattered out across the steps like the wings of some great, malignant bird. Martak leaned against the spear with his full weight. Malagor's flesh blackened with frostbite, and its froth became frozen slush. It glared at Martak, and he matched that gaze, even as he had before.

Then, with a frustrated whimper, Malagor flopped back and lay still. Martak shoved himself back, and stood. Down below, the fury of the beastmen was mostly spent. Martak watched with grim pleasure as Valten struck a minotaur, the force of his blow driving the monster to its knees. His second blow took its head completely off, sending it rolling across the cobbles. The surviving beastmen were beginning to flee.

Valten wheeled his horse about and rode back through the lines, speaking calmly to the soldiers. A joke here, a word of comfort there... The god in Martak watched in wonder as men who had only moments before been filled with fury and fear straightened their spines and locked shields once more. The ragged holes carved in their ranks by the beastmen vanished as fresh men moved to fill the gaps. Fallen standards were lifted high as Valten passed along the shield-wall, meeting the gaze of each man in turn. He began to speak, and his words were almost immediately drowned out by cheers.

What is he? Ulric murmured. Martak smiled. 'A blacksmith,' he said, softly. War was Valten's anvil, and, were the world a kinder place, perhaps he could have made something stronger from the raw materials the End Times had provided him. For a moment, Martak could almost see it... a world of shining towers, and prosperous peoples. Where no woman would have to abandon her deformed child to the forests; where no man would so fear the touch of tainted water that he chose a slow death by alcohol, rather than risk the waters of the Reik. Where the cities of men were not threatened by howling hordes of northmen or orcs.

Ulric growled within him, and Martak felt his smile slip. Such a world was not a pleasant thought for a god of war, winter and woe. 'Well, it's not as if we have to worry about it, eh?' he asked himself. 'The wheel of the world is slowing, and soon enough it will stop.'

Valten rode up to the bottom of the temple steps, and Martak went down to meet him. 'Do you hear the drums, Gregor? I think we've caught their attention,' Valten said. His eyes strayed to the remains of Malagor, and then he turned in his saddle, peering out across the square. 'Which is all to the good, I think. The men have had a victory. They'll be hungry for another.'

Martak followed his gaze. The horde gathered along the southern edge of the temple square had grown to massive proportions. It was a seething tide of black armour, cruel weapons and ragged banners. The latter stretched back into the gloom which dominated the narrow streets and crooked avenues of the Ulricsmund beyond. A wave of noise rose and spread from the ranks of the Chaos worshippers, tortured syllables crashing down and flowing over the men of the Empire. The raw surge of noise rose to mingle with the thunder that rocked the strange clouds overhead, to create an apocalyptic cacophony which drowned out all thought and sense.

Then lightning flared across the sky, and the horde fell silent. The sudden quiet was almost as bad as the noise had been. Martak felt

Ulric bristle within him, and he looked up, trying to catch a glimpse of the monstrous, ghostly shapes which moved behind the clouds. *They are here,* Ulric growled. *They come to watch.*

Eyes as wide and as hot as the sun washed over him, through a tear in the clouds, and Martak shuddered and looked away. There had been nothing recognisable in that gaze – nothing save an eternity's worth of hunger and madness. The Chaos Gods were not as the gods of men. They had known the world as dust in the aeons before creation, and they would know it as dust again before they were finished.

Out across the square, the host of the lost and damned parted like split wood. Chaos warriors, scarred tribesmen and squabbling daemons all pushed and thrust against their fellows to create a wide corridor. And down that corridor, riding at an unhurried pace, came the architect of all the world's pain himself.

Archaon, Lord of the End Times, had arrived.

Wendel Volker wished he had time for a drink. He wished he had time for anything. He stood amid the lines of the state troops, his armour stained with gore and his shield hacked almost to flinders. Brunner stood nearby, his falchion resting on his shoulder. The former bounty-hunter looked almost at ease, as if the carnage of only a few moments before had been nothing at all. The rest of Valten's men had spread out among the ranks, filling in gaps or simply seeking out friends and comrades to stand with. Volker had neither. Not any more.

He closed his eyes, and tried to relax. The worst was yet to come, and a Volker couldn't be found wanting. Behind him, he heard the murmurs of healers and warrior priests as they worked to stiffen spines and bind wounds. Servants of Sigmar, Ulric and even Ranald, all were present. Whether their gods were was another matter.

'He's a big one,' Brunner grunted.

Volker opened his eyes. The Chaos horde had fallen silent. Their master, the Three-Eyed King himself, had arrived. Volker lifted his visor to get a better look at the king of all monsters. Brunner wasn't wrong – Archaon was big, bigger than any of his followers, save for those who loomed over buildings. His armour shone with a terrible light, and the air about him shimmered as if the weight of his presence caused reality itself to stretch and fray. Archaon was *wrong*, Volker thought. He was the very essence of wrongness, of the foulness that crept in through the cracks in the world, and Volker felt his stomach twist in agonised knots as he watched the Lord of the End Times ride through his followers and into the square.

'How much do you think they'd pay me for his scalp?' Brunner said.

'They'd make you bloody emperor,' Volker said, not looking at him. Archaon was in no hurry. His daemonic steed pawed the ground as it moved forwards. The ground cracked and steamed where the animal's hooves touched. The Three-Eyed King was surrounded by a bodyguard of Chaos knights, each of them a monster in his own right. Archaon, his great sword balanced across his saddle horn, stared at the forces arrayed before the temple.

Volker fought the urge to shrink back into the ranks. He felt soul-sick and weary as Archaon's inhuman gaze swept over him. Overhead, the roiling clouds had thickened and darkened as the storm redoubled its fury. A hot rain had begun to fall, softly, slowly at first, and then with hissing fury. The sword in Volker's hand felt heavy, and his breathing was a harsh rasp in his ears. Archaon straightened in his saddle. His armour creaked like the wheels of a plague cart, and when he spoke, Volker felt each word in the marrow of his bones.

'I am the Final Moment made flesh. I stand here on this mountain, and I will sit on its throne. I will be the axis upon which the wheel of change turns, and the world will drown in the light of unborn stars.' Archaon looked up. 'Can you feel it, men of the Empire – can you feel the air tremble like a thing alive? Can you feel the heat of the fire that rages outside the gates of the world?' He lowered his head, gazing at them, his expression unfathomable, hidden as it was within the depths of his helm. 'The End Times are here, and there is no turning back. There is no past, no future, only now. Time is a circle and it is contracting about the throat of the world,' Archaon said, making a fist for emphasis. 'Why do you cling so to the broken shards of Sigmar's lie? There is no afterlife. There is no reward, no punishment. Only death, or life.'

Volker blinked sweat from his eyes. Men to either side of him shifted in obvious discomfort. Archaon's words ate at his resolve like acid, stripping him of courage and will. Archaon gazed at them for a moment, as if to let his words sink in, and then he began to speak again. 'Look to the sky. Look to the street. Cracks are forming in what is, and what was. That which shall be presses against the threshold of time itself. This world is, and always has been, but a moment delayed. A single drop of blood, hanging from the tip of a sword. And now, it splashes down.'

Archaon swept his blade up, and fire crawled along its length. '*This* sword. *Your* blood. Your age has passed. The pallid mask of human existence has begun to peel back, revealing the canker within. Why not rip it off at once, and glory in these final hours – shout, revel, kill, and taste the blood of the world as it dies.'

Men murmured. Fever-bright eyes blinked. Tongues caressed lips. Volker shuddered, trying to push his way through the numbing fog that had engulfed his thoughts. Archaon seemed to glow with a sour light, like a beacon calling all of the world's children home. Part of Volker wanted to follow it wherever it led, to give in to despair and rage and wash away the memories of Heldenhame and Altdorf in blood. He looked down, and caught sight of the crowned skull emblazoned on his cuirass, with the 'KF' sigil of Karl Franz.

The sound of hooves shook him from his reverie. Men stood straighter, and looked about, as Valten eased his horse through the press. He looked tired, the way they all did, but not weak. Not exhausted. When he spoke, his voice carried easily through the rain, and across the square, from one wing of the army to the other.

'He is right, brothers,' Valten said. 'All of history has come down to this place. Every story, song and saga, they have all led up to this day, this hour, this moment. We stand in the shadow of heroes and gods, and their hands are on our shoulders, urging us in one direction... or another.' As the words left his mouth, he turned towards Archaon.

'But it is up to us to choose who we listen to. We have been given this day to make our stand. To bar the door of the world against the beast that would devour everything we hold dear. We have been given this moment to show our teeth. To show our anger, and let it light the flames of the world's wrath.' Valten looked out over the massed ranks of soldiery. 'Let its heat warm you, and its light drive back the dark. Let that fire light the way to the ending of the world, if that is what the gods will. Let it scour the rock, and consume the stars themselves. Let the heat of our pyre scorch the Dark Gods cowering in the shadows, if that is the will of Sigmar.'

He paused. And smiled. It was a gentle smile. The smile of a blacksmith at his forge. 'But either way... let the fire burn, brothers.' The words were delivered quietly, but they carried nonetheless. Volker was not alone as a cheer ripped its way from his throat. Hundreds of voices rose, mingling into a single roar of defiance. The sky ripped wide, as if the cacodaemoniacal gods above had been driven into paroxysms of fury by the sound.

Archaon raised his sword. Lightning shrieked down, striking the blade and casting a sickly light across the square. The cheers ceased as the Lord of the End Times reminded them of his presence. Volker hunkered down behind his shield as stray sparks of lightning spat and crawled across the ground at his feet.

'This is the way the world ends,' Archaon rumbled. 'This is the way the world begins. Let my name ring out, and let the very mountains tremble. I have come for the rotten heart of your Empire, and I will not leave until I feel it grow still in my hand. Run and die, or stand and die, hammer-bearer, but die all the same.' He spread his arms, as if inviting attack.

'Death is a small price to pay for victory,' Valten said. He spoke steadily, with certainty, and his voice carried easily across the square. 'And our victory is writ in the heavens themselves. You are not the one to unravel the weave of the world. Ride home, ride back into the darkness.' He gestured with his hammer.

'I *am* home,' Archaon snarled. 'And I will not be denied.' He hauled back on the reins of his monstrous steed, causing the beast to rear. He raised his blade up and then swept it down, as if it were a headsman's axe and it were Middenheim's neck on the block.

With a roar to shake the Fauschlag itself, Archaon's army charged.

The moment the Slayer of Kings swept down, Archaon was in motion. Bent low in the saddle, the Lord of the End Times led the attack. Canto, surrounded on all sides by the grim, armoured figures of the Swords of Chaos, had no choice but to follow in his wake.

Canto ducked his head, and bent almost parallel to the neck of his newfound mount. The animal gibbered ceaselessly in what sounded like Tilean, spewing what were either curses or recipes as it pounded along, its hooves eating ground at a relentless pace. He'd tried hitting it, but that only made it talk more loudly, and it had tried to bite him to boot. He'd decided to settle for holding on and letting the beast do as it willed.

Holding tight to the reins, he risked a glance back. The rest of the Chaos horde was in motion behind the Swords. Chaos warriors from a hundred different warbands pounded after their warlord, shaking the square with the fury of their charge. Wild, yelling tribesmen ran alongside them. Packs of twisted, mutated hounds bayed madly as they loped across the cobbles, and daemons capered and gambolled in their wake. To the east, Canto caught sight of a massive slaughterbrute ploughing forwards, flinging aside unlucky tribesmen in its haste to get to the enemy. Gibbering Chaos spawn flailed about madly around its mighty form, screeching and screaming. Behind this vanguard came wave after wave of northmen, enough to bury all of Middenheim in corpses if that was what it took to win the victory.

He heard the roar of guns, and turned to see flashes of fire from the top of the temple steps. As soon as the horde had broken into a charge, the Empire guns had opened fire. Mortars thumped, cannons boomed and helblasters let out a staccato roar. To his right, a barrage of rockets slammed down amongst the remnants of the Headsmen, tearing his former comrades to pieces. Tribesmen fell as cannonballs pounded into the close-packed mass of bodies. Crossbow bolts hummed through the air like wasps, plucking riders from the saddles and catching leaping hounds in mid-air. Despite there being more room, it reminded Canto unpleasantly of his earlier march up the viaduct.

He jerked his mount to the side, narrowly avoiding a bounding pink horror as it was shredded into a pair of moaning blue ones in a spray of twinkling multi-coloured motes. Somewhere behind him, a Chaos-tainted giant gave a long, drawn-out death-howl as it toppled forwards like a felled tree. The ground shuddered beneath his steed's hooves as the great body crashed down, crushing a score of inobservant tribesmen.

But none of it mattered. There were simply too many bodies to be so easily thrown on the fire and forgotten. All around Canto, bellowing Kurgan, Aeslings and Tahmaks pressed forwards over the fire-torn bodies of the dead, climbing heaps and drifts of corpses in their eagerness to reach their foes. Snarling Dolgans, mounted on shaggy horses, galloped alongside Khazags and the horse-lords of the Kul. Kvelligs, Aghols and Bjornlings forced their way up, into the teeth of the enemy fire, their broad, brightly painted kite shields bristling with bullet holes and broken crossbow bolts. Too, masked cultists from the softer southern lands charged as wildly as their hardier northern allies, robes the colour of dried blood flapping as they smashed round shields with bronze-headed maces in terrible hymns to the Lord of Skulls.

The end was as inevitable as a storm in summer, or snow in winter. Canto drew his sword as his horse vaulted the broken body of a mutated ogre, and felt a cold weight in his gut. Either way, what happened here would determine the fate of all involved. *Death or glory,* he thought bitterly, as the Swords of Chaos galloped on.

Even as he drew close to the Empire lines, Canto felt an old, horribly familiar tingle at the nape of his neck. Somewhere behind the enemy, a whirling white vortex took form and rose above the heads of the soldiers. A figure clad in furs rose with it, long arms gesturing frantically. A harsh voice spat out jagged words of power, and a blizzard of shimmering ice-forms erupted from the swirling vortex. Canto heard a chill shriek and saw an immense flock of white crows, with beaks and talons of glittering ice, hurtle towards Archaon, and by extension, himself.

Riders to either side of him were torn from their saddles by the birds. He ducked his head, and felt talons scrape against his helm and cuirass. A skull was plucked from his pauldron. He'd lost his shield not long after entering the city, and he cursed himself for not claiming another. With a roar, he whipped his blade about his head in an attempt to drive the flapping ice-constructs back as he urged his horse on. He caught a glimpse of Archaon moments before the Lord of the End Times struck the enemy like a thunderbolt.

The shield wall exploded, as if it had been hit by a volley of cannon fire. Archaon could not be stopped or slowed, and wherever his head turned, men died. Canto and the others joined him a moment later, thundering home with a resounding crash. Screaming soldiers were smashed off their feet by the impact, while the blades of the Chaos knights cut through breastplates and shields or hacked off heads. Canto laid about him without enthusiasm, fighting on instinct. Every blow felt like the turn of a page, bringing them closer to the end. *But that's what you want, Unsworn,* he thought. *An end to this madness.*

It sounded like something Count Mordrek might have said. Under other circumstances, that alone might have made him dismiss it out of hand, but the act of killing brought with it a strange sort of clarity. Was it truly escape from this battle, from the eyes of the gods, which he desired, or was it an ending?

When he'd first chosen sides and taken up arms against his fellow man, it had seemed that he would never tire of battle, or of the rewards bought with blood. But a few centuries' worth of slaughter was enough to glut any man, especially the son of a spice importer from Nuln. He'd slipped off the wheel of fate, and hadn't looked back.

It had all seemed so clear, once upon a time. The triumph of the Dark Gods seemed a certainty. But he'd never stopped to ask himself what form that triumph might take. The gods weren't warlords or tribal chieftains, for whom land and slaves were the spoils of victory. The gods only desired souls and destruction. Neither of which appealed to Canto, particularly.

To the west the Empire lines suddenly exploded into a lurid disharmony of light and sound, and Canto was nearly jolted from his saddle by the reverberations. The air stank of magics, and with a great roar, a firestorm exploded above the Empire army's western flank. Men screamed as their clothing caught light and their skin ran like tallow. Weapons warped and curled, transmuted into horrible shapes or inert elements. The ripple of sorcerous destruction spread outwards, claiming the lives of any in its path.

But in the centre, the shield-wall still held, much to Canto's frustration. He found himself surrounded by grim Middenlanders and howling, sackcloth-clad flagellants. Flails and halberd blades struck his armour from all sides, and it seemed that no matter how many men he killed, there were always more. Suddenly, the knot of death about him began to unravel as the Three-Eyed King forced his way through. He met Canto's bewildered gaze with a terse nod. 'You'll have to fight harder than that, Unsworn. We have a ways to go, yet.'

Archaon's eyes bored into him, as if the Lord of the End Times could see his earlier thoughts and had found them wanting. Canto's sword arm twitched, and he saw an image of his blade sliding into the gap between the Everchosen's helmet and gorget. Shadow-shapes hunched and slithered at the edges of his vision, and he felt taloned hands on his shoulders and on his forearm, ready to guide his blade – where?

He felt a kernel of panic begin to grow in him, and he recalled how the air had tasted in that far-off, but never far away, moment when he'd had a man named Magnus at his mercy, and chosen obscurity over glory. He'd had a chance, once, to earn the rewards of the gods. He had chosen their ire and indifference instead.

He had another chance now. It was as if that same moment had hunted him down through all of the ages, and now it had found him. He could hear its howl of triumph as it stalked him over the points of spears and shaking standards. *Run and hide or stand and fight, Unsworn – your appointed hour has come round at last,* something whispered in his head. Was that his voice, or Archaon's? Was it a human voice at all, or something else?

And, more importantly, *what was the choice it wanted him to make?*

Archaon turned away, and began to fight his way forwards once more. His dreadful sword rose and fell with a sinner's wail, cutting short destinies and devouring hope. Canto looked down at the blade in his hand. Then, with a sharp cry, he drove his knees into his mount's flanks and charged in the Everchosen's wake.

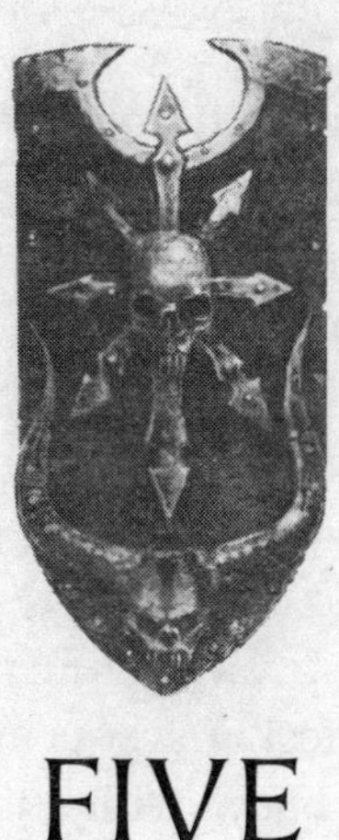

FIVE

The Temple of Ulric

Gregor Martak spun, and his ice-wreathed hands punched through the cackling daemon's soft belly. The pink horror shrilled as it began to split into two smaller blue ones, but Martak's fingers caught the creatures before they could fully form and filled their gaping maws with ice and amber. The daemons evaporated with tinny moans, as Martak turned his attentions elsewhere. Inside him, he could feel the godspark of Ulric raging and smashing against the confines of his soul.

To the west, the west, the god howled.

'Are there not enemies enough for you here?' Martak snarled. Ice and snow rose from his hands, sweeping forward to flash-freeze a slobbering Chaos troll. The brute toppled over and shattered into a dozen chunks. Northmen filled the gap left by the troll, and hurled themselves towards him with suicidal courage. Martak, mind reeling with the fury of the god nesting within him, hastily created a shield of amber and frost, blocking the first blow. At a gesture, the shield twisted and transformed, splitting into a multitude of stabbing lances. Several of his attackers were punched off their feet, and the rest were driven back. Martak stepped forwards, gathering his strength, and gestured again. The lances bulged, cracked and split, becoming shrieking hawks, raucous crows and even a few stinging hummingbirds.

The barbarians were forced back by the swarm of mystical constructs, even as he'd hoped. Breathing heavily, he staggered back too. The state troops closed ranks to his fore, buying him a few precious moments to catch his breath. He was tired - more tired than he'd ever been. Every muscle ached, and his body felt like a wrung-out wineskin. It was no easy thing to carry the weight of a god, and he knew, with animal certainty, that even if they won the day, he would be burned to nothing by the cold fire of Ulric's presence. Whatever happened here today, Gregor Martak was a dead man.

He smiled thinly. Then, his life expectancy had dropped to almost nothing the moment he'd been made Supreme Patriarch. And in a time of war, no less. He'd almost died ten times over in the first battle for Altdorf, and its fall almost two years later. He shook himself all over, like a dog scattering water, and sniffed the air. He caught the rank odour - like sour milk and spoiled fruit - of fell sorcery, and peered west, as Ulric had urged.

His eyes widened as he caught sight of the eldritch inferno sweeping across the western flank of the Empire's battle-line. He could hear the screams of men and the cackling of daemons, and knew that, unless whatever magics had been unleashed there were countered, the whole flank might collapse. He cursed and looked around for Valten.

The Herald of Sigmar sat on his horse nearby, with Greiss and the other commanders. His armour was dented and scorched, and his face was drawn and haggard. He had fought in the vanguard for those first terrible moments of the attack, but had been forced back behind the shield-wall by simple necessity. Now he was trying to organise a counter-attack with Greiss, Staahl and the remaining knights.

Martak hurried towards them. 'We ride through them, then,' Greiss was saying, as the wizard drew close. 'Middenheimers are bred hard, boy, and we don't balk at necessary sacrifice.'

'There's a difference between necessary sacrifice, and foolishness,' Valten retorted. For the first time since Martak had met him, the Herald of Sigmar looked angry. He seemed to loom over the knights. 'These are our men, Greiss, and you shall not treat them as mere impediments to your glory. They are not pawns to be sacrificed, or tools to be discarded,' Valten growled. 'They are men. *My* men.'

'Men die in battle,' Dostov said. It was obvious whose side the Grand Master of the Gryphon Legion was on. Then, the Kislevite wasn't unduly burdened by sentimentality.

'Men die, but they are not ridden down like dogs by their own commanders,' Valten said. He raised Ghal Maraz. 'And I will split the skull of the next man who uses the phrase "necessary sacrifice" to my face in such a way again.' He turned in his saddle, and looked down at Martak. 'Gregor, what-?'

Martak, about to tell Valten what he had seen to the west, felt his words die on his lips as a new sound intruded over the booming report of the artillery at the top of the steps above them. From within the confines of the temple came the scream of voices and the clash of weapons. These were mingled with the rapid chatter of gunfire and dreadful chittering. Even as Valten and the others turned to look up the steps, towards the great entrance of the Temple of Ulric, the artillery crews began to hastily pivot their guns.

'What are they doing?' Greiss snarled. 'The enemy is out here!'

Martak didn't bother to remind Greiss he'd said something similar before, and been wrong then as well. Blackened and bloodied soldiers, survivors of the temple garrisons, stampeded out through the great doors, hampering the efforts of the artillery crews. They were followed by hulking, armoured rat ogres, who tore into the fleeing soldiers and artillery crews both. Great cannons were upended and sent rolling down the steps. Gun carriages shattered to matchwood. Bullet holes stitched their way along Nuln-forged gun barrels, courtesy of the skaven ratling gun teams. Powder kegs were perforated as well, and the subsequent explosion rocked the temple to its foundations. The concussive blast killed men, skaven and rat ogres besides, and only Martak's quick thinking and magics prevented the explosion from reaching Valten and the others.

As his amber shield crackled and fell to pieces, Martak saw a fresh tide of ratmen sweep over the burning wreckage of the Grand Battery. Stormvermin and clanrats poured down the steps of the temple in a screeching flood. Valten cursed. He looked at Greiss. 'Hold the line. I'll deal with the vermin.' Without waiting for the surly knight's reply, he looked at Martak. 'Gregor, can you–?'

Martak shook his head. 'The western flank is collapsing. Daemon-fire is sweeping the square there, and I am needed.' He smiled bitterly. 'I was coming to ask for your help.'

Valten shook his head. He hesitated, and for a moment, Martak saw not the Herald of Sigmar, but the callow young blacksmith Huss had introduced him to, so many months ago. 'It appears our journey is coming to an end,' Valten said, fighting to be heard over the noise of battle. 'Since Luthor vanished, I have relied on your advice more than once. It has been a pleasure to call you friend, Gregor.' Valten bent low and reached out his hand. It was Martak's turn to hesitate. Then, he clasped forearms with the Herald of Sigmar. Valten smiled and straightened in his saddle. 'I do not think we will meet again, my friend.'

Then he turned, jerked on his horse's reins, and galloped up the steps to meet the coming threat. Martak hesitated again, for just a moment. Then, with a snarl, he turned to the west. He ignored Greiss's shouts as he began to push his way along, moving more swiftly than a man ought. He ran smoothly, his steps guided by Ulric, and in seemingly no time at all he was bulling through the ranks towards the daemon-threatened stretch of the line. As he moved, he reached out with his mind, snagging the errant winds of magic and drawing them in his wake.

I grow weak, son of Middenheim, Ulric murmured. *Soon my spark shall gutter out, and you will crumble to cold ash.*

'Then we'd best take as many of the enemy with us as we can,' Martak growled. 'Or would you rather crawl into a hole and die?' He heard the indignant snap of the god's jaws and bared his teeth in satisfaction. He shoved aside a pair of spearmen, and found himself staring at a hellish inferno of dancing, multi-coloured flames. Screams of terror filled the air as men burned and died, or worse, *changed*. Daemons leapt and shimmered beyond the flames, cackling and chanting.

As the line of soldiers around him fell back, Martak spread his arms, calling up what strength Ulric could spare him. The heat from the fires faded, and with a single, sharp gesture, Martak snuffed them entirely. He felt his body swell with power as he drew the winds of magic into himself, bolstering the strength of the fading godspark.

Martak threw back his head and howled out incantation after incantation. Daemons screamed as ice-coated spears of amber spitted them. Others were flash-frozen, or torn to shreds by icy winds. The daemonic assault faltered in the face of the combined fury of man and god, and for a moment, Martak thought he might sweep every daemon from the field.

Ulric howled a warning and Martak twisted around, freezing the air into a solid shield over him with a sweep of his hands as a wave of sorcerous fire lashed down at him from above. A gigantic avian shape crashed down, nearly crushing Martak. The wizard hurled himself aside, trying not to think about the men who still writhed beneath the immense daemon's talons. He scrambled to his feet.

Two pairs of milky, possibly blind eyes regarded him, and two cruel beaks clacked in croaking laughter. The daemon's two long, feathered necks undulated as its vestigial, yet powerful wings snapped out, casting the wizard into their shadow. He recognised the beast, though he had never seen it before. Kairos Fateweaver, dual-voiced oracle of the Changer of Ways.

'Ulric, man and god. We see you, wolf-god. We see you, cowering in this cave of blood and meat. Come out, little god... Come out, and accept the judgement of fate,' the daemon rasped, its voices in concert with itself.

Martak felt Ulric twitch within him. Even a god wasn't immune to accusations of cowardice. 'You are not fate,' he roared, though whether they were his words or Ulric's, he didn't know. 'You are its slave, as are we all.' Frost swirled about his clenched fingers. 'You are but the merest shard of a mad, broken dream. A cackling, senile shadow which schemes against itself because it is too myopic to recognise the wider cosmos.' He flung his hands out, releasing a blast of wintry power.

Kairos staggered, cawing angrily. The daemon's great wings flapped and its twin beaks spat sizzling incantations. The air about Martak took on a greasy tinge and strange shapes swam through it, passing through the fleeing soldiers as if they were not there. Motes of painful light swirled about, emerging and twisting about an unseen aleph.

'We have seen what awaits us all, wolf-god. It is a beautiful thing, and hideous, and it will unmake all and fashion it anew. The earth will crack, the skies will burn and all will cease, before beginning again. Why do you struggle and snap so?' the Fateweaver croaked.

A strange howling grew in Martak's ears and he staggered as unseen hands plucked at him, trying to draw him into the Realms of Chaos. If he had been as he was, he would have been lost. But he was more than he had been. And he was not alone.

Ulric roared, and Martak roared with him. His muscles bunched and he hurled himself away from the unseen hands. Claws of amber formed about his hands and he raked them across the

Fateweaver's wrinkled chest. The raw stuff of magic poured from the wounds and the daemon snarled. Twin beaks snapped at Martak, who stumbled back. 'What have you done, cur?' the Fateweaver cawed. 'You were supposed to die. We saw it!'

The daemon hefted its staff and swung it in a furious arc. Martak, his muscles filled with the power of the last god of mankind, caught the staff in mid-swing. He grinned into the teeth of the daemon's fury. 'What you saw, and what is, are not necessarily the same thing,' he said. Frost spread from his fingers, curling up the length of the staff. The Fateweaver squawked as it tried to rip its staff free of his grip. The unnatural flesh of its arms began to blacken and peel away from brass bones.

With a single, thumping beat of its wings, the Fateweaver hurled itself skywards. It paused for a moment, wings flapping, and glared down at Martak. Then, with a sound which might have been a frustrated scream, or a laugh of contempt, or even perhaps both, the Fateweaver vanished.

Martak stared upwards for a moment. Then he dropped his gaze to the remaining daemons. The creatures, deprived of their master and of their advantage, cowered back. He gestured sharply and jagged chunks of ice and swirling snow struck the closest of the creatures, as the soldiers of the Empire gave a great shout and surged forwards, their courage renewed. Martak stood unmoving as the line passed him, driving into the daemonic host. Ulric growled softly in his head as Martak turned east, where he knew that even at that moment, Valten was trying to drive back the skaven.

The god sounded as weak as Martak felt, and he knew that neither of them had much time left. But he was determined to make it count for something. Though the City of the White Wolf and its god might die today, the Empire would be preserved. Whatever else happened, Martak, and the spark of godly fury within him, could do that much.

* * *

The explosion had come as another unpleasant surprise in a day already full to the brim of them. Wendel Volker fought in the centre of the Empire lines, alongside Brunner and a few other familiar faces, including a number of dismounted Reiksguard and Knights of the Black Bear. They acted as a steel core to anchor the centre, but they rapidly became an island in a sea of panic as the Grand Battery ceased to exist and Archaon's forces attacked with renewed vigour. Volker cursed as crossbowmen fled past him, seeking the dubious safety of the temple. He thought he saw Fleischer among them, moving as quickly as her legs could carry her. He could hear screams echoing behind him, and the rising chitter of skaven.

A smaller explosion followed the first, and a keg of black powder, wreathed in flames, soared overhead. He looked up, watching it arc over the square. When it exploded, he instinctively raised his shield, and left himself open to a bludgeoning blow that catapulted him off his feet. He slammed into another knight, and they both fell in a rattling tangle. Wheezing, Volker looked up as a burly northman, wearing the shaggy hide of an auroch, swept his stone-headed mace out and drove another Reiksguard to his knees. The knight wobbled and was unable to avoid the next blow, which sent him spinning head over heels into the air. The northman spread his arms and roared, 'Where is the Herald of Sigmar? Gharad the Ox would crush his delicate bones in the name of the Lord of Pleasure!'

'Over there somewhere,' Volker coughed, forcing himself to his feet. 'Why not go look for him?' He was shoved aside as the man he'd slammed into got to his feet and lunged towards the Ox. The stone mace came down and pulverised the knight's head, helmet and all. Volker stared at the gory ruin of the man's skull for a moment, and then back up at Gharad. 'All right, then,' he muttered, raising his sword.

The mace whipped out and Volker stepped to the side, narrowly avoiding the blow. As the weapon whistled past his chin, he brought his sword down on the brute's arm. The blade chopped through meat and muscle, but became lodged in the bone. Gharad howled in pain, and his mace fell from his fingers. The northman clawed at Volker's throat with his good hand, while the latter tried to pry his weapon free.

Their struggle was interrupted by the sound of horns and the thunder of hooves. Volker dragged his sword free and hurled himself backwards as, with a mournful howl, the Fellwolf Brotherhood and the Knights of the White Wolf charged. Fleeing state troops were ridden down by the templars of Ulric as they galloped through the disintegrating centre line and smashed full-tilt into Archaon's advance. Empire and Chaos knights met with a mighty crash. Armoured steeds slammed together, crushing limbs and sending horses rearing in panic as their riders hacked and hammered at one another.

Volker scrambled away from the stomping hooves of the horses, one arm wrapped around his chest. Pain shot through him with every step, and it was hard to breathe, but he had to get clear of the press. Even his armour wouldn't save him from being trampled to death. He'd seen men die that way, and he had no wish to share their fate.

But, as he made to extricate himself from the situation, a large hand fastened itself around his ankle. He looked down, into the grinning, battered features of his opponent. 'Gharad is angry. He has been stomped on by many horses, little man,' the northman said, as he yanked Volker off his feet. 'Let Gharad show you how it feels.' Gharad slammed a bloody fist down on Volker's chest, denting his cuirass and driving all of the air from his lungs.

The northman tore Volker's gorget loose and flung it aside before fastening his thick fingers around Volker's throat. Gharad hunched over him as horses stomped and whinnied around them. Volker clawed at his opponent's wrists, trying to break his grip.

Gharad grinned down at him. 'Goodbye, little man. Gharad the Ox has enjoyed killing–' The northman's eyes crossed, and his grin slipped. With a sigh, he slumped over Volker, revealing a falchion, three throwing daggers and a hand-axe embedded in his back.

Volker heaved the dead weight off him, and looked up at Brunner. 'Thanks,' he gasped, as he rubbed his aching throat.

'Come on,' Brunner said, jerking his falchion free of the fallen northman.

'What?' Volker said, shoving himself to his feet. 'Where are we going?'

'Cut off the head, and the body dies,' Brunner spat. There was a dark stain on his side, and he grimaced as he pressed a hand to it. He jerked his chin towards Archaon. The Three-Eyed King was impossible to miss, despite the confusion. As they watched, he cut down a howling knight. 'Kill him, we get out of this alive.'

'I don't like our odds,' Volker wheezed. Something in his chest scraped. The blow from the northman's mace had, at the very least, cracked his ribs.

'I fought my way across half the Empire, through the walking dead, beastmen and worse things, all to get here,' Brunner growled. 'Never tell me the odds.'

Volker shook himself and looked around. The bulk of the Empire troops still held their place, despite the massed ranks of the enemy that pressed against them. But Volker had commanded enough men to see that the Middenheimers were close to collapse. The halberdiers still hacked and thrust at their enemies with grim resolve, but exhaustion was taking its toll, and Greiss and his fur-clad maniacs charging through the centre of their own lines hadn't helped matters. The enemy, on the other hand, seemed tireless, and without number. Every northman who fell was quickly replaced by two more; but there were no fresh troops to throw into the gaps growing in the defenders' ranks. What reinforcements there were, were busy trying to hold off the skaven pouring out of the Temple of Ulric.

That fact, in the end, made Volker's decision for him. If Archaon fell, the Chaos attack might disintegrate, easing the pressure on the embattled defenders. Evidently Brunner thought the same. He gestured with his sword. 'By all means, lead the way.' *You lunatic,* he added, in his head. Brunner smirked, as if he'd heard Volker's thoughts, and turned.

The bounty-hunter moved through the press of battle like a shark. His falchion snaked out left and right, cutting through legs or chopping into bellies. Volker did his best to keep up, smashing aside tribesmen with his recovered shield and sword, despite the pain in his chest. At times, through the smoke that now obscured most of the square, he caught sight of the battle going on atop the steps of the Temple of Ulric. Valten was there, his golden armour reflecting the light of the fires as he employed Ghal Maraz with lethal efficiency. The Herald of Sigmar had ploughed into the ratmen like a battering ram, and broken, twitching bodies flew into the air with every swing of his hammer.

'There he is,' Brunner shouted. He grabbed Volker and gestured with his bloody falchion. Volker peered through the smoke and saw their quarry. Archaon's horse reared as the Three-Eyed King chopped through a bevy of thrusting spears.

'What do we do?' Volker said.

Brunner smiled, pulled one of the pistols from his bandolier and fired. To Volker's surprise, Archaon tumbled from his saddle. 'What-?' Volker said.

'Wyrdstone bullet,' Brunner said, tossing aside the smoking pistol. A moment later, the bounty-hunter was ducking past the daemonic steed's flailing hooves, and arrowing towards its rider. Volker tried to follow him, but he found himself preoccupied by the attentions of one of the Chaos knights who made up Archaon's bodyguard. He caught a hoof on his shield, and felt a shiver of pain run through him. His sword sliced out, driving back a horse and rider. He saw Brunner's falchion flash down, only to be intercepted at the last moment by Archaon's blade.

Archaon forced Brunner back, and rose to his full height. Green smoke rose from the hole in his armour where Brunner's bullet had struck home. To his credit, the bounty-hunter didn't seem impressed. He lunged, and their blades came together with a barely audible screech. Volker saw Brunner's free hand flit to his vambrace, and then something sharp flashed and Archaon roared. The Lord of the End Times stepped back and groped for the throwing blade that had sprouted from between the plates of his cuirass. Brunner drew another pistol, his last, and fired. Or tried to, at least. There was a puff of smoke, followed by a curse from Brunner, and then Archaon lunged forwards, thrusting his sword before him like a lance.

The tip of the sword emerged from Brunner's back and he was lifted off his feet. Archaon held him aloft for a moment, and then, with seemingly little effort, swept the sword to the side and slung the bounty-hunter off. Brunner hit the street hard, with a sound that made Volker cringe inside his armour. He took a chance and darted through a gap in the press of battle, ducking a blow which would have removed his head.

Archaon was already climbing back into the saddle when Volker reached Brunner. He sank down beside the man, but he could see that it was already too late. And not just for Brunner – he heard a roar from behind him, and turned. He saw Archaon catch a blow from Axel Greiss, Grand Master of the White Wolves, on his shield. The Grand Master recoiled, readying himself for another swing as his stallion bit and kicked at Archaon's own mount. The White Wolves duelled with Archaon's knights around them.

Archaon swung round in his saddle, and his sword chopped down through plate mail, flesh and bone, severing Greiss's arm at the elbow. Greiss's scream was cut short by Archaon's second blow, which tore through the old knight's torso in a welter of gore. Volker looked away as Greiss's body slid from the saddle.

He looked down at Brunner. He realised that he'd never seen

the other man's face in the little time they'd known each other. They hadn't been friends. Merely men in the same place at the same time, facing the same enemy. Even so, Volker felt something that might have been sadness as he looked down at the dead bounty-hunter.

Panic began to spread through the ranks of the Empire almost immediately. The troops in the centre had held their ground against the worst Archaon could throw at them, but the death of Greiss was too much, even for the most stalwart soldier. Volker couldn't blame them. He knew a rout in the offing when he saw one, however, and he was on the wrong side of it, cut off from the obvious route of retreat by the fighting. Knots of defenders still battled on, most notably around the standards of the Order of the Black Bear and the Gryphon Legion, and to the east and west the flank forces still held, but the line had been broken.

Volker looked around desperately, trying to spot an avenue of escape. If he could reach someone – anyone – he could organise a fighting withdrawal. At the very least, they might buy themselves a few more hours. *Averheim,* he thought. *Save as many as I can – get to Averheim. The Emperor is at Averheim. The Emperor will know what to do.*

'Yes, he will,' a voice growled. Volker looked up into a pair of yellow eyes. 'Up, boy,' Gregor Martak growled. His furs were scorched and blackened, and his arms and face were streaked with blood. Volker knew, without knowing how, that it was not merely the wizard who regarded him, but something else as well. Something old and powerful, but diminished in some way. The wizard hauled him to his feet with ease, sparing not a glance for Brunner's body. Martak's eyes narrowed. 'Volker,' he rasped. 'One of Leitdorf's lot, from Heldenhame.'

'I–' Volker began.

'Quiet.' Martak's eyes were unfocused, as if he were listening to something. 'You survived Heldenhame, Altdorf and everything in between. You might even survive this, where braver men did not.' The yellow eyes looked down at Brunner. 'The time for heroes is past, Wendel Volker. Wolves are not heroes. They are not brave, or honourable. Wolves are survivors. The coming world needs survivors.'

Volker struggled against Martak's grip. The wizard shook himself and grinned savagely. 'It's the end, boy. You can feel it, can't you?'

Volker's lips tried to form a denial, but no words came. Men were fighting and dying around them, but no one seemed to notice them. Martak laughed harshly. He grabbed hold of Volker's chin. 'It's like a weight in your chest, a moment of pain stretched out to interminable length, until death becomes merely release.' His chapped, bleeding lips peeled back from long, yellow teeth. 'But not for you. Not yet. You must tell the Emperor what has happened. You must show him what I now show you.' Martak dragged Volker close. The fingers clutching Volker's chin felt like ice. 'You must claim my debt.'

Images filled Volker's mind – a shadowy shape creeping through the Fauschlag; the snuffing of the Flame of Ulric; and worst of all, a pulsing, heaving tear in the skin of reality itself. Volker screamed as the last image ate its way into his memories like acid. He tried to pull himself free of the wizard, but Martak's grip was like iron. He felt cold and hot all at once, and a cloud of frost exploded from his mouth. His heart hammered, as if straining to free itself of his chest, and he thought that he might die as his insides filled up with ice and snow and all of the fury of winter and war.

'No,' he heard Martak growl. 'No, you will not die, Wendel Volker. Not until you have done as I command.'

Panic spread like wildfire through the Middenheim companies, fanned to greater fury by the bludgeoning advance of the Swords of Chaos. Canto, still astride his cursing steed, could only marvel at the sheer, dogged relentlessness of Archaon's warriors. They fought like automatons. There was never a wasted motion or excess of force. As soon as one enemy fell from their path they moved on to the next without hesitation. They fought in silence as well, uttering no battle cries or even grunts of pain when a blow struck home.

Archaon, in contrast, was all sound and fury. He was the centre of the whirlwind, and he seemed to grow angrier the more foes he dispatched. Men were trampled beneath the hooves of his daemon steed, and banners were chopped down and trodden into the thick streams of blood which ran between the cobbles. One moment, he was amidst a desperate scrum of hard-pressed soldiers. The next, it had collapsed into a howling mass of terrified humanity, each seeking to get as far as possible from the roaring monster who had come to claim them.

The Everchosen spurred his mount through the madness, ignoring the fleeing soldiers. Canto knew who he was looking for and he spurred his own beast in pursuit, the whispers of the gods filling his mind. He tried to ignore them, but it was hard. Harder than it had ever been before. They were not asking that he follow their chosen champion – they demanded it. And Canto had neither the strength nor the courage to do otherwise.

So he galloped in Archaon's wake, and watched as the last defenders of Middenheim parted before the Three-Eyed King, or were ridden down. 'Where are you, Herald?' Archaon bellowed, as his horse reared and screamed. 'Where are you, beloved of Sigmar? I am here! Face me, and end this farce. How many more must die for you?'

Archaon glared about him, his breath rasping from within his helmet. 'Face me, damn you. I will not be denied now – not now! I have broken your army, I have gutted your city... *Where are you?*'

Canto jerked on his mount's reins, bringing it to a halt behind

Archaon. The latter glanced at him. 'Where is he, Unsworn? Where is he?' he demanded, and Canto felt a moment of uncertainty as he noted the pleading tone of Archaon's words.

'I am here,' a voice said, and each word struck the air like a hammer-blow. Canto shuddered as the echo of that voice rose over the square, and the sounds of battle faded. A wind rose, carrying smoke with it, isolating them from the madness that still consumed the world around them. 'I am here, Diederick Kastner,' Valten said. His words were punctuated by the slow *clop-clop-clop* of his horse's hooves.

'Do not say that name,' Archaon said, his voice calmer than it had been a moment ago. 'You have not earned the right to say that name. You are not *him*.'

'No, I am not. I thought, once, that I might be... But that is not my fate,' Valten said. 'And I am thankful for it. I am thankful that my part in this... farce, as you call it, is almost done. And that I will not have to see the horror that comes next.'

'Coward,' Archaon said.

'No. Cowardice is not acceptance. Cowardice is tearing down the foundations of heaven because you cannot bear its light. Cowardice is blaming gods for the vagaries of men. Cowardice is choosing damnation over death, and casting a people on the fire to assuage your wounded soul.' Valten looked up, and heaved a long, sad sigh. 'I see so much now. I see all of the roads not taken, and I see how small your masters are.' He looked at Archaon. 'They drove their greatest heroes and warriors into my path like sheep, all to spare you this moment. Because even now... they doubt you. They doubt, and you can feel it. Why else would you be so determined to face me?'

'You do not deserve to bear that hammer,' Archaon said. 'You do not deserve *any of it*.'

'No.' Valten smiled gently. 'But you did.' He lifted Ghal Maraz. 'Once, I think, this was meant for you. But the claws of Chaos pluck even the thinnest strands of fate. And so it has come to this.' His smile shifted, becoming harder. 'Two sons of many fathers, forgotten mothers and a shared moment.' He extended the hammer. 'The gods are watching, Everchosen. Let us give them a show.'

'What do you know of gods?' Archaon snarled. 'You know nothing.'

'I know that if you want this city, this world, you must earn it.' Valten urged his horse forwards and Archaon did the same. Both animals seemed almost as eager for the fray as their riders, and the shrieks and snarls of the one were matched by the whinnying challenge of the other. Canto tried to follow, but found himself unable to move. He was not here to participate, but to watch. The Swords of Chaos spread out around him, a silent audience for the contest to come. He felt no relief, and wanted nothing more than to be elsewhere, anywhere other than here.

Archaon leaned forward, and raised his sword. Valten swung his hammer, and Archaon's shield buckled under the impact. The Everchosen rocked in his saddle. He parried a blow that would have taken off his head, and his sword wailed like a lost soul as its blade crashed against the flat of the hammer's head. As they broke apart, Archaon's steed lunged and sank its fangs into the throat of Valten's horse. With a wet wrench, the daemon steed tore out the other animal's throat.

Valten hurled himself from the saddle even as his horse collapsed. He crashed down on the steps of the Temple of Ulric. Archaon spurred his horse on and leaned out to skewer the fallen Herald. Valten, reacting with superhuman speed, caught the blow on Ghal Maraz's haft. He twisted the hammer, shoving the blade aside. The daemon-horse reared up, and Valten surged to his feet. His hammer thudded into the animal's scarred flank. The beast cried out in pain, and it stumbled away. Archaon snarled in rage and chopped down at Valten again and again. One of the blows caught Valten, opening a bloody gash in his shoulder.

The Herald of Sigmar staggered back. Archaon wheeled his

steed about, intent on finishing what he'd started. His mount slammed into Valten, and sent the latter sprawling. As Valten tried to get to his feet, Archaon's sword tore through his cuirass.

Valten sank back down, and for a moment, Canto thought the fight was done. But, then Valten heaved himself to his feet, and he seemed suffused with a golden, painful light. Canto raised a hand protectively in front of his eyes, and he heard a rattling, hollow moan rise from the stiff shapes of the Swords of Chaos.

Archaon's steed retreated, shying from the light. It gibbered and shrieked, and no amount of cursing from Archaon could bring the beast under control. The Everchosen swung himself down from the saddle and started towards his opponent. As he entered the glow of the light, steam rose from his armour, and he seemed to shrink into himself. But he pressed forward nonetheless. Valten strode to meet him.

They met with a sound like thunder. Ghal Maraz connected with the Slayer of Kings, and Canto was nearly knocked from his saddle by the echo of the impact. Windows shattered across the plaza, and the Ulricsmund shook. The two warriors traded blows, moving back and forth in an intricate waltz of destruction. Archaon stepped aside as Ghal Maraz drove down, and cobbles exploded into fragments. Valten leaned away from the Slayer of Kings's bite, and a wall or statue earned a new scar. When the weapons connected, the air shuddered and twisted, and each time the Swords of Chaos groaned as if in pain.

Their fight took them up the steps of the Temple of Ulric. First one had the advantage, and then the other. Neither gave ground. Canto watched, unable to tear his eyes away, though the power that swirled and snarled about the two figures threatened to blind him. Two destinies were at war, and the skeins of fate strained to contain their struggle. The rest of the battle faded into the background... heroes lived, fought and died in their dozens, but this was the only battle that mattered. The future would be decided by either the Skull-Splitter or the Slayer of Kings.

Or, perhaps not.

A figure, reeking of blood and ice, clad in scorched furs, darted suddenly through the smoke. For an instant, Canto thought it was a wolf. Then he saw it was a man, and felt something tense within him. The man radiated power – dark, brooding and wild. He sprang up the steps of the temple, bounding towards the duellists. 'Stay your hand, servant of ruin,' he howled, in a voice which was at once human and something greater. 'This is my city, and you will despoil it no more!'

'Gregor – no!' Valten cried, flinging out a hand. The newcomer froze, half-crouched, like a wolf ready to spring. Magic bled from him, and the air about him was thick with snow and frost. 'This is my fight. This is the moment I was born for, and you well know it, Gregor Martak. And even if its outcome is not to your liking, neither you nor Ulric shall interfere.'

The air vibrated with a growl that came from everywhere and nowhere at once. To Canto, it was as if the city itself were a slumbering beast now stirring. Archaon hefted his blade in both hands and said, 'Growl all you like, old god. You are dead, and your city with you. And that shell you cower in is soon to join you, Supreme Patriarch or no.'

'Maybe so, spawn of damnation,' the newcomer growled, 'but even dead, a wolf can bite. And when it does, it does not let go.'

'Bite away and break your teeth, beast-god. My time is now,' Archaon snapped.

'No,' Valten said. 'Our time is now.'

Silence fell as the three men faced one another. Archaon slid forwards, blade raised. Valten moved to meet him. Canto longed to draw his sword, but he could not, nor did he know why he felt so. *Who are you planning to help this time, Unsworn? What god do you serve?* He pushed the thought aside. Something was happening on the steps. Something no one but him seemed to notice. He squinted, trying to see through the greasy envelope of smoke and the harsh light of the fire.

A sense of wrongness pervaded the air, as the shadows cast by the firelight seemed to congeal. A mote of darkness, which grew, like a rat-hole in an otherwise unblemished wall. Where before there had only been a conjunction of firelight, drifting ash and darkness, there was now something vast and verminous. It sprang too swiftly for Canto to get a clear look at it, but he thought it must be a skaven, although of great size. He caught only the glint of a blade. He could not even tell who it was heading for, whether its target was Archaon or Valten. His answer came a moment later.

'Valten, behind you,' Martak roared, flinging up his hands. With almost treacle-slowness, Valten and Archaon both turned. The triple blade hissed as it whipped through the air and struck Valten cleanly in the neck. The Herald of Sigmar made a sound like a sigh as his head tumbled from his shoulders. Archaon lunged forward and caught his body as it fell, roaring in outrage. From the darkness came a sound like the scurrying of myriad rats, and a whisper of mocking laughter. Then it was gone.

Archaon sat for a time, cradling the body of his enemy. 'He was mine,' he said. He looked up. The Eye of Sheerian flared like a dying star on his brow, and Canto felt a wave of incandescent heat wash over him. '*Mine.*' Archaon's rage was a force unto itself, burning clean the smoke and driving back all shadows. Above the city, the sky buckled and the clouds tore open as a bolt of sorcerous lightning slammed down. A portion of the temple dome collapsed with an explosive *boom*. Smoke billowed out through the temple doors and swept down the steps. Archaon set Valten's body aside and rose.

'He was never yours,' Martak rasped. He tapped the side of his head. 'This was never preordained, not in the way you think. It was a game. And it has been won.' His hands twitched and he stepped forward. 'But I have never been very good at games.' His hands flexed and the air ruptured as a great bolt of amber and ice shot towards Archaon.

Archaon split the bolt in two with his sword. More blades followed as Martak advanced slowly, tears streaming down his face. Archaon smashed them aside one by one. Shuddering, eyes white and hoarfrost crackling across his flesh, Martak thrust his hands out and a howling blizzard, composed of a million glinting shards of amber, enveloped the Everchosen. Shreds of his cloak slipped from its obscuring pall, and Canto felt his heart lurch in his chest.

Archaon emerged from the blizzard, hand outstretched. He caught Martak about the throat and lifted him high. 'The only game that matters is mine, wizard. Not yours, not that of the withered godspark in you which fades even now, and not even those of the Dark Gods themselves. Only mine. But you were right. It has been won.'

Martak twisted in his grip, howling like a beast. A knife appeared in his hand, and he thrust it into a gap in Archaon's armour, eliciting a scream. Archaon dropped him and staggered back, clutching at the wound, which smoked and steamed like melting ice. Martak rose up, eyes blazing. 'Even in death, a wolf can still bite. And what it bites, it holds,' he growled. 'You will not leave Middenheim alive, Everchosen. Whatever else happens, *you will die here.*'

Martak lunged. Archaon's sword slashed out, and the wizard's head, eyes bulging with fury, bounced down the steps. The air reverberated with a mournful howl as something left his body, and then all fell still. Archaon sank down onto the steps, his sword planted point-first between his legs. He leaned against its length.

'Yes, wizard, I will,' Archaon said softly, as he stared down at Martak's head. Nonetheless, his words echoed across the plaza. Canto, at last able to move, urged his horse forwards. The Swords of Chaos followed him. Around them, the battle was coming to its inevitable conclusion. The army that had stood with Valten was no more, its positions overrun and its few survivors fleeing through the streets, pursued by their victorious enemy.

Middenheim, the City of the White Wolf, had fallen.

PART TWO

The Last Council
Autumn 2528

SIX

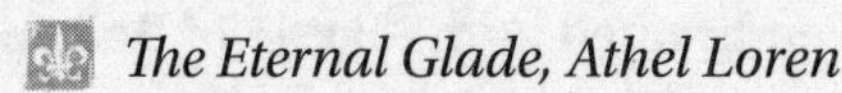

The Eternal Glade, Athel Loren

Jerrod, the last Duke of Quenelles, hunched in his saddle and steeled his mind against the creeping quiet of the Forest of Loren. Since childhood, he had feared the forest which clung to the south-eastern border of Quenelles. Over the years, it had been responsible for the deaths and disappearances of more friends and subjects than he cared to count. More than once, as a young lord, he had ridden to its edge on the trail of a missing peasant child, only to be forced to turn back in failure. It was a place of pale shapes and bad dreams. Then, the world itself had become a nightmare of late.

He closed his eyes, and wished yet again that the burden he now bore had not passed to him. That his cousin Anthelme had not perished in Altdorf, victim of a plague-stained blade. That Tancred, Anthelme's predecessor, had not fallen to the black axe of Krell. That he, Jerrod, was not the last of the line of Quenelles. But mostly, he wished that he was not here now, riding into the belly of the beast rather than fighting alongside his people in their hour of need – whatever remained of them.

Jerrod could still recall the smoke that lay thick on the horizon as he'd ridden hard through the pine crags, seeking aid for his beleaguered companions. The smoke that rose over the pyre that had been his homeland, and more besides. For there to be so much smoke, the whole of Bretonnia would need to be aflame, he knew.

What had happened, in the months since he and the Companions of Quenelles had ridden out alongside Louen Leoncoeur's crusade into the heart of the Empire, to bend their lances in aid of their oldest rivals, greatest enemies and occasional allies? What had befallen Bretonnia in that time? He opened his eyes and reached beneath his helmet to scratch at the week-old growth of beard covering his cheeks and jaw. Since his manservant had been brained at the Battle of Bolgen, he'd had no one to make him presentable.

If what was occurring in Bretonnia was anything like what was happening in the Empire, he feared to learn of it. The Empire had always seemed an unconquerable behemoth to him, a vast dragon with many heads, belching fire and ruin against its foes. To test oneself against that dragon had been the dream of many a young knight, himself included. But now the dragon had fallen, slain by a death of a thousand cuts, each more inglorious than the last. Then, when your enemy wielded plague, storm and fire as easily as a peasant wielded a cudgel, glory was the first casualty, as he and his Companions had discovered to their cost.

Barely a third of the men who had ridden beside him, first in the civil war against Mallobaude's wretches, and then later at La Maisontaal Abbey, and finally to Altdorf at the command of the Lion-Heart, still lived. Gioffre of Anglaron had died beneath Krell's axe at La Maisontaal Abbey. The cousins Raynor and Hernald had fallen beside Anthelme at Altdorf. Old Calard of Garamont had died on the walls of Averheim, sword in hand and a curse on his lips. Those who remained, however, were the cream of what Bretonnia had stood for – driven by duty and their oaths to the Lady to stand against evil wherever it might be found. And there was evil aplenty in the Empire.

First Altdorf, then Averheim, had become victims of the foulness seeping down from the north. The other cities of the Empire had fallen besides, but he had been at both Altdorf and Averheim, and had led the Companions in battle against the enemy alongside the Emperor Karl Franz himself, as well as the wild-haired Slayer King of the mountain folk, Ungrim Ironfist.

The thought of the latter only made the weight on his soul all the heavier. The Slayer King had died so that they might live, and escape the trap Averheim had become. While Jerrod knew little of dwarfs, he knew from the weeks they'd spent fighting beside one another that such a death had long been Ironfist's desire. That made it no less sorrowful, and he felt a moment of pity for the remains of the once-mighty throng which had followed Ironfist out of the Worlds Edge Mountains and into defeat. Like the Bretonnians, they too were the last gasp of a shattered people. And like the Bretonnians, they had no way of knowing the fate of those they had left behind.

He turned slightly in his saddle, to glance down at the heavy form of Gotri Hammerson as the dwarf runesmith stomped alongside Jerrod's horse. He was old, older perhaps than many a storied Bretonnian keep, Jerrod thought, and as hard as the stones of the mountains they now travelled through. He and the dwarf had not become friends – not quite – but they had fallen into a companionable routine. Their outlooks were not entirely dissimilar, for all that the dwarf mind was a thing utterly alien to Jerrod.

It was Hammerson who had seen them safely away from Averland, after the magics of Balthasar Gelt had plucked the battered remnants of their forces from the clutches of the Everchosen. Hammerson had led the Emperor and his motley assemblage of humans and dwarfs through the Grey Mountains by hidden dwarf roads. Indeed, it was only thanks to Hammerson that they had been able to proceed at all. Unguided, the army would have foundered, burdened as it was by the number of wounded.

Even with Hammerson's aid, the going had been difficult. Mindless dead clustered in the high crags, their only purpose to kill the living. Pools of suppurating wild magic had given birth to monsters and daemons. Too, the mountains were home to hundreds of orc and goblin tribes. Even the hidden dwarf paths had not been entirely safe. More than once, the battered group of men and dwarfs had been forced to defend themselves against greenskins which swept howling out of the crags. There, only Zhufbarak guns and Gelt's spellcraft had carried the day, a fact which proved no small frustration to Jerrod and his remaining knights.

While he respected Hammerson, his feelings for the wizard, Gelt, were mixed. The man, clad in filthy robes and a tarnished golden mask, made Jerrod's skin crawl. He stank of hot metal, and there was something… otherworldly about him. Jerrod had felt similarly when in the presence of the Emperor, who had wielded lightning at the Battle of Bolgen.

Unfortunately, whatever power had infused the Emperor now seemed to be gone, ripped from him by the hands of the Everchosen himself. He was nothing but a man now, in a time when men were all but helpless.

Jerrod sighed. He had seen two great nations consumed in fire and blood, and he longed to do something, anything, to achieve some small measure of retribution, no matter how futile. Nonetheless, even with guns and sorcery, it was invariably a close thing. The greenskins had ever frenzied forth in great numbers, but now, as the world came undone, they seemed particularly driven to madness. It was as if some unseen power had caught hold of them and set their brute minds aflame.

But even battle-maddened greenskins had been as nothing compared to what had come after. Even as the column of refugees had reached the pine crags that marked the northern boundary of Athel Loren, the wind had carried the sound of berserk howls. They had been pursued all the way from Averheim by an army of the Blood God's worshippers, and it was at the infamous Chasm of Echoes that they had been forced to make their stand. While Gelt and Hammerson's dwarfs had held the pass, Jerrod and the Emperor had ridden hard, braving the forest's dangers in an effort to make contact with Athel Loren's defenders.

Jerrod looked up towards the head of the column, where the Emperor walked alongside his griffon, Deathclaw. The animal was limping, but even so, it looked as dangerous as ever. It was a rare man who could ride such a beast without fear. Rarer still was the man who actually felt some form of affection for his monstrous mount. That Deathclaw seemed to reciprocate this affection was merely proof of Karl Franz's worthiness, and the rightness of Leoncoeur's decision to bring aid to the embattled Empire.

Jerrod had fought alongside the man for months. While at times Karl Franz seemed aloof and otherworldly, Jerrod had come to admire him, foreign sovereign or not. The Emperor inspired the same sort of loyalty in his men as the resurrected and re-crowned Gilles le Breton had in Jerrod's own countrymen. Especially his Reiksguard, the knights who acted as his personal bodyguard. Jerrod had got to know one of them quite well – Wendel Volker.

It was Volker who had brought the sad tidings of Middenheim's fall to the Emperor at Averheim. Volker was young, but his hair was white and his face worn like that of a man twice his age. His armour was battered and scorched, and he moved at times like one who was trapped in a dream. He was, like many men in these sad times, broken. He had seen too much, and endured more pain than any man ought.

Volker was walking beside the Emperor, one hand on the hilt of his sword. He had not left Karl Franz's side since arriving at Averheim's gates, leading a tiny, exhausted band of riders – the only survivors of Middenheim. How Volker had got them out, he'd never said, and Jerrod hadn't asked. They had arrived only days before Archaon's forces, and had ridden their horses to death to reach the dubious safety of the city walls. As if he'd heard Jerrod's thoughts, Volker slowed, turned and soon fell into step beside Jerrod's horse.

'Hail and well met,' Jerrod said, leaning down. He extended his hand. Volker took it.

'Never thought I'd see this place,' Volker murmured, without preamble.

Jerrod looked around. 'Nor did I.' He shivered. 'I wish there had been some other way.'

'You and me both, manling,' Hammerson grumbled. He looked up at Volker. 'It's no place for men nor dwarfs.'

'Few places are these days,' Volker said. He ran a hand through his frost-coloured hair. 'And fewer by the day.' He blinked and looked up at Jerrod. 'I'm sorry, Jerrod, I spoke without thinking.'

Jerrod smiled sadly and sat back in his saddle. 'We've all lost our homes, Wendel,' he said. He swept an arm out. 'We are all that remains of three mighty empires, my friends. The last gasp of a saner world. I would that it were not so, but if it must be, at least we die as the Lady wills, with courage and honour.'

'I'm sure Sigmar is of a similar mind,' Volker said, with a grim smile. He looked at Hammerson. 'And Grungni as well, eh?'

'I doubt a manling knows anything of the mind of a dwarf god,' Hammerson said sourly. He sniffed. Then, 'But aye... if death comes, let it come hot.'

'No danger of it being otherwise, given our rescuers,' Volker said. He pointed upwards, towards the sky, where the fiery shapes of phoenixes swooped and cut through the air. They were ridden by elves, Jerrod knew.

It had been by purest chance that he had found himself on the path to *Ystin Asuryan*, as their rescuers had called it. Fiery birds, white lions, and tall, proud elven warriors clad in shimmering armour had marched along its length, and gone to the aid of Hammerson and Gelt against the followers of Chaos. Now, the remains of that host escorted them deeper and deeper into the winding heart of Athel Loren.

All at once, Jerrod was reminded of where he was. Around them the trees seemed to press close, and strange shapes stalked through the gloom, watching them. This forest was no place for men. And there was no telling what awaited them within its depths.

Gotri Hammerson ignored the shadows and the trees and the whispers and concentrated on the path ahead, as Jerrod and Volker continued to speak. Let the forest talk all it wanted. He didn't have to listen. That was where the manlings always went wrong... they listened. They couldn't help it. They were curious by nature, like beardlings, only they never grew out of it. Always poking and prodding and writing things down. *And on pulped wood or animal skins at that,* he thought. *They trust their knowledge to things that rot... That tells you all you need to know.*

Still, they weren't all bad. He glanced at Volker, and at Jerrod, who sat slumped in his saddle. The Bretonnians were a hardy folk, and they knew the value of an oath. It was a shame that they had the stink of elves on them, but that was humans for you. Naive, the lot of them. You couldn't trust an elf, everybody knew that. Common knowledge in Zhufbar, that was. Couldn't trust elves, halflings or ogres. Not an honourable bone in any of that lot.

And you certainly couldn't trust a forest. That much wood in one place was unnatural. It did odd things to the air, and the light. And this particular forest was a wellspring of grudges, stretching from the time of Grugni Goldfinder to the present day. Many a dwarf's bones were lost beneath the green loam of the deep forest, their spirits trapped by the roots, never able to journey to the halls of their ancestors.

It was a bad place, full of bad things, like a pocket of old darkness in an abandoned mine. *At least we've got the ancestor gods on our side,* Hammerson thought. He felt a moment of shame, but pushed it aside. It wasn't the manling's fault, no matter what some among his dwindling throng might grumble. Still, there wasn't a dwarf alive who wouldn't be discomfited by the thought of one of their ancestor gods - and Grungni no less! - blessing a human so.

And there was no other explanation for it. Balthasar Gelt *was* blessed. How else to explain how runes flared to vigorous life in his presence? In the wizard's vicinity, gromril armour became harder than ever before and weapons gained a killing edge that no whetstone could replicate. Hammerson sniffed the air.

He didn't even have to look around to know that Gelt was near. The wizard glowed with an inner fire, like a freshly stoked forge. The air around him stank like smelted iron, and when he spoke, the runes that were Hammerson's to shape and bestow shimmered with the light of Grungni. Hammerson could feel the human's presence in his gut, and it bothered him to no end to admit that, even to himself.

Why had the gods gifted a manling with their power? And a wizard at that - a blasted elf-taught sorcerer, without an ounce of muscle on his lean frame and no proper axe to speak of. *And he rides a horse. With feathers,* Hammerson thought sourly. Couldn't trust a horse, especially one that could fly. A horse was just an elf with hooves.

And speaking of elves, and their lack of trustworthiness... Hammerson stumped ahead, one hand on the head of the hammer stuffed through his belt, to join Caradryan at the head of the column. The elf looked as tired as Jerrod, for all that he sat erect on his horse. His overgrown chicken was somewhere above them, turning the night sky as bright as day. Only an elf would ride a bird that burst into flame if you gave it a hard look. Caradryan, like Gelt, smelt of magic. He stank of wildfire and burning stones. It was a familiar odour to Hammerson.

'So you've got it then, have you?' he said, without preamble. He'd heard the Phoenix Guard weren't allowed to talk, so he was anticipating a short conversation. Or maybe just a nod, or grunt of acknowledgement. 'Ungrim's fire?'

Caradryan blinked and looked down. 'What?' he said, and his voice crackled like a rising flame. His eyes shone strangely, but Hammerson wasn't afraid to meet them. He'd got used to eyes like that, on the march from Zhufbar to Averheim. Ungrim had been like a flame caged in metal, sparking and snarling, aching to unleash its power.

'I thought you lot couldn't talk,' he said.

'We can speak. We simply did not. Asuryan commanded it,' Caradryan said. The elf's face twisted, and what might have been sadness filled his eyes.

'Nice of him to let you talk now,' Hammerson grunted.

'Asuryan is dead. And silence is no longer an indulgence we can afford,' Caradryan said.

'Just like an elf. Wouldn't catch a dwarf breaking a vow just because he misplaced his god,' Hammerson said, bluntly.

Caradryan's expression became mask-like. 'What do you want, dwarf?'

Hammerson looked up at him. 'Got a bit of godfire in you, elf. Don't deny it. Ungrim Ironfist had it, before he fulfilled his oath. I can feel it from here. Worse than that bird of yours. I'm surprised that horse hasn't died of heatstroke.' Hammerson looked away. 'Godfire or no, if you're leading us into a trap, I'll crack your skull.' He patted his hammer affectionately.

'Why would I rescue you, only to lead you into a trap?' Caradryan murmured. Hammerson frowned. He didn't like being reminded of that. He was no prideful beardling, and he knew that the presence of the elves had been instrumental in turning back the tide of blood-worshippers who had caught up with the dwarfs and their mannish allies in the pine crags. But it was impolite to mention it, and even an elf ought to know better.

'Who knows why elves do anything? You're all crooked in the skull,' Hammerson said, twirling his finger about alongside his head. 'And you didn't rescue us. Maybe you helped the manlings, but the Zhufbarak need no aid from your sort.'

'No?'

'No.'

'We didn't have to offer you our help, you know,' Caradryan said, frowning.

'Elves never offer help freely. There's always a price.'

'And your people would know all about that, eh, dwarf?' Caradryan said.

Hammerson looked up at him, and made to retort. But before he could, someone said, 'There is a price, and it is obvious, Master Hammerson. For we have all asked it, and paid it, in these past few months.'

Hammerson glanced over his shoulder, and saw the human Emperor striding along beside his griffon. Karl Franz had one hand on the beast's neck, and its striped tail lashed in pleasure as he scratched beneath its feathers. 'We fight for each other. That is the price and the paying of it, in these times. To fight alongside one another, and for one another, in defence of all that we knew and loved.'

Hammerson grimaced and turned back to the trail ahead. 'Aye,' he grunted. 'Doesn't mean we have to like it, though.'

The Emperor laughed. 'No, nor would I ask it of you. Irritable dwarfs fight better than content ones, I have learned.'

Hammerson opened his mouth, ready to deny it. Then he snorted, shook his head and looked up at Caradryan. 'And what about elves, then?' he asked.

'We fight better than dwarfs, whatever their disposition,' Caradryan said. The elf turned in his saddle and looked at the

Emperor. 'We are drawing near. When we arrive, you will accompany me into the Eternal Glade alone.'

'Not if I have anything to say about it,' Hammerson growled.

'You do not.' Caradryan didn't look at him. He spoke disdainfully, as if Hammerson were no more important than a pebble lodged in his horse's hoof. Then, that was elves for you. They thought the world danced to their tune. Even now, with everything that had happened, elves were still elves. But dwarfs were still dwarfs.

Hammerson stumped around in front of Caradryan's horse and extended a hand. As the horse drew close, the dwarf reached out and gave the animal a hard flick on the snout with one thick finger. The horse reared and snorted. Caradryan cursed and fought to control his steed. The whole column crashed to a halt behind him. White lions roared in consternation as horses whinnied and men shouted questions. Elves pelted forwards, bleeding out of the forest like ghosts. Hammerson ignored them, and the arrows that were soon pointed at him.

The runesmith crossed his brawny arms and smiled. 'Seems like I do, lad. Now, before we go a step further, I think we ought to decide who's going where, and who's invited to what.'

'Move aside, dwarf,' Caradryan said. The air grew hazy around his head and shoulders, and Hammerson could see the faint outline of flames. Hammerson shook his head.

'No.' Behind Caradryan, he could see the Emperor watching the confrontation, and Gelt as well. The latter looked as if he intended to intervene, but the Emperor stopped him with a gesture. Hammerson felt his smile widen. *Aye, leave it to the dwarfs, manling,* he thought.

'Move aside, or be moved,' Caradryan growled. He slid from the saddle and approached Hammerson. Flames crawled across his armour and his flesh was growing translucent, his every pore shining with reddish light. Hammerson held his ground, though every instinct he had was screaming for him to run. The elf wasn't really an elf any more, even as Gelt wasn't human.

There was a power there he didn't understand, and didn't want to. But that power was as nothing compared to the weight of the responsibility on Hammerson's shoulders.

'No. Whatever happens, from here on out, my people will be heard and will hear all that is said. We've earned that right, in blood and iron.'

'You've earned nothing, dwarf,' Caradryan said, in a voice like the hiss of flame across stone. 'That you still live, after being allowed so far into the last, most sacred place of my people, should be enough, even for your greedy kind.'

'If you think that, then you really don't know much about us. Whatever is said, it likely concerns us, and I would hear it.' The Zhufbarak, his warriors, his kin, were all that remained of Zhufbar. As far as he knew, they might be all that remained of the dwarf race. He had a responsibility to them, to see that their sacrifice wasn't in vain. To see that their enemies, at least, remembered them. To see that, whatever else happened, they had a say in how they met their end.

'I should have left you to die,' Caradryan growled. Hammerson wondered how much of the anger in his voice was him, and how much was the power that now resided in him. Ungrim had been much the same, in those final days. Angry at everything, and nothing.

'Would have been convenient for you, aye,' Hammerson said. He cut his eyes to Gelt, and then added, 'Without us to caution them, the manlings would fall right into whatever trap you've laid out for them. That's why you don't want us to hear it, eh?'

Caradryan frowned. 'You know nothing,' he snapped. Flames blazed to life around his clenched fists and crawled up his forearms. In their light Hammerson saw strange figures, part wood and part woman, slink through the trees, their bark claws flexing eagerly. More elves had arrived as well, these clad in the colours of the woods, and he felt a chill as he recognised the wild elves and dryads of the forest.

'Well that's why I want to hear all about it,' Hammerson said. He thought of home, of the Black Water, and of the huge waterfall that cascaded down the side of the chasm in which the hold was nestled. If he were to be burned here, he wanted that to be his last thought.

'Wait,' someone said, from behind him. Hammerson turned.

Several figures stood behind him, suffused by a soft light which threw back the darkness that clung to the trees. Three elves – a woman and two men, both of the latter armoured, one in black iron, the other in gold and silver. The woman stepped forwards, her forest green robes rustling softly. She wore a crown of gold, and her face was so beautiful as to be painful, even to Hammerson. Caradryan sank to one knee, head bowed. His flames flickered and died.

The Emperor moved then to stand beside Hammerson. He sank down slowly, arms spread, head lowered. 'Greetings, Alarielle the Radiant, Everqueen, Handmaiden of Isha. We come before you to humbly beg sanctuary and to offer our aid in these troubled times,' Karl Franz said. His voice carried easily through the trees. He looked up. 'Will you welcome us to Athel Loren?'

Hammerson lifted his chin in defiance as the woman's gaze passed over him. He knew of the Everqueen, and knew that she could incinerate him on the spot with the barest word. The runes branded into his flesh ached, and he could feel the power of her through them. But he was a dwarf of the Black Water, and he would not kneel before an elf.

Her eyes met his, and, after a moment, what might have been the ghost of a smile passed across her lovely features. She inclined her head. 'Be welcome, travellers,' she said. She raised her hand, and the elves lowered their weapons. The dryads retreated, slinking back into the forest. 'The world has changed, and old distrusts and grudges must be abandoned. You have done well, Caradryan.' Alarielle gestured for the Emperor to rise. 'Come. There is much to be discussed, before the end of all things.'

* * *

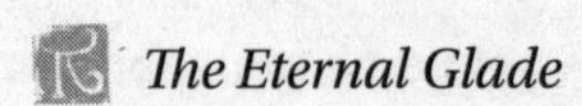

The Eternal Glade

Teclis, once-Loremaster of the now-shattered Tower of Hoeth, blood of Aenarion and Astarielle, sat beneath an ancient tree in the Eternal Glade, eyes closed, his head pressed against the staff he held upright before him.

To his mystically attuned senses, the heartbeat of the primordial forest of Athel Loren was almost deafening. The forest, and the Eternal Glade in particular, was a place of immense, incomprehensible power. It would have taken him an eternity to learn its secrets, if he had been so inclined. And then only if the forest itself had let him.

The murmur of voices rose and fell around him, beyond the barrier of his eyelids. Not just the voices of elves, more was the pity. There were men as well, and dwarfs. Athel Loren had become the final redoubt for the mortal races as well as the immortal.

When Caradryan, captain of the Phoenix Guard, had led a column of weary survivors into the Eternal Grove that morning, he had paid no notice to the furore it elicited in the inhabitants of the woodland realm. Instead, his mind had turned inwards, hunting, seeking, probing, trying to root out some clue as to the source of his failure.

Where did I go wrong?

He was not used to asking such questions. In him was personified both the capability and the arrogance of his people, and it was not without cause that some – including himself – thought he was the greatest adept produced by the folk of Ulthuan since the breaking of the world in those far, dim days when daemons had poured through the wounds in the world's poles. He was the first to admit it, and wore it as a badge of pride. Like his brother, Teclis was the best and the worst of his folk made flesh.

I made a mistake. Somewhere, somehow... What did I miss? What factor did I overlook? The thoughts spiralled around and around, like leaves caught in a stiff breeze. *Where did I go wrong?* He examined the moment again and again, from every angle and facet.

He could still feel the frustration of that moment – the winds of magic raging within the Vortex, even as Ulthuan crumbled beneath him, his ancient home sinking into the raging sea. He could feel the winds escaping, one by one, slipping through his grasp as quick as eels, and the mounting sense of loss. He had wagered everything on a single throw of the dice, and while he had not lost, he hadn't won either.

His hands tightened on his staff. He knew every groove and contour of it by touch, and he had worked magics into it since he had first taken a knife to the length of wood in which it had hidden. The staff was as much a part of him as one of his limbs. It was warm to the touch, and the pale wood shone with a soft light. The residual power of the lore of Light, the one wind until recently within his grasp, coiled within the core of his staff, where it had slumbered until he'd found the one on whom he would bestow it. The one whom he had resurrected and transformed into the Incarnate of Light, a living embodiment of Hysh, the White Wind of magic.

Oh my brother, what have I made of you? What have I done to you? What have I done for you? The latter question was easier to answer than the former. His sins in that regard were ever at the foreground of his thoughts. Tyrion, his brother, had died, consumed by the curse of their mutual bloodline, his body and soul twisted by the madness of Khaine. And it had happened by Teclis's design.

It had always been Tyrion's destiny to become the Incarnate of Light. But if he had done so while still bearing the curse of Aenarion, that power – the power necessary to redeem the world – would have become corrupted, and bent to the will of Khaine... or worse things. Thus Teclis had been forced to manipulate his own brother, to set the one he loved best on a path that would inevitably lead to his death. That such an outcome had been the only way of ensuring that the curse exhausted itself did not ease Teclis's guilt. Nor did the knowledge that Tyrion's resurrection as the Incarnate of Light was the lynchpin of his plan to throw back the *Rhana Dandra* – to win the unwinnable war. All that mattered was that he had killed his brother and doomed the world.

But Teclis had brought Tyrion back from death's bower; he had transported the frail, mummified remains of his twin across the world, from the shattered remnants of Ulthuan, leaving his people in the hands of Malekith.

He had come to Athel Loren, and watered the seeds of Tyrion-as-he-had-been within the Heart of Avelorn. When Tyrion had awoken from the slumber of death, Teclis had filled the emptiness left behind by Khaine's passing with the Flame of Ulric, filling Tyrion's still-weak limbs with new strength. He had damned a city and all of the innocents within its walls in order to give his brother a chance of survival, and he knew, in his heart, that he would make the same choice again. Tyrion had endured too much, and all of it at his brother's hands, for Teclis not to. And then, when he was sure that Tyrion could stand it, he had given him the power of Hysh, and stirred the ashes of destiny to life once more.

He had given his brother back his life, and in return Tyrion had fought alongside his fellow Incarnates, Malekith and Alarielle, to save the Oak of Ages from the depredations of Chaos's first-born son, Be'lakor, and those dark spirits he had twisted to his foul cause. Now, in the aftermath of that desperate battle, the few survivors of another, equally terrible conflict had come seeking sanctuary under the boughs of Athel Loren. And with them had come two more Incarnates.

Through the staff, he could sense the presence of the five Incarnates, their power grounded in frail flesh and bone, and the briefest trace of a sixth. The world hummed with the weight of them. Their every word sent shockwaves through his senses, and he could taste the raw power that seeped from their pores.

Slowly, his eyes still closed, he turned his staff, the gem set in its tip moving like a serpent's tongue, tasting the scent of each wind in turn. The gemstone was almost as old as the world itself, and it had taken him decades to work it and carve its facets to the proper shape. In his mind's eye, he saw the radiance of each – the blinding aura of Hysh, the constantly-shifting morass of Ulgu, the throbbing heat of Ghyran, the roaring hunger of Aqshy, the dense power of Chamon and, last and least, the faint thrum of Azyr, the Blue Wind of magic. Light, Shadow, Life, Fire, Metal and the faintest traces of the Wind of the Heavens. Only two were missing... Shyish, the Wind of Death, and Ghur, thc Wind of Beasts.

Of the two, he suspected he knew where the former had ended up – indeed, where else could it have gone? – but he had lost all hope of learning the location of the Wind of Beasts, or of the identity of its chosen host. The others, however, were here, right where they were supposed to be, and his regret was tempered by some small relief.

Nonetheless, he had failed. He had failed to control the Incarnates, failed to bestow the winds of magic on his chosen soldiers, and failed to bring them together in time. He had failed Ulthuan, he had failed his people, and now the world teetered on the knife-edge of oblivion. *What remains of it, at any rate,* he thought. The island-realm of the high elves was gone, lost to the swirling waters of the Great Ocean; the blood-slicked stones of Naggaroth were now little more than a haunt for cannibals and monsters; and Athel Loren was an inhospitable refuge for what remained of the elven peoples.

The elves were not alone in their doom, however. The ancient temple-cities of Lustria were no more, consumed in fires from the sky, the fate of their inhabitants unknown. The dwarfs had fared no better; their greatest holds had been all but overrun by skaven and worse, and those that remained had barred their gates in a futile effort to wait out the end of all things.

The realms of men had suffered as well. Bretonnia was a haunted wasteland, overrun by daemons and monsters despite the best efforts of its defenders. The lands of the south were gone, erased by the rampaging hordes of the ratmen. Kislev had been stripped to the bone by the hordes of Chaos, its people slaughtered or driven into the frozen wilderness to die. And the Empire, the last hope of the human race, was all but gone, its greatest cities taken by the enemy or reduced to plague-haunted ruins.

The enormity of it all threatened to overcome him, and would have, had events not conspired to bring the Incarnates together at last. He had doomed the world by his actions, his carelessness, but there was still a chance to salvage something. There was still a chance to weather the storm of Chaos, and throw back the Everchosen. And while there was a chance, Teclis would not surrender to despair. He could not.

'Teclis.'

Teclis opened his eyes. A ring of expectant faces met his sight. He took note of some of them – the newcomers had only been allowed a few representatives. The Emperor, Karl Franz. Duke Jerrod of Quenelles. Gotri Hammerson, runesmith of Zhufbar. Balthasar Gelt, wizard and Incarnate. And a white-haired knight, who was the Emperor's bodyguard. Something about the latter drew his attention. The man looked cold, as if he had been doused in ice-water, and when he caught Teclis looking at him, his face twisted, just for a moment, into a snarl. Teclis blinked, and the expression was gone. He hesitated, suddenly uncertain. 'What would you wish of me, Everqueen?' he asked, looking at Alarielle.

The Everqueen had been a living symbol of Isha, the mother-goddess of the elves, in better times. But her beauty had been transfigured into something terrifying since she had become the host for the Wind of Life. No more the nurturer, Alarielle had become instead the incarnation of creation and destruction, of life's beginnings and endings. The trees of the Eternal Glade shuddered and twitched in time to her heartbeat, her breath was in the wind, and in her voice was the rush and crash of the brooks and rivers.

'What I wish, Loremaster, and what I require are two separate things,' Alarielle said. Teclis knew she meant no insult, but even so, the coldness of her tone was almost too much for him to bear. Ever since she had given up the Heart of Avelorn to help resurrect Tyrion she had become withdrawn, as if the love she had once borne for his brother had become as dust.

'Not Loremaster,' he said. 'Not any more. Ulthuan is gone, and the Tower of Hoeth with it.' He spat the words with more bitterness than he'd intended. *You have no right to bitterness,* he thought, *not when your actions are the cause.*

'But you still live, brother,' Tyrion said, softly. '*We* still live. Our people survive, thanks to you. Ulthuan is gone, but while one asur lives, its spirit persists.'

'Oh yes, very pretty. And while one asur lives, or druchii or asrai for that matter, I am still their king, as much good as it does any of us,' Malekith interjected, his voice a harsh, metallic rasp. Like Alarielle, he had been bound to one of the winds of magic. In his case, it had been Ulgu, and the coiling, cunning lore of Shadows suited Malekith to his core. He was less a being of flesh than of darkness now, stinking of burned iron and radiating cold. 'And as king, I would have answers. Why do you come to us, human?' Malekith asked. 'Why do you dare to come to Athel Loren?'

'Where else is there to go?' Karl Franz said. 'The world has grown hostile, and sanctuary is hard to come by. Old allies find themselves equally hard-pressed.' He indicated Hammerson and Jerrod. 'Our greatest cities are in ruins, and our people are in disarray. Our last redoubt, Averheim, is dust beneath the boots of the world's enemy. I am an emperor without an empire, as are you,' Karl Franz said, looking at Malekith.

'Look around you, human... my empire still stands,' Malekith said. He stood and spread his arms. 'The enemy have broken themselves on it again and again. But we still stand.'

Karl Franz smiled. 'If this is what you call an empire, I begin to wonder why Finubar feared you.'

Shadows coiled and writhed around Malekith's form as he went rigid with anger. 'You dare...?' he hissed. 'I will pluck the flesh from your bones, king of nothing.'

'Yes, for that has ever been the way of your folk. The world burns, and you can think of nothing better to do than to squabble in the ashes.' Karl Franz gestured sharply. 'You would rather kill the messenger than hear the message. You would turn away allies, because in your arrogance you mistake strength for weakness and support for burden.'

'What would you know of us, human?' Alarielle said. Teclis glanced at her. Her features were perfectly composed, but he thought he detected the trace of a smile on her face.

'I know enough,' Karl Franz said. He turned, his eyes scanning the Eternal Glade. 'I know that what your folk call the "Rhana Dandra" has begun – indeed, it began several years ago. I know that Ulthuan is gone, and that the Great Vortex is no more.' His eyes sought out Teclis. Teclis twitched. The Emperor's gaze revealed nothing, but the elf felt a glimmer of suspicion.

Why had Azyr sought out Karl Franz? The winds were drawn to their hosts as like was drawn to like, but the Emperor had, to the best of his knowledge, never displayed the least affinity for the lore of the Heavens. Teclis forced the thought aside. It mattered little now, in any event. The power was gone, torn from him. Teclis shook himself and said, 'And do you know why?'

Karl Franz looked at him. 'No,' he said, and Teclis knew it was a lie.

'Oh, well, let Teclis illuminate you, eh?' Malekith said. He had sunk back onto his throne, his anger already but a memory. Teclis looked at him, and Malekith gestured sharply. 'As your king, I command you to tell the savages of your crimes, schemer.' Malekith laughed. 'Tell our guests how you gambled the world, and lost.'

Teclis looked at the thin, dark shape of the creature once known as the Witch-King, sitting on his throne of roots and branches beside the Everqueen. The creature he had helped crown Eternity King, and had gifted with more power than he deserved. Malekith met his glare, and Teclis knew that the former ruler of the dark elves was smiling behind his metal mask.

Teclis used his staff to help himself to his feet, and he pulled the tattered remnants of his authority about him. He looked at the newcomers. Despite being bedraggled and bloodstained, they did not look beaten, and for that, Teclis thanked the fallen gods of his people. They would need every ounce of strength that they could muster for what was coming. He cleared his throat, and made ready to speak.

Before he could, however, a snarl ripped through the glade. A snarl that was achingly familiar, and utterly terrifying. He turned, and his searching gaze was met by a yellow, furious one. Beast eyes those, and blazing with intent. The temperature in the glade began to drop.

'Thief!' the white-haired knight roared, in a voice not his own. The Reiksguard shoved past the Emperor, and hurled himself towards Teclis, fingers hooked like claws.

'Volker – no!' the Emperor bellowed, reaching for his guard. The man slithered out of his grip.

With a curse, the dwarf, Hammerson made a grab for Volker. 'Hold him back, lad, or it's an arrow to the giblets for the lot of us,' the dwarf roared at the Bretonnian as he wrapped his brawny arms around Volker's legs. The Reiksguard fell sprawling and Jerrod sprang on top of him, armour rattling. Volker thrashed beneath them, howling like a wolf. Teclis stumbled back, one hand pressed to his throat, his face pale with shock.

Volker was cold; colder than Teclis thought it was possible for a man to become and survive. The air around the struggling figures became silvered with frost, and the grass beneath them turned stiff and shattered. Jerrod's teeth were chattering, and Hammerson was cursing. Volker glared at Teclis, his eyes yellow and bestial. 'Thief,' he snarled again, and Teclis shuddered, pulling his cloak about himself. He had expected this, though he'd hoped it would be otherwise. Ulric was not the sort of god to pass quietly into oblivion, even if it would be better for all concerned.

'Yes,' he said hoarsely. 'Yes, I am a thief. And your moment has passed, old wolf. You are dead, and I will not let you sacrifice a life merely to take mine.' He lifted his staff, and the words to an incantation rose in his mind. But before he could speak, Karl Franz stepped between them. Though the Wind of the Heavens had been stripped from him, there was still something yet in him that made Teclis wary. A lurking strength, as unlike his own as Tyrion's was. He lowered his hands. 'I did what I had to do,' he said, without quite knowing why, as he met the Emperor's gaze. 'I did what was necessary.'

'And would you do it again?' Karl Franz said, his voice a quiet rumble.

Teclis hesitated. He glanced towards Tyrion. 'In a heartbeat,' he said.

The Emperor nodded slowly, as if he had expected no other answer. He turned and looked down at his bodyguard. The man thrashed and howled, fighting to be free of his captors. Veins bulged on his neck, and froth coated his lips. Karl Franz looked back at Teclis. 'Can you help him?' he asked.

Instead of replying, Teclis knelt. Volker's body twitched and his face seemed to elongate, becoming monstrous and unformed. Teclis stretched out his hand and plunged his fingers into the wet chill that obscured the man's face. He tried to grasp the shard of Ulric's essence that had made its home in the man, even as he had grasped the Flame in Middenheim. But this was different. It was no mindless flux of power, but rather a desperate consciousness, savage and determined. It struggled against him, and he heard Volker wail in agony.

Images flooded his mind. He saw Middenheim burn, felt the heat of the flames, and the blistering cold as the sliver of Ulric's might was pressed into Volker's soul. Fear, weakness, fatigue, all were buried beneath the cold, so that Volker might survive the sack of the city and escape to bring warning to Averheim. Even in death, the wolf-god had been determined to watch over his chosen people. Sigmar might have been their greatest god, but Ulric had been their first.

But now, with warnings delivered, there was one last task. Ulric had known that somehow, someway, Teclis would cross paths with the men of the Empire once more, before the end of all things. And he was determined to have his revenge. Teclis felt a sudden, stabbing pain, as if teeth were tearing into his flesh, and he jerked his hand back with a hiss. Steam rose from his blue-tinged flesh as he cradled the wounded limb to his chest. Alarielle and Malekith's guards started forward, but the Eternity King slammed a fist down on his throne. 'Be still,' he grated. 'No more of our people's blood shall be spent in payment of his schemes. Let him survive or fall on his own.'

Volker flung off his captors. 'You killed them, thief,' Volker snarled, lunging for him again. His voice echoed strangely amongst the trees, with a sound like ice-clad branches snapping. As he fell back, Teclis saw Tyrion start forwards, one hand on his blade. He waved a hand, stopping his brother before he could interfere. *This is my fight, brother, my burden,* Teclis thought. 'You killed my city – my people – you killed the world. For what?' Volker growled, in a dead god's voice.

'For him,' Teclis said, indicating his brother. 'For them. I sacrificed your people for my own, and I would do it again, a thousand times over, if I had to.' He extended his staff to hold Volker at bay. 'Malekith was right. I gambled the world. But I did not lose, for here you all stand... Incarnates, gods in all but name, ready to throw back the end of all things.' He made a fist. 'I tore apart the Great Vortex, and sought to ground the winds of magic in living champions, who would become mighty enough, as a group, to defy the Chaos Gods themselves.'

He saw Balthasar Gelt nod, as if a question had suddenly been answered. The wizard said, 'But not all of the winds are accounted for – what of the Winds of Beasts, and of Death?'

Volker threw back his head and howled, before Teclis could even attempt to reply. The air quivered with the sound. He ripped his sword from its sheath and swung a wild blow at Teclis. The sound of steel on steel followed the echoes of the howl, as the Emperor interposed himself, and his runefang, between the maddened knight and his prey. 'No,' Karl Franz said. 'No, the time for vengeance is done.'

'Who are you to gainsay me?' Volker roared. His eyes bulged from their sockets, and froth dotted his patchy beard. He strained against Karl Franz, trying to untangle their blades.

'I am your Emperor, Wendel Volker. And that should be all that needs to be said.' The Emperor spoke quietly as he leaned into the locked swords. 'Now sheathe your blade.' The two men locked eyes, and for a moment, Teclis wondered which would win out. Then Volker staggered back and slumped, his sword falling to the grass. He sank down, and the frost that coated his armour began to melt. The Emperor dropped to one knee and placed a hand on Volker's shoulder. Teclis could still feel the wrath of the wolf-god, or whatever was left of him, retreating, slinking back into hiding. It was not gone, but its fury was abated, for now.

Before anyone could speak to break the silence that followed, the trees gave out a sudden rattle, and a wind rose up, causing the leaves to make a sound like murmuring voices. Teclis stiffened. While he was no native of the forest, he knew well what that sound meant. It was a warning.

A moment later, a member of the Eternal Guard moved out of

the trees to Alarielle's side and whispered something into her ear. Her eyes widened and she stood quickly. She looked around. 'It seems that you are not the only refugees seeking sanctuary within the forest,' she said. Her voice was strained, and her skin pale. 'An army approaches the edge of the Wyrdrioth.'

Teclis's grip on his staff tightened. He could feel the presence of another Incarnate – and one far more powerful than any of those now standing in the Eternal Glade. Together, they might equal him, but separately, they stood no chance. Even here, in the living heart of Athel Loren, he could feel the malignant, suffocating pulse of Shyish – the Wind of Death – and the one who had become its host.

'An army?' Malekith snarled. 'Who would dare?'

'The Wind of Death,' Teclis said, before Alarielle could speak. He bowed his head. 'It is the Incarnate of Death.' He looked up, meeting the gaze of each Incarnate in turn.

'The Undying King has come to Athel Loren.'

SEVEN

 *The Wyrdrioth, Northern Edge of Athel Loren*

'Well, they appear to have prepared quite the welcome for us, I must admit,' Mannfred von Carstein said as he lounged insouciantly in Ashigaroth's saddle. The abyssal steed growled in reply. Mannfred patted the creature's armour-plated neck, and glanced around at his bodyguard of Drakenhof Templars. The armoured vampires sat astride their cannibal steeds, awaiting his orders. *Or so they wish me to believe,* he thought. His good humour evaporated. He turned back towards the forest and ran his palm over his hairless scalp.

If he'd been human, what he saw before him might have taken his breath away. Banners of all colours and designs were raised together as, for the first time in generations, elves, dwarfs and men prepared to fight as one. The battle-lines had been arranged before the tree line, barring the army of the dead from the Wyrdrioth.

If he'd had any intention of taking his forces into the forest, such a display might have annoyed him. He turned in his saddle, taking in the bleak host which was spread out behind him. The banners of the dead were thick among the pine-crags. An army of worm-picked bone and tattered wings, lit by baleful witch-fires, the dead had spilled down from the mountains in their thousands, their every step precise, guided by a single, crushing will. The will of Nagash.

Mannfred snapped his teeth in frustration. In the years since he had aided Arkhan the Black in resurrecting the Undying King, he had seen everything for which he had worked since his resurrection from the stinking mire of Hel Fenn turn to ashes. Every scheme, every triumph, gone like dust on the wind. All of it ground beneath the remorseless heel of Nagash, as the Undying King prepared for the final war.

Even Sylvania was no longer his – Nagash had given the blighted province over to Neferata to defend, while he marched to war with his remaining lieutenants. *Speaking of which... where is the bag of bones?* He twisted about, hunting for any sign of his rival. Arkhan was never very far from Nagash these days. Too, he seemed somehow... diminished by the association. As if Nagash's will had completely obliterated his own. In and of itself, the neutering of his old rival didn't bother Mannfred all that much. But the implications of it were unpleasant, to say the least.

I'd rather not become a mindless automaton, thank you very much, he thought. Such a fate was beneath him. Then, so was the current state of affairs. Still, reduced circumstances often meant increased opportunities. And there were plenty of the latter, in the wake of the destruction of the Black Pyramid.

He smiled thinly, relishing the memory. At the time, it had not been so enjoyable. But in the aftermath, with several weeks between then and now, he had come to see it for the opportunity it was. A sizeable Chaos army, composed of the rotting dead, giggling plague-daemons and howling barbarians, had smashed through Nagash's defences with a single-minded determination that put the Undying King's own forces to shame. Even worse, the enemy had been commanded by old friends and absent companions – the spectral abomination known as the Nameless, and Isabella von Carstein, newly resurrected and as unhinged as ever. One of them would have been bad enough, but the presence of both had made a bad situation all the worse.

The Nameless had ever been treacherous; the dark spirit was a thing fuelled by spite and treachery, more so than any vampire, and its questions and petulant demands had been a constant annoyance. Why Nagash had brought it back, when there were any number of appropriate champions to choose from, Mannfred couldn't say. The Great Necromancer could stir the waters of death and bring any spirit bobbing to the surface – why not bring back Konrad or one of the other von Carsteins? *Anyone other than Vlad,* he thought. But no, Nagash had seen fit to bend the Nameless to his will, and then forgotten about it until the creature had returned in the service of a new master.

And Isabella had come with it. *Hadn't that been a surprise,* he thought. Of all the von Carsteins he had certainly never expected to see her. Indeed, he'd half expected that Nagash had hidden her soul away in some phylactery somewhere, so as to better control Vlad. It was what Mannfred would have done, had he ever conceived of such a ploy. Unlike Nagash, however, he had no illusions as to just how uncontrollable Vlad truly was. *Or had been,* Mannfred thought, not without some amusement.

Sylvania had resisted the End Times until that point, inviolate and unchanged. Now, it was a reeking ruin, and what little life it had once had was gone, snuffed by the contest between Nagash and Nurgle. And more than one of Nagash's lieutenants had been claimed in that conflagration – Luthor Harkon, gone at last to join his treacherous kinsman Walach, and the mighty Vlad von Carstein himself, brought low by the woman he loved.

Mannfred couldn't restrain a laugh. *Goodbye, goodbye, parting is such sweet sorrow,* he thought gleefully. *So soon returned to the dust where you belong, old man.* How the Chaos Gods had got their talons in Isabella's twisted soul he didn't know, but she had been the most effective weapon they'd employed to date. She had distracted them all, even Nagash, while the skaven had burrowed beneath Nagash's nightmare pyramid and claimed a debt that the Undying King had owed them since the razing of Nagashizzar.

It had been a plan worthy of... well, him. He scratched his chin and chuckled, studying the ranks of the living. Of course, if he had been in charge, he would have made sure Nagash had been returned to his well-deserved oblivion, one way or another. Instead, all the Dark Gods had managed to do was stir the tiger from his lair. And now the predator had come to make common cause with his prey, against the fire that threatened to claim the forest around them. Not that the prey knew that just yet. The smell of fear on the wind was delightful.

'Ah Vlad, if only you could be here – at last, he follows your sage counsel. Too little, too late,' Mannfred murmured.

'You sound cheerful for one who has just had his territories stripped from him,' a familiar voice said. Mannfred twisted about in his saddle and looked down at Arkhan the Black as the latter pushed through the front rank of corpses. *'I thought you might make your move at last, when he made Neferata castellan of Sylvania.'*

Mannfred's smile faded. 'My loyalty is as solid as the bedrock beneath our feet, liche.'

Arkhan's skull tipped back, and a weird scuttling sound rose from his fleshless jaws. Mannfred's lips peeled back from his fangs. The liche was laughing at him. 'Oh, be silent, you withered husk,' he snapped.

'You are like a spoiled child, angry at having a favoured toy snatched from his grasp,' Arkhan rasped, staring towards the army of the living. *'And it is only fitting that Neferata rule... She was born for it, and it would take all four gods of Chaos to shift her. Besides which, there are now more Nehekharan nobles in your precious province than the backward Sylvanian aristocracy you*

and Vlad dote on. Nagash took the Great Land from them, and now they will have Sylvania in recompense.'

'Yes, because gods forfend that they should be discomfited in any way. A fragile breed, your desert princes,' Mannfred spat. Arkhan was right, which only made it worse. The customs of the kings and queens of Nehekhara were alien to him, and without Nagash there to quell them, they would revolt against him the moment he tried to impose his will. For now, at least. He pushed the thought aside and hunkered forwards in his saddle.

'Think of it, Arkhan. Few men, living or dead, can say that they have seen the green-vaulted reaches of Athel Loren. What secrets must linger in that wild wood? What secrets might you or I rip from it? All we have to do is...'

'Parley,' Arkhan said.

Mannfred snorted. 'Of course. Forgive me. For a moment, I forgot we had an army of but thousands at our back. So of course we must parley, lest their few hundred wreak unmentionable havoc.' He looked slyly at Arkhan. 'Why the sudden change of heart, you think? Why now, after all this time, does our lord and master stoop to address the cattle?' He smiled and tapped his nose. 'Vampires are very good at smelling weakness, liche. We can taste death on the air.' He leaned down, and met Arkhan's flickering gaze unflinchingly. 'Just how badly did losing the Black Pyramid hurt him, eh?'

'Why not ask him yourself?' Arkhan said.

'I thought I was,' Mannfred said. He turned away. 'In any event, who's it to be, then? Who'll act as herald, to bring word of our peaceful intentions to yon foemen?' He sat back. 'You, perhaps? Or one of your Nehekharan addle-pates? Perhaps that loud-mouthed fool, Antar of Mahrak? He's a favourite of yours, is he not?'

'You will do it,' Arkhan said, not looking at him.

'Will I?'

Arkhan said nothing. Mannfred sniffed, stood up in his saddle, and craned his neck, searching for the Undying King. Nagash was hard to miss – he stood at the centre of the army, a skeletal giant surrounded by a flickering corona that changed colour by turns, becoming green, then black, then purple. He was the corrupt heart and dark will of an army that was little more than a single, charnel entity. The hooded and cloaked forms of a dozen necromancers surrounded him as ever, each one lending his will to ease Nagash's burdens.

Nine heavy tomes, each filled with Nagash's darkest wisdoms, floated around him, pages flapping with a sound like the snapping of jaws. The grimoires were connected to Nagash by heavy chains, and they strained at them like beasts at the leash. Moaning spirits swirled about him, blending together and breaking apart in a woeful dance of agony. There were men there, and elves and dwarfs, as well as other races. To die at Nagash's hands was to not die at all, but instead be condemned to eternal servitude.

The wide skull, lit by its own internal flame, turned, and the blazing orbs that danced in its cavernous sockets brightened briefly. Nagash did not speak. He did not need to. Mannfred knew that Arkhan would not have spoken without Nagash's permission. He turned and snapped Ashigaroth's reins. The abyssal steed leapt into the air with a shriek, and hurtled towards the lines of the living.

He did not bother to attempt to conceal himself. As preeminent as he was in the sorcerous arts, those below were his match. The most powerful surviving sorcerers, wizards and necromancers in all the world, those not aligned with the Archenemy, were here in this place. The rest were dead, or hiding. Creatures like Zacharias the Everliving had perished, defying Nagash to the last, while monsters like Egrimm van Horstmann had been consumed by the ever-shifting tides of war and madness. Those who remained had chosen their hills to die on, and were gathering their strength for the storm to come.

Zacharias, at least, had made his end an entertaining one. He smiled as he thought of it – the sky had been wracked with spasms, and the Vanhaldenschlosse chewed to steaming wreckage by the confrontation between vampire and liche. Zacharias had held off Nagash's army alone with only his magics for days, before Nagash had bestirred himself to end the conflict. There had been something personal in it, there at the end, Mannfred thought. As if the two knew one another, and there was some grudge between them. In the end Zacharias had perished at Nagash's hands, strangled in the ruins of the Vanhaldenschlosse and his remains cast upon the pyre.

He leaned forwards, and Ashigaroth wailed like a lost soul as it hurtled over the heads of elves, dwarfs and men. Mannfred laughed as he let his steed indulge itself. Like him, the creature fed as much on fear as flesh, and there was precious little of the former left in a world so close to ultimate ruin. But while it lasted, he saw no harm in enjoying it.

He knew he was trusting in the curiosity, and perhaps even the misguided honour, of the living. And that trust was not misplaced. No arrow, bullet or spell assailed him as his abyssal steed dropped to the top of a towering boulder just before the line of raised shields. He sat for a moment, relishing the attention. He had moved in the shadows for so long, waging little wars, that he had almost forgotten what it was like to be the focus of so much fear. Once, long ago, he had faced men and dwarfs arrayed similarly. His enjoyment lessened as he recalled how the battle of Hel Fenn had gone. For all his power, he had been struck down in what should have been his moment of ultimate triumph.

And now, he was merely one nightmare amongst many. Mannfred shook his head, and smiled. 'Ah well,' he murmured. 'Best to be about it.' He straightened and said, 'So – who will it be, then?' His voice carried easily. The living were almost as silent as the dead. Mannfred grinned. 'Come now, don't be shy. We are all men of the world, and is not my presence a guarantee of good conduct? Who will it be? The Emperor without an empire? Or one of the exiles of fair Ulthuan, who now infest these shores like field mice? Come, come, step forward, and sign thy name into history as the one who stretched out a hand in fellowship to the Undying King,' he said. 'You have called, and we have come. Do not turn us away now, at light's last gleaming.'

It was a pretty speech, equal parts mocking and inviting. And it had the desired effect: a tall figure, clad in darkly gleaming armour, stepped forwards. 'Say what you have come to say, abomination, and then begone,' said Malekith. His armour's death-mask rendered his words strangely metallic, and Mannfred felt a chill. Here was one like Nagash, bound to some greater power. He could smell the raw essence of magic rising from the Witch-King, and for a moment, he felt his confidence waver.

Mannfred leaned in. 'And if I choose to tarry?' he spat.

'Then we will destroy you, and forget you,' said a second masked individual. Robes rustling, Balthasar Gelt stepped up to join Malekith. 'Your master has a surplus of puppets, vampire. One more or less will hardly change things.'

Mannfred smiled lazily. Though he could sense the power that now held Gelt in its glittering clutches, he was on firmer ground with Vlad's former pet. 'Ah, Gelt. Twice-traitor, first to your Empire and then to Vlad.' He shook his head. 'Poor Vlad... He could have used your help, you know. There at the end, I mean.'

Gelt stiffened, and Mannfred laughed. 'And now, here you stand.' He leered at Alarielle, who stood behind Malekith. 'I wouldn't trust him, my lady. Yon poltroon is the very best of serpents. Why, his heart is rotted clean through with guile and malice.'

'Something you would know intimately,' Karl Franz said. He didn't look at Mannfred as he spoke, and the latter knew, without turning to look, that the Emperor was staring at Nagash. And that, even more worryingly, Nagash was staring back at him.

Incensed, Mannfred glared at the man. 'I know only that you are a relic of a newly dead world. What use have you now, eh? A statesman without a state, a tyrant stripped of his power. A dead man would be more use than you, Karl Franz, last of the rotten house and failed potentate that you are. I dub thee Fumbler of the Faith and Lord Lackwit,' Mannfred said, making the sign of the hammer in mocking fashion. The Emperor looked at him, and Mannfred lowered his hand. Smoke rose from his fingers, and he shook his hand to disperse it. Even now, the symbols of Sigmar held some power over him.

'You have no power in that regard, thankfully,' Karl Franz said. 'Only one vampire was named elector, and he does not stand before me.'

Mannfred blinked. For a second, he was tempted to cross the distance between them and tear out the man's throat. But he restrained himself. Now was not the time to be drawn into foolishness. He licked his lips and looked at Malekith, pointedly ignoring the human. 'You commanded that I speak my piece, so I shall, mighty elf-king.' He swept out his arm to indicate the maggoty host stretched across the horizon. 'Great Nagash, Lord of the Underworld, Undying King and Supreme Lord of All Dead Things, wishes to parley.'

Arkhan the Black watched Mannfred confront the last rulers of the living world, and thought how, under different circumstances, the army spread out around him would be here for different reasons. Instead of a triumphal siege, however, they had come seeking allies in a last-ditch gamble.

The thought elicited some amusement. In life, he had been a notorious gambler, and a champion of debt; that was how Nagash had first caught him up in his schemes of empire. And here he was at the last, wagering what little he still had in one last great throw of the dice. He reached up and touched a charred spot on his robe. The black mark was in the shape of a hand – the hand of the Everchild, Aliathra of Ulthuan. In her final moments, before Arkhan had slit her throat, the elven princess had struck him. Something had passed between them, though he could not say what it had been. Whatever it was – curse, blessing or something in between – it was still within him. And it was growing stronger.

Arkhan looked up, examining the wheel of stars and the tortured heavens. They held no answers. The music of the spheres had become discordant and painful. Auguries showed only falsehood, and the oracular spirits spat gibberish, even when Nagash himself questioned them. The underworld was in disarray, and the gods of men were dead or diminished.

The Great Work was undone. An eternity of careful preparation, of strife and conflict, all for nothing. The thought did not weigh as heavily as he'd feared it might. In truth, it was worth it, if only to see the Undying King at a loss. Though his mind and soul had long been bartered away to Nagash, some flicker of the man he had been yet remained. Some sliver of that cynical, acid-tongued wretch, with his black teeth and gaudy robes, still lingered in the husk of him, and was, perhaps, growing stronger as Nagash's attentions were diverted to more important matters. And that fragment, that ghost of a ghost, was amused to no end by the predicament that Nagash had found himself in.

'Irony is a beautiful thing, if you are not its victim,' someone said, close beside him. Arkhan looked around. He was surrounded by a flock of robed and hooded adherents – liches, vampires, necromancers – all students of the Great Work. Mortuary priests, disciples of poor, dead W'soran, and those few surviving living practitioners of the Corpse Geometries, all gathered together now at his discretion. But the one who had spoken was none of those things – he was as unique as Arkhan himself.

He wore a hooded cloak, concealing his identity, but there was no hiding the warrior's build, or the aristocratic posture.

'I was never one to indulge in the misfortunes of others,' Arkhan said.

The hooded figure gave a bark of laughter. 'You forget – I have played dice with you, Arkhan. I know exactly what sort of man you were – and still are.'

'And what sort of man are you?'

'One who honours his debts.'

Arkhan turned away. *'It is a shame that you could not reach Averheim in time. You might have turned the tide.'*

The hooded figure looked at him. 'It is a shame that our lord and master failed to heed me when I suggested that we muster in defence of the Empire. And now look where we are. The last place any of us, especially him, wanted to be.'

'Which him are you referring to? Nagash... or your hapless progeny?'

'Both, I think,' Vlad von Carstein said. 'But Nagash especially. Mannfred knows that failure breeds opportunity as well as, or better than, success in the right circumstances. Nagash, I think, does not.' The vampire looked towards the towering shape of Nagash, his expression speculative.

'Nagash cannot conceive of failure. To fail would imply that he made a mistake. To admit that would unravel all that he is, was and will be,' Arkhan said.

'And would that be so bad?'

Arkhan leaned against his staff, skull pressed to its length. *'For better or worse, Nagash is as close to a god as remains to this dying world. To remove his certainty would be to cripple him, and by extension, condemn us all.'*

'Arrogance set him on his path, and arrogance will see him through,' Vlad said. He shook his head and sighed. 'More and more, I wonder if Mannfred is not his truest servant after all, given the similarities between them.'

'Mannfred is a fool. Nagash is not.' Arkhan looked at Vlad. *'Why have you not informed him of your survival? He believes that you met your end in Sylvania, at your paramour's hands.'*

'To be honest, I'm a bit surprised that he still thinks I'm dead,' Vlad murmured. He frowned, and for a moment Arkhan considered asking him about Isabella. That the Chaos Gods had brought her back was of little surprise to him. Nothing was beyond them, and such a resurrection was merely a parlour trick for such powers. But he decided against it. What Vlad thought of it was unimportant. All that mattered was that he served.

'He has never been very observant, where his desires are concerned. He wishes for you to be dead, and so you are,' Arkhan said. *'That is his greatest weakness, and greatest strength. His lies propel him on, fuelling the arrogance that lends him strength.'*

'Like Nagash,' Vlad said, with the smile of one who believes he's scored a point.

Arkhan shifted uncomfortably. He did not reply. Let the vampire think what he liked. In all the years he'd spent duelling with Mannfred, he'd forgotten how much more deadly the first von Carstein was. Mannfred, for all his faults, was not a philosopher. He was pragmatic, and focused on the material world. A craftsman of death, rather than an artist. For all his pretensions of nobility and all of his insistence that the world's throne was his by right of blood, Mannfred was still a callow, petty creature.

Vlad, on the other hand, was anything but. He had wrung knowledge from the writings of Nagash without the benefit of a tutor, learning through trial and error. He had fought for everything he claimed, and claimed nothing he had not shed blood in pursuit of. Mannfred schemed towards a single, final goal, like an arrow travelling towards its target. Vlad, however, was more like a sword, capable of more than simply carving out an enemy's heart.

'Was I ever as arrogant as Nagash?' Vlad asked. 'Was I ever as blind as Mannfred?'

Arkhan looked at the vampire. *'You tell me,'* he said, after a time.

'Neferata certainly thought so,' Vlad said, and chuckled. He rubbed the heavy ring that decorated his finger. 'Never could abide arrogance, that one.'

'No... she cannot.' Arkhan turned away from him. Vlad smiled.

'She and Isabella have – had – much in common. I thought, once upon a time, that I could mould her into the image of the queen. When she resisted, when she turned my arrogance back on me, hissing and spitting, I knew that there was no need. The first time she raised her voice to me in anger, I felt my heart ignite.' Vlad cocked his head. 'Was it that way with you, gambler? Prisoner, slave, lover... so many masks between you two. And now, shorn of all pretence...'

Arkhan said nothing. Vlad waited. When no reply seemed forthcoming, he sighed and shrugged. 'And that is the shame of it all. Love, that rarest of alchemies, is lost so easily when the wind shifts and the fire is sighted on the horizon. Luckily, for some, adversity only adds strength to that bond.'

Arkhan turned to see what Vlad was looking at. Behind them were arrayed the Drakenhof Templars. Loyal once to Mannfred, they had, by and large, honoured their oaths to serve the master of the von Carstein line, and had bent knee to Vlad upon his resurrection. Of the inner circle, only a few remained. Count Nyktolos had met his fate on the sands of the Great Desert; and the burly monster Alberacht Nictus, the Reaper of Drakenhof, had died defending that infamous pile, and the scores of huddled Sylvanian peasantry sheltering within it, against daemons more monstrous even than himself.

Of those he had known, and who had aided him in restoring Nagash, only two remained – Erikan Crowfiend, and Elize von Carstein. The morose Bretonnian, in his dark patchwork armour, sat close beside the crimson-haired von Carstein woman, both of them mounted on cannibal horses from the Sternieste stables.

He saw that their hands were not-quite touching, fingers barely intertwined. Love was not forbidden among the dead, for Nagash had little understanding of it, save as a goad. But it was rare. Vlad watched them surreptitiously, his eyes unreadable.

If he had been capable of it, Arkhan might have smiled. Instead, he let his gaze play over the other templars. Von Carsteins, most of them, though there were a few who bore on their faces the stamp of other primogenitors. Hard-eyed Blood Dragons, cunning Lahmians, even one or two brutal Strigoi, wearing tattered armour and cradling crude weapons. And one other, her face composed and so still as to resemble marble.

Eldyra of Tiranoc was an elf, or had been. She was the only survivor of Eltharion the Grim's doomed rescue attempt on behalf of the Everchild, she whose life essence had been used to quicken Nagash's spirit from its dark bower in those final moments at the Nine Daemons. She had fallen in that last, fateful battle, but Mannfred had been seized by one of his distressing whims, and had shown her mercy. Of sorts, at any rate.

Now, she sat astride her horse, as undead as the rest of the Drakenhof Templars, and as bloodthirsty as any of Mannfred's get. The elf noticed his attentions, and met his gaze. Her eyes held no hint as to her thoughts. As he watched, Elize von Carstein leaned over and murmured something to Eldyra, and the elf looked away.

'Not the first mistake Mannfred has ever made, but it might be his last,' Vlad said. Arkhan looked at him. Vlad gestured to Eldyra. 'Still, I am impressed that it was done at all. A rare thing, to see one of our sort crafted from alien flesh.'

'Your sort. Not mine,' Arkhan said.

'But even you have to admire the artistry of it. Men are born to die. They are well on their way to being corpses with the first, squalling breath that they draw. But to take a thing of life, a thing which will not know death, and to twist it so... Ah, well.' Vlad shook his head. 'Mannfred was always creative. For a limited value of the term.'

'Yes. And foolish. He is taunting them,' Arkhan said. Vlad followed his gaze, and frowned.

'Well, that's hardly a surprise, is it?' He chuckled. 'It has ever been his nature to be imprudent. That arrogance you mentioned earlier, I think. He cannot conceive of a defeat or a treachery of which he is not the author.'

'Then he is in for a rude surprise,' Arkhan said. He looked at Vlad, and then past him, at Nagash. The Undying King paid no attention to the living or the dead, instead communing with the roiling tempest of souls which had made him its aleph in the moments following his consumption of the gods of Nehekhara so many months ago. Arkhan cut his eyes back to Vlad. *'You are certain, then?'*

'If I weren't, I would have said nothing. I would not be hiding myself from him,' Vlad said softly. He frowned. 'Mannfred is a poison, and he always has been. He is treacherous and uncontrollable. He knows no master save ambition, and he listens to no counsel save that which is born in the black froth which passes for his mind. And he is the author of too much of the tragedy, too much of the grief which afflicts them. Though I am loath to admit it, Mannfred shook the pillars of heaven and earth. And the only way to patch the resulting cracks is... well.' He smiled sadly. The emotion, Arkhan noted, did not reach his eyes.

'He will be missed,' Arkhan said.

Middenheim, City of the White Wolf

Canto Unsworn rode through the ruined streets of Middenheim on his gibbering horse and tried to ignore the shrieks and screams that even now, a year after the fact, still rang out at odd intervals from the shadowed recesses of the fallen city. He also ignored the moans of the beaten, battered shape which he had dragged behind his horse across half of the city. Ignoring the former was easier than ignoring the latter.

A crackling bolt of sorcerous lightning hammered into a nearby building, causing a section of it to collapse and a cloud of dust to wash across the street. Canto looked up. The skies overhead still boiled with madness. The fury of the maelstrom above was matched by the destruction below. In the wake of the slaughter wrought by the victorious Chaos forces, the city had been scoured of what life it had once possessed. Archaon's forces ran riot through the ruins. Corpses had been piled into heaps in every square and plaza, unstable mountains of carrion that grew until they rivalled the city walls in sheer height. Many of these had been set on fire, and now a pall of stinking charnel smoke hung over sections of the city. Northmen, skaven and beastmen alike looted freely and with abandon.

Canto knew that it was only the will of Archaon which kept the disparate parts of the horde from turning on each other. For the servants of the Dark Gods, victory was as perilous as defeat, and the only safety was in battle unending. Already, the knives had come out; more than one ambitious chieftain or champion had made a try for Archaon's throat. Their bodies now hung above the city's gatehouses, beside the bodies of the Fellwolf Brotherhood, the Gryphon Legion and any others who had elicited the Three-Eyed King's displeasure.

The latter had been the last of the organised resistance within the city to fall. The hardy Kislevite knights, led by their Grand Master, Dostov, had holed up in the House of Coin, alongside the survivors of the various mercenary companies who had fought for Middenheim. Surrounded and besieged in an ill-provisioned prison of their own making, Dostov and his followers had nonetheless held out for several weeks. When the break-out attempt came, the Gryphon Legion – or what was left of it – had led the way, thundering towards the northern causeway and the viaduct beyond. Those who made it had found themselves fighting upriver against the warbands which were even then still streaming into the city.

Now Dostov hung from a stake on the northern gatehouse, beside what was left of the Grand Master of the Knights of the White Wolf, Vilitreska the so-called Lord of the Flux, Fregnus the Pallid, and the Pox-Knight.

Canto hauled back on his mount's reins, forcing it to stop as a pack of baying hounds loped across the street ahead. Through the smoke he thought he saw manlike shapes moving amongst them, and heard human voices mingled with the howling. Nearby, a nest of writhing tentacles and pulsing flesh that had once been a carriage house emitted a soft, wheezing moan, as if in mockery of the mortal wreckage Canto dragged behind him.

'Quiet, Ghular,' Canto said, as he twisted about in his saddle. 'Unless you want me to take your other hand.' The bedraggled shape shivered and fell silent. *How the mighty have fallen,* Canto thought. Ghular Festerhand, the Ravager of Loren, the King of Flies, and the Duke of Rot, was mighty indeed. Or had been, before Canto had taken off the blighted limb from which he had taken his sobriquet.

'You have only yourself to blame for this, you know,' he said, turning away. 'You saw what happened to the others, didn't you? The Pox-Knight? Cringus of the Thirty-Seventh Configuration? The Copper Princess? Do those names ring a bell, perchance? No? Of course not. Because if they did, you certainly wouldn't have planned to do what you were planning to do.' Canto shook his head. 'I understand the temptation, believe me. But did you really think the Everchosen wouldn't step on you like the disgusting maggot you so resemble?'

Canto kicked his steed into motion and rode on without waiting for an answer. The streets squirmed beneath the hooves of his horse, and ahead of him, a giant made from broken stones, splintered beams and masticated corpses staggered drunkenly across the Ulricsmund, roaring unintelligibly. Whole sections of the city had become distorted reflections of their former glory, transmogrified into screaming sculptures of living fire or revolving facets of impossible design and unknowable angles. Those that were left untouched by the warping power of Chaos had been claimed by petty chieftains or muttering cults, made over into personal lairs and fanes.

Granted, there weren't as many of the latter as there had been in the weeks following the city's capture. Archaon had seen to that, dispatching the detestable Curseling south to lay siege to Averheim. He'd sent the most enthusiastic and troublesome with the two-headed sorcerer, and as a result the city had quieted down nicely. For a time at least.

But then, the Curseling had gone and ruined everything. By the time Archaon had marched on Averheim, Vilitch had vanished. He wasn't especially missed, but his ineptitude had enabled the Emperor to escape into the mountains. Archaon had gone into a rage - denied the lives of both Valten and the Emperor, he'd butchered threescore of his lieutenants and tossed their skulls to the hounds. Canto had avoided that particular fate only by dint of luck; in the aftermath of the siege of Averheim, several plotters had chosen to take advantage of Archaon's fury to make their moves.

Canto had put himself between the Everchosen and the blades of his enemies. He had done so without thinking, and now reaped the rewards. He looked back at Festerhand. *Some rewards are better than others,* he thought morosely.

Archaon had taken Averheim as a message from the gods. He had returned to Middenheim, taking only such forces as were necessary. The rest, mostly worshippers of Khorne, he'd sent haring off to chase down the surviving enemy. Averheim had been left to the beasts. Some milky-eyed brute named Moonclaw ruled there now, the last Canto had heard of it. Now, Archaon sat brooding on his throne, conferring only with daemons, and marshalling his forces for... something.

And oversaw the excavation, of course. *Mustn't forget that, must we?* Canto thought, without amusement. Indeed, how could one forget a steadily growing chasm being gouged into the very heart of the Fauschlag by hundreds of slaves, both human and otherwise? At the very least, the massive heaps of spoil and slag which surrounded the ever widening scar were a constant reminder. Gangs of skaven scuttled past, keeping to the shadows. They lurked amongst the spoil and smoke, their chittering voices accompanying the screams of slaves and the hum of warpstone-powered devices.

Archaon had been quite put out with the skaven for a time, despite the alliance between his forces and those of the so-called 'under-empire'. He had become enraged when the ratmen had interfered in his duel with the Herald of Sigmar, and he had personally hunted down a number of the creatures in order to make them answer for their effrontery, including the creature which had first proposed the alliance – a whining, sneaky wretch of a rat called Thanquol. Now their bodies were displayed with the rest, and those that survived had quickly made themselves useful as overseers, foraging parties and slave labour.

When he reached the Temple of Ulric, Canto did not stop, but let his horse climb the steps. Besides being able to curse in four languages, the animal was quite adept at scaling stairs. That it could do both never failed to impress Canto. As it climbed, he gazed east, towards the excavation where it abutted the temple. Day and night, the Ulricsmund rang with the sounds of it, and he fancied his ears would never be free of it.

He rode past toppled statues of the wolf-god, and into the temple proper. The echo of his horse's hooves as he rode through the rotunda sounded strange, and slightly distorted. All around him was madness: busts and statues had been thrown down, or carved into hideous new shapes. Faces writhed and moaned along the walls. The vaulted ceiling had been hung with thick iron chains, from which dangled hooks and blades. On the latter were spitted the bodies of priests. All were present – the servants of Sigmar, Ulric, Shallya and more besides. Most were dead. Some were not.

Archaon was waiting for him, as ever, at the centre of his chosen throne room. The Everchosen had claimed the dais from which the Flame of Ulric had once burned as his own, and had placed his throne there. The throne was a monstrous construction, composed of brass and black iron, covered with stretched skin and skulls. Ghal Maraz sat at its apex, clasped in brass claws. A heavy shadow, black and stinking of hot iron, crouched behind Archaon's throne. It was massive, larger than any ogre or troll. As Canto approached, the shadow straightened with a sound like a bellows and great wings unfurled. He felt a wash of heat, as if from a smokeless fire.

He knew the daemon's name, though he wished that he did not. Ka'Bandha, the Skull-Smasher. Ka'Bandha, the right hand of the Blood God himself. Eyes like forge-fires gazed at him, burning him inside out. The air around the bloodthirster shimmered, as if the creature's very presence were a wound in reality. It eyed him with interest, as if sizing him up for a challenge. Canto ducked his head and tried to make himself smaller. Even Archaon himself would have been hard-pressed to survive an encounter with Ka'Bandha. Canto would have no chance at all. He kept his gaze averted, and relaxed slightly as he felt the daemon's disappointment wash over him. *No fun for you here, beast,* he thought.

The Swords of Chaos lined the way to the throne. Even now, having fought beside the black-armoured sentinels more than once, Canto could still feel the palpable menace which radiated from them. He hauled back on the reins and brought his disagreeable mount to a halt amidst a flurry of gutter-Estalian.

Canto waited, counting the moments. When Archaon did not stir, Canto cleared his throat and said, 'I come bearing gifts, my lord. As you requested.' He reached behind him and cut the straps that held Festerhand tied to his saddle. The champion, or what was left of him, flopped to the floor with a groan. His armour hung in ragged tatters from his maggot-like body, and his pale flesh was streaked with blood and bruises. He cradled the stump of his wrist to his sunken chest. Ka'Bandha chuckled. The sound was like scalding water hissing over stones.

Archaon looked up. He stared at the broken shape of the traitor for long moments, and then said, 'His hand?'

Canto reached into his saddlebag and produced a dripping sack. Something moved unpleasantly within. 'I thought it best to disarm him,' he said. He tossed the sack down.

Archaon didn't laugh. He rarely laughed. He pushed himself up, off his throne, and strode down from the dais, after gesturing for the bloodthirster to remain where it was. He stepped over the sack as if he hadn't seen it, and made his way to Ghular's side. He looked down at the broken creature. 'Grandfather Nurgle grows impatient. How many of his champions has he thrown in my path of late?' He looked at Ka'Bandha as he spoke.

'You do them honour, to call them champions,' the bloodthirster growled. Canto heard the clatter of brass chains as the shadowy mass moved about behind the throne. 'They are as blossoms, pruned from his garden, and as easily crushed.'

'Yes,' Archaon said. 'Fewer of them than the Schemer or the Prince of Pleasure, to be sure, but still... a not inconsiderable number. Is it vengeance for the Glottkin? Or something else?' The bloodthirster subsided into silence.

Canto knew Archaon wasn't expecting an answer. He followed Ka'Bandha's example and kept silent. It was always the same; Archaon spoke more to hear himself speak, than because he wanted replies. The Everchosen sank to his haunches with a creak of metal, and examined Canto's prisoner. 'Did he fight hard?' he asked.

That he expected an answer to, Canto knew. 'No harder than the others,' he said. 'I waited until he was looking the other way, and then cut his hand off. After that, he didn't have much fight in him.'

Ka'Bandha made a sound like a dog choking on a bone. The

heat grew intolerable, and Canto forced himself to look only at Archaon. The bloodthirster had a short temper, and it was made even shorter by such admissions. Simple murder was beneath the god of slaughter, apparently. 'Coward,' the beast gurgled, eyes shining like beacon fires.

Archaon stood. 'You are getting a reputation, Unsworn. They say you are my executioner.' Ka'Bandha made another disapproving noise, but Archaon ignored the creature.

'I am but your humble servant, my lord,' Canto said, bowing his head.

'Then come with me, O humble servant. I wish to look upon my great work, and see how it progresses,' Archaon said. Ka'Bandha rose to its full height, as if it intended to follow the Everchosen, but settled back at a gesture from Archaon.

Canto hesitated, watching the daemon warily, then slid out of the saddle and hurried after the Everchosen as the latter strode deeper into the temple. He could feel Ka'Bandha's eyes on him the entire way.

'What about the Festerhand?' he asked, as he caught up with Archaon. They were descending into the chill depths of the Fauschlag. Those who knew such things said that the skaven had bought their survival with a treasure that they had located deep in the mountain's guts, somewhere beneath the temple. And that treasure was the reason for the great excavation, as Archaon employed hundreds of slaves and gangs of sorcerers and daemons both in the endeavour, carving a path down through the heart of the mountain. Canto knew the truth of it, and knew that it was not a treasure, but something infinitely worse.

'What about him?' Archaon said. 'If he survives until I return, then I will kill him – or spare him, as the mood takes me. If he doesn't, the point is moot.'

'As you say, my lord,' Canto said obsequiously. He wondered what would get the Festerhand first... his wounds, or Ka'Bandha. Khorne had less use for beaten champions than he did for murderers.

Archaon stopped. Canto stumbled to a halt, just barely avoiding slamming into the Everchosen. Archaon turned. 'Do you disagree?' he asked. Canto hesitated. Archaon cocked his head. 'Do you know why I elevated you, Unsworn?'

A thousand witticisms sprang to mind and immediately turned to ash on Canto's lips. He shook his head slowly. 'No, my lord,' he said.

'I elevated you because I am not your lord,' Archaon said softly. 'Not really. You are a scavenger, a jackal, haunting the edges of eternity. You owe no fealty to any god or warlord. Like a thousand others, you are a man apart, with no loyalty or code to bind your words or mark your path. You do not seek pain, pleasure, pestilence or power. You seek only to survive. Of all the men and women who ride beneath my banners, you and your ilk are the most human. The most flawed, the weakest. But also the strongest.' Archaon turned away and continued walking. Canto followed.

Archaon continued talking. 'The followers of the gods burn bright, but burn swiftly. In every war, they die first, and at the pleasure of the gods. But your kind survives. You cling to this world like a barnacle, holding tight to what you once were, though it profits you nothing. Why did you never seek out the favour of the gods, Unsworn?'

You've already asked me that. You ask me that every day, Canto thought. What he said was, 'Fear, my lord. I feared losing myself.' It was the same answer he always gave, but it never seemed to satisfy Archaon. Then, few things did. The Three-Eyed King seethed with a cosmic frustration, as if the very air scraped his nerves raw.

'And would that be so bad?' Archaon asked. Canto looked at him. It was the first time Archaon had asked *that.* They had come to a massive cavern, its walls marked by skaven graffiti and piles of rotting bodies heaped in the corners. Chittering, red-eyed rats scattered as Archaon and Canto stepped into the eerie light cast by the iron and brass braziers set about the circumference of the cavern.

Before Canto could answer Archaon's question, a guttural voice bellowed a challenge. A trio of ogres, their flesh marked by tattoos of ownership and allegiance, and their arms and armour bearing all of the hallmarks of the daemonsmiths of Zharr Naggrund, stepped into view out of the shadows. The ogres bore heavy swords, and horned helmets that obscured their brutish features. Archaon raised his hand, and the ogres sank to their knees with much grunting and grumbling.

Archaon led Canto past the brutes, and into the gloomy chamber beyond the cavern. Something horrible and flickering occupied the bulk of the chamber – a black, glistening globe supported between two golden hemispheres. The globe was a blotch of shimmering darkness which seemed to draw all sources of light towards it. Canto staggered, struck, as always, by the sheer *wrongness* of the thing.

He had seen it more than once, but it never failed to cause his mind and what was left of his soul to tremble and cringe. He could hear a vast roaring of innumerable voices, and a thinner, sharper sound, like the scraping of rats behind the walls of the world.

Even worse, he knew it was but the merest tip of whatever monstrous eidolon was buried beneath the Fauschlag. Gangs of slaves worked day and night to uncover it, when Archaon's pet sorcerers weren't studying it, trying to unlock its power. Both slaves and sorcerers died in great numbers, their bodies left to rot at the bottom of the pit from which the thing rose. Soon they would have it fully uncovered, and they would pry it free of the mountain, like a pearl from an oyster.

Archaon moved across the chamber towards the dark globe, and the coven of robed cultists who were gathered about it. The cultists were muttering and invoking for all that they were worth. Which, Canto knew, wasn't much. The masked fools were little more than attendants. One of them, obviously the leader if one went by his golden mask, hurried towards Archaon, trying to run and bow at the same time.

'Can we proceed?' Archaon said, not looking at the coven leader.

'It stirs to life even now, mighty Archaon,' the man whimpered. He flung out a trembling hand. 'See how it shines, with the radiance of a thousand unseen suns. We have only uncovered the barest tip, and already it awakens.'

'Can we proceed?' Archaon asked again. There was a hint of menace in his voice.

The coven leader jerked upright in a flare of robes. 'If the gods will it,' he said. Archaon was silent. The man twitched and added, 'An offering of souls will be needed.'

'Then make it,' Archaon rumbled.

'My lord?'

'The slaves,' Canto interjected, unable to bear the coven leader's stupidity. 'Start feeding it the slaves.' He moved closer to Archaon.

'You never answered my question,' Archaon said softly, after a moment of silence. 'Would it be so bad, to lose yourself?'

Canto hesitated, and then said, 'Yes. Who I am, who I was, is the only thing I have left. To surrender it is to lose everything I fought for in the first place.'

'You value the life you had, then?' Archaon said. 'You cling to the past, afraid to face the future.' He swept out a hand towards the shimmering black globe. 'See, Unsworn, the beautiful thing which awaits all of us. It is not terrifying. It is life, and change, and growth. It is the life which springs from death. This world is dead, but a new one is growing here.'

'Mushrooms from a corpse,' Canto said.

Archaon lowered his hand. 'If you like. Maybe the world to come will be simpler, at that. Less burdened by the weight of history and failure. What I do know is that it will be stronger than this husk of a world we reside in now. There will be no weakness, no false morality or burdensome piety to chain men. The gods will sweep aside the old, and unmake the false foundations upon which the lie of this world stands.'

'And that will be better, will it?' Canto asked, without thinking.

'Yes.'

'For whom?' he asked. Archaon looked at him. Canto waited, then, when no punishing strike came, he continued. 'I never wanted this burden. It just came on me. I'm only a man,' he said softly. He looked at his hand, encased in black iron for gods alone knew how many centuries. 'I've only ever been a man. A wicked, evil man, who has done wicked, evil things. But I was never a monster. Never that.'

Archaon chuckled. 'And what would you be now, Unsworn? Man or monster?'

'I would be true to myself,' Canto said, though not without hesitation.

'There was one other who spoke like that,' Archaon said. 'His name was Mortkin. They called him the Black-Iron Reaver, and he carved his saga on the hearts of the gods themselves.' He glanced at Canto. 'He could have been the one standing here, once upon a time.'

'And why isn't he?'

'In the end, he remained true to himself. He was a man, Unsworn, not a monster.' Archaon turned back to the coruscating darkness of the globe. 'But I shed my humanity long ago. I cannot escape what is inside me, nor would I wish to. I have been in darkness for so long, that I fear I would find the light blinding.' He stared up at the globe, as if seeking something within its glistening depths.

'I am a monster and I have set the world aflame, so that I might watch it burn.'

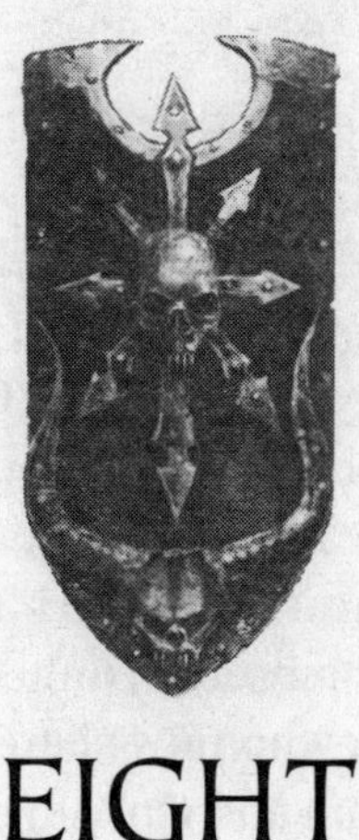

EIGHT

 *The King's Glade, Athel Loren*

It had been a week since the arrival of the dead on the border of Athel Loren, and what some were calling the Council of Incarnates had gathered in the King's Glade to at last discuss the ramifications of that arrival. The week had been one fraught with whispered discussions and late-night visitations as the influential vied against one another in preliminary debate. Too, it had taken a week to debate the truth behind Nagash's offer of parley. Some had sworn it was only a trick, meant to allow the Great Necromancer access to the Oak of Ages. Others had believed that Nagash himself was fleeing certain destruction and looking for protectors, rather than allies.

For his part, Duke Jerrod of Quenelles suspected that either possibility was likely, or that some other, even more subtle scheme was at work. He had argued fiercely against even allowing the creature into the forest, but, as was becoming clear to him, his voice counted for little in the debate. So, instead, he stood in silence beside Gotri Hammerson and Wendel Volker, and watched as those whose voices did count argued over the fate of the world, and of Nagash himself.

The council was an uneasy affair. Trust was not in ready supply amongst the powers gathered beneath the green boughs of the glade. There was discord amongst the elven Incarnates, though Jerrod couldn't say where it originated from. Too, none of the elves trusted Gelt or the Emperor, and Gelt, for his part, kept a wary eye on Malekith. The Emperor, as ever, moved amongst all of them, trying to reach an accord.

It wasn't simply the Incarnates who bickered, either. The elves were divided amongst themselves, united only in their disregard for the dwarfs and men who now shared the forest with them. The dwarfs were uncertain and tense in the trees, and Jerrod had no doubt that the strangeness of Athel Loren grated on them as much as it did his own people.

'Foolishness,' Hammerson muttered. He tugged on his beard. 'Look at it – standing there as if it has a right to exist. Fouling the air with its grave stink. Surrounded by flying books. Can't trust a book that flies, manling.' He gestured towards Nagash, who stood in the centre of the glade accompanied by his mortarchs, Mannfred von Carstein and Arkhan the Black. They stood within a ring of spears, surrounded by the Eternity King's personal guard. Malekith's Eternity Guard were amongst the finest warriors left to the elven race. They counted former members of the Black Guard, the Phoenix Guard and the Wildwood Rangers among them, and had faced daemons and beastmen alike in defence of their liege-lord. Despite the fierce pedigree of those guarding them, Nagash and his mortarchs didn't seem particularly intimidated.

Nagash was terrifying, even to one who had tasted the waters of the Grail. He was a hole in the world, an absence of life, heat and light. He radiated a cold unlike any that Jerrod had ever felt. It was the cold of the grave, and of hopelessness. Even here, in the heart of the forest, spirits whined and moaned as they swirled about the Undying King, caught in the maelstrom of his presence. Everywhere he walked, the grass died beneath his feet, trees withered, and the dead stirred.

'Is there any sort of book you do trust, Gotri?' Volker replied. The white-haired knight leaned against a tree, a jug of something strong and dwarfish dangling from one hand. Jerrod wondered where he'd got it. The dwarfs were stingy with their reserves of alcohol, especially given the fact that it was likely the last such in the world. Then, perhaps they'd thought it wiser to give Volker what he wanted without too much fuss.

Jerrod studied the knight. Sometimes, in the right light, Volker's eyes flashed yellow, and his face took on a feral cast. Mostly, it happened when Teclis was nearby. It was as if whatever force rode Volker were stalking the elf mage. Though, after the first incident, it seemed disinclined to attack. *And thank the Lady for that,* he thought. He'd heard the men of the Empire muttering the name 'Ulric' whenever they thought Volker was out of earshot, and wondered if the gods were truly gone, or merely biding their time.

Even as he thought it, his eyes swept the glade, taking in the faces of those who might as well be gods. The Incarnates were gathered together on the dais which held the thrones of the Eternity King and the Everqueen. They were speaking in hushed voices, intently and at times angrily. Of them all, only Balthasar Gelt paid any attention to Nagash. Though he could not make out the man's face behind his gilded mask, Jerrod knew that the wizard was glaring at the Undying King. Gelt's hatred for the creature had been plainly evident from the moment Mannfred von Carstein had brought word of Nagash's offer.

The Incarnates were not alone in the glade. Besides Jerrod, Hammerson and Volker, there were elves of every description, huddled in scattered groups, or standing alone, like Teclis, who watched Nagash like a hawk. Jerrod's eyes were drawn past Teclis, however, to the pale, radiant figure of the elf woman called Lileath, who stood nearby. It was not the first time he had found his attentions fixed on her. She was beautiful, but it was not her beauty which caught him. Instead, it was the vague, nagging sense that he knew her. That he'd always known her, somehow. Where she had come from, or who she represented, was a mystery. The elves seemed to defer to her, though she was no Incarnate.

'Stop staring at that *elgi* witch, lad. She'll have your soul out of your body like *that*,' Hammerson grunted, snapping his fingers for emphasis. Jerrod looked down at the runesmith.

'You know who she is, then?'

'Don't have to. She's an elf. Only two types of elves, manling... the ones that'll gut you, and the ones that will steal your soul before they do the gutting.' Hammerson crossed his arms. 'Heed me well, you stay away from that one.'

'Are we allowed to associate with any of them, then?' Jerrod asked, with as much innocence as he could muster. Volker snorted, stifling a laugh with the mouth of his jug. Hammerson glared first at the other man, and then at Jerrod.

'This is no laughing matter, manling. We're in their realm, and make no mistake – we're not guests. We might not be prisoners either, but that's only because they're more worried about him.' He pointed at Nagash.

Jerrod was about to reply when a hush fell over the glade, stifling each and every murmured conversation. Malekith rose from his throne of tangled roots, stone and metal, and said, 'Enough.' The word hung in the air like the snarl of an animal. 'Our path is obvious. We have the beast caged... Why not simply dispense with him once and for all? Let us scour this abomination from the face of the world, while we have the chance.'

He looked about him, as if seeking support from the other elven Incarnates. Caradryan remained silent, which didn't surprise Jerrod in the least. The silence of Alarielle and Tyrion, however, did. Only Gelt spoke up.

'I agree,' Gelt said. 'Nagash is as much a danger to us as the Dark Gods themselves, and he will turn on us in a heartbeat, if it suits him.'

'You're one to talk, sorcerer,' Mannfred said. Gelt flinched. The vampire smiled, and made to continue. He fell silent, however, as he glanced at Nagash, who had not moved, and did not seem inclined to do so.

Jerrod tensed, and his hand dropped to his sword. Nagash had said nothing, but Mannfred had obviously heard him nonetheless. The creature seemed disinterested in the debate, as if he were above the petty concerns of the living. Part of Jerrod longed to confront the beast – here was the living embodiment of the corruption which had so devastated his homeland, and he was barred from drawing his sword against it.

Frustrated, he drew his sword partway from its sheath and let it drop back with a rattle. He caught Lileath looking at him, and felt a flush of shame for his loss of control. Her eyes seemed to pull him in, and open him up. It was as if she knew everything about him, and somehow found him wanting. She looked away as the Emperor spoke up, and Jerrod twitched in relief.

'And if we destroy him, what then?' Karl Franz said. His voice carried easily through the glade. 'The foundations of the world crumble beneath us as we argue. We have no time for this. He is here, and his might, joined with ours, might yet win us the world.'

'Oh, well said, well said,' Mannfred crowed, clapping briskly.

Teclis spoke up. 'He is right, Malekith. It was only thanks to Nagash's theft of the Wind of Death that I was able to imbue you all with the powers you now wield. Though I wish it were otherwise, his presence is as necessary now as it was then. He is the Incarnate of Death, for better or worse. His destruction would serve only to weaken us,' he said. He looked at Nagash and met the Great Necromancer's cold, flickering gaze without flinching. 'And he knows, whether he admits it or not, that treachery will avail him nothing, save that he meets his ending sooner rather than later. Is that not so, O Undying King?'

Nagash said nothing. He merely stared at Teclis. Malekith, however, was in no mood for silence. 'Oh yes, and you would know all about treachery, wouldn't you, schemer? More even than myself, I think, and I am no novice in that regard.' Malekith laughed harshly. 'I never imagined to find myself here, the lone voice of reason in a world gone mad. The beast must die. This I command.' He sliced his hand through the air.

'Are you deaf as well as spiteful?' Teclis spat. 'Did you not hear me?'

'I heard,' Malekith said. 'I heard what you didn't say, as well. We need only the Incarnate of Death, not Nagash. The solution seems obvious to me.' He looked at Nagash. 'We slay him, and bind Shyish to another... Someone more trustworthy.'

'More tractable, you mean,' the Emperor said.

'And what if I do? Better a weapon under our control than a maddened beast which might turn on us at any given moment,' Malekith said. He looked at Teclis. 'Tear Shyish from him, wizard. We shall bestow it on another, of our choosing.'

'Aye, that's the way,' Hammerson muttered, nodding slowly. Jerrod looked down at the dwarf. Hammerson met his questioning gaze. 'My folk have grudges aplenty against the liche-lord. The spirits of our ancestors will know peace, once that skull of his is pounded into dust.' He blinked. 'Though, come to think of it, Malekith has just as many.' He frowned and shook his head. 'Isn't that always the way? The wolf-rat or the squig, which is worse? Both want to gnaw on your beard, so which do you kill first?'

'Squig,' Volker said, absently, as he stared at Nagash.

Hammerson and Jerrod looked at him. Volker shook himself and returned their look. 'What?' he asked.

'Why the squig?' Hammerson said.

'Bigger mouth, obviously.' Volker gestured to his face. 'Fit more of the – ah – the beard in, as it were.'

Hammerson was silent for a moment. Then his broad face split in a grin. 'Ha! I do like you, for all that you smell like a wolf den in winter, manling.' He gave Volker a friendly slap on the arm, almost knocking him from his feet. Jerrod shook his head and turned back to the debate.

Teclis stood between Malekith and Nagash. The elf looked tired. His robes were torn and faded, and his face was white with exhaustion. Jerrod felt a moment of pity – they were all worn down by constant battle, but something in Teclis's face told him that the elf's battles had started much, much earlier than their own, and that even here, he found no respite.

'There is no being in existence capable of containing so much death magic, who would not be as dangerous as Nagash,' Teclis said. He leaned against his staff. 'Human, elf or dwarf… it matters not. Shyish would change them, and for the worse, into something *other*. Also, like calls to like.' He looked at each of the Incarnates in turn. 'In each of you, there was something – some kinship – with the wind which chose you as its host. *Like calls to like.*' He glanced at Nagash. 'Nagash is the first, and the greatest necromancer the world has seen. Master of an undying empire, and ruler over the dead.' He glanced at Malekith. 'And all because your followers had the bad luck to wash up on the shores of Nehekhara so many centuries ago,' he added, waspishly.

'Necromancy can be taught,' Gelt said.

'And if it's the symbolism of the thing, we have plenty of dead empires about… including Bretonnia,' Malekith added. He gestured to Jerrod. 'Why, we even have the de facto ruler of that dead land here among us.'

'What?' Jerrod said. 'What are you saying?'

'You are a duke, are you not?' Malekith said. 'The only one amongst your barbaric conclave of horsemen, if I'm not mistaken. Your claim is superior.'

'Bretonnia is not dead,' Jerrod said. He looked around, seeking support. He found only speculation and calculation, in equal measure. 'My people still live. Else what is this for?' he asked, helplessly. Helplessness turned into anger, as Malekith gave a harsh caw of laughter.

'Hope is the weapon of the enemy, human,' the Eternity King said. 'Your land is ashes, as is mine, as is everyone's. A haunt for daemons and worse things. The quicker you accept it, the more useful you'll be.' His eyes glittered within the depths of his mask.

Jerrod's hand fell to his sword hilt. He heard Hammerson say something, but he ignored the dwarf's warning rumble. Malekith had said nothing that Jerrod himself had not thought a thousand times since the fall of Averheim. But to think it, to fear it, was one thing. To say it aloud – to make sport of it – was another. In that moment, he wanted nothing more than to draw his sword and strike. Hammerson was right: Malekith was as much a monster as Nagash. The world would be better off without him.

Cool fingers dropped over his hand before he could draw his blade. He whirled. Lileath released his hand and stepped back. 'No,' she said, softly. 'If you do, you will be slain in the attempt. And then where will your people be, Jerrod of Quenelles? Would you abandon your duties so casually? Is your honour so frail as to be torn by the words of such a spiteful creature?'

'You forget yourself, woman,' Malekith said. 'I am king.'

Lileath looked past Jerrod. 'It is you who forget yourself. King you might be, but I am Lileath of the Moon, and Ladrielle of the Veil, and it is by my will that you have survived to take your place on that throne. My power may have dwindled to but a spark, but I am still here. And I know you, Malekith. Deceiver and hero, arrogant and wise. The best and worst of your folk, housed in iron and forged in flame. You are as dangerous as the Sword of Khaine itself. But I was there when that sword was nothing more than a lump of metal, and I was there too when you were torn squalling from your mother's womb.'

She extended her staff and used it to gently push Jerrod back as she stepped forwards. 'If you do not put aside your differences, if you do not unite, then this world will be consumed. There is no time to pass petty judgements, or to exclaim in horror at the choices you have made, or the allies who offer their fellowship. The world is ending. The End Times are here. And if you would not be swept away like spent ashes from a cold hearth, you will heed me.'

Jerrod stared at her, wondering why her names struck such a chord in him. *Who are you?* he thought. He saw that Mannfred too seemed to recognise Lileath. The vampire's eyes met his, and the creature smirked, as if he and Jerrod shared some awful secret. Jerrod turned away with a shudder. Hammerson, in a rare display, patted his arm.

'He was lying, lad. That's what the elgi do,' the runesmith said. The words were scant comfort. Jerrod shook his head.

'No, Gotri. I don't think he was.'

Hammerson looked up at the knight, and felt a tug of sympathy. Despite what he'd said, he knew that what Malekith had said was more than likely the truth. Or some version of it, at least. From his expression, Jerrod felt the same.

It was no easy thing to lose kin or a home. To see all that was familiar torn away in an instant and reduced to ash. Hammerson glanced up at Volker, and saw a similar expression on the other man's face. Aye, the humans were now getting a taste of the bitter brew that his folk had been drinking for centuries. And the elves as well, come to that, though Hammerson felt less sympathy for them. They'd brought it on themselves, after all. The humans, though... Hammerson sighed. Humans had many, many flaws, as any dwarf could tell you. But they didn't deserve the ruination that had befallen them.

Then, who does? he thought. He looked at Mannfred. *Except maybe that one.* The vampire had a smug expression on his face, as if he were enjoying the bickering that surrounded him. Hammerson frowned.

He had been at Nachthafen the day that Konrad von Carstein had slaughtered the Zhufbarak. He'd been but a beardling, apprenticed to a runesmith, but he still had the scars from when Konrad and his accursed Blood Knights had attacked their position, overrunning it in moments. He remembered the king's fall, his throat torn open by the creature calling itself Walach Harkon, and he remembered the surging tide of corpses.

Mannfred was cut from the same grave shroud as Konrad. He'd waged war on Zhufbar as well, when he'd come to power, and many a dwarf had perished at his hands. If grudges had physical weight then Athel Loren would have long since sunk deep into the earth, between Malekith, Nagash and Mannfred.

No dwarf would ally himself with such creatures, even in the face of destruction. That, in the end, was the difference between his folk and the humans and elves. For a dwarf, better destruction than compromise, better death than surrender. *If the thing must be done, let it be done well,* he thought. It was an old proverb, but one every dwarf knew, in one form or another. All things should be approached as a craftsman approached his trade. To compromise was to weaken the integrity of that work. To allow flaws, to invite disaster.

Not for the first time, Hammerson wondered if he should simply take his folk and go. They would return to Zhufbar and see what remained of it, either to rebuild or avenge it. It was a nice thought, and it kept him warm on cold nights, staring into the dark of the trees, pipe in hand without even a good fire to provide light and comfort.

But that was all it was. If the thing must be done, let it be done well. And the dwarfs had made an oath long ago to the human thane, Sigmar, to defend his people for as long as there was an empire. And dwarfs, unlike elves, knew that an empire was made not of stone or land or castles, but of hearts and minds. Stones could be moved, land reshaped and castles knocked down, but an empire could survive anything, as long as its people still lived.

While one citizen of the Empire yet lived, be they soldier, greybeard, infant or Emperor, the Zhufbarak at least would die for them. Because that was the way of it. An oath was an oath, and it would be fulfilled, come ruin or redemption. Even if the humans chose to throw in their lot with the King of Bones himself, the Zhufbarak would stand shield-wall between them and the ravages of Chaos until the end.

Speaking of which, he mused, studying the giant of bone and black iron where he stood in an ever-widening circle of yellow, brittle grass. For a creature whose very existence was under threat, Nagash didn't seem altogether concerned. Which, to Hammerson's way of thinking, was worrying.

Malekith obviously felt the same. He was in fine form, arguing passionately with Lileath and Teclis. Hammerson could almost admire the Eternity King, if he hadn't been a deceitful, backstabbing kinslayer. Kings had to be harder than stone, and colder than ice, at times, and Malekith was both of those and no mistake. But too much cold, and even the hardest stone grew brittle.

He heard a hiss from Volker, and glanced at the knight. The white-haired man was staring hard at Nagash. Hammerson looked more closely at the liche and saw that the creature was stirring. One great claw rose, and silence fell over the glade. *'YOUR FEAR IS WITHOUT CAUSE,'* the liche said. His voice spread through the glade like a noxious fog. *'THE WORD OF NAGASH IS INVIOLATE. AND NAGASH HAS SWORN TO FIGHT FOR THIS WORLD.'*

Hammerson shuddered. The liche's voice crept under your skin like the cold of winter, and fastened claws in your heart. He wasn't alone in feeling that way. The Incarnates stared at the creature the way birds might regard a snake. Malekith reacted first. 'Any betrayer would say the same, if it suited his interest,' the Eternity King rasped, glaring down at Nagash from his dais. Nagash stared at the elf, as if sizing him up. Then he inclined his head.

'INDEED. AND SO I OFFER A GIFT, AS TOKEN OF MY INTENT.'

Malekith laughed. 'A gift offered by one such as you can hardly be considered proof of anything. I know, for I have used the same trick to great effect more than once.'

'I HAVE WRONGED YOU. YET THE INITIAL OFFENCE, THE FIRST LINK IN THE CHAIN, WAS NOT AT MY INSTIGATION,' Nagash grated. If a skeleton could look amused, Hammerson thought, then Nagash was it. The wide, fleshless rictus seemed to grow wider still, less a smile than a tiger's grin. *'THE EVERCHILD'S DEATH WAS NOT MY DOING.'*

Teclis flinched as the words rolled over the glade. He closed his eyes. He could feel the heat of Tyrion's rage beginning to build. Nagash's words had stoked fires that could never truly be extinguished. Malekith too must have sensed it, for he moved quickly to speak. But he fell silent, his words dying on his lips, as Alarielle rose from her throne.

'You speak of my daughter as if you were fit to say her name,' the Everqueen said coolly. Her voice was composed, and controlled, but Teclis could sense the fragility beneath. 'More and more, you insist on your own destruction.'

'MY DESTRUCTION WILL NOT BRING HER BACK. NOR WILL IT AVENGE HER.' Nagash looked around the glade. *'IT WILL ONLY BRING RUIN.'*

'Listen to the dead thing plead,' Tyrion snarled. He had not drawn his sword, but his hands were balled into fists, and the light within him was beginning to stir. 'We will not bargain for Aliathra's soul,' he spat. Alarielle looked sharply at him, but said nothing. Teclis could feel the Wind of Life beginning to stir as well. *Is this how it ends, even as it began... over the soul of the Everchild?* he thought.

His brother's sin, come home to roost. The child he'd fathered, against all logic, reason and tradition, the child who had been the hope of Ulthuan, and its destruction. Aenarion's curse made flesh, in a moment of passion and stupidity. Teclis's grip on his staff tightened. *Brave child. I failed you, as I failed your father and our people. But I failed you most of all.* Sorrow washed over him, leaving only numbness in its wake.

It seemed like only weeks ago that Aliathra had been sent to the dwarfs of Karaz-a-Karak as part of the Phoenix Delegation of Ulthuan. As royalty, and a sorceress in her own right, the Everchild was thought fit to treat with the High King, Thorgrim Grudgebearer. Aliathra had her mother's grace and poise and her father's courage, and the old alliances had been renewed and invigorated. But then, death had swept down on tattered wings and put paid to the plans of dwarfs and elves.

Teclis studied Mannfred von Carstein, taking in the sharp contours of a face that shifted constantly between regal indifference and bestial malicc. The name the creature went by was an assumed one, just another falsehood tacked on to the ledger that contained his crimes. Once, Teclis had sought to unravel that particular mystery – to find the source of the von Carstein bloodline and perhaps even eliminate it. Of all the vampiric infestations which blighted the world, theirs was the most militant, if not the best organised, and thus a potential threat to Ulthuan in the future. And of all the von Carsteins, Mannfred was the most dangerous.

His defeat of Eltharion the Grim in Sylvania proved that, if nothing else. The Grim Warden had attempted to rescue Aliathra at Tyrion's behest. The army he had taken into death with him had been sorely missed in the days and weeks which followed. Teclis could not say for certain that Eltharion's counsel would have ameliorated the tragedies that occurred after Tyrion had gone mad and their people had fallen to civil war, but his presence might have been enough to avert at least some of the anguish of those terrible days.

Instead, he'd died. And the hopes of Ulthuan had died with him. And now his killer stood smirking in the heart of Athel Loren, protected by an even greater evil. For a moment, Teclis wished that he were his brother, that he had even an ounce of Tyrion's fire in him, so that he might put aside reason and caution and drive his sword through Mannfred's twisted heart. But he wasn't, and he never had been. Instead, he watched and thought, and wondered why Nagash was offering anything at all.

When the answer occurred to him, he smiled. *Ah, clever. Of course. Why else insist on bringing the creature into the forest?*

Nagash faced Tyrion and Alarielle. Perhaps the creature judged them the greatest threat, or maybe he simply wished to enjoy their agony. *'YOU HAVE NO NEED TO BARGAIN. THE SOUL OF THE EVERCHILD IS NOT MINE TO GIVE. LIKE ALL OF YOUR KIND, SHE IS ALREADY FODDER FOR THE DARK PRINCE,'* Nagash said. Alarielle's hand lashed out, catching Tyrion in the chest, stopping him before he could lunge at the liche.

Teclis could feel the other Incarnates gathering their powers now. Malekith and Gelt would act first, before the others. Caradryan would act last, despite being bound to the most impulsive of winds. He would wait for Alarielle, or Tyrion. The Emperor, as ever, stood to the side. Teclis could almost see the wheels turning in the human's mind. The Emperor glanced at him, and gave a barely perceptible nod. He had figured out Nagash's ploy as well.

'INSTEAD,' Nagash went on, *'I WILL OFFER YOU THE ARCHITECT OF HER DEATH, TO DO WITH AS YOU WILL.'* As he spoke, Mannfred threw a triumphant look at Arkhan the Black. That look crumbled into abject horror, as Nagash turned and fastened one great metal claw on the back of the vampire's head, hoisted him from his feet, and tossed him towards Tyrion and Alarielle without hesitation.

Mannfred struck the dais with a resounding crack, and flailed helplessly for a moment, his face twisted in shock. 'No,' he shrieked. 'No, it wasn't me! I didn't kill her, it was...' Whatever he'd been about to say was lost as Tyrion's blade descended like a thunderbolt. Mannfred barely avoided the blow, scrambling to his feet, his own sword in hand. He whirled, looking for an exit, some avenue of escape, but a crackling flare of amethyst light rose and spread between the trees at the merest twitch of Nagash's talons.

'No, I've come too far, sacrificed too much to be your scapegoat,' the vampire snarled. He turned back and forth, blade extended, trying to keep everyone at bay simultaneously. He looked at Nagash. 'I served you! I brought you back, and this is how I am to be repaid?'

'YOU STILL SERVE ME, MANNFRED VON CARSTEIN. YOU HAVE SERVED ME IN LIFE, AND YOU WILL CONTINUE TO DO SO BY YOUR DEATH.' Nagash cocked his head. *'REST ASSURED THAT IT IS APPRECIATED.'*

Mannfred threw back his head and howled. He sprang from the dais, quick as a cat, and lunged for Nagash. His blade slammed down. Nagash caught the blow on his palm, and wrenched Mannfred from the air. The vampire tumbled end over end. He struck the ground, bounced, and lay still. Nagash held up the trapped sword, and his talons flexed. The blade shattered as if it were spun glass. The pieces fell to the ground in a glittering cascade, one by one, thumping into the dead grass.

Mannfred pushed himself to his feet. His eyes were empty, void of emotion. Teclis felt nothing. This was not victory of any sort or kind. It was a thing which had to be done for the greater good, and that drained it of any satisfaction it might have otherwise provided. Mannfred was to be but one more body for the foundations, rather than a conquered enemy. He met the vampire's gaze, and saw a spark in the blackness. A refusal to surrender to fate. In the end, that was all vampires really were. Survival instinct given form and voice.

Mannfred made to speak.

Nagash cut him off with but a gesture. Bonds of amethyst formed about the vampire, mummifying him in dreadful light. Soon, a cocoon of death magic hovered above the ground, occasionally twitching as its occupant tried to free himself.

A hush fell over the glade. Nagash stood silent and still, his gift hovering behind him, ready to be delivered into the hands of his prospective allies, if they agreed. No one spoke, however. Some were shocked by Nagash's actions. Others wondered if it were merely a ruse. Teclis wasn't shocked, nor did he believe it was a trick.

The liche's skull creaked as it swivelled to face him. The eerie light that flickered within Nagash's sockets flared. Teclis stared back, unperturbed, at least outwardly. He had faced Nagash twice before, once in the quiet of Nagashizzar, many years ago, when he had tried to enlist the Great Necromancer's darkling spirit as an ally against the growing shadow in the north. Nagash had refused then. Teclis wondered if the creature regretted that refusal now, when he was being forced to give up one of his servants as the price for what he could have once had freely. *No,* Teclis thought. *No, you regret nothing. Such emotions have long since turned to dust in the hollow chasms of your memory.* He smiled sadly. *Lucky for you, I have regret enough for all of us.*

Teclis looked at his brother. 'Well, brother?'

Tyrion glanced at Teclis, and then looked at Alarielle. He made as if to offer her his hand, but turned away instead. 'Honour is satisfied,' Tyrion said. Alarielle stared at him for a moment, and then returned to her throne.

'Honour is satisfied,' she repeated, softly.

Malekith, who had watched them in silence the entire time, gestured sharply and returned to his seat. 'Time itself is our enemy. As such, if... honour is satisfied, then I withdraw my objection.'

Teclis looked at Gelt. 'And you, Balthasar Gelt?' Gelt said nothing. After a moment, he nodded tersely. Teclis looked at the others. Caradryan shrugged. The Emperor nodded. Teclis sighed in relief. He turned his attentions to Nagash. 'You heard them, necromancer. Mannfred is ours, and in return, you will be allowed a place on the Council of Incarnates.'

'A PRETTY NAME. AND WHAT IS THIS COUNCIL, LOREMASTER?'

Teclis ignored the mention of his former position. 'That should be obvious, even to one as removed as you.' He met Nagash's flickering gaze directly.

'It is a council of war.'

NINE

 *Somewhere beneath the Eternal Glade*

Mannfred von Carstein cursed himself for a fool. It had become his mantra in the days following his betrayal and incarceration. He sat in the dark, constrained by a cage of living roots. The enchantments which had been laid upon his prison were a source of constant discomfort. He could not even muster the smallest cantrip.

This, he thought, *this is how I am repaid?* He had been loyal, hadn't he? Loyalty must run both ways, though. He had served faithfully and honestly, and how had he been repaid? With the loss of all that he had fought for, with betrayal and punishment for a crime he had not even committed. It had been Arkhan who had slit the elf maiden's throat, and used her blood to revive Nagash. Why hadn't Nagash dispensed with the liche instead? Arkhan had served his purpose – he was a shell now. Nothing but an extension of his master's will.

Maybe that was it. Neferata had said it herself – Nagash despised anything that wasn't Nagash. And what Nagash despised, he feared as well. *Do you fear me, Undying King? Even after all I have sacrificed on your behalf?*

For the first few hours of his imprisonment, he had raged and ranted, hoping to attract the notice of guards, or, even better, one of the Incarnates. He thought that if he could but tell them the truth of things, they would see how Nagash had tricked them. He couldn't say what he thought that might accomplish. He knew, now that he was imprisoned, he would not be freed, even if he proved his relative innocence. But to see Nagash defeated, or even destroyed, and Arkhan with him, was too tantalising a dream to relinquish.

But no guards came, if there even were guards. None of his enemies came, to gloat or to accuse. He was left alone in the dark, without the sorcery that was his birthright. Worse than his lack of magics, he could feel the very stuff of him draining away, as if the trees above him were drawing sustenance from his bones. The magics that permeated him were being siphoned off, and likely transmuted into new and vibrant growths above. *A vampire being vampirised,* he thought, and not for the first time. Under different circumstances, he might even have seen the humour of it all. As it was, he filled his days with plotting ever more savage revenge schemes for the day of his inevitable freedom.

And he would be free. That was the certainty which sustained him, even as his prison sought to suck the life from him. He had been buried before, more than once. Trapped in the dark. But he had always returned. Like Nagash himself, he had mastered death. It was not the end. He pushed himself to his feet. He looked up. 'Do you hear me? It is not the end! I still live, and while I live, I...' He trailed off. Someone was clapping. He whirled, a snarl splitting his features. 'Who dares mock me? Show yourself!'

'"Who dares mock me," he asks. Would you like a list?' Vlad von Carstein said, as he stepped out of the shadows and stood before the cage. He seemed healthy for a dead man, Mannfred thought. For a moment, he allowed himself to hope that Vlad had come to free him. Then common sense reasserted itself, and he took a wary step back.

'Come to gloat, old man?' Mannfred said. He glared at Vlad, wishing that he could kill with a glance. 'Or maybe you've come to finally put me out of my misery. Well, took you long enough. I was beginning to wonder how many assassination attempts it would take...'

'I'm not going to kill you, boy. The world has seen enough change, in my opinion.' Vlad leaned against the roots that made up the bars of Mannfred's prison and stared at him. 'You are only alive because I asked him to spare you.'

'Did you really?' Mannfred spat.

Vlad smiled. 'Well, not exactly. I pointed out that your suffering would make a better peace offering than your death. And Nagash, being, well, Nagash, thought that made sense.'

'Remind me to thank you at the first opportunity,' Mannfred said.

Vlad frowned. 'I did it for you, boy. Whatever you think, whatever self-deluding lie is even now burrowing into the sour meat of what passes for your brain, know that what I did, I did for you.' He leaned forwards, gripping the ancient roots. 'You are still my... friend. My student. Even now. Even here.'

'And that is all I will ever be, as long as you walk this world,' Mannfred said. He slid down the wall and sat. Hands dangling across his knees, he laughed bitterly. 'I will always be in the shadow of giants. You, Neferata, Abhorash... even that old monster W'soran. You carved up the world before I realised what was happening.' He smiled. 'I wonder where they are now.'

'Neferata is doing what she has always done, boy. She rules.'

Mannfred grunted. 'Yes. She rules the land we bought in blood and fire.'

Vlad chuckled. 'Such is the way of queens.' He leaned his head against the roots. 'W'soran is dead, I think. If such a thing can die. Otherwise he would be here, with us, scheming away.'

'And Abhorash?'

Vlad was silent for a moment. Then, 'Abhorash fights. But he fights alone. He will not serve Nagash, or any man. Even so, some small part of the world will survive the coming conflagration, thanks to him. Where Abhorash stands, the enemy will never triumph.'

Mannfred looked at him. 'You know where he is,' he said finally.

'I've made it my business to know where my people are. Especially him. Walach's bloodthirsty lunatics were but pale shadows of the Red Dragon. Even Krell would not be able to match him. There is nothing alive or dead in this world that can, I think.' He sighed. 'What I wouldn't give to fight beside him once more.' His gaze turned inwards, and his expression lost its mask of jocularity. Mannfred studied him in silence. For the first time in their long, often bitter association, Vlad looked his age – old beyond reckoning, and battered on the rocks of existence. 'We should, all of us, the last sons and daughters of Lahmia, be here. We were the first, and we should be here at the last.'

'Life's just not fair, is it?' Mannfred said, spitefully. Vlad glared at him. He pushed away from the cage, and shook himself, as might one who has just awoken from a long dream.

'No, it is not. It is a beast, and it is always ravenous. It eats and eats, but is never satisfied.' He tilted his head. 'Do you remember the day we met? Do you remember the first lesson I taught you?'

Mannfred said nothing. Vlad looked disappointed. 'The first lesson was this... nothing stays the same. No matter how hard we fight, no matter how much we struggle, the world moves on. The world will always turn, empires will rise and fall, and if we are not careful, we will be drowned in the ocean of time. We must adapt and persevere.'

'That is what I was attempting to do, before you came back and *ruined everything*,' Mannfred snarled. He shot to his feet and flung himself at the bars of his cage. He slammed into the roots and thrust his arm through, clawing for Vlad's face.

Vlad stepped back, out of reach. 'Whatever ruin has been wrought, it was not my doing, but yours. It was your foolishness that saw Nagash resurrected, that saw the elven realms thrown into turmoil, and the Empire weakened in its darkest hour. You pulled down this house of cards, boy, not me. The Dark Gods exploited your hubris, and now we all must pay the price.'

'From where I stand, I seem to be paying the price for us all.'

'You might be the safest of us, boy. Here, hidden away in your living tomb. You'll be safe from the fires that flicker on the horizon. It is my last gift to you.' Vlad pulled his cloak tight about him. He smiled. 'Rest now, my son. Your labours are over.'

'Vlad, do not leave me here,' Mannfred hissed. 'You *cannot* leave me here. You need me. Nagash needs me. I know things, Vlad – about your so-called allies, about our enemies – but I can't tell you if I'm trapped here!'

'Nor can you try and use those secrets to benefit yourself at the expense of everyone else. I know you, boy. I know what monster drives you, and I know that if we are to have any hope at all, you must be left here, and forgotten.' Vlad turned away. 'Close your eyes and sleep, boy. Dream, and learn from your mistakes.'

'Vlad,' Mannfred called out. Then, more loudly, 'Vlad!'

The elder von Carstein did not stop, or even glance back.

And soon, Mannfred was left alone in the dark once more.

 *The King's Glade, Athel Loren*

Vlad von Carstein flexed his hand, and admired the way the dappled light which dripped through the verdant canopy overhead played across his ring. He felt better than he had in months. His death and resurrection had cleansed his system of Otto Glott's blight, freeing him from the pain and weakness which had afflicted him since the Battle of Altdorf. The light stung his flesh, but he relished the clarity that came with such aches. It would help keep him focused in the hours and days to come.

He glanced up at Nagash. The Great Necromancer stood silent and still, as if he were some ancient idol, dug up from the sands of Nehekhara and carted to Athel Loren. Only the ever-shifting shroud of spirits which draped over him, and the flickering witch-light in his eye sockets, betrayed his awareness.

Arkhan, as ever, stood at his master's right hand. Equally immobile, he nonetheless gave the impression of being far more alert than the Undying King. Vlad smiled. Arkhan made for an effective watchdog. Though he'd been stripped of flesh, the soul of the man yet remained. He was no dull, dead thing, his senses muffled by time and Nagash's will. For all that he pretended otherwise, there was still enough of the back-alley gambler in the liche to make him dangerous. Much like Vlad himself.

His smile faded as he thought of Mannfred, buried down in the dark. *Ah, my boy, what a disappointment you turned out to be. Too ambitious to see the trap laid out before you.* Then, if it hadn't been Mannfred, it would have been someone else. The world was winding down, and had been for centuries. It could not be turned back. It could only be stopped – frozen at the last moment of the last hour, eternally poised on the precipice. But that was better than nothing. The world would survive, in some fashion.

He looked across the glade. As before, only a select few were present. The elven Incarnates, of course, and the Emperor as well. Teclis and the woman, Lileath. The Bretonnian duke, and the dwarf runesmith. And, of course, Balthasar Gelt. Vlad met the wizard's gaze, and inclined his head respectfully. Gelt too had cleansed himself, his mind and will no longer infected by the spiritual malaise which had been eating away at him when they'd first met on the Auric Bastion. Gelt had fallen, and been reborn as something new and powerful. Vlad smiled again, thinking of his own rebirth; the first, and the hundreds which followed, down the long road of years. He rubbed his thumb over his ring.

Gelt didn't return his nod. Then, Vlad hadn't expected him to. He let his attentions wander. He could hear the sounds of battle in the distance, to the west. That would be the elf-prince, Imrik, fighting against one of the many marauding herds of beastmen which threatened Athel Loren. The creatures grew bold, as the world weakened. They had penetrated the forest's defences, and got farther into its depths than ever before. The elves hunted them now, where they were not fighting them openly, and not alone. As a gesture of good faith, men, dwarfs and even Nagash had lent their forces to that effort.

The Emperor's man, Volker, led woodsmen from Middenland and Averland as well as foresters from Quenelles in daily patrols through those parts of the forest safe for human travel, and thus likely to be stalked by beastmen. Dwarf gyrocopters patrolled above the pine crags, and Vlad had set loose a few of his more over-eager followers, including Eldyra, on the hunt – a task which the elf-turned-vampire seemed to relish. He frowned. She was self-destructive, that one. Her new life did not sit well with her, and she was ever at odds with her fellow Drakenhof Templars. He had been forced to break up more than one confrontation in the past few days, and his patience with the former princess of Tiranoc was wearing thin.

Vlad glanced speculatively at Tyrion. The Incarnate of Light stood, as ever, near the throne of the Everqueen, one hand resting on his sword. Like Caradryan, Tyrion said little at these gatherings. Instead, he stared west, as if he could see the battle taking place there and longed to be at its forefront. From what Eldyra had told him of her old master, Vlad thought that the latter was exceedingly likely. He wondered if, perhaps, it might not be wise to bring master and former apprentice together once more. Eldyra would be of great help in the battles to come, but she needed focus. She needed to see that there was only one path open to her, and that path was Vlad's. Whatever the elf thought of the changes wrought in her, he would surely strive to aid her.

And in the lending of that aid, common cause might arise between Vlad himself and the elf-prince. Vlad had no illusions as to the disgust and mistrust his presence engendered among the others. It had ever been such, and it was no less than he expected. But if the Emperor could put aside his distaste, and even Gelt could be civil, then there might be hope yet. The time was coming when Nagash would dispense with him and return him to the dust from which he had been drawn. To Nagash, his champions were but tools, and easily disposed of.

Vlad had no intention of going back into the dark. Not now. Not while Isabella still walked the world, held in thrall to the Dark Gods. And not while the empire he was owed could yet be salvaged. He reached up and touched the tattered seal affixed to his cuirass – the official seal of Karl Franz, and the sign of an elector. Yes, he would speak to Tyrion and the Emperor both, and ingratiate himself to his enemies as only one who had manoeuvred through the adder-pits of the Courts of the Dawn could.

But later, I think, Vlad thought. When Nagash's presence was not such a sore point for the others, they might be more inclined to think charitably of him and his. His thoughts were interrupted by the sound of argument. It was a familiar sound, and almost depressingly so. Teclis and the others were, Vlad reflected, finding that forging such an assemblage of disparate powers was one thing, but getting them to work in harmony was another entirely.

Elven voices outweighed those of men and dwarfs here, and it was only thanks to the mediating efforts of Karl Franz that violence had not already erupted between the haughty exiles of Ulthuan and their guests. And the less said about Nagash, the better. Everyone had their own opinion as to what action the gathered Incarnates and their ever-dwindling followers must take next, but none could convince the others. The pendulum of discussion swung back and forth from civil discourse to squabbling arguments, and Vlad watched it all in amusement. This time, it was the sorcerer, Teclis, trying to sway the so-called Council of Incarnates to his strategy.

'The fate of the eighth wind is of the utmost importance,' Teclis was saying.

Lileath stood beside him, her face grave. She added, 'The Wind of Beasts is loose somewhere in the world, and while it is lost to us, your power cannot hope to match that of the Chaos Gods. If we are to have any hope of victory–'

'And what victory would that be? To save a world already infected by the taint of Chaos?' Malekith snarled. 'No, that is no victory at all.' He rose from his throne. 'With our powers we might yet seal the great breaches through which the winds of Chaos roar. Imagine it, a world free of Chaos, and of the tyranny of wild magic.'

'And without magic, what then?' Alarielle said. 'Our world only thrives because of it. Rather than dispensing with it, we should combine our abilities, and infuse Athel Loren itself with the very stuff of magic. We can return it to the splendour of ancient days, and make it a fitting final redoubt which might stand against the Dark Gods for an eternity.'

'No,' Arkhan the Black said. He stepped forwards, to the consternation of the others. Vlad hid a smile. Nagash rarely deigned to speak to the living, preferring that either Vlad or Arkhan handled such a tedious chore. The living undoubtedly considered it to be arrogance; in truth, Vlad knew that Nagash was ever at work attempting to bring the untold millions of mindless, unbound corpses which had wandered the world since his resurrection under control. Such a feat required every iota of Nagash's attentions.

'No,' Arkhan went on, '*Nagash shall not sacrifice that which is his by right. Not on behalf of the demesne of another.*'

'Indeed,' Vlad said, speaking up. He smiled and gestured airily. 'Especially when there are better ways to use such things.'

'You will be silent, leech. You are only here on sufferance,' Malekith snapped.

'No,' Gelt said. The wizard stepped forwards. 'Whatever you think of him, in his time Vlad von Carstein was a military commander without equal. For that reason, if no other, we should heed him.' Vlad hid his surprise. Gelt was the last one he had expected to speak for him, except for Hammerson, possibly. Vlad inclined his head.

'The lands from here to Kislev are swarming with the walking dead – bodies without life or consciousness, uncontrolled, but waiting.' He indicated Nagash. 'With the power of the other Incarnates added to his own, Nagash would be able to control the dead in their entirety. An army of billions, waiting to be utilised howsoever we see fit. Imagine it,' Vlad said, gesturing. 'The Everchosen may have armies aplenty, but they are not limitless, and with every battle, our numbers would swell.'

'Pah. Why bother with the dead at all? We should send emissaries to my folk,' Hammerson barked, pounding a fist into his palm. 'There are mighty holds yet in the mountains. Copper Mountain is but a few days travel east of here. My kin would open their doors to me – to us. And we would have an army capable of smashing us a path wherever we wish to go, or to hold these forests and crags indefinitely if that is your wish.'

'Hammerson is right,' Gelt said. He looked at the Emperor, as if seeking support. 'The dwarfs have always been the staunchest allies of the Empire, come what may. They would not abandon us now.' Hammerson nodded fiercely.

'Aye. But say the word, and I'll send my rangers into the crags. They'll use the dwarf paths, the routes known only to the dawi, and bring us back an army...'

'Time is short enough, without wasting it begging for aid from those who've already made their cowardice clear,' Tyrion said scornfully. Hammerson snarled an oath, and made as if to attack the elf, but Gelt held him back. Tyrion looked around, seemingly oblivious to the dwarf's mounting anger. 'Besides,' he continued, 'we have an army. The finest in the world – Aenarion himself would have been proud to lead it.'

'And you would know all about that, wouldn't you?' Malekith said.

The Emperor spoke up before Tyrion could reply. 'And what do you suggest we do with this army?' he asked.

Tyrion laughed. 'Isn't it obvious? We take back your Empire, my friend. We rally your folk, province by province. We drive the enemy back, back into the north, back into the void whence they came.'

'There are no provinces to rally, Tyrion,' the Emperor said, after a moment. His voice was rough with barely restrained emotion. 'There are no armies to raise, no sieges to lift. There are no embers of resistance to fan into rebellion.' He spoke slowly, as if every word was painful. 'The Empire that I – that Sigmar – built is done and dust. It has been ground under and made as nothing.'

Gelt hunched forwards, leaning against his staff. 'The Emperor is correct. The forces we have here are all that remain to us. To all of us.'

'All the more reason then, to take control of the limitless dead,' Vlad interjected. 'We can bury them in hungry corpses.' He looked at the Emperor. 'And perhaps take some measure of vengeance for the atrocities they have wreaked on our lands.'

'Not to mention the power that would give your master,' Caradryan said, speaking up for the first time. 'What would he do with that army, once our common foe was defeated?'

'Aye, the elf has the right of it,' Hammerson grated. He pointed a stubby finger at Vlad. 'The living cannot trust the dead. My people know that better than most. Bad enough that we must fight alongside elves, but at least the pointy-ears are alive.'

Vlad smiled and spread his hands. 'You think far ahead for one dangling from a precipice, Master Hammerson.' He looked around. 'There is no guarantee that even with the dead under our sway, it would be enough to throw back the enemy. Why worry about the future, when it is the present which is under threat?'

'Because it is for the future that we fight,' the Emperor said. He looked around. 'Survival is not enough, my friends. Nor is victory. One without the other would be a hollow triumph at best, and pyrrhic at worst.' His eyes met those of Vlad, briefly. Vlad stepped back, his pretty words suddenly so much ash in his mouth. 'This world is all that is, and will be, for our peoples. There is nowhere that can be made safe, nowhere that we can run.'

As the Emperor spoke, Vlad saw Lileath blanch and step back, her hand at her throat. He wondered idly what secret she hid that made her react so, even as he said, 'Then what are we even doing here?' He gestured about him. 'Beautiful as this forest is, I do not fancy it as a tomb.'

'Nor do any of us,' the Emperor said. 'Which is why whatever else is decided here, it must be unanimous. We must stand as one, or we will fall separately.'

Vlad glanced up at Nagash, and then away. He smiled and shook his head.

It was a pretty sentiment. But it was going to take more than sentiment to sway any of the gathered powers to a single cause.

Middenheim, City of the White Wolf

The Temple of Ulric rang with the sound of footsteps. Robed, huddled shapes scuttled into the dark, hissing and murmuring in abominable fashion. Strange, inhuman figures cavorted in the shadowed alcoves and aisles. Bestial forms clambered through the chains strung across the curve of the dome, feeding off the rotting bodies which hung there.

Pale shapes swayed and danced to the piping sound of flutes before the throne of the Three-Eyed King. They were clad in silks and damask, smelling of sweet oils and perfumes, and their hooves and claws were sheathed in gold. They sang and laughed as they danced, delicately clawing one another and scattering the blood about them as if it were rose petals. The pipers, slovenly, fat-gutted plaguebearers, crouched on the dais and played duelling melodies, as cackling pink horrors clapped and kept time.

Canto Unsworn strode forwards, through the silently arrayed

ranks of the Swords of Chaos. To the best of his knowledge, the Chaos knights hadn't moved since they had taken up their positions some weeks earlier. The daemonettes, in their dance, moved amongst them, but not a single one of the knights so much as twitched. Canto gestured sharply as one horned and cloven-hoofed beauty pirouetted towards him, and the creature dashed away, favouring him with a sulky smile as she spun past him. Her claws clicked across the side of his helm as he moved away.

As Canto drew close to the throne, he tossed the still-smoking helm of Nalac the Eschaton onto the floor. 'The Changer of Ways sends his regards,' Canto said, as the pipes went still and the horrors ceased their laughter. The helm, composed of millions of shards of tinted glass, caught the light in a thousand ways. It reminded him of another helm, belonging to another devotee of Tzeentch, long ago and far away. He pushed the thought away.

Archaon, heretofore slouched on his throne, sat up. 'Nalac. I do not know him.' He had Ghal Maraz across his lap. Even now, the hammer terrified Canto. No mortal hand would ever wield it again, but even so, it seemed to hunger for death and destruction. His death, and the destruction of those he served. Others had encouraged Archaon to dispense with it, to shatter it, or hurl it from the city walls. Their bodies now hung from the chains above, along with the others who had tested Archaon's patience.

'And you never will, my lord,' Canto said. 'He was one of Vilitch's disciples, and was trying to rouse the tribes occupying the Sudgarten District. I thought it prudent to – ah – head that off at the pass, as it were.' He gave the helmet a kick.

'Did he die well?'

'I'm not entirely certain. A flock of purple ravens burst out of his armour after I cut his head off. They flew off. I think that means I won.' He looked up at Archaon. 'The army grows restless, my lord.'

'The army eats itself, Unsworn,' Archaon corrected. 'Like a fire, swelling to fill a room and snuffing itself in the process. That is the nature of Chaos. Like the serpent eating its own tail, it feeds on itself, until there is nothing left to devour.' Archaon stroked the hammer gingerly, as if afraid it might bite him. 'And then, it begins again.' He shoved the hammer from his lap. It struck the dais and tumbled down the stairs. Daemons scrambled out of its path with shrieks and yowls. Canto stepped back as the hammer smashed into the floor at the foot of the steps. 'It always begins again,' Archaon said.

'Yes, my lord,' Canto said carefully, bowing his head.

When he looked up, Archaon was studying him. 'Have I thanked you yet, Unsworn? While I sit here, in my seclusion, you wield sword and shield in my defence. You fight battles so that I do not have to. Do you begrudge me, my executioner?'

Canto did not meet Archaon's gaze. He could feel its weight on his soul, and knew that his answer might determine his survival. Archaon had dispensed with most of his advisors and confidants in the days following the fall of Averheim. The lands of men were fallen, or of little consequence. The lands of the elves had sunk beneath the sea, and the dwarfs had retreated into the roots of the earth. The sour redoubt of Sylvania was ringed about by armies of beasts and daemons and skaven, and its crushing was of minor importance with Nagash's departure. There were no enemies left that Canto could see, save Archaon's own lieutenants.

Chaos feeds on itself, Canto thought. He lifted his head. 'I do not, my lord. I am content with my lot.' As he spoke, he hoped Archaon couldn't see that he was lying.

In truth, Canto had been preparing to leave for days. Every time he thought he might slip out of the gates and ride hell for leather for Araby or Cathay, some champion or chieftain got it into their head to cause trouble. If it wasn't a schemer like Nalac the Eschaton, it was a brute like Gorgomir Bloodeye, being spurred on by a suspiciously pale courtesan. Finding a vampire amongst the daemon-worshippers wasn't that surprising. There was at least one other in the city, to Canto's knowledge.

And a frightening creature she is, he thought. The Countess kept to herself, for the most part, and stayed within the plague gardens that had sprung up in what had been the merchant district. They said that she spent her days humming and singing to herself. On a whim, Sigvald the Magnificent had tried to hack his way into the gardens only to be put to flight, his tail between his legs.

'I do not remember what contentment feels like,' Archaon said. 'Maybe I never knew.'

Before Canto could even attempt to formulate an answer to that, the heavy oaken doors of the temple were smashed open. The sound of splintering wood filled the rotunda, silencing all else. Then, a thunderous voice boomed, 'You mock me!'

The temple shuddered as a heavy form entered Archaon's throne room, stinking of fire and blood. Ka'Bandha strode through the swirling daemonettes, scattering the handmaidens of Slaanesh as it strode towards the throne. One of the Swords of Chaos was caught a glancing blow from Ka'Bandha's axe, and fell. Before the knight could get to his feet, the bloodthirster sneered, raised one great hoof, and brought it down on the warrior's helm, pulping it. As if the death of one of their own had been a signal, the Swords of Chaos swept into motion. As one, they drew their swords and turned towards the daemon.

Canto took up his position on the dais, his own blade drawn. He doubted if he would last much longer than any of the others but there was no place to run that the daemon couldn't catch him, if it so desired. That was what he told himself, at any rate. Why else would he put himself between Archaon and the daemon? Better to stand with the Everchosen than perish. There was no telling what had driven the beast into a rage. The servants of Khorne longed for battle the way other beings desired food.

Archaon said nothing as the daemon thundered forwards. He

merely raised his fist, and, in eerie rhythm, the Swords sheathed their weapons and retreated to the chamber's perimeter. Canto hesitated, but then sheathed his own blade. There was no sense in making himself a target, after all.

'You forget yourself, daemon,' Archaon intoned as he slowly rose from his throne. 'I am the Everchosen, and I am the edge of Khorne's axe on this world. Would you approach his throne in so rash a manner?' His words echoed through the rotunda, and a ripple of daemonic titters followed in its wake as the watching daemons twitched in glee to see Ka'Bandha spoken to in such a manner. There was no love lost between the beasts, even here, united beneath Archaon's standard. They were worse than men, in some ways. 'Remember, daemon. In this world, you serve at my whim.'

'You are but a mortal speck,' Ka'Bandha snarled. 'I serve you only so long as you lead us to slaughter. But there is no slaughter here, Everchosen. Where is the ocean of blood we were promised? Where are the skulls you have tithed to the Lord of Carnage? I see nothing before me but the dried leavings of crows and jackals.'

The bloodthirster straightened, wings unfurling. A wash of heat billowed outwards, rippling from the daemon's form and filling the rotunda. The stones at Ka'Bandha's feet blackened and grew soft from that heat, and the chains dangling above its hunched shoulders turned white hot and dripped to the floor, link by link. 'You mock me, king of filth. You mock Ka'Bandha, and *make him an overseer for puling slaves,*' Ka'Bandha roared out, shaking the chamber to its foundations. The daemon smashed the flat of its axe against the brass cuirass which clad its hairy torso. The sound of metal on metal echoed through the temple and lesser daemons fled the sound of it, their paws pressed to their ears.

'Those slaves toil and die in the cause of the Four-Who-Are-All. What they uncover, what they feed with their broken bodies and blistered souls, will, when it awakes, spill more blood than all of the axes ever forged. But it must be excavated, and it must be fed.' Archaon paused. He cocked his head. 'Unless the great Ka'Bandha fancies excavating it himself.'

The bloodthirster lifted its axe and drove it into the ground, splitting stone and rocking the chamber. '*I will not be mocked,*' the creature roared, as it wrenched its axe free of the floor and lashed out, splitting one of the chamber's support pillars in two.

Stone and dust cascaded down as part of the ceiling collapsed. Canto ducked aside as a chunk of stone smashed into the dais. Archaon didn't so much as twitch, even as Ka'Bandha advanced on the throne. 'No. I see that,' Archaon said, as Ka'Bandha loomed over him. His hand fell to the hilt of his sword. He looked up at the daemon. Their faces were only bare inches apart. 'What is it you wish, then?' he asked quietly. 'Would you have me dispense with you, as I dispensed with the Fateweaver?'

Canto shivered. The two-headed daemon had grown agitated in the aftermath of the Emperor's escape from Averheim. It was a given that the Fateweaver had been working to undermine Archaon; treachery was second nature to the servants of the Changer of Ways. When the beast had openly challenged Archaon, demanding that he pursue the Emperor into the Grey Mountains, a confrontation which had been simmering for weeks occurred in the blink of an eye. There had been no speeches, no grand gestures. Merely a sword, flashing in the dark, and the sound of two monstrous heads falling to the floor. What was left had been fed to the thing in the depths of the Fauschlag.

Ka'Bandha was silent. For a moment, Canto wondered whether it might attempt to strike Archaon down. Part of him hoped it would try. Part of him hoped it would succeed. The creature glared down at Archaon, axe half-raised. Archaon waited. When no blow was forthcoming, he said, 'I am fulfilling your lord's wishes, Ka'Bandha. If you doubt that, then strike me down.' He spread his arms. 'Let us see whether Khorne rewards you... or punishes you.'

The bloodthirster snarled and took a step back. 'Blood must flow,' the daemon snapped. 'There is no blood here, Everchosen. Let the servants of lesser gods guard slaves. I would have battle.'

'There has been battle aplenty. Enough to glut even the King of Murder himself. The world drowns in blood, mighty Ka'Bandha. Only a single lone island resists the tide, and it matters little, isolated as it is.' Archaon lowered his arms.

There was something about his voice, his manner, which Canto found confusing. Archaon wasn't trying to calm the beast – no, he was trying to aggravate it. It wasn't just mockery. *What are you up to?* he thought.

'The Emperor escaped you,' Ka'Bandha growled.

Archaon shook his head. 'And so? What is a ruler with no land to rule? And what power he stole from the heavens, I stripped from him with my own two hands. His power, temporal or otherwise, is gone. He is broken, his armies scattered, his land... ash. The lie of him has been exposed to the world, as I swore to do. And now I shall fulfil my oath to our masters, Ka'Bandha. I shall crack the world open, so that they might feast on it at last. What is the Emperor, compared to that?'

Says the man who has spent weeks brooding because Karl Franz slipped through his fingers at Averheim, Canto thought. His eyes were drawn to Ghal Maraz, where it sat at the bottom of the steps. Even Ka'Bandha avoided it, and cast occasional wary glances at the weapon. Archaon was up to something – but what?

'It is a mistake to think him defeated,' Ka'Bandha rumbled. 'His skull belongs to Khorne.'

'Then, by all means... go collect it,' Archaon said, gesturing towards the doors to the temple. 'Karl Franz's life is yours. I give it to you freely, and without stipulation, save one.' He held up a hand, as Ka'Bandha growled. 'Let Khorne have his skull, by all means. But his skin is mine. Promise me this one small gesture, and I shall release you from my service, so that you might hunt your prey wherever he seeks to hide.'

The bloodthirster snorted. 'Aye, so it shall be. I shall collect skin and skull both. I shall drown the trees in blood, and bury the mountains in offal.' The creature threw back its head and roared in satisfaction. 'Let the Blood Hunt ride once more, before the end of everything!' The daemon spun on its heel and stormed from the chamber, smashing aside another pillar in its exuberance.

'Well, that's one way of handling it,' Canto said, as the dust cleared.

Archaon descended the steps, and sank down on the bottom one. He looked down at Ghal Maraz. He reached out, and traced the intricate pattern of runes which covered the hammer. 'Time... fractures, Unsworn. A thousand-thousand possibilities flare bright, and burn out before my eyes with every moment. But there are fewer and fewer of them with every passing hour. Our path grows narrow and thorny, and I am forced to play a game of death and deceit to ensure the proper outcome.'

The Everchosen picked up the hammer and held it out, as if weighing it. 'The hours grow short, and the shadows long. I would have vengeance, not because I desire it, but because it must take place, else what was it all for?'

Canto's hand fell to the hilt of his sword. Archaon was not looking at him. One blow, and he would be free. *Or dead,* he thought, as he lowered his hand. 'I do not know, my lord.'

'The beast will not succeed.' Archaon touched the shimmering gemstone set into his helm. 'I have seen its failure, spread across the skein of possibilities. The only question is one of time. When will the pieces fall? And where?' He spun Ghal Maraz gently in his grip. 'It must be here. There is a moment here, waiting to be born. It has weight, and draws every other moment towards it, like a stone drawing the man whose leg it is tied to down into the dark water. It will happen in Middenheim.' He glanced at Canto. 'The end must justify the means. The world is a lie, and the truth must out.' Archaon rose to his feet, Ghal Maraz in hand.

'I cannot rest until that is done, Unsworn. Even if I must defy the gods themselves, I will have the truth.' He climbed the steps slowly, the hammer dangling from his grip.

Canto watched the Everchosen sink back onto his throne, and thought of Araby.

TEN

 *The Silvale Glade, Athel Loren*

Duke Jerrod drove his blade down into the hairy back of the slavering beastman, severing the creature's spine. He wrenched the blade free and twisted in his saddle, lopping off the arm of another. The creature howled and staggered back, clutching at itself. His stallion whinnied and lashed out, killing the creature with a single blow from its hoof.

The beasts were wild with madness. The bloodlust so common to the minotaurs had spread to every gor and ungor loping beneath the trees. For days they had hurled themselves into death on the spear points and sword blades of the elves, and for every thousand that perished, another thousand prowled forth, slavering and berserk. For the most part the bulk of the enemy were held at bay by the elves, but some small groups had slipped through the wall of spears and shields to ravage behind the static positions. It was these isolated fragments of the horde that the Incarnates had roused themselves to destroy.

The elves, led by the Dragon-Prince, Imrik, were on the verge of exhaustion. But to give in, to surrender even a single glade, was to threaten the safety of the King's Glade. And that was too steep a price for even an hour's respite. But such was the fury of this latest onslaught, that even the Incarnates had been stirred from their interminable debate.

Or so it seemed to Jerrod, at least. Endless hours of argument, back and forth, accomplishing nothing tangible save to put folk who should be allies at each other's throats. It seemed inconceivable to him that such a thing was possible, that even now men and women broke and shattered beneath the weight of their own hubris.

Then, not everyone had the Lady to guide them onto the proper path as he and his knights did. Around him, the Companions of Quenelles fought with courage and honour, lances and swords red with the blood of abominations. He murmured a silent prayer as an axe hacked away one of the frayed strips of silk which decorated the crown of his helmet, and nudged his horse around. The flat of his shield caught the minotaur on the side of the head, knocking it aside. It stumbled, and then fell, as a spear erupted from its side. The beast collapsed onto all fours. Its hide bristled with arrows, and despite the spear in its side, it tried to struggle to its feet. An armoured boot caught it in the head, shoving it back down.

Wendel Volker caught the haft of the spear and jerked it free, before plunging it down through the minotaur's bulging, bloodshot eye. The Reiksguard looked up at Jerrod and smiled. It was a fierce, unnatural expression, lacking in humour. 'Much better than listening to all that bickering, eh?' Volker said.

'I never knew you to be so eager for a fight, Wendel,' Jerrod said.

Volker left his spear where he'd planted it. He drew his sword, and a single-bladed axe, from his belt, and hefted them meaningfully. 'What else is there?' he rasped. 'There's nowhere to run now. May as well take what I'm owed, before the end.'

Volker had changed much in the weeks since they had arrived in Athel Loren, Jerrod reflected. It was as if something grew within him, remaking him in its image. What that image was, and what form it would eventually take, Jerrod could not say. Whatever it was, it frightened him. The white-haired knight had always been a brave, if hesitant man, with too much love of the bottle for Jerrod's taste, but in the past few weeks he had become a fierce warrior, staying out on the borders of Athel Loren for days at a time, leading his band of foresters and scouts in hunting down any beastmen that slipped through the defences of the elves. The men who followed him included priests of Ulric and Taal, shrieking flagellants and howling, fanatical worshippers of the wolf-god. The mad and the lost, formed into a murderous pack that even the most bloodthirsty beast hesitated to cross.

Volker's eyes blazed, and Jerrod's horse whinnied nervously as the temperature dropped suddenly. He followed Volker's gaze, and saw that he was staring at the elf mage, Teclis. The mage fought beside Lileath, the elf-woman who was neither Incarnate nor noble, as far as Jerrod could tell. He could not, in fact, say what she was. Lileath of the Moon, and Ladrielle of the Veil – that was what she had called herself. But what did those names mean? Why did they sound so familiar to him, as if he had heard them before? *In a dream, perhaps,* he thought. Volker took a step towards them, weapons raised. Jerrod nudged his horse between them, blocking Volker's line of sight. 'Your Emperor has said that the mage is not to be harmed, my friend,' he said.

Volker grunted. 'So he has.' He twitched, and looked up at Jerrod. For a moment, his face was that of the man Jerrod had first met in Averheim, so many months ago. Then the mask was in place once more, and something feral looked out through Volker's eyes. He nodded to Jerrod and turned, raising his weapons. He howled. Jerrod's stallion stepped sideways in agitation as Volker's band of lunatics ghosted through the glade, following into step with their commander. They flowed smoothly towards a point where the elven battle-line was beginning to buckle, and smashed into the beastmen with howls and wild screams.

Jerrod saw the enemy reel from the sudden onslaught. *Another charge might put them to flight,* he thought. He signalled for one of his Companions to sound his horn. At the first quavering note, the Bretonnian knights broke off from the melee with an ease born of hard-won experience and formed up about him. Jerrod had lost his lance in the first crashing charge, but he wouldn't need it. Momentum, and the blessings of the Lady, would see him through. And if not, well... death would not find him a coward.

He spurred his horse into a canter and the Companions followed suit, falling into position behind him, arranging themselves by instinct without need for his command. The horses began to pick up speed as they drew closer to the main thrust of the battle. His blood sang in his veins as the canter flowed smoothly into a gallop. It had been too long since the Companions of Quenelles had ridden out and faced the enemy head on. There had been too much skulking behind walls or in glades; such was not the proper way of it, and he relished the chance to show the haughty inhabitants of Athel Loren how a true son of Bretonnia fought.

Elves turned as the thunder of hooves filled the glade. They had knights of their own, but their steeds moved with the grace and silence of a morning mist. The warhorses of Bretonnia on the other hand shook the earth and sky with their passing. They were not graceful or silent. They were a force of destruction, a mailed fist thudding home into the belly of the enemy. They were the pride of Bretonnia, and the sound of their hooves was the roar of a doomed people, proclaiming that they would not go meekly into the dark.

Jerrod hunched forwards in his saddle as the elven lines parted smoothly before them, as he'd hoped they would. And then the knights of Bretonnia smashed home in a rumble of hooves and a splintering of lances, driving into the ill-disciplined ranks of the beastherds with a sound like an avalanche. Those creatures unlucky enough to be in the front seemed to simply evaporate, torn apart or ground under hooves at the moment of impact. Those behind were dragged down seconds later, or else speared on the ends of lances. Those beasts closest to Jerrod were knocked aside, sent sprawling or trampled by his stallion as he hacked at the enemy. The knights pressed on, their formation spreading like a fist opening up. Behind them, the elves reformed their lines.

Jerrod laid about him until his arm ached and his heart shuddered in his chest. The beasts began to fall back, but not all at once, and not as he'd hoped. They were too disorganised for that, he realised. One herd cared little for what befell the next, and whatever fury drove them had yet to relinquish its hold on their stunted brains. Cursing, he made to signal for withdrawal. They could fall back, and charge again.

His horse reared as a number of ungors thrust spears at him. One glanced off his thigh, and another slashed through the strap of his saddle. Before he could stop himself, he was sliding ignominiously off his mount. He crashed hard to the ground, and was forced to roll aside to avoid being trampled by his own horse. Spears dug for his vitals and he flailed desperately, chopping them aside. Hairy hands grabbed for him, and cruel skinning knives or cut-down sword blades crashed against his armour as the creatures swarmed through the forest of stamping hooves and falling bodies.

A strong grip fixed itself on the back of his tabard, and he found himself dragged upright. An arm clad in black armour extended past him, clutching a long blade. An ungor spitted itself on that sword, and its malformed body withered and shrank within moments. The blade pulsed red for a moment and then returned to its original hue as its wielder ripped it free of the husk. Jerrod looked up into the smiling features of Vlad von Carstein.

'I thought you might require assistance,' the vampire said, as Jerrod parried an axe and opened its wielder's belly. 'I was nearby, and saw no reason not to lend it. You are from Quenelles, are you not? I thought I recognised your heraldry.'

'I am,' Jerrod said stiffly. He took a two-handed grip on his sword. He'd lost his shield in the fall, and his hip and shoulder ached. But the pain could wait; as long as he could move, however stiffly, he could fight. Vlad took up a position beside him.

'Ah, Quenelles... such a lovely land. I whiled away many a night there in the company of fine ladies. And the dumplings, ah...' Vlad kissed his fingertips in a gesture of appreciation. He beheaded a beastman with a casual swing of his blade. 'I taught young Tancred the proper way to hold a sword; this was the first Tancred, of course. Long dead now, poor fellow. Ran afoul of some detestable necromancer, I'm given to understand.'

Jerrod fought in silence. The vampire moved too quickly for his eye to follow. Vlad chopped through the neck of a beast and whirled to face Jerrod. 'You're the latest to bear the dukedom, I'm told. I too know the pain of being the last ruler of a fallen province.'

'Quenelles still stands,' Jerrod said.

'Of course it does, of course,' Vlad said. 'How could it not? But its people face much difficulty in the days to come, my dear duke. Have you considered the possibility of an alliance, for the days ahead?' He ducked beneath the wild swing of a club, and sent a beastman sprawling with an almost playful slap.

'With you?'

'Who better? We are both men of royal blood, are we not? And in the years to come, both the Empire and Bretonnia will need each other – humanity must stand together, Jerrod.'

'Humanity?' Jerrod blurted, as a beastman lunged for him. He stepped aside and brought his blade down on the creature's back. He heard the tramp of feet, and saw that the elves were moving forwards, spears levelled. They were taking advantage of the momentary lull the Bretonnian charge had caused, and were now moving to take back the ground they had lost. Jerrod raised his sword, signalling for his knights to withdraw.

'I was as human as you, once, and unlike some, I have never forgotten it,' Vlad said smoothly. He stepped back as the elves marched past them. 'Too, I am an elector of the Empire, and as such view it as my duty to put forth the idea of alliance, come our eventual victory.'

'You are so confident in our survival, then?' Jerrod said. His stallion trotted towards him, its flanks heaving, its limbs striped with blood. He stooped to check the animal, relieved that it had survived. Vlad watched him for a moment. He reached out, as if to stroke the animal's nose, but the horse shied away. Vlad let his hand drop, a tiny frown creasing his features.

'Of course,' the vampire said. 'As the Emperor said, we fight for the future. To countenance defeat is as good as accepting it. And I have come too far, and accomplished too much, to accept the ruin of it all.' He looked at Jerrod. 'The world stands, Duke of Quenelles.' He put his hand on Jerrod's shoulder.

'And I would see that it do so for many years yet to come.'

Gotri Hammerson clashed his hammer and axe together, summoning fire and heat. Beastmen fell, consumed and turning to ash even as they charged towards the Zhufbarak line. The runes of fire dimmed as he lowered his weapons. The dwarfs had taken up the flank, without asking permission. The elves had, in a rare display of sense, left them to it without protest. Now guns and good Black Water steel threw back the Children of Chaos again and again.

The beasts poured out of the trees in a disorganised mass. The giant, gangly shapes of ghorgons and cygors roared and smashed aside ancient oaks as they lumbered after their smaller cousins, and knots of bellowing minotaurs carved a path through their own kind to get to the dwarf lines. All of them were thrown back, again and again.

'Ha! We're hammering them just like the Ironfist did at Hunger Wood, Master Hammerson,' one of his Anvil Guard barked, his broad face streaked with powder burns and blood. 'They'll remember the Zhufbarak, sure as sure.' He swung his axe and beheaded an ungor as it scrabbled ineffectually at his shield.

'Aye, and if you don't pay attention, Ulgo, they'll be the only ones to do so,' Hammerson snarled. He smashed his hammer down, shattering a crude blade as it sought his gut, and gave its wielder an axe in the skull by way of reply. As he wrenched his weapon free, he raised his voice. 'I want a steady rate of fire. I want them pummelled into a greasy patch on the topsoil, lads, and an extra tankard of Bugman's best to whoever brings down that Grimnir-be-damned ghorgon over there.' The rhythmic snarl of gunfire answered him as the lines revolved, fresh Thunderers stepping forwards to take the places of those who had just fired. The Zhufbarak were a millstone, grinding over the enemy. They had plenty of powder and shot, and a sea of targets. Some beastmen inevitably made it through the fusillade, however, and when that happened, it was time for the rest of the throng to earn their ale.

The ground trembled. He craned his neck and saw Jerrod and his knights smash into the enemy centre like a hammer striking an anvil, and couldn't restrain a smile. 'Good lad,' he grunted. The Bretonnians fought like it was what they were bred for, and they hit almost as hard as a proper cannonade.

Something flashed at the corner of his eye, and he turned. His smile faded. Gelt stood at the heart of the battle-line, standing head and shoulders over the two dwarfs set to guard him – they were members of Hammerson's own Anvil Guard, clad in gromril armour and bearing heavy shields marked with runes of resistance and shielding. *Stromni and Gorgi, good lads,* he thought. Hard lads, like ambulatory boulders with as much brains between them, but once they'd set their feet and locked shields, nothing short of death would move them. Gelt was safe with them.

Not that he needs much in the way of protection, Hammerson thought, as a wave of shimmering light erupted from Gelt's hand and turned a number of beastmen to solid gold statues. Around Gelt, runes glowed white-hot, and the guns of the Thunderers seemed impossibly accurate. Axes hewed without going dull, and hammers broke through even the toughest armour and splintered the thickest bones.

A flash of runes caught Hammerson's eye. They lined the edge of a ragged cloak, which swirled about a figure who stood where the fighting was thickest. The dwarf was old, older even than Hammerson himself, to judge by the icy whiteness of his plaited beard. His features were hidden beneath the hood of his cloak, and he bore no clan markings on his armour. The axe in his hands hummed with barely contained power as it lopped off a beastman's head. The mysterious dwarf spun to smash a lunging beastman from the air, and his eyes caught Hammerson's as he did so.

For a moment, the din of battle receded, and Hammerson heard only the sounds of the Black Water, and the rhythmic crash of the great forges of Zhufbar. He heard the rolling work-songs of his clan, and smelt the forge-smoke. He saw the shimmer of a thousand clan standards gleaming in the sun, and the glint of rune-weapons raised in defence of ancient oaths and old friends. All of this and more he saw in the eyes of the white-bearded dwarf, and a name came unbidden to his lips.

'Eyes forward, Master Dwarf,' a smooth voice purred. Hammerson whirled, the name slipping from his mind as he came face to face with a bulky beastman. Its teeth were clenched and its eyes rolled wildly, but it had been stopped from reaching him by a quintet of pale fingers which were sunk knuckle-deep into the meat of its back, just between its shoulders. Vlad von Carstein smiled in a neighbourly fashion and then, with a wink, ripped a section of the creature's spine out. It toppled forwards with a single moaning bleat, and Hammerson instinctively crushed its skull with his boot.

The vampire bounced the chunk of bone on his palm for a moment before pitching it over his shoulder. 'I would have thought a warrior such as yourself would know better than to become distracted in battle, Master Hammerson,' he said.

'And I'd have thought you'd have the sense not to save a fellow who means you ill, vampire,' Hammerson grunted. Ulgo had noticed the vampire at last, and the Anvil Guard raised his axe threateningly. Hammerson glared at him until he lowered it. *Aye, and we'll be having a chat later, lad, about why it was the vampire who saved me and not you, eh?* he thought sourly.

'Still, and after I prevented that beast from braining you?'

'Who asked you to? I owe you nothing,' Hammerson said. He looked around, trying to spot the strange, white-bearded dwarf, but the old one had vanished into the eddies of battle. Hammerson shook his head, trying to banish the unease he suddenly felt.

'Perhaps I didn't do it for you, eh?' Vlad said. He stepped over the creature and smoothly took up position beside Hammerson in the shield-wall. The closest dwarfs looked askance at the vampire, and more than one gun-barrel drifted towards him. Hammerson gestured sharply. No sense starting a second fight when they were already in the middle of one. He signalled for those closest to fall back a step.

'Then why did you do it?' Hammerson clashed his weapons together again. Fire roared out, earning them a moment of respite. He looked at the vampire. 'And why aren't you with your master?'

'Which one?' Vlad asked. 'I am as much a son of the Empire as I am a child of death, Master Hammerson. And it is in my capacity as elector that I–'

'Who says you're an elector?' Hammerson snapped. 'Last I heard, electors carried runefangs – good dwarf weapons, those – and not whatever that monstrosity is.' He gestured towards the blade in von Carstein's hand.

Vlad smirked. 'I am an elector because the Emperor says I

am. And that means that we are allies, bound by old and sturdy oaths.'

Hammerson said nothing. Through the smoke, he saw Gelt slam the end of his staff down. The ground squirmed as great thorn-vines, composed of precious metals, rose from the earth and ensnared beastmen.

'He is quite talented, for a mortal,' Vlad said softly. 'He served me for a time, did you know that? And now he is redeemed and host to powers greater even than ours, runesmith.'

Hammerson hadn't known, and the thought didn't please him. Old doubts about Gelt, ones he'd thought he'd put aside, came back stronger than before. He looked at Vlad. 'What do you mean?' he growled.

'Things change, dwarf,' Vlad said. 'The world we pry from the jaws of destruction will not be the same as the one we remember. And old enemies might even be new friends, come that happy day.'

'Speak plainly, leech,' Hammerson spat.

Vlad sniffed. 'Fine. The Emperor is but a man. He will die, in time. Perhaps even in this war. As sole remaining elector, I will take his place. I would ensure that the ancient oaths between the Empire of man and the empire of the dwarfs are upheld, despite old grudges.'

Hammerson stared at him. Then he laughed. Great whoops of amusement tore their way from him, and he bent forwards, gasping with breath. Vlad stared at him in consternation. Ulgo and the others joined in, guffawing. The vampire turned, eyes narrowed.

'Oh, if that isn't the funniest thing I've heard in days,' Hammerson wheezed. He grinned at Vlad. 'And you accused me of paying too much attention to what might be. Ha! Trust a manling to start portioning out the stew before the pot's even warm. Even the dead ones, it seems.' The runesmith shook his head. 'Aye, vampire, we'll honour the old oaths, come what may. We'll defend the empire from *whatever* seeks to harm it.' He met Vlad's gaze and poked him in the chest with a finger. 'Be it living, or dead. Remember that, blood-drinker.' He turned away. 'Now be off with you. This is a time for fighting, not for talking. We have a battle-line to maintain, and I'll not have you flitting about, distracting my lads.'

Hammerson didn't bother to watch the vampire depart. He smiled grimly. *One battle at a time, Gotri,* he thought. *One battle at a time.*

'This is a waste of time,' Lileath said. She whipped her staff about, crushing skulls and splintering bones with a strength far beyond what her slight frame seemed capable of. Teclis stood at her back, his hands extended and the air sizzling with his magics. 'Every moment we stand undecided, is another moment lost,' she continued. Her staff shot forwards, puncturing the muzzle of a snarling gor in a spray of blood and broken fangs.

'I agree, but there is nothing to be done, my lady,' Teclis said. 'The others will not be swayed by pretty words or promises – especially not from me. Not now. My crimes are too numerous, my betrayals too fresh.' His sword hummed out, drawing blood and howls of agony from the enemy. He set his staff and lightning crackled from the tip, arcing out to smash into the ranks of beastmen. Contorted bodies were flung high into the air, to land smoking on the churned earth.

'Then you should have hidden your crimes better,' she snapped. Teclis almost snapped off a retort, but held his tongue. Though she had given the last of her power to slow the blight of Chaos, Lileath was still one of the ancient gods of elvenkind. And she was still the closest thing he had to a guide on the path he now trod.

In fact, it had been Lileath who had first set him upon that path. It was her staff he wielded, and her strength which had flowed through it, once, into him. As a goddess, prophecy had been amongst her gifts, and she had foreseen the End Times, and perceived the shape of their coming, long before his birth. It was she who had warned him of Aenarion's curse, and how it would twist Tyrion and doom their people. It was she who had convinced him of Malekith's legitimacy, and the need for the Incarnates. And it was she who had shown him how to bring Tyrion back from death, and what sacrifices would be required.

It had all been Lileath, and he had performed every task to her expectation save one – he had not been able to control the winds of magic. The shattering of the vortex had failed, and now the eighth wind was lost, somewhere in the east. If he strained his senses, he could feel it, just barely. It had found a host, he knew, though what sort of host he couldn't say. What he did know was that the Incarnate of Beasts was steadily moving west, pulled by the same sorcerous signal which had drawn the other Incarnates. But the host, whoever or whatever it was, would not reach them in time. Not unless they went out to meet it.

Then, united, the Incarnates could throw back Chaos once and for all. Or so Lileath had assured him. Even now, however, he wasn't sure. He watched her as they fought, studying her. Her determination was inhuman, greater than any save perhaps Nagash's, but was it truly bent in service to his cause? Was she truly fighting for the elves, or was there some other game being played? Some deeper purpose that the once-goddess had not seen fit to share with her servant.

His mouth twisted into a frown. Was that all he was now? A servant of fate? The thought did not sit well with him. Fate had ever been his enemy, from the first moment he had learned of the curse that had lurked in his and Tyrion's bloodline. Without thinking, he sought out his brother. As ever, Tyrion was deep in the maelstrom of battle, his form glowing brightly as he rode Malhandir through the press, striking down beastmen with every blow. The Emperor rode beside him on his screeching griffon, and though the human did not glow with power, his sword, and the claws and beak of his beast, took an equal toll.

The two were accompanied by Imrik and his fellow Dragon Princes, who crashed and swirled through the enemy ranks like lightning. The finest cavalry in all of Ulthuan, it was all but impossible to force them to maintain proper battle order. The Bretonnians too had joined with them, carving out a trail through the heart of the warherd. And above the massed charge flew Caradryan and his Phoenix Guard. The captain unleashed torrents of flame which burned only beastmen, and spared elves, men and trees alike.

And still, it was not enough. Teclis could feel the awful pulse of dark magics which hissed through the blood of the enemy. The Children of Chaos had ever been the fodder of the dark armies, and they had been called to Athel Loren in their thousands, united at last in common cause. They were not meant to succeed, he knew. They were but chaff, sent to die and keep the last redoubt under siege, until the Everchosen bestirred himself to launch a final attack.

The question was, why hadn't Archaon yet launched that attack? Why did he still sit north of the Grey Mountains, rather than flowing down and engulfing Athel Loren in fire and steel? Why not make an end of it?

There was something they were missing, some piece of the puzzle not yet fitted into place. Frustrated, Teclis whirled his staff over his head and brought it down. Crackling talons of lightning shot forth, catching nearby beastmen in their grasp. The creatures fell, wreathed in smoke. *What have we missed?* he thought. He heard the sound of a signal horn, and saw the Dragon Princes and the Bretonnians retreating. They flowed through the ranks of spearmen, who formed up behind them as the beastmen pressed forwards. He could hear elf nobles shouting out orders up and down the lines. They were buckling, and there was nothing anyone, even the Incarnates, could do. *And will we survive long enough to find out?*

He saw Imrik's standard bearer gallop past. The spearmen were falling back in good order, covered by bowmen and Alith Anar's Shadow Warriors as well as the dwarf Thunderers, but there were too many bodies in white and silver left behind. The battle-line was swinging inwards, folding in on itself as the press of the enemy became too great. Teclis set his staff, and readied a spell. It would not end here, but they would lose the Silvale Glade, and the enemy would draw ever closer to the heart of the forest-kingdom.

Then, a wash of cold, foul air filled the glade. The beastmen, once braying in triumph, began to edge back, suddenly uncertain. Teclis turned, and felt his blood turn to ice in his veins. Nagash had at last decided to act. The Great Necromancer had stood at the rear of the army, accompanied by Arkhan the Black, seemingly content to do nothing more than observe. But now, the Undying King moved slowly to the centre of the glade. The bodies of the dead twitched and stirred as he moved through them, and moaning souls were drawn in his wake. His nine books thrashed in their chains and snapped like wild beasts.

A minotaur charged towards him, roaring. Nagash's claw snapped out and caught the creature by the throat. Without slowing, or any visible effort, he broke the beast's neck and slung the body aside. Horns sounded and the elves retreated, streaming back from the liche. Teclis forced himself forwards. He doubted Nagash needed any help, and he wasn't inclined to offer it besides, but he was curious about what the Incarnate of Death was planning.

Nagash raised his staff in both hands, and brought it down. The ground groaned, and a circle of dead grass spread out from the point where the staff touched. Amethyst light blazed through ruptures in the soil. It grew brighter and brighter, and where it passed, beastmen died in untold numbers. Hundreds fell in moments, and fear swept through those who survived. Soon, those that the light hadn't touched were fleeing back into the trees. The herd was broken. Teclis released a shuddering breath.

Nagash lowered his staff and turned.

'IT IS DONE.'

'You... have our thanks,' Teclis said. Silence had fallen over the glade in the wake of Nagash's spell. Nagash strode past him without reply. Arkhan fell in step beside him. Vlad hesitated. He looked around, a slight smile on his face, and sheathed the sword he'd been holding. The vampire looked as if he'd participated in the fighting, at least.

'Well, I trust you're now seeing the benefit to our presence,' the vampire said. He grabbed Lileath's hand and bowed low. 'My lady,' he murmured. He released her and nodded to Teclis. 'Loremaster,' he said. Then he straightened, turned on his heel, and strode after Nagash.

'Though you did not choose him, I am forced to admit he is impressive,' Lileath murmured. She cradled her hand to her chest, and for a moment, Teclis wondered whether she was talking about Nagash or Vlad.

'I would be more impressed if he'd done that to begin with,' a harsh voice said. Teclis turned to see a familiar figure clad in blue and silver armour approaching, leading a horse in his wake.

'Well met, Imrik,' Teclis said. The Dragon Prince of Caledor looked as tired as Teclis felt, and worse besides. His once-proud bearing was bent beneath the weight of exhaustion, and his fine armour was hacked and torn and covered in gore. Imrik nodded curtly.

'The beasts are retreating, for now at any rate,' he said. His voice was hoarse from strain. He pulled off his helmet and ran a hand through his sweat-matted hair. 'They will return, though. In a matter of days, if not hours.' He turned his helmet over in his hands. 'There are more of them every time. It is as if every beast left in the world has gone mad, and come to Athel Loren.'

'You're not far wrong,' Teclis said. He looked up at the blistered sky, where the clouds seemed to congeal into leering faces which came apart as soon as he caught a glimpse of them. 'The Dark Gods muster their strength for some final blow – one which I fear will fall here, and soon.' He looked at Imrik. 'Can you hold them, if they come again?'

Imrik looked away, across the glade. 'Yes,' he said, after a moment. 'After that, however...' He trailed off. He shook his head. 'Your brother fought well, mage. He helped turn the tide here, as he did when the daemonspawn attacked the Oak of Ages. Hard to believe... what he was. It is almost as if it didn't happen.'

'Is it, Prince of Caledor? I find it all too easy to remember,' Teclis said. He watched as Tyrion picked his way through the carnage, sword held loosely in his hand. Even now, suffused by Light, he looked as if he belonged nowhere else.

'Aenarion come again,' Imrik said. 'And gone as quickly.' He looked at Teclis. 'Something must be done, mage. And soon... My forces are bled white while the Eternity King consorts with savages and worse things,' he muttered, casting a wary glance at Nagash.

'I know,' Teclis said. He leaned against his staff. His limbs felt like lead. 'I know.'

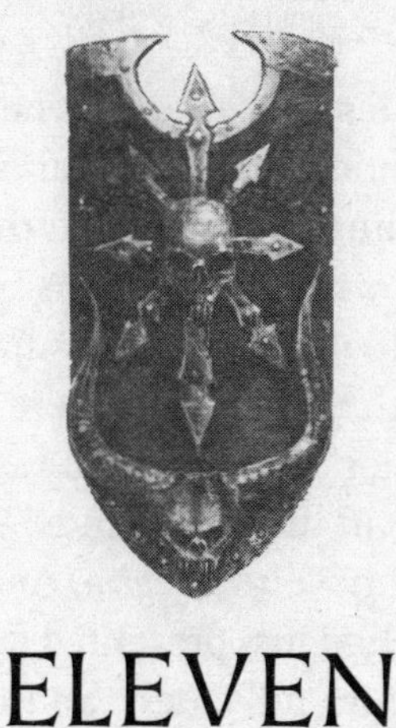

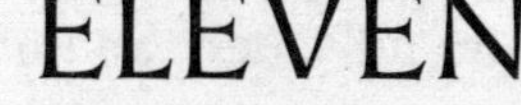

ELEVEN

 *Somewhere beneath the Eternal Glade*

Mannfred's eyes opened slowly. He had not been sleeping. His kind did not sleep, no matter how much it might have passed the time. He had been thinking, plotting his course should the opportunity for freedom present itself.

There were few paths open to him. Sylvania was a trap that would be his unmaking, if he dared cross its borders. Neferata would send his fangs back to Athel Loren without hesitation. The rest of the world was being consumed in a conflagration the likes of which even he had never seen, and he had no intention of dying alone and forgotten in some hole. No, there was only one route that promised even a hint of a chance at victory.

Middenheim, he thought bitterly. Middenheim, the heart of enemy territory. Having been rejected by his allies, he had no place to go but the arms of his former foes. Would they welcome him? He liked to think so. How could they not? Was Mannfred von Carstein not a pre-eminent sorcerer and tactician, a master of life and death? And did he not know many valuable secrets?

Indeed I do, he thought. So many secrets, including the

presence of the goddess of the moon herself. He smiled cruelly. His brief association with the branch wraith Drycha had yielded much, including the revelation that the Lady so assiduously worshipped by the Bretonnians was, in fact, the elven goddess Ladrielle, albeit in disguise. And since Ladrielle had kindly revealed that she and Lileath were one and the same, in the King's Glade earlier, it wasn't hard to see the weapon such information could be in the right hands.

But first, he would have to escape. And he judged that the opportunity to do so had just presented itself. A faint stirring of the air had brought him fully alert, and now his gaze roamed the shadows. There was a new smell on the air, indefinable but nonetheless familiar. Something was watching him. 'I smell you, daemon,' he said, acting on a hunch.

A shape moved out of the shadows on the other side of the bars. Great wings folded back as a horned head bent, and a voice like the grinding of stone said, 'And I smell you, vampire. You stink of need and spite.'

'And you smell like an untended fire-pit. What's your point?' Mannfred asked. 'I'd heard that the elves had chased you out of the forest with your tail between your legs, Be'lakor.' He gestured. 'They cast you out, as is ever your lot. It must get tiring, being thrown out of places you'd rather not leave. Shuffled aside and forgotten, as if you were nothing more than an annoyance.'

Be'lakor cocked his head. 'You are one to speak of being forgotten, given your current situation,' the daemon murmured.

'True, but you have fallen from heights I can but dream of,' Mannfred said. 'Be'lakor, the Harbinger, He Who Heralds the Conquerors, the Foresworn, the Dark Master. Blessed at the dawn of time by all four of the dark powers, you ruled the world before the coming of the elves. And now look at you... a shadow of your former glory, forced to scrabble for meaning as destinies clash just out of reach.' He smiled. 'One wonders what victory you seek here, in my guest quarters.'

'No victory, vampire. Merely curiosity,' Be'lakor said. 'And now that I have satisfied that, I shall take my leave.' The daemon prince turned, as if to vanish back into the shadows. Mannfred recognised the ploy for what it was. For an ageless being, Be'lakor had all the subtlety of a brute.

'Free me, daemon,' Mannfred said.

'And why would I do that, vampire?' Be'lakor asked. He stopped and turned. 'Will you promise to serve me, perhaps?' Obsidian claws stretched out, as if to caress the roots of Mannfred's cage. 'Will you sign yourself over to me, and wield those not inconsiderable powers of yours at my discretion?'

Mannfred laughed. 'Hardly.' He smiled. 'I know you, First Damned. I know your ways and your wiles, and our paths have crossed more than once. I saw you slip through the streets of comet-shattered Mordheim, and I watched from afar as you tried to break the waystones of a certain foggy isle in the Great Ocean. Your schemes and mine have ever been woven along parallel seams, though until now we have not met face to face.' Mannfred sniffed. 'I must say, I wasn't missing much.'

'You mock me,' Be'lakor rumbled.

'And you mock me, by implying that you would free me in return for my loyalty. We both know that such an oath, made under duress, would be no more binding than a morning mist.'

Be'lakor's hideous features twisted into a leer. 'Even if it were not made under duress, I would no more trust you than I would trust the Changer of Ways himself. You are a serpent, Mannfred, with a serpent's ambition. Power is your only master, and you ever seek it, even when it would be wiser to restrain yourself.'

'Ah, more mockery... Be'lakor, hubris made manifest, warns me of overreach. Did I not say that I know you, daemon? I have read of your mistakes, your crimes, and you are the last being who should warn anyone of the perils of ambition. There is a saying in Sylvania... grave, meet mould.' Mannfred chortled. 'I leave it to you, to decide which you are.'

'Are you finished?'

'I'm just getting started. I have nothing but time here, and nothing to do but to sharpen my wit. Shall I comment on your many failures next?'

Be'lakor growled. Mannfred subsided. He sat back, and smirked at the daemon. He'd planned to provoke the creature into attacking, and thus freeing him, but he had the sense that Be'lakor was too canny for such tricks, despite his lack of subtlety. 'No, instead, I think I shall offer thee a bargain. A titbit of some rare value, in return for thy aid in shattering the cage which so cruelly detains me.'

'And what is this bibelot, this morsel, that I should exert myself so?'

'Oh, something of great value, for all that it is but a small thing... a name.' Mannfred cocked his head. 'Much diminished, this name, but valuable all the same, I think.'

'Speak it,' Be'lakor said.

'Free me,' Mannfred replied.

'No. Why should I? What good is this name to me?'

'Well, it is not so much the name as the soul upon which it hangs. A divine soul, Be'lakor. One which has supped at the sweet nectar of immortality, but now is but a mortal. Helpless and fragile.'

'A god,' Be'lakor rasped. The daemon's eyes narrowed. 'The gods are dead.'

'Not all of them. Some yet remain.' Mannfred stepped back. He spread his arms. 'One, at least, is here, in this pestilential forest. Hidden amongst the cattle.'

'A god,' Be'lakor repeated, softly. The daemon's features twisted. Mannfred could almost smell the creature's greed.

'An elven god,' he said. 'One whose blood, mortal or not, contains no small amount of power, for one who knows how to extract it. I had considered it myself, but, well...' He motioned to the cage. 'I will gladly offer their identity in exchange for but the simple favour of cleaving these pestiferous roots which do bind me.'

Be'lakor was silent for a moment. Then, with a gesture, a sword of writhing shadows sprouted from his hand. He swept the blade across the bars, and Mannfred clapped his hands to his ears as he heard the trees which made up his prison scream in agony. He made to leave, but found the tip of Be'lakor's blade at his throat. 'The name, vampire.'

'Lileath, goddess of moon and prophecy,' Mannfred said, gingerly pushing the blade aside. It squirmed unpleasantly at his touch.

'Where?' Be'lakor growled.

'That was not part of the bargain,' Mannfred said. 'But, as I am an honourable man, I shall tell you anyway. The King's Glade. She sits on the Council of Incarnates, and listens to their bickering, no doubt plotting some scheme of her own.'

Be'lakor grinned. Then, in a twist of shadow, the daemon prince was gone. Mannfred sagged. Free of the deadening effect of the magics, he suddenly realised just how weak he truly was. Hunger gnawed at him.

He heard the rattle of weapons, and realised that Be'lakor's destruction of the cage had roused the guards. Mannfred smiled, and as the first elf entered the chamber, he was already in motion, jaw unhinged like that of a serpent and claws sprouting from his fingertips. He bowled the elf over with bone-shattering force and tore the spear from his grip. He hurled it with deadly accuracy, spitting the second and driving her back against the wall. With a growl, he tore the helm from the first guard's head and fastened his jaws on the helpless elf's throat.

Pain lashed across his back, even as he fed. He turned, jaws and chest stained with blood, and twisted aside as the sword came down again. The elf pursued him as he slithered away. Mannfred caught the blade as it stabbed for his midsection, and hissed in pain as the sigils carved into its surface burned his flesh. He drove the claws of his free hand into the elf's throat and tore it out.

He fed quickly, knowing that more guards were on their way. When he had supped his fill from each of the guards, he fled into the labyrinth of roots, taking care to keep to the shadows and to hide himself from the spirits which haunted Athel Loren. Freed of his cell, his magics had returned, and he had little difficulty in reaching the surface.

As he reached the open air, he tilted his head and sniffed. Escape was his most pressing concern, but he hesitated. He had been betrayed and humiliated. All of the plots and schemes he had concocted in his confinement came rushing back, and he savoured them. No, it wouldn't do to leave without saying goodbye. Nagash was beyond the scope of his powers. But he could still poison the well.

Which one will it be? he thought, as he glided through the trees, moving swiftly, conscious of the alarms which were even now being raised. The Incarnates were all, like Nagash, beyond him, though he hated to admit it. That left only certain individuals. And only one whose scent was close at hand.

Mannfred smiled as he set off in pursuit of his quarry. *How appropriate,* he thought. *Maybe fate is on my side after all.* If nothing else, it might prove amusing to take Be'lakor's prize off the table before the daemon got a chance to claim her. And if in doing so he could rend his faithless former would-be allies from a safe remove, all the better. Moving swiftly, he navigated the ever-shifting trails of the forest, avoiding the kinbands likely dispatched to bring him to heel, until he found the one he sought.

And then, with the surety of a serpent, he struck.

Duke Jerrod rose to his feet and spun, his sword flying from his sheath and into his hand. The point of the gleaming blade came to rest in the hollow of Mannfred von Carstein's throat. 'Do not move, vampire, or I will remove your foul head,' Jerrod said.

The Council of Incarnates was squabbling again, arguing over which course of action to take. He'd hoped that the battle with the beastmen would have seen them united at last, but such was not to be. Even as they'd returned to the glade, arguments had started anew. While Hammerson seemed to take a perverse pleasure in watching such rancorous discussion, Jerrod no longer had the stomach for it. It reminded him of the last days in the king's court, before Mallobaude's civil war. An enemy on the horizon, and all of them more concerned about getting their own way. Even demigods, it seemed, were not immune to foolishness.

He had been kneeling in the glade, praying to the Lady, asking for some sort of sign which might show him the way, when he'd heard a stick snap beneath the vampire's tread. Mannfred smiled and spread his hands. 'Why would I move, when I am where I wish to be, Duke of Quenelles?' He stepped back slowly, and bowed low. 'At your service.'

'I doubt that,' Jerrod said. He kept his sword extended, ready for any attack the vampire might make. His blade had been blessed by the Lady herself, and would cut through magic and flesh with equal ease. That said, he felt little confidence that he could do much more than distract the creature before him until aid arrived. Even in Bretonnia, the name of von Carstein was a watchword for savagery and death. 'I did not expect you to escape. Few make it out of the depths of Athel Loren alive.'

'Well, I'm not really alive, am I?' Mannfred said. His smile slipped. 'I am not much of anything now.' He paused, as if gathering his thoughts, and said, 'We are two of a kind, you and I... lords without lands, deceived by those we placed our trust in, and fought for.'

'We are nothing alike, vampire,' Jerrod said. A part of him screamed for the vampire's head. The creature deserved death for his crimes. But another part... He blinked. 'What do you mean "deceived"?' he asked, without thinking.

Mannfred pulled his cloak tight about him. 'You do not know, then. How unfortunate. But how in keeping with the selfishness of such creatures, that even now, when you have sacrificed so much, she still refuses to tell you.'

'She,' Jerrod said. He knew who the vampire meant. *Lileath,* he thought.

As if he'd read Jerrod's thoughts, Mannfred nodded. 'Yes, you know of whom I speak.' He frowned. 'I come now to warn you, Duke of Quenelles, as I wish I had been warned. A final act before I depart this malevolent grove, to perhaps rectify at least one wrong in my misbegotten life.'

'Say what you have come to say, beast.' Jerrod readied his sword. 'And be quick. I hear the horns of Athel Loren sounding in the deep glades. Your jailers will be here soon.'

Mannfred glanced over his shoulder, and then back at Jerrod. 'Lileath of the Moon, and Ladrielle of the Veil,' he said. 'I knew I had heard those names before, secret names for a secret goddess. A goddess of the elves... and of men.'

Jerrod hesitated. 'No,' he said, softly.

'Oh yes,' Mannfred said. He stepped close as Jerrod's blade dipped. 'They do like their amusements, the gods. How entertaining it must have been for her to usurp the adoration of your people, and mould you like clay.' He leaned close, almost whispering. 'Just think... all of the times you've sworn by the Lady, well, she was right there, within arm's reach. She heard every prayer, witnessed every deed.' Mannfred grabbed his shoulder. 'And said *nothing*.'

'No,' Jerrod croaked in protest. But it all made a terrible sort of sense. He could feel the connection between them, though he had not known what it was. And why else would the Lady have fallen silent, save that she was no longer the Lady, and had no more use for Bretonnia? He lowered his sword. For the first time in his life, he felt unsure. It was a strange feeling for him, for he'd never doubted himself before, not in battle or otherwise. But now...

He turned. Mannfred was gone. He shook his head. It didn't matter. The vampire wasn't important. Only the truth mattered. *He was lying, he had to be,* he thought as he hurried towards the King's Glade. But what he'd felt when he'd first laid eyes on her and every time since. The way she would not meet his gaze. The way she had stepped between him and Malekith. *Lying, oh my Lady, let him have been lying,* he thought.

No guards barred his way, for which he was thankful. He burst into the glade where the council was being held. His sudden appearance had interrupted Malekith's latest snarling rant, and all heads turned towards him. All save one.

'Lileath,' he said hoarsely. 'Face me, woman.'

Silence fell over the glade. Malekith waved his guards back to their positions. The Eternity King slumped back into his throne, and said, 'Well, face him, Lileath. Give the ape what he wants and maybe he'll slink back off to wherever he goes to hide when someone raises their voice.' Jerrod looked at him, one hand on the hilt of his sword. Malekith sat up. 'Ah, I was wondering when he'd figure it out,' he said softly, glancing at Alarielle. 'Such dim-witted beasts. Unable to recognise divinity, even when it is right beside them.'

'Be silent,' Hammerson barked. The dwarf stepped towards Jerrod, ignoring Malekith's sputtering outrage. 'Lad, what is it?'

'I know her name now,' Jerrod said. Hammerson frowned, but before he could speak, Lileath turned.

'And who told you that, Duke of Quenelles?' she asked.

'Is it true?' Jerrod replied.

'There are many truths,' Lileath said, after a moment's hesitation.

Malekith laughed bitterly. 'This is pointless. I shall have my guards remove the ape and the dwarf both. How are we expected to proceed with such distractions?'

'Proceed where?' Hammerson said. Thumbs hooked in his belt, the dwarf scanned the faces of the Incarnates. 'It's been weeks, and all you've done is given yourselves a pretty name. Even the great councils of Karaz-a-Karak move faster than this, when the enemy is on our doorstep. Distraction – pfaugh. I'd think you'd welcome it.' He patted the hammer stuffed through his belt. 'And I'll crack the skull of the first elf to lay a hand on me or the lad here.'

'There is no need for skull-cracking, Master Hammerson,' Lileath said. 'I shall speak to Jerrod alone, away from the council, if he wishes.' She looked at Jerrod and a wash of images flowed across the surface of his mind, memories and dreams, and for a moment, he was tongue-tied, humbled by her presence. He wanted to kneel.

Instead, he turned and began to leave. Lileath followed. They left the glade where the council met, and walked in silence to a nearby grove. For a while, the only sounds were those of the forest. The quiet shudder of branches, the rustle of leaves. And then, the sound of a sword being drawn from its sheath.

'Is it true?' Jerrod said.

'As I said...' Lileath began.

'No,' he croaked. 'No, do not play the mystic with me. I am only a man, and I would know whether or not my life has been a lie. I would know whether my people died for the games of a goddess not even our own.'

'Who told you this?'

'What does it matter?' Jerrod snarled. 'All you have to do is say that it is untrue. Say that you are not the Lady, and I will apologise. I will renounce my seat on the council, and we shall ne'er meet again. But *tell me*.'

Lileath was silent. Her face betrayed no anxiety, only calm. 'I do not deny it,' she said. Her voice was icy. 'Indeed, I am proud of it. I am proud of what I made of your primitive forebears.'

'You used us,' Jerrod said. 'We were but pieces on a game

board, dying for a cause that did not exist.' He raised his sword. 'We thought you were our guiding light, but instead you were merely luring us to our doom. Now the best of us are dead, and the rest will soon follow.'

'There was no other choice,' Lileath said. 'Prophecy was my gift, and I foresaw the End Times at the moment of my birth. I needed an army, and your people provided one.'

'Why us?'

Lileath looked away. 'Asuryan would never have countenanced the creation of a new race. Not after what was provoked by the crafting of the elves.' She turned and swatted aside his sword with her staff. 'I chose your forefathers to serve a greater purpose. I drew them up out of the muck, and gave them nobility and honour second only to that of the elves. Without the codes and laws that I gave you, your ancestors would have wiped each other out, or else been trampled into the muck by orcs or worse things.' She extended her staff, nearly touching his chest. 'Make no mistake, human. What you have, your honour, your lands, your skill, all of that is my doing. You owe me your life and loyalty, whether I be Lady or Ladrielle. And I make no apology for collecting on that debt.'

Jerrod heard a low, animal sound and realised it was coming from him. His sword arm trembled with barely restrained fury, and his blood thumped in his temples. The point of his blade rose. 'You are no goddess,' he whispered. 'You are a daemon.'

'No,' Lileath said. 'No, I am merely one who does what must be done.' She lowered her staff. 'It was necessary, Jerrod.' Her voice lost its ice, and became sorrowful. Her poise crumpled, replaced by resignation. 'The world is doomed. But that does not mean that hope is lost. There is a world – a Haven – where life may yet continue, even as this one is consumed in the fires of Chaos. Without Bretonnia's sacrifices, I could not have created it. Surely that is worth something?'

She stepped towards him. Her hand stretched out, and Jerrod

flinched back. 'Listen to me,' she pleaded. 'This war could never have been won. Not by you, or any of your brothers who died in service to the Empire, or in the civil war. But part of them, part of those who died, lives on in my Haven, protecting it from the evil which even now seeks to infect it. Even now, the spirits of your brothers, of all the knights who have ever died in service to the Lady – to me – fight on for a new world. A better world.'

'So even in death, you use us as weapons?' Jerrod said. A chill crept through him. 'Even our ghosts know no peace?'

Lileath dropped her hand. Her eyes were sad. 'What is a knight, but one who sacrifices for others?' she said, softly.

Jerrod stepped back. 'Small consolation, given that you were the author of that creed,' he spat. He shook his head. 'Is that all, then? Is that the story of us? Dogsbodies in life and death, serfs to immortal masters who see us only as weapons to be used and discarded?'

'Is that not what one does with serfs?' Lileath said.

Jerrod said nothing. He couldn't think, couldn't breathe. Why was he here? Had it all been for nothing? Lileath sank down to her knees, her skirts pooling about her. She bowed her head. 'If you do not believe me, then kill me, Jerrod, Duke of Quenelles. Kill me for what I have done. I ask only that after your honour – the honour I instilled in you – has been satisfied, you hold true to your oath and fight beside the Incarnates. Fight to hold back the darkness, so that a new world may be born.'

Jerrod hesitated. Then he raised his sword, taking a two-handed grip. He was ready, in that moment, to bring it down on Lileath's head. It was too much for him. The whole of his world, the philosophy by which he and all of his people had lived their lives, was nothing but a goddess's gamble. A game between inhuman forces, in which he and his were but pawns, raised up and spent with no more thought than a child might give to her toys.

'Why?' he croaked. 'Why did you do this to us?'

'I have already told you,' she said, softly. 'Saying it again will not help you understand. I made your people into the point of my spear, and used you as such. And now, you have turned in my hand, and your tip rests above my heart. Strike if you must.' Lileath looked up at him. 'But I would have your oath, before you do.'

'I... no,' he said. 'No, no more oaths, no more lies.'

'You will give me your oath,' Lileath continued, as if he had not spoken. 'You will swear to me, Jerrod of Quenelles, that you will fight alongside the Incarnates. That you will die for them, as you once might have died for me. You will swear this.'

'I will not,' Jerrod said. 'No more games of death on your behalf, or on the behalf of any other. You have broken us, ruined us, and my course is set. I...' He trailed off. The blade in his hand trembled. Before his eyes, he saw the faces of every slain Companion, and every fallen friend and family member. They had believed, and they had died, thinking that the Lady was watching over them. Instead, it had all been nothing more than a cruel hoax by a goddess who cared nothing for her people, or his.

But something held him back. Some tenuous strand of the man he had been, before Lileath had broken his certainties. Some small part which whispered to him that the deed he contemplated was unworthy of him. That to kill her, was to prove her right. To prove that her meddling and scheming had been necessary... That his people would never have found the light without her.

Jerrod looked down at her. He met her cool, alien gaze and said, 'You're wrong.'

Lileath blinked. Jerrod lowered his sword. 'You're wrong,' he said again. 'We owe you nothing. It is you who owe us, and you will not get out of our debt so easily.'

Lileath's eyes widened. She made as if to speak, but no sound passed her lips. She snatched up her staff and rose to her feet so quickly that Jerrod thought she meant to attack him. Then he heard the snap of great wings, and knew that Lileath hadn't been looking at him. He spun, and saw a dark shape explode from the shadows of the glade. Though he had never seen the creature before, Lileath clearly recognised it.

'Be'lakor,' she spat.

'Yes,' the daemon thundered as he charged forwards. 'I have come for you, fallen goddess. You denied me once, but now I will have both your soul and the Haven you boasted of for my own.' Wreathed in smoke and darkness, the daemon prince charged towards Lileath, shadow-blade raised, the glade shaking beneath his tread.

There was no time to think, no time to fear. Instinct took over. Jerrod stepped forwards, between the daemon and his prey. Be'lakor's sword smashed down against Jerrod's upraised blade, and the knight's arm went numb from the force of the blow. For all that the creature seemed barely substantial, it had a strength greater than any he'd ever known. Be'lakor's hell-spark eyes widened and his wings snapped, pushing him aloft. Leaves swirled about Jerrod, caught in the updraught as the daemon rose into the air.

He wished briefly that he'd thought to bring his shield. Then Be'lakor was dropping towards him, shadow-blade extended like a spear. Jerrod readied himself to meet the creature's attack but at the last second Lileath shoved past him, her staff in her hands. She raised it, and bolts of blinding light lanced from its tip to strike the approaching daemon. Or they would have, had they not passed through Be'lakor's form like arrows punching through fog. Jerrod reached out and grabbed the goddess by her shoulder, flinging her aside as Be'lakor swooped down over them.

He caught the creature's blow on his sword once again, and pain pulsed through his shoulder joint. As he stumbled, Be'lakor's free hand sliced towards him. The creature's black talons tore bloody furrows in his face and hurled him to the ground. Jerrod skidded backwards through the mud and fallen leaves. He slammed into a tree and rolled onto his face, struggling to suck air into his abused lungs. He was blind in one eye, and his cheek felt like a punctured water skin. Everything hurt, and thin rivulets of what could only be his blood crept across the ground.

With a groan, he levered himself up onto one knee. Using his sword, he tried to push himself to his feet, but his arms lacked strength. Be'lakor strode slowly towards him, trailing fire and smoke. 'Why do you fight?' the daemon prince gurgled. 'I heard all that passed between you, mortal. Your goddess has used you as badly as my gods once used me. She raised you up, and cast you down when you were of no more use.'

'While I can stand, monster, I will fight,' Jerrod groaned. He made to rise again, but his strength was gone. He toppled backwards. Be'lakor studied him for a moment. Then, with a grunt, the daemon lifted one clawed heel and slammed it down on Jerrod's left leg. Jerrod screamed as the force of the blow split his armour and pulverised the flesh and bone beneath.

'Now you cannot stand.' Be'lakor smiled. 'Do not feel obliged to interfere further, mortal. This is a matter for demigods.' Seemingly satisfied, the daemon prince turned away. Jerrod rolled awkwardly onto his side, and tried to pull himself towards his fallen sword as the creature closed in on Lileath.

Her eyes were closed, and spirals of glowing white energy began to form about her. Those spirals lashed out at Be'lakor as he drew close, and he bellowed in agony as wisps of his shadow thinned to nothing or were plucked from his body. Snarling, Be'lakor brought his blade down, smashing the staff from Lileath's hands and knocking her to the ground. 'You think to banish me?' Be'lakor roared. He smacked a fist into his chest. 'I am the First Damned, and older than any exorcism or rite of banishment. I have more right to stride this world than you, and I will not be cast out – not now, not ever!'

Jerrod's fingers closed on his sword. Biting back a scream, he plunged it into the ground and used it to haul himself upright. He lurched on his good leg, using the sword as a crutch, his eyes locked on Be'lakor's broad back.

Lileath scrambled away, her eyes wide. Be'lakor laughed. 'Is that fear I see in your eyes, little goddess? Prophecy was once your gift... Did you see this moment? Have you feared it all of this time? Is that why you offered your neck to the ape, so that you might escape your destiny?' He reached for her. 'Take it from one who knows, woman... There is no escaping destiny. There is only pain. Inevitable and unending.'

Lileath shied back from his outstretched talon, and Be'lakor leaned in. But he immediately reared back with a wail of pain as Jerrod lunged and slammed his sword into the daemon prince's back. Be'lakor thrashed wildly and Jerrod lost his grip on his sword, falling heavily to the ground. He rolled aside as Be'lakor's foot came down. The daemon prince's screams threatened to burst his eardrums, and he clapped his hands to the side of his head as the sound rose to agonising heights.

With a howl, Be'lakor finally tore the sword free of his back and flung it aside. But before he could move to finish its incapacitated wielder off, he was distracted by an ear-splitting roar that shook the trees to their roots. Large talons slammed into the daemon prince and knocked him sprawling.

The black dragon landed in the middle of the glade, giving vent to a second roar, louder than the first. Jerrod saw Malekith perched on the beast's back, sword in hand and a shroud of shadows curling about his lean frame. Be'lakor scrambled to his feet with a snarl and whirled as if to flee, but a thunder of hooves made him hesitate. A figure glowing as brightly as the sun hurtled into the glade and cut off the daemon's path of retreat.

Jerrod stared as Tyrion urged his horse up. The light which poured from the elf-prince incinerated the shadows which made up Be'lakor's form. The daemon prince reeled, and his body shrank and twisted, losing mass. Be'lakor lunged away from the newcomers and dived towards the welcoming shadows beneath the trees.

Malekith gave a sharp, mocking laugh and gestured. The

shadows about Be'lakor seemed to twitch and stretch, and the daemon prince snarled as he was dragged backwards. He fell, clawing at the ground for purchase, but to no avail. Even as he struggled, chains woven from light snagged him by his limbs and wings and horns, imprisoning him. The daemon was like a child before the power of the Incarnates, and soon, Be'lakor, who had thought to seize a goddess, had himself been made a prisoner.

Jerrod saw Lileath running towards him, and he wanted to speak, but no words came. Darkness crowded at the edge of his vision, and he fell back into oblivion, accompanied only by the frustrated shrieks of the First Damned.

TWELVE

 *King's Glade, Athel Loren*

Gotri Hammerson chewed on his cold pipe and stared into the dark. The sounds of celebration had died away quickly after Jerrod had entered the vast glade where the Bretonnians and the other refugees from Averheim had made camp. Now, there was no noise at all, as people retired to their cold meals or ragged tents and the glade fell into darkness. But it was no darker than a mineshaft, and so Hammerson sat and thought.

The duke had survived, but only thanks to the efforts of Athel Loren's healers. Even so, he was crippled, missing a leg and an eye. And all to save an elf woman who was not what she seemed. Hammerson sighed and adjusted his posture. He'd waited to welcome the lad back with the rest, after hearing of his heroism. But Jerrod had been in no mood for celebration or exultation. He had taken his men and retreated to the far edge of the glade, away from the other refugees and the Zhufbarak. Now the great camp was quiet, and Hammerson sat in the dark, wondering what had happened.

It was the elf's doing, he knew that much. Whatever else, he knew he'd been right to warn Jerrod away from her at the start. You couldn't trust elves, especially ones who claimed to have been goddesses. He tugged on his beard, wondering what he should do, or if he should do anything at all. Was there even anything he *could* do?

His hand fell to his hammer as he smelt warm metal and forge-smoke. He didn't look around as someone eased out of the dark to sink down beside him. 'The manling will live, then?' a rough voice asked. It was a voice such as the mountains might have spoken with.

'He will,' Hammerson said, after a moment.

'That is good.' There was a flash of heat, as a pipe was lit. 'They're fragile, humans.'

'But brave.'

'Aye, they are that. Too brave. Too rash.' Hammerson's companion puffed quietly on his pipe for a moment before continuing. 'Then, maybe these are the days for the foolhardy among us. The days of sealed holds are done. There will be no barred gates strong enough to resist what is coming, I fear.'

Hammerson turned to look at the white-bearded dwarf. Even now, a hood obscured his features, and he had his great, single-bladed rune-axe balanced on his knees. 'Is this to be it, then? Is there no hope, old one? Are our people to vanish into the hungry dark, unmourned and unremembered?'

'Aye,' the old dwarf said, softly. Then, he smiled and reached out to clap a heavy hand on Hammerson's shoulder. 'But we'll not go alone, lad.' He heaved himself to his feet, axe in hand. 'We'll march proudly into the dark, son of the Black Water, axes sharp and shields raised. We'll make the enemy pay for every inch of ground, and water the roots of the world to come with their blood, young Hammerson. That I swear.'

And then he was gone, as if he'd never been. Hammerson did not look for him. Grombrindal went where he wished, and no dwarf, daemon or god could hinder or follow him if he did not wish it.

'Who was he?' a voice asked.

'Who was who, manling?' Hammerson turned. 'I was wondering where you were. Not in a celebratory mood?' he asked.

'Not as such,' Wendel Volker said. 'I think they're planning to leave.'

Hammerson looked at the man. 'And why would you think that?'

'I heard Jerrod say as much, when I was eavesdropping,' Volker said. He held up a small cask as Hammerson glared at him. The little barrel was some unlucky dwarf's personal supply of drink, designed to hang from his belt or the inside of his shield. 'I didn't mean to. I was just going to get this,' Volker said, shaking the cask.

Hammerson's glare intensified. 'Is that one of ours?'

Volker popped the plug on the cask and took a swig. He smacked his lips. 'Yes,' he said, handing it to Hammerson. 'I got it off poor old Gorazin, after that last fight with the beastmen. He wanted me to have it.' The dwarf shook his head and accepted the cask. He took a long pull and handed it back.

The liquid burned going down. 'Gorazin knew his Bugman's, I'll say that for him,' he muttered. 'Not done, giving an ancestral cask on to a manling, though. Remind me to admonish him, when we get to the halls of the ancestors.'

'How am I going to do that? Seeing as I'm not a dwarf, I doubt I'll be going to those particular halls, lovely as they sound.' Volker took another swig.

'You've drunk enough Bugman's over the past few weeks to be a dwarf. I think the gods will overlook your abnormal height,' Hammerson said. He stuffed his pipe back into his armour and added, 'Did you come out here just to get a drink, or did you have something to say?'

'The council requires your presence. Or so the wizard says,' Volker said, stuffing the plug back into place. He belched and rose to his feet. 'Gelt convinced the rest of them that the daemon should be interrogated. The wizard thinks knowing what

Archaon's up to might help the council come to some sort of decision. They're about to question the beast. Gelt thought you'd like to be there for it.'

'Aye, that I would,' Hammerson said. He rose to his feet and gestured. 'Lead on.'

When they reached the King's Glade, Be'lakor had already been brought before the council. The daemon prince had traded his chains of light for shackles of silver and starlight, and he looked the worse for wear, surrounded by the levelled halberds of Malekith's Black Guard. Be'lakor knelt at the centre of the ring of heavily armoured elves, his body shrunken and battered. His wings had been clipped and broken, and one horn had been smashed. The elves had not been gentle on their captive.

Not that I blame them, Hammerson thought as he and Volker joined the Emperor and Gelt. The dwarfs too had their stories of the Shadow-in-the-Earth, and his fell deeds were carved into the record of grudges for many a clan and hold. It was said that Be'lakor had been responsible for the destruction of Karak Zhul, among other crimes.

Malekith reclined on his throne, Alarielle beside him. Tyrion stood to the left of them, and Caradryan to the right. Teclis and Lileath stood at the foot of the dais. The latter looked hale and healthy for a woman almost stolen away by a daemon, Hammerson thought. Then, maybe the gods of the elgi were made of sterner stuff than gossamer and moonbeams. Nagash, as ever, stood away from the rest, accompanied only by Arkhan the Black and Vlad.

'I heard the other vampire escaped,' Hammerson murmured, looking at Gelt. 'Slipped clean away in all the confusion.'

'He can't have got far,' the Emperor said. 'Athel Loren is a trap from which there is no escape, I'm told.'

Gelt shook his head. 'You don't know Mannfred. He's escaped, otherwise Vlad wouldn't be here,' he said, nodding towards the vampire. 'If Mannfred were still loose in this forest, Vlad would be on his trail. That he's here instead...' He shrugged.

'What's one more monster loose in the world, eh?' Hammerson said. He fell silent as Malekith rose from his throne.

The Eternity King looked down at Be'lakor. 'Well, beast. What have you to say for yourself? I would have thought that you'd have learned your lesson when you came for the Oak of Ages and we sent you scuttling off back into the dark.'

Be'lakor looked up, eyes smouldering with hatred. 'Did you ever learn from your many, many attempts to conquer Ulthuan, Witch-King?' Be'lakor looked at Teclis. 'Or did you have to wait for someone to do it for you?' The daemon prince laughed.

'At least I accomplished it in the end,' Malekith said. 'You, unfortunately, have been descending ever further into cosmic irrelevance with each passing century. Look at you – you're barely a ghost now. Just a flickering blotch at the corner of my vision, a whisper easily ignored.'

Be'lakor looked at the halberds pointed at him. 'You do not seem to be ignoring me.'

'No,' Alarielle said. She did not rise, but her voice commanded immediate attention. 'You have made that impossible, beast. You must be dealt with.'

'And yet here I kneel,' Be'lakor growled.

'Destruction is far too merciful for a creature like you,' Malekith said. He glanced at Lileath as he spoke. 'Besides, who knows how long you've been flitting about, listening to our councils? Why send you back to the Realm of Chaos, where your dark spirit would merely inform your masters of what you've learned?' Malekith gestured derisively. 'No, I think we can do better than that.'

Be'lakor laughed. 'I do not fear you.'

'THEN YOU ARE A FOOL,' Nagash said. *'LONG HAVE I BEEN CURIOUS AS TO THE DURABILITY OF CORPOREAL MANIFESTATIONS SUCH AS YOURSELF. HOW MUCH IS FLESH AND HOW MUCH IS THOUGHT? I SHALL DISCOVER THE ANSWER AT MY LEISURE. AND YOU? YOU WILL HOWL.'*

Be'lakor stared at the liche, as if trying to gauge the truth of his words. Then he laughed. The sound was a bitter one, full of malice but also resignation. It was the laugh of a master who had met his match. 'I know you, Nagash of Khemri. I saw you place yourself on your father's throne, blood still wet on your hands. And I know that you will do as you say, and worse besides.' He looked at Malekith. 'What must I offer, to escape the tender mercies of the Lord of the Charnel Ground?'

Gelt stepped up. 'Information, daemon. We wish to know why the Everchosen sits in Middenheim, and allows beasts to lay siege to this place. Why has he not come himself?'

'Perhaps you're just not that important,' Be'lakor said. Malekith gestured, and the shadow-stuff which made up Be'lakor's form writhed for a moment. The daemon shrieked and shuddered. Malekith lowered his hand, and Be'lakor sagged, panting. The daemon prince laughed weakly. 'It is the truth,' he hissed. He looked at Gelt. 'Three times, I have sought to pre-empt the Everchosen's successes with my own, and three times I have failed. But there will not be a fourth. So I will speak. I will tell you all that I know.'

He shoved himself to his feet. The Black Guard stepped back as one at Malekith's gesture, giving the creature room. Be'lakor looked around. 'Archaon has no reason to come to Athel Loren, for he already has what he desires – what the gods themselves desire. You think them directionless. You think them to be mad, idiot intelligences, but they are anything but. There is purpose in the random, and direction in the storm. The destruction of your petty Empire was never the goal,' he said, leering at the Emperor. The latter didn't so much as bat an eye, and Hammerson felt his respect for the human grow.

'The gods care little for the slaughter of nations, or the deaths of kingdoms. Oh, they dine well on the souls offered up so, but Middenheim is the true prize. Middenheim, and what lies beneath it,' Be'lakor continued. His eyes strayed to Volker and the daemon twitched back. Volker shuddered and made a low sound in his throat, but the Emperor placed a hand on his shoulder, calming him. Be'lakor blinked, and said, 'There is an artefact there, a device from an earlier age, before the coming of Chaos. Even now, Archaon works to excavate it.'

'What sort of artefact?' Teclis demanded, voice hoarse. Hammerson was startled by the elf's expression. He had never known one of that race to ever show such raw horror so openly before. The mage was white-faced and trembling.

'One which, if certain rites are performed, will detonate. It will create a rift in the fabric of your colourless reality. A rift to equal those which occupy the poles of this broken world.' The daemon prince smiled. 'So you see, you are not important, for you have already lost.'

'Well, I don't see it,' Hammerson blurted out. 'What is this overly talkative soot-stain hissing about?' He looked at Gelt, who shook his head helplessly.

'It means the end of everything, dwarf,' Teclis said. 'The end of the world.'

Teclis sagged. He felt as if his strength were but a memory. Everything he had done, every sacrifice he had made... all for nothing. He felt Lileath reach out to steady him, but he flinched away from her. He forced himself up, and looked around. Every eye was upon him now, waiting for answers only he could provide. Answers that he did not wish to provide. He closed his eyes and cleared his throat. 'The Loremasters of Hoeth theorised that our world only survived the coming of Chaos because a terrible equilibrium formed between the two polar rifts. They cancelled one another out, and became stable. But if a similar rift is opened in Middenheim, with no counterbalance...' He trailed off, unable to get the words out.

'THE WORLD WILL BE CONSUMED,' Nagash said.

'It might take years, or days or mere moments,' Teclis said. 'But if that rift is called into being, if it hasn't already been called into being, the end is certain.' He looked around. Horror and fear was etched onto every face.

I did this, he thought. If he hadn't taken the Flame of Ulric, Middenheim might have withstood the siege. Tyrion would be dead, but the world might have survived. He had sacrificed everything to resurrect his brother, and now it was all for nothing. The world was doomed regardless. He closed his eyes and pressed his head against his staff. *My fault,* he thought. *Forgive me, please.*

When he opened his eyes, he saw the man, Volker, staring at him. The human's eyes had gone yellow, and something terrible and lupine was superimposed over his own features. It was invisible to the others, he knew, save perhaps Lileath and Nagash. But the godspark was there, crouched in the dark of Volker's soul, waiting. The wolf-god met his gaze and licked his chops. Teclis shuddered and looked away. No wonder the god persisted. Teclis had bet the world and lost, and now his debt was fast coming due.

'THE ARTEFACT MUST BE SEIZED,' Nagash rasped.

'Middenheim is too far, liche,' Malekith said. 'Too much territory to cover, and too many enemies between us and it. The worldroots have withered, and we do not have the manpower to make such an invasion feasible.' The Eternity King sank back into his throne. 'The daemon is right. We lost this fight before we even drew our blades.'

Silence fell. Teclis tried to think of something. He had always had a plan, even in the darkest moment. But nothing came to him now. There was no path to take that did not lead to destruction. He felt a hand on his back, and turned as Lileath stepped past him. She was shaking slightly, and he wondered again what had passed between her and Jerrod, before Be'lakor's attack. He had had no time to ask, and he doubted she would tell him.

'Impossible or not, it must be accomplished,' she said, her voice cold and hard. 'The artefact must be destroyed. Together, you have the power to do it, and to thwart this madness before it overtakes us all.'

'Were you not listening, woman? There is no way,' Malekith snarled. He thumped his throne with a fist. 'We do not have the troops or the time.'

'Then use magic to make up for both,' Lileath said coolly, not looking at him.

'I know such magics – I used them to help us escape Averheim – but I cannot transport so many such a distance,' Gelt said. 'And even if I could, to unleash such magics in close proximity to the rift might prove disastrous. We might precipitate the very catastrophe we hoped to stop.'

'Nonetheless, it must be done,' Lileath said. 'There are no more options. There is only this path, this certainty – if we do not act, the world dies.'

'The world is already dead,' Be'lakor said. 'You merely seek to postpone its burial.' He looked up at Malekith. 'Well, Witch-King? Have I bargained for my life satisfactorily?'

Malekith sat silently for a moment. Then he laughed harshly. 'Oh yes, I'd say so. You will have life, of sorts.' He gestured. 'You shall be broken on the Anvil of Vaul, daemon, and sealed in ithilmar.' He looked at the Everqueen.

Alarielle reached up, and plucked a ruby from her crown. She handed it to Malekith and said, 'This ruby shall be your cell. The essence of you shall be sealed within its facets, once my... husband has cracked your bones and stripped you of your flesh.'

If Malekith had noticed Alarielle's hesitation in referring to him as her husband, he gave no sign. Instead, he held up the ruby and continued, 'Thus bound, you shall be sealed away, deep beneath the Glade of Starlight, in a prison of root and stone which shall outlast even the Rhana Dandra. You shall live, in the dark and the quiet, while the world lives or dies about you.'

Malekith leaned in. 'Your story is done, daemon. It has come to its final ignominious conclusion.'

Be'lakor snarled and made as if to lunge up the dais, but the halberds of the Black Guard flashed and the creature fell, squealing. He cursed and screamed as he was dragged away, Caradryan and Malekith following in his wake to see to his imprisonment. Teclis watched them go. The council had broken up without making a decision, but he had expected as much.

'Fools,' Lileath said, watching as the Incarnates drifted away to discuss events with their advisors and allies. 'Can they not see what is made plain?'

Teclis did not reply. He took a deep breath. The air was thick with the dry smell of changing seasons, as winter overtook the forest. Finally, he said, 'You told me that we could win. Is that still the truth?'

Lileath looked away. 'No.'

'Was it ever the truth?' Teclis asked softly.

Lileath looked up. 'I knew from the first that this doom would come upon us.' She laughed bitterly. 'What sort of prophet would I be otherwise?'

'You lied to me,' Teclis said, fighting to keep his voice even.

'You told me once that you could not fight without hope,' Lileath said. She looked at him. 'So I gave it to you. I needed you, Loremaster.'

He felt sick. 'It was all for nothing then.'

'Not at first,' Lileath said. She spoke hurriedly, her words clipped and forceful. 'By the sacrifices you made, I wrought a great working – a Haven. A place of safety that would have seen your people – *our people* – through the coming storm.' She smiled sadly. 'But... I cannot feel it any more.'

'What happened to it?'

She turned away. 'I do not know. Maybe it still exists. Maybe the Dark Gods found it, and have already consumed it and the untold souls within, including my brave Araloth and... our child.

My daughter.' Her voice cracked. 'I cannot feel my daughter, Teclis.'

Teclis stood helplessly as she began to weep. Then, without a word, he turned and walked away.

'You will not stay, then?' the Emperor said, as he helped Jerrod onto his horse. 'Your sword will be missed, Duke of Quenelles.'

It had been several days since Be'lakor's interrogation and imprisonment. The elven healers had done what they could in that time for Jerrod, but the marks of the daemon's claws remained. His face was a ruin, one eye covered by a ragged length of cloth torn from a standard. His leg was almost useless, a lump of dead meat held together only by his armour. Even so, Jerrod felt he had got off lightly.

Jerrod looked down at the other man, and smiled sadly. Volker and Hammerson were there as well to see the Bretonnians off. The dwarf looked glum, and Volker looked drunk. Jerrod thought it was appropriate, seeing as they'd looked much the same when he'd first met them. He shook his head. 'We cannot stay. I have told you why.' He looked out at the western edge of Athel Loren, where the trees grew thin and gave way to the vastness of Quenelles, and felt his heart grow heavy.

'I know,' the Emperor said. He reached up and clasped Jerrod's forearm. 'And I do not begrudge you your anger. I hope... I pray that you find some sanctuary in this world, Jerrod. I hope your people survive and flourish, and that one day, we again feel the ground tremble beneath the hooves of the true sons of Bretonnia.'

'Thank you, my friend,' Jerrod said. The Emperor nodded and stepped back. Jerrod looked at Volker and Hammerson. 'Goodbye, my friends. It has been an honour to fight beside you. Both of you.'

Volker clasped his hand, and stepped back to join the Emperor without speaking. Hammerson glared up at Jerrod for a long moment. Then, with a sigh, he said, 'If you ever have need of the Zhufbarak, lad, you have my oath that we will come. So long as your kith and kin exist, we shall stand at their side.'

'And will you lead them, then?' Jerrod said, smiling.

'If I don't die in the next few days, certainly,' Hammerson said. He hesitated, and then patted Jerrod's leg. 'Maybe I'll even make you a new leg, eh?'

Jerrod laughed softly. 'I look forward to it, Master Hammerson.'

Hammerson nodded tersely and stepped back. Jerrod watched the three of them return to the forest, and did not feel slighted at their departure. There were plans to be made and a war to be won or lost. But it was not his war, not any longer. The elves had lied to them, and no knight in his company wished to fight alongside those who had used them so.

Before he could set his horse into motion, however, he heard the drumming of hooves, and turned to see four riders approaching out of the dark. He tensed as he recognised Vlad von Carstein in the lead. 'Well met, Duke of Quenelles,' the vampire called out, as he drew close. 'Might I have a word, before you leave?'

'A quick one,' Jerrod said brusquely.

'I wished to impart a story I heard, not long after my resurrection,' Vlad said, dismounting as his steed drew up beside Jerrod's. 'I think you'll find it interesting.'

'I do not have time for stories, vampire.'

'You have nothing but time,' Vlad said. 'And this is no ordinary story. It is about a monastery.' Jerrod blinked in confusion, but said nothing. Vlad leaned forwards. 'There is said to be a monastery, somewhere in the Grey Mountains, where Gilles le Breton has decided to make his stand,' he murmured. 'I had it from the mouth of one who rides with us now – a mad creature, whom your folk knew as the Red Duke.' He turned and gestured to one of the other riders. Jerrod looked past him, and met the malignant gaze of a nightmare out of legend. The Red Duke sat proudly in the saddle of his skeletal steed, one hand on the pommel of his infamous blade. At first, he scowled at Jerrod, but then, after a moment, he dipped his head in a gesture of respect. Jerrod returned the nod before he could stop himself. He looked back at Vlad.

'In that place, it is said that your king fights beside a knight garbed in crimson, in defence of what remains of your people,' Vlad went on.

'A red knight...' Jerrod murmured. He looked at Vlad. 'He is one of your kind. Like... the Duke. Like you.'

'No. Not like that sad, mad warrior or like me. Abhorash is the best of us,' Vlad said softly. 'He owed a debt to your king, and swore an oath, and while he fights, Bretonnia lives. In some small corner of your shattered land, the heart of all that was Bretonnia *survives*.'

'Why do you tell me this?' Jerrod asked hoarsely.

'Because I know that it was Mannfred who broke your faith, and set you at odds with Lileath. And because I too know what it is like to lose everything. To lose your home, your people, even your gods.' Vlad turned away. 'I would not wish it on anyone.' He looked back at Jerrod and smiled. 'Even a man who, under other circumstances, would be doing his level best to remove my head.' He stepped back. 'The Red Duke knows the way. He will lead you to your people, if they yet live. And two others will go with you, to see that you and your men arrive safely, and that your guide does not... get out of hand. Erikan Crowfiend and Elize von Carstein, a daughter of my blood and a son of the Bretonni. They are old, and strong in the ways of our kind.'

Jerrod looked at the other two vampires, on their mummified steeds. One was a haughty-looking, crimson-haired woman, the other a dishevelled, broad-faced man. Their steeds stood so close together that the knees of their riders touched. As Jerrod watched, the man took the woman's hand. He blinked, and looked down at Vlad.

'You can trust them. And when you reach your sanctuary, tell Abhorash that...' Vlad hesitated. He laughed and shook his head. 'Tell him that he was right, in the end.'

'About what?' Jerrod asked, without thinking.

Vlad chuckled and turned away, pulling his cloak tight about himself. The vampire hauled himself into the saddle and rode away, leaving Jerrod staring after him. After the vampire had vanished, Jerrod turned. His people waited. He looked at the Red Duke.

'Well?' he asked, softly.

The creature turned his skeletal steed about. 'West,' he growled. 'To the fires beyond the horizon, and into the mountains.' With a shout, the vampire kicked his mount into a gallop. The other vampires shared a look, and then followed suit.

Duke Jerrod, the last son of Quenelles, inhaled the clean air of Athel Loren one last time. Then he spurred his horse into motion. And the knights of Bretonnia followed.

 *The Winterglade, Athel Loren*

'I should not be here,' Eldyra of Tiranoc said. Even marred as it was by a predator's rasp, her voice was still a thing of beauty. Measured and graceful, more so than any human could hope to mimic. 'I have no right to this place.' She looked from side to side slowly, staring at the trees and the shadows. 'Not any longer.'

'And who told you this?' Vlad said, softly. He walked beside her, hands clasped behind his back, seemingly at ease. In truth, he was as nervous as she, for Athel Loren contained dangers even for creatures like himself. Nonetheless, he felt a sense of satisfaction. After the revelations of the council, it felt good to accomplish something, anything. Even if it was only honouring an old debt.

He wondered if the Bretonnians would make it. He hoped so. There was little enough nobility in the world, and for it to pass away entirely was not something he wished to see happen. *What might you have made of them, Abhorash, if you had not made that oath?* He smiled. What might he make of them still?

Too, it was good to know that at least one of his bloodline might survive the coming conflagration. Whatever else happened, the von Carstein name would not die. *Oh Isabella, you would be so proud of your little Elize,* he thought, and then frowned. He rubbed his neck where Isabella's blade had hacked his head from his shoulders, only a few months before, and thought of his loving paramour and the twisted fate which had befallen her. The gods were cruel, and cunning. They had snatched Isabella's soul from Nagash's grasp, and brought her back. They had bound her tortured soul up with that of a daemon of plague and pestilence, in an act equal parts malice and mockery, and set her loose on Sylvania.

It was that attack which had roused Nagash, and convinced the Undying King that he required allies. And it was that attack which had convinced Vlad of his course. In order to save Isabella, he had to save the world. And that meant making alliances, and binding together the separate strands of the remaining forces opposed to the Ruinous Powers, whether they liked it or not. And the only way to convince them to stand together was to give them hope that there would be a world, come the morning.

Of course, it would be helpful if I believed that, he thought sourly. In the attack, he and Isabella had met, and she had killed him. Granted, it wasn't the first time Isabella had stuck something sharp in him, but it was the first time she'd done so with such an excess of malice. He growled softly, and pushed the thought aside. The Dark Gods wanted him to agonise over her fate, to falter and hesitate. But he was not one to crumble beneath the pangs of loves lost or imperilled. He loved her, and he would do what he could to save her. He would free Isabella one way or another, even if he had to take her head to do it.

That was one lesson Mannfred had never bothered to learn.

Loyalty went both ways. He owed as much to those of his bloodline as they did to him. Thinking of Mannfred gave him pause to wonder where his former disciple had vanished to. That he had escaped Athel Loren was obvious. As to where he had gone, well, he had had several days to get there. Vlad pushed the thought aside. Mannfred was a problem for another day, if another day ever dawned.

'No one had to tell me I wasn't welcome here,' Eldyra hissed. She wheeled about, perfect features cracked and uncertain. The beast poked through her bones. Then, it was never very far from the surface in elves. They were as savage as any barbarian hillman, for all the airs they put on. Perhaps even more so. He smiled.

She had been waiting at the edge of the forest while he saw the others off. Given the events of the council, he'd thought it best to clear up all lingering questions, debts and worries. One needed to be free of mind to properly enjoy a cataclysm, after all.

'Then how do you know? Does your flesh burn? Does your soul cringe? If not, then there is no bar to your presence here. Indeed, I had hoped that a walk through these woods might even soothe your unquiet spirit somewhat.' Vlad gestured airily about him.

Eldyra stared at him. She opened her mouth to speak, but instead turned away, hugging herself. Vlad frowned and reached for her. She whirled and slapped his hand aside. She hissed, eyes red and wild. Vlad backed away, hands held out in a pacifying gesture. 'You have not fed. The beast is harder to control when you are starving.'

'Blood will never cross my lips,' she spat.

'It already has, otherwise you wouldn't be in this situation, my dear,' Vlad snarled, letting his own mask slip. 'And if you continue down this path, you will lose what little sanity remains to you.' He spread his arms. 'We do not die of starvation, princess of Tiranoc. We merely shed our skins, like snakes, losing all pretence of humanity. *Vargheist*,' he said. He gestured. 'Too much feeding, the same. Varghulf, then. The beast is always lurking, just below the skin. It rages like a fire, and like a fire, it requires careful tending.'

'Better to snuff it entirely, then,' she croaked. She looked down at her hands. 'I will not be a slave to darkness.'

'You are not a slave. You are one of night's dark masters,' Vlad said. He held out his hand. 'Take my hand, and I will teach you, as I have taught so many. You have been given a gift, and I would not see it go to waste.' Eldyra strode past him. He laughed and caught up with her. She needed to be taught, even as Isabella had. As they all did. And he had brought her here, so that she might speak to the only man who might help her learn.

They found Tyrion in a clearing, but he wasn't alone. The Emperor stood beside him. They were speaking quietly as they watched the burning sky. He held up a hand, and Eldyra halted. Her eyes were fixed on Tyrion, and she trembled slightly. Vlad gestured for her to remain silent. Despite the distance, he could hear their conversation as clearly as if he stood beside them.

'I see little cause for hope,' Tyrion said.

'Meekly spoken, for one who has returned from the dead,' the Emperor said. Tyrion glared at him. Vlad smiled. *A point for the man without a kingdom,* he thought.

'It will take more than clever words to survive the coming doom,' Tyrion said. 'Even for you, god-king.' Vlad blinked. Had that been a turn of phrase? If so, it was surely an odd one. Vlad cocked his head, considering. There was something about the Emperor, it was true... Vlad felt a vague sense of unease whenever he drew too close to the man. As if there were some force within him which threatened the vampire's very existence. Until now, he'd put it down to the lingering traces of the magic which had reputedly been torn from the Emperor. But what if it were something else?

'That is why you and I must persuade the others to go to Middenheim,' the Emperor said. 'Lileath is right. Archaon must be stopped. At any price.'

'The city lies many weeks' march away, through territory swarming with foes. Do you honestly believe that we can prevail against such odds? Even with the aid of our... allies, it will be almost impossible.'

The Emperor grunted. 'I shall not sit back and wait for death.'

Tyrion was silent for a moment. Then he shook his head. 'No. Nor shall I. To Middenheim we shall go, then. And whatever fate awaits us there.'

'Not immediately, one hopes,' Vlad said, smoothly.

Tyrion and the Emperor turned, and Vlad winced. The elf glowed with an internal light that was almost impossible to bear. He heard Eldyra whimper, and clamped a hand on her shoulder. 'Stand, for his sake, if not your own,' he murmured. Still clutching her, he bowed low. 'My Emperor, I have come before you, seeking a boon.'

'I was under the impression that your master was Nagash,' the Emperor said, with what might have been a slight smile on his face.

'Ah, but a man may have many masters,' Vlad said, straightening. 'Some, even, by choice.' He smiled ingratiatingly. 'I am Elector of Sylvania, am I not? Indeed, I fancy I am the last elector, besides your gentle self, my lord.' Vlad's smile turned feral. 'Aye, if you were to die I would, by default, become emperor, would I not?'

'No, you would not,' the Emperor said.

'No?'

Karl Franz smiled. 'The emperor must be elected by a majority of electors.' His smile turned hard and cold. 'The dead, unfortunately, do not have a vote.'

Vlad frowned. He was about to reply, when Tyrion said, 'Why are you here, vampire?'

'I believe you know my companion, O mighty prince,' Vlad said, stepping aside. Eldyra twitched, as if she might flee.

'Eldyra,' Tyrion said, softly. She froze, quivering. She took a hesitant step. Tyrion, his face sad, held out his hand. 'I feared you dead, sister of my heart.'

'I am dead,' she hissed. Her fangs flashed in the moonlight. 'I died in Sylvania. I failed and died, cousin. And now I pay the price.'

Tyrion said nothing. He merely held out his hand. Eldyra hesitated. Then, she reached out and took his hand. Vlad watched as Tyrion led her off, out of earshot. The Emperor looked at him. The human showed no fear, no disgust. Only curiosity. Vlad was impressed. The Empire had improved the calibre of its aristocracy since he had last walked abroad, he thought. 'Why did you bring her here?' Karl Franz asked.

'What else could I do?' Vlad said. He shrugged. 'She is of no use to me as she is. Maybe he can make her see sense.'

'Meaning to accept her fate,' the Emperor said, looking at Tyrion and Eldyra. 'To surrender to the curse which has been thrust upon her. To give herself up, like a lamb to the slaughter.'

'No,' Vlad said. 'To fight. To live!' He shook his head. 'We all must make sacrifices if we are to survive. She has only two paths before her - acceptance or madness. And the world is mad enough already.'

'There are always other paths,' the Emperor mused. Vlad made to reply, when he heard the sound of a sword being drawn. He turned, and his eyes widened. Eldyra knelt before Tyrion, her head bowed. Tyrion stood over her, sword raised, his face expressionless.

'No,' Vlad snarled. He reached for his sword, but froze as he felt the edge of the Emperor's runefang slide beneath his chin. Karl Franz had drawn the blade so swiftly, so silently, that Vlad hadn't noticed.

Before he could react, Tyrion's blade fell. Vlad closed his eyes and looked away. Anger pulsed through him, but he fought it down. He looked up, at the Emperor. 'Why?' he growled.

'She asked me to,' Tyrion said. Vlad turned to him.

'You had no right. She was mine,' Vlad hissed. 'She was of my blood.'

Tyrion sank down beside the body, which was beginning to smoke and crumble into ash. He drew his fingers through it, and sent it swirling into the air. 'She was my friend,' he said, after a moment. 'How could I refuse her?' He looked at Vlad, and the vampire turned away, raising his cloak to cover his face as the light seared him. 'Go now, Vlad von Carstein. You have my thanks, for what it is worth.'

'I do not require your thanks,' Vlad spat.

'You have it, all the same,' the Emperor said. He sheathed his blade. 'You will find us in the King's Glade tomorrow, as ever.'

Vlad backed away. 'Yes, another day of acrimonious indecision ahead of us. How thrilling.' He stopped as the Emperor looked at him.

'No. No, one way or another, tomorrow will see the path ahead made clear. I expect to see you there, Elector of Sylvania.' The Emperor turned away, and placed his hand on Tyrion's shoulder.

Vlad hesitated. He had seen something there, a shadow-shape superimposed over the man's frame, a giant made of starlight and the sound of clashing steel. Part of him wanted to kneel and swear fealty to the thing. Another part, the oldest part and the wisest, wanted nothing more than to run away.

Vlad listened, and fled.

THIRTEEN

 *The Silvale Glade, Athel Loren*

Prince Imrik, once of Caledor, now of Athel Loren, coughed as the tainted smoke clawed at his lungs. Smoke from the pyres stained the sky, and a film of ash clung to everything in the glade. As fast as they burned the bodies of the beastmen, new pyres had to be lit. The creatures came again and again, heedless and mad.

Nagash's display had only scared them off for a few days. They had returned, in greater numbers, driven forward by inhuman impulse. The entire glade stank of that madness, and whole seas of blood had been spilled. Whatever else happened, the glade would never recover from the carnage which occurred beneath its boughs.

How did it all come to this? The same thought had rattled in his mind since Ulthuan had broken apart and vanished into the hungry ocean. Could it have been prevented? Could any of it have been changed?

Imrik did not think so. At least not by him. He knew who was to blame, whose schemes had unravelled the very thread which bound their world together. But there was no refuge in recrimination. And revenge - well, there was no time for that either. Whatever Teclis had done, he had done because it had seemed the right thing to do. Imrik knew what that was like well enough. He had made similar decisions himself.

He had joined Malekith's side during the war for the promise of dragons, and unity in the face of the storm seeking to devour them all. He had sacrificed his own ambitions on the altar of necessity, on the advice of a ghost. Caledor the First had spoken to him in his dreams, and showed him what must be done. Tyrion had gone mad, his mind and soul subsumed by Khaine. Malekith was the lesser of two evils, and whatever else, he was the true heir of Aenarion. Too, he had glimpsed chinks of nobility gleaming through the calloused soul of the Eternity King. In those moments, he knew that Malekith was the only one who could lead the elves into a new, better world.

Unfortunately, the world seemed to have other ideas. Horns sounded, and he signalled his men to regroup. The beasts were coming again. 'Archers to the rear, spears to the fore,' he roared. The tactic lacked elegance, but it had served them well so far. Arrows thinned the herd, and the spears did the rest. He and his knights would break any knot of beastmen too strong to fall to arrow or spear. *Like Vaul at his anvil,* he thought, with grim amusement. He readied himself, testing the weight of his lance. He looked around at his knights.

They were the finest knights in the world, survivors of the battle at the Isle of the Dead. To an elf, they looked tired, worn down. Only duty sustained them. Imrik had long ago run out of words and speeches. He met the eyes of the closest of the knights, and said, 'Princes of the Dragonspine, ride with the speed of Asuryan, and fight with the valour of ages.'

He turned back to the battle as the first herds burst from the treeline. They pelted full-out, with no discipline or order or hesitation of any sort. Arrows flew, and those first herds died. Imrik sat up in his saddle. There was something different this time.

There was something on the air, some thickening of the light and stink of battle. He looked up. Red clouds roiled above the trees, as they had for weeks. Some said that they could see faces in those clouds, but thankfully, whatever lurked in the sky had never revealed itself to him. His horse grew restive, pawing at the earth. Its eyes rolled in fear. He reached down to stroke the animal, and found it was trembling.

The din of battle grew muted and faint, but a new sound quickly intruded. It was as if all sound and fury had been drawn to a single point and squeezed into a throbbing pulse. Imrik saw an arrow take a beastman chieftain in the throat. As the arrow sank into the hairy flesh, it seemed to reverberate with a sound like thunder.

And then, with an ear-splitting crack, the world burst asunder.

The ground churned as the blood-soaked meadows ran like water drawn into a whirlpool. Trees were uprooted and smashed, and beastmen exulted as they were swept away by the bloody tide. Those elves closest to the writhing vortex of blood and darkness tried to scramble back, out of reach of the ground that snagged and grasped at them. Some made it, some did not. 'Fall back,' Imrik roared. 'Fall back!'

The beastman assault had ended, but he could feel the earth screaming, and knew that something much worse was coming. His horse stamped and whinnied in terror, but he held tight to its reins. Whatever it was, it would not find Imrik of Caledor a coward.

Horned figures, red and lanky, burst from the roiling firmament and threw themselves at the collapsing battle-line of the elves. They were joined by baying daemon-hounds, and behind them came shapes even more monstrous – larger than any minotaur, with wings and horns and great roaring voices which called down the blessings of the Blood God.

Imrik shouted orders, but it was no good. There was no discipline, only fear, and his army bent in two and broke as the daemonic horde smashed through their centre like the tip of a blade. He urged his horse forwards, through the broken ranks of fleeing elves. *King's Glade, they're heading for the King's Glade,* he thought. He had to stop them, though he knew not how. His knights followed, picking up speed as the army dissolved around them. Imrik lowered his lance and pointed his charger towards the largest of the daemons.

His lance splintered as it struck the creature, and it reeled with an angry bellow. But before his steed could carry him past, Imrik found himself smashed from the saddle by a fist the colour of dried blood. He hit the ground and rolled, his body convulsing with pain. He coughed blood as he tried to rise, but his legs refused to work. He struggled to draw air into his bruised lungs as he clawed weakly for his sword.

A heavy weight came down on his back, pressing him flat to the ground. He was enveloped in the stink of butchery and slaughter, and could only glare up at the being holding him down. 'You are not the one I seek, little elf,' the bloodthirster growled. 'And anyway, the Lord of Pleasure has claim on your pathetic soul. But you struck a blow, and for that, I give you your life, such as it is. Take it and run, and do not seek to put yourself between the Blood Hunt and its prey.' Then, with a triumphant roar, the beast sprang into the air, its powerful wings flapping.

Unable to move, wracked with pain, Imrik could only watch in horror as the daemonic tide flooded towards the King's Glade.

The King's Glade, Athel Loren

'Then we are decided. Middenheim must be taken,' Lileath proclaimed. The elf woman stood in the centre of the glade, staff in hand, the focus of every eye and thought. 'Even if it costs our lives to do so.'

Gotri Hammerson let out a sardonic cheer. He had anticipated another day of acrimonious wrangling, but had been pleasantly surprised to find that the Incarnates were, for once, of one mind.

Even Malekith and Nagash had no objections to raise. Privately, Hammerson wondered whether it had been the departure of the Bretonnians which had motivated the accord. The absence of Jerrod and his men further reduced the forces available to the council, should the need for battle arise. They couldn't take the chance that others – like the Zhufbarak – might follow suit.

You might have done us a favour, lad, though you'll be sorely missed, he thought. He glanced up to find the Emperor looking at him. The man had a slight smile on his face as he turned away, and Hammerson shook his head. He knew for a fact that Karl Franz had visited most, if not all, of the Incarnates the night before. *Was that why you didn't stop him from leaving, then? Did you need a pair of tongs to stir the fire with?*

He was a cool one, was the manling Emperor. He moved people like pieces on a board, and was always two or three moves ahead. Not that it had helped him at Averheim. Nonetheless, he was more formidable than the dwarf had expected. Hammerson looked at Vlad von Carstein where the vampire stood, as ever, beside Nagash. He recalled what the creature had said in the Silvale Glade, and he snorted. *You'll have a hard time supplanting that one, blood-sucker, elector or no. He's already divided your loyalties, and you don't even realise it.*

Suddenly, alarm-horns sounded from the outer glades. Hammerson looked around, one hand following to his hammer. The air in the glade grew thick, and he could taste smoke and ash in the back of his throat, though he was nowhere near a fire. He saw Gelt stagger, and reached out to steady the human. 'What is it, lad?' he growled.

'My... my head,' Gelt said, cradling his skull. 'I can feel it – feel them!'

Hammerson whipped around as Alarielle screamed and fell from her throne, to collapse on the dais. Both Malekith and Tyrion went to her side. 'What in the name of Grimnir is going on?' he snarled.

The glade was filled with a sound like tearing metal, and then a body flew into the glade. It crashed down, broken and bloodied. Hammerson recognised it as having been one of the ceremonial guards stationed outside the glade. Even as the body struck the ground, the air was filled with the stamp of cloven hooves and howls of eagerness. Nightmares made flesh streaked into the glade, before the dead guard's body had even settled or the echoes of Alarielle's scream had faded.

The daemons loped towards the dais, steaming blades bared, seeking flesh. And then they combusted into crackling ash as Tyrion rose to his feet, drew his blade and seared them from the fabric of the world with a blinding wave of light. Caradryan was the next to act, his halberd spinning in his grip, creating a vortex of hungry flame which enveloped another group of daemons and reduced them to greasy motes on the air.

Even before the ashes of the Incarnates' victims had settled, a chorus of howls announced the arrival of a second, larger wave of daemons. The creatures burst into the glade from all sides, tearing through the undergrowth. Black blades glistened in the crimson hands of the hissing bloodletters as they loped towards their intended prey.

Caradryan flung out a hand and a wall of flame roared to life, catching a score of bloodletters in mid-leap. Some of the daemons survived the flames, however, and they came on, skin aflame. Caradryan set his feet and swept out his Phoenix Blade, killing one even as the rest bowled him over. Hammerson was about to go to his aid, when he heard a screech and saw the elf's firebird plummet into the glade like a flaming comet. The great bird tore the daemons from its master, flinging them across the glade, and Caradryan sprang onto the animal's back as it swept back towards him.

'Master Hammerson, to your left,' the Emperor shouted, as his runefang snaked out to block a blow that would have taken his head. Hammerson turned and caught a descending blade on the crossed hafts of his weapons.

He forced the bloodletter's blade aside and rocked forwards, slamming the front of his helmet into the creature's snarling features. The daemon shrieked and fell back, clawing at its face. 'Why bother putting runes on your helmet, Gotri?' Hammerson said, mimicking the voice of the runesmith who'd trained him. 'That's why, you old goat,' he spat, as he cut the bloodletter's legs out from under it and crushed its skull with his hammer.

The Emperor fought beside him, his steel caked in daemonic ichor. The human fought in silence, moving with the precision of a hardened veteran. Though the power he'd once wielded had been ripped from him, he was no less a warrior. Hammerson felt a moment of pride as he watched Karl Franz fight, and knew that he had made the right choice in staying. This was a man who was worthy of a dwarf oath. Even if he did ride an oversized buzzard.

Hammerson glanced at the dais as lightning flashed over his head. A nimbus of light played about Tyrion's head and rippled from his blade to scour daemons from existence. Beside him, Teclis swept his staff out, wrenching lightning from the air and sending it snarling outwards to throw back the encroaching daemons. Near the twins, Malekith wielded his own magics, shadow-claws tearing at daemonic flesh.

As the tide of daemons pressed in, intent on reaching the Incarnates, the three were forced to fight back to back to protect the unconscious form of Alarielle. In that moment, all differences, all past conflicts, were forgotten and the last of Aenarion's bloodline fought as one against an enemy as old as time itself.

Hammerson shook his head and smashed a leaping daemon-hound from the air, before he spun to crush the skull of another with his axe. 'Come on, filth! Come and taste the steel of Zhufbar!' he roared, clashing his weapons. 'Though the Black Water might have fallen, her people still fight – come and take what you've got coming to you.' The runes on his weapons flared and the air became as hot as a forge, to burn and blacken the flesh of the scuttling daemons. They fell twitching and squealing, and he finished them off quickly.

More took their place. They charged towards him, howling out hissing prayers to the Lord of Skulls, and Hammerson felt a twist in his gut. There were too many for him to fight alone. But he set his feet and hunched forwards. 'You want me? Come and get me,' he muttered. Before the first of the creatures could reach him, however, he heard a scream and felt a breeze. A massive wing smashed the daemons aside as the Emperor's griffon, Deathclaw, landed in the glade. Hammerson glanced nervously up at the beast as it prowled past him, tail lashing. That nervousness faded as he saw more daemons bounding forwards. The griffon crouched, and Hammerson knew that even with the beast at his side, they'd be hard pressed. He looked up as a shadow fell across him, and saw Arkhan the Black, mounted atop his monstrous steed.

The liche seemed unconcerned with the battle raging below him. 'A little help?' Hammerson bellowed. Even as he spoke, he knew his words were futile. To such a creature, he was likely more use dead than alive. Arkhan turned away, as if the conflict below bored him. A knot of daemons burst past Deathclaw and flung themselves at the runesmith. Hammerson was knocked sprawling, his weapons flying from his hands. He drove a bunched fist into a leering face, and felt a flush of satisfaction as fangs snapped and the creature pitched back. But the others bore him down.

As his back hit the ground, however, the weight of the daemons vanished. He looked up and saw the creatures turning to dust. As they dissolved on the breeze, he saw Arkhan the Black looking down at him. The inscrutable liche held his gaze for a moment, and then turned away. Hammerson snorted and retrieved his weapons.

'Don't expect me to say thank you,' he grunted, as he clashed his weapons and readied himself to face the next wave of foes.

* * *

Vlad von Carstein did not wait for Nagash's permission before he leapt into battle. Let the Great Necromancer do as he saw fit; Vlad wanted nothing more than to lose himself in combat, if only for a little while.

He was frustrated and angry, and the daemons paid the price. He whirled and stamped, fighting with all the fury of an Arabyan dervish one moment, and then with the blunt force of one of the war-monks of Cathay the next. He slid from style to style, indulging in the raw physicality of combat. His sword flashed as he recalled lessons in peach orchards and vineyards, on dusty training grounds and ice-floes.

The bloodletters responded, coming for him like flies to spoiled meat. He spun, parried and thrust, using their numbers and his speed to his advantage. As he fought, he heard again the sound of Tyrion's blade striking home, and the soft whisper of Eldyra's essence fading. Again and again, he saw it, heard it, felt it, and his rage grew.

He knew why she had done it. Indeed, he was surprised she hadn't done it herself. But he did not understand, and he cursed himself for a fool. If he had not taken her into the grove, then she would have lived. Unhappily, perhaps, but she would not have tossed away her life to no purpose. That, in the end, he could not forgive.

Fool, he thought, *you had the power to make a difference. The power to set your world right, and instead you threw it away and for what – honour? Disgust? Fear?* Mannfred should have known better than to allow his servants to turn Eldyra and give her their dark gift. Elves were too fragile, at their core. Too enamoured of their life as it was, to see the glory in becoming something else. Like the dwarfs, they were stagnant, trapped in themselves.

Thinking of Mannfred, he wondered where his student had fled to. He had set the Drakenhof Templars on his trail, but Mannfred had eluded them all. Now he was loose in the world, doing who knew what. *I wish you well, boy. May you at last have learned something from your mistakes.*

Vlad bent backwards with serpentine ease, avoiding the sweep of a black blade. He righted himself and drove his sword home, impaling the daemon. It folded over his arm, clawing at him weakly. He shoved it aside with a disdainful sniff.

He heard the screech of metal on metal and turned to see another of his former protégés, Balthasar Gelt, fighting side by side with Lileath. They had joined their magics, unleashing a molten storm of metal on the pack of flesh hounds bounding towards them. Several of the creatures were torn apart by the storm, but still more made it through, the brass collars about their necks glowing white hot. One of the slavering hounds leapt for the former goddess, jaws wide. Its pounce knocked her sprawling, and Gelt was too distracted to lend aid.

Vlad was at her side in an instant. He snatched the daemon from the air and dashed it down. As it struggled to right itself, he thrust his blade through its throat. He tore the sword free and spun, slashing a second hound in two in a single motion. As one the remaining hounds bayed and loped towards him, ignoring Gelt and the elf-woman, as Vlad had hoped.

He dispatched them efficiently and quickly, moving among them like a bolt of dark lightning. Wherever he struck, a flesh hound fell dead. When the last sank down with a querulous whine, he stepped back, and helped Lileath to her feet.

'You... saved me,' she said.

'One does what one can, in these trying times,' Vlad said. He inclined his head to Gelt. 'And are we not allies? Sworn to defend one another, against a common foe?'

'And what about your master?' Gelt said. The wizard swung his staff out in an arc and the air was filled with glittering shards of silver, which plucked a bevy of bloodletters off their feet and sent them crashing down some distance away. Vlad turned.

Nagash stood alone, at the heart of a writhing amethyst vortex, surrounded by heaps and piles of withered, steaming daemon corpses. Fragments of broken bone and torn flesh swirled about him, dancing upon the unnatural winds he had called into being. The air about him was thick with wailing spirits, and at his merest gesture, daemons fell.

'Nagash needs no aid,' Vlad said, with a shrug.

'No,' Lileath murmured. She looked pale, and Vlad could smell the fear on both her and Gelt. Even his fellow Incarnates, it seemed, were not immune to the horror that was the Undying King. 'Nor is he alone in that.' She looked up. Vlad followed her gaze.

Above them, Malekith's black dragon twisted through the air, breathing dark, poisonous fumes wherever daemons clustered. And where the dragon's shadow touched, blackfire constructs in the shape of Malekith himself rose to howl across the glade, immolating any creature which stood against them.

Then the air was stirred by thunder and heat, and Vlad could taste the coppery tang of blood in his throat as roaring shapes, larger than any bloodletter, dropped towards the glade from above, crashing down like the fists of Khorne himself. Vlad was nearly knocked from his feet by the force of their arrival. Lileath fell with a cry, and Gelt was only able to remain standing thanks to the support of his staff. 'Bloodthirsters,' the wizard said, as Vlad hauled Lileath to her feet once more. The wizard whistled sharply, and the sound was answered by a shrill whinny as his pegasus darted through the upper reaches of the glade.

'More than that,' Lileath hissed. 'It is the Blood Hunt – bloodthirsters of the Third Host.'

'You say that as if I should care,' Vlad said. 'One daemon is much the same as another.'

'The same could be said of vampires,' Lileath said.

Vlad looked at her. He smiled. 'I stand corrected. I– Look out!' He caught hold of her and jerked her aside as Caradryan's firebird crashed down into the glade, its body entangled in the whip of one of the bloodthirsters. The Incarnate of Fire was hurled from the saddle, and skidded through the carnage.

'One side,' Gelt said. The wizard caught hold of his pegasus's mane and hauled himself into the saddle as the animal galloped past Vlad and Lileath. With a snap of its great wings, the pegasus thrust itself into the air and hurtled towards the fallen Incarnate, even as daemons pressed close about him. Vlad was tempted to join Gelt in his rescue attempt, but there were enemies aplenty, closer to hand.

Besides which, it was clear enough to him that Gelt had matters under control. The wizard cast chains of gold and air about the bloodthirsters as they descended on his fellow Incarnate, and held them back through sheer force of will. Caradryan rose to his feet, halberd in hand, and flames rose with him, reaching out to incinerate the roaring daemons where they struggled against Gelt's magics.

Vlad stepped back as a bloodletter lunged for him. The creatures reminded him of the more feral of his kind, all brute instinct and no skill or finesse. Back to back with Lileath, his sword reaped a deadly toll on the bloodletters that careened towards him without an ounce of self-preservation between them. Lileath thrust out her hand and bolts of cold moonlight speared forth, causing daemonic flesh to smoulder and sear where it touched.

'Well struck, my lady,' Vlad laughed. 'We might win the day yet!'

'We are outmatched, brother,' Teclis said, as he caught a daemon's blade on his staff and forced it aside. As the creature staggered, off balance, he drove his sword into its side and angled the blade to catch its foul heart. The creature came apart like a fire-blackened log as he pulled his sword free. His arm ached from the force of the blow, and sweat stung his eyes. 'There are too many of them,' he panted. He couldn't catch his breath.

'And what would you have me do? I'm killing them as fast as I can,' Tyrion snapped. He beheaded a bloodletter with a swipe of his sword and turned, pressing two fingers to his mouth. He whistled sharply.

'Calling for your steed, then? Planning to leave us so soon?' Malekith growled. 'I never thought you a coward, whatever else you were.' Shadow tendrils lanced from the Eternity King's form and speared a pack of howling flesh hounds as they loped up the dais.

'No – he's right,' Teclis said, forcing himself to stand up straight. 'There are few of us, and many of them. We must keep moving and spread out, unless we wish to be overwhelmed. Make them divide their forces, and draw them to the strongest Incarnates. We will destroy them piecemeal.'

Malekith grunted. He looked down at Alarielle. The Everqueen was still unconscious. 'What of her?' he asked, his voice softening, though only slightly.

'I shall guard her with my life,' Teclis said.

The Eternity King looked at him and laughed hollowly. 'I am sure she will appreciate it.' He raised his hand, and with a roar that shook the glade, his dragon swooped towards him. Malekith shot skywards on a column of twisting shadows, and was in the saddle moments later. The dragon roared again and Malekith laughed wildly as the beast crashed into one of the newly arrived bloodthirsters, coiling about it like an immense black serpent.

Two more of the bloodthirsters raced towards the dais, their mighty hooves churning the soil. One leapt into the air with a single flap of its leathery wings and flew towards them with a bone-rattling bellow. 'This one's mine,' Tyrion said. He extended his sword and a burst of cleansing light shot from the blade, clipping the daemon's wing. The bloodthirster smashed into the dais with a startled roar. Before it could recover, Tyrion reversed his blade and leapt, driving the sword into the beast's skull with both hands. As he tore the blade free, the second hurtled past him, towards Teclis.

Teclis gritted his teeth and smashed the end of his staff down. Magic flowed through him, and out, assailing his opponent. All eight winds were his to command, and he did so now, battering the daemon with amber spears, thorny growth, blistering starlight and searing flame. Blinded, bleeding and burned, the creature crashed down onto the dais, and did not move again. Teclis met Tyrion's gaze, and the latter nodded curtly.

Tyrion turned as his steed, Malhandir, galloped through the press of battle, bowling over flesh hounds and trampling bloodletters. He vaulted into the saddle, hauled on the reins and turned the horse's head east, towards the spot where the Emperor and Hammerson fought. Teclis silently wished his twin well.

Every muscle in his body ached and he could feel his strength beginning to ebb. The Incarnates had reserves of power he did not possess, and he was drawing near his limits. He looked down at Alarielle. There was no telling why she had collapsed, but he thought it likely had to do with the eruption of a daemonic portal so close to the heart of Athel Loren. As the Incarnate of Life, she was tied body and soul to the living world. The opening of such a portal would have felt much like a red hot blade being driven into her flesh.

A shadow fell over him, and he looked up in horror as another bloodthirster dropped towards he and Alarielle. His exhaustion forgotten, he raised a hand and hurled a bolt of cerulean lightning at the daemon. The creature roared as the bolt struck home, but it did not fall. It landed on the dais, the ancient white wood cracking and warping beneath the touch of its hooves. The beast loomed over him, reeking of blood and offal. He thrust his staff forwards, calling forth more lightning.

The bloodthirster shrieked and stomped up to him, hacking at him with its axe. The blow smashed into the dais, narrowly missing him. Teclis tumbled backwards. Before he could get to his feet, the axe was descending on him again. Hastily, he interposed his staff, knowing that it wouldn't protect him even as he did so.

The axe halted, bare inches from him. The bloodthirster gave a strangled cry as it staggered back. Teclis's eyes widened as he saw thick tendrils of plant life coil about the beast's wings, legs and arms. And beyond it, he saw Alarielle on one knee, her palm pressed to the dais. The wood buckled and ruptured as more roots thrust through it and snagged the struggling daemon. The creature bucked and thrashed, snarling, but for every tendril it ripped free, more tightened about it.

'This is my domain, beast,' Alarielle said, as she rose to her feet, 'and you are not welcome here.' She made a fist, and the bloodthirster screamed as the roots suddenly burrowed into its flesh. As its roars reached a crescendo, she opened her hand, splaying her fingers. A moment later, the bloodthirster convulsed and then was torn apart by the flailing roots. As chunks of daemon pattered down, Teclis climbed to his feet.

'Alarielle, I–' he began.

'Quiet,' she said. She turned and surveyed the ruin that had been made of the glade. Her features contorted into an expression of grief and anger. 'The forest is screaming. It is caught in a nightmare which does not end. It must awaken,' she snarled. 'Do you hear me? Awaken.' She raised her hands, and swept them out as she spoke. '*Awaken and fight!*'

And before Teclis's disbelieving eyes, it did.

It happened swiftly. At first, there was only the sound. Deep and sonorous, it was akin to the rumble of a distant avalanche. Then, all around the glade, trees began to move, their roots tearing free of the clammy ground as their bark flexed and twisted into half-remembered shapes. In ones and twos the ancient guardians of Athel Loren were jarred awake by the cry of the Everqueen. The ground shook with a fury unseen since the days before the coming of the elves as the forest began to move.

Ponderous at first, and then faster and faster, the gnarled feet of the newly awakened treemen thudded home into the sod, propelling them into battle with the ravening daemons. They erupted from the forest on all sides, hurling themselves at the enemy with creaking roars. Bloodletters and flesh hounds alike were smashed aside or trampled underfoot and brass-fleshed juggernauts were crushed like tin as the ancient guardians of the forest roared into battle with the invaders. Daemons scattered like dead wood caught in a gale.

Teclis watched in awe as Athel Loren awoke for the first time in millennia. It was as beautiful as it was terrifying, for the forest unbound was as powerful in its own way as the Dark Gods, and equally as deadly.

Only where the treemen clashed with the bloodthirsters did their advance slow. The greater daemons were shards of Khorne's rage made manifest, even as the treemen were splinters of the great soul of Athel Loren. Not since the first incursion of Chaos had such a battle been waged. Lesser daemons were crushed as the titans battled, and even the Incarnates were not immune to the fury of the creatures. Teclis saw Arkhan nearly swatted from the air by the wing of a bloodthirster, and a moment later, his brother was almost crushed by a toppling treeman.

A roar sounded, echoing above the din of the colossal battle. Teclis looked up, and saw a black shape, vast and terrible, dropping towards he and Alarielle. One of the treemen climbed the dais and sought to ward off the new arrival, but the ancient was no match for the newcomer. A great hammer, covered in ruinous sigils, thudded down, and the treeman's arm evaporated into a cloud of charred splinters. As the guardian reeled, an axe hacked deep into the thick bark. The treeman fell with a groan. A moment later, its head vanished beneath the hoof of the bloodthirster as it climbed the dais to confront Teclis and Alarielle.

'Ka'Bandha of the Third Host, Huntsman of Khorne, bids you greeting,' the creature rumbled. 'The Lord of Skulls has laid claim to this forest and every scalp within it, and it is my pleasure to claim them on his behalf.' As it spoke, the creature drew closer, until it loomed over them. It raised its hammer.

'Prepare thyselves, for thy doom is come...'

FOURTEEN

 *The King's Glade, Athel Loren*

Teclis stared up at the beast, and felt fingers of dread claw at his heart. He knew the name Ka'Bandha, for it was associated with many dread prophecies and dark futures. The Huntsman of Khorne stalked his prey across the vast sea of infinity, and had last trod the world during the previous great war against Chaos, when Teclis had helped the human leader, Magnus, escape the clutches of the Blood Hunt.

As he had done then, so many centuries ago, Teclis called up the lightning and cast it into the leering face of damnation. Jagged bolts of crackling energy struck Ka'Bandha; hissing magics crawled across the daemon's armour, and sparks played over the runic crown it wore. Ka'Bandha laughed gutturally, and bore down on them.

Two more treemen moved to cut the daemon off. They bounded up the dais with great, creaking leaps. Ka'Bandha cut down the first one without slowing, but the second caught the daemon a blow on the back with both of its fists, dropping the brute to one knee. Ka'Bandha roared and swung to face its attacker, ignoring the lightning that Teclis continued to hurl at it. The treeman caught the daemon's thick wrists in vine-laced fingers.

For a long moment the two creatures stood almost motionless, straining against one another. Teclis knew that the contest would not last forever. Strong as the guardian was, the daemon was stronger. He reached out, trying to grasp the faint strands of Ghur which permeated the glade. Though the Wind of Beasts was not strong here, it could still be manipulated, if he but had the strength. Catching it, he sent it flooding into the treeman, giving the guardian new strength. He staggered, and Alarielle caught him.

Ka'Bandha roared in baffled fury as it was slowly pushed back by its opponent. The bloodthirster opened its fanged maw and vomited a torrent of deep and ruddy flame into the treeman's face. The ancient guardian was consumed in moments, and Ka'Bandha ripped its arms free in an explosion of charred wood. The bloodthirster whirled on Teclis and Alarielle, burning spittle dripping from its jaws. 'I will have your skulls for such effrontery, little elves,' Ka'Bandha growled.

Teclis stared at the beast in growing horror. He had faced untold daemons over the course of his life, and he had bested them all. But this beast seemed resistant to everything he hurled at it. *Is this it, then?* he thought, as the creature's shadow fell over him. *Is this my debt come due at last?* It seemed fitting – an elf could only taunt the gods for so long before they turned their full attentions upon him.

Ka'Bandha's axe flashed down, and Teclis reacted on instinct, interposing his staff. The force of the blow drove him down, and pain thrummed through his arms and shoulders. His magics could protect him, but not for long. He glanced over his shoulder, intending to tell Alarielle to run.

The Everqueen ignored his panicked exclamation, and set her staff. The stuff of life itself writhed about her in a shimmering halo of all colours and none. Thorny vines burst from the cracked expanse of the dais and sought to snare Ka'Bandha, as they had the other bloodthirster. But unlike the earlier beast, Ka'Bandha easily tore itself free of the constricting plant life, heedless of the many wounds it caused itself.

The bloodthirster's hammer slammed down towards Alarielle. Teclis threw out a hand, and a shimmering shield of magical energy coalesced between the Everqueen and the daemon-weapon. Teclis bit back a groan as his body began to quake with the strain of his sorcery. Ka'Bandha lifted its hammer for a second blow.

'It speaks ill of the Lord of Skulls that his Huntsman is so easily distracted from his true prey,' a voice called out. Ka'Bandha stepped back, and turned. Teclis's eyes widened as Deathclaw landed heavily on the steps of the dais. The Emperor sat astride the griffon, and he gestured at Ka'Bandha with his runefang. 'It is known that you once came for Magnus the Pious, but failed to claim him. Did your god punish you for that, beast?'

Ka'Bandha snarled. 'Yes, I failed to claim the skull of one human emperor. But yours shall suffice as a replacement,' the bloodthirster hissed, gesturing at the Emperor with its axe. Before it could do more than gesture, however, Deathclaw was already hurtling forwards like a feathered cannonball at the Emperor's behest. The griffon crashed into the daemon and the animal's beak tore at Ka'Bandha's throat, even as its talons sank into the bloodthirster's arms.

Teclis pulled Alarielle aside as the two creatures careened down the dais, roaring and snarling. The Emperor clung grimly to his saddle and stabbed down at Ka'Bandha with his sword. 'Fool,' Teclis muttered. 'Without the power of Azyr, he's no match for that creature.'

'He is a fool, but a brave one. He is buying us time, and we must make use of it.' Alarielle raised her staff. 'I can feel Durthu – he is less than a league hence, and drawing near,' she said. Teclis felt a chill. If there was any creature in Athel Loren which could match

Ka'Bandha for pure hate, it was the ancient treeman known as Durthu. Powerful beyond measure, despite the old scars which covered its frame – a legacy of a long ago confrontation with the dwarfs – Durthu was the rage of the forest given form.

Alarielle continued, 'Durthu will not be coming alone. We have three armies in this forest, and by now they will all know that something is occurring. We must simply hold out until they arrive.'

Teclis looked at her. 'And how do you propose we do that?'

Alarielle didn't answer. Instead, she lifted her staff over her head. Teclis flinched back as the Wind of Life churned about her, and he felt a hum deep in his bones as she once again called out to the forest. All across the glade, those treemen not currently engaged with the enemy began to move towards the centre of the clearing. Those already there sank their roots deep into the soil and locked their limbs, creating a living palisade.

Other treemen moved to join them, and along the way, they plucked up those Incarnates or their advisors who were not lucky enough to be riding a steed, or able to fly. Teclis saw a treeman scoop up the dwarf, Hammerson, and, ignoring the runesmith's virulent cursing, carry him to the dubious safety of the growing bastion. Teclis grabbed Alarielle's arm. 'Come, we must go,' he said urgently.

'What of the human?' she asked.

Teclis turned, seeking out the Emperor. He cursed as he saw that his worst fears were confirmed. Ka'Bandha had recovered from the griffon's attack and had wounded the animal, driving it back and nearly spilling the Emperor from his saddle. Before he could move to help, however, a roiling cloud of shadow enveloped the bloodthirster. Each mote of darkness pierced the daemon's flesh, eliciting a startled shriek of pain from Khorne's Huntsman. As the bloodthirster staggered, flailing blindly at the shadows, Teclis saw Tyrion galloping towards the daemon, sword in hand. There was a flash of light, and the daemon screamed again as Tyrion swept past, his blade trailing a line of ichor.

Teclis gestured to the Emperor as the man glanced his way. Karl Franz hesitated, as if reluctant to leave the fight, but then nodded. He hauled on the reins, and forced his snarling mount to swoop away from its opponent and towards them. Deathclaw spread its talons and scooped the two elves up as it sped over the dais.

As they flew towards the living palisade of treemen, a crash of timber heralded the arrival of the last of Ka'Bandha's forces. Teclis watched in horror as great engines of shimmering brass and impossible heat, all thumping pistons and fang-muzzled cannons, burst into the glade, belching fire and ruin. Treemen were torn apart by howling barrages, and the forest itself was set aflame. Alarielle writhed in Deathclaw's grip, wracked by agony as she experienced Athel Loren's pain as her own. The palisade shuddered around them as Deathclaw landed.

The Incarnates were still scattered, Teclis saw. A column of pulsing amethyst light marked where Nagash still fought alone, uncaring of the greater struggle. Vlad von Carstein struggled to free Hammerson from the twisted wreckage of the treeman which had been carrying the dwarf. The guardian had been struck from behind by a roaring bloodthirster, and the vampire fought desperately against the daemon. Lileath was nowhere to be seen.

With a shrill whinny, Gelt's pegasus crashed to the ground and rolled awkwardly, kicking futilely at the daemons which clung to it. The bloodletters shrieked and hissed as Gelt, pinned beneath his thrashing steed, incinerated them with a spray of molten metal. Teclis hurried to aid the wizard. Above them, Caradryan's firebird cut a sharp turn, as the Incarnate of Fire turned his attentions to the wave of daemons already clambering over the palisade of treemen. Teclis hauled Gelt to his feet with one hand as he sent a cerulean bolt of mystical energy smashing into a knot of bloodletters.

'We're out of time,' the Emperor said, shouting to be heard over the rumble of daemon-engines and the death-shrieks of trees. 'If we do not escape, then we have lost everything. Even if we survive the battle, the world will be doomed.'

'What would you have me do?' Teclis snarled.

'Use your magic! Get us to Middenheim, while some of us can still fight,' the Emperor said. He gestured with his sword. 'Even a few of us might be enough to prevent the Everchosen from ending everything.'

'I told you before, I lack the power to do that. And even if I could, such an expenditure of magic that close to Middenheim might cause the very catastrophe we seek to prevent,' Teclis said. 'It cannot be done!'

'Then what do you suggest we do?' the Emperor growled. 'The daemons will just keep coming until this forest is ash, and us with it. We have no more time, Teclis. It must be now, or never.'

'I – I...' Teclis hesitated. He shook his head. He was tired. So tired. The world pressed down on him from all sides, and his mind worked sluggishly. There were so many things he had not anticipated, so many missteps he had made. What if he made another? In trying to save the world, would he only hasten its demise? He looked at Alarielle, but she shook her head, her face pale and strained. There was no help there. He tried to catch sight of Tyrion – his brother would know what to do. Tyrion was always certain of the right path.

Only he's not, is he? He never was, a voice whispered in his head. *It was always you, in the end. Your decisions, your morals, your certainties. But your cold, fathomless logic has failed you at last, just when you need it most.*

The battle raged about him. He glimpsed scenes of heroism and despair as he turned, searching for some answer in the confusion. He saw Nagash stand alone and unbowed against hundreds of squalling daemons, like a pillar of black iron in a crimson sea. He saw Tyrion and Malekith, still locked in combat with Ka'Bandha. Through the thickening wall of the palisade, he saw Caradryan vault from his saddle and plummet onto the hull of one of the daemon-engines, his halberd sweeping down to pierce the brass and send a gout of cleansing flame into its interior. He saw newly arrived elves die, even as they rushed to the defence of the Eternity King. A treeman sank down, groaning, its ancient soul snuffed by the fiery barrage from a daemon-engine.

He felt a hand on his arm, and turned. Lileath, her face streaked with blood and soot, smiled gently at him. 'There is a way,' she said. 'My body is mortal, but the power of a god still flows in my veins, and in my spirit. With them, you could do what must be done.'

Teclis stared at her. From behind him, he heard the Emperor mutter, 'Innocent blood...'

Lileath laughed harshly. 'I have not been innocent for a long time, king of the Unberogens. Neither have you, or indeed any of us. We are here at this moment because we are the only ones strong enough to withstand the storm.' She reached up and gently stroked Teclis's cheek. 'I have lied, and committed treachery. I have condemned the innocent to death, and sent brave men to their doom, all to prevent the end now unfolding around us. I have done what is required, and if my heart's blood is the key to victory, then that shall be given as well.'

'You will die,' Teclis croaked. He grabbed her hand.

'We are all going to die, son of my son. It is the Rhana Dandra, the end of all stories and songs. And better I die for a purpose, than drown in horror.'

'You are Lileath of the Moon. Your voice has guided me since I was but a child. When I try to remember my mother, it is your face I see. Your voice I hear,' Teclis whispered. 'Do not ask this of me, my goddess. Are my hands not stained with enough blood?' He closed his eyes, and held tight to her hand. The sounds of battle grew dim, and seemed to fade.

'If you truly love me, my beautiful Teclis, you shall grant me this final boon,' she said. He saw that there were tears in her eyes. 'I cannot feel my daughter, or my love, Teclis. I have lost everything. I would know peace.'

'He will do it,' the Emperor said.

Teclis released Lileath and whirled, lightning crackling about his clenched fists. 'You do not speak for me, master of apes. If your folk had done as they were meant to do, none of this would be happening.'

'The same might be said of yours,' Lileath said. Teclis turned back to her, helpless. 'He is right. There is no time. You know, in your heart, that this must be your path.'

He wanted to argue. But his words were lost in the scream of one of the guardians which made up the palisade. It was uprooted and flung back by a gout of flame from a daemon-engine, to crash down nearby, twitching and smoking. The sound of battle rolled back in on him, and he could hear it all, in its terrible glory. It was the sound of a world ending. 'What must I do?' he asked.

Lileath pressed a dagger into his hands and sank to her knees. 'It cannot be swift,' she said. 'When my spirit flees, so too will my divinity, and any advantage you might gain with it. My death must be slow. It must be perfect.' She caught his hand, and guided the dagger point to a spot just to the left of her breast-bone. 'There,' she said softly. She looked at him, and smiled sadly. 'Are you ready?'

'No,' Teclis rasped. Then he rammed the blade home with every ounce of strength he could muster. Lileath stiffened and moaned. He sank down to catch her as she toppled forwards. Blood stained his robes, and her breaths, shallow and rasping, were loud in his ears. The fading spark of her divinity danced across the dark of his mind as he reached out to catch it before it could flee. Several times it slipped his grasp, and he panicked. Then, he felt her hand reach up and rest on the back of his neck, and he grew calm. A moment later, a hand found his shoulder, and he heard a calm voice murmur encouragement. New strength filled him, and he hurled his mind and spirit at the slippery spark of power.

Bolstered, he seized the fading power and bound it to himself, drinking it in greedily. As it suffused him, driving aside all doubt and weakness, he felt her hand slide away, and her body shudder once, and grow cold. For a moment, his mind soared high above Athel Loren, and he could see the embattled mortals as flickering pinpricks of light, struggling against an all-encroaching ocean of darkness. The Incarnates showed more brightly still, the light of their power almost blinding. Nagash alone shone with a darkness almost as complete as that of the creatures he fought.

Teclis saw Gelt sheltering beneath a shield of gold as a bloodthirster hammered at it. He saw Nagash pluck another from the air, and crush its thick bones to powder in his unyielding grip. He saw Ka'Bandha tear his way free of the magics of Tyrion and Malekith, and Alarielle, and charge towards Vlad and Hammerson.

And he saw himself, kneeling, cradling Lileath's body. The Emperor stood behind him, one hand resting on his shoulder, and he knew the origin of that calming voice, and the sudden surge of strength. Something lurked within Karl Franz's frail envelope of flesh, something akin to both Lileath and the strange, fierce godspark in the man Volker, but more powerful than either. The Emperor looked up, and Teclis knew that the man could see him.

No, not the man. Karl Franz had not been a man for some time, Teclis knew. The Emperor nodded slowly, and Teclis turned his thoughts from mysteries to Middenheim. His mind and spirit stretched out, and pulled the disparate strands of the winds of magic to him. Without thinking, without even truly understanding, he began to weave them together, moving swiftly. The last spark of Lileath's power was already beginning to fade, and the magics he'd harnessed threatened to overwhelm him.

Pain shot through him, such as he had never felt before. He worked feverishly, fighting against the pain and the fatigue that came with it. The spell he was weaving was already beginning to unravel, even as he crafted it. Desperately he reached out with his magics, and carefully gathered up the motes of light which were the Incarnates and the others and enfolded them in the tapestry of the spell. One he had to reach further for, across vast distances into the east, and it struggled mightily in his grip, but it too joined the others.

They will not be enough, he thought.

They will have to be, the Emperor's voice replied.

Even as the man's voice echoed in his head, the spell, at last complete, tore loose from his weakening grasp and hurtled away from him, towards the distant darkling light of Middenheim. Then, overcome at last, Teclis slumped forwards, and collapsed into darkness.

 *Somewhere Else, Some Time Later*

'Wake up, elf.'

Teclis groaned. A sudden flare of pain ripped through him, and his eyes shot open. He lurched awake, a scream on his lips. He blinked back tears and looked up as a familiar figure carefully extracted his claws from Teclis's thigh.

'There we are. Back among the living, then?' Mannfred von Carstein said, smiling genially down at Teclis as he licked blood off his talons. 'I'd wager you thought you saw the last of me, eh?'

'Hoped, more like,' Teclis mumbled. He was not so much surprised to see the vampire as he was disgusted. After the creature's escape, he had feared that Mannfred would turn up again at an inconvenient time. And, true to form, it seemed he had.

Mannfred laughed and kicked him. Teclis grunted in pain. 'Where am I?' he wheezed, after a moment. He was lying face-down on cold stone. Manacles bit into his wrists, keeping him from standing. The only light came from guttering torches placed somewhere above his head, and the air stank of blood.

'Where do you think, elf?' Mannfred spread his hands. 'Can you not feel it? You are in the shadow of cataclysm itself.' The vampire grinned. 'Middenheim, mage. You are in Middenheim.'

'And why are you here?' Teclis asked. He knew the answer well enough. It was Mannfred who had started this chain of events, however unwittingly, and fate was not so kind as to deprive the beast of his final reckoning. *You are here because you have no choice. None of us do. We are all caught in the storm,* Teclis thought.

'How could I not be here? To witness the end of those who so cruelly betrayed me – me, who came in good faith, with heart open and hands empty.' Mannfred leered down at him. 'I knew there was only one place you would come, elf. I knew, as surely as I knew Be'lakor would allow his greed to overrule his judgement.' He sank to his haunches and caught Teclis's chin. 'But just how you got here, well, that was interesting... You crashed right through the roof of the Temple of Ulric, and smashed down before the throne of the Everchosen himself. I never suspected that you had that sort of power. Too bad it seems to have deserted you...'

'Silence, leech,' a voice rumbled. Its owner was hidden in the shadows which dominated the farthest reaches of the great chamber. Mannfred flinched and stepped aside. He bowed low, pulling his cloak tight about himself.

'Of course, my lord. Do forgive thy most unworthy of captains for his zealotry. Mine heart was overcome with adder's venom, and I sought to–'

'I said be silent,' the voice said. This time, Mannfred fell quiet. Teclis heard the rasp of armour on bone, and then, 'Well?'

'The elf is powerless, my lord,' a third voice said. Teclis looked up as a hooded figure stepped out of the shadows, the twisted metal of his mask gleaming in the torchlight. His tone was obsequious, his posture locked in a permanent half-bow, and he stank of dark magic. Teclis noted with some distaste that the sorcerer held his own purloined staff and sword. 'His magics have deserted him, as is the fate of all such false creatures.'

Despite what the creature said, Teclis was not wholly powerless, not that he planned to admit it. He could feel the presence of the Incarnates still, and felt a thrill of bitter satisfaction. He had transported some of them, at least, to Middenheim, along with many of their followers. Unfortunately, the spell had slipped from his control in the last few moments, and scattered them across the city.

Too, he could feel a new element. The Wind of Beasts was close at hand. He had feared at the time that he might have imagined its presence, but now he knew for certain that all eight Incarnates were accounted for. All eight Incarnates were in Middenheim.

'Not entirely, I think,' the first voice said. It sounded amused, and Teclis resisted the urge to shrink back from it. The sorcerer turned slightly to peer into the dark.

'I told you, fool,' Mannfred said, sneering at the sorcerer.

'Quiet, leech, or I shall stake your body out for the crows.' Through the shadows, past the pit of hissing, seething blood, on the throne of skulls which sat at the chamber's far end, a heavy figure reclined. As Teclis watched, the figure rose, and the eyes within its golden helm were unreadable. 'You have travelled a long way to die, elf,' Archaon said. 'But do not despair. The world shall not long outlast you.'

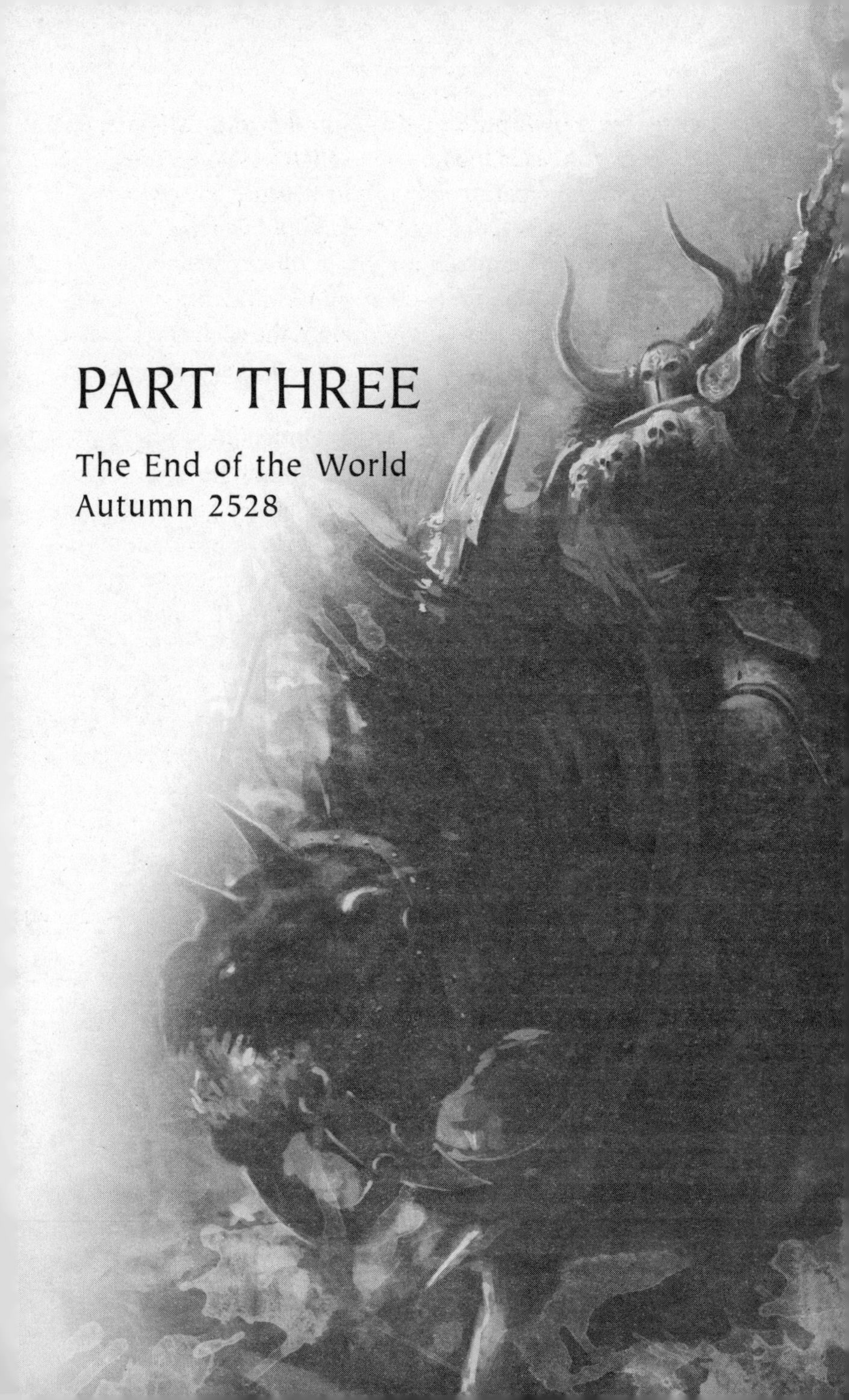

PART THREE

The End of the World
Autumn 2528

FIFTEEN

 *The Ulricsmund, Middenheim*

An angry red dusk had fallen over the Fauschlag. Strange lightning carved the sky into facets, and the streets boiled with activity. War had again come to Middenheim; only now it was the servants of the Everchosen who found themselves under siege, and on multiple fronts.

The heart of the Ulricsmund, within sight of the Temple of Ulric, was one such front. Caradryan, Incarnate of Fire and Chosen of Asuryan, had not wasted time wondering how he had come from Athel Loren to the blasted streets of a human city, or what had happened to the other Incarnates. Indeed, there had been no time to even consider it.

Scarcely had the storm of magic about him and those elves who found themselves at his side ebbed when they found themselves under attack from the axe-wielding, black-armoured Kurgan they now faced. Wreathed in fire, the Phoenix Blade hissed as it smashed home into the chest of a howling northman and sliced him into two blackened halves. Before the edge of the blade could strike the blood-smeared cobbles, Caradryan had reversed the stroke, pivoted, and removed the head of a second northman.

Fire crawled along his lean limbs, and his hair crackled like a halo of flame as he fought. He'd lost his helmet during the battle in Athel Loren, but it was of no matter. He moved swiftly, the Phoenix Blade an extension of his arms. The haft slid through his grip as he raised the ancient halberd and spun, letting it sing out to its full length. Northmen fell back in a bloody tangle as he completed the turn. He retracted the weapon, pulling it in tight even as he came to a halt, before punching it forward to spit a slavering Chaos hound in mid-leap.

The captain of the Phoenix Guard tossed the dying beast aside and fell into a defensive stance as he retreated back towards the other elves. The sutras of Asuryan ran through his head as he gauged the strengths and weaknesses of the enemies who pressed close about him, pursuing him. *Chaff before the wind,* he thought. It was not arrogance which prompted that conclusion, though once it might have been. He had been arrogant in his time, possessed of a certainty in his own superiority. It had taken a god to humble him, to show him the truth of his place: to show him that just because he was alive, that didn't mean he truly lived, and that just because he could speak, that didn't mean he should.

You must crawl before you can walk, boy, Asuryan had said, his voice rising from the flames in the holy Chamber of Days. *I will teach you, though in time, you might wish I had not.* And he had. His lessons had begun that day, and a callow, spiteful brat had become, if not a better elf, at least a more tolerable one.

He signalled silently for the archers among his miniscule host to let loose a volley. Arrows hissed overhead, and the front ranks of the Kurgan fell. The rest retreated in disarray. Now that the initial impulse to violence had been curtailed, the northmen seemed to be coming to grips with the fact that an enemy force had materialised in their very midst. They wouldn't remain hesitant for long, he knew. Then they would come again, and he and his small band would be overwhelmed.

He looked west, towards the slag-heaps and spoil piles which had been at his back when he'd arrived. Immense clouds of smoke and soot rose into the air above the area, and he recalled Be'lakor's taunts about the artefact Archaon was looking for. He frowned, wishing that the voice of Asuryan still whispered to him. But he did not. Asuryan, like all of the gods, was dead. But his servants would do what they could, in his absence and in his name. Even if that meant nothing more than dying well.

Roars and shouts rippled from between the ruined buildings which loomed above and around them. The Kurgan were regrouping. Chieftains and champions would be restoring order, and in a few moments, the enemy would be upon them again.

Never before had his fate weighed so heavily on him. Even the power caged in his body was no guarantor of his survival; after all, that power, the raw fury of Aqshy, had consumed Ungrim Ironfist in the end. *Is that my end, then?* he thought. *To be consumed in flames, like Ashtari?*

He looked up, and saw the firebird swoop low over the elves. The great bird shrieked. His kind had long dwelt amongst the Flamespyres of Ulthuan, laying their eggs amongst the great alabaster pillars of rock, where magical flames flickered eternally. Now, with Ulthuan's destruction, there were no more Flamespyres, and there would be no more firebirds. A wave of sadness swept through him as Ashtari's shadow passed over him, and the cry of the bird reverberated through his bones. No, there would be no more firebirds.

But they could burn brightly one last time, before the end.

Yes. We can all burn. The thought passed across his consciousness as Asuryan's whispers had once done. For a moment, it was as if the god were still alive. *Fire does not diminish as it is divided,* he thought. *Instead, it only grows stronger.* He almost laughed for the simplicity of it. What good was caging the fire in one warrior, when it could lend its strength to many? He raised the Phoenix Blade, and felt Aqshy struggle within him, seeking its freedom. He reversed his halberd and drove it down, blade-first, into the ground. *Now you are unchained,* he thought, *go, spread and avail them of your strength.* The fire rose around him, licking out to engulf those elves closest to him, even as the Kurgan mounted their charge.

As the northmen thundered towards them, Aqshy blazed forth, the flames growing and dividing a thousandfold. It spread through the ranks of his tiny army, and flames flickered to life along the edges of blades and in the eyes of his warriors, whether they had been born in Ulthuan, Athel Loren or Naggaroth. Fatigued bodies straightened with new strength, and warriors shouted, their spirits renewed. Caradryan rose to his full height, the Phoenix Blade held out before him. He watched the enemy draw close, and the last captain of the Phoenix Guard smiled.

'In the name of Asuryan,' he said, pitching his voice to carry for the first time in centuries, 'and for the fate of our people... *charge!*'

 *The Wynd, South-east of the Ulricsmund*

So, you yet live, eh? Malekith thought, as he caught a glimpse of the fire suddenly rising above the rooftops of the Ulricsmund. In Malekith's opinion, of them all, Caradryan was the least suited to wield the powers he had come by. Better by far that it had been given to one more suited to such things.

Still, one must make do, he thought, as he guided Seraphon through the reeking air above the city, towards the distant smoke. He recognised the telltale sign of an excavation immediately, having overseen similar enterprises in his life. How many magical baubles had he dug out of the mountains and ice-floes, forced to grub about like a dwarf while seeking an easier path to the power so long denied him? 'Pity I never thought to simply rip it out of the Vortex, eh, Seraphon?' he said, and stroked the dragon's long neck. The black dragon screeched and unleashed another searing cloud of fire into the tangle of streets below.

Malekith leaned forwards in his saddle and peered down at the battle taking place below. His forces, such as they were, swept through the narrow streets and drove the skaven before them. The ratmen had been surprised to see the enemy on their doorstep and Malekith had seized the advantage, driving his cohort on, the Eternity Guard at the fore. In the tangled streets the skaven could not bring their numbers to bear, and his warriors harried them mercilessly.

The skaven were detestable creatures, barely worth unsheathing his sword for. He contented himself with sending his shadow-shapes to draw blood in his place, while he sat safely astride Seraphon. The dragon screeched again, and incinerated another squalid nest. Skaven ran shrieking into the open, their greasy fur alight. Malekith laughed.

His laughter faded as he looked up at the sky. Things pressed heavily against the clouds, half visible but wholly incomprehensible. He felt all mirth drain from him. It was as if the skin of the world were stretched too tight over some gangrenous wound. He could smell the foulness of it on the wind, and feel it in his blood.

Memories of another moment and another sky like that crashed down on him, and the Eternity King shuddered in his armour. He had stepped into the realms of Chaos once, in a desperate gamble, and fought his way free only by dint of luck and willpower. The sky in that dread country, where time and space had no meaning save that which was given them by the whims of deranged gods, had looked the same.

'The world is dying, Seraphon,' he murmured, stroking the dragon's scales. 'All of our striving has come to nothing, it seems. Even as my deceitful mother swore.' He smiled beneath his mask. 'So be it. I am king, and I will face the end as a king.' He leaned back in his saddle, his cloak of shadows rippling about him as he gazed up at the roiling sky. 'Heed me well, you puny gods. Malekith, son of Aenarion, last true lord of the elves, has come to meet you on the battlefield. And as my father before me, I shall carve my name into your mind, so that you might shudder at the mere thought of it for all eternity. I shall break your fragile schemes, throw down your blood-soaked champions, burn your halls of decadent indulgence and scour the plague-ridden earth with cleansing fire.'

He drew his sword. 'You will win in the end, because that is the way of it. But I shall poison your victory with my last breath. Do you hear me?' he roared, casting his words into the howling winds. 'I shall not go lightly into destruction. I shall burn like a black sun, and you shall know fear before my standard is cast down. I will break this world before I let you claim it. This I swear.' He swept his blade out as magical lightning slammed down around him, shattering buildings and casting the bodies of the dead high in the air. The sky twisted in on itself, and the red light grew darker.

Malekith paid it no mind. He bent over, urging Seraphon to greater speed. Let all the gods stand in his way, if they dared. He was the Eternity King, and this world was his. And he would not lose it now, not without a fight.

 *Neumarkt*

Arkhan the Black watched in satisfaction as Krell and the Doomed Legion brought the gift of death to the enemies of Nagash. It had been but the work of moments to lend his sorcerous might to the great spell Teclis had woven in Athel Loren. Another power, too, had been there, lending aid, and between them, they had bolstered the reach of the spell so that more than just those in Athel Loren were caught up in its folds.

Almost the entirety of Nagash's army had been plucked from the pine-crags and transported to the streets of Middenheim to join their master for the final battle. And it was the final battle. Arkhan could feel it in his bones. It was like an ache, edging towards true pain, and he welcomed it. He reached up to touch the Everchild's mark on his chest. Would her curse reveal itself soon, he wondered? Would it even get the chance? The very bedrock of the world was shifting beneath his feet, and he felt that soon it might swallow them all. Even Nagash himself might not survive. He pushed the thought aside, even as it occurred to him.

Oblivion, he thought. *To sleep at last, no more to be awoken, no more to be set on the war-road.* He watched as the northmen, heavy with sleep and ale, died swiftly beneath the axe of Krell. *Do you welcome the end, as I do?* he wondered, watching the wight wade through the enemy with obvious glee. Krell was an enigma to the living, but to Arkhan he was a brute, barely chained by Nagash's sorcery, a creature not wholly one thing or another. Now he fought those he once might have led, and without hesitation. No, he decided. No, Krell would not welcome an end to his days of slaughter.

Nor would others, Arkhan suspected. Vlad was in this city somewhere – he could feel the vampire's black soul, pulsing like a ghost-light – and he had no intention of succumbing to oblivion. Vlad was as treacherous as Mannfred, and, worse yet, far wiser than his protégé. When the end came, when the Great Work at last came to its resolution, Vlad would pit himself against Nagash; else why would he seek to curry favour with humans and elves alike?

And he was not the only one. Neferata too would rally her followers, and set her standards in opposition to the Undying King. Arkhan felt some slight satisfaction at the thought... He had counselled Nagash to leave her as castellan of Sylvania for that very reason. Let Neferata cull the more treacherous elements of the dead for her own armies. Best to know who the enemy was, when the time came.

'COME,' Nagash said. Arkhan looked up at his master. Nagash surveyed the carnage as if it were of no more import than a squabble for table scraps between dogs. The Great Necromancer started forwards, almost floating as the spirits of the dead

rose to join the throng which surrounded him. Arkhan followed in his wake, lending his spells to those of his master as they drew those slain by Krell and his wights back to their feet and added them to the already substantial horde. Nagash, it seemed, intended to drown the city in an ocean of corpses.

It was an effective tactic, if lacking in finesse. Arkhan glanced at his master. Then, the Undying King had never been one for finesse. But once, at least, he had understood subtlety. Now, even that seemed to have been discarded. In his own way, Nagash was just as much a brute as Krell – he was not human, not any more. Nor was he the liche who had resurrected Arkhan to serve him in Nagashizzar. He had become something else, something far closer to the gods of old Nehekhara. A vast, irresistible force aimed at a distant target.

Cries filled the air. Arkhan looked up. Few buildings still stood in this part of Middenheim, and those that were in evidence had been repurposed into slave pens. Arkhan saw that many, if not all, of the captives were clad in the ragged and faded uniforms of a number of provinces. As the northlanders flooded past the ramshackle gates of the pens, the slaves had begun to cheer, but those cheers became screams as they saw the dead shambling in their captors' wake.

'Should we free them? Such chattel might be useful, in the coming fray,' Arkhan said, looking up at Nagash. The other Incarnates, he knew, would look kindly on such an action. Such small mercies were the way to bind their unwilling allies to them all the more tightly.

'YES. WE SHALL FREE THEM,' Nagash intoned. He reached out a hand, and Arkhan felt the Winds of Death rise. Amethyst light played about Nagash's outstretched claw, and then a darkling fire washed across the stinking pens which covered Neumarkt, choking the life from all it touched. The screams rose to a fever pitch, and then, all at once, fell silent.

But they did not stay silent for long. Soon, every corpse in

Neumarkt was rising to its feet, and making to join the still-shambling throng. They smashed from their pens, and rose from the streets, and fell in with the horde, which continued on through the city and into what had once been the Great Park. Arkhan said nothing as the dead swarmed. Nagash was his master, and Arkhan's will had never been his own. Better to argue with the storm, than with the Undying King.

There, amongst the burned-out trees and bald earth, the enemy had chosen to make their stand. The horde lurched to a stop at a simple gesture from Nagash. Arkhan took in the thick ranks of steel shields which lined the park's eastern overlook, and the warriors who crouched behind them. Behind this bulwark, sorcerers chanted loudly, tracing strange sigils in the air, and the air grew hot and foul as fell sorceries were worked.

Nagash laughed. The distant chants faltered and fell silent, as the sound of it crawled across the park and into the ears and hearts of the enemy. It was a terrible sound, like the crackle of ice-covered bones as they were trod underfoot.

Nagash looked down at Arkhan, his eyes glowing balefully. He swept out his staff to indicate the followers of Chaos. *'LOOK, MY SERVANT. MORE SLAVES TO BE FREED.'* Nagash set his staff and set the dead to moving again with but a thought.

'LET US SHATTER THEIR CHAINS.'

 *The Palast District*

Vlad von Carstein caught the northman's chin and wrenched his head to the side. There was a sharp pop as the man's neck snapped, and the vampire sank his fangs into the dying man's throat. When he had finished, he shoved the body aside to join the others, and dragged the back of his hand across his mouth. The blood tasted foul, but it was nourishing enough.

The group of northmen, clad in reeking furs and black iron, had been as surprised as he when he'd appeared suddenly in their midst. He'd felt the magics that Teclis had invoked, but had not grasped their intent until he had been surrounded by startled warriors. He'd recovered his wits first, and then butchered the lot. He looked around. He recognised the Palast District easily enough, though it had been substantially redecorated since he'd last visited Middenheim.

'Ah, Jerek, my old friend, you would weep to see your city treated so,' he murmured as he took in the sheer, bewildering scope of the desecration which had occurred. Even Konrad, bloody butcher that he had been, would have been in awe. The gardens and palaces he had once known so well were now lost beneath a charnel shroud.

Lacerated offerings to the Blood God hung from gore-slicked trees, or lay chained in fountains given over to bubbling blood. Bodies hung from gibbets or crow-cages, or were impaled on fire-blackened stakes. Some of the victims of these tortures still lived, mewling pitifully, their eyes gouged out and their tongues cut loose from their moorings. Even Vlad, who thought he had seen the worst the world could offer up in his centuries of life, was disgusted by it all. There was no artistry here, no purpose to the pain, and thus it was all a monumental waste. And if there was one thing Vlad could not abide, it was waste.

This was what awaited the world, if the Incarnates failed. He shook his head, more determined than ever to see this affair put to rest. He passed through the blood-sodden gardens like a ghost, delivering the mercy-stroke more than once on his way. Sounds of battle echoed through the district, and every figure he observed – be it armoured northerner or, more disturbingly, feral, pale-fleshed elf woman – was running south.

He followed them at a safe distance, killing only when necessary to hide his presence, and keeping to the walls and rooftops when he could. He was certain, given the sounds of battle wafting back towards him, that he would find allies at the end of his journey, though whether they would be in any state to aid him was another matter. He pursued the horde to the heart of the Middenplatz, where a scene of impressive carnage met his eyes.

Perched atop the northern gatehouse, he watched as treemen traded booming blows with bestial giants, and braying gor-bands hewed at shrieking dryads with crude axes. Whistling arrow volleys raced across the red skies, thudding into horned skulls and twisted bodies. The elves and their allies were surrounded on all sides by a seething ocean of madness. Beastmen, blood-cultists and daemons all were in evidence, and no matter how many fell, more took their place. As Vlad watched, one howling berserker cut through his own bestial allies to reach the elves, only to be smashed aside by a treeman a moment later.

He saw Alarielle at the battle's heart, jade life-magic flowing from her hands, healing wounds and restoring her fallen warriors to fight anew. Even so, it was plain enough to Vlad that Alarielle was growing weaker. She was pale and drawn, and her limbs trembled with fatigue... or perhaps pain. He suspected that she would have fallen long since, had the ancient creature fighting at her side not supported her. The vampire recognised Durthu easily enough – the treeman was hard to forget. The indomitable creature stood like a breakwater against the forces which lapped about them, and his mighty fists and gleaming sword brought death to any who sought to harm the Everqueen.

Vlad had commanded enough armies in his time to recognise when one was doomed. Alarielle's forces were being steadily ground down, and even his power was not so great as to turn the tide. An army was required, and he was but one man. He sank to his haunches and watched. He could not save them, and he had no intention of dying with them, but even so, he could not make himself depart. Alarielle fought on, despite her weakness, and Vlad could not help but be enthralled.

It might be possible, he thought, to save her. Her warriors were doomed, but if he were fast enough, he might be able to extricate her from the slaughter. She would not thank him for it, he suspected, but the other Incarnates certainly would. He readied himself to lunge into the fray, but before he could so much as twitch, the air was split by the roar of cannons and the entire eastern wall of the Middenplatz blew apart. Chunks of jagged stone flew across the square, pulverising beastmen and bloodcultists in their dozens.

Vlad was nearly knocked from his perch by the force of the explosion. As he regained his balance, he heard the crack of gunfire. Bullets punched through the spiralling dust and gromril armour gleamed in the smoke. Dour and dolorous voices erupted into song, and the sound of heavy boots on the march filled the air.

Alarielle and her forces had needed an army, and it seemed an army had come. Vlad smiled as he recognised Gelt, standing tall among the runic banners of the Zhufbarak. Hammerson was with him, looking none the worse for wear. That they both had survived was a surprise, but a pleasant one. Vlad drew his sword and readied himself to join the fray as, with a great shout, the armoured ranks of the dwarfs started forwards, and battle was joined.

The Sudgarten

Wendel Volker threw back his head and howled. His sword flashed, cutting down a skaven in mid-leap, and he led his followers forwards. Tears rolled down his cheeks as he caught glimpses of what had befallen Middenheim in his absence. The air stank of ash and ruin, and rage warred with sorrow in him as he led his motley band of priests, flagellants, foresters and knights into the heart of the skaven horde to avenge the city he had fought for and failed.

Teclis had brought them back, somehow. The last Volker recalled, he and his men had been hurrying towards the King's Glade, to lend aid to the embattled Incarnates. Now they fought through the tangled streets of the Sudgarten, against ratmen rather than daemons. He and his men loped in the wake of the Emperor and those knights who still had horses to call their own – banners bearing the emblems of the Reiksguard, the Knights Griffon and the Knights of the Twin-Tailed Comet rose above the wedge of armour and horseflesh that charged into the teeth of the jezzail-fire. Clouds of gun smoke rolled across the street, momentarily obscuring the enemy battle-line. A bullet plucked a howling flagellant off his feet and knocked him sprawling. Volker felt a shot whizz past his cheek, but didn't slow.

He longed to lose himself in battle, to join the ghosts he saw swirling about him everywhere he looked. Goetz, Dubnitz, Martak and others, including faces he had not seen since the fall of Heldenhame, like the brutal Kross or old Father Odkrier. They watched him from the windows and doorways, from behind the enemy ranks and just out of the corner of his eye. They coalesced in the smoke, and their faces rose through the blood that trickled between the cobbles. They spoke to him, but he could not hear them. Ulric's snarls drowned them out.

The fury of the wolf-god burned in his breast, driving him on through the stinking powder smoke despite his fatigue. Gregor Martak's parting gift had been less a blessing than a curse. Volker had not slept since he'd escaped Middenheim the first time, leading those survivors he could to the dubious safety of Averheim, thanks to the godspark nestled within him. Most of those he'd saved were now dead, so perhaps it hadn't mattered either way.

He felt his bones shudder in their envelope of flesh, and knew Ulric was lending him strength. He pivoted as the god growled a warning, and caught the crashing blow of a rat ogre on his shield. The force of the impact drove him to one knee. A burst of light blinded him as he readied himself for a second blow. He heard the rat ogre shriek, and saw it turn and rear back, pawing at its eyes, as a golden, glowing shape rose up before it. A blade flashed, and the creature toppled like a felled tree.

The elf, Tyrion, galloped past, shining like the sun, and behind him came the knights of the elves, moving more quietly, but no less swiftly, than their human allies. The elves had appeared near the western gatehouse of Middenheim alongside the Emperor and his followers. Now they fought side by side, as they had centuries past, against the forces of another Everchosen. Volker rose to his feet and turned, Ulric muttering in his head. *He cannot be trusted,* the wolf-god snarled. *He is the thief's brother!*

'Shut up,' Volker hissed. A crude spear dug for his vitals and he smashed it down with the bottom of his shield, before driving his sword into the throat of the skaven who held it. He drove forwards, forcing skaven aside with his shield, and cutting down those who would not be moved. Around him, men and elves moved up, whether on horseback or on foot, and the skaven steadily retreated, falling back through crossroads and squares.

You dare? I am Ulric!

'You're bloody annoying is what you are,' he muttered. The god had been in his head since Martak had given him up, and he hadn't shut up since. Sometimes, Ulric talked so much that Volker had trouble telling which thoughts were his, and which belonged to the wolf-god. Every day, there was a little less of the man he had been, and a little more of the thing Ulric was turning him into. The wolf-god had eaten him hollow.

He heard the scream of the Emperor's griffon and saw the beast swoop low over the melee, scooping up skaven in its talons as it went. It dashed the unlucky ratmen against the cobbles as it banked and turned. The Emperor clung to the beast's back and swung his runefang out, lopping off limbs and crushing skulls.

He is tiring, Ulric rumbled. *He is but a man, with a man's frailties.* Volker felt a moment of panic, and muttered, 'Is that what you were waiting on, then? To jump from me to him, the way you left Martak?' He knew, without knowing how, that if that occurred, he would die not long after. Part of him was even looking forward to it.

I did not leave Martak. I died with him. As I will die with you, Wendel Volker. I have split myself again and again, until I am but a sliver of the god-that-was, all to survive, to reach this moment, when I might sink my fangs into the flesh of the one who took my city – my people – from me. I am Ulric, the god of battle, wolves and winter, and I will have my vengeance!

'For all you know, Teclis is dead,' Volker growled. He hacked down on an armoured stormvermin, knocking the black-furred skaven off its feet. It lashed out at him with a heavy, serrated blade. He felt the tip scrape across his cuirass, and dodged back. Before the skaven could get to its feet, his sword hammered down to split its skull. 'And if he's not, we might need him,' he added, desperately.

I will have vengeance, Wendel Volker. Whether the world lives or dies, Middenheim will be avenged. You will be avenged, Ulric growled.

Then his head ached with the mournful cry of innumerable wolves, and he threw back his head and howled again and again, as he fought on. And as he fought, Wendel Volker's tears turned to ice on his cheeks.

 *The Merchant District*

'Waaagh!'

Orcs spilled through the streets like a green tide of violence, and unprepared northmen and panicked skaven drowned beneath them. They hacked, thumped and head-butted their way through the ruins of Middenheim's merchant district and with every foe who was pulled down by the brawling horde, be they armoured Chaos warrior or skittering skaven jezzail team, the war cry only grew louder. It was a deep, feral rumble that rose and spread ahead of the onslaught, louder even than the sounds of battle.

'Waaagh!'

Crude blades smashed down through iron shields and crumpled steel helms as the orcs hacked at their foes with a wild abandon, inflamed by a force beyond their comprehension. They chopped at the enemy until their blades blunted and broke, and then continued to pummel their foes with bloody fists.

The greenskin warlord fought at the head of the horde, his axe spinning like a bloody whirlwind about him as he bellowed challenge after challenge. Massive, broken-toothed and clad in battered armour, where Grimgor Ironhide went, the enemy shield-walls split and Chaos champions died, the names of their gods still on their lips. Monstrous beasts, strong with the stuff of Chaos, fell dismembered, and their remains were trodden into pulp as the horde rampaged on through the streets, tireless and relentless.

Grimgor caught a northman by his bone-bedecked beard, and yanked the unlucky man forwards. Their skulls met with a resounding crack and the northman slumped back, his skull cracked open like an egg. Grimgor licked blood and brains from his lips as he shoved the body aside and drove his axe down on an upraised shield covered in writhing, shrieking colours. He split the shield, releasing a wailing prismatic spray, and reached through the ruins to grip the throat of its bearer. 'Get over 'ere,' he growled. He flung the brawny warrior into the air, and roared, 'Lads, catch!'

Behind him, his Immortulz cheered as they hacked at the fallen human, painting themselves with his blood and howling with laughter at his screams. Ahead of Grimgor, the humans were falling back, retreating through the close-set streets, keeping their shields between themselves and the orcs. He'd fought them long enough now that he knew what they were planning. The horse 'umies, on the plains, would scatter and reform – it was like trying to bash rain. But these were the iron 'umies... They'd fall back and form a shield-wall, and wait for their bosses to send for reinforcements. He knew from experience that iron 'umies could hold out for a long time. If they didn't want to move, they didn't.

For some reason, that wasn't as pleasant a thought as it might normally have been. He felt an itch, just to the left of his skull, and knew Gork wanted him to keep moving. *Go fasta,* the god growled, *fastafastaFASTA!*

Grimgor threw back his head and bellowed in frustration as Gork's words cascaded across his brain. Why couldn't the 'umies just take a kicking? They had to know that they couldn't get away from him, or resist him. They were worse than the bull-stunties, with their armour and fire and whips.

A grin split Grimgor's grotesque features as he recalled how the stunties had wailed as he'd torn down their city of pillars and pits, freed their slaves and toppled their statues. That'd teach them to break their staves on his hide. That'd teach them to try to make Grimgor a slave. The grin faded, and the old anger came back, hotter and fiercer than any stunty fire-pit. He lifted Gitsnik and pressed the flat of the great axe to his brow. His gnarled frame was a patchwork of scars, most earned properly, in the heat of battle. He'd fought stunties - both kinds - and rats and gits and big-bellies aplenty in the past few months, but it had always come back to the bull-stunties and their fire-pits. Their whips and chains and iron staves.

They had given him his first scars when he'd been no more than a runt. And he owed them for that.

Gork had shown him favour, filling him with strength enough to kick over the stunties' towers and turn their ziggurat of black obsidian into rubble. But first, he'd broken skulls and taken heads and put together the biggest Waaagh! around - orcs, goblins, even ogres. After Gork had blessed him with his strength, he had crushed Greasus Goldtooth's skull with the ogre's own mace. In the years that followed, he had broken the back of the Necksnapper and shattered the lodgepoles of the Hobgobla Khan. He had cracked the Great Bastion, and burned the dragon-fleets of Nippon. The East was green, and it was his. But it hadn't been enough. Something was pulling him west. Gork, maybe, or Mork, drawing him towards a bigger fight. A better fight. He could feel it in his veins, thrumming along, like that time Gitsnik had got hit by a lightning bolt.

He'd thought, at the time, he'd found that fight in the city of the bull-stunties, but the gods hadn't even let him enjoy the krumpin' he'd given them before they'd scooped him up, and all his boys with him, and deposited him into the middle of a fight. A big fight, bigger than any he had ever seen. There were 'umies, rats, stunties, point-ears, and bone-men – every flavour of opponent. For a moment, Grimgor thought he'd died and gone to Gork's hall, but then he'd got an arrow in the head and realised that they were in a human city. He reached up to scratch the wound. The arrow had got dislodged somewhere along the way, and the wound had already scabbed over. Gork clamoured in his head and Grimgor shook his head in irritation.

He lowered his axe and eyeballed the northmen. He grunted and turned. Gork wanted him to get to the heart of the city, and fast, and Grimgor wasn't of a mind to argue with the gods... not yet anyway. This situation called for a bit of... Morkishness. 'Oi, Wurrzag!' he bellowed, punching his Immortulz aside to clear a path. 'Get up here, ya git.' He knew the crazed shaman would be close. Wurrzag was never very far away these days, not since Gork had reached down and given Grimgor a flick on the noggin.

Orcs and ogres made way for a capering, tattooed figure, wrapped in badly stitched hides and wearing a wooden mask decorated with feathers. Wurrzag wobbled to a halt before Grimgor, twitching in time to some internal rhythm. Grimgor grimaced. The air around the shaman sparked and crackled with energy that made an orc's blood fizz and his flesh itch. Wurrzag shook his staff under Grimgor's nose. 'All hail da once and future git,' the shaman warbled. The shaman hesitated in mid-hop. 'Werl, one o' dem, anyways.'

'Yeah, shut up wiv' that nonsense and go do that fing you do, right?' Grimgor snarled, gesturing towards the enemy with his axe. He wanted to plant Gitsnik right in the middle of the shaman's stupid mask on general principles, but Wurrzag was too valuable. 'They is in my way, and I want 'em gone. Gork wants me somewheres else, and I intend to go there. But that ain't here, so go blast 'em.'

'Yes, oh mighty git,' Wurrzag squawked, shaking his staff.

'And stop calling me a git,' Grimgor roared, as the shaman twitched past him. He turned and raised his axe. 'Golgfag, get over 'ere,' he snarled, as he caught the ogre's attention. Golgfag muscled aside a couple of orcs, and only had to thump one of them. They were scared of the ogre, and Grimgor didn't like that. The only thing his lads ought to be scared of was him. 'Get your lads up here,' he bellowed at the ogre. 'Me and you are breaking that shield-wall. You got a problem with that?' He glared at the ogre challengingly. Golgfag and his ogres had joined the Waaagh! as it crossed the Worlds Edge Mountains, and he'd come close to killing the mercenary more than once. Every time, Gork had whispered to him and quelled his anger.

The big ogre had proven more useful than most of his greedy kin – he was as smart as any runt, and dead sneaky when he needed to be. It had been Golgfag who had got the gates of Zharr Naggrund open, so Grimgor's lads could barrel in. The ogre had held the great iron gates open, despite having half a dozen stunty crossbow bolts in him. He and Grimgor had fought side by side and back to back up the steps of the black ziggurat, and had toppled the massive statue of the stunties' bull-god, alongside Borgut Facebeater and Wurrzag. That had been a good day, even if he'd had to kill ol' Borgut later, on account of him trying to make himself boss. He missed Borgut. Not at the moment, but in general.

'Got no problems, boss,' Golgfag rumbled. He wore a heavy horned helm that added to his already considerable height, and for an instant, Grimgor considered cutting him off at the knees. He didn't like standing in the ogre's shadow. 'Happy to bash whoever, wherever, whenever.'

'Good,' Grimgor grunted. He heard the air sizzle behind him, and felt his skin prickle. The light turned green, and cast weird shadows on the buildings around them. All around him, orcs, ogres and goblins set up a caterwauling and men screamed. He turned to see Wurrzag dancing a madcap jig as the shield-wall crumbled beneath a storm of crackling emerald lightning. Grimgor felt the strength of Gork rising in him, an elemental fury that outstripped even his own boiling anger. He grinned and Golgfag stepped back warily.

'Let's get to bashing then,' Grimgor snarled. He lifted his axe and waved his Immortulz forwards. Golgfag roared out for his followers, and the mingled wedge of black orcs and ogres took the fore as they thundered towards the enemy lines that Wurrzag had softened up. Grimgor sped up, wanting to get the first lick in. He caught Gitsnik in both hands and lifted it. 'I'm gonna stomp you ta dust, and break your bones,' he roared, hurling his words towards the faltering shield-wall. 'I'm gonna pile yer bodies in a big fire and cook 'em good! I'm gonna bash heads, break ya faces and jump up and down on the bits that are left!'

And when I get where Gork wants me ta go, I'm gonna get really mean, he thought in satisfaction. Then, he was upon the enemy, and there was no need to think at all.

SIXTEEN

 *The Temple of Ulric, the Ulricsmund*

'How tedious. Surely we are all capable commanders. I do not need my hand held, even if I were intending to commit myself to an afternoon of carnage,' Sigvald the Magnificent groaned, one arm flung over his head as he reclined on the steps of the dais which led up to Archaon's throne. 'Dechala, my love, please inform the Everchosen that I am afflicted with ennui and will be unable to sully my fingers with the grime of battle today.' He flapped a hand at the serpentine shape of the daemon princess known as Dechala the Denied One.

Dechala possessed the upper body of the beautiful elven princess she had once been, and the lower body of an immense serpent. She hissed at Sigvald. Whether it was a sign of annoyance, or some form of flirtation, Canto could not say. He watched as she slithered closer to the manacled form of the elf mage, Teclis, where he lay huddled next to the dais. His robes were filthy and blackened and his face was turned away from the gathering, but Canto knew he was still paying close attention, even so. He was a cool one, was the elf, and he stank of powerful magics.

Even though he was a prisoner, Canto knew it was best not to get too close to him. Dechala, however, seemed unconcerned. She caressed him gently, as if trying to tease a lover awake, and leaned close, her tongue flickering.

She caught Canto watching her, and wrinkled her nose in a fashion that had him momentarily forgetting the six arms and the spiky bits. *Don't even think it, Canto,* he thought. Those who knew such things said that Dechala's embrace was a moment of pleasure, followed by an eternity of pain. She had been in Ind, he knew, alongside Arbaal, bringing the wrath of the gods down on that far land, until she and her rival had been scooped up by whatever dark forces were responsible for such things and brought to Middenheim.

He turned away as one of the others he'd brought to the temple at Archaon's behest made his feelings known. 'Cease your prattling, Geld-Prince,' Arbaal the Undefeated rumbled. 'The gods have called us here to do battle with their enemies. Would you deny their wishes?'

'And are you so arrogant as to know the wishes of a god not your own?' the horned, winged creature known as Azazel, the Prince of Damnation, purred as he sauntered out from behind Archaon's throne. The daemon prince's talons clicked across the haft of Ghal Maraz, where it was mounted above the throne.

Arbaal growled wordlessly and hefted his axe. A large, scaly paw pressed itself to his cuirass, stopping him from hurling himself at Azazel. 'None of us know the will of the gods,' Throgg, the self-proclaimed King of the Trolls, rasped. 'At least not until it is too late.' The troll was larger than any other of his kind that Canto had ever had the misfortune to run across. And his eerie self-control was equally as disturbing as Dechala's sinuous attempts at seduction. They said the troll had been plucked from Kislev by the whims of the gods, and that he bore the marks of battle on him. Canto wondered who would be insane enough to go toe-to-toe with Throgg. Then, he wondered whether they had survived.

'All I know is that I was enjoying the finest flesh Parravon had to offer, before I was whisked back to this inglorious termite mound,' Sigvald said. 'I am without even my sword-boy, or my mirror-eunuchs. How am I expected to perform without my mirror-eunuchs?'

'We all have our burdens to bear, Geld-Prince,' Mannfred von Carstein said. The vampire examined his talons, not looking at Sigvald, or, more pointedly, at the shrouded figure of Isabella von Carstein, who stood well away from the creature who shared her name. The two vampires had studiously ignored one another since Mannfred's arrival.

Canto watched Mannfred warily. He still didn't understand why Archaon had allowed the beast, or, for that matter, creatures like the renegade dark elf priestess Hellebron, into the city. They were treachery incarnate, and if they knew what the Everchosen was planning – indeed, if any of the gathered champions knew – they would turn on him in an instant. 'And in any event, eunuchs are easily replaced,' Mannfred continued.

'Are you volunteering, prince of leeches?' Sigvald purred. 'I believe I have just the paring knife for you...'

Mannfred laughed. 'Would that I could, barbarian.' The vampire turned his red gaze on Sigvald. 'Would that I could match my strength against yours, but... well. We have enemies enough, I think, and on our very doorstep.'

'Our doorstep, vampire?'

Canto stiffened as Archaon's hand fell on his shoulder. 'You have brought them all?' the Everchosen said, gazing at the assemblage.

'As many as weren't already engaged, my lord,' Canto said, as Archaon stepped past him. 'Hellebron has already brought the foe to battle in the Palast District, and only a few of the skaven are not currently hard-pressed,' he continued, gesturing to the tiny knot of skaven who stood near von Carstein. The ratmen looked nervous, as well they should have – they were not well liked by their allies. 'Harald Hammerstorm will do as he wills, as ever. And the other warlords send their regrets, I'm sure.' Not that there were many of the latter left. Most of the champions and warlords worth the name had already gone to join the gods, in one fashion or another. Those that hadn't died in the taking of the city, or during the assault on Averheim, had crossed Archaon and paid for that temerity with their lives.

'What of the Broken King?' Archaon asked, his amusement evident.

Mannfred and Isabella were not the only dead things in Archaon's service. The Broken King was another – a foreign potentate, ruler of a dead land, clad in shattered vestments and filthy wrappings. He was one of the skeletal princes of far Nehekhara, though which one, he had never revealed, even as he prostrated himself before the Everchosen's throne in the months after the destruction of Averheim.

'He has already gone to confront the enemy,' Canto said. In truth, he did not know where the Broken King was, or what he was up to, and he did not feel like hunting the creature down to ask it. Let it live or die, as it wished.

Archaon said nothing for long moments. Then he shook himself slightly, and murmured, 'Monsters and fools. How fitting.' He looked around. 'We are besieged. You all know this, and you know too that this is the last roll of the dice for our enemies. This is the last gasp of the civilised lands, and when this battle is done... the gods will reward us.' Archaon made a fist. Canto felt a chill streak through him, and he glanced upwards, towards the red sky clearly visible through the shattered dome of the temple.

The gods are watching, he thought. But he didn't think they particularly cared who won. He looked at Archaon. *You don't either. Not really. Because you think you've already won. It's a foregone conclusion to you...* Because it wasn't about battles or enemies for Archaon. Not now. Now it was all about time and fire. While the rest fought, he contented himself with stoking the flames. Canto gripped the hilt of his sword and wondered how one might escape those flames when one was already in the pot.

Archaon was still talking. 'The enemy are scattered, for now. If we are quick, we might be able to destroy them piecemeal. If not, well...' He spread his hands. 'Such is the will of the gods.' He gestured to Arbaal. 'Most important are those closest to hand. A host of elves is on our doorstep, just east of here. Their skulls are yours, should you wish.'

Arbaal nodded silently. Archaon looked at Dechala. 'You will take the south – the Sudgarten. The enemy muster there as well.' As the elf-snake hissed her agreement, Archaon motioned to Isabella. 'And you, countess... you shall reinforce Hellebron in the Palast District. Catch the enemy between the engines of blood and pox, and crush them.'

Isabella, face hidden behind her veil, gave no sign that she'd heard. Instead, she simply turned and strode away, accompanied by Arbaal and Dechala. Canto looked towards the dais and saw that Azazel was gone as well, though the daemon prince had been given no orders. Archaon didn't seem concerned for such trivialities. He turned to the skaven. 'Darkendwel,' he said, addressing the large shape which crouched above the knot of skaven warlords, perched high on a broken statue.

The shadowy shape of the skaven verminlord twitched as Archaon spoke its name. The squabbling warlords and seers gathered about it fell silent as the Everchosen turned to face Darkendwel. 'The orcs in the merchant district. Do they fight alongside the others?' Archaon asked. 'Have our enemies grown so desperate as to elicit the aid of mindless savages?'

'No, O most mighty King-With-Three-Eyes,' the verminlord chittered. It hesitated, and then added, 'Or such does not appear to be the case.'

'Then find out,' Archaon rumbled. 'Lead them towards... the Wynd, I think. Let us see if they prefer the elves as playmates.'

Archaon cocked his head, as if in thought. Then, 'I was sorry to hear that your fellow verminlord, Visretch, fell to the blade of the elf-prince, Tyrion. I had much I wished to discuss with him, when the time came.' Canto smiled as Darkendwel tensed. One of the verminlords had been responsible for killing Valten, against Archaon's wishes. The Everchosen hadn't found out which one had struck the blow, but it wasn't for lack of trying.

'He died in your name, O most magnificent god-king,' the verminlord intoned.

'Then you can do no less,' Archaon said. He turned and pointed at Sigvald. 'The dead are yours. I want the skull of this so-called Undying King for a drinking cup, Geld-Prince.' Archaon glanced at Throgg. 'You will take your forces and join him. Sigvald will require assistance.'

'I require no such thing,' Sigvald said, pushing himself to his feet. 'And I will not share my glory with an ape in a crown.' He gestured dismissively towards Throgg. 'I can barely tolerate his smell... How do you expect me to fight alongside him?'

'I do not,' Archaon said simply. 'I expect you to die beside him. Perhaps I am mistaken. I am curious to see which it is.'

Sigvald gaped at him. The Geld-Prince's hand strayed towards the hilt of his sword, but Throgg reached him first. One scaly hand clamped down hard, trapping Sigvald's hand and wrist. The troll-king grinned unpleasantly. 'Come, beautiful one. We have carrion birds to feed, and dead men to set to rest,' Throgg rumbled. Sigvald jerked his hand free of the brute's grip and hurried away, Throgg trailing after.

'And what of me, O mighty Everchosen? What are your commands for me?' Mannfred said, bowing obsequiously, as they left. Archaon climbed the dais and took down Ghal Maraz before he glanced at him.

'Go where thou wilt, and die as you wish, leech. I have no commands for you, save that you remember whose side you have chosen, and that the gods have your scent, and they will harry you to destruction, should you forget.' Archaon gestured dismissively with the hammer.

Canto smiled slightly, pleased. Mannfred annoyed him. *Only room enough for two lickspittles in this court, I'm afraid,* he thought. As if the vampire had heard his thoughts, Mannfred turned a red-eyed glare on him. Canto's hand fell to the hilt of his sword, but Mannfred stormed past him, trailing shadow and the stink of old blood in his wake.

'I'm going to have to kill him, I think,' he said, without thinking.

'Possibly,' Archaon said. He still held Ghal Maraz in his hands. 'Then, possibly, it shall become unnecessary before long. It is all winding down, Canto. Can you not hear it? The wind which howls through the streets is the dying gasp of this sad world. The tremors which shake this mountain are but its death-shudders. Soon, it will all be done. All lies revealed, all gods thrown down, and the earth and sky made one.'

Canto shivered in his armour. His hand was still around the hilt of his sword. *One blow, that's all it would take... One swift blow, and then... Cathay,* he thought. Only there wasn't a Cathay any more, or an Araby, or anywhere that wasn't here. Still... just one blow...

'It would take more than one, Canto, and you know it,' Archaon said, softly. He did not turn around. Canto froze nonetheless. 'You had your chance once, to change the fate of all things, and you squandered it. You ran, rather than make a choice. In the end, it all comes down to choices, Canto. You chose to remain a man, in a world fit only for monsters. And now you face another choice.'

Archaon turned, Ghal Maraz swinging loosely in his grip. 'The gods are always of two minds, Canto. One mind says strike, and the other says hold. The gods see all possibilities and none, and they are blinded by this wealth of knowledge. So they plot within plot, and scheme against themselves, even in their moment of victory. For if I succeed, the game ends. The world ends and their playthings are but ashes on the cosmic wind.' He lifted the ancient hammer, turning it slightly in his grip, as if to admire the way the light glinted off the runes which marked its surface. 'Like this hammer, the Dark Gods are both creator and destroyer, and they cannot make up their minds as to which they are in any given moment.'

He swung the hammer experimentally. 'They are idiot gods, Canto – they are more powerful than you can conceive, but in truth, they are little better than giggling imbeciles, drawing shapes in the mud. They will crush this world into dust and blow it away, and then move on to some other world, some other place where the game begins again. That is the truth of it.' Archaon tossed the hammer aside carelessly, and it thumped down with a hollow clang. 'In a way, you were wise not to pledge your allegiance to any of them. That alone has given you the will to decide your own fate. The others will fight, because their gods demand blood. But you have a choice. Indeed, you have so many choices that I cannot help but envy you. I have no choices left to make, and am bound to my path.'

Canto shook his head. 'What... what choices?' he croaked.

'You could kill me,' Archaon said. He spread his arms. 'It might be enough to halt what has begun. With me dead, the gods would certainly turn away, though whether in satisfaction or anger, I cannot say. Or you could run. You could flee, and live for however long the world remains. I will not stop you.' Archaon crossed his arms. 'You could fight. You could be Unsworn no more, and perhaps even gain some measure of power in these final hours. Become a demigod like Azazel or Dechala, eternal and inhuman.'

Canto stared at him. After a moment, he said, 'None of those sound particularly enjoyable.' He looked down at his hand, clamped tight to the hilt of his sword, and, not for the first time, thought of Count Mordrek and the way he'd died. *An ending, that's all any of us are after,* he thought.

'Nonetheless, the choice is upon you at last. What do you wish to do, Unsworn?' Archaon asked. 'Which road will you take? Once, you showed some small touch of mercy, and spared the world its due punishment. Now, you have that chance again. Will you show it mercy a second time?' There was something in Archaon's voice which made Canto hesitate. A note of pleading perhaps, or resignation. It was the voice, not of a conqueror, or a great champion, but a man tired unto death, and wanting only oblivion.

Run and hide or stand and fight, Unsworn – your appointed hour has come round at last, he thought. He'd thought it had passed, but Middenheim, Averheim... it had all been a single moment, stretched over weeks and days. But now it was done, and he could no longer avoid it. He could only choose, as Archaon had said.

Canto's sword was in his hand, before he knew he had drawn it. There were no voices in his head, no whispers, only the sound of a tortoise of iron and crystal as it trudged on and on, into endless wastes, searching for something that could never be found. His sword slashed down towards Archaon's head, and then there was a flash of light, and pain and he was falling back – back onto the ground.

'I hoped you would run,' Archaon said solemnly. The Slayer of Kings hung loosely in his hand, its edge red with blood. It had cut through Canto's armour as if it were nothing. 'If you had run, I could have spared you this, for a few hours more. You have served me well, and without complaint, and I would have liked to have given you that much.'

Canto couldn't breathe. There was a fire in his belly, and it was consuming him from the inside out. Even so, he still managed to laugh. 'I... am running,' he wheezed. 'Death is the only escape from... from what's coming.' Pain swelled in him, choking off his laughter. Archaon knelt beside him.

'Do you fear the truth so much, then?' Archaon asked. He sounded regretful, and confused. *You aren't bound to your path, you just never bothered to look for another,* Canto thought, through a haze of agony. *Were you too scared? Is that it? Are you afraid, Everchosen? And here I thought I was the coward...*

'Whose truth?' Canto said, his voice barely a whisper. Archaon twitched, as if struck. The world was going red and black at the edges, and the pain had faded, leaving only a leaden weight on his limbs and heart. Canto closed his eyes. 'I'll not be forced to choose between dooms,' he slurred. 'Let the gods catch me if they can. I remain true to myself.'

Archaon said something, but Canto couldn't hear it. He could hear nothing now, save the distant laughter of thirsting gods, and the slow, soft wheeze of the tortoise as it walked on, towards the edge of the world.

Canto ran after it.

Teclis watched Archaon rise to his feet, sword still in his hand. He left the body of the Chaos warrior where it lay, and turned towards his captive. Teclis had not caught everything that had passed between them, but he thought he understood it regardless, and he cursed the warrior, whoever he had been, for not killing Archaon when he'd had the chance. The moment had passed now, and it would take more than a blade in the back to topple the Everchosen from here on out.

'He was the world's last hope,' Archaon said, as he turned towards Teclis. 'I thought, for a moment, he might... but no matter. The way is clear and my path assured. Let the skies weep and the seas boil. Let us be free, at last, of the hideous weight of life.'

Teclis gathered his legs under him as Archaon strode towards him. 'Not all of us think it a burden,' he croaked. Archaon raised his sword and shattered the chains which connected the elf to the dais, as Teclis shied away instinctively. Archaon reached down and grabbed the chains, hauling Teclis upright.

'I do not care what you think, mage. I care only what you see. Come.' Archaon dragged Teclis up through the temple, onto the ancient battlements which surrounded the shattered dome. Teclis nearly stumbled and fell many times, but Archaon kept him moving with sharp tugs and cuffs about the head and shoulders. When they reached the open air, Teclis gulped it in, trying to clear his mouth and nose of the taste and smell of the foulness within the defiled temple.

Archaon paused at the top of the battlements. The Everchosen gazed out over the city, watching the play of light and shadow stretch across the ruins. Even from here, Teclis could hear the sounds of battle, and see the smoke. He could hear the boom of guns, and the raucous cries of the orcs. *And wasn't that a surprise,* he thought sardonically. It made a strange sort of sense. The Wind of Beasts had gone east and found a suitably bestial host. Appropriate, if unanticipated.

Archaon tugged on the chains. 'What do you see?' he rasped.

Teclis looked at him, and a dozen different answers sprang to mind. *What should I tell you? That the Incarnates are bound together by bonds of magic, and those same bonds are drawing them here? That it is fate, that it has come down to this, and that even the Ruinous Powers are but children in the hands of destiny?* But no. Archaon didn't want to hear any of that. The question had been rhetorical. The Everchosen was no longer a man, but merely a mechanism... a toy, wound up and set loose by irrational beings.

The elf sniffed. 'I see the end of all you have planned, and the fall of the Dark Gods.'

Archaon laughed. The sound set Teclis's gut to churning. 'Such defiance. Do you not fear me?' the Everchosen asked. There was no threat there. Only a question.

'What does it matter?' Teclis said. He examined the Everchosen, studying the stained armour, the ragged furs and the expressionless helmet. Once, he thought, the man before him could have been something else. There was a whiff of destiny deferred about him. It reminded him of Tyrion, in a way. Archaon could have, once upon a time, become the guiding flame for humanity, leading his folk out of the shadows and into glory.

Instead, he had become nothing more than a black fire, blazing at the heart of a world-consuming inferno. *You could have been a hero,* Teclis thought, and felt a wave of sadness sweep through him. *But you didn't even try, did you? Did you even have the chance?* He shook his head and looked out at the city. 'My life and death are irrelevant. I have played my part in this sorry affair.'

'Let me tell you what I see,' Archaon said, hauling Teclis close. 'I see a battle already won, and the dying spasms of a world already ended. Whether your allies win or lose, I win. Or were you hoping one of them might turn the tide? Your brother, perhaps?' Archaon shoved Teclis back.

Teclis fell to his knees on the hard stone. He ignored the pain, and glared up at the Everchosen. *So certain, are you? So assured of the outcome that it has blinded you to any other possibility. You made your choice, and you expect the world to fall into line with it.* He snorted. *You are more like my brother than I thought.* 'Armies are not the only expression of strength. And my brother is not who you should fear. It is the Emperor.'

'Karl Franz is a weakling. A mortal serving a false god in the name of a nonexistent empire,' Archaon said. 'I tore his magic from him, and sent him running.'

Teclis allowed himself a wintry smile. 'I did not say the Emperor is Karl Franz.' He looked away, out over the city. He could see the lights of the Incarnates, drawing close. And one in particular attracted his eye. He could feel Archaon's eyes boring into him. 'Karl Franz died in Altdorf, at the hands of your servants. He was a man, and he died a man's death. But an empire must have an emperor, and one came who answered the call.' He smiled. It had taken some time to puzzle it all out.

'What are you saying?' Archaon said.

'Did you really believe that the Heldenhammer would do nothing while you annihilated all that he built?' Teclis said. He turned and met Archaon's black gaze without flinching. 'Sigmar is coming, Everchosen. Even as he came for your predecessors. And with him, all of the fury and fire of this world which you so casually claim is dying.'

Archaon lashed out with a fist, and knocked Teclis sprawling. 'Sigmar is a lie,' he snarled. He grabbed Teclis's chains and jerked the elf to his feet. 'He is a lie!'

Teclis grinned through bloody lips. 'I hope I get to see you tell him that face to face.'

Mannfred cursed loudly and steadily as he stormed out of the Temple of Ulric and flung himself into Ashigaroth's saddle. The great beast groaned as it flung itself into the air at his barked command. Mannfred snarled uselessly as he flew over the rooftops of the Ulricsmund. It was all going wrong; he could feel it. The wind was shifting, but he couldn't tell in which direction. *This is not as I foresaw,* he thought. Victory had seemed so certain, then. Now, there was no certainty save that the end was fast approaching.

When he had arrived in Middenheim a few days earlier, Archaon had readily accepted his offer of fealty, even as he had that of the renegade elf priestess, Hellebron, and, even more surprisingly, Settra the Imperishable. The former king of Khemri was the last individual, living or dead, that Mannfred had expected to see here of all places. He'd thought the ancient liche reduced to dust and scattered across the sands of his beloved Nehekhara, after his refusal to serve Nagash as a mortarch.

The Everchosen had seemed amused by these turncoats more than anything. And the Everchosen's other champions had wasted no opportunity to remind Mannfred of his new place in the scheme of things. He had been forced to defend himself, and his place in the pecking order, more than once. Such efforts had hardly been worth it, however.

He already regretted coming to Middenheim. This disrespect was the last straw. He would not fight for Archaon. Servitude to a jumped-up barbarian was no less galling than being Nagash's slave, and he had no taste for either. Let them fight one another. He would keep clear, and be ready to take advantage of what remained.

Ashigaroth hurtled on through the sky, as Mannfred turned his attentions to the battles taking place throughout the city. Somehow, Teclis had managed to drag the Incarnates and their followers to Middenheim, but he had not done so in any organised fashion. Nevertheless, they were moving steadily towards the Temple of Ulric, and Archaon. It would not take them long to smash aside the few obstacles Archaon had set in their path.

Mannfred glanced over his shoulder, back towards the temple. *What is your game, Everchosen? Why are you not making a more concentrated effort to stop them? What am I not seeing?* Since arriving in the city, he had attempted to uncover the reason for Archaon's seeming unwillingness to abandon the city. What was so important about Middenheim that Archaon would trap himself here?

Thus far, no answers were forthcoming. Archaon had shared his intent with few beyond his inner circle, most of whom were now dead by the hand of that fool, Canto. Archaon's executioner was nothing special – just another barbarian. But the others had deferred to him, as if he held some special place in Archaon's esteem. Mannfred's lip curled. As if a creature like that could be important.

Ashigaroth screamed and reared in mid-air. Mannfred fought to remain in the saddle as the beast bucked and shrieked. He twisted in the saddle, searching for what had disturbed his mount, and saw the sky over the Grafsmund split open, and spit out something like a falling star. He urged Ashigaroth closer, even as the falling thing slammed into the street and shook the city. Badly battered buildings collapsed all about the circumference of the newly made crater, filling the air with smoke and ruin. Northmen streamed through the streets below him, hurrying to confront the new arrival. Curiosity compelled him to follow suit.

The fallen rubble shifted and slumped as the monstrous form of a bloodthirster rose to its feet. The daemon was badly hurt, its unnatural flesh scorched by fire and marked by dozens of wounds, but it did not lack for strength as it tore its way free of the crater. The charging northmen had stumbled to a halt, and, as Mannfred watched, they sank down to their knees before the bloodthirster. As the smoke cleared, the vampire caught a good look at the beast, and he jerked on Ashigaroth's reins, pulling his mount up and away. Mannfred had studied the servants of the Dark Gods, and had familiarised himself with such entities as the Fateweaver and the Plaguefather. He knew Khorne's Huntsman when he saw him, and he wanted to be nowhere near such a ravening engine of destruction.

What the beast was doing here, he could only surmise. Archaon had sent Ka'Bandha to claim the skull of the Emperor – perhaps the daemon had simply followed his prey with the single-minded determination that so characterised the followers of the Blood God. The daemon unleashed a roar fraught with almost tangible frustration, and lashed out with the hammer it clutched in one claw, pulverising a number of the kneeling humans.

Ka'Bandha roared again. The surviving northmen, overcome by the daemon's bloodlust, threw back their heads as one and unleashed a warbling, communal howl. As the daemon strode away, the northmen followed, running on all fours as often as on two legs.

Mannfred shook himself. While he was immune to the daemon's presence, even he could feel the heat of the creature's rage. He urged Ashigaroth away, towards the Palast District. The more distance he put between himself and the daemon, the better. As he passed over the blood-soaked ruin Hellebron's cultists had made of the Middenplatz, a flash of movement below caught his attention. Something black, streaking across a rooftop.

Mannfred blinked. *Vlad,* he thought. *So, you've come as well. I thought you were smarter than that. Then, you could never resist a grand moment, could you?* He urged Ashigaroth in pursuit, and loosened his sword in its sheath. There was little chance, given the powers involved, that he could sway the battle one way or another. The thought galled him, but he was pragmatic enough to admit when he was outmatched. But he could accomplish at least one thing in the meantime.

Nagash should never have brought you back, old man, he thought. *And I'll see you sent back into the dark before this world ends.* Mannfred smiled cruelly as he hurtled in pursuit of the other vampire. Whatever else happened, whatever fate awaited Mannfred or the world he'd sought to claim, Vlad von Carstein would die.

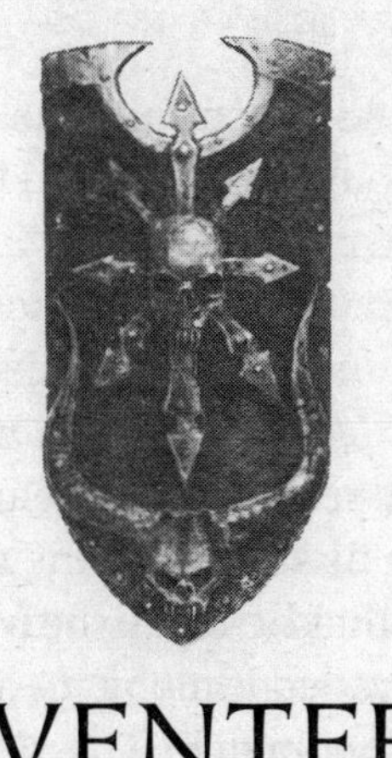

SEVENTEEN

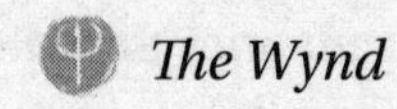

The Wynd

Malekith cursed as the eastern flank of his forces began to buckle beneath the weight of the orc assault. The ruins shook with savage cries as the greenskins barrelled through the thinning ranks of the fleeing skaven and crashed into the elves. The elves fought with all of the discipline and fury of their race, but they could not match the pure, bestial ferocity of the newcomers. He tugged on Seraphon's reins, drawing the dragon through the air towards the collapsing lines. Below him, elves on horseback galloped to bolster the flagging flank.

He couldn't say where the greenskins had come from, nor did he particularly care. That they were here now and attacking his forces was all that was important. It had all been going so well. The skaven had been driven before them, fleeing like the rodents they were. But even as the elves had pressed forwards, the orcs had been lured onto a collision course with Malekith's forces. He could see the cunning pattern now – the ratkin had ever been willing to sacrifice thousands of their own kind in order to secure a minor victory. He cursed himself for not being more wary. Now he had a more persistent foe to contend with, and he knew, though he could not see them through the fog of war, that the skaven were likely regrouping. They would not have led both armies here, if they did not have some–

The thud of jezzail shots and the crackle of warp-lightning cannons interrupted his thoughts, and confirmed his suspicions. Seraphon caught an updraught and reared to hover in the air as, below, jezzail-shot thudded into the melee, gouging bloody trails of dead and wounded through the press of battle. Poisoned wind mortar shells burst open along his lines, claiming the lives of many elves, including the fierce corsairs of the Krakensides.

Of course, he thought. *Why draw one foe into a trap, when you can draw two? Cunning vermin.* Malekith snarled in frustration and jabbed his spurs into Seraphon's scales, urging the dragon on.

With a shriek, the great beast undulated through the air, eastwards, in search of the hidden skaven positions. Malekith hunkered low in his saddle as green lightning arced from a crumbled second-storey archway, and at his command, Seraphon tucked its wings and plummeted towards the ruins like a diving falcon. The black dragon smashed into the ruins hard enough to shower the streets below with debris, and its head snaked forwards, jaws agape. Thick, black smoke spewed from its maw, and filled the ruin. Dying skaven staggered into view, collapsing even as they tried vainly to escape the noxious poison.

Malekith summoned flames of shadow and sent them roaring into the depths of the ruin, searing those skaven whom Seraphon's breath had not reached. He laughed as the vermin burned, and longed to do the same to the whole city. Let it all burn, and be lost to darkness, so that the enemy might know the futility of standing against the Eternity King.

He heard a squeal from above him, and twisted in his saddle. Shapes dropped towards him from the upper reaches of the ruin, wielding curved blades that glistened with poison. Even as he raised his blade, he knew that he would not be able to stop every blow.

Something flashed in the dark, and spun past him. Several of the assassins went limp, like puppets with their strings cut, and smashed into the ground below. The remaining skaven landed on Seraphon's back and leapt towards him, only to die with his sword in its skull. As he swept the twitching carcass away from him, he turned to see a dwarf axe embedded in the stonework nearby. Whoever had thrown it had done so with consummate skill, killing two assassins in mid-air with a single throw.

'You never were any good at watching your back, were you?' a rough voice rumbled, from somewhere nearby. Malekith froze. He recognised the voice, though he had not heard it in millennia. Not since those dim, distant days before elf and dwarf had discarded all oaths of friendship, and gone to war. 'Just as well I was passing through.' He caught a glimpse of gleaming armour and a flash of white beard, and felt his heart lurch in memory of a pain he'd thought long forgotten.

'Snorri,' Malekith whispered. 'My friend – I...'

But the speaker, whoever they had been, was gone. He turned and saw that the axe was gone as well, as if it had never been. Malekith shook his head. He knew the legends, and had heard the stories from the lips of slaves and captives, but he had never believed... not until now. He smiled. *Go in peace, my friend, and meet your doom as is fitting.*

Even as the eastern knot of skaven guns fell silent, so too did those situated to the south. Malekith pushed aside old memories and regrets as he peered into the darkness and glimpsed the glint of golden murder-masks there – the Chaindancers had found new prey. Malekith's smile turned cruel as he heard the screams of the ratkin, and silently wished the sisters of slaughter luck in their hunt. 'Such hubris these vermin display, to believe that we are prey, eh, Seraphon?' he murmured, as he gave the dragon's reins a tug. The beast flung itself back into the air, wings pumping.

As he passed over the heaving sprawl of battle, a dull ache began to grow in his skull. It was a familiar sensation – the tug of strong magics, of the great winds of the Vortex striving against one another. He felt it most strongly when another Incarnate was close by. He peered down, and saw a war-hydra fall, its coils split by the bite of a crude axe. A burly figure bounded through the writhing death-spasms of the beast, and crashed into the close-packed ranks of the Phoenix Guard. Amber energy sparked and snarled around the orc, as if the creature were the eye of a storm.

'The eighth wind,' Malekith hissed. And bound to the body of a brute at that. Suddenly, the presence of the orcs made sense – this was Teclis's fault. *Much like everything else,* he thought sourly. *And like everything else, it is up to me to see to the rectification of this colossal blunder.* The orcs were uncontrollable, and filled with the power of Ghur. They would ruin whatever slight chance of victory the Incarnates possessed.

'No, best to let the Wind of Beasts seek out a more fitting host,' he said, as he urged Seraphon into another dive. 'Once we have freed it from its current shoddy shell, of course.' The dragon roared, as if in reply, and dived down towards the orc warlord.

Improbably, the brute ducked beneath Seraphon's grasping talons. Malekith cursed as the dragon turned, jaws wide. The orc whirled and charged towards them, axe raised. The dragon spewed poison smoke, but the orc plunged through it heedlessly. Malekith blinked in shock, as the orc suddenly bounded from the cloud of poison and crashed down onto Seraphon's spined skull. Before the dragon could do more than issue a startled snarl, the orc was scrambling up Seraphon's ridged neck, towards the Eternity King.

The orc was even more monstrous up close, Malekith thought, even as he drew his blade to block a blow from that lethal axe. One eye blazed fiercely from a green, scowling face pitted with scars. The black armour was tarnished and piecemeal, but sturdy, and the orc's arms bulged with thick knots of muscle. There was a flare of light as their blades met, and Malekith grunted in pain as the force of the blow jarred his arm. The orc was strong; far stronger than he'd assumed. 'Grimgor is gonna gut ya,' the orc snarled, spraying spittle all over Malekith. 'Gonna rip out yer spine and beat ya to death wit' it. Gonna squish yer heart like it were a squig, and suck it dry!'

'You'll do nothing except scream, brute,' the Eternity King hissed. Malekith's hand snapped out, the clawed tips of his gauntlet sinking into the orc's arm, eliciting a bellow of pain. The orc rocked and his broad skull slammed into the faceplate of Malekith's helm, almost buckling it. Nearly jarred from his saddle, and dazed by the blow, Malekith slumped back, releasing his hold on the orc. The creature grinned and hefted his axe for a killing blow, but a sudden undulation from Seraphon as the dragon launched itself back into the air sent the brute tumbling away, back to the street below.

Before Malekith could attempt to spot where his foe had landed, a great chittering shriek rose from the north, and he turned to see a host of armoured skaven ploughing through the ruins of a burnt-out guildhouse, straight towards his already embattled forces. 'No,' he spat. 'No more of this foolishness.' Even as he spoke, however, the sound of more orcs arriving reached him. Hundreds of orcs were spilling through the rubble of storehouses and shops, an unyielding wave of green violence, seeking to sweep his embattled forces from the field. Giants and ogres lumbered amongst them, and squealing, snorting boar riders careened through the streets ahead of the rest.

His host was caught in the jaws of a trap, and there would be no escape. Not through force at any rate. His elves were too few, and even his own power, great as it was, could not prevail over so many enemies. *Is this it, then? Is this my fate – our fate? To be drowned in violence by uncomprehending savages or cowardly vermin? Am I to preside over ignominious defeat? Is that to be my legacy?* he wondered, as his heart sank and his warriors died.

No. No, this was not his fate. He had struggled too hard, fought too long to give it all up now due to the error of another. He was Malekith. He was supreme. He had survived the Flame of Asuryan not once but twice, and forged two nations in his lifetime. He had beaten daemons, and matched his will to that of the Dark Gods themselves and emerged whole and triumphant.

But there had ever been one common element to his victories. One foe that had to be defeated first, in every case. *Pride, damnable pride.* It was pride that drove him; he knew it and accepted it. It was pride that lent him strength, and pride too which had endangered his every plan and scheme. Pride told him that he needed no aid; pride murmured that he could find a more fitting host for the Winds of Death and Beasts; pride demanded that he fight to the last, against those he deemed inferior.

And it was with a single twist of his limbs that Malekith dashed pride to the ground, and dropped from Seraphon's saddle. He landed lightly, despite the weight of his armour, borne to the street by coiling shadows. The orc still lived, and was hacking his way through the Phoenix Guard with a single-minded determination that put Malekith in mind of Tyrion. *Brutes of a feather,* he thought, as he strode towards his opponent.

The orc roared as he caught sight of Malekith. Several of his followers made as if to charge the Eternity King, but the orc cut them down without hesitation. Malekith smiled. The beast would allow no other to claim his victory. *Pride is not the sole province of Asuryan's children,* he thought as he drew close to the rampaging orc. Amber light sparked and snarled about the orc warlord, illuminating him with a pale glow.

Well, now to see whether I am right... or dead, Malekith mused, as he swiftly sank down to one knee, bowed his head, and extended his sword hilt-first towards his opponent. 'I yield,' he said, loudly.

The orc, axe raised over his blunt skull, blinked. Malekith said, 'I yield, in my name, and in that of the elven race. We are your servants.'

The orc hesitated for a moment. Then a slow, cruel snarl of triumph spread across his features. The orc raised his axe and turned towards his brawling followers. '*Grimgor is da best!*' he bellowed. He pounded his chest with a closed fist, and his followers added their voices to his victorious roar.

'No,' Malekith said.

The orc whirled about. 'What?' the brute growled.

Malekith matched the beast's gimlet stare with one of his own. 'I - we came to this city to defeat one who claims that title for himself.' He flung a hand out to indicate the skaven. 'They serve him, as do the northmen. They say he is the best, the strongest warrior in the world. So strong that he intends to crack it, and drown what's left in fire.' Malekith inclined his head. 'How can Grimgor be the best, if Archaon kills the world?'

'Archaon,' Grimgor rumbled, drawing the Everchosen's name out like a curse. Amber sparks danced in the brute's good eye. The beast turned north, towards the Temple of Ulric. 'Archaon... thinks he's better than me?'

'I doubt that he thinks of you at all,' Malekith said.

'Take me to him,' Grimgor snarled, shoving the flat of his axe beneath Malekith's chin. 'I'm gonna bash 'im, and then I'm gonna stomp 'im, and then we'll see who's best.'

'It would be my pleasure,' Malekith murmured, rising to his feet. Grimgor snorted and turned. At a single bellow, his orcs began to flow around the elves, and towards the skaven. Malekith could almost admire the iron control the beast had over his simple-minded followers. But he still intended to plant his sword between the brute's shoulder blades once the day was won. He'd sacrificed his pride on the altar of necessity, but that didn't mean that matters between them were resolved.

I hope you survive what's coming, beast. If only so you can witness my supremacy first-hand, when your services are no longer required...

* * *

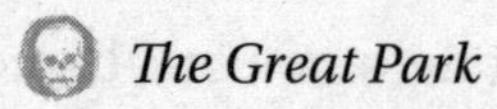

The Great Park

Arkhan the Black pinned the northman to the ground with a sweep of his staff, and watched disinterestedly as the savage convulsed and withered to a lifeless husk. It joined the others that surrounded him in an ever expanding ring of death, and he paid the body no more notice. It wasn't even worth raising to fight anew.

From around him rose the clangour of battle, as barrow-blade crashed against ensorcelled steel in a monotonous rhythm. Nearby, the wights of the Doomed Legion fought against the black-armoured reavers of the Wastes, both sides trampling the bodies of Kurgan and northmen beneath their heavy treads. With a gesture, Arkhan re-knit broken bones and rebound wicked spirits to their mouldering bodies, dragging those wights who had fallen back to their feet to rejoin the fight.

The sky had gone from red to black, and squirmed like a carcass full of maggots. The few remaining trees in the Great Park had been set alight by witch-fires as the battle surged back and forth. The living had been joined by a cavalcade of daemons – graceful, dancing shapes which moved with impossible quickness across the field. One such bounded towards Arkhan, her lilting song playing across the grave-whisper of his thoughts. Faces flashed in his mind's eye – Morgiana, Neferata, others, women he had loved and lost in his sorry life – but he ignored them easily enough. His will was not his own, and could not be broken so lightly. The vast, black bulwark of Nagash's thoughts steadied his own, and he interposed his staff as the daemonette's claws snapped shut inches from his skull.

The daemon hissed at him and he twisted to the side, throwing the androgynous creature to the ground. Before it could rise, he had drawn his barrow-blade and severed its head from its neck. He turned, blade still in hand, and scanned the park. Wailing spirits hurtled through the ashen air to the south, ripping the life from Kurgan warriors, even as the latter fought on beneath their skull-topped banners against a lurching, fire-blistered horde of zombies. He heard a rasping roar, and turned to see Krell's axe crash down on the mirrored shield of a creature he recognised as Sigvald the Magnificent. Arkhan had only crossed paths with the Geld-Prince once before, in Araby, but he knew that the Chaos champion was a deadly opponent, despite being a preening brat.

Arkhan extended his staff, unleashing a crackling amethyst hurricane of death-magics at the daemonettes who capered past Sigvald and Krell, unbinding them and reducing them to motes of glittering dust. Through the cloud, he saw Sigvald driven back by Krell's whirling blows, each of which bled seamlessly into the next.

Again and again, Sigvald lunged at Krell, his flickering blade skittering across Krell's ancient armour, but the wight gave no ground, and continued to drive his opponent before him. Krell launched a wide blow, meant to decapitate Sigvald, but the Geld-Prince ducked beneath it. The blow shattered the scorched husk of a tree, showering both warriors with cinders and ash. Sigvald lunged, and his sword punched through Krell's breastplate with a screech of metal and a puff of dust.

Krell staggered back, a dry, death-rattle laugh echoing from his fleshless jaws. He pivoted, wrenching the sword from Sigvald's grip, and backhanded him, sending the Chaos champion flying backwards. Arkhan nodded in satisfaction. All was as it should be.

Suddenly, a throaty roar split the cacophony of battle. Arkhan looked towards the overlook of the park and saw a vast, lumpen silhouette clamber over the hill. A tattered red cloak flapped about the beast's shoulders, and a tarnished crown pulsed strangely on its brow. Arkhan raised his staff warily. This creature too he recognised, though he had never before laid eyes on it. Arkhan had heard the stories from his agents in the north, of

Throgg and his ice-palace in the ruins of Praag. Of the capture of sorcerers and mages of all races and descriptions; of Throgg's obsessions, and his fall at the hands of a one-eyed dwarf. *It seems that fall was not so long as one might hope,* Arkhan thought.

For now, it seemed as if the Wintertooth, the so-called King of the Trolls, had come to Middenheim, and he had not come alone. Trolls, giants and mutants of the northlands flooded down the overlook, smashing into both the dead and the living without regard to whether they were friend or foe. Feral minotaurs slaughtered Kurgan warriors as the ghorgons of the Drakwald tore through the massed ranks of zombies.

Arkhan wove spells of strength and recovery with all the speed his dead limbs could muster, trying to hold the army of corpses together. He could feel Nagash's displeasure ripple through him, and with a twitch of his staff he summoned the surviving morghasts from the angry skies. The osseous constructs hurtled down like birds of prey, their spirit-bound blades chopping into bestial flesh. But for every dozen brutes and beasts that fell, a morghast was pulled down from the sky, to be hacked apart or torn limb from limb.

Though it took almost every iota of concentration he could muster to reform the destroyed constructs and fling them into battle once more, Arkhan kept one eye on the duel between Krell and Sigvald. If the wight could manage to dispatch the champion, it might tear all heart from the surviving Kurgan and put them to flight. With them out of the way, the beasts would be easy prey. Or so he hoped.

That hope, however, proved to be in vain. Arkhan watched, disconcerted, as Sigvald lunged to retrieve his sword, still stuck in Krell's chest, and Krell's axe whistled down to shatter the mirror-shield the man held. Sigvald staggered back, sword in hand, face bloody. The axe had bifurcated the shield and gashed the Geld-Prince's handsome features, reducing one side of his face to a ruin. Sigvald clapped a hand to his mangled flesh and wailed like a dying cat. The champion lunged, still shrieking, and launched blow after blow at Krell.

Krell staggered back beneath the rain of wild blows. His axe lashed out in reply, scarring Sigvald's gleaming cuirass or scoring his flesh, but the Geld-Prince was too far gone to feel the blows, Arkhan realised. The two warriors whirled and clashed through the melee, smashing down any creature, living, dead or otherwise, unlucky enough to get between them. Arkhan considered lending Krell aid, but dismissed the idea even as it occurred to him. He had his own battle to fight – a roaring giant stretched a wide hand towards him, as if to scoop him up. Arkhan ducked under the grasping fingers and lashed out with his sword, slicing through the creature's wrist. The giant howled and retracted its limb, as Arkhan thrust his staff out and spat a killing word. The great beast staggered as its mighty frame began to shrivel and sag. It turned to dust even as it fell.

Arkhan heard a crash and spun. Sigvald, broken sword in hand, had borne Krell to the ground. One of the wight's arms was missing, and as Arkhan watched, Sigvald braced his knee against the other, pinning Krell. The champion was howling unintelligibly as he battered at the wight with his broken sword and bleeding fists. Krell's armour crumpled beneath the maddened Geld-Prince's blows, and Arkhan could feel the wight's spirit slipping loose from its husk. He took a step towards them, but found his path blocked by a massive shape.

Throgg roared and smashed his club down, narrowly missing Arkhan. The troll-king wrenched his weapon up, scattering cobblestones, and swung it again. Arkhan twisted aside and hacked a bloody trench in the troll's side. Throgg staggered, clapping a hand to the steaming wound. His club found Arkhan's hip, pulverising the bone. Arkhan stumbled, and it was only thanks to his staff that he stayed upright. He dragged himself out of reach as his bones re-knit, but Throgg didn't follow. Instead, the troll seemed captivated by Sigvald and Krell's confrontation.

Arkhan shuddered as he heard the fading scream of Krell's ancient, black soul, and he glanced over his shoulder. Sigvald sat back on his heels, panting and bloody-faced, staring blindly down at the shattered remains of Krell. The Geld-Prince threw back his head and screamed, though whether in triumph or in mourning for his ruined features, Arkhan couldn't say. Regardless, the scream was cut short a moment later by Throgg, who split Sigvald's head open with his club, dashing his brains across Krell's carcass.

Throgg turned, a smile on his grotesque features. 'He was a fool, and a wastrel,' the troll rumbled. Arkhan was startled by the troll's voice. It was not that of a beast, but of a man. A man in agony. For a brief moment, Arkhan felt a strange kinship with the creature – they were both but pawns in the designs of others, their own hopes and dreams but sparks lost in the grand conflagrations of those they served.

'And you are neither, I suppose,' Arkhan rasped.

'No. The gods sent me here to die on your sword, so that my body might tangle your feet and delay you,' Throgg said. He looked around. More bellowing creatures – monsters of all shapes and sizes – spilled down from the overlook with every passing moment. What was left of the Doomed Legion was already being swept away, and only the southern stretch of the Great Park was still firmly in the hands of the dead. The battle was going badly, Arkhan knew. He could feel Nagash's growing frustration, and the heavy tread of his approach.

'A TASK FOR WHICH YOU AND YOUR HORDE ARE SINGULARLY WELL SUITED, APE,' Nagash said, as he stepped over the burning carcass of a chimera. Blood stained his robes and armour, but the nine books still thrashed and snapped at the ends of their chains, and his captive spirits still wailed. *'BUT I HAVE NO TIME FOR SUCH DISTRACTIONS. I HAVE GODS TO SLAY.'*

Throgg hefted his club. 'Make time, carrion-bird,' he roared.

'I have been denied an empire, but I will not be denied victory.' The troll surged forwards, brushing Arkhan aside as if the liche were no more substantial than a spider-web. 'I will wear your skull as an amulet, and the gods will grant me all that I wish!'

Nagash's great blade looped around, and chopped through the club. Throgg lurched to the side, off balance, and Nagash's free hand snapped forwards, talons digging into the troll's throat. Nagash dragged the troll close. *'THE GODS GRANT NOTHING YOU DID NOT ALREADY POSSESS, FOOL. THEY ARE LIARS AND THIEVES. I WILL DRAG THEM SCREAMING FROM THEIR NIGHTMARE WOMB AND FLAY THEIR SECRETS FROM THEM. SERVE ME, AND I WILL GIVE YOU ALL THAT YOU MIGHT DESIRE.'*

Throgg pounded uselessly on Nagash's arm, trying to break his grip. The troll glared at Nagash. 'Better death,' he snarled, in his almost-human voice. 'Better death than service to such as you. The gods might raise us up, or dash us down, but there is a chance there, at least. There is no hope, not in you.'

'AS YOU WISH,' Nagash intoned. His great blade, death-energy writhing along its length, plunged down, through the troll's thick shoulder and into his torso. Throgg screamed and sank down, clawing at Nagash's robes. The Undying King held the sword in place, and the magics in that fell blade did their work, chewing through the troll's mutated body like acid. Throgg collapsed slowly, falling in on himself, until there remained only a pile of char and ash, and a tarnished crown, which rolled slowly away across the cobbles to fall flat at Arkhan's feet.

'And thus do the unworthy fall,' a voice as dry as the desert sands rasped. Arkhan looked up from the crown, and turned. A familiar form, ancient bones shrouded in tattered ceremonial wrappings and broken armour, stepped towards them, khopesh in hand. *'Will you join him in oblivion, Usurper?'*

'SETTRA,' Nagash said.

'I have walked across half of this world to find you, Usurper.

You broke me and scattered me, but Settra is deathless. Settra is eternal. And so Settra returned, and now he stands here, sword in hand, and he denies you, Usurper. He stands between you and triumph,' Settra croaked. He lifted his khopesh and pointed it at Nagash, who regarded him as if he were less a threat than a curiosity.

'I DID NOT BRING YOU BACK, LITTLE KING,' Nagash said.

'No,' Settra said. *'You did not.'* The khopesh dipped. *'They did. The jackals of the smokeless fire, the howlers in the Wastes. They dared to offer Settra aid.'*

'HOW FOOLISH OF THEM,' Nagash said.

'They offered Settra victories, and empires and life unending.'

'AND WHAT DID THEY ASK IN RETURN, LITTLE KING?'

'That I serve them and kill you.' Settra looked down at the remains of Throgg, and then, quicker than Arkhan could follow, lunged. Nagash lurched aside, but Arkhan realised that Settra had not been aiming for the Incarnate of Death. Instead, the ancient king's blade chopped into the scaly torso of the dragon ogre which had been preparing to smash its enormous axe down on the back of Nagash's skull. The beast roared in agony, but Settra did not give it time to recover. He tore his blade free and slashed upwards, separating the monster's head from its shoulders. It toppled over like a felled tree, and Settra turned.

He extended his khopesh towards Nagash. *'Settra does not serve. Settra rules.'* He strode past them, towards the horde of monsters. *'Go, prince of Khemri. Settra will forgive your trespasses if you but make the jackals howl. Teach them that the kings of the Great Land cannot be bought and sold like slaves. And then, when it is done, Settra shall take your head, and take back his people.'*

As the last words left his mouth, Settra the Imperishable broke into a run, slashing out at a snarling giant even as the great beast reached down for him. His khopesh removed its fingers, and then its lower jaw in rapid succession. A moment later, he was lost to Arkhan's sight as he plunged into the heart of the battle.

Arkhan looked up at Nagash. The Undying King gazed in the direction Settra had vanished for a moment longer, as if bemused. Then he turned to look down at Arkhan. *'MY SERVANT,'* he said.

'What would you have me do, master?'

'I MUST REACH THE ARTEFACT, OR ALL IS FOR NAUGHT. TAKE TWO HOSTS OF THE MORGHASTS AND HOLD HERE, UNTIL YOUR LAST STRENGTH IS GONE. DO NOT FAIL ME.'

Arkhan didn't flinch. He had fallen before, as had Krell. It was never the end. No matter how often he wished it were so. Settra's reappearance was proof enough of that. And Nagash was right. They could not break away from the enemy here. Even though Throgg was dead, and Sigvald too, their foes were too numerous and too far gone in their bloodlust to be so easily shifted, even by one as mighty as Settra. For Nagash to make his escape, someone would have to stay behind and keep the remaining Kurgan and the monstrous horde occupied. And since Krell was no more, that left him. *'Yes, master. Do you have any further commands?'*

Nagash hesitated. And for the first time, Arkhan the Black felt a flicker of hope. He had never known the Great Necromancer to hesitate, even in the face of defeat. It was as if, for the first time in centuries, the Undying King was uncertain of the ultimate outcome. Nagash looked down at him and said, finally, *'DIE WELL, MY SERVANT.'*

Then Nagash stalked south, leaving Arkhan to face the enemy alone. Arkhan turned away, and set his staff. The remnants of Throgg's army that weren't currently being occupied by Settra rampaged towards him, shaking the ground beneath his feet. Arkhan tightened his grip on his sword, and thought of a long-forgotten alleyway, where he'd first set his feet on the path to eternal servitude. A path that had, at long last, reached its end.

He thought of the feeling of sand across his cheeks, and the smell of Cathayan spices on a sea breeze. He could taste blood, and the black leaf, and the kisses of a queen. He looked down at his fleshless hand, clasped about the hilt of his sword, and then up, at the crawling sky.

If Arkhan the Black had been capable of smiling, he would have.

The Palast District

'*Fire!*' Gotri Hammerson roared, chopping the air with his axe. The ensuing volley punched through the ranks of the beastmen, dropping many. The rest came on, braying coarse-tongued battle cries as they charged heedlessly into the dwarf shield-wall. 'Ironbreakers – to the fore!' Hammerson bellowed, as he signalled for the Thunderers to retreat.

The Ironbreakers, clad in gromril and bearing runic shields, stumped forward, accompanied by Balthasar Gelt, as the dwarf line fell back around them. The Incarnate of Metal planted his staff, and the runes inscribed on the ancient armour of the dwarfs glowed with power. A moment later, the beastmen crashed into them, hacking at flesh and armour with frenzied abandon. The dwarfs held firm, and soon the last of the creatures was slumping into the dust or scattering in flight. Hammerson caught Gelt's eye, and nodded sharply.

They had come to the aid of the elves, but almost too late. Alarielle's forces were outnumbered and surrounded by an ever-expanding ring of foes. And unlike the beastmen, these didn't look as if the thought of dwarf bullets filled them with much dread. Witch elves, howling blood cultists, and daemons swirled about Alarielle's elves and tree-spirits, and only where Durthu and the remaining treemen fought was the battle not going badly.

Hammerson knew that wasn't going to last. He could see a massive cauldron-shrine grinding slowly across the plaza towards Alarielle, and perched atop it, the fugitive Blood Queen, Hellebron. The wiry witch elf spat and railed, issuing orders and threats in a voice twisted by madness. She clashed her blades and gesticulated wildly, as if overcome by the same frenzy which possessed her followers. He'd heard that she had fled Athel Loren before the arrival of the refugees from Averheim, and had learned enough about her proclivities to know that she meant Alarielle ill.

'We must rescue her,' Gelt said, as he hurried towards Hammerson. His golden mask was dented and tarnished, but his eyes glowed with power. 'If Alarielle falls, so too will the world,' he continued. He gestured with his staff towards the cauldron-shrine, as its heavy wheels ground over the broken dead and laughing witch elves came leaping in its wake.

'Aye,' Hammerson grunted. 'I have eyes, lad. I know.' He raised his axe. 'Zhufbarak – shield-march,' he shouted. 'Let's go give the tree-huggers a hand, lads.' The Ironbreakers locked shields and started forwards, as the clansmen and Thunderers followed suit. A dwarf throng on the march was akin to one of the Empire's steam tanks, capable of rolling over almost any enemy. Clansmen on the flanks used their shields to provide cover for the Thunderers, who unleashed volley after volley, reloading as they moved. The Ironbreakers formed the wedge, smashing aside any enemy who sought to stand in the throng's path. And there were plenty of those. Hammerson and Gelt took the point of the wedge for themselves, unleashing their respective magics on the foe.

Hang on woman, we're coming, he thought, as he summoned runes of fire and swept aside a shrieking witch elf. *Not that I have any clue how to help you, when we get there. Or if you'll even live that long, with the way you're looking...*

From his few glimpses of her, as she fought in the shadow of Durthu, the Everqueen looked less radiant than cadaverous. It was as if she had aged centuries in moments, and her movements were faltering. Nonetheless, she fought on, her magics reaching out to snare and break the enemy at every turn. Hammerson had no real fondness for the elves, but he knew bravery when he saw it. And he was determined not to let it be in vain.

The Zhufbarak throng advanced at a glacier's pace, with all the relentless inexorability that implied. Salvoes thundered forth, flinging bodies into the air and throwing the already anarchic ranks of the enemy into complete disarray. The great, coiling war-horns of Zhufbar groaned so loudly as to shake the rubble, and where bullets and steam did not reach, axes and hammers served to split Hellebron's host in two.

At a gesture from Gelt, golden light danced across the weapons of the dwarfs, awakening the full power of the ancestral runes. Gromril armour flared and shone like the stars that had once shone in the skies above as it was struck by enemy blows. Hammerson raised his axe and gestured east. With his other hand, he motioned west. The dwarf shield-wall split with perfect synchronicity, and two lines of clan warriors turned outwards around a hinge composed of a doughty core of Ironbreakers, one to the east, the other to the west. Hammerson gestured to Gelt. 'Take the west, lad. I'll see to the east,' he growled. 'Let the enemy break themselves on good dwarf steel. Give the elgi a chance to catch their breath. We'll collapse the wall when we've earned some space, and squeeze the enemy between us, like grist beneath a millstone.'

Hammerson watched Gelt go, and then turned to study the turmoil they had wrought in their wake. He grunted in satisfaction as he saw that their intervention had destroyed any momentum the enemy possessed. They'd cut Hellebron's forces in two, with the Blood Queen herself caught on the wrong side of the shield-wall and trapped between dwarfs and elves. Then, that didn't seem to bother her all that much. She was exhorting her followers to greater efforts, ranting and shrieking loudly enough to wake the dead. The elves would have to hold out until the dwarfs could fall back to their position.

Hammerson glanced back at Alarielle. *I hope you can handle her, woman, because we've got our hands full,* he thought. A thunderclap shook the Palast and rattled his teeth in his jaw, and he turned to see the followers of the Blood God slam into the western shield-wall. Axe-blades chopped over shield rims or hooked dwarf legs, and the wall wavered, but only for an instant. Rune-axes carved red, efficient arcs through the packed ranks of the enemy, as the Zhufbarak gave their foes their fill and more of skulls and blood.

'Hold them, lad,' Hammerson growled. He looked around at his warriors, as they strained against the enemy. 'And you, you great wattocks... that goes for you as well!' he roared, clashing his weapons together. 'Hold!'

The ancient treeman gave a cry, like the splintering of a great oak, and collapsed. Alarielle whipped around, the pain of the world's dying a drumbeat in her temples, and stared in shock as Skarana, eldest of the oldest, toppled down into death. The bloodthirster roared in triumph and ripped its axe free of the treeman's body, scattering charred splinters across the heads of the wailing dryads which flung themselves on the daemon's followers. The daemon charged towards her and Durthu, wings flared, arms wide, as if inviting them to meet it in battle. She could feel her protector stiffen in anticipation, and then relax.

Durthu would not leave her side willingly. Not while only a thin wall of spears separated her from Hellebron's maddened servants. The treeman did not trust the dwarfs to reach her in time. But he was the only one among them strong enough to dispatch the daemon even now charging towards them. She placed a hand on the rough bark of his wrist. Durthu was the greatest of Athel Loren's children. In his mighty frame was the strength of the forest itself, and the blade he carried had been forged by the gods.

'Go,' Alarielle said. Durthu looked down at her, silently. Alarielle frowned. 'Go, Durthu. Go begrudgingly, or willingly, but go. Do as I command. I will be here when you return.' Durthu reached out, and brushed a lock of hair from her face. Then, with a sound like an avalanche, the treeman turned and strode to meet the daemon.

Durthu picked up speed as he moved past the spear-wall of the defenders, and his great root-feet trampled the enemy as he charged towards the approaching daemon, his massive blade held out behind him. He reached out with his free hand, and roared with all the fury of Athel Loren as he smashed into the bloodthirster, sending the daemon staggering sideways into the Middenplatz wall. There was a crackle of snapping bone as the force of the impact shattered the daemon's wings, and the beast howled in agony.

Durthu didn't slacken his assault. Even as the bloodthirster tried to rise, the treeman swung his Daith-forged blade up and drove it down through his opponent's breastplate and into the unnatural flesh beneath. The bloodthirster shrieked and grasped the blade. It hauled itself up and smashed at Durthu with its axe, hacking deep grooves into the treeman's bark. Durthu ignored the frenzied assault and twisted around, wrenching his blade free of the bloodthirster's chest. Without pausing, he whirled about, bringing the sword about to chop clean through the daemon's thick neck.

The treeman stepped aside as the daemon collapsed, but Alarielle did not see what happened next. Her attentions were dragged back to her own predicament, as one of her warriors gave a shout. Alarielle grimaced as the corpse impaled on the woman's spear abruptly flopped into motion and pulled itself off the point of the weapon. Others began to rise as well, slipping and sliding in their own blood as they struggled upright. Alarielle hissed in pain as the Winds of Life recoiled from the abomination taking place before her. She raised her hand, ready to sweep the risen dead aside with her magics before they could attack, when a sudden shout stayed her hand. A familiar form had dropped from the Middenplatz wall and into the battle, laying about him with a deadly blade.

'Take heart, dear lady,' Vlad von Carstein called out as he sprinted past her warriors, accompanied by the staggering forms of the newly slain, who stumbled in his wake. 'Your champions are legion, be they man, dwarf or heroic tree-stump. Your burying place is not here, and not today. So swears Vlad von Carstein, Elector of Sylvania,' he shouted, flinging himself into battle like a dark thunderbolt. Where he moved, the enemy fell, only to rise again at his command. With every corpse that rose, a jagged thorn of pain cut into her heart. But those pains were but pinpricks compared to the agony she felt with every breath. The world itself was coming undone, collapsing in on itself like a rotten tree, and she could feel the sharp ache of the artefact Archaon was employing to accomplish the unmaking.

The vampire slithered into the heart of the ranks of the bloodthirster's followers, his sword flickering like lightning. He employed finesse and brutality in equal measure, and moved with such grace that Alarielle thought even Tyrion might have looked upon him with envy. He employed the risen dead like ambulatory shields, using them to create opportunities for his kills. She shook her head, grateful and disturbed in equal measure, and turned her attentions to her own battle.

Despite the aid of the dead and the dwarfs, Hellebron's forces had reached the ring of dryads who protected Alarielle, sacrificing their lives to keep her safe. She felt every death, every mangling blow that afflicted the tree-spirits, and it was all she could do to stay on her feet. She watched in dull-eyed horror as dryads flung themselves up the iron stairs of the cauldron-shrine that steadily bore down on her. The spirits attacked Hellebron, who hacked them down with shrieks of laughter. Alarielle closed her eyes. She felt every blow, and her body shuddered as each spirit fell. Hellebron bounded off the cauldron, her lithe shape covered in blood and sap. 'I see you, queen of weeds and maggots,' she screeched, gesturing with one of her cruelly curved blades. 'I see you, and I will wear your pretty skin as a cloak.' She darted forwards, and two of Alarielle's guards moved to intercept her. Without slowing, Hellebron swept her blades out and removed their heads.

Alarielle stepped up. Her asrai fell back at her command, clearing a path. She wanted no more of them to die in a futile attempt to stop the Blood Queen. Hellebron danced towards her, grinning madly, and Alarielle wondered how it had come to this. What had set the Blood Queen on this course? She had come to Athel Loren with Malekith and the others, but her loyalty to her people had faded like a morning mist, leaving only this... thing which now capered and shrieked at her in challenge. A challenge that she would meet, though she was no warrior. Though she had learned blade-craft from the finest warriors in Ulthuan, the Everqueen was a creature of peace, rather than war, and even with the power of Life Incarnate, she was little match for the former ruler of Har Ganeth.

'We looked for you,' Alarielle said, 'after Be'lakor's attack on the Oak of Ages. We thought you had been slain.' She waited for Hellebron, trying to conserve her strength.

'That would have pleased you to no end, I'm certain,' Hellebron cackled. She pulled the edges of her blades across each other, filling the air with their shriek.

'If you think that, then you are truly demented,' Alarielle said. 'You were welcomed into Athel Loren, sorceress. You and your followers both, despite your foul ways. You are of the asur, despite your predilections, and I would not see you dead.'

Hellebron grimaced. 'You lie,' she spat. Her grimace twisted into a manic grin. 'And now, you die!' She lunged, and Alarielle interposed her staff. The cobblestoned street ruptured as a writhing thicket of thorn-vines burst upwards to ensnare the leaping form of Hellebron. The Blood Queen shrieked in pain, but did not stop. Her blades flashed out, chopping through the vines, and a moment later, she was free. She snarled and drove one of her blades into Alarielle's belly.

Alarielle screamed as Hellebron jerked the blade free, and clapped a hand to the wound in her stomach. She slumped to her knees, the pain overwhelming her. Her staff rolled away, forgotten. The world seemed to shudder around her, as if in sympathy, and she bowed her head, trying to concentrate through her own internal din. She could feel the essence of Ghyran trying to mend her torn flesh, but she was too weak. The world's pain, added to her own, was too much to bear. Nonetheless, she could not give in. Too much counted on her. She tried to focus her own magics through those of Ghyran, to bolster her flagging body.

Out of the corner of her eye, she saw Hellebron's second blade descending towards her neck, as if in slow motion. The Blood Queen's features were distorted by rage, triumph, and something else. *Fear,* Alarielle realised. Hellebron was afraid. Of what, she couldn't say, but that fear was driving the Blood Queen to attack like a wild animal. The Wind of Life whispered in Alarielle's mind, and in that instant, the Incarnate of Life knew what was required of her.

Alarielle forced herself to her feet and caught Hellebron's wrist as she rose, halting the blade a hair's breadth from her neck. She forced her opponent back and tore her hand from her wound. The green energy of life crackled between her bloody fingers as she pressed her hand gently to the side of Hellebron's contorted face. The magics flowed into the dark elf, and centuries of madness and frenzy were washed away by the healing tide of Ghyran. The fractured psyche of the Blood Queen became whole, for the first time in a thousand or more years, and with lucidity came understanding. For a moment, a different woman entirely looked out through Hellebron's bulging eyes, saw what she had made of herself, and the witch elf moaned in horror.

Alarielle met Hellebron's horrified gaze and said, 'I'm sorry.' Then, grabbing hold of her opponent's wrist with both hands, she forced

Hellebron's own blade up into its owner's chest. The deadly blade passed through Hellebron's ribs and its curved tip found her heart, and the horror in her eyes faded as her contorted features slackened into something resembling peace. She slumped against Alarielle, and the Everqueen sank back down, blood pouring from the wound in her belly. She slipped down beside her fallen opponent.

She felt cold, and the dark crept in at the edges of her vision. She heard the screams of Hellebron's remaining followers and the agonised shouts of her people, and wanted to weep for the uselessness of it all, but lacked the strength to do anything but lie still. *Is this death, then?* she thought. She did not fear it. Aliathra's face swam before her eyes, and she reached up, hoping to touch her daughter's cheek once more, to say at last all the things she should have said. *I will tell you of your father, and how he tore me from my silk pavilions and slew any who stood in his way, the day that Malekith came for me. I will tell you how we hid in the forests of Avelorn, and what occurred there. I will tell you everything, at last... You are so like him, my daughter. Brave and foolish and proud... I–*

A shadow fell over her. Heavy, rough hands picked her up, and a voice like the curling of roots through the hard-packed earth spoke gently to her. Durthu. The treeman cradled her close, and the last thing she heard before oblivion swept her under was his roar, as it shook the Middenplatz down to its foundations.

Vlad watched in consternation as the treeman, still cradling the broken form of the Everqueen, wrenched the cauldron-shrine from its frame and, swinging it by its broken chains, hurled it at the remaining blood-worshippers. Then, with another bone-rattling roar, the ancient spirit uprooted its sword and stalked into battle, killing any who dared stand against it, be they elf, human, beast or daemon.

Too little, too late, brute, Vlad thought, as he blocked a blow from his current opponent, a hammer-wielding berserker who'd announced himself as Harald Hammerstorm, as if Vlad either knew or cared as to his identity. If the Incarnate of Life was dead, that boded ill for their chances to see off whatever apocalypse Archaon was brewing in the bowels of Middenheim. He snarled in frustration. To have come so close, only to fail now, was unacceptable. He had lost Isabella, Sylvania, even Mannfred... He would not lose the world as well.

'Die, beast,' Hammerstorm roared. He struck out with a looping blow, which Vlad easily avoided. His riposte glanced from the Chaos warrior's shield, and they circled one another, each searching for an opening in the other's defences. Why the warrior had singled him out, Vlad couldn't say, but he was getting bored. Hammerstorm was tenacious, and annoyingly difficult to hurt. Vlad grinned as the warrior surged towards him, shield tilted, hammer swung back. It was the first mistake his opponent had made, and Vlad intended to make it his last. He slid forward to meet the Chaos warrior, rather than retreating, and let his blade glide across the face of Hammerstorm's shield. The point of his sword pierced Hammerstorm's visor, even as the warrior's hammer caught him in the ribs and knocked him sprawling.

Vlad rolled to his feet with a hiss of pain, one arm pressed tight to his side, as Hammerstorm took a faltering step towards him, hammer raised for another blow. Blood was pouring down the Chaos warrior's visor. He took another step, a third, and then toppled forwards. He crashed down, and his hammer clattered from his grip. Vlad rose to his feet with a wince, and saluted his fallen enemy.

The wind shifted, and a familiar, if foul, stench invaded his nostrils. He whirled and cursed as he caught sight of the diseased host that crashed against the dwarf line, even as the last of the blood-mad berserkers died. Plaguebearers wielded rusty, pus-encrusted blades against the ragtag shield-wall of the Zhufbarak, and where they struck, metal rusted, leather rotted and flesh turned black and swollen. The golden light of Gelt's magics warred with the malignant wind of putrefaction as the weary dwarfs met their foes with stolid determination. Even as Vlad hurried towards them, he saw his zombies begin to rot and collapse, even as they had in Sylvania so many weeks ago, and he knew, even though he could not yet see her, that Isabella was near.

'Hello, wife,' he murmured. A plaguebearer lurched towards him. Vlad blocked a blow from its mottled blade and snatched a flapping length of intestine from its bloated belly. With a jerk, he tore its guts from its thin body, and decapitated it as it fell to its knees, off balance. 'Do not hide your pretty face from me, my love... Where are you?'

'Behind you, my love, my darkling light,' a voice breathed in his ear. The words faded into the buzzing of flies and he twisted about as a blade tore through his cloak, scraping sparks from his cuirass to mark its path. The swarm of biting, stinging flies enveloped him and he staggered as the insects covered his eyes and nose and mouth, as if seeking to burrow into the meat of him. 'Come, give me a kiss, Vlad. Open your mouth and let me in,' Isabella purred, her voice coming from every direction and none.

Vlad slashed out blindly, and the swarm scattered. His zombies were all fallen back into the arms of death, and he stood exposed and alone, caught between the dwarfs and the daemons. He cursed and sprang out of the path of battle, bounding from fallen statues to the tops of fire-blackened stakes and finally to the crumbling ramparts of the Middenplatz wall. Isabella would follow him, he was certain. If she did, their confrontation might give Gelt and Hammerson a chance to defeat the daemons. Without Isabella to guide the beasts, they would be easy enough to banish back to the realm of Chaos.

As he cleared the ramparts, however, a shadow fell over him, and he looked up to see an abyssal steed swoop low over the wall before alighting on a crumbled tower, just out of reach. He glared up at the creature and its rider in annoyance. 'Hello, boy. Come to help, or to hinder?' Vlad asked.

Mannfred sneered. 'Neither, if it's all the same to you. I merely wanted to come say goodbye before your inevitable messy end, old man.' The other vampire leaned back in his saddle and clapped his hands together. 'It's a better one than you deserve, I'll say that for you.'

'What you know about what anyone deserves could fill a very small jar,' Vlad said, suddenly weary. 'I see you've chosen a new side to fight for. How egalitarian of you.'

'Any port in a storm,' Mannfred said. He frowned. 'And the only side I'm interested in fighting for is mine, Vlad. I fight for myself, and no other.'

Vlad smiled, and looked up at the dark sky. 'I was right. You are like Nagash. More like him than the rest of us, even old Arkhan.'

'I am nothing like him,' Mannfred snarled, hammering a fist into his mount's neck, eliciting a snarling squeal from the beast. 'Nothing!'

'No, you're right. Nagash at least has a will to match his monstrousness. He is true to himself, whatever else. But you are a tyrant, just as he is.' Vlad shook his head, and looked down at the battle below. 'A true ruler believes in something greater than himself, boy. A nation, an empire, an ideal. Something...'

'Oh, spare me,' Mannfred growled. He flung out a hand. 'Do you think I'm a fool? You have never done anything out of largesse, old man.' He smacked his fist against his breastplate. 'Even me – you only took me under your wing because you needed me.'

Vlad grunted. 'Not so.' He smiled thinly. 'I took you in because I pitied you.' He cocked his head. 'In truth, I always preferred Konrad. Dumb as a stone, but honest.'

Mannfred drew himself up, his eyes blazing with hate. Vlad tensed, readying himself for his former protégé's attack. But

Mannfred did not attack. Instead, he shook himself and looked away. Vlad frowned. 'If you're not here to plant a sword in my back, boy, why are you wasting my time?'

'Maybe I simply wanted to indulge in the conviviality of a family gathering once more, before I go to forge my own destiny,' Mannfred said. Vlad blinked, and then turned towards the gatehouse tower behind him, where he could hear the humming of flies. Isabella, ragged skirts flowing, stepped onto the ramparts.

'Greetings, husband,' she said. Her musical tones were overlaid with the guttural growl of the daemon that possessed her. 'Will you not embrace me?' she continued. She extended her hand, like a proper noblewoman looking to dance.

'Yes, Vlad, by all means... embrace her,' Mannfred said.

Vlad glanced back at him. 'Leave, boy.'

'And if I choose to stay?'

'Then I will kill you after I kill him,' Isabella said, softly. She drew her sword and extended it. 'This is not for you, Mannfred. You do not belong here, and you will not sully this moment with your rancour and spite. Run away, little prince. I will find you before the end, have no fear.'

Vlad smiled and shrugged. 'You heard her, boy. This is a game for adults, not conceited brats. Go bother the elves, eh? I understand Tyrion would like a word or three with you.' He flapped his hand loosely. Mannfred snarled in frustration and jerked on his steed's reins. The creature took to the air with a shriek, and Vlad watched it depart. He turned back to Isabella. 'I won't let you kill him, my love. Foul as he is, the little prince is still bound to me, and I owe him my protection.'

'And what do you owe me, my love?' Isabella said, stepping gracefully towards him.

'More than that,' Vlad said softly. 'I owe you life, and happiness, and eternity. That is what I promised you, once upon a time.'

'You lied,' Isabella said, drawing closer.

'No. Not to you. Never to you,' Vlad said, readying himself.

'Lies,' Isabella hissed. She came for him in a rush, faster than even he could process, and it was only through luck that he parried her blow. They fought back and forth along the rampart, trading blows that would have killed any normal human, or even many vampires. It was all Vlad could do to keep up with her – the daemon in her soul gave her unnatural strength, as well as twisting her mind. Isabella had always been mad but the daemon made it worse, and he cursed it and the gods it served as he fought.

In his mind's eye, he could still see her as she was on that first night, leaning over her father's deathbed as he gasped his last. 'Do you remember the night we met, my love?' he said, as they crossed blades. 'The night your father died, and your deceitful uncle attempted to usurp your claim? Do you recall how the stars looked that night?'

'There was a storm, and no stars,' Isabella snarled. 'And you murdered my uncle!'

'Only with your permission,' Vlad said, as they broke apart. She screeched and came at him, forcing him to back-pedal. 'I loved you then, and I love you now...'

'Lies,' she hissed, and her sword slashed down, nearly severing his hand at the wrist. His blade fell from nerveless fingers and he staggered back against the ramparts, clutching his wounded wrist. Isabella smiled cruelly, and for a moment, he saw the gloating face of a daemon superimposed over her own. Beneath his grip, he could already feel the ring he wore employing its magics to knit his torn flesh and muscle.

She stretched out her hand, and took a step towards him. 'I will enjoy seeing your flesh putrefy and slough from your cankerous bones, husband. It is all that you deserve.'

'Maybe,' Vlad said. 'I left you, my poor Isabella. I swore that I would stay by your side forever, and I... lied. I died. And then you...'

She paused, mouth working. He saw the daemon again,

snarling silently. Isabella shook her head, and he knew that she was still in there, somewhere. 'I... died too,' she said, not looking at him. 'I died.' She looked at him. 'I *died.*'

'But you live now, and I live, and I will not let you die again, even if it means that I must,' Vlad said hoarsely. He thought of his dreams, and hopes, of the Empire he'd hoped to rule and serve, and of old friends he'd hoped to see again before the end. And he thought of a young woman named Isabella von Drak, and the way she'd smiled at him in the moonlight, and touched his face without fear, when the beast in him was awakened. And just like that, Vlad von Carstein knew what to do.

He flung himself forwards as she hesitated, and smashed the blade from her hand. As she lunged for him, he grabbed her arms and twisted them up behind her back. Where her hands touched his, his flesh began to moulder and rot, and he snarled in agony, even as he slid the von Carstein ring from his finger and onto hers. Then, grabbing hold of her, he shoved them both towards the edge of the ramparts with the last of his fading strength.

As they fell towards the fire-seared stakes below, Vlad laughed. *This feels unpleasantly familiar,* he thought, in the moment before they struck one of the stakes at the foot of the wall. The point of the stake punched through Vlad's heart an instant after Isabella's. He felt her go limp beneath him. He felt no pain, or regret, and as his body came apart, he caught her head and pressed his lips to hers. Then she was gone, and what was left of Vlad von Carstein slumped into oblivion on its stake.

Balthasar Gelt shouted an incantation, and felt the Wind of Metal surge through him. The air coalesced about the plaguebearer that had been about to strike down one of his bodyguards, and the daemon was suddenly encased in silver. Steam spewed from the tiny gaps in the sheath of blessed metal as the daemon was sent howling back into the void. The dwarf reached out with his hammer and nudged the statue over. He caught Gelt's eye and grunted wordlessly, as he hefted his battered shield and moved back into the fray.

'It was my pleasure,' Gelt said. He wasn't entirely sure which of the two Anvil Guard it was – whether it was Stromni he'd saved, or Gorgi. It didn't matter, in any event. They weren't the most talkative duo, and didn't seem to know his name either, calling him variously 'manling,' 'wizard' or the more ubiquitous 'human.'

He swung his staff about, unleashing a crackling surge of magic. More daemons were erased from existence, ripped apart by golden bolts or shredded by tendrils of thrashing iron. But for every chortling plaguebearer that fell, two more took its place. The daemons were without number, and without fear. They crashed again and again into the ragged and ever-shrinking shield-wall of the Zhufbarak like a limitless tide of filth. The air was thick with flies and screams. Not even his magic could hold them back indefinitely.

The knowledge didn't weigh as heavily on him as it once might have. As far as he was concerned, he was living on borrowed time. He had cast his soul into the blackest depths, and it was only by chance that he had been saved from damnation. *If this be doomsday, I will not flinch from it,* he thought, and then smiled at his own pomposity. *It's not like I'll have the time, at any rate. The world is coming apart and it will take greater powers than mine to hold it together.* He tossed his staff from one hand to the other and drew his sword, parrying a blow from a pox-riddled blade. As their weapons scraped apart, Gelt rammed his staff into the plaguebearer's belly and sent a pulse of magic thrumming through it. The plaguebearer twitched in consternation, and then exploded as a thousand thin spikes of gold tore it apart from the inside.

Gelt swung his staff about like a morning star, and sent the ever-expanding sphere of spikes hurtling into the packed ranks of the enemy. The sphere exploded into a thicket of thrashing tendrils, and at his shouted command, the dwarfs took the opportunity to fall back while their foes were otherwise occupied. As dwarfs streamed past him, Gelt set his staff and roused the hidden deposits of ore in the bedrock of the Fauschlag, summoning them to the surface. Great barricades of molten metal flowered into being between the Zhufbarak and the plague-host.

'That won't hold them long.'

Gelt turned to see Hammerson stumping towards him. The runesmith had lost his helm, and his face and beard were streaked with blood and soot. Nonetheless, he was smiling grimly. 'Good plan, though. Give us a minute to have a wee drink, at any rate.'

'I think we're out of Bugman's,' Gelt said. 'You'll have to settle for water.'

'I'll die thirsty then,' Hammerson said. 'Out of Bugman's... it really is the end of the world.' He tossed his head, indicating the remaining elves. 'The elgi woman, Alarielle... she's dying, lad.'

Gelt turned and looked towards the ragged ring of elven shields that sheltered the fallen Everqueen. Her remaining warriors surrounded her, fighting alongside the dwarfs. The treeman, Durthu, loomed over the Everqueen, killing any daemon which drew too close. As Gelt watched, the ancient spirit spread its arms and roared so loudly that a semi-ruined wall nearby collapsed, filling the air with dust.

'What is he doing?' Gelt muttered, as Durthu hurled its sword into the leering, bloated face of a great unclean one, spitting the greater daemon like a hog over a fire-pit. The treeman shoved Alarielle's defenders aside and sank down beside her limp, pale form. Gelt started forwards, but Hammerson grabbed him.

'Don't even think about it, lad. Whatever he's doing, it's only bound to help, and you'll only rile him up if you interfere,' the dwarf said. Gelt subsided, but continued to watch, unable to look away. As he watched in awe, the treeman's bark-flesh withered and cracked, and leaves fell like dust from his shoulders and head. Gelt could feel the power flowing between Durthu and Alarielle, and knew, without knowing how, that the treeman was giving of his own life to restore the Everqueen.

The calcified and crumbling husk of Durthu collapsed in on itself as Alarielle's form swelled with light and life. She rose, her flesh unmarked, her eyes clear. She gently touched the crumbling remains of Durthu and then turned. The light of Ghyran crackled in her eyes, and she spread her arms and threw back her head to sing a single perfect note.

Gelt and Hammerson threw up their hands to protect their eyes as white fire, crested with green, filled the Middenplatz and roared hungrily through the Palast District. It passed over the heads of the remaining elves and dwarfs harmlessly, but where it struck the hordes of daemons, it wreaked a terrible destruction. Hundreds of daemons were reduced to ash in a matter of moments, but thousands more pressed forwards, through the sooty remains of their fellows. To Gelt, it was as if the Dark Gods were determined to prevent them from reaching the centre of the city at any cost.

And why wouldn't they be? That is where Archaon is, and his devilish artefact, and that is where the true battle is. Not here, Gelt thought, looking around. They were cut off. Surrounded on all sides... save one. The northern gatehouse had been cleared by Alarielle's fire. As she moved to join he and Hammerson, he looked at her. 'We must get to the Temple of Ulric,' he said. She frowned, one hand pressed to her head.

'Yes... I can feel it. That is where the artefact is,' she said, wincing as if the thought pained her. 'But we have no time. Our forces cannot...'

'No,' Hammerson grunted. 'We cannot. But we can hold the way clear, and buy you time.' The runesmith gestured and Gelt saw one of Hammerson's Anvil Guard lead his pegasus, Quicksilver, towards them. His heart leapt at the sight of the proud animal.

It had been hurt during the battle in the King's Glade, one wing badly scorched. But though the animal couldn't fly, Quicksilver was still the fastest stallion this side of the famed stables of Tiranoc. Or would have been, had either the stables or Tiranoc still existed.

'I do not wish to ask this of you,' Gelt began, as he looked at Hammerson. He reached out, without thinking, and placed his hand on the dwarf's shoulder. Hammerson twitched, as if to knock the hand aside, but in the end, he merely shook his head.

'Then don't. No time for long goodbyes, lad,' Hammerson rumbled, placing his heavy hand over Gelt's. 'We made an oath, and we'll not break it now.'

Gelt hesitated, trying to summon the words. Hammerson nudged him impatiently, poking him in the belly with the flat of his hammer. 'Go on, lad. Get moving, the both of you. There's work to be done, and it's best done well. Don't let the elgi and that tottering tower of bones mess it up.' The runesmith grinned. 'We'll see to things here, one way or another.'

Gelt nodded and turned away. He caught hold of Quicksilver's bridle and hauled himself into the pegasus's saddle. The animal whinnied and reared, as Gelt extended his hand to Alarielle. She climbed into the saddle behind him, without hesitation. 'We must ride swiftly, wizard,' she murmured as she wrapped an arm around his midsection. 'They will pursue us.'

'Let them try. Quicksilver has outpaced daemons before. Aye, and worse things besides,' Gelt said confidently. At a tap of his heels, the pegasus began to gallop towards the northern gatehouse. He did not look back as he felt the twinge of Hammerson's magics on the wind, and heard the crack of gunfire. Alarielle pressed her face to his back as her people moved around them, elves and dryads fighting and dying to clear them a path.

Daemons bounded forwards to block their route, but Gelt thrust his staff out, over Quicksilver's head, and swept the creatures aside with a gout of shimmering energy. Then they were past the northern gatehouse and galloping through the streets beyond, in the direction of the Ulricsmund and the Temple of Ulric.

As they rode, Gelt whispered a silent prayer to whatever gods might still be listening that the other Incarnates would be there to meet them.

Hammerson watched Gelt ride away, and smiled sadly. 'A good lad, that one, for all that he's had a rough path to walk.'

'Aye,' Grombrindal rumbled. Hammerson could not say where the white-bearded dwarf had come from, or when he had arrived, but he was here now, and that was all that mattered. If this was to be the last war of the dwarfs, it was only fitting that the White Dwarf himself be there to fight alongside them. Grombrindal hefted his axe, and ran his thumb along the edge. 'But he and the elgi woman are best out of it, eh? This is dwarf work.'

'Aye, that it is,' Hammerson said. He no longer felt tired. Though Gelt's enchantments were fading, his warriors looked as fresh as the day they'd set out for Averheim, so long ago. It was as if the presence of the revered ancestor had renewed their strength.

He looked past the shield-wall and saw that the Chaos hordes, daemons and mortals alike, were readying themselves to charge once more. If they were allowed to get past the Zhufbarak, the Incarnates would pay the price. Hammerson raised his axe. 'Plant the standards, lads,' he bellowed. 'I want to fight in the shade.'

With a loud rattle, the clan standards were stabbed into the ground, creating a makeshift forest of gold and steel. Hammerson looked up at them, and knew that he was seeing them for the last time. 'I forged some of those myself,' he said.

'Good runework,' Grombrindal said.

'Not worth doing, otherwise,' Hammerson said.

Flesh hounds howled, and bloodthirsters roared. Bloodletters shrieked and mortal warriors added their chants and screams to the daemonic clamour. The dwarfs ignored the noise. Hammerson nodded in satisfaction. 'I wish Ungrim were here. He'd love this.'

'He is here, lad,' Grombrindal rumbled. 'They're all here, standing with us, in this moment. All the kings and their clans, be they thane, clansman or Slayer, they are with us now. Can't you feel them? They are crying out for vengeance. Today is a day for the settling of all grudges, great or small.'

As the White Dwarf spoke, Hammerson thought he could see them. The ghosts of his ancestors moved through the ranks of the living to fill the gaps in the shield-wall. And not just the dead of storied centuries, but those more recent. He saw Thorek Ironbrow, and Ungrim Ironfist. He saw Thorgrim, the Grudgebearer himself, and others besides. Faces and names from history and recent days. It was as if the entirety of their people had come to witness this final act of defiance.

He saw Grombrindal standing upon a broad shield, supported on the shoulders of a one-eyed Slayer and a tankard-carrying ranger. The good eye of the Slayer met his own, and Hammerson felt his growing sadness washed away in a moment of anger. Anger that it had come to this, that all the great works of his people were now as nothing. The fate of the world would be decided elsewhere, by the hands of humans and elves.

For the dwarfs, there was only this. The whole of their history, brought to this point. Hammerson met Grombrindal's gaze, and the White Dwarf nodded slowly. *If it must be done, let it be done well,* Hammerson thought. Whether they were dead or alive, that was the only way dwarfs knew how to do anything.

On the other side of the shield-wall, the Chaos horde had jolted into motion at last. Hammerson lifted his weapons. 'We make our stand here,' he said, trusting in his voice to carry to every ear. 'No more running. We stand here, for the Black Water, for every hold, and the world entire. Do you hear me, sons of Zhufbar? Like the stones of the mountains... *we will hold.*'

EIGHTEEN

 *The Ulricsmund, Middenheim*

Caradryan spun his Phoenix Blade, blocking the deadly bite of the axe as it flashed towards him. The Chaos champion known as Arbaal the Undefeated roared in fury and hacked at the Incarnate of Fire again. Nearby, Ashtari shrieked in fury as he tore at the scaly body of Arbaal's flesh hound. The daemon-dog wailed in frustrated rage as the firebird drove its beak into the beast's flesh again and again.

'I have slaughtered armies of elves,' Arbaal roared. His axe reeked of hot blood, and it left trails of crimson smoke in its wake as he brought it slashing down towards Caradryan's head. 'I have broken the backs of dragons, and eaten the hearts of sea-leviathans.'

'Your culinary practices are no concern of mine,' Caradryan snarled, parrying the blow. His arms ached, but he whirled the halberd about as if it were as light as a feather. He twisted and spun, driving the Chaos champion back. 'It does not matter to me how many you have murdered, monster. It ends here.'

Quicker than thought, Caradryan lunged, slashed and jabbed,

striking Arbaal again and again. He knew that were he not host to Aqshy, he would have no hope of standing up to such a foe, let alone defeating him. But with the fire raging in him, he felt as if there were no battle he could not survive. It was a dangerous feeling. He had spent centuries honing his mind and body, and learning to control the rage that was the curse of every elf. But the fire called to that primal part of him, and lent it strength. He wondered if this was akin to what Tyrion had felt, when the fury of Khaine had driven him into madness and despair. There was a freedom in it that called to him, and that he longed to embrace. Instead, he whispered the mantras of Asuryan, trying to maintain focus.

Arbaal swatted the Phoenix Blade aside, ripping it out of Caradryan's hands. The elf cursed himself for his momentary lack of focus and threw himself over Arbaal's next blow, his hands reaching for the halberd's haft. He caught the weapon and rolled to his feet, turning just in time to block a blow that would have split him in half. Shattered cobbles shifted beneath his feet as Arbaal put all of his weight behind his axe, and forced the elf back.

Caradryan wrenched his halberd to the side, trying to twist the axe out of his opponent's grip, but Arbaal was ready for such a tactic, and he drove a fist into the elf's belly. Caradryan staggered back, and lurched aside as Arbaal tried to smash him from his feet.

The axe gashed his arm, and Caradryan bit back a scream. His blood hissed and bubbled as it splattered Arbaal's cuirass, and the Chaos champion hesitated, giving Caradryan a chance to put distance between them. As he retreated, Caradryan cursed himself for a fool. If he hadn't moved when he had, Arbaal's blow would have taken his arm off. He could feel the fire within him, demanding to be let out. But to do so would be to doom his warriors to certain death. Arbaal charged towards him, axe ready. The weapon howled as it came around. *Only one chance,* he thought.

Caradryan spun about and leapt backwards over the sweeping blow. He tumbled through the air and dropped down behind Arbaal. Even as the champion whirled to face Caradryan, the Phoenix Blade slashed out. Ancient armour, crafted in Khorne's own forges, ruptured as the fiery blade tore upwards through it. Arbaal sagged backwards, clutching at the wound. He raised his axe, but Caradryan hacked his arm off at the elbow. Arbaal screamed in fury and lurched towards the elf, groping for him with his remaining hand.

Caradryan stepped back, out of reach, and pivoted, hammering the edge of his halberd into the space between Arbaal's collar and the bottom of his helmet. The white-hot blade tore through the champion's neck, and his head tumbled free to roll away across the cobbles. Caradryan sank back against a wall, panting. He placed a hand to the wound in his arm, and winced as his touch cauterised the bloody slash.

He looked up. Proud princes of drowned Caledor swooped fearlessly through the increasingly agitated skies on their dragons, braving the lightning and sorcerous fire that rained from the bloated clouds in order to drive back the enemy. As he watched, a dragon was struck by a Chaos-birthed bolt of emerald lightning and its smoking corpse plunged from the sky to demolish a row of ramshackle houses.

Below them, plunging recklessly through the plazas and streets of the Sudgarten and the Ulricsmund, came the remaining knights of Ulthuan, the Empire and even chill Naggaroth – Reiksguard galloped alongside Silver Helms and the shrieking, scaly shapes of Cold Ones. The wave of armour and horseflesh swept over and smashed down the enemy wherever they struck. And at their head rode the shining figure of the Dragon of Cothique, his blade searing the darkness and all those things which sought to hide in it. It was the greatest cavalry charge in the history of the world, led by the greatest hero the elven people had ever produced. And he was not alone – the Emperor was there as well, on the back of his griffon, Deathclaw. Where the great beast pounced, blood and horror ensued for the followers of Chaos.

Around Caradryan, his host battled on against the enemy as well. His warriors were cloaked and shielded by fire, and it spilled from their weapons to consume northman and daemon alike. And there were plenty of both to feed the growing conflagration. Even with the forces of Tyrion and the Emperor, they were hard-pressed. The closer they drew to the Temple of Ulric and the great excavation which marked it, the harder the servants of the Ruinous Powers fought. *But they fight in vain,* he thought.

Already, the less fanatical of the enemy were beginning to fall back. Especially those who had witnessed the defeat of Arbaal. The champion had slaughtered a score of Ulthuan's finest before Caradryan had reached him, and like as not, he could have carried the day by himself. With his fall, his warriors were starting to retreat, and the daemons who had accompanied him were wavering into instability, their always-tenuous hold on the world slipping. Too, he could feel the presence of the other Incarnates, not just Tyrion and Karl Franz, but Nagash and the others as well, all drawing closer. They would be here soon, and if Teclis was to be believed, no power in the world could stand against them. Victory seemed not only possible, but imminent.

A bellow, deeper and more powerful than the loudest roll of thunder, pierced Caradryan's burgeoning hopes and swept them aside. It echoed down from the sky and rose from the ground; it shivered through the bricks and tore through alleyways and escaped from cul-de-sacs. The sound reverberated through every cobblestone and he clutched his head in agony, even as he turned, seeking out the author of that cry.

A moment later, the sky erupted in fire. Blazing meteors pierced the clouds and smashed home amidst the battle, killing warriors from both sides indiscriminately. The cry continued, growing impossibly loud as more and more meteors hammered down, levelling buildings and pummelling streets into ruin. Caradryan swept his halberd out, summoning a shield of flame to protect those few of his warriors that he could reach. But it was to no avail. His flames were snuffed, and elves died. Caradryan snarled in fury and whistled for Ashtari. The phoenix rose from the corpse of Arbaal's flesh hound with a single beat of its crimson wings and swooped towards him, dodging through the rain of burning debris. He caught hold of the bird's harness and hauled himself up onto its back as it streaked past.

His warriors followed him as he flew on, each one knowing, even as Caradryan did, that to stand still, or to seek shelter, was to die. So they followed him, plunging through the fleeing ranks of the enemy and carving themselves a path towards their goal. The Temple of Ulric was within sight, and nothing – not the enemy, or the wrath of the Dark Gods themselves – would deter the sons and daughters of Ulthuan from reaching it.

Tyrion swept Sunfang out in a shimmering arc. The daemoness the Loremasters knew as Dechala, the Denied One, parried the blow, shrieking and cursing him in the ancient tongue of his people as her coils tightened about he and Malhandir. The battle swirled on around them, as the finest warriors of three kingdoms fought and died against the forces of the Dark Gods, and the sky wept fire. Nearby, what had once been a tavern exploded, filling the air with burning chunks of wood and stone.

Dechala's many arms flailed at him as she rained blow after brutal blow down, but he blocked each of them with a speed which shocked even him. He could feel the power of Hysh flowing through him, lending him speed of body and mind. *Whatever you have done to me, brother, wherever you are, thank you,* he thought. The daemoness had come at him suddenly, out of the press of battle, striking like an adder. It was as if she had been hunting for him alone, but he suspected any Incarnate would have done. He caught sight of Deathclaw, swooping low over the battle, and saw the Emperor's runefang flash and remove a bloodletter's head as he passed it. Despite the situation, he was glad the daemoness had found him, rather than the human. Whoever or whatever he was, he was still no match for a creature like Dechala.

Dechala chose that moment to lunge for him, swift as the serpent she resembled, her beautiful features contorted with hate. Her jaws spread wide, and he was forced to catch hold of her chin with his free hand. The poison dripping from her fangs hissed and sputtered where it dripped onto his gauntlet. Tyrion shoved her head back, and her flesh began to smoulder where he touched it as his aura of light started to burn away her cloak of darkness. She shrieked and squirmed, tail lashing. Malhandir whinnied in pain as her coils tightened convulsively.

Tyrion parried a blow meant to gut him, and his riposte was swifter than even the daemoness could follow. Sunfang was a blur of light, and it pierced Dechala's chest before she even had a chance to scream. The Denied One slumped, smoke rising from her, and her coils loosened and flopped quivering to the ground, to be trodden into ruin by Malhandir's hooves. Tyrion urged his horse on, and the animal reared and lunged away from the dissolving ruin of the daemon princess even as a fiery meteor obliterated the spot where she had fallen.

He heard a familiar shriek from above, and saw Caradryan hurtle towards the Temple of Ulric in the distance, his host following in his shadow. Flaming blades and spears cut the host a path through the disorganised rabble of the Chaos forces. Tyrion grinned. *Leave it to the silent one to lead the way,* he thought. He hauled on Malhandir's reins, and the stallion pawed the air with a whinny.

'Ride,' Tyrion roared with all the strength he could muster, to those of his warriors still fighting around him, whether they were human or elf. 'Ride and fear no darkness. Ride, for the world, and the breaking of the gods!' Even as his steed's hooves struck the ground, the animal was in motion, charging in Caradryan's wake. Those who could fell in behind him, as fiery ruin continued to hammer the cursed city from above. Knights of Stirland, Altdorf and Ostland, of Cothique and Caledor, of Ghrond and Hag Graef, galloped in his wake. The proud survivors of three kingdoms, who looked to him for orders and inspiration.

Tyrion felt the weight of that responsibility keenly, even as he found joy in the sound of thundering hooves and the rattle of lances. He knew, in his heart, that this was the last charge of the world's defenders. Even if they won, even if the Dark Gods were cast back, the flower of elven *ithiltaen* and of human chivalry would fall here, never to ride again. Win or lose, the pillars of his world had been broken. *And we must see that it was not in vain,* he thought. He leaned forwards, over Malhandir's neck, and hacked down a northman standard bearer as he swept past.

The Temple of Ulric rose into sight as Tyrion galloped through the cramped streets of the Ulricsmund. The building was a shell of its former glory. It had been defiled and shattered by the servants of the Ruinous Powers. Tyrion recalled how Teclis had spoken of the city, when he had made common cause with the human Magnus against the forces of Chaos. Tyrion himself had been occupied fighting the druchii, after the battle of Finuval Plain. Teclis had said that Magnus had been a small man, and unimpressive at first glance, but filled with an inner fire that had been matched only by the Flame of Ulric itself. The same Flame that now coursed through Tyrion's blood, and lent its strength to his own.

He heard a snarl, and looked over his shoulder to see the Emperor's bodyguard, Wendel Volker, riding hard at his elbow. The Reiksguard looked almost as monstrous in that moment as their enemies, his eyes as yellow as a beast's and his lips peeled back from teeth which were too long. Then the moment passed and he was but a man again. Tyrion turned away. He did not know for certain what force lurked in the human, but whatever it was, it made him as savage as any of the great lions of Chrace.

Malhandir whinnied, and Tyrion snapped out of his reverie with a curse. They were within sight of the great excavation which marred the side of the Temple and marked where the artefact Be'lakor had spoken of was housed, but even as they drew close, a blaze of crackling warpflame suddenly roared to life, blocking off their advance. Tyrion hauled back on Malhandir's reins, bringing the horse to a sudden stop.

'Can you do anything?' a voice called down from above. Tyrion looked up as the Emperor's griffon landed nearby. The human looked as exhausted as Tyrion felt, but he still gripped his sword firmly. 'We are running short on time.'

'I… don't know,' Tyrion said. He urged Malhandir forwards, aware that as he did so, he could hear a growing war-chant echoing from the north. The enemy had found their courage, now that the rain of fire had slackened, and were regrouping. Tyrion felt Hysh rise within him as he extended Sunfang towards the crackling flames. Through the multicoloured haze, he could see the robed shapes of Chaos sorcerers and capering daemons.

Light flared, rising from his every pore, driving back the dark all around him. The flames quavered as the light struck them, and recoiled for a moment before reforming, even stronger than before. Tyrion climbed down from Malhandir's saddle and strode forwards, blade still extended. The flames gave way before him, but then roared up, as if to envelop him.

A gleaming halberd slid into place alongside Sunfang. Tyrion glanced aside, and saw Caradryan take up a position beside him. The Incarnate of Fire smiled thinly. 'Let us face the fire together, heir of Aenarion,' Caradryan rasped. Tyrion nodded tersely, and then turned back to the flames. Together, the two Incarnates drove their power against the warpfire barrier, trying to snuff it. Beads of sweat rolled down Tyrion's face as he summoned the light and sent it frenzying forth to sear the unnatural flames. Beside him, Caradryan's own flames burned hotter and brighter than the colourful daemon-inferno. But still, the warp-fire barrier held.

Behind him, Tyrion could hear the Emperor shouting orders, reforming the ranks of the combined armies to face the attack that was imminent. The human was a commander without equal. But he also knew that this was no longer a battle for mortals... It was the Rhana Dandra and only gods could hope to keep their footing in the torrent of blood to come. He almost turned back, to lend his aid, when Caradryan grabbed his shoulder. He glanced at the former captain of the Phoenix Guard, and nodded. *You are right, my friend... If these flames are not snuffed, we will all perish this day.*

The howling grew louder and louder, until it beat at his ears. Tyrion risked a glance, and saw a nightmare horde burst through the streets and dash pell-mell towards the combined armies of men and elves. Northland hounds, lean and athirst, loped ahead of savage brutes which had once been men, before some fell power had driven all reason and humanity from them, reducing them to feral monstrosities. The berserker wave slammed into the allied lines, and died in droves. But not all of them, and some managed to drag a knight from his horse, or pounce on a spearman and bear him to the ground, their teeth in his throat.

Tyrion instinctively turned, his blade sweeping out. Light speared forth, and a group of howling barbarians were immolated in an instant. Before he could turn his attentions back to the barrier of flame, however, Caradryan shoved him aside. Tyrion hit the ground and rolled to his feet as a monstrous shape slammed down onto the street where he'd been standing. Tyrion raised his sword as the bloodthirster rose to its full height and turned towards him. The beast gestured with its hammer. 'Ka'Bandha has come, elf,' it roared. 'You thought to escape me, mortals, but the Huntsman of Khorne will not be denied!'

'Running wasn't my idea, I assure you,' Tyrion snarled. He

darted in, and threw himself beneath the daemon's first blow. As its hammer smashed down on the street, he was already on his feet. Sunfang whipped out, carving a trail of fire across the bloodthirster's back. Ka'Bandha reared back and roared. It whipped around, and Tyrion was forced to leap back as the axe it clutched in its other hand crashed down, carving a gouge in the street. Before he could launch another attack, the daemon wrenched its weapon free of the street and reared back, slamming one massive hoof into his chest. Tyrion skidded backwards, his chest aching and no air in his lungs.

Before Ka'Bandha could take advantage of his predicament, however, the Emperor was there, his runefang singing as it carved through one of the bloodthirster's wings, eliciting a shriek of fury. That shriek rapidly became a snarl of triumph, as Ka'Bandha whirled and smashed Deathclaw from the air with the flat of its axe. 'You... Your skull is mine, human,' Ka'Bandha roared, as it closed in on the fallen animal and its rider.

'And yours is mine, hound of carnage,' Caradryan grated, as Ashtari swooped around the bloodthirster's head. The Phoenix Blade flashed and Ka'Bandha staggered as flames roared about it, singeing its unnatural flesh and scorching its brass armour. But the beast did not fall, no matter how many wounds Caradryan opened in its hide.

Ka'Bandha bellowed and swung its hammer out, catching the phoenix as it dived past. The great bird fell with a scream and the bloodthirster was on it in an instant, with fatal results. The daemon's hammer rose and fell with deadly precision, and the last phoenix of the Flamespyres died. Caradryan, who had fallen from his saddle, hacked at the daemon in a fury, and his halberd, wreathed in white-hot flames, crashed down on Ka'Bandha's skull hard enough to shatter the brass crown the daemon wore, and to open its scalp to the bone.

Ka'Bandha, blinded by its own ichor, lashed out wildly, trying to drive the Incarnate back. As Tyrion dragged himself to his feet, he saw one wild swing of the hammer catch Caradryan in the legs, and he heard the snap as the elf's bones were shattered by the impact. Caradryan fell heavily, striking the hard rock of the Ulricsmund with crushing force, and his halberd was jarred from his hand as the bloodthirster bore down on him.

Tyrion, one arm wrapped around his side, staggered towards them, but was too slow. Ka'Bandha lifted one hoof high, over Caradryan, who strained to reach the haft of his weapon, which lay just out of reach. The daemon stamped down onto the Incarnate's chest, and, with a thunderous crunch, Caradryan, captain of the Phoenix Guard, servant of Asuryan, died. Tyrion watched in horror as sparks of flame burst from the shattered corpse and took root in the bloodthirster's flesh, running hungrily across its limbs, until no part of the daemon was not aflame. Ka'Bandha wailed and thrashed in obvious agony as it felt the wrath of Aqshy. Even so, the beast did not fall.

Tyrion saw Deathclaw hurtle towards the daemon once more, the Emperor clinging to his saddle, his blade sweeping out. But before his blow could land, Ka'Bandha lashed out, even as it had before, and struck the griffon from the air with its hammer, driving the beast into the rubble of the temple nearby. The Emperor was flung from his saddle by the impact, and thrown high through the remnants of a stained glass window and into the temple beyond. Tyrion's heart sank as the bloodthirster turned towards him, grinning through the flames that ate at its bestial features. Though the fires burned it, its lust for battle had not dimmed.

'Flee, blood-speck, and I shall save your skull for another day,' Ka'Bandha gurgled, as it glared down at him. 'Flee, little elf, and do not seek to come between the Huntsman and his prey this night.'

Tyrion straightened, and felt the fire sing in his veins. The light around him began to glow, and the daemon winced. It raised a hand, as if to shield its eyes. Tyrion raised Sunfang. 'I do not bargain with daemons,' he said. 'I kill them.'

Then, with a yell, he launched himself towards Caradryan's slayer.

The Temple of Ulric

The Emperor awoke in darkness, his face sticky with blood and his body a mass of aches and pains. *Forgot what that was like,* he thought sourly, as he pushed himself to his feet. The air was heavy, and a slaughterhouse stink was thick in his nostrils.

He looked around warily, hands flexing. He'd lost his runefang somewhere between here and Ka'Bandha's hammer, and he scanned his surroundings for something to take its place. He peered into the darkness, marking the body of a Chaos warrior nearby. The man's sword was to hand. Though he was loath to touch it, beggars couldn't be choosers. As he started forward, he took note of the corpses hanging from the ceiling on heavy chains and hooks.

With a start, he realised he was under the great dome of the temple. For a brief heartbeat, rage pulsed through him to see this most holy of shrines defiled so, but he regained control of himself quickly. 'Work first, mourn later,' he muttered.

'Same old Sigmar.'

The voice slithered out of the dark. The Emperor froze, and then turned, following the echoes of laughter. He saw a throne of skulls and flayed skin rising above a dais of bones, and at its base, a familiar gleam of bronze. 'Ha,' he murmured. No cleansing flame, no sunlit morning, had ever seemed as beautiful as the sight of his hammer, gleaming in the dark. He stepped towards it, hand reaching out, but stopped as the laughter echoed again.

'Yesssss, it *is* you. I knew it from the first. I smelt your stink on the wind the moment that fool elf freed you from the Vortex, Unberogen. For two thousand years, this world was free of you, but here you are, hiding in a dead man's skin.'

Sigmar looked up as the alabaster-skinned figure climbed atop the back of the throne and spread great black wings. Eyes like polished opals shone as the horned head twisted about. 'It has been a long time, my old friend,' the daemon prince murmured. 'Centuries since last we spoke, eh, Sigmar?'

'Gerreon,' Sigmar said. He felt the old hate welling up again, like a wound that had never properly healed. A woman's face passed before his eyes, and receded into memory. This thing before him had been his friend, once upon a time. Now, it was a plaything of Chaos.

'Azazel,' the daemon prince corrected, gently. 'Alas, no time to catch up, I'm afraid. No time to speak of better days, of loves lost and won. Time is speeding up, and the world judders to pieces in haste. I thought... well. One last moment, before the end.' Azazel pointed at the fallen shape of Ghal Maraz, where it lay amidst the refuse of barbarity. 'You want that filthy thing, cousin? Then come and take it, if you dare.'

Sigmar lunged for the hammer. Azazel gave a wild shriek of laughter and flung himself towards his prey, drawing a blade covered in ruinous sigils as he did so. The blade slammed down, inches from Sigmar's head. The Emperor rolled aside. Azazel rose, wings stretching out. He stood between Sigmar and his weapon, and spread his arms as if in invitation. 'A good effort, but not good enough. Not for this,' Azazel said. He took a step towards Sigmar. 'I wish that we had more time, my friend. I have been waiting so long to see you again.'

'Can't say the same, I'm afraid,' Sigmar said.

Azazel laughed. 'Oh, how I have missed you,' he said. Then with a single snap of his wings, he hurtled forwards. His blade hissed as it whipped towards Sigmar's neck. Sigmar twisted aside and flung himself towards his hammer. Even as he caught the haft, he heard the boom of Azazel's wings. He rolled onto his back, and just managed to block the daemon prince's blade with the haft of Ghal Maraz. For a moment, Azazel crouched above him. The blade writhed like a thing alive in his clawed grip. 'Do you ever think of her, brother of my heart?' Azazel purred, as he forced the blade down. 'Do you recall her scent in lonely moments, or the way the light caught her hair? Do the memories press down on your heart, when you recall Ravenna? Do you spare even a thought for dear Pendrag?' Azazel chuckled. 'I know I don't.'

'I think about them always, Gerreon. As I have thought about this moment,' Sigmar said, from between gritted teeth. He felt stronger than before, as if some part of him which had been missing up until now had returned. It wasn't simply the presence of Ghal Maraz, but something else – as if a weight had been lifted from him. He heard the clash of steel in his head, and the song of distant stars. He pushed back against Azazel. The daemon prince's eyes widened.

'What are you–?' Azazel began. Sigmar shoved the haft of the hammer up, and Azazel screeched as the edge of his own blade gashed his chest and throat. He tumbled backwards, wings flailing. His blood hissed as it burned the flagstones. Sigmar swept his hammer out, and inhuman bone splintered as the force of the blow tore the daemon prince's sword from his grip. The sword wailed like a wounded cat as it was sent skidding across the floor.

Sigmar kicked him in the head as he tried to rise. The daemon prince yowled as the Emperor trod on his wings, pinning him in place. Sigmar raised Ghal Maraz over his head. 'You said it yourself, Gerreon. There is no time. And so I send you back to the forge of souls more quickly than you deserve.'

'No!' Azazel shrieked. His eyes bulged in fear as he tried to tear himself free, to no avail. The hammer came down with thunderous finality. The great wings twitched once, and then fell still. Sigmar Unberogen looked down at the rapidly dissolving ruin of a man he'd once called friend, shook himself, and strode away, towards the sound of fighting.

There was a war to be won. And a world to be saved.

NINETEEN

 *The Ulricsmund, Middenheim*

Wendel Volker grunted as his sword became lodged in the skull of a snarling northman, and he released it as the body slumped. He reached down and snatched up the axe of a fallen White Lion and spun it experimentally. Somehow, the axe, despite not being made for human hands, felt more natural in his hand than any sword ever had.

An axe is a warrior's weapon, Ulric growled softly. Volker ignored the god and turned to chop a leaping Chaos hound out of the air, sending the dying beast crashing down nearby. He whirled back, and smashed aside a brass-faced shield before cleaving through the breastbone of its owner. He tore the axe free and spun, seeking more foes. He'd lost his horse in the first charge, but he'd never been comfortable with the animals. As far as Volker was concerned, being on a horse made you a target. Ulric seemed to feel the same way.

Anarchy reigned wherever Volker cast his gaze. Bellowed war cries and the clash of steel echoed across the city. All around him, men and elves were hard-pressed by the savage northmen.

The latter seemed tireless, driven beyond all reason and discipline and into a red rage that ended only in death. They came again and again, hurling themselves at the dwindling ranks of the Empire and the elves, dying in droves but pulling down warriors in their death-throes. Even worse, the northmen were not alone in their assault. The clamour of battle was drawing enemies from all over the city, including beastmen and skaven.

A flare of light startled him, and he turned to see Tyrion still locked in combat with the bloodthirster. The elf was holding his own, but only just. The bloodthirster had already killed one Incarnate, and though it was wreathed in flames and bleeding from dozens of wounds, it didn't seem to be slowing down. And Tyrion was beginning to tire.

A knight, bearing the bull emblem of Ostland on one pauldron, staggered into him. Volker grabbed his arm, and the knight tried to pull free. His armour was scorched and dented, and he'd lost his helmet. 'Let go of me, damn you,' he cried.

'Get back in line,' Volker snarled. The man paled and stumbled back.

'The Emperor is dead,' he shouted. 'We cannot win!'

Volker tensed, and Ulric snarled within him. Before he could stop himself, he swung his axe and decapitated the knight. *Cowardice is like a disease,* Ulric growled, *and it spreads as swiftly as any pox.* Volker saw other men, knights and halberdiers, woodsmen and handgunners, staring at him in shock and fear. His fellow Reiksguard, whom he'd been fighting among, edged away from him. His gut churned, but he lifted the bloody axe high and bared his teeth. 'Fight or die, men of the Empire,' he snarled. He could feel the god adding his strength to Volker's voice, making sure he was heard by every human ear on the field of battle. 'I do not care which, but do it bravely, and do it well. Fight, in the name of Sigmar, who forged our Empire. Fight, in the name of Ulric, who forged our people! Fight and rend the enemy like the wolves who birthed you!'

A northman charged through the press towards him, bellowing incoherently. Volker spun the axe in his hands and brought it down in a two-handed grip, cleaving the barbarian from pate to jowl. He tore the axe free and gestured towards the enemy. 'Fight, you Unberogens! Fight, you Teutogens, Jeutones and Brigundians, fight, sons of Ulric all! Fight until the Fauschlag quakes and the Dark Gods hide in fear,' he roared. And they roared with him. He could feel the panic and dismay giving way to anger and determination as he charged towards the foe, his people at his back, and felt Ulric's contented growl roll through him. Whatever else happened here today, the men of the Empire would not falter.

A new sound pierced the clangour of combat then, even as Volker led his people into battle. It rose from the south, spiralling up into the smoky air, and set the hair on the back of his neck to dancing. Through the madness of battle, he caught sight of green shapes flooding into the plaza. 'Orcs,' he muttered, as he slammed his shoulder into a bloodletter's gut and flipped the daemon over his back. 'As if things aren't mad enough.'

Not just orcs, Ulric roared, *elves as well. The Incarnates approach. Allies, Wendel Volker. Or if not allies, then those who come to make war on our enemies.* He shuddered as the god-spark howled within him, joyously this time. *War, man, war so as to shake the pillars of heaven itself! See them, Wendel Volker, see how they come, scenting the blood of our prey!*

Volker shook his head, trying to ignore Ulric's howls and concentrate on the fight at hand. He heard someone shout his name, and jerked back as the Chaos warrior charging towards him was suddenly transmuted to gold. He turned and saw Balthasar Gelt riding towards him, the Everqueen sitting behind him on the pegasus's back. 'Volker, where is the Emperor?' the wizard shouted. Volker signalled for his fellow Reiksguard to fall in around Gelt and Alarielle, and the remaining knights did so swiftly.

'That... thing struck him down. I don't know where he is, and there's no chance of finding out, not with the enemy hemming us in,' Volker said, gesturing towards the spot where Ka'Bandha and Tyrion still fought as Gelt helped Alarielle down from the pegasus. 'If you've got any magic that can find him, now's the time to use it,' he continued.

Before Gelt could answer, an ear-splitting screech sounded over the din of the battle. The two Incarnates and Volker turned to see the bloodthirster reel back, away from Tyrion, its axe a twisted ruin. It tossed the smoking weapon aside and reached for Tyrion. It smashed his sword down, and knocked him from his feet. The daemon loomed over the elf, its hammer raised for a killing blow.

'No,' Alarielle hissed. She started forwards, but Volker stopped her, even as Ulric howled a warning in his mind.

'Wait – look!' he said. A sudden gale sprang up, sweeping across the Ulricsmund. And with it came a charnel stink that hung heavy on the air. A moment later, a swirling black cloud, roiling and pulsing with dark energy, burst out from between two buildings. The street shook beneath the tread of something monstrous as the cloud rolled forwards. Where it passed, combatants fell dead, their skin desiccated and cracked, their weapons and armour crumbling to dust. The cloud of death made no distinction between orcs and elves, skaven and northmen. It claimed them all.

The cloud drew close to Ka'Bandha, who stared at it in bewildered rage. As it got within arm's reach, it split open to reveal an immense, skeletal figure standing amidst the thinning vapour. Nagash had come, at last. And death came with him.

Volker cringed back as Nagash drew his great, serrated blade and hewed at the bloodthirster. The daemon interposed its hammer at the last moment, and the two baneful weapons connected in a shower of sparks. Nagash gave a death-rattle of frustration and launched another blow. Ka'Bandha swatted it aside with a roar. The two beings slammed together and broke apart, their duel scattering the combatants around them as it shook the street. The remaining windows in the temple shattered as sword and hammer met again, and even the warpflames shied away from the duel.

Through the smoke and dust thrown up by the confrontation, Volker saw a horse galloping towards them, the slumped form of Tyrion on its back. Alongside Alarielle, he caught the elf as he toppled from the saddle. 'Does he live?' she asked.

'I live,' Tyrion coughed, reaching up to stroke her face. She caught his hand and held it. Volker turned away, uncomfortable. *Battle is no place for such things,* Ulric growled petulantly.

'Quiet,' Volker murmured. He could hear something. Like a rattle of spears and a rumbling of drums, or the snap of distant flames. He turned, to ask Gelt if he'd heard it, and saw that the three Incarnates were staring up at the sky. Gelt was shaking in his saddle, and the elves looked bewildered.

Lightning slammed down, not the blood-red lightning of the Chaos-cursed skies, but something brighter and purer. It struck the dome of the temple, and shook the Fauschlag down to its core. Ka'Bandha and Nagash both shrank back from the light, their fight forgotten in the face of such overwhelming elemental fury.

Tyrion laughed.

'Welcome back, my friend,' he said.

Sigmar strode through the dust and the smoke, lightning crawling across his form, Ghal Maraz in his hand. He had cast off the remains of his cloak, and his helmet. For the first time in a long time, he felt whole. Complete.

He had been reborn in the broken body of Karl Franz as the Glottkin had ravaged Altdorf, called to a man of his blood by the winds of magic and fate, and perhaps even necessity. An empire, even a dying one, needed an emperor. *I was the first, and so I will be the last,* he thought sadly. Then he looked out at the massed ranks of friend and foe, and smiled. *Or perhaps I will be the first again, come what may.*

But he had not been reborn whole. His power had been split, even as Ulric's was, between himself and the man called Valten. But what had been in Valten had coiled waiting in the hammer he now held after the youth's death, waiting for the hand of its true owner. Now, reunited, the power of the heavens was his once more, and Sigmar Unberogen was whole.

He raised his hammer, and it began to glow with a cerulean light. As he passed Deathclaw's broken form, the griffon stirred and clambered to its feet with a groggy scream. 'Up, you lazy beast,' Sigmar murmured, stretching out his hand to stroke its feathered neck. 'Up. We have a war to win,' he said. The beast made to follow him, but he waved it back. He strode towards Nagash and Ka'Bandha. The liche met his gaze and, after a moment's hesitation, inclined his head.

'UNBEROGEN,' Nagash said.

'Monster,' Sigmar said conversationally. He swept Ghal Maraz out, and Nagash flinched back. 'Step back, Nagash of Khemri. This one is mine.' Sigmar stared at Ka'Bandha. The bloodthirster was still warily watching Nagash, even as the liche slunk back. 'Turn, hellhound.'

Ka'Bandha turned, a smile creeping across its distorted features. The daemon's nose wrinkled. 'Ahhhh. I smell the stink of a broken soul. You have defeated the Prince of Damnation.' The bloodthirster's smile widened, in its mask of flames. 'Good. That saves me the trouble.'

'I didn't do it for you,' Sigmar said, stepping through the rubble. 'He was an obstacle. A stumbling block, set on the path of fate by your masters. They fear me.' He lifted Ghal Maraz. 'They fear this.'

'I do not fear you,' Ka'Bandha growled.

'No. But then, you aren't important. Just another obstacle.'

Sigmar leaned his hammer across his shoulder. 'You've done your part, beast. And now the story goes on, without you.'

'I will have your skull,' Ka'Bandha snarled, raising its hammer.

'No. But I will have yours,' Sigmar said.

Ka'Bandha roared and swung its hammer down. Sigmar ducked under the blow as it sizzled through the spot his head had occupied, and leapt onto the fallen statue of a forgotten hero. As Ka'Bandha turned, roaring, Sigmar was already in the air, his hammer clasped in both hands. The weapon seemed to glow for just a moment as it descended, and then with a thunderous crash, it slammed home. Ka'Bandha's roar was cut short as the rune weapon crumpled Chaos-spawned bone and tore steaming flesh. Sigmar landed in a crouch, and Ka'Bandha crashed down beside him, its body already unravelling as the dark spirit of Khorne's Huntsman fled back to the abattoir of souls from which it had been plucked.

Sigmar rose slowly to his feet. As if that had been a signal, a great cry rose from the ranks of the Chaos horde, and, almost as one, they at last faltered. Some howled and fled, others dropped to the ground and cowered. Some fought on, but they were quickly overwhelmed by the brawling mass of orcs. Even as Sigmar joined the other Incarnates, the remainder of the Chaos horde broke and fled into the city, pursued by the greenskins and ogres. All save for a burly one-eyed orc, and his bodyguard.

Sigmar eyed the beast as it stumped towards them, its broad form suffused with what he knew to be the Wind of Beasts. *Well, that explains that,* Sigmar thought. He hid a smile as the brute gestured curtly for Malekith to step forward. The Eternity King looked as battle-worn as any of them, and his eyes were hard behind his mask. 'Grimgor, Boss of the East, demands that he be allowed to challenge the Everchosen,' he said, his tone making it clear that he would brook no humour at his expense. 'If you have a problem with it, he wishes it known that he will – ah – crump you.' Grimgor nodded and glared about challengingly.

'IF THE BEAST WISHES TO TRY ITS LUCK, LET IT,' Nagash said. The uproar of battle had faded, and now the only sound was the eerie crackle of the warpflame barrier. Sigmar looked at it, stroking Deathclaw's neck.

'He will not try it alone,' Tyrion said, sheathing his sword. 'It will take all of us to win this battle.' He frowned as he said it, and glanced sidelong at Nagash. 'Even those we would rather not fight beside.'

'YOUR PREFERENCES ARE OF LITTLE CONCERN TO ME, ELF-PRINCE. I WOULD HAVE THIS AFFAIR DONE WITH,' Nagash said. The liche stalked towards the barrier, amethyst magics crawling along his limbs as he focused his powers on the wall of daemonic flames.

'We must aid him,' Sigmar said. 'All of you – turn your power upon the barrier. We must act as one, if we are to accomplish what we must.' As he spoke, he thrust out a hand, and a bolt of lightning streaked from his palm to strike the barrier. One by one, the other Incarnates followed suit, and soon, the warpflames were assailed by the dichotomic onslaught of light and shadow, of life and death, lightning and shards of gold. The flames died back and surged forth, redoubling in strength even as the Incarnates smote them.

Grimgor alone did not unleash the power that had made him its host. Instead, the orc hefted his axe and bellowed a wordless challenge at the pulsating barrier, before rushing in to strike the flames with a wild blow. Sigmar smiled as the barrier collapsed at last, and the orc staggered through. Grimgor spun wildly and decapitated one of the sorcerers responsible for the flame-barrier, even as the backwash of the broken spell consumed the others and reduced them to ash.

Beyond the flames, Sigmar could see the great excavation and the smoke rising from its depths. He could feel the pull of those depths, and his hand tightened on Ghal Maraz's haft. The Fauschlag gave a shudder, and he stumbled, feeling a hollow sensation in the pit of his gut. He looked around. 'We must hurry. The artefact has awakened.'

'How can you tell?' Tyrion said.

'How can you not?' Alarielle said, striding past him. Her face was pinched and tight with pain. 'It is like a wound which will not heal – the world is screaming in agony.' She stumbled, and Malekith solicitously caught her arm.

'THE WORLD IS DYING,' Nagash said.

'And that is why we must hurry,' Sigmar said. He looked around. 'The fate of the world is in our hands, my friends,' he said softly. 'And we cannot afford to fail.'

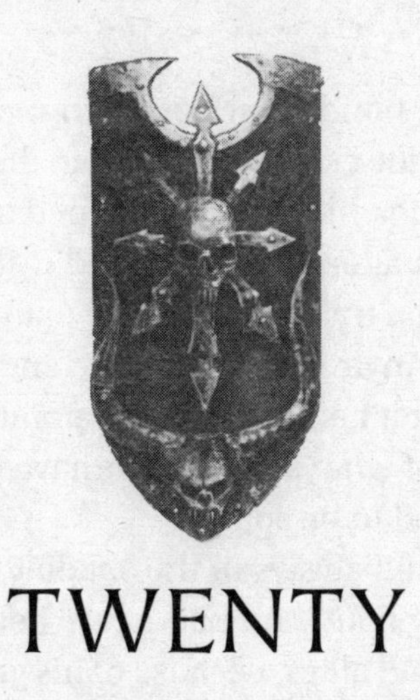

TWENTY

 *The Depths of the Fauschlag*

Teclis opened his eyes as the cavern shook. Great fangs of rock fell down from the roof of the chamber to smash across the ground, and dust choked the air. Whatever was going on above, its echoes were reverberating through the mountain Middenheim was built on. Or perhaps it was not the battle above but the abomination below that was causing the Fauschlag to shudder so.

The warp-artefact shone ominously at the centre of the rough-hewn chamber, its surface rippling with hateful colours. He squinted against its cold light, trying to make out the shapes that dived and swam within it, but gave up after a moment. Sorcerers clustered about it, uttering harsh chants to coax the thing to life.

Learned as he was, he only recognised a few of the incantations being shouted. Even those he knew were archaic, older even than the elves themselves, and had likely not been spoken aloud since the time of the Old Ones. As he watched, a sorcerer toppled over, smoke rising from her mouth and eyes. Her body joined those of the others who had been overcome by the power they were seeking to manipulate.

Teclis tested the bonds that held him moored to the cavern wall. Despite the wide cracks that now ran the width and breadth of the walls and floor, his chains remained taut. His wrists were raw from previous attempts, and blood dripped down his fingers. He did not stop trying, despite the pain. There was nothing else to do but try. Anything else was surrender, and now that he was here, now that it had come to this point, Teclis had discovered wellsprings of what some might have called courage, but which he suspected to be spite.

The spite of a child always in the shadow of his stronger sibling. The spite of a man who had never been trusted by those he called friends and allies, because of his gifts. The spite of one who had been forced to sacrifice everything for a chance at victory, only to find himself falling short yet again, despite his best efforts. And it was the spite of a gamesman without any moves left, as much as anything else, of one who had been outmanoeuvred and outplayed. So Teclis hauled on his chains, strengthened by bile, and anger, and frustration; there was hatred in his heart, and he would not, could not yield. He did not know what he would do if he got loose, but he would do something. Anything.

That he could feel the wellspring of magic which filled the cavern only added to his frustration. It had been drawn from the rock and the air by the thousands of blood sacrifices Archaon had ordered conducted. The bodies of those unfortunates lay strewn about the chamber like a carpet of abused flesh, and the smell of their dying hung thick on the air. The magics roared about like a wind, caught in the pull of the warp-artefact, but Teclis could not manipulate even the slenderest thread, thanks to baleful runes etched into his manacles.

Where are you, brother? he thought. *Do you still live? Do the others? Or was it all for nothing?* He threaded his thin fingers through the links and turned, trying again, as he had so many times before, to pull the chains free of the rock. As he did so, he looked around, taking in the silent ranks of the Swords of Chaos, and their master on his hell-steed. Archaon stared up at the oily surface of the artefact as if captivated. He had not looked away from it since they'd arrived, save to occasionally check that Teclis was still safely bound.

You should have killed me, Teclis thought, bracing his foot against the wall. Pain screamed through his shoulders and arms, but he ignored it. *But you need an audience, don't you? Like a petulant child, waiting to throw his tantrum until his parents are close by. You need me to see what you have done.* His muscles throbbed with weariness and a bone-deep ache, but he strained backwards regardless. Blood welled around the edges of his manacles, and he could not restrain a grunt of pain.

Another quake shook the cavern. Stalactites speared down, shattering on the ground, filling the air with debris. Gold gleamed in the cracks above his head, and not for the first time, he wondered about the true nature of the Fauschlag. *Not that it matters,* he thought. Yet, the part of him that was still a loremaster remained curious. More stalactites rained down, and several of the chanting sorcerers were crushed into messy pulp. Those closest to them made as if to flee, but returned to their labours at a simple gesture from Archaon. They feared the Everchosen more than a death by falling rock, and Teclis couldn't blame them.

A faint sound tugged at his ears. Faint, but growing louder. He recognised it instantly, and smiled suddenly, fiercely. *Brother. I knew you would not let me down. I knew it!*

Teclis licked his cracked and bleeding lips, and cleared his throat. 'Do you hear that, Everchosen?' he called out, letting his chains fall.

Archaon did not turn.

Teclis smiled. 'Do you hear the sound of the drums, Archaon? The crash of steel, the tread of feet? Those are the sounds of battle, Three-Eyed King. You asked me earlier what I saw, Archaon. Well, I saw the future – your future – and it is not pretty.' He hurled the words at Archaon, taunting him. Words were all he had left, and he intended to expend his quiver.

'Silence,' Archaon said. He turned in his saddle, his eyes glowing eerily within his helm.

'Do you remember what I said, on the ramparts?' Teclis continued. 'Sigmar is coming, Archaon. No... he is here. Do you hear him? Do you feel him?'

'Sigmar is a fairy tale. A myth for children, the mad and the blind,' Archaon rumbled. 'Which are you, elf?'

'I don't know. Which are you, human?' Teclis spat. *Child,* he thought, *I am a child. Or mad, but I have seen too much to be blind.*

Archaon wheeled his horse about, and his hand hovered over the hilt of his sword. For a moment, Teclis wondered if the Everchosen would strike him down. The chamber shuddered again, and Archaon laughed softly. He glanced over his shoulder, up at the flickering warp-artefact. As Teclis watched in horror, the artefact's gleaming surface abruptly swelled, doubling in size. Those sorcerers closest to it were sucked into its depths, their screams echoing through the cavern. Vast, pain-wracked faces bulged from within it, pressing against the oily skin of the artefact, and whorls of colour contracted and broke apart in dizzying fashion. Terrible lights gleamed up through the cracks in the cavern floor, and a strange, sickly sweet smell filled Teclis's nostrils as the air wavered, suddenly full of shapes which were not quite in synch with the world. They moved too swiftly, or too slowly, about him, and he shied away from leering faces and insubstantial gripping talons.

Daemonic whispers filled his mind, clawing at the walls of his soul. The sphere increased in size again, and the whispers grew louder. He thrashed in his chains as the daemons tore at his will and sanity. The end was mere minutes away, he knew. The sphere was growing exponentially, but it could only grow so big before it at last imploded. And when it collapsed, the Fauschlag, and all within it, would be wrenched into the Realm of Chaos, as the rest of the world was slowly, but surely torn apart.

'It is beautiful, is it not?' Archaon said, as the wraith-like shapes of daemons swirled about him as if he were the eye of a storm. 'Here is the doom of all mankind, come round at last.' He raised a hand, and daemonic shapes coiled about his arm and fingers like serpents. 'These are the last moments. Glory in them, Teclis of Cothique, for after this, only horror awaits you.' Archaon spread his arms.

'A great and beautiful horror awaits us all.'

Wendel Volker watched in awe as the Emperor, Tyrion and the orc, Grimgor, carved a savage path through the horde of squealing skaven. Though the fighting was not confined to them, they bore the brunt of the red work being done in those tunnels. The skaven died in their hundreds, and their bodies carpeted the cold bedrock of the calcified catacombs where they'd chosen to make their stand, but there were always more of them.

Volker, axe in hand, hauled a wounded elf archer to her feet and shoved her back towards her fellows as armoured stormvermin burst out of a side tunnel and charged towards the small force of men and elves. Before he could shout for his fellow Reiksguard, Gelt stepped forwards and gestured sharply, sending a hail of golden shards hammering into the ratkin. He watched in disgust as the newly dead skaven twitched upright a moment later, dragged back to their feet by the will of Nagash. He cut his gaze towards the swirling black cloud which surrounded the Undying King, and felt Ulric snarl within him.

He knew how the god felt. It was one thing to ally with elves, or even orcs, but the liche was something else entirely. He was as wrong as Chaos, in his way, and he cared nothing for the lives of his allies. Nagash ranged ahead of them all, moving swiftly, killing himself a path through the enemy with magic, sword or choking cloud. No skaven monster or war machine could stand against him, and they had faced plenty of both after descending into the Fauschlag. The deeper they went, the more fierce the resistance became.

The Incarnates had been forced to combine their efforts, fighting together for the first time since they had all gathered in Athel Loren. Malekith's shadow-constructs harried the enemy, driving them squealing into the path of Gelt's shards or Alarielle's thorns. Tyrion and the Emperor guarded Grimgor's flanks as the orc and his Immortulz bulled ahead, taking on the worst the skaven could send against them with enthusiasm rather than strategy.

From behind him, Volker heard the rasping intake of breath that heralded Malekith's dragon preparing to breathe its reeking smoke into another set of tunnels. The great beast, and Deathclaw, had had a tough time of it at first, for neither beast would be parted from their respective masters and they'd had to squirm and scrape through the upper tunnels. But once those manmade tunnels had given way to the cavernous natural corridors, the dragon had flared its wings and lent its might to the advance.

Tough beast, Ulric murmured, admiringly.

'Glad it's on our side,' Volker said. He spun his axe, and chopped through a spear as it sought his belly. He slashed out, killing the skaven who'd wielded it, and then those behind it. Ulric had some strength yet, and the god lent it freely. Volker was not equal to the Incarnates, but he was more than the man he had been.

The Fauschlag continued to shake and shudder about them, and more than once, Volker heard the scream of a man or elf as they vanished into some crevasse, or were crushed by rocks tumbling from above. The moans of the wounded pursued them all down through the tunnels. Those who were trapped, or could not walk, were left behind to survive as best they could. That which was still the man he had been cringed in horror at the thought, but the wolf in him, the part that was ice, knew that it was necessary. Time was of the essence, and there was none to spare for those who could not march.

A strange light played across the blade of his axe as he swung it and swept the head from a skaven's shoulders. As the body fell, he saw that the ratmen were fleeing, scuttling for their holes. *Do you smell it, Wendel Volker? We are here,* Ulric thundered in his head. The wolf-god gave a joyous howl. *We are here and our prey is at last within reach! Blood is on the air, and the sounds of battle fill our ears. Rend and slay, tear and smash! Vengeance!*

Volker shuddered as the godspark twisted and writhed in agitation within him. Blood poured down his skin as white hairs grew from his pores, and his bones cracked and shifted. He closed his eyes, trying to fight past the pain. Suddenly a cool hand pressed itself against the back of his grimy neck, and he felt a cleansing wind blow through the cold runnels of his soul. He turned and saw Alarielle. The Everqueen smiled sadly, and stepped back as he flinched away from her. 'I – thank you,' Volker said. He could taste blood in his mouth. He didn't know what she had done, but the pain had lessened.

'Do not thank me,' the Everqueen said. 'Fight, son of the Empire. Fight hard, and die well, if it comes to that.'

'Which it almost certainly will,' Malekith said. The Eternity King glared at Volker. 'Whatever lurks within you, man, see that it does not seek to hinder us. We have arrived at the precipice and I would not be sent over the edge by mistake.' Malekith gestured with his sword, and Volker turned back towards the strange light. He smelt an acrid stink, and Ulric growled, *Daemon-spoor.* They had come to a wide, high cavern, which rang with the shrieks of daemons and the grinding of shifting rock. And the light as well, which burned and chilled at the same time, the way the sun was said to do in the far north.

Before them was arrayed the full might of the Lord of the End Times. Daemons of every size and description blocked their path to the artefact, and they surrounded a core of black iron – Archaon, Volker knew, and his Swords of Chaos. 'There are thousands of them,' someone muttered. Similar mutters ran through the ranks, and hands tightened on weapons as men and elves faced the army of the End Times.

'More than that,' Volker said. *If I were still a gambling man, I wouldn't bet a farthing on our chances,* he thought. He felt strangely calm, and wondered whether that was Ulric's doing, or Alarielle's.

'No wonder the vermin ran,' Gelt said hollowly. 'I wouldn't want to get caught in the middle of this either.' The Incarnate of Metal sounded tired, and Volker knew how he felt. Wherever he looked, there were bloody bandages, bound limbs and exhausted faces.

Volker looked to the Emperor, and saw him sitting rigid in Deathclaw's saddle, his hammer across his lap. He stared across the cavern, and his face was placid, as if he were deep in thought. *That was always his problem,* Ulric growled. *Too much thinking. What is there to think about? The enemy is here, we are here, there is only one choice. There is no more time for cleverness. There is only time now for blood, steel and will!*

As if in reply to the wolf-god's muttering, Grimgor threw back his head and gave a wild bellow, which drowned out even the raucous howling of the gathered daemonic hosts. The orc spread his arms, and his Immortulz gave voice to their own cries. Then, with a rattle of iron, the greenskins charged. 'Well, that's torn it,' Volker said.

The daemons reacted instantly, surging forwards like a sea of infernal fury to meet the Incarnate of Beasts and his warriors. Bloodletters bounded up, hissing Khorne's praises; horrors of all hues and shades laughed uproariously and hurled torrents of writhing magic without regard for friend or foe; plaguebearers shambled into battle, pox-blades ready; and the handmaidens of Slaanesh danced in, claws snapping. And behind them all came the greater daemons, driving their lesser manifestations on with lash and bellowed order.

The Emperor lifted Ghal Maraz, and, as one, the Incarnates and their remaining forces started to advance. There was no grand strategy or battle-order. There was only the raw press of the melee, strength against strength, and human muscle and will against daemonic caprice. Volker began to run as, around him, knights galloped into battle. Silver Helms and Dragon Princes joined the charge, shouting out the battle cries of fallen Ulthuan and Caledor. Arrows arced overhead, and Malekith's dragon uttered a scream of rage and anticipation as it launched itself into the air. The dead bodies of skaven, elves and men lurched past Volker as he ran, stumbling into battle with broken blades and empty fists.

Volker ducked under the slash of a bloodletter's black blade, and hammered his axe into the daemon's gut. The creature folded over him, its fiery ichor scorching his armour. He tore the axe loose and turned. *There,* Ulric snarled. *There he is – the thief!*

He saw the ragged shape of Teclis chained to a wall across the cavern, and he snarled deep in his throat. Volker hefted his axe and began to lope towards the prisoner. Icy strength flooded his limbs, propelling him faster and faster. Daemons lunged at him out of the press of battle, and he hacked them down. He leapt over the body of a burning elf as a salvo of coruscating sorcery enveloped a number of Malekith's warriors, and chopped through the gangly arm of a pink horror as it sought to snare him.

As he ran, he saw the orcs crash into the wild, pirouetting daemonettes. The shrieking laughter of the latter rapidly turned to screams as the black orcs proved uninterested in anything save slaughter. Volker was forced to leap aside as the pearlescent hoof of a keeper of secrets slammed down nearby. The daemon strutted into battle against Grimgor. The orc launched himself at the creature with a roar, and his axe smashed down into the distorted, bovine skull, filling the air with ichor. The orc's roar of triumph followed Volker as he continued on, arrowing towards his prey.

A plaguebearer rose up before him, and he smashed his axe into its bulging side, tearing it out the other in a welter of foulness. The daemon sagged, its blade falling from its rubbery fingers as Volker stepped over it. The air was cold around him. He looked down at Teclis, and said, 'Hello, thief.' But it wasn't his voice. It was the deep, rough growl of the godspark within him. 'Your debt has come due.'

'Well, wolf-god, if that is who and what you are,' Teclis murmured, through bloody lips, 'I am helpless at last. Your prey hangs before you, throat bared. What will you do?'

Volker glared at him. Everything around him, the noise of the battle behind him, the constant keening wail of the shimmering black sphere at the centre of the cavern, all of it fell away, lost in the howling of wolves. He was cold inside and out, and despite the heat of the cavern, his breath frosted on the air. He raised his axe. Teclis closed his eyes.

Volker hesitated. Teclis cracked one eye. The elf smiled. 'Then, perhaps I am not your prey after all, despite your howling.' He grimaced, as a spasm of pain rippled through him. 'Am I your enemy, Wendel Volker? Or are we at last allies in this last hunt?'

Volker shook his head. He lowered his weapon. The Fauschlag shook, and Volker closed his eyes for a moment as the howling grew too much to bear. In his head, he heard the voice of Gregor Martak. *You will not die, Wendel Volker. Not until you have done as I command.* 'No,' he said, softly, as he looked at Teclis. 'You are not my quarry.' He turned. He spotted Archaon, galloping through the press of battle, and Ulric howled within him. *Yes, yes!*

And then, axe in hand, the last servant of the wolf-god went on the hunt.

* * *

Sigmar Unberogen saw the battle as if through a prism – scenes and vignettes of heroism and struggle flashed across his eyes. He saw Malekith, once more astride his dragon, shadows flaring about him like a dark cloak, hurtle into battle against two malevolent lords of change. He saw Alarielle, pale and weak, the world's pain battering at her body and mind, snare a gambolling beast of Nurgle in a web of thorns and tear it to slimy shreds. He saw Gelt unbind the enchantments that bound together daemonic weapons, and loose swarms of flesh-rending shards to tear scores of daemons apart. He saw Nagash, lurid amethyst fires boiling in his eye sockets, stalk forwards, his spells and legion of corpses driving the enemy before him.

Strange times, he thought, as he watched the liche do battle with the world's foes. There was a strange sort of nobility there, buried beneath the murk and madness. A will that rivalled his own, a drive for victory that was second to none. Nagash would fight to the end, for he could not countenance defeat. As he watched, the liche swung his blade and opened a bloodthirster's belly, scattering burning ichor through the air.

Deathclaw's screech brought him back to himself and Ghal Maraz lashed out, smashing the malformed skull of a plaguebearer. Around him, the remaining members of the Reiksguard fought from horseback, or on foot, as they slowly pushed their way towards the warp-artefact. Sigmar watched as the men – his men – fought on, and thought, *once, I would have known your names. I would have known who you were, and we would have shared wine and blood. I do not know you now, and I am sorry.*

He jabbed his hammer out, and sent a bolt of cerulean lightning smashing into a pack of flesh hounds as they loped towards Grimgor. The orc was oblivious to his peril, being too occupied with trying to shove his axe down the throat of a great unclean one. The beasts were hurled back, or up into the air, their scaly bodies blackened and broken. *Saving an orc,* Sigmar thought. *What would Alaric say?* He smiled. *He'd probably be annoyed all of his runefangs have gone missing.*

The air throbbed as the artefact at the chamber's heart pulsed, and as Sigmar turned towards it, he saw it expand to almost four times its previous size. Jagged lesions appeared on its outer skin, spreading like stress fractures in a pane of glass. A brilliant white light shone from the growing wounds, dazzling and painful in its intensity. The Fauschlag gave a sudden, jarring lurch, and Sigmar knew that they were out of time.

Great slabs of rock crashed down from above, pulverising zombies, daemons and even a few luckless elves. Sigmar jerked Deathclaw into motion as he saw Tyrion's horse go down amidst the rain of debris, its leg broken. The griffon barrelled in with a shriek and snatched both horse and rider out of the path of a stalactite. The elf looked up at Sigmar and nodded his thanks as he and his wounded steed were deposited nearby. Sigmar didn't waste words on inquiring after the elf's health. Hurt or not, Tyrion would fight on. He urged Deathclaw back towards the centre of the cavern, hoping he might reach the artefact. *Though what I'm going to do when I get there is another matter entirely,* he thought, as his hammer crashed down on a bloodletter's flat skull.

He spotted Malekith as he hurtled through the rain of falling stones, and gestured towards Teclis's bound form, hoping the Eternity King would understand. There was no way his voice would carry through the cacophony of the collapsing cavern. Fortunately, the Incarnate of Shadow seemed to have grasped his meaning, and he nodded tersely as his dragon wheeled about in the air to swoop towards Teclis, ignoring the rocks which bounced off its scaly hide. Sigmar looked around, trying to spot the other Incarnates.

He saw the great unclean one Grimgor had been attempting to throttle struck by an immense chunk of rock, and it burst under the impact, foetid liquid spurting free from the torn prison of unnatural flesh to spatter all who fought around it. The orc dodged aside at the last moment and now stood alone almost in the centre of the cavern, his Immortulz spread out around him, locked in combat with the fallen daemon's servitors.

As Grimgor turned towards the light of the sphere, Sigmar saw Archaon, still sitting astride his horse before the artefact, raise a fist. The Swords of Chaos lowered their lances as one, and started forwards. The Chaos knights picked up speed, and soon they were galloping towards the orcs, Archaon at their head.

'Faster, old friend,' Sigmar shouted, as Deathclaw lunged. But even as the griffon careened towards the centre of the cavern, Sigmar knew he would be too late. Grimgor caught sight of Archaon and roared in delight. The orc charged to meet the oncoming knights, his bodyguard loping alongside him. The greenskins crashed into Archaon's warriors and carnage ensued. Grimgor beheaded a horse with a wild blow, and dragged a knight from his saddle as the man sought to ride past.

The Incarnate of Beasts swung the hapless Chaos knight like a bludgeon, battering at the latter's comrades with more enthusiasm than accuracy. He hurled the limp body aside and whirled to meet the charge of the Lord of the End Times. Archaon bore down on the orc, intending to ride him under, but Grimgor was too fast. He slid aside, avoiding the thrashing hooves of the hellsteed, and lunged at its rider. His axe slammed into Archaon's shield, buckling it and knocking the Three-Eyed King from the saddle.

Sigmar felt a thrill of hope as he watched the orc stalk towards the fallen Everchosen. Of all of them, he had thought the brute the least likely to strike the killing blow. But fate, it seemed, had other plans.

'I will not be felled by a beast,' Archaon snarled, his voice carrying over the clamour of battle. He surged to his feet, even as Grimgor reached him. 'I am Archaon, and I am the end made flesh,' he shouted. He slashed out, nearly opening the orc's belly. 'What do you say to that, animal?'

'Grimgor says shut up and die,' the orc roared. Axe crashed against sword, as the brute hurled himself at Archaon with wild abandon. Back and forth, they reeled through the melee, trading blows that would have felled dozens of lesser opponents. The orc's axe scored red lines across Archaon's armour, and Archaon's blade drew blood again and again.

Finally, axe met sword and the two weapons became tangled, and their wielders strained against one another, using every ounce of strength that they possessed to hold their ground against their foe. For a long moment they stood, head to head, the Lord of the End Times and the Once and Future Git, the Three-Eyed King and the Boss of the East. Then, with a guffaw, Grimgor's skull crashed against Archaon's helm. Sigmar saw the strange, flickering gemstone set in the Everchosen's helmet shatter, and realised that Archaon was the Three-Eyed King no more. The Everchosen would have to make do with the two he'd been born with – what was left of the Eye of Sheerian speckled the broad expanse of Grimgor's brow.

The blow broke the stalemate, and the two warriors staggered apart. Archaon reached up to touch the crumpled face of his helm, and he howled in rage. A strange energy suddenly illuminated the blade of his sword and rippled up his arm, and then he was striding in with liquid grace. Grimgor met his advance, and each time they traded blows, black lightning streaked from the point of impact, until at last the orc's axe succumbed and shivered apart in his hands. The orc staggered back, eyes bulging.

He didn't stay off balance for long, however, and he tossed aside the remains of the useless weapon and leapt for Archaon, hands reaching for the Everchosen's throat. Archaon rolled into the collision, and his sword's point erupted from between Grimgor's shoulder blades in an explosion of blood. The orc staggered, and slumped with a guttural sigh. His thick fingers clawed uselessly at Archaon's cuirass as he slid to the ground, and a writhing amber haze rose from his form, to coalesce briefly in the air before collapsing into wisps of light which were drawn towards the shimmering void growing within the warp-artefact.

Grimgor's warriors uttered a communal howl of fury as their boss fell, and flung themselves at the Swords of Chaos with redoubled ferocity. Archaon beheaded one as the orc clawed at him, and turned to meet Sigmar's gaze as the latter leaned forwards in Deathclaw's saddle. The griffon hurtled across the cavern, the Reiksguard galloping in his wake. Behind him, Sigmar heard the death-scream of a dragon, but he could not afford to take his eyes off his enemy. 'Archaon,' he roared. 'Face me, Destroyer.'

Chaos knights hurriedly interposed themselves, and died beneath Deathclaw's talons. Sigmar smashed Ghal Maraz down on upraised shields and shattered thrusting swords. Axes and swords hacked into the griffon's limbs and flanks, and its shrieks of pain and rage filled Sigmar's ears, but he could not afford to retreat, not now, and never again. He caught sight of elves and zombies to either side of him, fighting against the daemons that sought to envelop his desperate spearhead. He heard the crackle of magics, and saw screeching daemons evaporate as they swooped towards him.

Deathclaw gave a great shudder and lunged with a heart-wrenching cry, to slam into a rearing steed. Sigmar was flung from the saddle, as was the rider of the horse, and as he rose to his feet, he saw that he was face to face with Archaon.

Sparks flew as Ghal Maraz smashed against the Slayer of Kings. Lightning rippled along the hammer's rune-etched head, vying with the dark fire that swirled about the Everchosen's daemon-blade. Nearby, Deathclaw and Archaon's steed fought savagely, and the rocky ground was spattered with blood and ichor as the two animals clawed and bit one another. 'I beat you once, follower of lies,' Archaon roared, thrusting out a hand. 'I ripped your lightning from you, and shattered your last redoubt, and I will do it again...'

Sigmar grinned fiercely as nothing happened. Blood streaked his face and beard, but he felt no weakness. Not now. He batted Archaon's hand aside and slammed Ghal Maraz down on the Everchosen's pauldron, knocking him back. 'Well? What are you waiting for?' he said. He thrust the hammer forwards like a spear and caught Archaon in the chest. 'Take my lightning, Everchosen.'

Archaon staggered back. 'I – what?'

Sigmar tapped his own brow. 'We're on an equal footing now, boy. Just me and you.' He swung the hammer again, and Archaon barely parried it. Each punishing blow bled into the one that followed and Sigmar pushed his opponent back, until Archaon slashed at him, gouging his armour and cutting the flesh beneath. Behind him, the warp-artefact gave another blinding pulse, and the cracks in its surface grew wider. He heard Deathclaw utter a shrill cry, and saw the griffon fall, tangled with Archaon's mount in its death-throes. The latter gave voice to a final whinny before Deathclaw's talons tore out its throat, and then both beasts were still. Sadness swept through him as he bashed Archaon's sword aside and drove his hammer into the Everchosen's cuirass, turning one of the skull tokens hanging there to powder.

The griffon had known he wasn't its master, though he wore the man's skin. It had served him regardless, and it had served him well. He had not known Karl Franz, though he wished he had. That the beast had loved him so, enough to fight on as it had, spoke well of the Emperor. Scattered memories, not his own but those of the body he had taken possession of, filled his mind, and he saw the Imperial Zookeeper hand over an egg to a youth on the edge of manhood. He saw the first faltering steps of the cub, as Karl Franz fed it morsels from his own fingers. And he saw their first battle, and felt a savage joy as the griffon defended the body of its wounded master. *I am sorry,* he thought. *I am sorry for it all.*

'You will fall here,' Sigmar said, fighting for breath. His strength was ebbing. 'Whatever else happens, you will fall.' He felt the ground tremble beneath his feet, and he saw that the warp-artefact was no more – it had been completely consumed by the swirling void it had given birth to. The roiling surface of the sphere ate away at the cavern around it, and a crackling, empty void of white was left in place of the churned rock. His heart sank.

'It doesn't matter,' Archaon said. 'Nothing matters. I've won. This world will burn, and something better will rise from the ashes.' He launched a flurry of blows that Sigmar was hard-pressed to block. He was moving slower now, and the entire right side of his armour was slippery with his own blood. Archaon didn't seem to tire, but Sigmar, for all his power, knew he wasn't so lucky. His heartbeat hammered in his ears and his lungs burned, but despite it all, despite the danger, he knew he wouldn't have traded places with anyone.

This is where I was meant to be, he thought. Despite the fury of battle, he was calm. *This is my reason for living, this is why I was born. This moment is mine.* Out of the corner of his eye, he saw a white-furred shape lope towards him, and he smiled. *Hello, old wolf. You told me once I would come to a bad end, and here we are.*

Archaon's sword slipped past his flagging guard and smashed into his cuirass. Sigmar fell back, off balance. He struck the ground hard, and Ghal Maraz was jolted from his hand. He stared up at Archaon, as the latter lifted his blade in both hands.

'To think, they believed that you could save them,' Archaon said.

'To think, I once thought you might do that yourself,' Sigmar said. Archaon hesitated. Sigmar smiled sadly. 'Diederick Kastner, son of a daughter of the Empire. You could have been the sword that swept my land free of Chaos forever. In a better world, perhaps you have. But here and now, you are nothing more than another petty warlord.'

'You know nothing about me,' Archaon said, still holding his sword aloft.

'I know you. I saw you born and I saw you die, again and again. I saw your soul twisted all out of shape by the honeyed words of daemons, and I saw you turn your back on me. I saw and I wept, for you, and for what I knew you would do.'

Archaon lowered his blade. 'No...'

'You made yourself a pawn of prophecy,' Sigmar said. 'You set your feet on this path. The daemons helped, but it was you who walked into the darkness. It was you who fled the light, Diederick.'

'You are not Sigmar. The gods are all dead, and he was a lie,' Archaon grated.

'Are they dead, or are they a lie? Make up your mind,' Sigmar said. He could see Ghal Maraz's haft, just out of the corner of his eye. He stretched a hand towards it.

'You are lying,' Archaon roared. He lifted his sword, but before he could bring it down, there was a flash of white fur, and then Wendel Volker was there. Axe and sword connected with a screech, and the former exploded in its owner's hands. Volker staggered, and Archaon's sword chopped down, through his shoulder and into his chest. Archaon tore his blade free and the Reiksguard fell. Sigmar rolled over and reached for the hammer, but Archaon kicked it aside. 'No! No more distractions. No more lies,' Archaon howled. 'You die now, and your Empire dies with you.' He made to move after Sigmar, but something stopped him. Sigmar looked down, and saw Volker clinging to Archaon's legs.

'I told you once, Everchosen. When a wolf bites, he does not let go,' Volker croaked. 'And I told you that you would die here, whatever else.' Archaon looked down in obvious shock, and Volker grinned up at him. 'This is *my* city, man, and you will not take it!' Ice began to spread across Archaon's greaves, and he roared in anger and pain as the cold gnawed at him. Then the Slayer of Kings flashed down, and Wendel Volker, bearer of the godspark of Ulric, was no more.

Sigmar saw Volker slump, and heard, deep in his mind, the death-howl of the god he had worshipped in his youth. He had no time to mourn, for even as Archaon tore his blade free of the body of the last of the Reiksguard, the Everchosen pivoted and brought the howling daemon-blade down. But Volker and Ulric's sacrifice had given him the time he needed to recover, and call up the lightning that was again his to command.

Sigmar thrust his hands up, and felt the blade crash against his palms. Lightning crackled between flesh and the hungry bite of tainted steel, and Sigmar slowly closed his fingers tight about the blade. Then he pushed himself erect, driving Archaon back with every step. The Everchosen tried to push back, but the Emperor was too strong.

And then, with a scream that was of joy as much as it was of pain, the Slayer of Kings shattered in Sigmar's grip. Archaon reeled as smoking shards of the daemon-blade tore into his armour. Blinded, dazed, he stumbled back. Sigmar lunged forwards and drove his fist into Archaon's featureless helm, buckling the metal, and driving him back, over the precipice, and into the maelstrom of shadows.

Archaon, Lord of the End Times, vanished into the darkness.

TWENTY-ONE

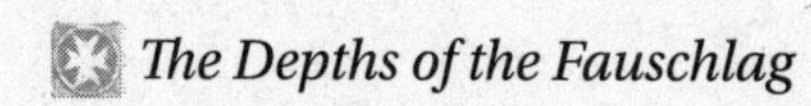

The Depths of the Fauschlag

Sigmar shoved himself to his feet and, Ghal Maraz in hand, backed away. The sphere shuddered like a sick animal. A moment later, it shattered and collapsed in on itself, leaving a swirling rift of energy in its place. The white had become black, and it hurt Sigmar's eyes to look upon it. Howling winds sprang up, buffeting all those who remained in the chamber and pulling them towards the writhing void. Sigmar saw that he and the other Incarnates, along with Teclis, were the only living beings in the cavern; every elf and human who'd descended into the depths with them was dead. Sadness warred with relief. Better death than what would have awaited them in the void. The powers of the Incarnates protected them from the energies now filling the cavern, but mortals would have been swept away within moments of the rift's explosion.

All around him, the remaining daemons began to shudder and come apart. Their flesh ran like melted wax, and they were pulled, drop by drop, into the maw of the void. The fitful pulses which had marked the sphere were gone, replaced by an ominous rumble whose intensity grew with every passing moment. Sigmar turned away from the rift and began to force his way towards the other Incarnates, fighting the pull of the wind with every step.

The rock beneath his feet ran like water in a whirlpool, its hue and shape changing from one second to the next. Leering faces formed in the shifting stone, and vanished as soon as he looked at them. All around the chamber, the laws of nature were coming undone as the raw stuff of Chaos leaked into the world through the rift.

'We were too late,' Malekith snarled as Sigmar reached them. The Eternity King had to shout to be heard over the wind. He supported Teclis, and one of the mage's arms was flung over his shoulder.

'No,' Gelt shouted. 'No, we have not lost, not yet.'

'What can we do?' Alarielle screamed. She leaned against Tyrion, and Sigmar could tell from her face that she felt every single one of the torturous changes the cavern was undergoing. 'It is but a trickle now, but it is growing stronger with every passing moment. We cannot hope to contain it!'

'WE MUST. WE WILL,' Nagash thundered, facing the void. *'THIS WORLD IS MINE. NAGASH WILL NOT FALL. NAGASH CANNOT DIE. I WILL NOT. NOT AGAIN.'*

'He's right,' Sigmar said. He looked at Teclis. 'If we combine our magics, as we did against the warpflame barrier, will it be enough?'

'I – I do not know,' Teclis said, shaking his head. The elf struggled to stand on his own, and pushed away from Malekith. He held his staff and leaned against it. 'The Winds of Aqshy and Ghur, they are lost...'

'They are not lost,' Tyrion said. 'I – we – can all feel them still. They are here, with us.' He looked at his brother. 'We must try, brother. Else what was it all for?'

Teclis stared at his brother in silence for a moment, his robes rippling in the shrieking wind. Then he nodded. 'You are right, brother. You are always right.'

'Except when I'm wrong?' Tyrion said, smiling.

'Even then,' Teclis said, grinning. He shook his head. 'You know what to do. The winds know their task, and they will guide you in the doing of it. I will try to bend Ghur and Aqshy to it as well. Even without hosts, they will be of some use.'

Sigmar looked at the others, and then, as one, they spread out, moving to the edge of the void. As they approached the roaring maelstrom, each Incarnate summoned the last vestiges of their power, and flung it forth, seeking to cage the uncageable. Sigmar groaned as the lightning crackled from him to spend its fury on the swirling rift. The void sought to draw the power from him, as Archaon had done at Averheim, and it took every ounce of his remaining strength to prevent it. He clutched Ghal Maraz in both hands and drew the lightning tight, focusing his will through the ancient hammer.

He saw Teclis set his staff, at the centre of the line, and begin to draw the Winds of Fire and Beasts into himself. He was not a suitable host for either, let alone both, and the winds struggled against him. Sigmar watched helplessly as the elf's flesh began to boil and peel. What Teclis was attempting was a death sentence, but they had no other choice. *Our lives for that of the world. That's a fair bargain,* he thought. He gritted his teeth against a sudden surge of pain. A light was growing in the chamber, as each of the winds was pitted against the audient void. And then, against all probability, the rift began to shrink.

We're doing it, Sigmar thought. *Gods of my fathers, wherever you are now, help us last just a little longer. Give us all strength.* His body shuddered, and he felt as if the meat of him might separate from his bones. Smoke rose from the head of Ghal Maraz as he poured bolt after bolt of celestial lightning into the yawning abyss.

Something flickered, just out of the corner of his eye. He

twitched his head to the side, and his eyes widened as he saw a familiar shape detach itself from the dark at the edges of the cavern and rush forwards silently. Sigmar flung out his hand. 'No!'

Balthasar Gelt turned at Sigmar's cry, but his reply was lost as Mannfred von Carstein's sword erupted from his chest. The wizard was lifted off his feet by the vampire's blow, and a beam of golden light sprang from his limp frame and vanished soundlessly into the void. 'Mine,' Mannfred howled. 'The power will be mine. Even as this world is mine.'

Teclis, seeing the loss of Chamon, stretched out a hand, as if to grasp the Wind of Metal and haul it back from the abyss, but the effort was too much for him. Sigmar watched in horror as Teclis of Cothique, High Loremaster of Ulthuan, was ripped apart by the triumvirate of magical winds, and reduced to swirling ash. Even as Teclis perished, the rift gave an ear-splitting shriek and, in a flare of inky black light, tore free of the Incarnates' control. Sigmar was flung back across the cavern, and he struck the ground hard. The other Incarnates had suffered similar fates, or had retreated at the first convulsion of the rift.

As Sigmar picked himself up, he saw that only Mannfred and Nagash were left standing next to the rift, and the vampire gesticulated at the liche, his feral features twisting in triumph. 'Vlad told me to pick a side, and I have, master. Better to be the right hand of anarchy, than the slave of Nagash. Walach was right, the blood-soaked fool. Aye, and Kemmler as well. You are nothing but a disease, Nagash… a plague on all the world, and with this power, I shall drive your midnight soul into the void forever. And it shall be me who rules this world, and rides its corpse into eternity. The world shall have a new Undying King, and you shall be forgotten!'

The vampire spun towards the rift, and, as Teclis had, he thrust out his hands, as if to draw the winds to him. Instead, however, it was the raw substance of the rift which answered his call. It washed over him, and Mannfred's laughter degenerated into a scream as he staggered back, his flesh smoking.

The rift flared and Sigmar added his screams to those of Mannfred, as did all of the remaining Incarnates. The void tore the winds loose from their hosts and drew them into itself. Sigmar thrashed as the celestial magics of Azyr were dragged from him a second time, and sucked into the nightmare abyss. He collapsed, his body trembling, and his strength gone. He saw the other Incarnates fall, one by one.

Nagash was the last. For long moments, the Undying King stood unbowed against the howling void and his own dissolution, as the magics that had given him form slowly unravelled. He fought against the void, as if determined to wrench back the Wind of Death through sheer will. Then, at last, the Great Necromancer threw back his head and screamed desolately one final time before he suffered Teclis's fate and was torn apart by the swirling energies.

As the ashes of his former master were swept into the void, Mannfred staggered blindly away from the rift, clawing at his seared flesh. He ranted and railed in a language Sigmar did not recognise, and called out for people who were not there. Sigmar tried to push himself to his feet, but he lacked the strength. He heard the scrape of steel on stone, and turned to see Tyrion lurch to his feet, sword in hand.

Mannfred did not notice Tyrion's approach until the last moment, and as he whirled, fangs agape, Tyrion slammed his sword up through the vampire's belly and into his black heart. Mannfred screamed and clawed at Tyrion's arms as the elf lifted him off his feet. Sunfang flared as the magics forged into the blade awoke, and Mannfred thrashed as he burned to ashes from inside out. Tyrion jerked his blade free, and what was left of Mannfred von Carstein collapsed into ashes, to join those of Teclis and Nagash in the void.

As Tyrion stepped back, the cavern gave a great crack. The walls shifted and sickly yellow blood dripped down from the cracks. Vast sections of the cavern floor fell away, into nothingness.

Boulders and stalactites fell like rain. Sigmar looked up as a great spill of rock tumbled down towards the Everqueen, and he shouted to Tyrion, who whirled about, but too late. The Everqueen would have perished there, had Malekith not lunged forward and thrown her clear, towards Tyrion's reaching arms. The Eternity King vanished amidst the thundering downpour of rock a moment later.

Sigmar shoved himself to his feet, and took a staggering step towards the fallen rocks. If there was even a chance that Malekith might be saved, he intended to try. But as he drew close to the expanding edge of the rift, a dark shape rose out of the void and smashed into him.

He turned as Archaon lurched into him, the Everchosen's fingers scrabbling for his throat. The Lord of the End Times roared incoherently as he battered at Sigmar, his words lost in the howl emanating from the ever-expanding rift. Sigmar smashed him down with Ghal Maraz, but he was on his feet a moment later, reaching out to grab the haft of the hammer. The two men struggled for a moment on the edge of the void.

Then, they were gone, lost amidst the swirling darkness.

EPILOGUE

Autumn 2528

Neferata stalked through the ruins of Middenheim, as the world died around her, and wondered why she had come. She had left the uncertain safety of Sylvania, left her new kingdom in the hands of her greatest rival and only friend, Khalida, and made for the certain doom of Middenheim. She had flown through the tortured skies, urging her abyssal steed on to greater and greater speed for reasons she could not articulate. Her armour was scorched and scarred, and wounds marked her flesh, but she felt no pain. There was no more time for pain, or fear, or anything save sadness. She looked up, and watched the sky burn. Her steed screeched in agitation where it crouched on the northern gatehouse.

You were right, Khalida, she thought. *It is the end, and nothing we have done means anything any more. All our petty grievances and spiteful schemes are as dust before the doom that is coming to claim us all.*

A whimper caught her attention and she turned, seeking out

its source. She saw a woman, clad in ruined armour, crouched nearby, amongst rubble and the bodies of elves, dwarfs and northmen. Neferata sniffed, smelling Vlad's blood on the woman. She moved towards her, sword in hand. The woman had been beautiful once, and might have been again, if there had been time.

'But there is no time,' Neferata said, softly. 'There is *no time*.' The end had come and gone, and all that was left now was for the carrion birds. She could feel it on the air and beneath her feet. She looked down at the woman, pondering. Then, hesitantly, she stretched out a hand.

'Her name is Isabella.'

Neferata whirled, her heart thudding in her chest. Arkhan the Black staggered towards her, through the smoke and fire, leaning on his staff, his ragged robes swirling about him. When he reached them, the liche looked down at Isabella. *'Vlad must have saved her somehow. He was always a determined fool.'*

'Not a fool,' Neferata said softly. She sank down and cradled Isabella, as if the other woman were a child. 'Just a man.' She looked up at him. 'You survived.'

'I did. Thanks to Settra.'

'Settra,' Neferata said, unable to believe her ears. She shook her head, dismissing the thought, and asked, 'Nagash?'

Arkhan extended his hand. Neferata's eyes widened, as she took in the slow dissolution of Arkhan's skeletal fingers. *'The Undying King is gone, and his magics with him. Soon, I will join him. The Incarnates have failed, and the world is coming undone beneath our feet.'*

Neferata looked up. 'We will all join him. The world is done,' she said. Isabella whimpered, and Neferata murmured comforting nothings to her. 'All our striving, all our pain... for what?'

Arkhan was silent for a moment. He looked down at her and then placed a hand on her shoulder. *'For the chance at something better,'* he said. He took her hand and pressed it to his chest. *'Do you feel it, Neferata?'*

She jerked her hand away. 'Feel what?'

'One last roll of the dice,' Arkhan said.

'Spoken like a gambler,' Neferata said. She hugged Isabella close and stroked the whimpering vampire's matted hair. Crimson tears rolled down her cheeks and plopped into the dust. Arkhan reached out and wiped them away, before he turned away, to face the growling dark that crept through the streets towards them. *'The End is here, my queen. The all-consuming black fire of the empty spaces between worlds. I see it, even as Nagash must have seen it. It will devour the world, bit by bit, until nothing is left. Until our world, our history, is but dust on the cosmic wind. When they have finished toying with the remains, the Ruinous Powers shall turn away. They will turn their attentions to other worlds, other times, and it will be as if we never existed.'* Arkhan extended his hand without looking at her. She took it, and he hauled her to her feet. She still held Isabella. The city trembled around them, and a strange light rose from the cracks in the street.

'But I see something else, in the void... I see a figure, shining with the power of light and the heavens, swimming through the dark, determined to stir the embers of our passing and free the seeds of a new world, and new life,' Arkhan went on, his rasping, creaking voice filled with something she thought might be wonder. He touched his chest, and she saw a light shimmering through the rents in his robes. He glanced at her. *'There may yet be hope, though that word feels strange to say.'* He looked down at his chest, and touched a black mark on his robes, in the shape of a hand. '*I thought she had cursed me, but I think she knew, in the end, that it would come to this. I see a figure, small in the darkness, but it will grow stronger, and I will help, even as oblivion claims me.'*

Neferata looked at him. Questions danced through her mind, but she could not speak. She wanted to tell him to abandon whatever mad fancy had seized him. She wanted to tell him that her powers might sustain him, that together, they could hold off the end of everything. But the words turned to ash on her tongue. Arkhan turned fully towards her, and caught her chin in his crumbling fingers.

'Run, Neferata. Run and perhaps you may yet outrun the end. Perhaps you may survive, to flourish with those seeds of life I will help plant in the world to come. Run to Sylvania, fly back to our people, and lead them, in these final hours. Lead them into death, and into the new life the old gods of the sands once promised us.'

'Arkhan...' Neferata murmured. She caught his hand, and kissed his mouldering bones, and then stepped back. 'I will lead them.'

'I will buy you what time I can. It will not be much, but it will be all that I can give. Go, quickly,' Arkhan said, turning back to face the destruction. Neferata turned without another word and ran, Isabella cradled to her chest. Behind her, Arkhan extended his arms, as if he might bar the doom of all the world through sheer determination. Amethyst energy crackled along his bones and leaked out through the cracks in the same. His robes flapped about him as he lifted his staff high, and spat the words to every spell and incantation he knew that might hold back the tidal wave of destruction.

She could almost imagine him smiling, in those last few moments as she fled Middenheim on the back of her abyssal steed. A flash of purple from behind her and the crack of splitting air told her of his fate, and she closed her eyes to weep for the only man she had ever loved.

The world died around her, as she fled. Middenheim fell first, consumed by the nightmare forces awakened in its depths. The hungry darkness crept outwards from the void where the Fauschlag had once stood, and crawled across Middenland, consuming the Middle Mountains and the Drakwald. It was at once empty and full of squirming, abominable shapes, like vast serpents or the writhing tendrils of some immense, unseen kraken. Riots of colour and sound filled it, only to vanish and reappear.

The keening of a thousand daemons washed across the stricken land ahead of it.

Beastmen stampeded out of the Drakwald in their thousands, fleeing before a doom that called out to them, even as it drove them mad with fear. Neferata saw them below her as she flew, vast hordes of panicked animals, and the Children of Chaos were soon joined by others – humans, orcs and even ogres, all fleeing before a doom they could not understand, and had no hope of escaping.

The darkness grew, devouring one province and then the next, over the course of the days and weeks that followed. Talabecland vanished, and then the Reikland, swallowed up by the cacophonous void birthed in the heart of Middenheim. Averland fell next, and then the others, one by one. In their mountain holds, the remaining dwarf clans saw nothing of the end, and would not have fled, even if they had.

The Grey Mountains crumbled, and even its staunchest defenders could not prevent the wave of desolation from washing over what remained of the kingdom of Bretonnia. The great forest of Athel Loren vanished, as if it had never been. The new-born over-empire of the skaven followed, and no burrow was deep enough to hide the scurrying hordes of terrified ratmen from obliteration.

The world shuddered down to its roots as it was consumed. In Sylvania, what was left of the peasantry, as well as refugees from Averland and the Moot, sought safety in the ruins of Castle Sternieste, where the dead made ready to protect them as best they could. By the time Neferata reached her lands, the sky had gone black from horizon to horizon.

Her abyssal steed smashed into the battlements of Sternieste, its form wreathed in smoke. It groaned and shuddered as Neferata hauled Isabella off its twisted form, and lifted the nearly comatose vampire up. Her retainers met her on the battlements, their eyes wide with fear. 'Mistress, what–?' one began.

'The end,' Neferata snarled. 'Where is Khalida? Where are the liche-priests? Where are the necromancers? Summon them all! Gather them here, so that we might–'

'We might what, cousin? Escape our fate, one last time?'

Neferata turned, and saw Khalida, once High Queen of Lybaras, and once her cousin, standing nearby, staring out at the encroaching darkness. Even now, her thin limbs wrapped in crumbling wrappings and her ceremonial vestments tarnished with age and battle, she was the very image of a queen. Neferata snarled in frustration. 'And you would meet it gladly, then?' She shook her head. 'I will not go like a sheep to slaughter. Not now, not ever.'

'You speak as if we had a choice, cousin,' Khalida said.

'There is always a choice,' Neferata began, but the words died in her throat as she saw the distant shape of the great bone wall raised by Mannfred in the year before Nagash's resurrection crumble like sand. The darkness swept over it, and Sylvania shuddered like a dying beast. Below, in the courtyard, the surviving humans screamed and wept in fear. Neferata shook her head. 'Too late,' she muttered. She looked down at Isabella and kissed the other vampire on the brow. 'I am sorry, little one. I was not fast enough.'

'Yes,' Khalida said. She turned towards Neferata. *'Time has caught up with us at last, cousin. The Great Land is dead, and soon we will join it.'*

Neferata laughed sadly. 'Maybe it is past time. But I will not do so cowering in a hole.' She looked at her cousin and smiled. 'We are queens, cousin. We are daughters of the Great Land, which was old when the world was young. Let us die in a manner befitting our station.' She extended a hand. 'Will you join me, Khalida?'

Khalida stared at the proffered hand, and, after a moment of hesitation, took it. Down below, the warriors of Lybaras, Khemri, and Sylvania raised their shields, as if bronze and steel might be enough to resist the destruction sweeping towards them. Frightened humans cowered behind skeletal warriors and armoured vampires, seeking protection from those they had once feared.

And then, the final darkness swept the last of the old world away.

The world came apart and the hungry dark stretched out towards the stars, unsated. The raw stuff of Chaos consumed the heavens in an orgy of uncreation. Stars flickered out one by one, until only darkness remained. It might have taken moments, or millennia, but the Dark Gods were not bound by the flow of time, and did not mark its passage.

But even as the ashes of the shattered world settled in the void, the powers and principalities of Chaos moved away, already bored by their triumph. The four great powers turned upon one another, as they always did, and mustered their forces for war. The Great Game began again, on new worlds, and the Dark Gods broke off from the swirling void at last. Had they not done so, they might have noticed a mote of light, within the dark.

The tiny pinprick of light tumbled through the dark. It had once been a man, though it had forgotten its name. It fell for what might have been centuries, until it came to a shard of the world that had been. Desperate, it reached out and caught hold of the shard with a grip that could shatter mountains, saving itself from the storm of nothingness.

As it slumped, exhausted, thought and memory returned, and soon, its strength as well. And with strength came memory – a name. And with that name came purpose. Gathering what remained of his strength, he stretched out a hand.

And then a miracle took shape in the void...

ABOUT THE AUTHORS

Guy Haley is the author of the Space Marine Battles novel *Death of Integrity*, the Warhammer 40,000 novels *Valedor* and *Baneblade*, and the novellas *The Eternal Crusader, The Last Days of Ector* and *Broken Sword*, for *Damocles*. His enthusiasm for all things greenskin has also led him to pen the eponymous Warhammer novel *Skarsnik*, as well as the End Times novel *The Rise of the Horned Rat*. He has also written stories set in the Age of Sigmar, included in *Warstorm, Ghal Maraz* and *Call of Archaon*. He lives in Yorkshire with his wife and son.

Josh Reynolds is the author of the Blood Angels novel *Deathstorm* and the Warhammer 40,000 novellas *Hunter's Snare* and *Dante's Canyon*, along with the audio drama *Master of the Hunt*, all three featuring the White Scars. In the Warhammer World, he has written the End Times novels *The Return of Nagash* and *The Lord of the End Times*, the Gotrek & Felix tales *Charnel Congress, Road of Skulls* and *The Serpent Queen*, and the novels *Neferata, Master of Death* and *Knight of the Blazing Sun*. For Age of Sigmar he has written the Legends of the Age of Sigmar novels *Pestilens* and *Black Rift* and several audio dramas including *The Lords of Helstone*. He lives and works in Northampton.

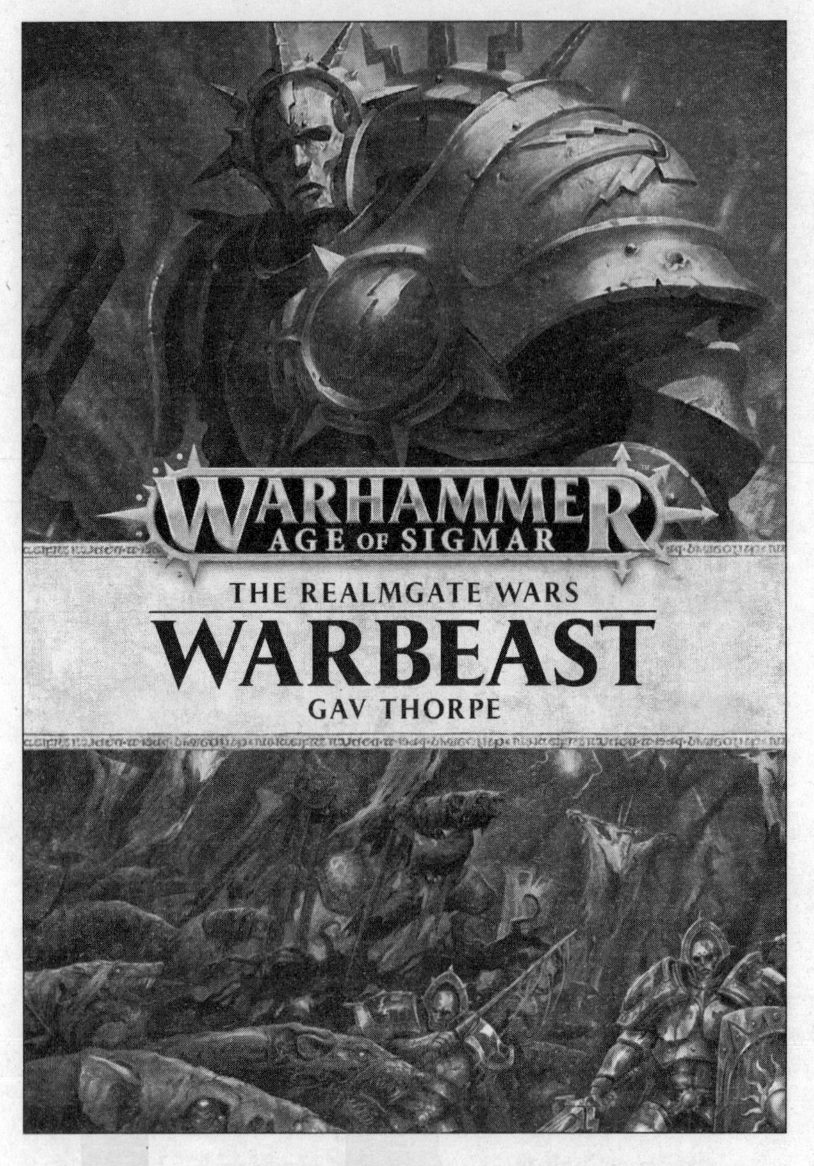
WARHAMMER
AGE OF SIGMAR
THE REALMGATE WARS
WARBEAST
GAV THORPE

READ IT FIRST
EXCLUSIVE PRODUCTS | EARLY RELEASES | FREE DELIVERY
blacklibrary.com